THREE GREAT NOVELS
Turnham Malpas Tales

Also by Rebecca Shaw

REBECCA SHAW

Three Great Novels: Turnham Malpas Tales

The Village Show
Village Secrets
Scandal in the Village

ORION

First published in Great Britain in 2003 by Orion,
an imprint of the Orion Publishing Group Ltd.

The Village Show Copyright © 1997
Village Secrets Copyright © 1998
Scandal in the Village Copyright © 1999

A CIP catalogue record for this book
is available from the British Library.

ISBN 0 75285 645 6

Typeset at The Spartan Press Ltd,
Lymington, Hants

Printed in Great Britain by
Clays Ltd, St Ives plc

The Orion Publishing Group Ltd
Orion House
5 Upper Saint Martin's Lane
London, WC2H 9EA

Contents

The Village Show

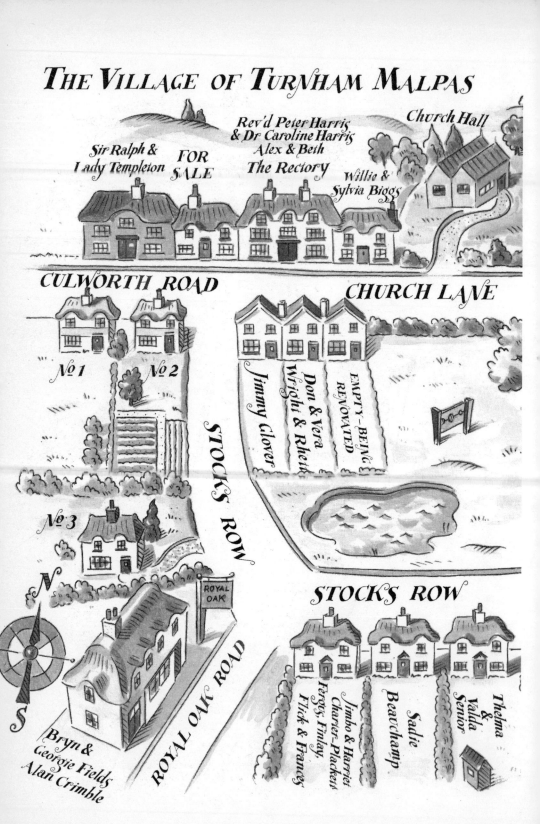

Inhabitants of Turnham Malpas

Sadie Beauchamp	Retired widow and mother of Harriet Charter-Plackett.
Willie Biggs	Verger at St Thomas à Becket.
Sylvia Biggs	His wife and housekeeper at the rectory.
Sir Ronald Bissett	Retired trades union leader.
Lady Sheila Bissett	His wife.
Louise Bianca Bissett	Their daughter.
James (Jimbo) Charter-Plackett	Owner of the village store.
Harriet Charter-Plackett	His wife.
Fergus, Finlay, Flick and Fran	Their children.
Alan Crimble	Barman at The Royal Oak.
Pat Duckett	Village school caretaker.
Dean and Michollo	Her children.
Bryn Fields	Licensee of The Royal Oak.
Georgie Fields	His wife.
H. Craddock Fitch	Owner of Turnham House.
Jimmy Glover	Taxi driver.
Revd. Peter Harris MA (Oxon)	Rector of the parish.
Dr Caroline Harris	His wife
Alex and Beth	Their children.
Linda	Runs the post office at the village store.
Gilbert Johns	Archaeologist and Choirmaster.
Barry Jones	Estate carpenter.
Mrs Jones	His mother.
Jeremy Mayer	Manager at Turnham House.
Venetia Mayer	His wife.
Michael Palmer	Village school headmaster.
Greenwood Stubbs	Head Gardener at Turnham House.
Sir Ralph Templeton	Retired from the Diplomatic Service.
Lady Muriel Templeton	His wife.
Vera Wright	Cleaner at nursing home in Penny Fawcett.

1

Caroline slammed the rectory door behind her and tramped through the snow to the church hall. They were holding the first committee meeting for the Village Show tonight, and if she knew anything at all about village committees, it was bound to be a lively evening. Now that the kitchen there had been renovated, she didn't mind quite so much having volunteered to make the coffee. She shuddered when she remembered the old kitchen with its antique water geyser and smelly cupboards – and one never-to-be-forgotten night when she'd found a mouse nesting in the cardboard box they kept the packets of biscuits in!

While the kettle boiled she went through the members' names, counting them off on her fingers to make sure she had enough cups out. People so soon took umbrage if they felt you'd forgotten them. There was Jeremy from Turnham House ('the Big House') in lieu of Mr Fitch who couldn't find the time, Jimbo from the Store who'd be doing the food, Michael Palmer from the school for the children's entertainment, Barry Jones, the estate carpenter, in charge of building and erecting the stalls, Bryn from The Royal Oak, Caroline herself representing the church, Sheila Bissett for the flower, fruit and vegetable competitions – she'd need to be kept in check or she'd be telling everyone what to do – Linda for the first-aid tent, and last but not least Louise as she called herself now, as the secretary. So that made nine.

The kettle was coming briskly up to the boil as Caroline heard the sound of early arrivals. It was Sheila Bissett with Louise, stamping the snow from their boots before they came in.

'Mother, please! I'm the secretary – I *do* know what I'm doing. I have taken notes before.'

'I just want things to go well, dear. It'll reflect on you if it isn't properly organised.'

'Well, it will be, so there. And don't forget *please* about my name.'

'I don't want to change it. I've always loved the name Bianca.'

'I haven't *changed* it, Mother, I'm simply using my first name. I've never known why you called me by my second name. Louise is so much nicer.'

'Well, it'll take me ages to get used to it after all these years.'

'You must, Mother, otherwise no one else will use it.'

Sheila tried to imprint the name on her brain. 'Louise. Louise. Louise. Heaven knows what's made you decide to do it.'

'New place. New start. I've always wanted to do it and now's the right moment. I need an entirely new persona,' Louise pleaded quietly. 'It matters to me, it's really important.'

'All right, then I'll remember. By the way, if there's any talk about the sizes of the marquees, don't forget I want a really big one for the competitions. I shall need lots of space for displaying the exhibits, you see. That Mr Fitch has plenty of money so he can dig deep for this Show.'

'The marquee for the food will be the biggest, I expect.'

'Oh well, naturally, what else can we expect? Some people, namely Jimbo, have more influence than is good for them. But let's face it, the competitions will attract the most people; they won't come all the way to the Show just to eat Jimbo's food, good though it is.'

Caroline came out of the kitchen carrying a tray of cups and a big pot of coffee. She put it down on a table. 'Hi! Would you like coffee? Milk? Sugar?' Sheila and Louise went to collect their cups.

Sheila sipped her coffee and to fill the silence said, 'Your parents have gone home today, Caroline?'

'This afternoon.'

'I met them in the Store the other day. You're so much like your mother, I didn't realise she was a doctor too.'

'Oh yes, I just wish I had half her energy. I think Peter's quite glad to see her go! She's been in his study trying to reorganise his files. He's really very patient with her.'

'They were saying how much they'd enjoyed staying with you.'

'They love seeing the children. Our two are their only grandchildren so far, you see. Their complaint is they don't see enough of them with living so far away.'

'Pity the weather wasn't a little better for them while they were here.'

'They don't really mind. Just glad to have a rest, if you can call it a rest, living in the same house as two two-year-olds!'

Sheila laughed. 'I see your point! I'm really looking forward to this Show. Such a good thing for the village, Mr Fitch coming – isn't it, Caroline?'

'It is. He's certainly stirring us up! First the Bonfire Night Party and now the Show. Before we know where we are, Mr Fitch will be thinking he's Lord of the Manor.' The three of them laughed, but they each acknowledged there was a ring of truth in what Caroline had said.

A cold draught announced the arrival of Jeremy. He waddled in swathed in a huge mackintosh and heavy leather boots, which made him appear more mountainous than ever. 'Hello, hello, ladies. Ah, coffee! Just what I need.'

Caroline handed him his cup and said, 'Jeremy, I don't think you've met Louise Bissett, Lady Bissett's daughter. She's agreed to be secretary for the Show. Brave girl!'

Jeremy extended his fat, sweating hand to Louise. 'Good evening, nice to meet you. Brave indeed! Having a taste of country air for a change, eh?'

'Something like that. You're Mr Fitch?'

'No, no, wish I was. My wife Venetia and I run the Big House on behalf of Mr Fitch's company. He uses it as a training centre for his staff.'

'I see. So you employ secretaries and the like?'

'Yes, we do. Is that what you are?'

'Well, I'm in banking really but I've got secretarial skills. So think of me if ever you need anyone. I'm organising the rector at the moment, lending a hand here and there, you know.'

Jeremy laughed and patted her arm. 'Lucky man to have such a charming assistant!'

Caroline agreed. 'Yes, he is. Louise is doing a sterling job with the church magazine. She's also just started distributing the new church telephone directory which she's compiled. We must let Jeremy have a copy, mustn't we, Louise, then if he needs any of us, he has the numbers to hand.'

'I'll drop a copy in for you tomorrow.' She beamed at him.

'Thank you kindly. Thank you very much. Show you round if you like when you come up.'

'Lovely! I've only seen the house from a distance; it'll be great to see inside it. Thank you.'

They chose chairs next to each other and Sheila sat on the other side of Louise. The outside door opened and in came the rest of the committee – Bryn Fields deep in conversation with Michael about the merits of being a Free House, Barry talking to Jimbo about the marquee for the food and Linda from the post office bringing up the rear on her own.

'Coffee, everyone, before we start.' They gathered round exchanging pleasantries, and then finally settled in their chairs to begin the meeting.

'As secretary, and due to the fact we don't appear to have elected a chairperson, shall I take the lead?' Louise looked round the group, meeting everyone's eyes and waiting for an affirmative. They all agreed with nods.

Louise cleared her throat, and in a decisive voice opened the meeting. 'Firstly and most importantly we have to decide on a site. Mr Fitch, who initiated this idea, has decided that he wants it on the lawns in front of the Big House and in Home Farm field. He'll open up an adjoining field for car parking, he says. Frankly, I don't think we have any choice, do you?'

Michael Palmer agreed. 'Let's face it, there isn't anywhere else at all where the ground is level enough nor where there is such good access.'

'There's always Rector's Meadow,' Bryn suggested.

'Rector's Meadow – where's that?' Louise asked.

Jeremy supplied her with the answer. 'Part of the estate. It borders Pipe and Nook Lane behind the rectory, and runs along the back of the gardens at the rear of the Big House. It would be a good-sized area, but the access is so poor. Pipe and Nook is very narrow – let's face it, it's only an access road for the garages at the back of the rectory and the other houses. And there's no proper road from the other side, only a cart-track. At least down the main drive cars can pass each other.'

'Rector's Meadow? Isn't that where the village cricket pitch used to be, Jeremy?'

'I wouldn't know, Jimbo, sorry.'

Louise looked round the committee for enlightenment but no one could answer so she again suggested the grounds of the Big House. 'All in favour?'

'Unanimous!'

Linda giggled. 'Let's hope they clear all the cowpats away before the big day! There be dozens of cows in there at the moment.'

Jeremy frowned. 'I'm quite sure that matter will be attended to long before the day. Mr Fitch doesn't want anything to spoil the Show, he's set his heart on it being the success of the year.'

Caroline and Sheila exchanged a smile.

'Now we must settle the date. Mr Fitch suggests the tenth or seventeenth of July. Any opinions?'

Jimbo checked his diary and said he preferred the seventeenth.

Michael Palmer said he thought that by then a lot of the children would have gone on holiday. He preferred the tenth.

'It's too soon after Stocks Day,' Sheila commented.

Michael disagreed. 'Well, there's not much work associated with Stocks Day and it'll be a good chance to advertise it, won't it?' he responded. 'All those people coming for Stocks Day, we could hand out leaflets.'

'It's agreed then, the tenth?' Louise waited for a show of hands, and the decision was carried seven to two. She made a note on her pad and then expanded on Mr Fitch's ideas. 'This Show is a huge responsibility. There hasn't been one the size of this ever before, not even the ones they had before the Second World War. He wants a really big Show – an arena with events going on all afternoon, competitions displayed in a marquee, another marquee for teas and the like,' she nodded at Jimbo who inclined his head in acknowledgement, 'stalls which charities could man, ice cream, beer, you name it. He wants a Show with plenty of get up and go, not some kind of damp squib which will fizzle out halfway through the afternoon. It's got to be the show of shows, to put Turnham Malpas on the map once and for all.'

Michael Palmer said, 'Well, the school's contribution will be a display of Maypole dancing. I know it's not May Day but it looks so colourful and we have enough children for two Maypoles. Then we shall have a gym sequence by the Top Juniors, followed by country dancing. Somehow we'll need to rig up a piano and a microphone for Mrs Hardaker to accompany it.'

'I'll make a note of that.' Louise jotted down a memo.

'I'm also willing to run a children's fancy dress competition. That will bring plenty of parents.'

'Thanks, Michael, that sounds great. You're just the right person for that. Do we have any other ideas?'

Bryn proffered an idea he'd been mulling over for a long while. 'I thought one of the events we should have in the arena could be a tug-of-war – you know, The Royal Oak throws down the challenge to The Jug and Bottle in Penny Fawcett or something – and I'd give a barrel of beer as the prize. I'd organise it. It would encourage the Penny Fawcett people to come, wouldn't it?'

Raising her voice above the babble of conversation Louise said, 'A very good idea. That's what we want, things to draw in the crowds. Could you be in charge of overseeing *all* the events in the arena, Bryn, do you think? We need someone to coordinate it all. You'll need to liaise with the organisers.'

'Well, I'm a comparative newcomer – perhaps there might be someone else who would prefer to do it? Michael?'

'To be honest I think I'll have enough to do keeping an eye on the children, and when you look round this committee, apart from Barry I'm the only person who *isn't* a comparative newcomer, so I don't see it matters. You go ahead, Bryn.'

When the question of the marquees came up, Jeremy's advice was requested.

'Well, I have the name and address of the chappie who did the marquee for the Bonfire Party we had. He was excellent, very helpful and really quite reasonably priced. I'll see to that, if you like. How many and how big?'

Jimbo asked for one the same size as the one they'd used for the Bonfire Party. 'I'm not very good at measurements, but the chap will have it in his records, won't he? That should be big enough.'

'For the competition tent, I'm afraid I shall need one much bigger than that.' They all looked at Sheila.

'Bigger than that?'

'But it was enormous.'

'Surely not!'

'It's not Chelsea Flower Show, yer know.'

Barry scoffed, 'Come off it, Sheila, what the heck! You could have got three double-decker buses in that marquee Jimbo had. Half the size'll be big enough. Next thing, Linda'll be wanting one that size for her first-aid tent.'

Linda giggled and said, 'Yes, if you like. You never know, there might be an outbreak of food-poisoning and I'll need loads of space for beds!'

Jimbo protested sharply. 'There won't be *any* food-poisoning if I'm catering, believe you me!'

Linda blushed. 'I was only joking, Mr Charter-Plackett. Me of all people should know how careful you are about food hygiene.'

'So I should think.'

Sheila turned indignantly to Barry and scathingly commented, 'And what do you know about it, Barry Jones? Nothing. If I say I want a bigger marquee, a bigger marquee I want. So write that down, Louise.' She pointed energetically at her daughter's notepad.

'Got the chairperson in your pocket, have yer, Sheila? Favouritism, that's what it is. Favouritism. We'll have a vote.' Barry raised his arm and bellowed, 'All in favour of Sheila having a marquee the same size as Mr Charter-Plackett's.'

Sheepishly everyone's hand went up, apart from Louise and Sheila.

Furious at losing, Sheila retaliated with, 'Very well then, but don't blame me if the tent is so crowded, visitors faint with the heat. Some people,' glaring at Barry, 'have no understanding of these things. The flowers will wilt and the vegetables will be dried to a crisp. I had such plans . . . But as we are democratic and it's gone to the vote, then so be it.'

Caroline intercepted the look Sheila gave Barry as she spoke. She could tell the matter wasn't really closed as far as Sheila was concerned.

'The next item on the agenda is the stalls,' Louise announced. 'Barry, would you like a word about your plans? I understand Mr Fitch has spoken to you about them.'

Barry stood up, took a piece of folded paper from his trouser pocket, and after examining it closely he began to speak. 'Yes, I've had a consultation with Mr Fitch and he says I've to go ahead with my own ideas and he'll fall in with whatever I've planned, keeping in mind a certain amount of restraint regarding cost. Which really means I've to account to him for every penny *before* I spend it. The idea I've come up with is that all the stalls shall be the same size—'

Sheila interrupted him. 'Oh no, that would look boring. They want to be all different.'

'Just let me finish, please. As I was saying, the stalls will all be the same size and will all be done up as if it was a medieval Show. They'll have small roofs over them and be decorated with crêpe paper all the same colours and quite close together. *Not* spread out all over the field. If yer spread 'em out, people won't bother to walk to some of 'em and those ones won't take much money, but if they're together in, say, three sides of a square they'll look more effective. We'll have flags flying on top of the stalls and that. The estate will make them all and then store them somewhere for next time. I'm recruiting some boys from the village to help put them up during the week before, so there's no need to worry about that.' Barry sat down and waited for some response.

Sheila spoke first. 'Well, I'm sorry but no. It won't do. All the charity people running the stalls will want to do their own thing . . .'

Barry interrupted. 'And a right mess they'll be, too. The only thing I intend letting them do is providing a sign across the front to say who they are – and even that'll have to be to my measurements. Believe me, they'll be glad to be relieved of the job of decorating them.'

Jimbo came down on Barry's side. 'Frankly I'm in wholehearted agreement with Barry, and my marquee shall be just how you want. Tell me the colours you're using for the stalls and I'll do the same with a bit of variation here and there.'

'Boring, boring, boring.' Sheila tugged indignantly at her skirt, pulling herself more upright in her chair. 'You must be mad, Barry.'

'Yer only getting back at me because I balked you from having a bigger marquee than Jimbo here. You know it makes sense.'

Louise called the meeting to order and Michael Palmer in his most conciliatory voice said quietly, 'I've been to lots of Shows of this kind over the years, and the standard of decoration on the stalls has been quite appalling. They've just no idea. If Mr Fitch is willing to pay for all this, then I suggest we fall in with Barry's plans. It will look very stylish.'

Hastily Louise said, 'All those in favour?' It was passed unanimously with the exception of Sheila who folded her arms and looked everywhere but at the other members of the committee.

Bryn broke the silence by saying, 'What about my beer-tent? Nobody's mentioned that.'

Sheila indignantly came to life. '*Beer*-tent? Who said anything about a beer-tent? Common, that's what that is. We need to keep some standards!'

Jeremy tut-tutted his impatience. 'Mr Fitch *wants* a beer-tent, and if it's a hot day it'll be a necessity. That doesn't trespass as far as you're concerned, does it, Jimbo?' Jimbo shook his head and Jeremy continued by saying, 'Could you minute that, Madam Chair, please? A smaller marquee for Bryn for a beer-tent.'

In a quiet voice Linda said, 'I've a friend in Culworth who runs a hot-dog stall by the station in the evenings. Would it be an idea if I asked him to come for the afternoon? He could park his van by the beer-tent and the two things would kind of work together, wouldn't they?'

Startled by Linda's thoughtless treachery, Jimbo protested loudly: 'Linda! Kindly remember who employs you. *I'm* paying for the food concession. I do not want a hot-dog van taking my trade. If I have the food concession, then I have it and no one else. If the committee would allow it, I would provide a separate ice-cream outlet or even perhaps two if the weather's hot. How about that?'

Sheila rushed to support him. 'What a good idea, Jimbo. Much more tasteful than a hot-dog stand.' Linda shrank back into herself and vowed not to say another word. For two pins she'd give up her job in the blasted post office – that would show Mr Charter Plackett he couldn't ride roughshod over her just because he employed her – but what with the wedding and things and jobs being so scarce she really couldn't afford to resign. She'd just have to swallow her pride.

Louise took the lead again. 'Right, I've noted all that and will let you have a copy of the minutes as soon as I've typed them up. What I should like is a list from Barry of how many stalls he's proposing to construct . . .'

'Twenty.'

' . . . Oh right, and which charities he's contacted . . .'

'Don't know about that, 'cos I'm better with my hands, I am. You'll have to do all that asking people if they want a stall . . .'

'Oh, right then, I will. I'll ask the Scouts, Guides, Red Cross, et cetera – any charities I can think of. If you know any who might want to participate, please let me know. I also need to know things like classes for the competitions, food available, a list of the entertainments like the tug-of-war that we're putting on in the arena, and the timings,' she nodded to Bryn and he gave her the thumbs-up, 'what displays the children from the school are doing,' Michael raised his hand and acknowledged what she said, 'and anything else we can mention in the publicity. I'm sure Peter will let me use the rectory computer for doing the advertising, it's so much more powerful than mine,' she looked at Caroline for confirmation and got it, 'and all we have to do now is arrange the date of the next meeting, by which time we shall all have a lot more input.'

Jimbo raised his hand. 'I say, just a minute, I've had an idea. Don't you think we need more in the way of entertainments? Something to keep people really interested in staying at the Show and spending until they've no more money left.'

'How about a firework display?' Linda said, hoping to get back into his good books.

There was a chorus of, 'What a good idea!'

Jimbo shook his head. 'Sorry, but that would mean going on until dark and the whole project would take far too long. In any case, we might have reached saturation point with my fireworks; time I gave them a rest. My idea is – what about trips in a hot-air balloon? I have friends who are real enthusiasts. They'd come, I'm sure, when they know it's for charity. What do you think?'

Everyone's faces lit up with enthusiasm as they took the idea on board.

Louise was highly delighted at his innovative idea. 'Brilliant, but we should have to be specifically insured for it. Mr Fitch is taking out insurance obviously, but hot-air balloon trips are a whole new ball-game. I'll have a word with him about it, and I'm certain his insurers will come up with something. It's a wonderful idea though, Jimbo. They'll be a really big attrac—'

The door opened abruptly. Peter was standing there looking at Caroline, his face as white as the snow outside. He didn't need to speak; they could all tell by his demeanour that something had happened which none of them would want to hear. Caroline studied his face, the colour draining away from her cheeks even before he spoke. 'Darling, I'm afraid you'll have to come home. There's . . . there's been an accident. You must come.'

2

Caroline went towards him walking stiffly, her muscles paralysed by fear. He held out his hands, clasped firmly hold of hers and led her outside into the snow. The ice-cold wind took away her breath and she gasped for air.

'Peter, for God's sake – what is it?'

Still holding her closely to him, he said quietly, 'I'm afraid it's your mother and father. They were driving—'

'Are they all right? I mean, are they injured or . . . is it worse than that?' She pulled away from his arms and put her head back so she could see his face. In it she read the message she dreaded to hear.

'Oh God, please God, no?'

'Not dead, darling, no. Badly . . . badly injured. I don't know what to say. I really don't. Come home, please, out of the cold.'

He helped her walk back to the rectory. When they got there, Sylvia was waiting with the brandy bottle and a glass on the table beside the sofa. Peter sat her down and poured her a glass. 'Here, darling, drink this. It'll help.'

'No, I shan't, not till I hear what you have to say. Tell me now. Right now!' She shook his arm as she spoke, to emphasise her urgency to face the truth. 'Go on, tell me. No matter how hard it is. *Tell me.*'

'Well, it was Ginny who rang – she telephoned from a hospital in Newcastle. Apparently they were about twenty miles from home, and with the snow and the driving conditions being so bad, I'm afraid they came off the road and went smack into a tree, and rolled down an embankment. The car turned over several times, I understand. They're both still unconscious.'

Caroline sat without speaking, quite still, quite silent, stupid silly little memories flooding into her head. Memories of seeing her mother standing by the river watching them swimming and desperately disguising how anxious she was about them all. Her mother on prize-giving days, trying hard not to look superior to everyone else when her girls won prizes. Her pride when she, Caroline, had qualified as a doctor. Her father, respected and loved by all his patients, his dark hair always tousled, his suit baggy, his tie askew. She wouldn't cry. No, she wouldn't. She absolutely wouldn't cry.

There were things to be done, like phoning the hospital, and arrangements to make so she could go up to see them. Yes, of course. She, more than any of the other three, would know the score.

'Peter, I'll have to go home, won't I?'

'Of course, my darling, of course. Drink your brandy. Please. That's an order.'

Caroline sipped it slowly, her mind racing with chaotic thoughts. Someone appeared in the doorway and Caroline couldn't think who on earth she was. Peter seemed to know her because he said, 'That's fine, Sylvia, thanks for your help. We'll make some plans tomorrow first thing. Yes, fine. Thank you. OK. Good night.'

The person came right into the room, and taking her hand she said gently, 'Don't you worry about a thing. The rector and Willie and I will see to everything here. We'll make sure the children are well cared for, so don't you fret. I'm so sorry.'

She realised it was Sylvia. 'Thank you, thank you, I know I can rely on you. I'm so grateful to have you.' When Sylvia had gone Caroline said quietly, 'Peter, did Ginny say what injuries they had?'

'No, they hadn't told her when she rang. All she knows is that it's serious, very serious.'

'I'm ringing the hospital. Right now. Use my influence. Yes, that's what I'll do.'

Peter nodded. 'Right.'

At three o'clock in the morning, she had told him she would drive herself home, but Peter had said no. 'If I'm to stay here with the children, then you're certainly not driving yourself and most definitely not in this weather.'

'Peter, *I can drive.* I've not lost my senses.'

'Not in this state you can't. All that way to Northumberland? No, absolutely not. I cannot allow it.'

'I'm not a fool.'

'I know. But it would be a foolhardy thing to attempt. You've got to think of the children, darling. They need you. You must not take stupid risks, not now you have children.'

'Oh yes, of course, Alex and Beth.' She got up out of bed. 'I'll go and check they're all right.' She padded away into the nursery. Beth was sleeping on her back, her right thumb close to her mouth, the blankets pushed to one side, her nightgown round her waist. Caroline made her comfortable and tucked the blankets around her firmly. Alex was sleeping on his side, well tucked in. She really would have to see about him going into a bed. He was so much taller than Beth and the cot was definitely on the brink of being uncomfortable for him. She stroked his head, expressing with her hand all the love she had for him. As she did it, she half-remembered the touch of her own mother's hand in the night, once when she had a temperature and her mother felt concerned for her. The caring bond was never broken, and now it was her turn to care. She returned to bed, snuggled into Peter's protecting arms and fell into a troubled sleep.

It was Malcolm the milkman who spread the news round the village about where Caroline had gone. 'Just leaving the milk when they came out of the rectory. Sylvia Biggs was holding on to them twins and the rector and her, that is Dr Harris, was getting into the car. He's taking her to the station, yer see. Can't drive all that way in that state. It's 'er parents – them what went 'ome yesterday. Bad crash on their way back. Terrible it is.'

Pat Duckett, hurrying to get ready to go over to the school and open up, said: 'I didn't know – I'd no idea. How awful! She will be upset. They were so nice; I met them out with the twins when they were here. Such nice people. Just like her, no edge.'

'Yer right, 'er mother is lovely. I cut mi hand last week on a broken bottle, and I'd wrapped it up with a bit of rag till I finished the round. But she came to the door with the weekly money, saw the rag and made me go in the rectory where she cleaned it up and put a proper dressing on it. And she was waiting for me next morning to 'ave another look, make sure it was going on all right. Really kind, just like Dr Harris.'

'Them poor little kids, they will miss their mum.'

'She'll miss 'em too – devoted to 'em, she is.' Malcolm put down the crate he had in his hand and propped his shoulder against the door-frame, preparing for a long chat. 'Sylvia Biggs was saying she won't have no swearing, no talking about guns an' killing an' that. Right particler she is.'

'Quite right, too. I'll go round when I've done the school, see if they need a hand. Thanks, Malcolm.'

'How yer liking it here then, Pat? Big move up for you, ain't it? Four bedrooms and all mod cons. Bet your dad's pleased to 'ave got a job like this. Gardener and a house thrown in. Liking it, are yer?'

'Lovely. Just lovely. Never been as well off in my life.'

'All yer need now is a man to keep yer warm at nights!'

'You offering your services, are yer?'

Malcolm backed off the step. 'No, no. Not me. I'm well fixed-up.'

'Over the brush, I understand.'

'None of your business.'

'No, and my private life is none of yours.'

'Saw Barry Jones with yer at the Bonfire Party. You could do worse.'

'Marriage bureau your latest sideline, is it? The scams you get up to would fill a book.'

Malcolm chuckled and tapped the side of his nose. 'No. No. I'll be off then.'

'Yes, get off.' She punched his arm playfully. 'Mind 'ow yer go, Malcolm, take care.'

Michelle and Dean eating their breakfast right behind her in the kitchen contemplated an aspect of their mother's life they had never thought of before.

Michelle swallowed her mouthful of Corn Pops and said, 'Mum, are you really thinking of marrying Barry?'

'Of course not. Three drinks last November doesn't mean wedding bells, does it?'

'I like Barry.'

Dean pushed back his chair; he'd noticed the time and needed to be off. 'I like him too. He's a great bloke. If you married him he'd make us some nice cupboards and that. Yer keep saying you could do with some.'

'Yer don't marry for the sake of some nice cupboards, our Dean. And would you want his mother for a grandmother? I ask yer!' Dean pulled a face, laughed and disappeared upstairs.

Rather wistfully Michelle said, 'Mum, I'd quite like having a dad.'

Pat smiled indulgently at Michelle. 'It would be nice for yer, love, with not remembering yer own dad, but that's not the right reason for getting married, is it?'

'No. I expect yer've got to marry for L-O-V-E. I can hear Grandad coming down. He'll need a fresh pot, you know what he's like.'

'Yes – demanding, like all men.'

Pat called at the rectory as soon as she'd finished at the school. Peter hadn't yet returned so it was Sylvia who answered the door on her way back from the study where she'd been taking a coffee in to Louise.

'Good morning, Sylvia. Just heard about Dr Harris's mum and dad. Thought you might need a bit of 'elp and that, in the circumstances. Come to offer my services, I thought.'

Sylvia caught Alex just as he was about to leap over the threshold into the road. 'Come back, Alex, there's a good boy. Thanks for calling in, Pat, we've got everything organised for now but if I do need any help then definitely I'll give you a call. Louise is here today so she's answering the telephone.' Sylvia pulled a face and then carried on saying, 'Perhaps you could sit in one night if the rector needs to go out?'

'That would be great. Glad to be of help. I've always been fond of the twins. Any news from Northumberland this morning?'

'Dr Harris called the hospital before she left. Still critical, I'm afraid. They've got terrible injuries. They're both being operated on today. Look, come in or I shall be losing these two before the morning's out.' They stood in the hall while Sylvia listed their injuries. 'So all told, they've broken bones, internal injuries and serious head injuries. So I don't know when things will be back to normal.'

'Still, once they've turned the corner she'll come home, won't she? These two'll miss her; 'spect they'll be playing up no end, poor little things.'

Sounds of a furious argument in the kitchen made Sylvia terminate the conversation. 'Must get on, Pat. Thanks for calling and I'll let you know.'

Pat stepped out into the road, waved and left, calling out from the lane, 'Don't forget to ring! I'm on the phone now since we moved.'

Sylvia nodded her thanks and raced back into the kitchen. 'No, Beth, that is Alex's car; this one is yours. Here you are. Now no more shouting, please.'

But the children wouldn't be pacified and Sylvia was relieved to hear Peter's key in the lock.

'Now, Rector, caught the train all right?'

'Yes, we did. Caroline's promised to ring as soon as she has any further news. It's been a terrible shock for her. She's the eldest, you see – she's always felt responsible for them all, so they lean on her.' He turned to the children. 'Now my little ones, what's all this noise?'

'They're very upset, Rector. They're not used to her leaving them and they're missing her already.'

'So am I.' He stooped down to pick up the children, one on each arm, and he kissed them both soundly. 'No more arguing, you've both to be good. Daddy misses Mummy too, and I'm not shouting and being cross, am I?'

Louise stood in the doorway, her coffee cup in her hand. She strode forward and placing her hand on Peter's, said, 'Don't worry, Peter, I'll do the best I can to help. Anything, anything at all. I'll come in every day if need be.'

Peter thanked her and said he thought that between Willie, Sylvia and himself they'd manage. 'But if we do have a crisis, I shall know who to call on.'

Sylvia said, 'Pat Duckett's been already. I expect she'll be the first of many. As soon as everyone knows, we'll be inundated with offers of help, so don't worry yourself, Louise. You confine your efforts to the computer – after all that's what you're best at.' And Sylvia went to unload the washing machine, leaving Peter surprised by the sharpness of her tone.

'Right then, children, down you go. Louise and I have a lot to do this morning. Be good.'

Caroline rang that night to say both her parents had come through their major operations that day, and although they still weren't out of the woods, things were looking a little more hopeful. She described the operations in so much detail she made Peter almost wish he hadn't married a doctor. She knew far too much for his liking. 'Mother's opened her eyes and spoken to me, but Dad's only looked round and then fallen asleep again. He didn't know me really.'

'Well, he always has been a bit vague, hasn't he?'

'Peter!'

'Well, he has. Remember that time when we came back from our honeymoon and he mistook me for a patient? I mean! His own son-in-law.'

'He'd been on call all night and he was exhausted, OK? Darling, how are the children?'

'Noisy and fractious. Missing their mother, like I'm missing my wife. Loads of parishioners have called to offer their services. Sylvia's got so many promises of walks and minding and things, she's having to keep a roster. I probably shan't see the children at all. Louise has promised to come in every day . . .'

'Naturally.'

'Caroline, please! What she does is out of kindness. After all, she's not getting paid.'

'I know. I know. However, I've got something better to talk about than her. Like how much I love you, and I wish you were here.'

'Look, would you like me to come up?'

'Absolutely no. You're better to be at home giving the children security. There's nothing you can do anyway. Just pray for them, darling, please.'

'I have been.'

'Thank you.' There was a pause. 'Thank you for that. I'm exhausted, I've just got to get to bed.'

'Of course. Take care, my darling, and good night. My love to Mum and Dad tomorrow when they can talk. Have the girls got there?'

'Oh yes. Peter, I'm so worried! There's nothing I can do and I wish there was.' There was a moment's silence and then she said shakily, 'My love to you. I'll ring tomorrow night.'

'Good night, darling. Sleep tight. God bless you.'

Peter put down the receiver and went to look out of his study window. He'd always admired his parents-in-law. Stout-hearted Northerners, down-to-earth, tough, humorous, compassionate and latterly so forgiving of him. He hoped more than anything that they would pull through.

Just before he fell asleep that night it occurred to him to be careful where Louise was concerned while Caroline was away. He'd have to watch his step. The parish wouldn't stand for any more nonsense from him; one foot wrong and that would be it. He couldn't think of any possible reason to stop her helping with the parish work and she'd been a boon, no doubt about that. But helping with the children, no, definitely not. God's work, yes, but not his. He thought about Caroline sleeping in Northumberland in her old bed and wished she was home in Turnham Malpas in his.

3

'Mother, have you seen that file for the Show? You know, the red one. It's got a blue label with "Show" written on it?'

'No, dear, I haven't.' Sheila emerged from the kitchen, her stocky figure swathed in her latest negligée, pale pink with little bouquets of white flowers on it. Ron thought it too thin for decency, but he was no expert. Underneath she wore a matching nightie. Since she and Ron had restored, to use Ron's words, 'diplomatic relations', she'd endeavoured to bring a touch of excitement to his life by wearing tempting nightdresses. 'I'll look in your room, dear. It can't have gone far.'

Louise, head down in the bottom drawer of her desk, shouted triumphantly: 'Eureka!'

Sheila flinched. 'I don't think that's a word suitable for the drawing room, dear, do you?'

'Mother, for heaven's sake! Thank goodness I've found it. I can't think why I put it down there in the bottom drawer when it's so urgent. I'll just put these lists in the right place and then I'll be off.'

'How they managed before you came I shall never know. Peter must be really grateful for your help.'

'He is. She isn't.'

'Don't say that. I've a very soft spot for Caroline Harris.'

'Can't think why. I can feel she doesn't like me every time I see her. And those clothes! Who does she think she is?'

'Well, she was a doctor before the twins arrived, so she would be earning good money and then I have heard on the village grapevine that Peter has a private income, so he doesn't have to rely on his stipend, you see.'

Louise pretended disinterest. 'Oh well, that accounts for it then. Now, where does this go? Oh there. Gilbert Johns says he knows some Morris Dancers. I've wondered about asking them to come to the Show.'

'Oh, that would be *so* colourful! We've been in Turnham Malpas five years now and there's never been Morris Dancers here, not even on Stocks

Day. That would be a real draw! I thought you weren't speaking to Gilbert since he's being so awkward about having you in the choir?'

'I'm not, but he doesn't seem to have noticed. In any case I haven't given up the idea at all. Just letting it lie dormant for a while till I get another chance. It's perfectly ridiculous to refuse to have a woman in the choir. But then what else can you expect?'

Sheila, who had been busy spraying leaf-shine on her rubber plant while she talked, stopped and looked at Louise. 'What do you mean?'

'Well, he's always so mild and kind of soft, he wouldn't know how to cope with having a woman in the choir.'

'He's always been very much the gentleman as far as I've been concerned.'

'It doesn't mean because he doesn't make waves that he can't be a gentleman as well, Mother.'

'No, I suppose not. He never socialises at all, does he? Never stays for coffee after the service or anything. You never get to know him any better however many times you talk to him.' She glanced at the clock under its glass dome, its little brass weights steadily rocking back and forth. 'Look at the time, Louise, you're going to be late at the rectory. How are they managing without Caroline?'

'Pretty well. The children are being farmed out all over the place. They're very naughty at the moment, you can't leave them for a minute.'

'Missing their mother, I expect. Well, she's not really their mother, but you know what I mean.'

Louise swung round from the mirror, her top lip lipsticked and the bottom still awaiting her ministrations.

'Not their mother?'

'I thought you knew. They're his but not hers.'

'Haven't they been married long, then?'

'Oh yes. A good long time like seven years or something. But those twins are his by someone who used to live here. It was quite a scandal at the time, but the village closed ranks and no one let on. She left immediately the twins were born. We never mention it now. I thought you knew.'

'You mean he was unfaithful to her and they then adopted the twins?'

'Yes.'

'God! I didn't think he could be tempted away. They're so lovey-dovey with each other. Kiss here. Hug there. Darling this, darling that. Well, well! This puts a whole new light on the matter.'

'On what matter?'

Louise turned back to the mirror. 'Oh, nothing. Just a figure of speech.' Her hand trembled ever so slightly and she had to wipe away the lipstick on her bottom lip and apply it again.

Louise studied her reflection in the mirror. She'd tried to soften her strong features, so like her father's, by lightening her hair to a kind of ash-blonde, and she'd had it cut short in a severe bob to give her a more youthful look. She wore mascara to enhance her eyes but sometimes wondered if they were her best feature, after all. Fancy Peter Harris doing that . . . She could understand completely how someone could be attracted to him, but imagine a man of the cloth allowing such a thing to happen! And twins too! That seemed to make it worse, somehow. So Caroline hadn't got as much of a hold over him as Louise had imagined. She pondered about how many times adultery had taken place; though she supposed it only needed once to conceive. She patted some powder over her lips. She hated shiny lips, they looked too aggressive. Then she imagined his arms around her, her hands caressing his wonderful red-gold hair, his strong athletic body pressed close to hers, inch for inch, his lips lingering in her hair, listening to him whispering . . .

'Good morning, Louise. You're up bright and early.'

It was Dad. 'Morning, Dad. I'm off – they need me at the rectory. You've promised to be the starter of the races at the Show, haven't you, Dad? The tug of war and the children's races? That's what I've put you down for, anyway. See you. Shan't be home for lunch, Mother. I've promised to give Sylvia a hand with the twins. They're wearing her out. Where's my briefcase? Oh, there it is. I'm off.'

'I shan't be here anyway. Dad and I have promised ourselves lunch at the pub.' As Louise slammed the cottage door, Sheila smiled indulgently. 'How Peter managed before she came I don't know. I've never seen her so enthusiastic, have you?'

'No. Where's my breakfast?'

'Won't be a minute.'

'I don't like you wearing that . . . thing about the house. It's all right for the bedroom but not downstairs.'

'All right, keep your hair on. I'm not walking down the street in it, am I, only sitting in my own drawing room.'

'And don't encourage Louise so much with all this voluntary work. She needs a proper job. Money doesn't grow on trees.'

Louise hastened on winged feet across the Green to the rectory. Fancy the twins not being Caroline's. She found it hard to believe. Amazing what you learned about people. Everything all wonderful on the surface but under-neath . . . Today she had the opportunity to help him, to make herself indispensable – yes, that was it, indispensable while Caroline was away. She knocked impatiently on the door.

It was Peter who opened it. 'Good morning, Louise. Snow's going at last. I like it when it first comes but then after a while one wishes it anywhere but where one is.' He took her coat and hung it in the hall cupboard.

Louise noticed that before he shut the door he smoothed the back of his hand down the sleeve of a coat of Caroline's. She could have burned that coat there and then. He opened the door to the study. 'I've dictated a lot of stuff but you'll soon whizz through it. If you've work to do for the Show, today could be the day.'

'Don't you worry about that, I'm staying for lunch to help Sylvia, we arranged it yesterday.'

'I really don't want to put on you any more than I have to. I thoroughly appreciate what you do for the parish and I'm sorry the church can't afford to pay you for doing it, but I really can't have you spending time looking after my children. It simply is not right. Thank you all the same.'

Louise blushed bright red. Partly with anger and partly with disappointment. 'But I've promised Sylvia. She has no chance to get her housework done now with Caroline being away.'

'The twins are going to Harriet Charter-Plackett this afternoon straight after lunch, so Sylvia will be able to catch up then. The twins love playing with baby Frances. They're staying there for tea.'

'When was this arranged?'

'Sylvia organised it yesterday afternoon, why?'

Louise left the study and went to find Sylvia. She was upstairs stripping the two cots and putting clean sheets on. Alex and Beth were playing with some old soft toys they'd found stored away in the nursery cupboard.

'Loo' Lulu, it BooBoo, Beth's BooBoo.' Beth held up a tatty well-worn rabbit with one ear missing for Louise to see, but she hadn't time for her.

'Look here, Sylvia,' she burst out, 'we had it all planned. I was going to stay for lunch and look after the twins this afternoon. You knew all about it. Now I hear they're going to Harriet for the afternoon.'

Sylvia picked up Beth's counterpane from the carpet and without pausing in her work to look at her said, 'I know, but Mrs Charter-Plackett offered and it was the most convenient day for her so I said yes.' Sylvia finished smoothing the counterpane on Beth's cot and turned to look at Louise. 'Let's face it, you really much prefer the computer to children. I know exactly why you want to take care of the twins, don't I?' Sylvia stared meaningfully at Louise, who glared back.

'What exactly do you mean by that remark? Speak plainly, I don't like innuendos.'

'Very well then. I know you want to look after the twins to usurp Dr Harris's place here while she's away . . .'

'Well, really! You're being ridiculous! Why should I want to do that?'

'I can't put it plainer than that, and I won't have it. Come, children, help Sylvie put these toys away and then we'll go to the Store. Mr Charter-Plackett says he'll have that *Jungle Book* video in he promised.'

Louise protested. 'All I'm doing is trying to help while this family is in difficulties. I can't think what can be wrong with that.'

Alex slammed the toy-cupboard door shut and shouted, 'Sylvie, done. Come on, Sylvie. Bimbo's Bimbo's.'

Sylvia bent down to pick him up. 'In future the only domestic thing you may do is make your own coffee and that's that. I'm sorry.' She called Beth and the three of them went off down the stairs.

Louise took a deep breath and followed them down. She found Peter keeping a low profile in his study.

'Peter! Sylvia has deliberately arranged for Harriet Charter-Plackett to have the children later today when she knew we'd arranged for me to help her look after them. I'm very hurt. They know me, and they'd be quite happy with me. I'm only trying to help.'

'I know you are, and I'm grateful for all you do, but the house and the children are Sylvia's responsibility whilst Caroline is away, and well . . . that's how it must stay.' He looked pleadingly at her and her heart melted. The poor dear man, dominated by two bossy women. What some men have to put up with. If he was hers he'd have the last word on everything. If he was hers . . .

In his gentlest voice, Peter said, 'So shall we get on with what we know you do best, which is relieving me of having to plod slowly along for hours with my two-finger typing?'

'Yes, of course. I'm here to help you in any way I can – and you mustn't hold back from asking me for anything, however difficult.' Louise smiled sweetly at him, and switched on the computer.

While she sorted out the work he'd done for her to type he worried about how to broach the subject of her joining the church choir. Gilbert Johns had spoken to him about her on Sunday evening after the service.

'You see, Peter, she persuaded me to give her an audition. Fine. I didn't mind, not at all. Didn't take long.' He sighed. 'I hate to cause pain to anyone and I'm telling you and only you because I know I can rely on you not to gossip, but you see although Louise has a powerful contralto voice, and can read music perfectly, her singing is ever so slightly, and I mean ever so slightly, out of tune. A mere soupçon, that is all. But to someone with an ear like mine it is discernible and makes me wince. So even if I had females in the choir I wouldn't have her. Can you tell her for me, discreetly, please? And not mention she's out of tune?' Gilbert had begged so charmingly that Peter had agreed to do it. But how? Better tackle it now. Clear the air.

'By the way, Gilbert Johns spoke to me on Sunday evening. I'm afraid the answer to your being in the choir is still no. He's absolutely adamant. He's had another discussion with the men in the choir and they wish to stick to tradition and keep it all-male. So I'm afraid there's nothing more to be said.'

'Oh, did he really consult them? I bet! It's ridiculous that in this day and age they won't have women in.'

'Well, I'm sorry but there it is. You see, he has a waiting list of boys wanting to join, a position most village choirs would be exceedingly glad to find themselves in, so . . .' The telephone rang and saved him from having to pursue the matter with Louise. By the time he put down the receiver Louise was immersed in her typing. Just as he had become absorbed in his own work, the computer fell silent and he realised Louise was crying.

For a few minutes he ignored her, hoping the crying would stop and he could pretend he hadn't noticed. But it didn't. He put down his pen and said quietly, 'Can I help?'

His gentle enquiry made her sob.

'Please tell me, it may help.'

Louise wiped her eyes and said, 'It's always the same. I'm all right for typing and administration and office work, but when it comes to something personal no one wants to know.'

Peter perceived there was more to the problem than what had happened that morning with Sylvia and Gilbert's refusal. 'I don't think it's just this morning, is it, that's made you say this.'

Louise shook her head. 'No, it isn't. I . . . I . . . that's why I'm here.'

'In Turnham Malpas, you mean?'

'Yes. If I tell you, can I rely on your confidentiality?'

'Of course. Absolute secrecy, I promise.' He turned his chair to face her and waited.

'I worked at a bank, as you know, and I was in charge of helping people who were starting up new businesses. I listened to what they had to say, saw their business plan and commented on it. If it wasn't right I helped them to put it right, decided if it was viable, talked to them about a loan and the conditions of repayment, took the whole thing to my manager, thrashed it out with him and with his approval agreed it, then kept a watching brief through the first critical years. I was doing well, really well till one day . . . till one day this man came in. He was utterly charming. Polished upper-class accent, like yours,' Louise smiled at him, 'well-mannered, not good-looking but . . . Anyway, he had a good business plan – well-presented, not on a scrap of paper like some of them did – and I worked on it, though there wasn't much to do. The manager was on holiday and I should have waited until he got back, but somehow it all seemed so genuine and the client was so keen, and so open and friendly. If I shilly-shallied, he'd lose the opportunity so I contacted the area manager instead. Of course, to him the sum involved was peanuts in comparison to the figures he dealt with every day, and because he had confidence in me he gave the go-ahead.'

'And it didn't work out?'

Louise shook her head. 'I was completely taken in. We started having our business discussions while taking lunch together, then it became dinner, then I . . . began to fall in love with him. After that, I was no longer behaving rationally where his loan was concerned. Anyone else and I would have been alerted, but in the circumstances . . . Look you don't want to hear all this. Sorry.' Louise turned back to the keyboard.

'If it makes you feel any better, I am here to listen – that's fifty per cent of the job for a clergyman.' She looked at him. He smiled.

Louise almost choked with gratitude. 'Well, I gave my notice in at the bank at his suggestion and was going to join him. General factotum, secretarial work, learning the business so that I should become his partner and not just in the business. I couldn't resist his charm. I began helping weekends and evenings while I worked out my notice, and I have to admit I could think of nothing else but him. Then I'd a day's holiday to come so I thought I'd take the opportunity to get ahead with the spread-sheets I was doing for him, so I'd be free at the weekend. I walked in the office early and there was this blonde, all legs and . . .' She paused. 'It wouldn't have been so bad if he hadn't been so cruel. Searingly cruel. I couldn't for the life of me tell you what he said.'

'I'm so sorry. It must have been dreadful.'

His sympathy made her tremble. 'I . . . I'm not telling anyone, not even you, what he said. It was staggeringly hurtful. I stormed out and drove like a maniac. I don't know to this day why I didn't have an accident, I really don't.' She wiped her eyes. 'I spent an horrendous weekend and on the Monday went to the bank and straight to his file and began working through it. Of course his references turned out to be forged; the whole story had been a complete fabrication. I had to go to the manager and tell him. If I hadn't already given in my notice I would have been sacked on the spot. You see, I should have delayed authorising the loan until my manager had come back from holiday, and what was worse I had involved myself with the man. Should have kept it entirely on a business footing. I, who thought I had a head for business, had ignored all my training. He had me absolutely fooled.'

'I'm so sorry.'

'So not only had he made me lose my job, he'd also broken my heart. I can't forgive myself for being so taken in. How could I have been such a fool? I loved him, you see. He behaved like a gentleman, said he valued me too much to anticipate our marriage.' Louise stopped while she regained control over her sobs. 'Said he wanted our relationship to be on the right footing, and I admired him for that; it made me feel cherished as well as loved. But it was all a sham. A total sham. It was because he didn't want *me*. I was all right, you see, for getting the loan and doing the work, but not for a relationship. That's how it always is. Good old Louise. My parents think I was made redundant, so please don't tell them, will you? I couldn't bear for them to know the whole story.'

'Of course I shan't tell them. You know, when something like this happens, one has to pick up the pieces and plod on and eventually one gets through the maze.'

'You're so kind. So understanding. Thank you. I really do appreciate you listening to me. I feel so much better now, having confided in you. It's wonderful to have you to talk to, just wonderful and you're such a sympathetic listener. You have this gift, you know, of helping people to speak the truth and—'

To his relief there came a knock at the door. It was Sylvia back from the Store with the video clutched in her hand.

'Only me, Rector. I need a word. Is it convenient?'

'Of course, come in.'

Sylvia nodded her head in the direction of the kitchen. So Peter stood up and followed her in there.

'Rector, I've told Louise she's not to interfere with our domestic arrangements. I won't have it. Yesterday she coerced me into agreeing that she could look after the children, and you've no idea how relieved I was when Mrs Charter-Plackett rang up offering to have them both. I won't have it and I know Dr Harris wouldn't want it either. So that's it. I won't desert my post in her absence, but if I have any more interference then as soon as Dr Harris returns I shall give in my notice. She and I work beautifully together and I would regret doing it – I've never had a job I've enjoyed so much – but the sooner that woman finds herself a proper job, the better it will be for us all.'

Peter said, 'Now see here, Sylvia, I know that you're under pressure without Caroline, but please don't allow yourself to get so upset. Louise is no threat to you; in fact, it's all rather sad and I feel rather sorry for her. But I have told her myself she must confine her help to the parish and that our domestic arrangements are off-limits. So we are both on the same side. Please don't even contemplate giving in your notice, because if you do Caroline will have me hanging from the highest branch of the royal oak for all to see.'

Sylvia laughed. 'Oh sir, I'm sure she wouldn't, oh no. So long as you and I have an understanding then we shall both act accordingly. She mustn't be encouraged. Right, children, drink and biscuit-time, I think, while we watch *Jungle Book*. Your Sylvie needs her coffee, and I expect Daddy does too.' Sylvia went to put on the kettle, shaking her head in amusement.

Friday lunchtime in The Royal Oak dining room was always busy. There was a hint of the freedom of the weekend coming up, and besides retired people enjoying their well-earned pleasures, there were plenty of villagers intent on enjoying themselves too. As they had already promised, Ron and Sheila had arrived for lunch, breathlessly later than they had intended so they were having to wait in the bar while a table became free. Ron was standing talking to Bryn with one foot on the bar rail and in his hand a pint of Bryn's homebrewed ale. Sheila was sitting at one of the small round tables in the window sipping her gin and tonic. She was scrutinising Ron and comparing him with other older men in the bar. He'd weathered quite well really, considering. Now he'd lost weight his stomach had been reduced to more manageable proportions and the fat around his throat, which had wobbled when he spoke, had disappeared.

The door opened and in came Sir Ralph with Muriel. She never could get used to calling her Lady Templeton. After all, Muriel had only been a solicitor's secretary before she married Sir Ralph. My, but he was handsome. All that thick white hair and his tanned skin and that aristocratic haughty nose. Class. Yes, definitely class. Sheila waved eagerly to Muriel and she came across.

'There's room for the four of us if I move my handbag. Here, do sit down. It's so busy in here today, isn't it?'

Muriel sat down, eager to be friendly. 'Hello, Sheila. It's a little warmer today, isn't it? I'm so glad the snow has almost gone. How's Louise? Has she got a job yet?'

Sheila laughed. 'No, not yet. She's looking round though. Wants the kind of job she can get her teeth into. Though how she's going to find the time I don't know. She's so busy at the rectory now, especially with Dr Harris being away.'

'Of course. I haven't heard today. Do you know how things are?'

'Well, they've both had their operations and it's simply a question of waiting to see. Six hours in the operating theatre, they say. Of course, at their age it must have been the most tremendous shock.' Ralph brought Muriel's drink across and then went to rejoin Ron and Bryn. 'Louise's helping all she can. She's having lunch there today and looking after the twins for Sylvia this afternoon.'

'She's certainly keeping very busy. I understand she was hoping to join the choir. Has she done anything about that at all?'

'Well, yes.' Sheila drew closer to Muriel and quietly said, 'She persuaded Gilbert Johns to give her an audition, which of course she passed, but he's said no way will he have women in the choir. She's very upset about it, but she's not given up on him yet – oh no, not my Louise.'

'Well, if Gilbert Johns has said no I don't see how she will change that. He's a very quiet man but very determined where his choir is concerned. We're really very lucky to have him, you know. He's made it such a wonderful choir and when you think about it, for so small a village we are very privileged.'

Ralph came across, glass in hand. 'Hello, Sheila. Everything all right with you and yours?'

'Yes, thank you, Sir Ralph. Everything's hunky dory. I hear Mr Fitch is opening the Village Show. Pity it couldn't be you.'

Muriel saw Ralph's lips press together with annoyance but his answer came out cordially enough. 'We shall be abroad when the Show is taking place, Sheila, so the matter doesn't arise.'

Muriel quickly decided she needed her lunch. Anything to stop Sheila putting her foot in it any more than she already had done. Sheila was renowned for annoying Ralph.

'I think we'll go in for lunch, Ralph. We booked for half-past one, didn't we? If you're ready, that is.'

'Of course, dear. Of course. Will you excuse us, Sheila?'

To Muriel's distress, Sheila and Ron followed them into the dining room and asked if they could share their table as it looked as if all the other diners had become glued to their chairs.

'Would it be a bother?' Sheila asked.

Ralph stood up, pulled out a chair for her and said, 'Certainly not. We shall be glad of your company.' When they had got seated they discussed the menu. Ralph said, 'I'll order, this is on me.' Under the table Sheila tapped Ron's knee with a newly lacquered bright red fingernail and he agreed to Ralph's suggestion and thanked him for his offer. Ralph went to the food hatch and placed their orders.

They chatted about village affairs and the Show and the annual Stocks Day and how nice it was having somewhere decent in the village to eat lunch. When Ralph returned to his seat, Ron mentioned the houses Ralph was having built. 'So glad you got permission for them. The price of houses around here is astronomical. Renting out your properties will inject new life into the place – encourage families and such. This snow has held things up though, hasn't it?'

'Unfortunately it has, but with luck they'll all be completed by the middle of the summer.'

'Have you got any tenants yet?'

Muriel eagerly explained the situation. 'Alan here,' she nodded her head in the direction of the barman, 'and Linda are having one, though it won't be ready in time for their wedding, and three of the others are already promised. So that leaves us with four tenants to find, but we've had lots of enquiries, haven't we, Ralph?'

'Yes, we have. I'm being a bit particular about the tenants. I don't want the houses being rented by people who don't actually *need* housing in the village. None of this business of using them as weekend hideaways. The houses must serve a definite purpose. I haven't, or rather *we* haven't had them built just to make money.'

Sheila, impressed by Ralph's good intentions, said, 'Well, I think it's wonderful. The village needs those houses – we're losing so many young people because they can't afford to buy. I hear Mr Fitch is trying to snap up any cottages going spare. He's bought Pat's and he's put in a bid for one of the weekenders' cottages, but I don't suppose he'll be as high-minded as you are, Sir Ralph.'

Just as Ralph was about to thank Sheila for her compliment, the dining-room door burst open and Louise stood on the threshold looking around. She spotted Sheila and Ron, smiled sweetly when she saw with whom they were dining and went to join them. Ralph stood up, and belatedly Ron did too after another dig from Sheila's sharp fingernail.

As Sheila moved her chair closer to Ralph's to make room for Louise, she asked, 'Why aren't you having lunch at the rectory? You said you were.'

Teetering between tears of disappointment and an outburst of temper, Louise said between gritted teeth: 'They're going to Harriet's straight after lunch for the afternoon. Sylvia arranged it. I'll go and order my food.' She pushed her chair back so roughly that it almost fell over, but Ron caught it adroitly and stood it up for her.

'Well, really! She does seem annoyed,' Sheila whispered. 'I wonder what made Sylvia decide to do that? It seems awfully rude.'

Trying to pour oil on troubled waters, Muriel suggested that maybe Sylvia had got her plans confused. 'She must have so much to do with Caroline being away and the telephone to answer and things, I expect she's got mixed up. And the children will be missing their mother, so I suppose they'll be more difficult than usual, which won't help. They are such dear little things but so . . . inventive!'

Ralph wholeheartedly agreed with Muriel, and Ron said, 'Yes, I expect so. One at a time was enough for us. Two must be murder!'

'Looks to me as if our Louise could commit murder. That Sylvia is getting too big for her boots, you know. But still, Louise loves working for Peter and he's so appreciative of what she does. She's completely reorganising the quarterly magazine, and of course you'll have got your copy of the parish telephone directory?'

Muriel nodded her agreement. 'Oh yes, we have. A very good idea, that. I didn't realise we had so many people connected with the church. I just wish they all . . .'

Louise returned, and as she sat down again she said, 'I've been told I'm to keep to the secretarial side and have nothing to do with the children or the house. I'm permitted – *permitted*, mind – to make myself a coffee when I want as Sylvia has too much to do to be waiting on me, she says.'

Muriel grew increasingly uncomfortable at Louise's outburst. When she'd finished speaking, Muriel said quietly, 'I think Sylvia is overwhelmed with the responsibility and all the work, and—'

'Oh no, Lady Templeton, it's because Caroline has told her not to let me have anything to do with the children.'

Ralph decided to intervene. 'Louise, I'm quite sure you're mistaken. Caroline's not like that.'

Louise retorted sharply, 'Peter would be delighted for me to help with the twins, but Sylvia's put her foot down and he's got to go along with it, or he'll catch it in the neck from Caroline if Madam Sylvia gives her notice in.' Louise said how sorry she felt for Peter with two women dominating him; it wasn't fair to him, not fair at all. He certainly didn't deserve all the harassment he got. So engrossed was she in her sympathy for Peter, she didn't realise that her eyes and her face glowed with love.

Muriel read the signs only too well. So did Ralph. So too did Ron. But Sheila blundered on with, 'Well, of course he's so lovely, so kind, he'll let them ride roughshod over him. You're so perceptive, Louise, trust you to put your finger on the problem. You ask him again, he's bound to let you help.'

Ron cleared his throat and firmly intervened. 'Louise, you'll not meddle in other people's affairs. Accept the situation. After all, since when have you enjoyed children's company? You're better with computers and things. That's the best way for you to help.'

'Please don't be telling me what to do, Dad. Haven't you noticed I'm a grown woman now?'

'In that case then, you should have more sense and behave like one. Finished, Sheila?'

'Well, yes, but I want . . .'

'Thank you, Ralph and you too, Muriel, for a very nice lunch. We'll do the same for you sometime. Come along, Sheila, we've lots to do.'

'Lots to do? What have we got to do then?' But Ron took her by the elbow and hurried her out. Louise gulped down the remains of her meal and after a quick, 'Goodbye,' she too left.

Ralph finished the last drops of his coffee, put down his cup and said, 'I'm afraid there's a big problem there. Let's hope Peter knows how to deal with it.'

'I'm sure he does.'

'Well, we'll see. "A woman scorned" you know . . .'

4

Jimbo was unable to attend the next meeting of the Show committee, due to a severe cold. He'd been determined to go, but Harriet had insisted that he go to bed. 'Next week is absolutely hectic, so if you don't take care *this* week then it's a sure thing you'll be too ill to do anything *next* week. Ask Pat to go instead. After all, she's in charge that day.'

'Brilliant! Of course – ring her up. She'll enjoy all the gossip. Tell her she'll need to call round for my file with all my notes in.'

When Pat called Jimbo was in bed so Harriet gave her the notes and wished her good luck. Pat asked if there was any more news from Northumberland.

'I babysat for them last night and Peter said Caroline's parents were beginning to come round though they were still not out of the woods, obviously. Slight improvement, I understand. Caroline's hoping to come home next week. She's missing the children, to say nothing of Peter.'

'Oh well, that's good news. Them children are missing her and not 'alf.'

'They are. If you don't mind me saying, you're looking very smart tonight. I love your suit.'

'I saw this in a closing-down sale and it fitted. Glad you like it. I didn't really want to dress in the Oxfam shop but I'd no alternative before. I'll make notes of anything important and let Jimbo have these back.' She waved goodbye with the file and pushed her bike up Stocks Row.

There was plenty of laughter coming from The Royal Oak. A while since she'd been in there. If the meeting finished in good time she'd call in. See if Vera and Jimmy were in. She missed her chats over the garden wall with Vera. Pat glanced across to her old cottage as she crossed Church Lane. They'd put new windows in now. Double glazed, too – now that would have been nice. Still, not nearly as nice as where she lived now. She wouldn't change, not for a king's ransom. She wheeled her bike to the dark side of the church hall and put the lock on it. Yer never knew these days, not even in Turnham Malpas. The lights were on and Louise was making the coffee.

'Hi there! Milk and sugar?'

'Yes, please. One sugar.'

'I'm doing the coffee with Caroline being away.'

'She's hoping to be back next week.'

Louise swung round quickly, almost spilling the coffee she was handing to Pat. 'Is she? How do you know?'

'Harriet told me.'

'I see.'

Barry was the next to arrive. 'Two sugars, Louise, and plenty of milk. Make it strong. A man needs something to give him stamina!' He accepted his cup and went across to sit next to Pat. 'Hello, Pat. You're looking great tonight.'

'Thanks, you don't look so bad yourself. New jumper?'

'Yes, Mum bought it me for Christmas. Haven't seen you around.'

'No, well, I've been busy getting the house straight.'

'Any problems, ring for Barry. I shall be only too pleased to pop round and have a coffee in that nice kitchen of yours.' He put his arm around her shoulders and gave her a good squeeze.

'Barry!'

'Go on, give us a kiss!'

Pat pushed him off though at the same time she was quite enjoying his attentions. 'Give over! For goodness sake, what yer thinking of?'

'A kiss, that's what. A kiss from the best girl in the world.'

'Barry!'

'Go on! It'd liven up the meeting, wouldn't it, Louise?'

'I don't know about that.'

Pat chuckled. 'You've kissed the blarney stone, you 'ave.'

'There's not a drop of Irish blood in my veins. It's you, yer get me going.'

'Well, you're not getting going with me, Barry Jones. Just you watch your step.' It was a long time since any man had paid attention to Pat in that kind of way, and though she wouldn't have admitted it for the world she quite enjoyed his banter. His arm still lying nonchalantly across the back of her chair felt comfortable. She hitched ever so slightly closer to him and he squeezed her shoulder in recognition.

'Coming for a drink in the pub if we finish in time?'

Pat hesitated, then shook her head. She made the excuse that it would be late when they finished and she didn't like cycling up the drive in the dark when it got late.

'Tell yer what, I'll put yer bike in the back of the van and drive you home. How about that? That's worth a drink, isn't it?'

'You still driving that disgusting old van?'

'My Ferrari's being serviced.' He grinned and at such close quarters she could see his beautiful white teeth, evenly spaced and shining, and she sniffed the antiseptic smell of mouthwash on his breath with pleasure.

Pat dug him in the ribs. 'You daft thing.'

'Well?'

'All right then. One drink, that's all.'

Barry held out his empty cup to Louise. 'Here you are, thanks. Let's get this meeting speeded up tonight, I've other fish to fry.'

'Hmmmph!' Pat retorted. 'First time I've been likened to a cod.'

Barry laughed loudly and she could see he hadn't a single filling in his mouth. Somehow that seemed to put him in a class of his own. There weren't many men so careful of themselves that they hadn't got a single filling by the time they reached forty.

Louise called the meeting to order. She tapped the end of her pen on her saucer and said loudly, 'Can we begin, please? There's a lot to get through. Thank you. Good evening, everybody. Firstly, apologies via Peter for Caroline's absence. I understand her parents are showing some improvement at last, though they are still very ill and will be in hospital for some time yet. Also from Jimbo, who has a severe cold. Pat has come in his stead. Give him our best wishes, Pat, please, when you see him. Now, you've all received a copy of the minutes of the last meeting. Are there any matters arising?'

Bryn asked about the hot-air balloon situation. Had anything been done?

Pat nervously spoke up. 'In 'is notes Jimbo says the friends of 'is who 'ave the balloon are willing to come. They'll charge £5 a head for a turn. It sounds an awful lot of money, doesn't it, but the cash they take will be donated to a charity.'

Michael Palmer thought that seemed very reasonable. 'I'd give £5 for a turn. Never tried it, but I'd like to. I wonder how many passengers they can take at once?'

Pat studied Jimbo's notes. 'Don't know – it doesn't say. He's given me a list of the food and the prices he'll be charging. There's a copy for everyone.' She passed the pile around the circle and they each took one.

Sheila Bissett was horrified. 'Fifty pence for a cup of tea? At our flower-arranging society we only charge twenty-five pence. That's outrageous. You can see what he's done. Paid a small amount for the concession and then he's charging prices like this. Shameful. It is for charity, after all.' She scanned further down the list. 'And look at this – fifty pence for a sausage roll!'

Pat leapt to his defence. 'Yes, and if you went into one of them posh cafés in Culworth, what would you pay there? Ninety-five pence for a small pot of tea. Nearly a pound for a scone with butter and jam. I think his prices are quite reasonable in the circumstances.'

'And what circumstances are those, pray?'

'Proper tables and chairs to sit at. Proper cups, not those blasted paper things that burn yer 'ands and make the tea taste like cardboard. Nice knives and spoons, not them blessed plastic things, and serviettes. And you've got to take into account the losses he stands from people nicking the cutlery. I reckon someone took enough for a whole set when we did the catering for a company "do" in Culworth. Six of each. Just wish I'd caught 'em at it. Besides which, you have nice smart pleasant waitresses serving at the counter and clearing the tables. I know 'cos I shall be organising 'em.'

'And what do you, with your education, know about arranging such matters?'

Barry, who had been slowly coming to the boil during this attack on Pat, now rose to his feet, crossed the circle of chairs and stood feet apart, pointing his finger in Sheila's face.

'Any more lip from you and we'll start talking about *your* education and *your* past, shall we?'

Michael quickly intervened. 'I say let's cool it, this isn't right.'

Jeremy tut-tutted and suggested Barry sat down.

Bryn shook his head and Linda blushed.

'I will when she's apologised. I'm waiting.'

Pat, embarrassed at his defence of her when she was quite capable of defending herself, muttered. 'It really doesn't matter, you know. I don't care.'

'No, but I do. Well? I'm still waiting.'

Louise quietly said to her mother, 'There's no call for that.'

Linda, who had never liked Sheila because in her opinion Sheila always treated her like something that had crawled out from under a stone, piped up with, 'I don't know what education has to do with it. If Mr Charter-Plackett has asked Pat to be in charge then he must think she's capable, and I myself think the prices are very reasonable.'

'So do I,' Bryn said, having grown weary of Sheila challenging every decision. 'Sit down, Barry, do and let's get on.'

Remembering that he wanted the meeting to finish in reasonable time so he could take Pat for a drink, Barry reluctantly agreed and sat down, putting his arm across the back of Pat's chair again as though that was where it belonged. Pat shuffled away from him a bit and he removed his arm and looked glum for the rest of the meeting.

Bryn said, 'Well, we've organised the food and the hot-air balloon rides, now I'm going to talk about the events in this arena Mr Fitch wants. I've scheduled things to happen so they don't clash, and so we don't get similar events following on after each other. First there's the fancy-dress parade, then the tug-of-war between the two pubs – I've put that early so they can compete before they've all had too much to drink. I'm donating a barrel of beer for the winners, as you know.'

There was a general murmur of thanks for his generosity which he acknowledged with a nod of his head. 'I understand that Sir Ronald,' he nodded his head in the direction of Sheila, 'will be starting them off. Best of three, I think. After that there's the school display, then the Morris Dancing.' He nodded enquiringly at Louise who agreed it was all in hand. 'Then the police motorcycle display team have agreed to come on. Oh – and to finish, there'll be the children's races. Thought that would keep the kids and their parents there all afternoon. I think that about sums it up.'

'Excellent! Well done!' Jeremy complimented Bryn.

'Absolutely, Bryn, that's great! Thank you very much indeed. What a lot of hard work.' Briskly consulting her list, Louise suggested they got on with the business in hand.

Bryn nodded and said, 'By the way, I'll leave *all* the children's fancy-dress competition to you, Michael – classes, prize, age groups, et cetera?'

'Of course.'

'We'll definitely have that as the first event in the arena then. Otherwise the costumes will be ruined if they have to wait. We'll do a grand procession round the Show, finishing in the arena. Could you sort some judges out, Michael?'

Briskly Louise pushed on through the agenda, and much to Barry's delight it closed within another half an hour, leaving him plenty of time to take Pat for a drink.

'Good night, everybody. See you on the twelfth of next month.'

'Not the twelfth, Barry. It's Friday the thirteenth!'

'Oh you, that's right.'

While Barry was putting her bike in his van, he said, 'I could have strangled that Sheila.'

'Oh, don't worry, she's always like that. Oh Gawd, me bell's dropped off. Did yer hear it? Just a minute while I look for it. Here it is – rusted away it has, I'll have to get a new one.'

Barry put it in his pocket. 'I'll fix it for yer, Pat, leave it to me. Come on, hop in and we'll drive round.'

They parked the van in the car park behind the pub and walked round to the saloon door. Barry held it open for Pat and she popped in under his arm. As she straightened up she saw, sitting at her favourite table, Sylvia and Willie and opposite them Jimmy, whom she hadn't spoken to in a long while.

'What will yer 'ave?'

Pat hesitated and decided she'd get more trendy than in the past. 'I'll have a gin and tonic, please. Shall we go and sit with Jimmy and them?'

Barry didn't want to, but on the other hand he might be pushing things along too fast if he insisted they sat alone. Make too much of a point of his intentions in front of everyone.

'Yes, fine, I'll get the drinks.'

When Sylvia saw Pat coming across she slid further along the settle to make room for her.

Jimmy grinned at her. 'Well, Pat, long time no see. Too posh are yer nowadays then?'

'Enough of your cheek, Jimmy Glover. I've been far too busy getting straight as you well know. Just because I'm living in the Garden House doesn't mean I've given up on me friends. Hello Sylvia, hello Willie.'

She plumped down on the settle making sure she wasn't creasing her skirt.

'Must say you're looking smart, where've you been?' Jimmy commented.

'To the Show committee meeting in place of Jimbo, he's got a shocking cold and Harriet wouldn't let him go. Right meeting we've 'ad and not 'alf.'

Jimmy, always ready for a bit of gossip, said, 'Let's get your drink in and then yer can tell us.'

'That's all right, thanks, Barry's getting mine. Will yer mind if he sits with us?'

There was a chorus of, 'Of course not,' just as Barry came to the table with the drinks.

Jimmy greeted him with, 'Evenin', Barry. Don't see you in here much.'

'No.' Sylvia moved up a little further and Barry squeezed in beside Pat. 'I'm a Jug and Bottle man myself, but this was the nearest tonight. It's quite nice in here, isn't it? I might change my allegiance.' He smiled at Pat, showing those lovely white teeth again, and she smelt the mouthwash. She'd never known before that mouthwash could be so . . . so . . .

Willie urged Pat to tell them what had happened at the meeting.

'Sheila Bissett's put her foot in it again.'

Barry banged down his glass and said, 'Bloody woman! Needs her brains examining, saying Pat couldn't run the refreshment marquee! For two pins I'd have throttled her.'

Pat chuckled. Jimmy, unable to resist making a comment about Pat's escort, gave Barry a sly look and then said, 'It'll be a long way up that drive this time o' night on yer bike, Pat.'

'Mind yer own business, Jimmy.'

'It *is* my business. Me and Willie 'ere have been guarding your interests for a long time. We don't want you cycling up there in the dark, do we, Willie?' Willie agreed. 'Can I offer yer a lift in me taxi?' Jimmy asked.

Pat felt a fool. She blushed.

Barry laughed. 'Yer can stop digging for clues – *I'm* taking her home. Her bike's in my van right now.'

'Oh well then, I'm relieved. I know she'll be in capable 'ands with you, Barry. Oh yes, very capable hands. Very capable . . . hands.'

There was something about the twinkle in Jimmy's eye and the smirk on

Willie's face which made Pat question what Jimmy had said. 'What do you mean by that?'

Jimmy jerked his thumb in Barry's direction. 'Ask 'im.'

'Well?'

'I don't know what he's talking about. Take no notice, Pat.'

'Why have you gone red then?'

'I haven't.' But he had. Bright red and very embarrassed.

Willie chuckled. 'Casanova. That's what he is. Casanova.'

'He's had more girls in the last twenty years than I've had hot dinners,' Jimmy sniggered.

'That wouldn't be difficult, seeing as it's mostly pork pie and a bag of crisps for yer dinner,' Pat retorted. Oddly she felt quite pleased Barry was inclined that way. It would make life more exciting. Her Doug had been about as sexually active as a monk. She never did quite understand how she had ever managed to conceive twice.

'Come on then, Barry, if yer've finished yer drink. I've an early start in the morning, and it was already beginning to freeze when we left the meeting.' Barry squeezed out from the settle followed by Pat. Behind Barry's back Jimmy gave her the thumbs-up and Sylvia flashed her a wink.

Barry shouted, 'Night all,' as they both left.

As he helped her climb up into the van, he said, 'Take no notice of what they were saying in there.'

'Doesn't matter to me. You're only giving me a lift 'ome. Why should I worry?'

'Oh I see.' She was glad when he shut the doors. The air was freezing cold. In the short time they'd been outside her nose had gone cold and she was shivering.

'No heater in this old wagon, I expect?'

'No. I'm a hot-blooded man meself, don't need no heating.'

'Hot, are yer? So it *is* true?'

'Look! They were only pulling yer leg. OK, I haven't reached forty without having been around a bit. You wouldn't have it otherwise, would you?'

'No, I suppose not. I like a man to be a man. Anyway, it doesn't matter to me.' The slush of the last few days had now become treacherous ice. The wheels made crisp crunching sounds on the hardened ruts and ridges of the road surface. As they turned into the drive gates the van slewed across the road and almost slid into the stone pillars.

'Mind out, Barry! Watch it!'

'OK. OK. Keep yer hair on!'

Barry parked the van close to the estate tractors and the two motor mowers. Across the yard Pat saw Grandad's light was still on. She could pick out the pattern on his curtains. My, they were lovely. They were

Michelle's choice, she had a good eye for colour she had. She saw Dean's light go off. Time she was in bed too.

'Thanks for the lift, Barry. How d'yer open this door?'

'Yer can't from the inside. There's something the matter with the lock.'

'Is that your idea of a joke?'

'Certainly not. Try it for yerself.'

She did and it wouldn't open.

'There's a price to pay. Give me a kiss and then I'll open it.'

'I should cocoa. I'm out of practice. Seven years since my Doug died, and I 'aven't kissed a man since. Not that I kissed him all that much when he was here. He wasn't the kissing kind.'

'I am. There's nothing like kissing a good woman, specially one who's nicely rounded like you. I prefer something to get hold of. Don't fancy stick-insect women. Come on, let's have a go.'

The idea was more tempting than he would ever know. Inside her, there welled up feelings she'd been ignoring for years. The touch of someone who appreciated her, her as she was, simply her. Pat. Pat Stubbs that was. 'You are daft. Go on then. Just a little peck and then I'm off in.'

'I've got you in my clutches and besides, I've also got yer bike. There's no escape, Pat Duckett. Come 'ere.'

Her handbag was in the way, and Jimbo's file dug relentlessly into her thigh. It must have dug into Barry's too because he thrust it impatiently onto the floor amongst the oily rags and toffee papers and the sawdusty bits around her feet. She opened her mouth to protest but he closed his lips on her open mouth and kissed her like she'd never been kissed before. She didn't respond, didn't eagerly give back what he was giving her, but she liked it. Oh yes, she liked it. She couldn't release her feelings but they were there, they had surfaced. A few more tries and she might give as good as she got. His hands began wandering . . .

'That'll do, Barry Jones. You've had yer kiss now let me out.'

As she waited for him to lift her bike out, she looked at the house and thought she saw Dean's curtain flick back into place.

'Good night, Pat. By jove, we could be good together, I can feel it. I'll be round for coffee tomorrow morning. See yer.'

5

Barry turned up for coffee the morning after the Show committee meeting, just as he'd promised. Pat hadn't believed he would but she'd made sure when she got back from school that her hair was brushed – she was growing out her frizzled perm so it was difficult to make it look good, but she did her best. She'd changed from her school trousers and jumper and was wearing a skirt and sweater she'd spent a fortune on in M & S. It wasn't really meant to be for every day, but just in case he meant what he said she'd put it on. There was a pile of ironing to do so that seemed to be the easiest rather than him finding her sweating over cleaning the windows or something.

She snapped the board open, banged the iron on it and plugged it in. Now she'd two men to iron shirts for, the weekly ironing seemed to take an age. Barry didn't seem to wear shirts – well, not proper shirts, just T-shirts and things under thick sweaters. She thought about his abundant black hair, nearly like an Arab's, and those laughing brown eyes. Doug had been gloomy, Barry was jolly. Barry oozed sex; Doug had oozed sweat. When she thought about it, in her darker moments she'd often wondered why on earth she'd married him in the first place. Liked the idea of a wedding day, she supposed. The excitement of showing off an engagement ring. The thrill of walking arm in arm with a man, and it had seemed a good escape from that dreary job in the café . . . She was just finishing the last of her father's handkerchiefs, when she heard Barry's van skidding into the yard.

Pat tried to remain unconcerned, but her heart skipped a beat and that strange feeling she'd experienced when he'd kissed her surfaced again.

The back door shot open.

'Morning, Pat. Got the kettle on? I've only got fifteen minutes.' He was standing in the doorway laughing at her. Pat bent down to unplug the iron.

'Not for you I haven't, but I'm having one.'

'Aw now, Pat. You promised.'

'No, I didn't. You said you were coming, I didn't promise anything.'

'Come on, Pat, do a fella a good turn. I've been working since just after seven, and it's half-past ten, OK?'

Pat grinned. 'OK. Just this once, but don't make a habit of it.'

They sat at the kitchen table where Barry had already envisaged he'd be having his bowl of porridge one day. 'Nice kitchen this. Very nice.' He looked round appreciatively. 'I told you this was the right spot for the table, didn't I?'

'You did.'

'Pat!'

'Yes?'

'There's a new theme park opened, have the kids been to it?'

'No. Got no transport.'

'How about it then?'

'Well, I can't go, can I? There's no bus, and what's more I can't afford it.'

'I mean, shall I take you all?'

Pat took a deep breath and said, 'I don't know about that.'

'We'd go in my car, not the old van. Yer dad can come as well. I like yer dad. He's a skilled craftsman and I've a lot of time for people like him.'

'So are you. He'd never come. By the time he's done a week's hard graft gardening up at the Big House he's ready for his chair and the racing weekends. I'll ask the kids, see what they say. Dean's getting a bit old for gallivanting with his mother.'

Barry drank the last drops of his coffee, put down his cup and said, 'There's a chance, then?'

'Perhaps.'

'Saturday, I thought. I'm a real kid at those sort of things. I have a go on everything that moves, every blessed thing there is.'

'OK. We'll see.'

'I'll call tomorrow and you can tell me what you think.'

'OK.' For the first time since he'd entered the house Pat looked directly at him. She'd never noticed how long his eyelashes were, nor how strong his hands looked, resting tensely on the table, locked tightly finger to finger. This morning there was a faint smell of aftershave. He stood up, leaned across and kissed her. He tasted of sweetness, and kindness, and security today.

'Any coffee going, Pat?' It was Dad calling from the back door, as he stopped to pull off his boots.

'I'll be off. Persuade Michelle to come. Morning, Greenwood.'

'Morning, Barry. Jeremy's looking for you. Old Fitch is on the warpath, been on the phone from London for nearly half an hour. If I were you I'd look busy and be quick about it.'

'Right. Bye, Pat!'

'Bye.' Pat went to the cupboard to get a mug. 'How's things, Dad? You don't usually come in for coffee.'

'No, well, I saw his van, and I knew Jeremy was looking for 'im. They're getting him a mobile then he won't be able to sneak off. Got in the habit of calling to see 'er at Home Farm, before that the Nightingales.'

'The Nightingales? God! As if she isn't busy enough with that brood of hers.'

Greenwood looked wise. 'Ah, well. Yer'd better watch out, if he's started calling here. My coffee ready? I 'aven't got all day.'

After Dad had gone Pat went back to the ironing. She was in two minds. Furious with herself for not knowing what Barry got up to, but at the same time captivated by him. Well, blow it. So long as he didn't get her into bed why shouldn't she have a fling? Someone to take her out in his car, someone to laugh with – and heaven alone knew, there'd been little enough of *that* these last years. She'd browbeat Michelle into going to the theme park come Saturday – she'd *pay* her to go, anything so long as Barry took them out. Why shouldn't she have some fun? Why ever not? Right, Barry Jones, you're on. Oh no! Half-past eleven. She unplugged the iron again, threw on her coat and wool hat, grabbed her bike and fled down the drive to the school.

After the school dinner was finished and the children were out at play, Mr Palmer left Mrs Hardaker in charge and disappeared into his house for half an hour's break. Pat, needing some more cleaning materials, went across to the schoolhouse to interrupt his rest and ask for some petty cash.

'Hello-o-o, Mr Palmer! Hello! Anyone at home?' She knocked on the door but getting no reply, pushed it open and called down the passage. 'Hello! It's only me!' The sitting-room door was partly open so Pat pushed it wider and saw Mr Palmer standing by his sideboard with a silver photo frame in his hand and what appeared to her to be a daft expression on his face. She cleared her throat. 'Excuse me – I did knock.'

Mr Palmer jumped and hastily put away the frame in the open sideboard drawer and slammed it shut. 'You made me jump, Mrs Duckett. What can I do for you?'

'Well, Mr Palmer, I'm needing petty cash for cleaning materials. I'm a bit short this week otherwise I would have got them and then asked for a refund. Sorry to disturb you. I did shout but you didn't hear me.'

'No, no. Sorry. Right. I'll get the petty cash out. Ten-pound note be enough?'

'Oh, yes. I'll bring the change back. It's bleach for the lavatories and the kitchen sink, and polish and window cleaner.'

Mr Palmer disappeared into the kitchen. Pat knew he'd be a few minutes, he kept the petty cash well locked up. She tiptoed across to the sideboard and after one quick check at the kitchen door, slipped the drawer open and found herself staring at Suzy Meadows. She swiftly shut the drawer and went back to where she'd been standing, her head racing with thoughts. He'd kept *that* quiet. Who'd have thought . . . Mr Palmer came back.

'Oh thanks, Mr Palmer. I'll be back with the bill and the change.'

'I'll be in school when you get back, so bring it to me in my office.'

'Right-ho.'

Suzy Meadows. Well! She wouldn't believe it. No one had heard a thing about her since the rector and Dr Harris had adopted the twins. Just fancy if the rector knew! Or more so, if Dr Harris knew! The crafty monkey, he must have been in contact with her all this time. Over two years since she'd left. Must be, 'cos the twins were born beginning of December and they were over two now. Wait till she told Jimmy and them, they'd be amazed. Then she thought about how kind Mr Palmer had always been to her, and how much she'd liked Suzy Meadows when she'd lived in the village, and how lovely Suzy's three girls had been. Stupid names – Daisy, Pansy and Rosie. Beautiful girls, though.

The bell on the door of the Store pinged joyously as Pat pushed it open.

'Hello, Jimbo! Am I glad to get inside. It's still so cold. Hope this blessed slush will be gone soon. Can't be soon enough for me. Cold better?'

'Not much, but thanks for asking. Meeting go all right?'

'Yes, thanks. Usual arguing and gossiping. I've brought you up to date in your file. Here it is.'

'Oh good! Must press on. I'll look at it later.'

The Store was busy. People who'd put off coming out shopping while the snow was at its worst, had now decided they couldn't wait any longer and were busy stocking up. Barry's mother was the centre of a small group exchanging news, thankful of an outlet at last after being incarcerated by the snow.

Barry's mother had to move to allow Pat to reach for the bottle of bleach. Pat made a pretence of studying the different brands on offer to give herself an opportunity to find out what they were talking about.

Barry's mother put down her wire basket, and folding her arms said, 'So, he's been seen with 'er by our Terry *and* our Kenny when they went there to the races at New Year.'

'No!'

'True as I'm 'ere. With 'er *and* 'er girls. Course, I'm saying nothing. I'm drawing no conclusions.' She drew herself up self-righteously and looked round the attentive group. 'It doesn't do to gossip, does it? But really! She's third-hand and not half. Bet the rector, God bless him, 'ud be surprised if he knew!'

By mistake, Pat knocked Barry's mother's arm as she reached for the bleach.

'Oh sorry, Mrs Jones.'

'Hello there, Pat. We're just talking about your Mr Palmer. Right sly old fox he is, don't yer think?'

'It so happens I have the greatest respect for Mr Palmer. He's a very nice person to work with. And if you're gossiping about 'im then I don't want to hear.'

Barry's mother gave her arm a nudge. 'Oh come on, Pat, don't tell us you don't know. You must. He's seeing Suzy Meadows. Thick as thieves they are. It's all round the village. Bet you could tell us a thing or two.'

'I couldn't and I wouldn't. You should watch your tongue. One day you'll get sued for what you say, you will.'

'Listen who's talking! Whiter than white are we? Huh! You've passed on some rare bits of gossip in your time, Pat Duckett. Gone all hoity toity now, have yer, since yer've gone to live at the Garden House.'

'No, I haven't, but I don't pass scandal on about someone who doesn't deserve it.'

'That's cheek, that is, Pat. Accusing me of stirring it. Don't come to me when you want to know the latest. Giving yerself airs!'

Pat shrugged her shoulders and went to the till. 'Give me a bill, will yer, Jimbo? It's for the school.'

Over the shelves Pat heard Barry's mother say, 'Listen to 'er! Jimbo this and Jimbo that! Who does she think she is?'

Jimbo winked at her. Pat chuckled and left.

Mr Palmer was in his little office when she got back to the school. Everyone called it his office but all it really consisted of was a desk, a chair, and a wash basin, with a curtain across one corner for the teachers to put their coats behind. If a parent came to see him, they sat in his chair and he propped himself on the wash basin.

Pat put her head round the door. 'There you are! Here's the change and the bill. I'll be off now. See yer later, Mr Palmer. Snow'll soon be gone, thank goodness.'

As she mounted her bike out in Jacks Lane, Barry passed in his van. He pulled up with a shriek of brakes and the slush in the road sprayed wildly about, catching Pat's boots and bike wheels. She jumped to one side as best she could.

'Eh, Barry! What yer doing? Watch out!'

Barry leaned out of the window. 'Sorry! It was the shock of seeing you – got my blood racing. How's things?'

'Same as they were when I saw yer last. Middling!'

'Don't forget to ask your Michelle, will you? I'm looking forward to it. One whole day in your company!'

'I'm looking forward to it as well.' She put her hand on the edge of the open window. 'I haven't asked our Michelle, not in school-time. I'll ask her tonight. I'm sure she'll say yes.'

He leaned out of the window and tried to kiss her, but Pat dodged away. Barry laughed, bunched his fingers, kissed them with a flourish, put the van into gear and drove away, taking the corner into Church Lane with more speed than sense. Neither Pat nor Barry had seen his mother standing at the corner of Shepherds Hill and Jacks Lane watching them. Neither of them saw her lips press firmly together in annoyance. As everyone in the village knew to their cost, Barry's mother's displeasure was something to be taken seriously.

6

Peter took the children with him when he went to pick up Caroline from the station. They'd been awake since six. Having no one at home to care for them while he said his early-morning prayers in the church, Peter had had to abandon his half-hour prayers and his three-mile morning run with Jimbo until Caroline got back, so he'd been containing them and entertaining them that morning for what seemed like half a year. The need for re-establishing his life pattern was growing; his routine of having Caroline around him, of breathing her scent, of holding her, of knowing she was there picking up the pieces. God, he'd be glad to have her back. He'd taken to touching her coat in the hall cupboard whenever he had to open it and sometimes when he didn't need to. He just deliberately held the door open and absorbed the feeling of Caroline by holding her coat. It was the longest time they'd been apart since their wedding day.

At the very least her return would sort out the problems with Louise and Sylvia. What a fortnight it had been! Placating one, confiding in the other. He couldn't manage without either of them, with Caroline away. But he had to finish with Louise, even if she did make his life easier and free him for the parish. Caroline would see to everything, that was for sure.

In his rearview mirror he spotted Alex trying to undo the fastening on his safety seat. 'Alex, no! Leave that, please. We shan't be long, the station's only five minutes away.'

Peter found a place in the station car park, and with a twin firmly gripped in either hand, he marched to the station entrance. Beth took fright at the size of the station concourse and had to be picked up. She clung to him, her soft cheek against his own, her eyes closed, her breath fluttering rapidly on his neck. He checked the arrival screen and mercifully he'd got there on time. 'Platform seven it says, children. We've got to go over the bridge. Come along, Alex. Hurry. Big steps. Up! One, two, three.' Beth struggled to get down. 'Me, me.' She climbed the steps too, her sturdy little legs trying to keep pace with Peter's.

As they reached the platform on the other side, Caroline's train drew in.

Passengers came pouring off. For a moment Peter couldn't see Caroline and then he did. His heart bounded with joy. 'Look! There she is, children! There she is! There's Mummy!'

As she walked towards them, Peter rejoiced in her strong determined walk, her dark hair blowing in the wind which swirled so cruelly along the platform, her sparkling eyes, the sheer joy the sight of her gave him. Caroline put down her cases. The children clung to her legs with cries of delight, Peter kissed her, she kissed him, she kissed the children and then Peter again, then hugged the children close. 'Darlings! I'm so glad to be home. I'm sure you've grown. Alex, you've had your hair cut!'

'Yes, he has. It kept falling into his eyes and annoying him and I knew you wouldn't like that. And, yes, I think they *have* grown. Are we glad to see you. You take the children, I'll carry your cases. How's things at the hospital?'

'Well, both Mother and Dad are improving every day. Mother's got this mad idea she's going to discharge herself. Which of course is ridiculous as she has both legs in plaster and a fractured skull and three broken ribs and terrible bruising. She's making their lives hell in there. Dad keeps trying to calm her down and constantly reminds her that she's the patient and not the doctor at the moment, but it's no good, she won't behave herself. In some ways I'm quite glad I've come away, she's so embarrassing!'

'Sounds as though she's on the mend.'

'She is. Oh yes, she is. I may go back up there when they both come out, just for a few days. But that won't be for some time yet. Hurry up, I'm longing to get back home and catch up on all the news.'

When Peter unlocked the front door of the rectory, he called out: Sylvia, we're back!' Alex and Beth ran straight to the kitchen, shouting 'Sylvie, Sylvie, Mummy come. Mummy come on train.' But there was no reply.

On the kitchen table was a note.

Welcome home. Glad you're back. Thought it would be nice for you to have the place to yourselves for a while. Casserole and jacket potatoes in oven. Fruit pie in fridge. Kettle just boiled. Cake in cake box. Messages in study. See you 8 a.m. tomorrow.

Yours, Sylvia

'Isn't that lovely of her? She's so thoughtful. I don't know what we'd do without her.'

It wasn't until they were in bed that night that Peter confessed how close they'd come to losing her.

'Her notice? I don't believe this. How could you let it happen?'

'I didn't let it happen. It just nearly did.'

'If she goes, then I've had it. I won't cope.'

'We'd get someone else.'

'There's no one like Sylvia. She and I understand one another. She can't be replaced.'

'Don't worry, darling. She's still here. You mustn't fret.'

'It was Louise interfering, wasn't it?'

'Well, yes.'

'I knew it. The woman's a menace.'

'She's a tremendous help to me. She's so efficient and full of bright ideas. I don't know how I managed before she came.'

'I see. Has she got a proper job yet?'

'No.'

'I see. Has she been for any interviews?'

'No.'

'I see.'

'You keep saying "I see". You must have a very clear picture in your mind by now.'

'Oh, I have. I always have had about her. The way she feels about you is there in her face whenever she looks at you.'

'What *do* you mean?'

'Peter, you are an absolute darling! You never notice, do you, that Louise actually glows when she looks at you. She tries hard to disguise it, but she can't – not from *me* anyhow. However, there's one thing I'm sure of – it isn't *she* who's in bed with the handsomest man there ever was, but *me*, so we're going to enjoy ourselves. It's been such a long time . . .'

Over breakfast, Caroline told Peter he should tell Louise she was not needed any more. 'After all, losing Sylvia would be a greater loss than Louise going, believe you me.'

'In my own time, Caroline, in my own time. I have absolutely no justification for asking her to stop working for me. She's in the middle of the quarterly magazine and saving me hours of typing time. I'm sorry, I can't dismiss her out of hand. Just allow me to do it gradually. Please. This is my area, after all.'

'Agreed. It is. Sorry, I forgot. But I won't brook any interference in my domain. What's sauce for the . . .'

'Right.' He looked at her, enjoying her early-morning look, and the dampness of her hair fresh from the shower. 'Love you. Last night . . .'

Caroline put her hand on his as he reached out to her across the kitchen table. 'I know. Love you.' Their brief moment together was split apart by Beth, who had crammed her mouth with toast and was quietly choking. 'Oh, heavens above!'

They were in his study going over the notices for the following Sunday so Caroline would be up to date, when Peter couldn't resist holding her tight and kissing her. Neither of them noticed that Sylvia had been to the front door to let Louise in. The first they knew was the study door opening and Louise saying, 'Good morning, Peter . . . Oh, sorry!'

Caroline was furious with herself for allowing Louise to catch them embracing, but on the other hand perhaps it would serve to emphasise that there were no grounds for thinking she might make progress with Peter.

'Good morning, Louise. How's things?' Caroline said.

'Very well, thanks. Nice to have you back. We've managed to keep things going, haven't we, Peter?'

He nodded in reply. Louise asked after her parents and then Caroline excused herself and went to attend to the children.

'Now let's get down to work.' Peter smiled his devastating smile and Louise's insides flipped. Oh God, he was gorgeous. She felt a powerful jealousy of Caroline and her intimacy with him.

'The magazine is nearly ready for putting together. Just needs my letter for the inside page and then you can finish laying it out. After that there'll be the photocopying and the collating and stapling. From then on I can't take advantage of you any longer. You must have time to concentrate on getting a new position.'

'Are you saying you don't want me to come any more?'

'Not that, no. I'm merely being considerate to you. No one can manage nowadays without a regular income, and I'm trying to give you the time to attend to that.'

'But I *want* to help. I can go for interviews any time. Who'll do the weekly *Parish News*? Who'll collect the material for the magazine? Who'll type all the parish correspondence? You can't, you've enough to do.'

'Somehow or other I'll manage. There must be lots of people who would be glad to assist. Your help has been invaluable, but my conscience won't allow me to let you do it any longer.'

'Don't let your conscience worry you.' Louise turned swiftly in her chair and staring straight at him with an angry face said, 'Is this because of Sylvia? Has she said something?'

'No. Certainly not. I make my own decisions.' Louise was tempted to ask if it was Caroline who had queered her pitch, but quickly changed her mind. That would alienate him and she couldn't face that. The sun was coming in through the study window, catching the red-gold glints in his hair, making, as she saw it, a halo around his head. He looked so handsome, so . . . charismatic. She could feel his strong vibes reaching her from across the room. Perhaps one day she would be stroking that wonderful head of hair and . . . Then she remembered someone saying that Peter had looked so penetratingly at them, they genuinely believed he'd read their thoughts. What if he was reading hers right now?

Swamped by her emotions and quite unable to control her feelings for

Peter, Louise burst into tears and fled from the study. Startled by her reaction Peter called for Caroline.

She appeared at the study door, her arms full of clean laundry. 'Yes?'

'It's Louise, have you seen her just now?'

'No.'

'She's burst into tears and run out.'

'Run where?'

'I don't know. Somewhere. You go and find her – please. I mustn't.'

'Right. What have you been doing to her, I ask myself.'

'Absolutely nothing. As you well know.'

Caroline grinned, put down the laundry on the hall table and went in search of her. She noticed the front door slightly ajar. Panicking, she shouted, 'Sylvia! Have you got the children?'

'They're both here with me, cleaning your bathroom.'

'OK, thanks. Peter, she must have gone home. She's left the front door open. Has she taken her bag and things?'

'Her bag's here.'

'Give it to me.' Her coat had gone from the hall cupboard, so Caroline put her own coat on and taking Louise's bag set off for the Bissetts' cottage.

The snow had gone completely now and the sun had broken through the clouds. The sight of the cottages ranged round the village green, the pond and Jimmy's geese, brought joy to Caroline's heart. How she loved living here. Timeless, beautiful, welcoming, enriching . . . she couldn't find enough words to describe how much it all meant to her. You could keep all your big impersonal cities, with their high-rise flats and their smoke and their traffic. There might not be much happening hereabouts, but it nourished her soul.

She tapped briskly on the door of the Bissetts' cottage. No one came. She tapped again and then after a moment the door opened. It was Sheila, looking upset.

'Good morning, Sheila.'

'Good morning, Caroline. Come in.' She opened the door wider and Caroline stepped in. It was the first time she'd been in Sheila's cottage, and somehow the décor didn't take her by surprise. It was just how she had imagined Sheila would have decorated it. Sweetly pretty, overdone with frills and furbelows, pretty, non-controversial water-colour prints lined up on the walls and artificial flower arrangements placed in every conceivable spot.

'Terribly sorry, Sheila, but Louise seems to be upset. Has she come home?'

Sheila nodded.

'She's left her bag and things. Here they are. We don't know . . .'

'She won't tell me.'

'Should I see her?'

'If you like.' They'd conducted their conversation in stage whispers, but now Sheila said in a voice slightly louder than normal, 'Do come in, Dr Harris. I'm sure Louise will be pleased to see you.'

She was sitting scrunched up in a corner of Sheila's sofa, desperately trying to look as though nothing was the matter. But her eyes were red, her cheeks blotchy. When she saw Caroline she straightened herself up and attempted to give herself more presence.

'Louise! I'm so sorry. Can you possibly tell me what has upset you? Peter's distraught that it might be something he's said.'

Louise swallowed hard. 'Oh no, it's nothing he's said – no, not at all. He's too kind to say anything to upset *me*. Well, not intentionally anyway.'

'So what's caused all this? It's not like you. Is it the time of the month? If so, Peter will understand.'

Sheila froze with embarrassment; she was scandalised. Rectors shouldn't know about private things like that.

Louise flushed and said, 'Oh no, it's nothing like that. It's just that Peter said after the magazine was finished he wouldn't be needing me any more. He only said it out of kindness, I know, because he's anxious I have time to get a job. But I do so love coming across to the rectory and helping. It feels really worthwhile. Such a lovely atmosphere to work in. A real home. A truly welcoming place to be, and I would miss it.'

She looked up and gave Caroline a trembling smile. The compliment about her home won Caroline over despite all her wariness of Louise, and before she realised it she was saying, 'Look, if you like working for Peter, well, that's fine by me. After all, you only come three mornings. That gives you plenty of time for interviews and things, doesn't it? Peter does appreciate your help. He's so slow at typing and I'm worse than him, so it's no good me trying to help. I'm just sorry the church can't afford to pay you, but it can't. Don't let what's happened upset you too much, Louise. Stay at home this morning and we'll start with a clean slate on Wednesday. How about that?'

'Thank you very much. I do appreciate you asking me. You're really kind. I'll be in on Wednesday then. A clean slate, like you said.'

'Good. I'll be off then.'

Sheila asked if she'd like to stay for coffee. 'No, thanks, I've a lot to do this morning – just got back, you see. Another time, perhaps. I'll let myself out.'

Caroline went home to the rectory unable to believe that she'd agreed to, no actually *invited* Louise to continue working there. She considered herself to be either the biggest fool this side of the Cul, or the very best kind of Christian ever.

In the Bissetts' cottage Louise couldn't believe her good luck. She kept dabbing her eyes so her mother wouldn't realise how pleased she was at the turn of events. Underneath, her triumph made her want to burst out laughing. Out of the ashes of her disastrous, ridiculous exit she had got exactly what she wanted. Caroline, not Peter, but *Caroline* asking her to go back to the rectory. What she'd said to make it happen she didn't know, but it had.

'Well, there you are, dear. You see? I told you how lovely Dr Harris is. She *must* like you going there. I heard the rector saying what a great help you are to him. I did tell you how nice they both are.'

'Indeed you did, Mother, indeed you did.'

7

Pat went to get her bike out from under the shed where her father kept the mowers. If she didn't watch out she'd be late for opening up the school. Thank Gawd the last of the snow was gone. A bright winter sun was striking through the trees, and Pat felt a certain lift to her spirits. Truth to tell, she'd felt full of good spirits ever since Saturday. What a brilliant day they'd had. Barry certainly knew how to have a good time. Him going with them had persuaded Dean to go too and they'd had a lovely family day out. Michelle went on everything Barry and Dean went on, and Pat had to admit it was all wonderful: Michelle hand in hand with Barry, Dean opening up and talking more than he'd done for years. He needed a man, did Dean.

Where the blazes was her bike? It was no great prize, but it was all she had. Blast it! Someone had pinched it. She'd have to walk. She turned away cursing the light fingers of someone who could find her old bike worth stealing. Then she noticed propped against one of the mowers a bike which didn't belong to her. There was a luggage label tied to the handlebars. It said:

Dear Pat,
Have mended your bell. Here it is attached to your new bike.
With love, Barry.
P.S. Hope you like it.

It wasn't absolutely brand new, but near enough. And there, neatly fastened to the handlebars, was her old bell, well-oiled and cleaned up. Shining as all bicycle bells should. Pat couldn't believe it. It was no good, she'd have to give it back. She'd use it today and then . . . yes, and then give him it back. Let's hope he hadn't thrown her old bike away.

The saddle needed a bit of adjustment; her feet wouldn't reach the ground.

'Dad! Come here a minute.'

'I'm having my breakfast.'

'Never mind yer breakfast, come here and sharp.'

Grandad came grumbling out of the back door. 'What's so urgent I can't fini— Aye Aye! What's all this then? I didn't know you'd got a new bike.'

'Neither did I. I'm using it today and then it's going back.'

'Who's it from?'

'Guess who?'

'Not Barry?' Pat nodded. 'I warned you about 'im, didn't I?'

'Look, I need it right now to go to school on, then he's getting it back, believe me. Lower the saddle, will yer, Dad? It's getting late. I don't want to let Mr Palmer down. Be sharp.'

'All right. Hold yer horses.'

Michelle came out. 'Oh Mum, a new bike! Where did yer get it from?'

'Barry, and it's going back.'

Michelle was horrified. 'Mum, yer can't give presents back. He'll be ever so upset.'

'I don't care, he's got a cheek.'

'No, he hasn't, Mum, it's your present. He's only being kind. Please don't hurt his feelings.'

'Well, I shall.' Michelle burst into tears and ran inside.

'That it then, Dad? That's better. Thanks. Be nice to her, tell her I can't accept presents from him, no matter what.'

'OK. Off yer go, then.'

She'd be going to the Show committee tonight; she'd tell him then. They weren't at the stage for giving big presents. He'd ruined it all. She whirled along down the drive amazed at how far the bike went with such a small amount of effort. It definitely put her old bike in the shade and not half.

As she swung round into the schoolyard, Mr Palmer was coming back from the Store with his newspaper.

'Morning, Mrs Duckett. New bike, I see.'

'Not for long. It's going back.'

'Why? It looks great.'

'It is. It's the giver who isn't great. However, nice morning, isn't it? See yer later.'

When she'd finished her morning efforts at the school she went to the Store to pick up a few things she needed. A card for Dad for his birthday, some meat for tonight, four pints of milk and a couple of nice bread rolls for Dad at lunchtime. She propped her bike in the stand Jimbo had provided and wandered in.

Linda was concentrating on her accounts behind the post-office grille and Harriet was by the till.

'Hello, Pat. All right?'

'Yes thanks, Harriet. Jimbo's away at the conference today?'

'That's right. Back tomorrow night. Don't let on but Fran's in the back with Mother. Our part-timer's got the flu so I'm having to fill in. Jimbo would explode if he knew.' Pat tapped the side of her nose with her forefinger and promised not to tell.

She went between the shelves looking for the things she needed. She was just choosing her Dad's card when the little brass bell jangled angrily and the door slammed shut with a loud bang. Pat heard Barry's mother's voice. 'Would you mind telling me whose bike that is outside?'

Harriet said, 'Well I don't know really. Lots of people put their bikes there, sometimes even when they're not coming in here.'

Pat popped her head round the end of the card display. 'Someone wanting me?'

'Me.' Barry's mother tapped the lapel of her old brown anorak with a sharp finger as she marched towards Pat. 'Me, that's who. It's yours, is it?'

'Well, in a manner of speaking, yes.'

'I'll have you know that was *my* bike. What are you doing with it?'

Pat fumbled in the bottom of her bag and brought out the luggage label Barry had tied to it. Barry's mother snatched it from her but didn't have her reading glasses.

'I'll read it for you.' Pat took it back and read the words out loud. Harriet turned her back, to hide her laughter. Barry's mother all but exploded.

'He bought that bike from me for a song. I'd no idea he was giving it to *you*.' She became red in the face and for once was speechless.

'Don't you worry, you'll be able to give him his money back, if you haven't already spent it, 'cos he's getting it back tonight. I'm not having him giving me presents.'

'Well, at least you're showing more common sense than I gave you credit for; even so, our Barry's too good for the likes of you.' Harriet gasped. Linda pressed her handkerchief to her mouth in horror. But Barry's mother didn't realise she'd met her match.

Pat went white as a sheet. 'Considering your Barry's past history, I think it's me who's too good for him.'

'Past history?'

'Yes. If all I've heard is true, I'm the one who's in the position to be picking and choosing, not Barry.'

'Well, I never. Not one of my sons . . .'

It was Pat's turn to tap the brown anorak. 'Just a minute, what about your Kenny and that dodgy car? The police couldn't prove it but we all knew. And what about your Barry and his trips up to Nightingale Farm, eh? Or your Terry and that barmaid from The Jug and Bottle – it was her husband who blacked his eyes and broke his nose that time, wasn't it? Don't start denying it or I might remember some more juicy bits about the three of 'em.'

Unable to deny what Pat had said, Mrs Jones tried another method of attack. 'And what have you had to do to get that bike?' she sneered.

At this Pat drew herself up, turned her back on her and stalked out of the store.

Harriet was appalled. So rude. So hurtful. She felt proud of Pat, though; she was the first person she'd ever heard stand up to Mrs Jones. Jimbo would have given his right arm to have been here and heard all that.

'Anything I can get for you, Mrs Jones?' Harriet asked in her sweetest tones.

'No.' And she marched from the store, earrings swinging, breathing fire and intending to give Pat further lashings with her tongue. But she was too late to catch Pat, she was already disappearing up Stocks Row, pedalling furiously. If Mrs Jones could have seen her face she would have seen tears – and Pat hadn't cried in a long time.

It was a cold crisp night, and Pat was well wrapped up for her cycle-ride down the drive to the meeting. She'd debated all day as to whether she should keep the bike to spite Mrs Jones or hand it back like she'd first intended. Michelle was so upset. And Dean had put his pennyworth in, coming down on Michelle's side. 'Mum! He gave us a lovely day out, did Barry, he's really kind. I liked him. Don't be nasty to him.'

'Look, our Dean. You're old enough to understand about grown-ups. I don't want to encourage him. When you get to my age you need to take things steady. It's not like it is with these young things who hop into bed the first night they meet.'

'They're not all like that, Mum.'

'Well, I know, but I need to go steady, and giving me a nearly new bike is rushing his fences.'

'Tell yer what, Mum, I wish I'd seen his mother on it. That'd be a right laugh.' Pat couldn't help smiling at the thought.

By the time she reached the church hall she still hadn't decided what to do, but left the bike in the dark behind the hall well locked up.

Louise was making the coffee tonight, and Pat was the first again.

'Hello, Louise.'

'Hello, Pat. You take sugar, don't you?'

'Yes, please, but only half. I'm trying to lose a bit of weight.'

'It's a slow process, isn't it? I keep trying but it's such hard work when you've got a sweet tooth.'

Pat covertly eyed Louise's figure and secretly agreed she did need to lose weight. 'Chocaholic, that's me.'

'Me too.'

Barry was the next to arrive, his face alight with the anticipation of hearing Pat's gratitude.

'Evening, Pat.' He stood, legs apart, arms folded directly in front of her, waiting expectantly. 'Well then, what d'yer think to it?' His handsome vigorous face was so appealing in its childlike eagerness that Pat couldn't ask him to take it back.

'Well, Barry, I . . .'

'Go on then.'

'I owe you a big thank you. It's the best present I've had in years.'

'Aw Pat, that's great. 'Ere, give us a kiss.' He reached out with both arms, gave her a hug and kissed her cheek in front of the rest of the committee just arriving together.

'Barry!'

'Never mind them, they won't mind. D'yer like it really?'

'It's lovely. It goes so fast. One turn of the pedals and I'm halfway down the drive. It's wonderful. What have yer done with my old one?'

'It's still in the back of the van. Daren't throw it away in case you wouldn't keep yer new one.'

'Our Michelle's dead impressed.'

'Does she need a new bike?'

'No, no, I've bought her one already.'

Barry looked disappointed. 'Anyway, so long as your bike pleases you, that's what counts. Couldn't let you go on any longer with that old thing of yours.'

Linda, sitting on a chair drinking her coffee, put down her cup and said, 'After what went on in the Store today, I'm surprised Pat hasn't thrown it in the beck.' Barry spun round to face her. Pat tried to shut her up, but she was too intent on her story to notice. 'The way your mother treated her, it's a wonder Pat's still speaking to you, Barry Jones. It was a disgrace.'

'What's this all about?' Barry asked Pat.

'Look, I'll tell yer later, all right? Not now. Give me a lift 'ome and then.'

Louise called the meeting to order. 'Can we begin, please? Are we all seated? Right. You have the minutes of the last meeting; are we all agreed to take them as read?' She looked round the circle and they all nodded their assent. 'Right then, matters arising.'

'I'm short of men for the tug-of-war team for The Royal Oak.'

'I need help with the competitions in the flower tent. It's impossible to do it all by myself, much as I try.'

'What are we doing about prizes for the fancy dress?'

'I've got far too many people wanting to have stalls. I'll never get them made in time.'

'Who's going to find all the money for everything? We have no advance funds, only what comes in at the gate on the day.'

'Who's opening it – Sir Ralph?'

'No, he's away all that month.'

'I'm planning for the children's display to last ten minutes. Is that long enough, do you think?'

The problems and queries seemed to last an age and Barry, who was so upset that his lovely idea had apparently been spoiled, scarcely noticed the progress of the meeting.

He only came to life when Louise gave them the date for the next meeting. He stood up. 'Right, that it then? We're off.'

He put Pat's bike in the van alongside her old one, and helped her in. They drove to the Garden House without saying a word. He never even offered her a drink in the pub. When he'd switched off the ignition, he turned towards her and said, 'Well?'

'She was annoyed, very angry in fact, that you'd given her bike to me.'

'I paid her for it.'

'She said you'd got it "for a song".'

'That's not true. I'll tell you something, Pat. I've realised just lately that all I ever do is go after women who are already well-married. That way, you see, they're unobtainable. That way, there's no chance I shall be in a position to commit myself to anything at all. And do you know why?'

'You don't like the idea of being tied down?'

'Well, I suppose it's partly that, but in truth it's because of my mother.'

Pat laughed. 'Come on, Barry, if yer under her thumb that much you can drive off into the sunset right now. We'll call it a day.'

'Our Kenny and our Terry, we're all the same. She rules our house with a rod of iron. Nobody would think we were grown men. Dad's given up, he can't fight any longer. She rules him too. She's no intention of any of us getting married and leaving home. Good money coming in and a purpose in life, that's what it is, and she thinks no one's good enough for us. I'm sorry. I expect she was a complete bitch. But the reason is, you see, you're available, aren't you?'

'Don't know about that.'

'Well, yer know, able to get married if you choose.'

'Avril Nightingale and her at Home Farm certainly weren't available.'

'If you've heard tales about me and Avril you can forget it. Right?'

'Right.'

'Just a bit of fun. Livens up the day.'

'Now we've got that straightened out, I'll be off in.'

'Friends again, then?'

'OK.'

'Take you out Saturday night. Just you and me?'

'Not Saturday, I'm working for Jimbo.'

'Give you a lift there and back?'

'Jimbo takes me. Another night.'

'OK. Coffee next week? Your kitchen?'

'Yes, if yer want. Thanks again for the bike. It's lovely. Good night.'

'That's all right, Pat. Glad I could be of service. I'll get it out for you. Next time my mother picks on you, ignore her. She's a jealous old bitch.'

'Thanks. Good night.'

Dad was waiting up. 'Did yer give him yer bike back then?'

Pat flung her coat and bag on a chair and flopped down beside her dad on the sofa.

'No, I didn't. He was so delighted with himself I couldn't disappoint him.'

'Michelle'll be glad. A dad would be nice for her, and for Dean too.'

'I know. I know. But yer don't marry just to give yer kids a father, do yer?'

'No, but it is a plus, isn't it? And bringing up Dean isn't easy. A good dad would be a help. He'd fit in here. Me with me own room and that.'

'You wouldn't mind then?'

'No. We're two of a kind, Barry and me. Craftsmen, who take pride in our work. Yer could do worse. He has a generous nature.' Dad laughed.

'That story about Avril Nightingale isn't true, right?'

'OK. OK. Right, I'm off to bed.'

'Good night, Dad.' She sat ten more minutes before the fire watching the dying embers. It was no good. She wasn't having all that again. Bed and that. She'd got used to being on her own. No point in upsetting the applecart.

8

The quarterly magazine had reached the stage when several hours had to be spent photocopying all the pages. The copier was squeezed into a spare corner of the choir vestry so Louise, having been forewarned by Peter, always so thoughtful, put on her warmest trousers and sweater and was getting organised for heading off to the vestry one cold Saturday morning.

'Look, take a flask.'

'Mother, please. I'm not a child. If I get cold or thirsty I'll pop into the rectory for a drink. I don't like Thermos coffee, as you well know.'

'All right, dear, I'm only trying to help. You know your Dad's sorry you haven't been getting any interviews. Aren't you beginning to worry?'

Louise put the finishing touches to her face powder before she replied. 'No, not yet. A job will come in its own good time.'

'Yes, dear, but all your savings will be disappearing, won't they?'

Louise patted her mother's arm. 'Don't fret yourself, I'm all right. It's not your problem.'

'Well, I know, but Dad and I haven't got a bottomless pit. He gets a generous pension from the union, and there's his TV and speaking fees and that, but it'll only stretch so far.'

'Tell Dad not to worry. I know what I'm doing.' She bundled some papers into her briefcase and hurried away across the Green.

She knew for a fact that Caroline and the children were visiting a friend's house for the day, which left Peter in the rectory all by himself. Sylvia didn't go in at the weekend, unless it was an emergency, and as it was supposed to be Peter's day off, she had high hopes of a quiet hour with him all to herself.

The choir vestry was empty so Louise set about the copying. She needed to be methodical, because she was copying on both sides of the paper and she wanted it to be absolutely perfect. That was her way. Whatever she did had to be perfect. Sometimes she wished she wasn't like that, wished she was more laid back, gentler, more appealing – softer, more casual. But always people relied on her for perfection, always expected it of her and she'd come to want it herself more than anything.

The front cover had come out really well. That friend of Caroline's had done an excellent design job on it. It was ten o'clock. She decided she needed coffee. She took a copy of the front cover to show Peter. He answered the door as she knew he would.

'Oh, hello. How's it going?'

'Just fine. Look, I've brought you the front cover hot off the press, so to speak. What do you think?'

'Come in. Why, it's brilliant. Really good. Your idea of the yellow paper for the spring edition has worked out beautifully, hasn't it? However did we manage before you came? I'm just making coffee – would you like some?'

'Well, I didn't really expect it, but yes I will. That's most kind. It's so cold in that vestry.'

'Not for long. They start work next week on the central heating.'

'Really? Where have you found the money for it?'

'Mr Fitch at the Big House gave it to us.'

Louise whistled. 'My word. How generous.'

'It certainly was.'

Louise spent a blissful half-hour sitting with Peter in the kitchen, talking about this and that. There were no interruptions, no children calling for Daddy, no wife looking askance at her, no housekeeper looking daggers, no telephone ringing. Just the meeting of two beautiful people.

He looked different in his casual clothes; jeans, the collar of a checked shirt showing at the neck of his black sweater. She admired his big strong hands wrapped round his mug of coffee. All of six feet five, but gentle and vulnerable. Broad-shouldered but needing support. Physically powerful but such a sensitive man. Louise swallowed hard. Her excitement at being alone with him almost overwhelmed the tight rein she had on her emotions; she mustn't let her feelings ruin this wonderful opportunity.

'You must be glad of a day by yourself. The children can be very trying, can't they?'

'I wouldn't be without them for the world. Until one has children of one's own, one doesn't remotely understand how deep the bond between parent and child goes.'

'Caroline does wonderfully with them, doesn't she, considering they're not . . . her . . . own.' She could have bitten her tongue out. The moment he'd realised what she was going to say, a shutter had come down over his face and he'd immediately withdrawn to some place she couldn't follow.

Desperate to retrieve the situation, she hastily added, 'Please forgive me.' She reached across the kitchen table and took his hand. 'I'd no business to say that. I'm so sorry. I have such respect for her, and for you. If I've given offence, please forgive me.'

Still holding his hand, her feelings for him surfaced and her eyes glowed with love, which she quickly veiled when his eyes opened and he said, 'You only spoke the truth. But never, never, *ever* mention the matter again.' He smiled sadly at her as though apologising for his curtness. Her heart went out to him.

Peter stood up and said, 'I promised myself some study-time today while the house is quiet. Would you mind if I got on with that now?'

Louise stood up also. 'Of course. I'll wash up the mugs and then I'll be off. There's still a lot to do.'

She might have overstepped the mark with her choice of subject, but she knew they'd moved closer together through having experienced that delicate moment. She'd certainly touched a raw spot.

The vestry was occupied when she got back. Gilbert Johns was there. He was kneeling down in front of the choir cupboard sorting through his sheet music.

He looked up as she came in. 'Hello, there. Will it be annoying if I look through my choir music while you do that?'

'Of course it won't. Just hope you're warmly dressed for it, though. It doesn't get any warmer in here.'

'The sun never gets round to these windows, does it? I've put an extra sweater on under my jacket.'

Still excited by her half-hour alone with Peter, Louise's hand trembled as she set the copier zinging again; the sound of its rythmic pulsations filled the vestry. She stood silently watching the sheets filing steadily from the machine, trying to bring common sense to the situation in the rectory kitchen. It wasn't the time for letting him know how she felt. Not yet. Instinct would tell her the right moment.

Gilbert carried on sorting through his music without speaking. He had little social chitchat, she knew, but he could at least say *something*. Without any warning, just then a whole shelf-ful of music fell from the cupboard, scattering all over the floor as far as Louise's feet and under the machine.

'Damn and blast! Oh, sorry. I do beg your pardon.'

'Here, let me help you pick it up. This lot could well do with cataloguing, couldn't it?'

'How right you are. It's one of those jobs I've kept promising to do for almost five years and haven't got round to.'

'I can't bear things not to be organised. Wouldn't it make life easier if it was all put in order?'

'Well, it would. I promise faithfully I shall do it this very next weekend.'

'Look, Gilbert. As you know, I'm not working at the moment . . .'

'So I heard.'

'If I sorted it all out, would I be doing you a good turn?'

He stood up, hands full of music, and looked intently at her. 'Do you mean that?'

'I wouldn't say it if I didn't.'

'You must be one of life's angels.'

Taken aback by his compliment, Louise didn't reply for a moment. Then: 'Not really, just someone who can't stand mess.'

'I don't wish to be impertinent, but would you know how to do it?'

'Well, as you are aware, I *am* a singer,' Gilbert looked embarrassed – and so he should, she thought, 'so I would have some idea. Though there may be a query or two.'

'I would be glad to advise.' He bowed graciously. 'I've never actually got to the bottom of all this music. One tends to have favourites, so I never have had all the stuff out. It could prove quite interesting.'

The copier interrupted them. It had ground to a halt from lack of paper. Gilbert stacked the piles of music he and Louise had collected on to the shelf, brushed his hands together to get rid of the dust, and with a brief, 'Thank you,' and a quiet, 'Good morning,' he put a sheaf of music in his music case and left the vestry.

She'd done it again; let her organising ability be made use of once more. If she kept on like this, when would anyone see her as anything other than a person obsessed by tidiness? She'd organised the rectory files, redesigned the quarterly magazine, put the parish directory together, revamped the weekly *Parish News*, done all the lists and the minutes for the Show, and now she'd be tackling a job someone had left undone for five years. After she'd completed cataloguing the music, that would be it. She wouldn't volunteer ever again to organise anything at all. Then perhaps people would see her as she wanted to be seen. In fact, as she really was. Passionate, loving, spirited, artistic.

She caught a glimpse of herself in the mirror, which for centuries rectors and choirmen had used to check their appearance before going into the church for a service. What she saw was strong, almost masculine features, with a straight, sharply cut hairstyle that did nothing to flatter her face. Though its colour was softer than it had been, she knew in her heart of hearts that Peter would prefer a more natural look. Even her grey sweater, neat and restrained, its polo neck covering her right up to her jaw, was merely serviceable but not alluring. There was nothing about her to tempt any man, least of all someone like Peter. Perhaps if she dressed more gently, in softer colours with more feminine styling, he would notice her. Yes, that was it! Forget the power dressing and the practical clothes. She'd re-vamp herself. *That was it!* She'd finish the copying and then she'd rush into Culworth and do something positive. This was where she'd been going wrong all these years, and like a stupid fool had never realised it. Yes, she'd dress more like . . .

Willie came in, a huge bunch of keys in his hand. 'Wanting to lock up if that's possible. You nearly done?'

'Oh yes, I have. In fact, I'll stop now and do the rest on Monday morning.'

'Sorry to rush yer but we can't leave the vestry unlocked with the church open to the public. Me and my Sylvia are going out for a couple of hours, so I want to lock the vestry up. Specially with the copier being in 'ere. You're doing a grand job with the Show and all this typing for the rector. You're good at your job, Louise, I'll give you that.'

What Willie said put fire into Louise's decision. She stopped only long enough to make everything tidy and then rushed away across the Green.

'Mother! I'm off into town.'

'Oh, good! Can I come too?'

'Sorry. Another day. I shall be ages.'

Sheila was disappointed. 'Oh well, all right then, but collect your father's suit from the cleaners. I'll give you the ticket before you go.'

'I might not have time.'

'Take it just in case.'

'I'll not wait for lunch.'

Curls, yes, restrained curls and waves. Not sculptured, like it was now. Yes, that's what she'd have. Coloured brown like her hair really was, but curly.

9

That Saturday night, Pat and Barry went for a drink in The Royal Oak. They'd taken Michelle to the cinema in Culworth earlier in the evening, dropped her off at the Garden House and left her sitting in Grandad's room having a drink of tea and biscuits with him before she went to bed.

'Nice kid is Michelle.'

'She thinks you're the best thing since sliced bread.'

'Does she? That true?'

'It's true.'

'And Dean?'

'Oh, he's quite keen 'cos he'd like some cupboards in his room and he thinks you'd build them for him if . . .' She looked away, embarrassed by what she'd nearly said.

'I'll build them anyway.'

'It's not my house, you know. You'll only be improving it for Mr Fitch.'

'I dare say, but you'd have the use of 'em. I've plenty of wood I can scrounge. Nobody'll miss it. Cost next to nothing. I'll start next weekend.'

'Barry! Your mother already thinks there's something going on.'

'She'll be wrong then. Another gin?'

'Oh thanks. Let me pay for this.'

'When I need financial help I'll let you know.' He stood up and went across to the bar. Bryn was serving.

'Evening, Bryn. Where's that charming blonde bombshell of a wife of yours tonight then?'

'Wedding bells. Alan and Linda got married this morning and Georgie's been up there. We couldn't both go, and Georgie does like a good wedding, so she's representing The Royal Oak as yer might say.'

'I'd forgotten that. Funny chap.'

'He has his good points. First-rate cellarman.'

'Well, that's what you need in this business. Same again, please. You'll have heard the news about the sewers?'

'Sewers?'

'Yes. They've got to put sewer pipes in at the Big House. Been using septic tanks all these years and they're no longer adequate. All those people living there all week long's causing havoc with the plumbing, and the health people say there's to be a proper sewage system put in. Got to connect the house to the main system. And guess where they're going? Straight across the front lawns and then across Home Farm field and into the main road. There's been a long holdup because they've to be very careful where they dig, you see. County Hall has plans of the area all round here and there's ancient sites that the trench for the sewers will have to avoid. So they've been backwards and forwards with detailed plans making sure nothing's disturbed that shouldn't be disturbed. Course, that's what's taken the time and made the starting date so late.'

'God! How long will all that take?'

'Old Fitch says it's to be done like yesterday. Could be weeks, he's blazing mad. The phone-lines and the fax have been buzzing like nobody's business. He's kept fending them off but the day of reckoning has arrived.'

'But what about the Show? What are we going to do?'

'Exactly. With a bit of luck and a following wind, if you get my meaning, they might be finished in time. They start on Monday. Let's pray for fine weather, then they won't get held up.'

'All the effort we've put in . . . I can't believe it.'

'Neither can Mr Fitch. The Show was one way for him to get back at Sir Ralph. Yer know, all this Lord of the Manor stuff. But they can't put it off. Things is really serious, not to say disgusting, in the plumbing department up there.'

'Does Louise know?'

'Not yet. They only agreed it yesterday. Thought she might be in here tonight. Old Fitch is going mad about the damage to the lawns. They're his pride and joy. Spent pounds on bringing 'em up to scratch. Like bowling greens they are. "Manicured" I think is the word. Anyways, they'll be a right mess when they've finished digging. He tried to persuade them to take a different route and go out the other side of the estate, but that would be twice the distance and twice the cost so that's not on.'

'Serious for once, are you?'

'I'm not pulling yer leg, it's true.'

'No-o-o-o, I mean . . .' Bryn nodded his head in Pat's direction.

Barry looked across at Pat. She was wearing her new suit – a dark blue with a lovely soft flowered scarf in the neck. Her new haircut suited her, and the half-stone she'd lost had revealed the bone structure in her face. He liked what he saw. She caught him watching her, grinned and waved.

'Could be, Bryn, could be.'

'Since she started going out with you she's knocked ten years off her age. Could be moving to the Garden House has helped too.'

'Perhaps.'

'You're playing your cards close to your chest tonight.'

Barry laid his hand on his heart, grinned from ear to ear and said, 'There are some things lay too close to the heart for words. See yer.'

As he handed Pat her drink she said, 'What was Bryn saying?'

'What a glamorous beauty I was escorting tonight.'

'Don't be daft. I'm no beauty.'

'It's amazing what love can do.' He toasted her with his glass and then took a long drink of his beer.

'Yes, like a good thump round the head, and that's what you'll be getting before you're much older.'

'Be serious, Pat.'

'I am.'

'No, yer not. You pretend to be tough, but inside you're all marshmallow. Being tough's kept you going all this time – well, now you can stop the pretence.'

'It isn't a pretence. I *am* tough.'

'I'm going to find the marshmallow bit in you.' Barry took her hand in his and holding it firmly took it up to his lips, then he grinned and said, 'Oh God, disinfectant. Pat – for goodness sake!' He pushed her hand away and pretended to cough. Playfully she slapped him round his ear.

'I'll give you disinfectant! It's my new handcream. I'm fed up having hands that look as if they've been scrubbing floors with carbolic all week. Anyways, it doesn't look good to be serving food with chapped hands and broken nails.'

'You like working for Jimbo, don't you?'

'I do. It's like a new world opening up for me. For the first time in my life I'm becoming somebody. Not just a skivvy but *somebody*. I've never really thanked you for the bike. I do love it, Barry. Thanks ever so much. It's made such a difference.'

'I'm glad. Pat I've been thinking how about if . . . oh, there's Louise.' Barry waved to catch her eye, and beckoned her over. 'Come here, Louise. Got something to tell you.'

Louise gave him the thumbs-up and went to the bar to buy herself a dirnk.

Pat whispered to Barry, 'What in heaven's name has she done with herself? She's dyed her hair again. And she's changed the style.'

'Must say she looks different.'

'Different! That's to put it mildly. And new clothes. What the heck.'

Louise came across to their table. She put her drink down and seated herself next to Pat.

'Hello, thanks for asking me across. I'm supposed to be meeting someone but they haven't turned up yet. You wanted to tell me something?' The brown hair certainly suited her skin tone better, more like her own possibly, thought Pat, and the pale crushed-strawberry sweater with the soft neckline was certainly a more feminine style compared to the one she usually wore, but it was the cut of the black trousers which Pat had noticed as Louise walked across to them. They must have cost a bomb. Louise took a sip of her Cinzano and lemonade and looked enquiringly at Barry.

'Yes. Bad news, I'm afraid. On Monday they're starting digging to put the new sewer pipes in at the Big House. Right across the lawns, over Home Farm field and out into the main road.'

'*What?* Are you kidding me?'

'God's truth. Old Fitch has been trying to play for time, but the Health say do it now or we close you down. So he's got no alternative.'

'But they won't be finished in time, will they?'

'Good summer, let's hope so.'

'What a mess. All the work we've put in. The Morris Dancers, the police team, the hot-air balloon, the competitions.' She took a sip of her drink and then something else occurred to her. She sat bolt upright and for once spoke without considering every word she said. 'The printing – we've had the printing done! All that money. I'm expecting all the leaflets and posters to arrive this week. It's far too far advanced to cancel that. What are we going to do?' Some of the customers sitting close to their table heard Louise's raised voice and the news passed round the bar in a trice.

'Show cancelled, you say?'

'Never!'

'Well!'

'New sewers? Not before time. Our Melanie works in the kitchens, says them lavatories is a disgrace. They gurgles and don't flush properly, according to her.'

'Health have too much power. Shut 'em down, indeed! What business is it of theirs, I say?'

'Exactly. It's like living in a police state.'

'It is, yer right.'

'Time this government got their comeuppance.'

'Exactly. Give me yer glass, I'll get 'em in this time.'

Louise recovering from the first shock-waves, said, 'Still, two and a half months . . . that's a long time with these modern diggers and things, isn't it? We shall be all right, shan't we?' There was a request for reassurance in the tone of her voice.

'I expect so. Well, I hope so.'

'I shall go up to the Big House on Monday and have a word with Mr Fitch in my capacity as Show secretary.'

'Won't do much good. He's in Toronto and won't be back till next weekend.'

Pat, who hadn't spoken a word since Louise joined them, said how much she liked Louise's new hairstyle.

Louise looked pleased. 'Oh, thank you. I had it done this afternoon. Not had curly hair before.'

'New clothes too.'

'Yes. Not before time.'

Pat was puzzled at the back of her mind. There seemed to be something familiar about the clothes, and she couldn't think why.

They talked for a while longer and then Pat pushed back the cuff of Barry's jacket and looked at his watch. 'Time I went home, Barry. We'll love you and leave you, Louise. Hope yer friend turns up.'

'Friend? Oh yes. Right. Good night. Let's hope the sewers get done in time. I think I'll still go up there on Monday and have a word with the men. Chivvy them along a bit.'

'Good idea. Good night.'

Barry and Pat left the saloon, and after they'd gone heads got together and they became the subject of speculation.

'Just 'ope she knows what she be doin'.'

'All alike, them Joneses. Sex mad.'

'Talk about spreading it about.'

'Remember that time . . .'

'She wants to watch her step. Just got herself nicely sorted with that big house and that, and then he turns his sparkling eyes on her.'

'Cor, he's got something though, hasn't he? Those thighs! Gawd! Wouldn't mind a bit of it meself.'

'You devil you.'

'He's a bit of all right, is Barry.'

'Can't think what he sees in '*er*.'

There was no friend coming to join Louise, and she sat alone until her drink was finished and then she left.

'Before you go up to bed, Dean, I'll have a look to see where you want your cupboards putting.'

Dean leaped off the sofa. 'Do yer mean that? Are you going to make me some?'

'Your mother says I can. If that's all right with you.'

'Come up. I'll be your apprentice if you like.'

'OK.'

Pat put the kettle on and got out the cups and saucers. She found a crumpled tray cloth at the back of the tablecloth drawer and smoothed it out on the tray, anchoring it with the teapot and the sugar basin. Somehow she wanted to give a good impression. She didn't know why, but she did. She found some chocolate biscuits which Dean had missed and laid them out on a plate.

Barry came down, he was scribbling on a piece of paper he'd torn from the pad Dean used for his essays.

'There, that's it. I'll have it done in no time at all.'

'You're too kind. Don't do it if you're too busy.'

'Nonsense! He wants cupboards and cupboards he'll get. He could do with encouraging. Boys need a man about.'

He sat beside her on the sofa. She poured the tea, giving him a heaped teaspoon of sugar, the way she remembered he liked it.

'He's going to do well at school, isn't he?'

'Yes, but I don't know where he gets it from. Used to be a tearaway and now he's working all hours. School says when he's done his GCSEs, which isn't for a bit yet, he should stay on and do A-Levels and go to University. Doug would have been that proud.'

'Still miss him, Pat?'

'No.' She offered him the biscuits.

'Thanks. Once bitten, twice shy?'

'Don't know.'

'Come here. Give us a kiss.'

'Dad'll be in.'

'I've paid him to stay in his room.'

'You haven't, have you?'

'No. But he was young once.' Barry kissed her and this time she kissed him. She'd taken her jacket off when she'd come in the house, and as he kissed her Barry smoothed his hands up and down her bare arm to where her sleeve began, and then more adventurously he slipped his hand inside her blouse and was caressing her collar bone as they kissed. Then her neck and then he slid her bra strap from her shoulder and began kissing the hollows at the base of her neck.

'Mmmm . . . you smell good.'

'Barry, that's enough. Please.'

'Come on. Come on. You know you're beginning to enjoy it . . .'

And she was, but she was afraid. Afraid of wanting him to go on. Afraid of enjoying it too much. Afraid of going too far, from which there would be no stepping back. And anyways, Pat Duckett didn't do things like this and *enjoy* them. There wasn't room in Pat Duckett's life for enjoyment. All the same, it did feel . . .

'That's enough, you two. Anybody'd think you were teenagers. Is that tea still hot?'

It was her dad. Pat struggled to sit upright, hooking her bra strap back up and straightening her hair. Barry laughed. 'Come on, Greenwood. You're a spoilsport.'

'Spoilsport my foot,' Greenwood said. 'Your reputation goes before you, Barry. You're not spreading it about round here. I want her treated with respect, and your past record doesn't lead me to believe that's what you'll do.'

'Come off it! That's the first time we've really had a go.'

Humiliated, Pat snapped, 'Dad, be quiet. I'll get you a cup.' She disappeared into the kitchen.

'And I'll tell you something else, Barry. You don't mess her about and then float off to pastures new. She's had a rotten life with that fool she married. I'm not having her hurt again.'

'Cross my heart and hope to die, I'm not messing about. Honest.'

Pat came back.

'Oh, I see. Cup and saucer tonight. Usually it's a mug. Thanks, Pat. I'll say good night.' He nodded curtly to Barry, took his cup of tea from Pat and left.

'You'd better go. Thanks for the drink tonight.'

'That's all right, my pleasure. I've been thinking, Pat. I know someone who has a big residential caravan. I did some jobs for 'im a while back and he said any time I wanted to borrow it, so long as he wasn't needing it, I could. A week, he said. It's quite close to the sea and there's a river with trout fishing. I could take my rods and Dean could fish. There's places to visit. I know Michelle likes to look round gardens . . .'

Pat put up her hand to stop him. 'Oh no! I'm sorry, but no. I've got too much respect for my kids to have them knowing I'm . . .'

'Pat! Let me finish. There's three bedrooms. It's huge. Dean and me could have one, you and Michelle the other and Greenwood could be on his own. How about that?'

'I'm sorry, beg yer pardon for misunderstanding. It's a wonderful idea, but I'd have to talk to them about it. I'll let you know. We'll have a family conference and see. It would have to be when the schools break up. Our Dean can't miss school at the moment, and our Michelle will want to be there, seeing as it's her last term.'

'Of course. I understand that. I'll make enquiries then, just in case. Say yes, please. Goodnight, Pat.' He left without giving her a kiss and she felt quite let down.

Before she went to sleep, Pat thought about the evening and how much she'd enjoyed it. A week by the sea would do them all good. But she couldn't understand the game Barry was playing. What with Avril Nightingale and the woman from Home Farm, and all the tales she'd heard, 'cos Jimmy and Willie knew what he was like, it didn't fit in that he wanted a holiday with two kids and a grandad. Still, she liked the bedroom arrangements and with Dad there he couldn't, could he?

As she was falling asleep she found the answer. It sprang into her mind in a flash, just when she was thinking about Barry's lips on her collar bone. Of course. *That was it.* It was as plain as the nose on yer face. *Louise was trying to look like Caroline.*

10

On the Monday morning, instead of heading straight for the rectory, Louise went up to the Big House to see what was going on. Quite by chance she met Jeremy Mayer out on the front lawns. He was standing with his bulky legs apart, his pocket watch in his hand.

'Good morning, Jeremy. Nice day.'

'Good morning, Louise. To what do I owe this pleasure?'

'Sewers.'

'Ah, yes. They should be here by now, but they're not. Eight o'clock start they said, and it's now half-past nine.'

'It's all very well you know, but what about the Show? We can hardly run it if there's diggers and trenches in the way.'

'My very thoughts. Mr Fitch is steaming over there in Toronto. In fact, I'm amazed he hasn't been on the buzzer yet.'

'The leaflets and the posters are being delivered this week. I don't know what to do.'

'My dear young lady – and you're looking dashed handsome this morning, I must say – if Mr Fitch has anything to do with it, we shall *all* have spades in our hands before long, me included.'

He patted the sleeve of her new suede jacket with his white podgy hand. She adjusted the Jaeger scarf at her neck and said, 'Do you mean that?'

'He hasn't got where he is today without making things happen. But this time he seems to have come up against something even he can't fix. Believe me, if paying everyone to get behind a spade will speed things up, he'll do it. This Show's important, you see. It's all part of establishing himself in the village. Shouldn't be saying that but it's true and they all know it, but he doesn't realise they all know it.'

'So basically the committee have to keep their fingers crossed?'

'Exactly. But things don't augur well, do they, when the men haven't even turned up. Try not to worry.'

'We've arranged so many events,' Louise fretted. 'I haven't the courage to confirm things, but I'll have to pretend it's going ahead and keep my fingers crossed.'

The receptionist came out of the front door. 'Mr Mayer – it's Toronto!'

'Oh God! Pray for me. Coming, Fenella.' As fast as he could, considering his bulk, Jeremy scurried back inside.

Louise drove back along the drive, feeling in two minds about the Show. One half of her wanted to take the gamble that it would go ahead, the other cringed at the thought and wanted to cancel the whole thing. Peter might have a few ideas – she'd consult him. While she waited at the drive gates for an opportunity to get out into Church Lane, she looked at herself in her rearview mirror and liked what she saw. Minimum of make-up, brown curls, the Jaeger scarf adding a touch of colour to the dark, dark brown of her suede jacket. She'd spent a fortune. Thank heavens for little plastic cards. But the day of reckoning would surely come, she knew that. In fact, the idea of getting a job began to loom in the furthest corners of her mind. As Mother said, and she didn't say much of significance very often, money didn't last for ever. But she looked good. Oh yes. Depending on the atmosphere at the rectory, today could be *the day*. She was brought down from the clouds by a loud tooting behind her. It was Barry Jones wanting to get out of the gates.

She twinkled her fingers at him through the open window and with a quick check turned right into Church Lane. Barry Jones . . . He gave off that extra bit of something she couldn't quite define. A kind of manly vibrance. A sexuality which excited. Still, Pat was welcome to him – though what he saw in *her* she couldn't imagine. She, Louise Bissett, had her sights on higher targets than an estate carpenter.

She put on the handbrake, picked up her new leather handbag and her briefcase and leaped out ready for what could be the best day of her life so far. Because today things would happen. She was vague about exactly what, but today she was taking a big step forward of some kind.

When she opened the door in response to Louise's knock, Caroline was taken aback but strove not to show it.

'Good morning. Isn't it lovely today? Like the hair. What a transformation. Makes you look completely different!'

Louise hung her suede coat, with the new scarf tucked down the sleeve, in the cupboard and smiled. 'Thought it was time I smartened up, seeing as I shall be going for interviews soon. Don't want to look like a country bumpkin.'

'Absolutely not. They couldn't think that about you before and certainly not now. You've got interviews then?'

She couldn't downright lie so she said, 'In the pipeline, thank goodness. I'll do an hour and then go and finish the photocopying. Has Peter shown you the front cover?'

'Yes, I'm so pleased with it. When the magazine's finished I'd like a copy to send to my friend.'

'Of course. That design on yellow paper has worked really well. We make a good team, don't we, Peter and I?'

Tongue in cheek Caroline agreed and said, 'Sylvia's making coffee. I'll ask her to bring it in.'

Caroline was constructing a tent for the children with a couple of blankets and the kitchen table when Sylvia returned from taking Peter and Louise their coffee.

When Caroline emerged from under the table Sylvia said, 'There's your coffee, Dr Harris, on the corner by your rocking chair. I'll sit in the other one, otherwise we'll spoil the tent.'

Usually Caroline and Sylvia chatted while they had their morning break but today Sylvia was silent. The only sound in the kitchen was the slight creaking of Caroline's chair as she rocked and the chattering of the children having their own drink and biscuit in their makeshift tent.

'Is there something the matter, Sylvia? Have I upset you or something? You're awfully quiet today.'

'You haven't upset me, no.'

'Well, then are you not well? I'm sure we can manage if you'd rather be at home.'

'I'm quite well, thank you.'

'I see.' Caroline looked at her over the rim of her mug and pondered on the cause of Sylvia's silence. She'd come to rely on her for bits of information about the village that she ought to be aware of, and drinking their morning coffee was one of the best times for talking.

'Has someone else upset you then?'

'Nothing no one's said, if that's what you mean.'

'What then? Come on, you can tell me. I'm the soul of discretion.'

Sylvia reached across and placed her mug on the corner of the Aga. 'If I tell you I could upset several people. But I can't keep quiet. For your sake I can't keep quiet.'

'Well, then spit it out.'

Sylvia cleared her throat, hesitated for a moment while she found the right words and then said, 'Since the first day she walked in here, into this rectory, it's been as if a time bomb's been waiting to go off. I can't put it more strongly than that. A time bomb. You know it. I know it. The only one who doesn't is the rector, bless 'im. And now this.'

'This what?'

'Haven't you noticed anything different this morning with Louise?'

'She's had her hair done and bought some new clothes. I thought she looked quite good.'

'That's right – she does. But have you realised what she's doing? I noticed it in church yesterday.'

'Brightening herself up, I suppose. Ready for going to interviews.'

'No, Dr Harris, she's copying you.'

Caroline was astounded. 'Copying *me*? Really, Sylvia, I know you've never liked her but this is ridiculous.'

'Is it? Dark brown suede jacket, expensive scarf, Jaeger skirt and blouse not exactly like yours, but the same colours. Saw her in church, wearing a pale pink jumper and black trousers very, very similar to yours – and her hair has now gone brown and curly. Believe me, I'm right.'

'I never realised that, but you could be right . . . They *are* similar, aren't they?' Sylvia nodded. 'But what would she want to do that for?' Caroline said slowly.

'Think about it. It's not because she admires *you*, is it?'

Caroline put her mug down on the table and sat deep in thought. Then she said, 'I'll leave the children with you for a while, if I may.' She stood up and left the kitchen by the back door. Sylvia could see her walking in the garden; to outward appearances she was checking her plants but Sylvia, who knew her well, guessed rightly that she was searching in her mind for an answer to the problem.

Louise came in with the empty coffee mugs from the study before she left to finish the photocopying.

'Thanks for the coffee, I'm off now. Caroline not about?'

'No. She's not.'

'I wanted a word.'

'You can leave a message.'

'Tell her . . . tell her . . . Never mind, I'll see her next time I come.' As Louise went towards the door into the hall she half-turned and smiled oddly at Sylvia. The back door opened and in came Caroline.

'Louise! I'm glad I've caught you. I wanted a word.'

She returned to the kitchen. 'Oh right. Yes?'

'Flattering though it is for me to find that you have chosen to copy the way I dress, I don't like it.'

'The way you dress? What *do* you mean?'

'What you're wearing today. It's tantamount to a complete copy of my clothes.'

'You're being ridiculous. Why on earth should *I* want to copy *you*?'

'I don't know – you tell me.'

'You're totally mistaken. That was never my intent at all.'

'I don't like it, I'm afraid. However, I've said how I feel – I can't do any more.'

'You certainly can't. I repeat, you're quite mistaken. These clothes are my choice and nothing whatsoever to do with your taste in fashion. If I wanted to copy anyone, it would be Harriet Charter-Plackett, not you.'

Angry beyond belief at the manner in which Louise was speaking to Caroline, Sylvia interrupted: 'You know full well why you're doing it. We're not idiots in this village, though I know you think we are. You're doing it to get a response from the rector – and don't deny it!'

'Who do you think you are, speaking to me in that tone?'

'Someone who sees more clearly than you would like. If you're trying to win him for yourself, you're barking up the wrong tree. The rector wouldn't even *look* at you, even though you're dressed like Dr Harris. He only has you here to work and for nothing else.'

Louise turned to Caroline. 'Are you going to stand by and allow a . . . *servant* to shout at me? How can anyone possibly think I see Peter as anything other than my spiritual advisor? When have I ever done anything to make anyone think otherwise?'

Sylvia didn't allow Caroline time to answer. 'Dressing like you are today, and when I saw you yesterday in church. If you never came back in this house again it would be too soon. I know exactly what you're up to. The rector, bless him, can't see it, because he never thinks ill of anyone, ever. But I can see straight through you, oh yes! Now buzz off and don't come back.'

By now the children, sensing that their mother and their beloved Sylvie were upset, had crawled out of the tent and had become very agitated, crying, 'Mummy, Mummy!' They clung to Caroline's legs, begging to be lifted up.

Caroline, in an attempt to calm the situation said, 'Sylvia! This won't do. Please leave it to me.'

'I can't, because you won't say what has to be said. I saw clean through her the first day she came here. I knew her little game. Well, it's to be stopped before it goes any further. I won't see this family broken up and stand by and say nothing. So, off you go.'

Not one of them noticed that Peter had heard the arguing and come from his study and was now standing in the kitchen doorway. Louise, seething and fast losing control of the situation, said the one thing she knew cut right to the heart of her intention. 'Broken up? This family broken up? As if I would do such a thing to these two little children.' She looked lovingly at the twins as they stood clinging to their mother.

' "These two little children?". You don't care *that* much for 'em.' Sylvia clicked her fingers as close to Louise's face as she could. 'You only pretend to care to keep in the rector's good books. They're his and Dr Harris's and don't you forget it.'

Louise finally lost her self-control. 'Hers and Peter's? Oh yes?' There was a scornful note in her voice which stabbed straight at Caroline's heart. She went ashen, and her hands began to shake. The children fell silent.

Sylvia stepped forward as though she would strangle Louise. 'Get out! Go on, get out. Never *ever* come back here. Do you hear me? Never!'

Peter's voice at its loudest would have stilled a storm and he used it now, overriding Sylvia's shouting, every word couched in cold implacable anger. 'I will not have this arguing in my home. Your behaviour is disgraceful. Both of you should be ashamed. Absolutely ashamed. Not another word. Sylvia, please leave. And you too, Louise. Out! Your behaviour in front of my wife and our children has been quite unforgivable.' Neither of them moved. 'I'm waiting.' His face was deathly white with temper, and he smashed a fist against the palm of his other hand as he repeated, 'I'm waiting!'

Louise suppressed the urge to speak to him, recognising that she had gone far too far, and would probably never retrieve the status quo again. Sylvia, fearful of his anger, quietly went into the hall, took her coat from the cupboard and rushed home to the comfort of Willie's arms. Louise had no such arms in which to shelter; she went home to weep alone.

Peter stood quite still for a moment breathing heavily and attempting to regain his self-control. Alex and Beth were still crying, so he picked them both up and sat each of them on a kitchen chair. He opened the cake tin and gave them each a piece of flapjack, and with shaking hands poured some juice into their beakers. Having spoken reassuringly to them, he turned his attention to Caroline. She was standing apart, tears silently pouring down her cheeks, one hand pressed to her forehead shielding her eyes, the other gripping the back of the nearest chair.

'Caroline, come.' Peter opened wide his arms and she went to him. A safe anchorage was what she needed and that was what she got.

'My darling girl. I'm so sorry. So very sorry. I'd no idea things had gone that far.'

'But Peter, I did say.'

'Yes, and I was easing her out but you invited her back.'

'I know. I know.'

Peter wiped her eyes for her and kissed her eyelids. 'No more crying. The matter is finished or it will be when I've dealt with it.'

'She said how much she loved coming to our house because it was so welcoming and warm, and of course that won me over. I couldn't believe it when I heard myself saying she could come back.'

Peter groaned. 'I was even so blind that I complimented her on her clothes this morning.'

'You're too kind. I couldn't stop Sylvia; she was so wild she wouldn't listen to sense. She was like a terrier.' Caroline took out her handkerchief and wiped her eyes again. 'She's no fool, she saw through Louise from the word go. Peter, what are we going to do? You've lost your secretary and I've lost my housekeeper.'

'Come and sit on my knee.' He seated himself in Caroline's rocking chair and she perched on his knee. With her head on his shoulder and his hand caressing her arm, he said, 'I shall deal with Madam Sylvia after lunch when tempers have cooled. Don't worry, Willie and I will sort it out. We've a good understanding, him and me.'

'Will you sort Louise too?'

Peter gave her a grim smile. 'I'll have to work at that. She's harder to solve than Sylvia. Can't leave it as it is now, though.'

'There's going to be no end to the pain, is there? I think the answer is for us to leave here and make a fresh start somewhere else, where no one knows. But it would break my heart to do that. I love it here.'

Peter gripped her tightly and gently shook her. 'So do I. So do I. But, I promise you faithfully here and now, if things get too bad for you, Caroline, then move we shall. The decision is entirely yours.'

'Oh Peter, I wish I was a million miles from here, right now, just for a while.'

'I wish you were too. Well, I mean all of us together a million miles away. Never mind, not long now and we *shall* be away. For two blissful weeks.'

'Devon, here we come. I won't have Louise back. I'm sorry, I know I'm trespassing, but I won't.'

'Neither will I. That's it – finished. I must have been a complete fool not to have noticed the way things were going. Sorry.'

'I'm sorry for her at bottom. She must be desperate.'

Peter kissed her. 'You're so kind, Dr Harris.'

'So are you. What a mess. I feel drained. Such a scene in my own kitchen. It will be a while before I get over this, and the children too, they were so upset. I'm glad they're still too young to understand. However, must get on. I'll start lunch. Finished, my little ones? Come on, then, down you get.'

'They are your little ones, Caroline, they truly are.'

'I think so myself sometimes.'

'Don't doubt it. They went into shock when you were away. So difficult to handle. Sylvia did wonders but they wanted you.'

'Whilst I make the lunch, you'd better occupy your mind with how we'll get Sylvia back. That's the phone – will you take it or shall I?'

He tipped her off his knee and went to answer it.

After he'd eaten lunch, Peter went next door to apologise to Sylvia. He knocked at their cottage door and Willie answered it.

'Ahh, Rector. Just having a bite of lunch with my Sylvia. In need of some company, she was.' His look held an element of disapproval.

'Good afternoon, Willie. Come to make sure you've found the details for the grave that has to be dug. I left them in your tray. It's an old one, not been opened for more than fifty years.'

'I know that one, sir. My father was the last one to open it. It's nearer sixty years. Leave it to me. Now the weather's warmed up, 'spect we shall have a few more graves to dig. It always 'appens. Freezing weather, they all stay alive. Warms up and Bob's yer uncle, they drop like flies.'

Peter whispered, 'Can I speak to Sylvia?'

'She's very upset and so am I. She was only defending Dr Harris.'

'I know, it's all such a mess. But can I speak to her – to apologise?'

'I'll ask.' Willie went back inside and Peter thought he could hear some agitated whispering. He strained to listen but couldn't make out the words.

After a few moments Willie came back. 'Yes, sir, Sylvia's in.' He gave Peter the thumbs-down sign, which he acknowledged with a rueful grin. 'I'll be off then, Rector, and leave you to it.'

Peter bent his head and went in. The ceilings in Willie's cottage were much lower than in the rectory, and he had to keep his head bent. He found Sylvia in the sitting room, in an armchair, twisting her handkerchief round and round her fingers.

'May I sit down? It's so uncomfortable for me to stand.'

'Of course. Yes, of course.'

Simultaneously they both said, 'I want to apologise for—'

Peter raised his hand to stop her speaking. 'No, Sylvia, I've come to apologise. You were only guilty of putting up a spirited defence of my wife and our children. I was so angry at the whole situation and even more angry with myself for not having realised the way the wind blew. You didn't deserve what I said. So I'm here to apologise most sincerely to you and to ask if we can let bygones be bygones and, please, will you possibly be able to consider coming back to the rectory?'

'I don't even have to consider it. Of course I'll come back. Working for Dr Harris is so . . . well so . . . She's a lovely person to work for and I love your children, I really do. They help to make up for not having any of my own, even if they are little devils!'

'Which they are, I have to confess.'

'But – and it's a big "but".'

'Go on.'

'I won't come back unless I have your absolute firm promise that Louise doesn't come near the rectory. If she does, I shall probably throttle her. Please, sir, if you value your family, don't have her back. I know I've no business talking to a clergyman like this, you're much too clever to need advice from me, but I've got to say it. She's trouble.'

'You have my solemn promise.'

'In that case then I'll be back. I'll just get my coat.'

'No, don't do that. Leave it until tomorrow. Have the rest of the day to yourself. And thank you for accepting my apology. I can't bear for Caroline to be hurt, and she was hurt, badly hurt.'

'I know. And I'm sorry. Very sorry for the way I behaved, but I was so angry.' Sylvia stood up. 'I won't keep you. So long as we have an understanding, that's all that matters.' She smiled at him. 'I didn't know you had such a temper. It was quite a revelation.'

'Sorry.'

'Thank you for coming round.'

Peter came out of the cottage and went to stand by the pond on the Green. Jimmy's geese came hustling forward in the hope that he would be feeding them.

'Sorry chaps, no bread today. I envy you your uncomplicated lives. How I envy you. Still, with a brain the size of a walnut, or it could even be the size of a pea, I suppose I can't expect you to solve problems like mine. I've solved one and now I'm off to sort out another. Do you have any advice to offer?' They honked busily. 'No, I didn't think you would have. I shall have to leave it to the Lord to help me find the right words.'

The door of the Bissetts' cottage was slightly ajar when Peter knocked. 'Hellooo! Peter here, from the rectory. May I come in?'

11

The story of Peter turning Louise and Sylvia out of the rectory was round the village in no time at all. By the middle of the afternoon, the main topic of conversation in The Royal Oak was what on earth had taken place to make him do such a thing. A peace-loving man like him, chucking the two of them out? Well, they knew he had a temper. Look at the time he confronted them all when they were stoning Beryl and Gwen's house. Or that time they turned against Alan Crimble when he ran Flick Charter-Plackett down and she was laid almost lifeless in Church Lane. But even so . . .

Most likely it was to do with Sylvia running the cake-stall at the Show for the Red Cross. That Louise wasn't half bossy if she took a mind.

Jimmy Glover knew different. 'I reckon that Louise has gone crackers. When she rushed across home after she'd been turned out she was wearing Dr Harris's clothes.'

'Don't be daft. How could she be?'

'Well, I saw 'er and she was. True as I'm 'ere, or if they wasn't Dr Harris's they was a dead spit.'

'Well, we all know she 'as her eye on the rector. Perhaps fancied looking like Dr Harris to tempt him.'

'Take a lot more than looking like Dr Harris to make anyone be tempted with her!' The speaker chuckled into his beer.

'I reckon that's why she volunteered to help him, 'cos she fancies him.'

'Anyways, let's face it, he wouldn't be tempted by '*er*!'

'No, course he wouldn't. It's her doing the running, that's what. Desperate for a bit of that there 'ere and she fancies him, made her feelings plain and Sylvia's 'ad a row with her.'

'Good at her job though. Made a right improvement to the weekly church newsletter, and I hear the magazine's been hyped-up no end.'

'Not saying she isn't good at her job, but she's no business stirring it at the rectory.'

'Wonder what he said to her when he went across there this afternoon?'

'Didn't know he'd been.'

'Oh, he has. He went to Willie and Sylvia's then across to see her. There quite a while he was.'

'What you been doing then all afternoon? Sat looking out the window?'

'Day off. Felt like a rest, but it's been that busy with the comings an' goings I might as well 'ave been working.'

The conversation turned to the Show and who would win the prizes in the vegetable section. They plumped for Willie winning the beans and Barry's mother the Victoria sponge and the cut flowers like usual.

Peter was in his study thinking over what he'd said to Louise.

When he'd first gone there and called through the open door, it was Sheila who'd come to speak to him.

'Good afternoon, Sheila. I was hoping for a word with Louise. Is she in? I see her car's outside.'

'Oh, good afternoon, Rector.' Peter knew he was in trouble if Sheila Bissett called him 'Rector'. 'Coming to make things straight with her, are you?'

'I'd like to talk, yes.'

'She's very upset and she won't tell me what's happened – except she keeps blaming you. After all she's done for you and not a penny piece in return, all voluntary and she comes home in that state! It wasn't right.'

'Is she in? Can I have a word?'

'I'll go and see. I think she's in bed. Wait there.' She left him standing in the little hall, while she went upstairs. After a few minutes, she came back down and said, 'Louise won't come down, but she says will you go up?'

'I don't think so. If she wants me to wait while she dresses then I will, but it's imperative I speak with her.'

Sheila climbed the stairs again. After a few minutes she returned, followed by Louise who was wearing the clothes she'd had on earlier in the day. Her hair was well-brushed and combed, her make-up meticulous and she was looking subdued and cautious as though afraid of saying the wrong thing yet again.

'Good afternoon, Louise. Can we sit down somewhere?'

'Of course, how nice of you to come to apologise.' She led the way into the sitting room and pointed to the largest and most comfortable chair in the room. 'Sit here, it'll be better for you with your long legs.'

Louise seated herself in a smaller chair quite close to his own and waited. Peter had realised instantly that this could prove to be the most difficult conversation of his life.

'Firstly, Louise, I have not come to apologise. Not for losing my temper, not for turning you out, not for anything at all. I *have* come to say that I am afraid I cannot permit you to come to the rectory any more. What you said this morning – well, the bit I heard – was the truth. What was unforgivable was for you to say it in the manner you did and in front of Caroline and our children.'

'Just a moment. Have I got this right? What I said was true but it had to be left unsaid?'

'Yes. Positively yes. Caroline and I shall decide when the time is ripe to tell the children. Also, this business of dressing like my wife . . .'

'That was not my intention at all. It was pure coincidence, but of course I shan't be believed. You prefer to believe someone who is only a servant.'

'Sylvia is not a servant, nor is she a fool. Even I, when it was pointed out to me, recognised that this was what you had done. It's just not on, Louise. Someone in my position has to be very circumspect . . .'

'Of course you have. I wouldn't want it otherwise. I know a clergyman must be very careful not to compromise himself in any way, so I have never given you one moment's cause for concern.'

'No, I suppose that is true. You haven't, but there is this feeling . . .'

'Don't worry, Peter. I know how difficult it must be for you, sandwiched as you are between two domineering women. It must be very hard for such a gentle person like yourself. You need to keep the peace with Caroline, and if that means hanging on to Sylvia then that is what you must do.' Peter tried to protest, but Louise rushed on with what she had to say. 'You and I will sort it out. First, I have a word-processor here in my room which I could quite easily use for doing the church typing. You leave the tapes here, with your little machine as you so charmingly call it, I'll do the work and you can collect it. How's that for an idea? Just because things are difficult at the rectory it shouldn't mean that you miss out on secretarial help.'

'If you get a job, then . . .'

'I can always do it in my spare time. Don't you worry about that.' As she spoke Louise allowed her hand to rest on his knee for a moment. Because his mind had been scrabbling around for reasons why this scheme wouldn't work, Peter hadn't drawn away immediately and through his cassock he'd felt the warm pressure of her hand. He'd sensed there was more to it than sympathy and he knew he had to make a stand.

He moved his leg away from her hand, but Louise continued speaking in the same vein. 'Two intelligent human beings like us, you see, have found a solution, haven't we? You and your family are very dear to me, Peter. I wouldn't dream of doing anything to disrupt your family life. Not at all. And I mean that. Let's try out our new scheme and see how it goes. A little adjustment on both sides and it should work splendidly.'

At this point Peter stood up. 'I'm afraid not. It won't do. I want to thank you for all you've done these last couple of months – no one has been more grateful than I for your efforts – but I have to call a halt. I'm sorry but there it is. I'll say good afternoon now. I sincerely hope that this little misunderstanding will not affect your coming to church. I would be very upset if it did. You have a splendid contribution to make to the life of this village and I hope you'll go from strength to strength. Thank you, Louise.' He proffered his hand for her to shake. She held it with both her own.

'I can't believe you're saying this to me. Not after all we've meant to each other. I'm indispensable to you and well you know it. You're allowing Caroline, and Sylvia too, to dictate to you against your better judgement. It all stems from their jealousy of me. All I've ever wanted is to be useful to you in whatever capacity you need.'

Peter extracted his hand from her tight grip and said, 'There's nothing more to say. I'm going now. Perhaps when you've thought it over you'll realise I've made the best decision. Pray about it. That way you'll come to terms, and understand why I have said what I have, I'm sure you will.'

'I shan't. Not ever.'

Sheila was dusting her ornaments in the hall as Peter left.

'Good afternoon, Sheila. I think we've got the position clear now. See you in church on Sunday. Bye bye.'

'Bye bye, Peter.'

He walked home and went immediately to his study. He'd done all he could, but he had an uneasy feeling that this was not the end.

The moment he'd shut the door, Sheila raced into the sitting room to have a word with Louise.

'Well, what did he say?'

Louise stretched as though she hadn't a care in the world. She laid her head back against the cushion and smiled. 'Right now he's doing exactly as those two women have said he should. But I haven't worked closely with him all these weeks not to know him through and through. He doesn't want to do as they say. He wants me to stay working for him in his study. He relies on me, you see, Mother. Just wait another day or two, a week at most, and when the work starts piling up, he'll be back. The poor man, I feel desperately sorry for him.'

'Oh, I do too. He's such a lovely person. So charis . . . what's that word?'

'Charismatic.'

'That's it. Charismatic. You feel so drawn to him. He only has to hold your hand and look at you . . .'

'That's just what he did.'

'Did he really?'

'Yes. He looked really deeply into my eyes, you know like he can sometimes and you feel as if your soul is being stripped bare . . .'

'Oh yes, I know, it makes me do the right thing even when I don't want to. I can't help myself.'

'Well, he looked at me like that and said I had a great contribution to make to the life of the village and he hoped most sincerely that this little fracas wouldn't stop me from going to church. He would be very upset if it did.'

'Really?'

'Believe me, all I have to do is wait and I shall be back at the rectory before dear Caroline knows where she is.'

Suddenly Sheila felt things weren't quite right. There was something disquieting about Louise's attitude, almost as if she was seeking revenge on Caroline. Sheila decided to warn Louise about the unpredictability of the villagers if they decided things weren't as they should be.

'The whole village will know by now. You'd better be careful. They're not past stoning, you know. Quite mediaeval, they can be. If they don't like what's happening, something comes over them and they all band together. I've seen it, I know.'

'Mother, you're going daft. Stoning – honestly!'

'It's true! It happened only two years ago – Peter had to come out and stop it. Terrifying it was, but he was wonderful.'

'He can be very masterful.' Louise sounded dreamy. 'He seems so gentle, but there's always that feeling of power there. Well, I shan't let stupid tales about stoning stop me. I shall go about my affairs as normal.'

'I'd stay at home for a day or two before you venture out. You could pretend to have a cold.'

'Sometimes, Mother, I wonder about your sanity, I really do. I need some chocolate.'

'I'll get it for you, dear. Let me go, I shan't be a moment. What would you like – fruit and nut?'

'No, I'm going myself. I want to choose.' Louise strolled up Stocks Row and into the Store. There was something very uplifting about the Store. It felt such a good place to be, as though going in and shopping there was a very fashionable and well-judged thing to do. She supposed Jimbo had deliberately planned it that way. The Store was very busy and the noise-level quite high, but as she walked in the hubbub died. She picked up a basket and began to wander round the shelves thinking that she'd buy herself some chocolates, she deserved a treat after all she'd been through. She might even purchase some of those special Belgian chocolates which Jimbo said were sold only in Harrods and in his store. That took a bit of swallowing but . . . then someone jerked her elbow quite savagely. The basket almost flew from her hand.

In an exaggeratedly polite voice Barry's mother apologised. 'Oh, I'm so sorry, *Dr Harris*. Oh, it's not Dr Harris – it's you, Miss Bissett. What a silly mistake to make. Did I catch your elbow? Are you keeping well?'

'Yes, thank you. I'm fine.'

'That's a good thing then. Busy at the rectory today, are you? Just popped out for something for their tea? We know how much they love you . . . popping in and out.'

Louise wanted to retort sharply but she quickly sensed the nature of the attack and sweetly smiled instead. A ripple of giggles followed her as she made for the glass counter where the continental chocolates were displayed. Harriet came to serve her.

'Hello there, can I help?'

'I'll have half a pound, please. Mainly hard centres and I like pralines and some of those fresh cream ones, please. Oh, and I'd like a couple of marzipans too.'

While Harriet busied herself putting on plastic gloves and making up one of the gold cardboard boxes to put the chocolates in, Louise looked about her.

There was a knot of women gathered around Barry's mother. They kept glancing in her direction and smothering explosive laughter. She ignored them as best she could, but their malicious interest in her became hurtful, so she watched Harriet tucking the chocolates into the box instead. Harriet, aware that Louise was being mocked, did her best to keep her attention. After all, Louise was spending money and it wasn't for Harriet to treat her badly just because she disapproved of what she did in her private life.

'There we are, Louise, I've put in a selection of the ones you asked for, and then filled up the odd corners with others. If it's a present, would you like me to gift-wrap it with ribbon et cetera, and a little card?'

It wasn't a present except to herself, but she nodded her assent. Perhaps by the time Harriet had finished, those women would have gone. But they hadn't and she had to run the gauntlet to the till.

'Prezzie for Dr Harris, is it?'

'Don't be silly. It's for the rector!'

'I hear you haven't got a job yet?'

'Devil finds work for idle hands!' A gale of laughter followed that remark and Louise fled from the Store with as much dignity as she could muster. Her mother for once was right – she'd stay at home for a few days. Then she remembered the Show committee meeting. Well, she'd go to that, but that was all. It was just a question of waiting for Peter to ask her to help him again. Peter the rock. Her rock, on which she would build her life. Quite how it would happen she wasn't sure, but it would. She'd see it did. Somehow.

12

Caroline had decided that she must let bygones be bygones where Louise was concerned and turn up for the Show committee meeting as though nothing had happened. She wasn't exactly relishing the idea, but there was no alternative. If she gave her excuses, they'd all know the reason why and it would make them more determined than ever to ostracise Louise for what had happened at the rectory the previous day.

She decided to get there early to forestall any discussion of Louise's behaviour before it had a chance to start. Whether by design or not, Louise arrived early too.

'Hello there, Caroline. Making the coffee? Oh good! Just what I need.' Louise's tone was friendly but respectful, when Caroline had expected her to be belligerent.

'Yes, I promised I would,' she replied neutrally. 'Here you are – black, no milk, no sugar. Right!'

'How clever of you to remember! Jimbo's not here again tonight. Pat is not really a very good substitute; he's always so full of good ideas whereas she has none.'

'Pat's all right. I like her.'

'You've got to like people. Being the rector's wife, you've no alternative.'

'Oh, I do have an alternative. Believe me, I have.'

Louise dared to speak his name. 'Peter all right?'

'Shouldn't he be?'

'Oh no, I didn't mean anything by that, just wondering how he was coping.'

'I see. Well, he's fine, thank you.'

'Sitting in tonight?'

'Yes.' Caroline thought that with all her years' experience as a doctor she understood people pretty well, could sum them up, see beneath the surface, work out their motives . . . but Louise had her foxed. What was the woman up to?

They were saved from continuing this painful conversation by the arrival of Barry. 'Pat not here yet?'

'No, not yet.'

Louise archly remarked that they seemed to be an item nowadays.

'An item – what's that?'

'Well, I mean kind of pairing off, sort of.'

'Anything the matter with that? We are both free agents, and I'm not trying to steal her from anyone, which is more than can be said for some people not a million miles away from me.' He took his coffee from Caroline and went to sit on a chair, carefully putting his papers on the one next to him to make sure he could keep it for Pat. Louise sat down and avoided meeting anyone's eyes. Trust Barry Jones to be crude. People like him were so basic, they'd no subtlety at all. None. She sorted out her files and rehearsed in her head her opening speech. But what Barry had said kept coming between her and the words. Damn and blast him. Besmirching a beautiful relationship. Typical. He'd better not say anything in front of Mother when she came, or else . . .

Before the meeting, most of the members had been up to see the progress of the new sewer pipes over at the Big House. Jeremy and Barry saw it every day and so did Pat, but the others made separate journeys to see what hope there was of still being able to hold the Show.

Barry came down on the side of optimism. 'I've great hopes it'll all be completed. No problem. Don't you think so, Michael?'

'Oh yes, I'm quite sure. It'll be a close run thing but yes, I'm sure you're right.'

Sheila disagreed. 'I don't know about that. I think we should postpone it for two weeks, just to be on the safe side.' The others looked horrified.

Pat was appalled. 'Postpone it? How can we do that? All the printing's done and everything, and they're all timing their flowers and veg to come to their peak at the date we've fixed. If we delay for two weeks I don't know what they'll do. Willie Biggs has got some brilliant beans and you should see his roses – coming on a treat they are. Jimbo's sweetpeas are gorgeous too. I reckon he'll take the prize this year.'

'He'll have to go some to beat Mrs Beauchamp's. Saw hers last week – cor, the size of 'em! Asked her what she fed 'em on but she just tapped the side of her nose and refused to say. Special seed she got from a big specialist near London,' Linda put in sagely.

'Jimmy's entering some eggs. His are always the brownest ones you'll ever see.'

Sheila looked up surprised when Pat said that. 'Eggs? There'll be no classes for eggs.'

'No classes for eggs – why ever not? Proper shows always have them – the biggest, the brownest, best-matched six all displayed on a doily in a basket . . . Course there's classes for eggs!'

'There aren't. Couldn't fit them in.'

'Well, Jimmy doesn't know.'

'He should. I distributed the advance lists weeks ago.'

'I wouldn't like to be in your shoes when he finds out. They always have eggs. Jimmy'll be real disappointed, he will.'

Louise checked the official printed list. 'No eggs. Sorry.'

''Ere, let me look at that.' Barry almost snatched the list from Louise. He ran his eye down both sides of it and said, 'She's right, there isn't. What yer playing at? Them at Nightingale Farm have them Welsummer hens, brilliant eggs they lay. They're planning to enter.'

Sheila drew herself up, patted her hair and answered firmly. 'Not this year they won't. It's all produce.'

Michael Palmer murmured, 'But what are eggs if they're not produce?'

'I mean growing produce like beans and flowers and things.'

It suddenly dawned on Linda what the reason was for the egg classes being omitted. 'Let me look at that schedule, Barry.' She scanned the list and quickly counted, as swiftly as she counted the stamps in the post office. 'I thought so. There's almost twice as many flower classes as produce classes. Well, I never. I wonder why?' She looked accusingly at Sheila. 'Obvious who's planned this.'

'You all saw the list before it went to the printers and you all approved it.'

'Yes, but you've added classes since we saw it, and crossed out others.'

'I never, Linda Crimble. I never have. Getting married's done you no good at all. You've developed a suspicious side to your nature.'

'Well, really. Just wait till my Alan hears what you've said.'

Louise, seeing her mother under siege, decided to interrupt. 'Now really, this won't do. My mother is guilty of no such thing. That's the list as you saw it before it went to the printers. Believe me.'

Pat decided to have her say. 'Oh yes? There weren't no class for flower arrangements with a seaside holiday theme. Definitely, 'cos I would've remembered that.'

Sheila triumphantly answered Pat's suspicion with, 'Seeing as you go away every year to the sea you'd be bound to remember.'

Caroline, who'd taken no part in all the wrangling, decided that things were getting far too personal. 'Shouldn't we deal with important matters like who's going to be in charge of keeping the money safe and who's going to be on the platform with Mr Fitch and who'll be at the gate to take the ticket money? Surely the eggs can be dealt with later.'

Sheila hurriedly agreed with this piece of sound common sense, mainly because she *was* guilty of adding flower classes after the schedule had been approved. These people had no idea what was style and what was not. Eggs indeed!

'You should have had a bigger marquee for the competitions. I did say so at the time, but I was overruled. If it had been bigger there would have been room for eggs.'

''Ere, just a minute. What's happened to the cake competitions? There's none for adults, they're all for children. My mum'll have something to say about this – she's a miracle with a Victoria sponge.' Barry glared at Sheila. She swallowed hard. There seemed to be no end to the unpleasant discoveries tonight.

Pat looked down the schedule Barry was holding. 'Shortbread's my thing and there's no classes! There's always shortbread classes. Look 'ere, Sheila, you've overstepped the mark.'

Jeremy, who'd had to come to the meeting before he could have his supper, swore under his breath; hunger always made him short-tempered. 'I've something better to do than sit here listening to arguments about shortbread and eggs. Let's get on with it. Mr Fitch has suggested that I take charge of the money and lodge it in the office safe until we have time to count it. He'll make sure he's here to open the Show and he wants room on the dais for three guests; he suggests we choose three of us to represent the committee. So that'll be seven in all – quite enough. Two of his guests will be ladies and he would like them to be presented with bouquets. Large ones.'

Michael proposed that Caroline, Louise and Pat should sit on the dais.

Caroline declined. Louise agreed and Pat agreed and then realised she'd be too busy at that juncture and she'd look a fool in her waitress uniform anyway. She'd have to propose someone fast, anyone to stop Sheila preening herself up there in front of everybody. 'I can't accept as I shall be too busy then in the food marquee. Don't you think we should have a man on the platform, otherwise Mr Fitch will be the only one. What about Louise, Bryn and Mr Palmer?'

Bryn nodded his agreement. 'That's settled then. Louise, write down me, you and Michael.'

Sheila protested at the unfairness of this. 'But what about me? I've done a lot for this Show! It's not right. I ought to be on the platform.'

A deathly hush fell. Faint hearts looked at their shoes, stronger ones at a point somewhere west of Sheila's shoulders. As no one backed her up she said, 'Oh right. That's how it is, is it? You can organise your blasted Show as best you can. I'm having nothing more to do with it.' She picked up her bag and began stuffing her papers into it.

Jeremy said, 'Now see here, Sheila, we never meant to upset you.'

Pat muttered, 'Didn't we?'

'This little contretemps can soon be resolved, can't it?' Jeremy looked meaningfully round the circle of members. Michael took it upon himself to volunteer not to be on the platform.

'Seeing as the fancy-dress parade is the first in the arena I shall really be too busy supervising the children to have time to sit on the platform, so please, Lady Bissett, have my place. I'm sure you'll grace the platform far more decoratively than I shall.'

Wryly Pat whispered to Barry, 'He's right there. Her outfit will be Buckingham-Palace-Garden-Party-here-I-come standard, you'll see.'

Sheila, with her back to everyone as she zipped up her bag, stopped midway, beamed triumphantly and then, changing her face into an excellent impression of a woebegone spaniel, sat down again and said, 'Well, all right then. Seeing as you've asked me so nicely, I will sit on the platform – though how I shall find the time I really don't know, I shall be so busy.'

Pat jumped in quickly at this hint of doubt. 'In that case then we'll ask Dr Harris again, shall we? You'd do it, wouldn't you?'

'No, thank you.'

Louise said, 'That's settled then. Bryn, me and Mother on the platform. I've made a note about the bouquets, Jeremy – I'll order those. Now, shall we continue? Who's going to be on the gate?'

Jeremy solved that by offering two estate-workers who'd been press-ganged by Mr Fitch into giving a hand. 'They're both big and beefy so you'll have no trouble with gatecrashers trying to get in for nothing.'

After they'd cleared up several more points Louise was just arranging the date of the next meeting when Barry said, 'Before the meeting closes I think we should sort out this question of the classes which have been scrubbed. No good sweeping it under the carpet. Can we have an extra sheet printed, or something, so that the egg classes and that are back in?'

Sheila took a deep breath intending to enter the fray before things got out of hand but she felt a sharp dig in her ribs from Louise, so she kept quiet.

Michael answered him. 'I think that would be a very good idea. After all, we are doing this for the sake of the village, profit is not our prime motive, and if that's what the village expects then that's what they must have. A few eggs are not the stuff of crises, are they? Nor indeed are some more cake classes. Can we ask Lady Bissett to amend her lists please, before it causes trouble? We can blame it on a printing error.'

Linda agreed with him. 'I second that.'

'So do I. I've done two lots of shortbread to make sure I get me hand in before the day, and I think I'm on a winning streak. What do you say, Louise?' Pat looked hard at Louise as she said this. 'Well?'

'OK then. I'll type an amendment, photocopy it and slip it in each programme. Won't bother the printer – he'll only charge the earth.'

Michael stood up. 'May I offer a word of thanks to Louise for all this unpaid work she is doing for us? We all go away with a few jobs to complete but she has to keep her hands on everything that's going on. We're really most grateful to you for your wonderful organisation. All your lists and meticulous attention to detail, we're very lucky to have your services. You're doing an excellent job. Thank you.' He looked round the circle and putting his hands together, waited for the others to do the same. They all began clapping. Louise looked embarrassed.

Pat muttered, 'If only she'd stick to her lists we'd all do better.'

'What did you say, Pat?' Sheila broke off from clapping. She'd heard what had been said, and still smarting from Pat's victory over the cake classes was determined to show Pat up for what she was.

'I said it's good she sticks to her lists, that way nothing gets missed, does it?'

'That's not what you said.'

'If you knew what I said, why did you ask me to repeat it?'

'It was a nasty remark you made. It's not fair, she's working really hard.'

'All depends what she's working *at*, doesn't it?'

Caroline stood up and said, 'We've arranged the date for the next meeting, so shall we all go? Willie will be wanting to lock up.'

Ignoring Caroline's calming remark, Sheila stood up and said with a threatening look on her face, 'And what do you mean by that?'

'She knows what I mean only too well.'

Caroline said, 'Pat, please,' in a pleading tone.

'It has to be said, Dr Harris.' Pat looked directly at Louise. 'We each of us know what you've been up to – well, you'd better put a stop to it right now, 'cos we won't stand for it.'

Louise stood up and looking directly at Pat said, '*I* have done nothing to be ashamed of. Nothing.'

Pat stood up and hands on hips said belligerently: 'You're not suggesting the rector *encouraged you?*'

Barry took her arm. 'Now Pat, be careful.'

'Careful? It needs saying. She's doing an excellent job with the Show, but heaven help us! She's causing trouble and it's got to stop.'

While Pat had been speaking, Sheila had been saying, 'What does she mean? I don't understand.'

Linda, seeing an opportunity to get back at Sheila, and indirectly at Louise for her condescending treatment of her at the post office counter, jumped in with support. 'No good trying to kid us that you've had *encouragement* at the rectory. That's enough to make a cat laugh.'

'Encouragement? What *are* you women talking about?' Jeremy had now finally run out of patience. 'If there are no more committee matters to discuss, then I for one am going home. I want my supper. Good night.' He marched for the door. Michael and Bryn wanted to do the same but both felt they should stay, just in case.

Caroline, normally so in control of herself and of events, tonight found herself quite unable to take command of the situation.

Barry said quietly to Pat, 'Leave it, leave it, there's going to be too much said that should be left unsaid.'

Pat ignored him and drove home her attack. 'Dressing like Dr Harris indeed! We all noticed. Think we're blind or something? Stick to what yer know best, lists and computers and things.'

'I don't have to put up with this kind of attack. All this malicious gossip, it's so unfair and quite unwarranted. Here,' she handed Pat her file and when Pat didn't take hold of it she dropped it on the floor, 'take that and you can be secretary seeing as you know so much. We'll see what kind of a good job you can make of it.' Louise picked up her bag and left, very close to tears because of Pat's attack. Wherever she went, whatever she did it always came back to the same theme. All she was fit for in other people's eyes was administration and organisation. Nothing else. Surely to God there was more to her than that . . . wasn't there?

Sir Ronald was at home watching the football in the sitting room. When the front door banged open he leapt guiltily out of his chair. He called out, 'Kettle's boiled, the tea won't be a minute.' As he crossed the hall to the kitchen he realised Sheila was crying.

'Now then, old girl, what's the matter?'

'I don't know. Ask her.' She jerked her thumb at Louise and then burst into fresh storms of weeping.

'What have you been saying to her, eh?'

'Nothing, Dad, nothing. It's me who's been hurt, not Mother. There's nothing to blame me for.' Louise flung down her bag and made to go up the stairs.

'Just a minute, madam. You may be an adult but while you're under our roof you owe me an explanation of why yer mother's so upset.'

Sheila stopped crying long enough to blurt out, 'She's resigned from the Show committee.'

'Well, you nearly did too,' Louise sniffed.

'But that was because of the classes. I don't know why *you* nearly resigned. What was it Pat was meaning? And Linda? She said about the "rectory" and "encouragement". What did she mean?'

Louise pressed her lips tightly together. Her father saw the child in her and remembered the fierce arguments they'd had when she was young. Give him their Brendan any day. He barked at her, 'I'm still waiting for an explanation and I don't care if it takes all night. What have you been doing?'

'I've been doing nothing. It's other people who've been "doing", not me.'

Sheila remembered. 'Is it something to do with Caroline? She was very white-faced. Was it her? Have you been arguing with her?'

'We don't like each other, but it's not her.'

Sheila wiped her nose again and then asked, 'Sylvia then?'

'It's not Sylvia.'

Sir Ronald groaned inwardly. 'That only leaves the rector.'

Louise, with eyes downcast said, 'Don't blame me, I've done nothing.'

Sir Ronald persisted with his quest for the truth. 'Then if *you've* done nothing, what's all the fuss about?'

Louise took a deep breath to control her tears. The truth. She couldn't tell them the truth no matter what. She couldn't admit to rejection once again, not again. 'They all . . . well, Pat Duckett seems to think I've been making overtures to the rector. I haven't, of course not, for heaven's sake, but that's what they think.'

His eyes widened. 'You don't mean the rector's been . . . Lovely chap though he is, and I wouldn't have a wrong word said against him, he does have a certain reputation which probably you don't know about. I can understand he's very attractive to women. Oh yes.'

'I refuse to say anything which might damage his reputation. Now can I go to bed? I'll have my tea in bed, Mother, and I'll have one of those plain biscuits as well . . . please.' Her parents watched her walk up the stairs and when they heard her bedroom door close they looked at each other.

'Ron, I ought to believe her, I am her mother after all, but I don't.'

'You don't?'

'No. I think she's been making all the running and he's been backing off as fast as he can, but she won't let go. There's something strange happened at the bank which she won't tell me about.'

'But she got made redundant, she said so.'

'I know she did, but there's more to it than that.'

'She doesn't usually lie. What do you think happened, then?'

'I don't honestly know anything, it's just a feeling I have.'

'Woman's intuition, eh?' He put an arm around her shoulders and gave her an understanding hug.

Sheila wiped her eyes, dropped the tissue in the metal waste-basket she'd decorated with flowered fabric and trimmed with gold fringe, and whispered, 'Oh Ron, whatever are we going to do? What she really needs is to meet a nice man.' Sheila's eyes glowed. 'That's it! I bet that was it! There was a man involved at the bank.'

'The sooner she gets a job and moves away the better.'

'Amen to that!'

13

'Craddock Fitch here, I need to speak to Miss Bissett.'

Sheila's hand trembled as she held the phone. After the upset last night she'd hardly slept a wink and wasn't really braced sufficiently at this early hour of the morning to conduct a conversation with someone so prestigious as Mr Fitch.

'Er, oh yes, er, it's Lady Bissett speaking, yes, I'll get her for you, can you hold the line?'

She raced up to Louise's bedroom, and knocked agitatedly on the door. 'Louise, Louise, it's Mr Fitch on the phone, hurry up! Don't keep him waiting.'

Louise appeared in a second, still in her nightdress, sleep heavily obvious around her eyes, her hair uncombed. Sheila watched her run downstairs to the phone. No, she thought, the rector wasn't at fault. It was all Louise's overcharged imagination, that's what it was. Well, Ron had said she had to deal with it; he'd said after all it was women's talk. Her heart quaked at the thought, and there came a mysterious throbbing in her ears. Oh dear, had she got high blood pressure? If she hadn't now she would have by the time this was all over. She could hear, couldn't avoid it really, Louise saying, 'Yes, of course, Mr Fitch. Certainly. Twelve noon. Of course. Certainly. Oh, how lovely. Thank you. Looking forward to it. Bye bye.'

The receiver went down and Louise came charging up the stairs. 'That was Mr Fitch, he wants to see me at twelve about the Show. He's driving down from London this morning. Twelve o'clock, he said, and then stay for lunch. I'm having a bath and washing my hair. Mind out of the way.'

'But you've resigned!'

'Oh God – so I have! The file! I'll need the file! Damn and blast it!'

What she'd hoped would be a relaxing soak in perfumed water planning how she would impress Mr Fitch, changed into a frantic charge through several rehearsals of how she would extract the file from Pat, without admitting she wanted to be back as Secretary to the committee. Why did he have to ring at such an inopportune moment? A few more days and she could have resolved it, got the file back, been reinstated and carried on as before. Without being on the committee and without the rectory visits she had nothing left and would definitely have to find a job. There was no further excuse. She could make a start on sorting out Gilbert's music, but that would really bring little reward. Though she had promised she would do it. Yes, she'd do it and then that would be that. Louise put a stop to her meanderings. This wasn't working out how to get the file back from Pat without too much loss of face.

A decision to leap out of the bath and get round to the school before Pat left meant Louise was out in Jacks Lane by twenty minutes past nine. She found Pat in the school kitchen hanging up some tea towels to dry on a little rack above the sink. Louise could hear the babble of children's voices, but didn't smile like others did when they heard it; she was too preoccupied searching for the right words.

Pat turned to see who had called her name.

'Oh, it's you! Well, what now?'

'Could I possibly have my file back? I think I must have left some private correspondence in there and I need it, this morning, right now. Please.'

'Not got it, I'm afraid.' She finished hanging up the cloths, then began drying her hands on the kitchen roller-towel.

Startled, Louise asked sharply, 'Not got it? Where is it then?'

'Dr Harris took it. I certainly wasn't going to take over, not on your Nellie! So if you want it you'll have to go to the rectory for it.'

'I see.' Louise swallowed hard. 'I'll have to go there then.'

'You will. Though how you've the cheek to knock on their door after the rector's turned you out, I don't really know. Glad I'm not in your shoes.'

'Mmmmm. Right, well, I'll get round there.'

'See yer then.'

Louise didn't notice the glee on Pat's face, nor did she see Pat dance a little jig right there on the red tiled floor.

She walked slowly out of the school and across the playground, then stood for a few moments in the gateway watching the builders working on the houses in Hipkin Gardens. They were glazing the windows already. How many months had she been at home? Too many. What on earth was she going to do? It was such a feather in her cap for Mr Fitch to want her to go for lunch and discuss the arrangements for the Show, that she couldn't, honestly couldn't, miss out. She'd promised him anyhow, and at least he wouldn't know what the gossips in the village were saying about her. They just didn't understand how she felt. She could make darling Peter so happy, so very happy. There were no two ways about it; she'd have to face up to going to the rectory. It might not be a bad thing, after all; she might even get a chance to have a word with Peter on his own. She'd go home first, have a coffee and a think and then walk across and request the file.

At the rectory the file was on Peter's desk, where he'd left it the night before, after he and Caroline had gone through it when she'd got back from the committee meeting.

'Give credit where it's due, she's an amazing organiser, isn't she, Peter? I can't see how I could possibly be as detailed as this. All these notes, cross references, all this detail. All these coloured stickers, red for this, yellow for that. Brilliant! If she went under a bus tomorrow we'd be able to carry on as if nothing had happened.'

'Caroline! What a thing to say!'

'Well, we would – it's true. But whichever way you look at it, I've got to get her back as secretary again. I simply haven't the time to take all this on, nor am I the kind of person who could keep such immaculate records.' She waved her hand over the file, closed it up and said, 'What a pity her private life is in such a mess. All she needs is a good—'

'Caroline!'

'*Man* I was going to say – a man who loves her for what she really is. After all, there must be more to her than all this.' She waved her hand over the file again. 'Who could we find for her?'

'Michael Palmer springs to mind.'

'Yes, that's a good idea – we could give them those opera tickets you were sent. We're not opera people, but Michael is and she would be, if it meant going out with a man. Yes, we'll give them the opera tickets and follow it up with a post-Show dinner party. That would make a good start for them, don't you think?'

'Caroline! I don't want her anywhere near the rectory, thank you, unChristian though that might sound.'

When the doorbell rang Peter was impatient at the interruption. Caroline had taken the twins into Culworth to buy new shoes and meet a friend for lunch, and Sylvia was using up some holiday which was due to her. He was in the rectory all on his own and taking the opportunity to finalise an article he'd been asked to write for the local paper. As he crossed the hall, he put a welcoming smile on his face and opened the door.

'Ahh! It's you, Louise. Good morning. What can I do for you?'

'Good morning. May I come in?'

Peter had a rule that anyone and everyone was welcome at the rectory whatever the time of day or night. Reluctantly he held open the door and asked her in. However, instead of inviting her into his study as he would normally have done, he stood waiting in the hall to hear what she had to say.

'Actually it's the file, the file for the Show. In a moment of . . . extreme stress I gave it to Pat last night. I don't know if Caroline . . .'

'Yes, she did.'

'Is she in? Could I have a word?'

Peter said she was out, sorry.

'Oh, I see. Do you happen to know where she put it? I need it to get some things out, personal papers I left in by mistake.'

Peter gave her one of his deep searching looks. Louise lowered her eyes and stared at the carpet. Why must he look at her like that right now? She couldn't tell lies when he looked at her like that. 'Well, the truth is, the truth is, I want it back . . . because I want to be . . . oh God! The truth is . . .' Suddenly out of nowhere, abruptly and thoughtlessly she blurted out, 'It's you. Oh, Peter! I can't bear not seeing you, can't bear it.' She took her handkerchief from her pocket and wiped away the tears welling in her eyes.

'Now see here, Louise, you know it's not possible. Simply not possible. We agreed on that.'

'No, you agreed to it with Caroline and Sylvia, you *told* me.'

'Quite right I did. What I said still stands though.'

'Why can't I see you? Why ever not? Just you and me, we work together so well. I wouldn't ask to look after the children. Think how well-organised your parish work would be with me helping you. Oh Peter!'

'I . . . I . . . There's no way this conversation can proceed. I'll get the file and you can take it away. Caroline really rather wished you'd be secretary again. She didn't feel up to the job herself, not when she saw how complicated everything was.'

'No, you see, that's it. That's all everyone ever sees me as – a highly efficient administrator. But I'm not like that underneath. Underneath I'm . . .'

'I'm sorry.' Peter backed away. 'Please, whatever it is, leave it unsaid. There's nothing to be done about it.'

'But there is. You could solve it all for me, for us. You and me. I'm brimming with ideas for helping the parish, to increase the congregation, to reorganise the giving, even ideas for different services. I've given it such a lot of thought. It would be brilliant. I'd see to it that it was, believe me.' Eyes brimming with tears, she looked longingly at him, her soul stripped bare for him.

Peter glanced away. 'I'll get the file.' He made to go to the study, intending she should stay in the hall, but she followed him in and shut the door.

'Why not? I don't understand why not? We work together so well, you and I. We've grown so close, and I've . . . I've . . . Oh, Peter, Peter, please!'

Peter stepped back to avoid her clutching him. God, what a mess! 'I desperately don't want to hurt you. I have the greatest respect for you, you see, but frankly I have no intention ever . . . again . . . of doing anything that would hurt Caroline. Me seeing you and working with you, would endanger my relationship with her. The first day I met her I knew how it was to be. I love her very deeply. We are married for *life*. There is *nothing* that I would do to jeopardise that. I made my promise before God and that promise I shall keep till the day I die.'

He watched the tears begin to pour down Louise's cheeks. When Caroline cried it broke his heart. Seeing Louise cry caused a sick feeling in the pit of his stomach: not pity, nor pain, nor distress, but revulsion. He strove to keep his feelings from his face, but it was his way to be truthful and to expect, and receive, the truth from others, so he was unsuccessful in hiding how he felt. She wiped her eyes and looked up at him again, intending to plead just one more time. He'd misunderstood, he didn't realise she was offering herself to him, but she saw the look on his face and recognised the truth; her tears revolted him.

He handed her the file. She snatched it from him, flung wide the study door, and ran away. Out through the open front door and across the Green to home. If her mother spoke one word to her when she got in she'd kill her. But she did. And they had the row to end all rows. And her father was home too, and said his piece. And Louise wept, desolate, unloved and thirty years old. At a quarter past eleven she remembered she still had Mr Fitch to see. When he saw how efficient she was, he'd appreciate her even if no one else did. She'd drag the last remnants of her self-respect together and get up there and show him what she was made of.

14

Pat, still chuckling about Louise's dilemma, didn't bother to cycle between the school and the Store. She left her bike in the school-shed and walked round. Barry was coming tonight for a meal. Dean and Michelle had persuaded her to invite him. It was a thank you for Dean's cupboards, a talk about arrangements for the holiday, and a chance to get to know each other better. Grandad had agreed to go on holiday with them so long as he had a room of his own, and Dean was so delighted to be going away he'd not complained about sharing with Barry.

What was she to cook? Jimbo might have some ideas. She pushed open the door and picked up a wire basket. Jimbo was behind the meat counter sharpening a large carving knife.

'Morning, Jimbo. Can yer knock off for a minute and let me pick yer brains.'

'Just the person I want to see. I'll pick yours first. What on earth happened at the meeting last night? I've just seen Louise racing across the Green, crying buckets, clutching to her ample bosom that file she always takes to the meetings. Is there something I ought to know?'

'Well . . .' Pat told Jimbo the details of the upset. 'So this morning I told her to go to the rectory if she wanted it.'

'I say, what can have happened?'

'Crying, you said? Serves 'er right.'

'Yes, and running like hell.'

'Blimey! He must have told her straight. Only right he should. Anyway, I'm making a special meal tonight. For five. Can you give me any ideas? Not too expensive, but just a bit special.'

'Special meal?' Jimbo eyed her speculatively, his eyebrows raised, his head to one side.

'Now look, Jimbo, I know you like to know everything that goes on, but this time it's secret.'

'Won't stay secret for long, not in Turnham Malpas.'

'Maybe not.'

They discussed the meal at length and when Jimbo had packed her shopping for her and she was paying him, he said, 'He's all right, is Barry, a nice chap. Does the noble parent like him?' He grinned at her and she couldn't be angry.

'Old Mrs Thornton that 'ad this place before you was a gossip, but you're ten times worse.'

'Such fun though and quite harmless. Sorry! I didn't mean to pry.'

Pat settled her forearms on the ledge in front of the till and didn't notice the doorbell jingle. 'Yes, I'm asking him as a thank you for putting up some cupboards in Dean's bedroom. I might as well tell you the rest. He's going on holiday with us to Devon . . .' Jimbo coughed significantly and winked. Pat turned round to find Barry's mother breathing fire down her neck.

'Is that my Barry you're talking about?'

'It is.'

'You're no better than you should be, Pat Duckett. Going on holiday with him when you're not married. Disgusting! Wait till he gets home.'

'And what do you propose to do about it? He's a grown man, he can do as he likes.'

'Not when he's under my roof he can't.'

'Well, he is going on holiday with us, and that's final. First holiday my kids have ever had, and nothing's going to spoil it for 'em. Not you, not anybody.'

'I don't know who you think you are, speaking to me like that.'

'Same as you, ordinary. To put your suspicious mind at rest, your Barry's sharing a room with our Dean, not me. Satisfied?' Pat picked up her shopping and with a brief nod to Jimbo walked out.

It was after ten by the time she'd finally got Dean packed off to bed. Grandad had helped to wash up and then taken a cup of tea up to bed to watch the football in his room.

'Do you want to watch the football, Barry?'

'No, thanks, not tonight. Come and sit next to me here.' He patted the cushion beside him and put his arm along the back of the sofa. He smiled up at her and her heart flipped.

Barry patted the cushion again. 'Thanks for a lovely meal, it was smashing. You're a good cook.'

'Makes a difference when yer can afford the ingredients. Before Dad came, it was egg and chips, beefburger and chips, or jacket potatoes for ever and a day.'

'Been hard for you then.'

'Yer can say that again.'

'I'd like to make life easier for you.'

Pat turned towards him and said, 'You are doing that already by taking us all away. I need to sort out the money for that. Can't let you pay for everything, petrol and that. I'll bring plenty of food with us.'

'There's a supermarket on the site. As far as the money's concerned, petrol's my responsibility and the caravan's free so there's only the food and the entertainment to pay for. Yer dad said he wants to chip in with that so I reckon it won't be that expensive.'

'You been talking to Dad about it then? When?'

'One day, when we met.'

'He likes you.'

Barry asked, 'D'you like me? That's the big question.'

'Yes, I do. You're house-trained, clean, smart and healthy, and you've got all your own teeth.' She grinned at him.

Deflated he said, 'Make me sound like a dog, you do.'

Pat laughed. 'What did you expect me to say? That you put me in mind of Clark Gable, or Rex Harrison or someone?'

'I'd rather you said Harrison Ford or Kevin Costner.'

'I couldn't match up to them! No, they'd be no good.'

'Give us a kiss. Come on.'

'I'm not much good at kissing.'

'I'll teach you, I'm an expert.'

'It is true then – you an' all those girls?'

'No, no. All talk. Kissing's instinct really. All instinct.'

'Is it?'

'Go with the flow as they say.' He hitched himself closer to her and taking her in his arms he vigorously set about kissing her cheeks, then her eyelids, and then several small kisses around her lips. It was Pat who opened her mouth and encouraged him to kiss her 'for real' as she called it. It was Pat who groaned her pleasure at his kisses, it was Pat who moved closer still and it was Pat who didn't object when he opened the buttons at the neck of her dress and began touching her neck and her throat with rapid exciting kisses.

'Oh Barry . . .'

'God, Pat, we'd better stop.' He sat upright and didn't look at her, anywhere but at her. His hands were twisting together as though battling with themselves. She rebuttoned her dress, and sat rigidly upright away from him, not touching him, puzzled by his reaction and disappointed that he didn't find her exciting.

Barry muttered quietly, 'Sorry about that. Really sorry.'

'Why?'

'I'd better go.'

'Go – why? Is it because . . . I didn't do it right?'

'No, no, you were great. This time it's . . .' He took a deep breath. 'Always before it's been sex first and last. This time I'm getting it the right way round. This time it's important to me. You're important to me, that is. Don't know why, but you are. I've always gone for the tarts before, all high heels and boobs. But this time it's different. More real. I want to get it right.'

'I see. I think that's how I'd like it too.'

Barry stood up. Looking down at her, he said, 'You mean you might take a liking to me?'

Pat nodded. 'But there's the kids. I come with baggage as yer might say. And there's Dad.'

'I know. But I like your kids. Really nice they are. Not at all cheeky and wanting things all the time. You've done a good job there.'

'I've tried. They're not always good.'

'Wouldn't want 'em to be. I'll say good night. Take no notice of Mum, by the way.'

'If you say so.' She stood up and went to see him to the door. 'Good night and thanks, Barry.'

He waved good night and then turned back. 'I just want to say this. Men yer know, at work, talk about the women they've been with the night before. Their girlfriends and their wives too – go into all the detail, for a laugh and to boast, yer know how it is. I did it too. I want you to know I don't talk about you. OK?'

'Right, thanks.'

Pat felt a million dollars. Yes, a million dollars. Beneath all his flirty talk he was a decent bloke. She locked the back door and began to make herself a drink to take to bed.

The kitchen door opened and Michelle was there. 'Mum, I'm thirsty, can I have a drink?'

'You not been to sleep yet then?'

'For a bit, but then I woke up feeling funny.'

'Sit there and we'll 'ave a cup of tea.'

'Mum?'

'Yes.'

'I do like Barry.'

'Good.'

'Do you?'

'Yes, I think so.'

'You know L-O-V-E? Well . . .'

'Yes, go on.'

Michelle stirred her tea. 'Does Barry L-O-V-E you?'

'Not yet, but perhaps he might.'

'I thought there was a big bang and you knew you were in love.'

'Sometimes there is, but when you get older sometimes it happens slowly.'

'I hope you love him. I'd like him for a dad. Could I be a bridesmaid? I've never been one.'

Pat laughed. 'We'll see. He hasn't asked me yet.'

'No, but he will. I can tell the signs.'

'Michelle!'

'I've talked to Grandad. He says the same. He says Barry's smitten, 'cos he's different with you. I think he likes me too, don't you? I should like him to like me. Could I call him Dad?'

'Only if we married.'

'Well, hurry up then. When he proposes will you tell me all about it? What went on and that. I need to know for when I grow up.'

'Cheeky face!' Pat kissed her and the two of them went off to bed.

When she got into her own bed, she stroked the pillow next to hers. She'd kept the bed her and Doug had bought when they first got married. Pat tried to imagine what it would be like to have Barry going to sleep there every night. Feel funny. Been alone for eight years she had. If, and it was a big if, they married she'd have a new bed – one of those big ones, the really big ones, then there'd be plenty of room. She wouldn't want any more kids though. They'd have to have an understanding about that. Not when she was knocking on forty and the other two so old. No more kids. He'd have to understand. Pat took a last look around her bedroom before finally closing her eyes and going to sleep. She admired the flower pictures Dean had bought her to put on the wall over the radiator. She leaned out of bed and dug her fingers into the tufts of the carpet she'd chosen in that big carpet warehouse outside Culworth; she patted the bedspread, pretend patchwork quilt like them American quilts, and finally she switched off her bedside lamp – now that was a luxury. Before, she'd always had to get out of bed to turn off the light.

Yes, things were definitely looking up. One whole week beside the sea, like a real family, and to top it off she was determined she'd win the shortbread prize, because this year was her year.

15

The bar in The Royal Oak was packed. Saturday evening, hot summer weather, and the world and his wife were there. The tables outside in Royal Oak Road were filled, and the overspill had taken their drinks out on to the Green and were sitting on the grass, enjoying themselves. Willie and Sylvia were at their favourite table in the saloon, with Jimmy and Vera.

'Pat not coming then?' Vera asked.

Jimmy shook his head and said, 'No, Vera, she's got other fish to fry. That Barry's taking up a lot of 'er time.'

'Good luck to her, I say. He's a nice chap, all that flirting he does though, it's scandalous. Cor, he's had some girls in his time. Got caught in the hayloft at Home Farm few years back. Talk about a carry on, that was. There was mention of a shotgun, but he managed to escape.'

Sylvia put down her gin and tonic to say, 'Well, he seems to have steadied down now. The whole lot's going on holiday together after the Show.'

'No! Grandad as well?'

'Yes.'

'Well, that's a turn-up for the book, that is. Wouldn't ever have thought Barry would be taking two kids and a grandad with 'im. What a laugh. He must be serious! Any news from the church we ought to know, Willie?'

'Not from the church, 'cept the rector's away. Gone to Devon today for two weeks. Time they both had a holiday. That's all really. But there is news from the school. Did you know Mr Palmer's given his notice in?'

'Mr Palmer given his notice in?' Jimmy couldn't believe it. 'After all these years? Whatever for?'

'Got a new job miles away. Head of a big primary school. Hundreds o' kids.'

'Bit different from ours then.'

Sylvia said she couldn't think what on earth had made him move.

Vera agreed. 'Neither can I. He's been here nearly twenty years, must have been. Yes, twenty at least. He's going on for forty-five or thereabouts.

Wonder what's made him do it? I've always thought of him as a permanent fixture, like the school boiler or something.'

'It'll be a big wrench for 'im anyways.'

'Pat always thought him and Suzy Meadows would make it up. Very pally they were when she ran the playgroup at the school.'

'That poor girl must have had enough of men one way and another.' Sylvia felt Willie's knee nudge her under the table as she spoke. She tried to change the subject. 'Still, new fields to conquer and all that. You planned your holidays yet, Vera?'

Vera's mind was still dwelling on Mr Palmer. 'You know, it would have been great for Mr Palmer and her to get together. A readymade family with them three girls, and lovely girls they are too. He's too old to start a family of his own, it would have been just right.'

Jimmy suggested he'd never have the guts to ask her in the first place. 'When his wife killed herself he switched off. Good with the children but dead as a dodo otherwise. Don't yer think?'

'Well, he never does have much to say about anything except school. That's the only time he comes alive. Sad, very sad.' Vera gazed gloomily into her empty glass.

''Nother drink, Vera?'

'Oh, thanks, Jimmy. What it is to have a wealthy neighbour.' She giggled at him. 'Same again, please. We'll drink to Mr Palmer, wish him good luck in his new job. It takes some believing.'

When Jimmy got back with the drinks they toasted Mr Palmer and his big decision to move away from Turnham Malpas, and then had an in-depth discussion on the likely winners of the prizes at the Village Show.

Jimmy summed up the situation in a nutshell. 'Well, yer can all say what yer like but I reckon when all's said and done the Templeton Cup for most points in the produce classes will be won by Willie.' He paused to take a long drink from his glass and then volunteered a piece of information that none of them knew about. 'There's going to be another cup this year.'

'Who says?'

'Louise-know-it-all-Bissett. She's persuaded old Fitch to present a cup for the most points in the flower classes. 'Spect it'll be as big as the FA Cup knowing 'im. The Fitch Flowers Cup it's to be called. The conditions'll be on that amendment sheet they're 'aving to put in 'cos of the classes that got left out by the printer – so Louise says, but we all know it was Sheila Bissett left 'em out on purpose. I'd 'ave 'ad something to say if there'd been no egg classes. My 'ens are laying like nobody's business now they're getting fed better. That new 'ouse of theirs suits 'em a treat.' Jimmy downed the last of his beer and said he'd got to go. 'I'm off to Culworth; there's always plenty of business for a taxi on Saturday nights. I've got a living to earn. Be seeing yer.'

'You shouldn't be drinking when yer driving.'

'I've only 'ad two halves. I'll suck a couple of mints on the way. Nobody'll know.'

Vera shook her head. 'He'll never improve, he won't. Right turn-up for the book about Mr Palmer though, isn't it? Just wish he could find a right nice little wife, not too flighty, but quiet like 'im. Wonder if they've got a replacement? Poor fella, right upheaval it'll be.'

Michael Palmer lay soaking in the bath in the schoolhouse, unaware that he was the subject of speculation in the bar. He'd left the bathroom door open so he could hear the sound of his CD player in the sitting room. There was no pleasure more enjoyable than lying in the bath, alone in the house, listening to good music.

He must remember to feed his roses before he went to bed. This year, his last year, he was determined he'd win something. He'd tried beans and marrows and won nothing, but this year he was trying roses. A Highly Commended would please him greatly – a final fanfare before he left. He sat up to turn the hot tap on for a while. As the comforting hot water passed his feet and began creeping up his legs, he thought about his new school. Three hundred children compared to thirty-eight. What a difference. What a decision. The most decisive step he'd taken in years. He turned off the tap and lay down again.

He still had to tell Suzy. He should have told her before he accepted the job, but somehow he knew he couldn't face a possible rebuff. The school was only fifteen miles from where she lived. Near enough, but far enough away, so if she didn't want to see him any more then they wouldn't be bumping into each other and it wouldn't be embarrassing. On the other hand . . . he did love her. She brought joy with her and gave it to him, joy like he'd never known. The final chords of the symphony bombarded his ears, and as the notes died away he became aware of the telephone ringing. Michael got out of the bath, wrapped a towel round his waist and went to answer it.

'Hello, School House, Michael Palmer speaking.'

'It's me – Suzy.'

His heart leaped. 'Hello, how are you?'

'I'm fine, thanks. I've been thinking.'

'Yes?'

'I haven't seen you for a long time.'

'Four weeks and five days.'

'Is it? That's a long time. I wondered if there might be a possibility you could come over. Next weekend perhaps?'

'I'm sorry, I can't. I've sold my car today.'

'Oh, that's good news. You didn't think you would.'

'No, well, I did and my new one won't be delivered until a week on Tuesday, so I've no transport at the moment.'

'Oh, I see. I am disappointed.'

'So am I. But it can't be helped. It would have been lovely to see you.'

'Michael . . .'

'Yes?'

'I could come to you, I suppose. No, of course I can't, because I wouldn't want to meet . . .'

'Oh, but Caroline and Peter won't be here. They'll be on holiday. You could come. We don't have to advertise the fact. Keep a low profile et cetera. It wouldn't matter, would it?' He'd begun to sound eager.

'Really?'

He controlled his eagerness. 'I don't want you to get the wrong idea. I mean . . . what I wanted to say was, I'm not putting pressure on you . . .'

'Oh no, I know you wouldn't.' He thought he heard Suzy sigh.

Michael rushed on with what he had to say. 'There's the spare bedroom, you see. You could have that.'

'Yes, I suppose I could. Shall I come then?'

'Yes, please, I'd like that. That would be lovely.'

'I'll come Friday night after school and leave first thing Sunday. Can't expect Mother to have the girls all weekend.'

'I'm really looking forward to seeing you.'

'Right, Friday night it is. What will the village say?'

'Plenty. But I don't care. After all, I'm—'

'What?'

'Nothing. Nothing at all. I'll see you Friday night then. I'll give you a ring during the week to confirm. Good night, Suzy.'

'Good night, you dear man.'

Michael, now shivering from head to foot, put down the phone, and dashed back into the bath. He put the hot tap on and warmed up the water again. He felt as though he'd taken a big step. The second big step in the last few weeks. This coming weekend could be the one when he proposed. On the other hand, was he doing the right thing? Yes, he was. Nothing ventured, nothing gained. She did want to come. She was willing to risk a lot to see him, so she must be interested. Yes, definitely, this coming weekend could be one of those turning points.

He was still joyful in school on Monday morning. He couldn't keep the happiness from his face. Pat noticed it. As she slipped her feet into her old school shoes she said to him, 'My word, Mr Palmer – you won the lottery? Million pounds, was it?'

'No, of course not, Mrs Duckett.'

'Well, I don't know what's caused it, Mr Palmer, but you're like a cat who's been at the cream.'

Michael wagged his finger at her and said, 'I'm not the only one. Since you moved to the Garden House, you've been on top of the world, and I don't think it's only the move that's done it.'

'Well, no, you could be right there.'

'I'm glad for you, Pat.'

Pat looked up from the cupboard under the sink where she was searching for a duster. 'My word, something's up. This summer I shall have worked 'ere in this school seven years and that's the first time you've called me Pat. It's always been Mrs Duckett this and Mrs Duckett that. What's up then?'

'Nothing, nothing at all. It must be the weather.'

'Weather my foot! I reckon I'm not the only one who's courting. It's not that Louise Bissett, is it?'

'Good God, no!' The words slipped out without thinking and he looked so appalled by his rapid, thoughtless answer to Pat's question that she burst out laughing.

'Gawd 'elp us, I 'ope not! Desperate she is for a man, so yer'd better watch out.'

'Mrs Duckett! That's most unfair. Not at all kind.'

'Well, just mind you're not *too* kind to her yerself. She's after anything in trousers, she is. The poor rector's having a right time with her. Mind you, I'm not surprised – he *is* lovely. Wonder he's not had trouble with women chasing him before this. Course, he did have, didn't he?' She glanced at him as she picked up the polish from the draining board, and saw he'd clamped down and gone back to how he used to be. Withdrawn and unapproachable. Gawd! That was it. The photo in the drawer. He was moving to be near her. Of course. She'd right put her foot in it this time.

'The windows in the playgroup room – when you have a moment, they need cleaning, Mrs Duckett.' He turned on his heel and left the kitchen. Mr Palmer deserved some happiness. You'd got to grab it while you could. In fact, no one in their right mind should turn down the chance of happiness. Life could be Gawd-awful lonely at times, even if yer 'ad kids, which he didn't.

He made Suzy a cup of tea as soon as she arrived. He'd boiled the kettle three times while he waited for her coming. His expectation was she'd be there by about eight, but it was nine before he saw her car. He watched as she slid it carefully into the narrow parking space by his house wall. In 1855 they didn't build school premises to accommodate cars. He'd taken a deep breath and gone to open the door. Bag in hand, she stood there smiling. She was wearing a dress the colour of wild cornflowers, and with it a matching blue headband holding back her hair from her face. His photo-graph didn't do justice to the blue of her eyes, nor to her silver-blonde hair, nor the delicate roundness of her cheeks. She seemed smaller than when he'd seen her over five weeks ago, more vulnerable, more hesitant. There was a tremor in her voice when she said, 'I've come as I promised.'

'Come in, come in.' Michael was conscious of being hale and hearty to cover how he really felt. Was he never going to be able to speak the unspeakable? To ask the impossible? Why should this delightful creature want him? He was ten years her senior and not remotely good-looking. Even her husband for all his faults had had a certain air. But he, Michael Palmer, had nothing to offer. His heart sank and he wished this weekend had never begun.

They talked the whole of the evening, Michael putting off the dreaded moment when he had to show her her bedroom and use the bathroom and . . . How would he get over the awkwardness of it all?

He proposed over breakfast. Broke the news first about moving from the village, said how excited he was by the challenge of the bigger school, the urban environment, and mentioned that it was about fifteen miles from where she lived. He'd have to buy a house, though he'd rent first and give himself time to look around and . . .

'Michael! What amazing news! I never thought you'd leave here.'

'I should have left when Stella . . . when Stella died. But I didn't, couldn't face my daily life here, never mind moving away on top of it all. At least everything was familiar here.'

'Something important must have made you decide to move away from here, something quite mind-blowing.'

He put down his spoon, and stared at the remains of his Shredded Wheat. 'Yes, something did. I unexpectedly fell in love.'

Suzy picked up her cup, and before she drank from it, she looked at him over the rim. 'Who's the lucky woman?'

Michael didn't answer immediately. His eyes strayed to the kitchen window and then back to his Shredded Wheat. He picked up his spoon again, filled it with cereal, lifted the spoon halfway to his mouth, put it down again and said so softly she had to strain to hear, 'You.'

'So did I. Fall in love. Unexpectedly.'

He took her to his favourite high point. They sat close together bracing themselves against the strong breeze blowing briskly over the fields below.

'I love this place. It's mine. I come here when I'm unhappy.'

'But you're not unhappy today of all days, surely?'

'No, not today. Today I could be on the brink of happiness. Yes, the brink of a lifelong happiness.' He turned his head to look at her, the second time that day he'd looked frankly and openly at her. He asked her bluntly a question he'd formulated a thousand ways in his mind but had never found the courage to ask.

'Peter Harris. Where do we stand about him?'

Suzy snatched her hand from his, and looked away.

He persisted. 'We must have it clear, quite clear, and then it won't be mentioned again.'

'My word, Michael, you're coming right out from behind the parapet today, aren't you?'

'There are times when one must. I can't hide any longer.'

'Neither can I. Seeing as we're being honest . . .' Suzy pushed her hair away from her face and tied the long length of it with a ribbon she took from her shirt pocket. 'I needed comfort and love the day they found Patrick dead. Peter was there, and for the moment he needed me. No, *wanted* me. To his dying day he will regret what happened. I shan't, though. It was a momentary attraction, which by the grace of God, gave Peter and Caroline the children they wanted. Nothing more, nothing less. You need have no worries about regrets or anything, Michael. My only regret is that it's taken me so long to come round to knowing how much you mean to me.'

Michael recaptured her hand, put his arm around her shoulders and hugged her close. The sun went behind a cloud. Suzy shivered and rubbed her arms. She smiled at him. 'It's getting cold. Time to go back to your house. I'll cook tonight, right?'

'Right. Race you to the bottom.'

Suzy laughed. 'Honestly, who am I marrying – a man or a boy?'

'A man, believe me – a man.'

Peter slowed right down when they came to the sharp right-hand bend by the sign to Turnham Malpas. Caroline glanced at the children strapped in their safety seats. 'It's all right, they're both still asleep. What a nightmare journey! I'm so sorry, darling, that we've had to come home. Who'd believe it – chickenpox! I really think the other guests believed they had the plague.'

'We couldn't have stayed. They're much too ill and much better off in their own beds, safe at home. We'll have another holiday later in the year, I promise. Only two more miles and we'll be back.' Peter patted Caroline's leg. She took his hand and squeezed it. 'Thanks for being so understanding,' she said. 'I really did wonder if I was being too "parenty" and worrying too much.'

'Indeed not. Coming home was by far the best decision.'

'Oh Peter, isn't it lovely having children? We'd got very self-centred, you know, before they came. Debating about whether to go to South Africa or the Rockies or whatever. And here we've had one week making sandcastles on a Devon beach and I've loved every minute of it.'

'Same here – every minute. But we mustn't get too smug with ourselves, or we might become dull.'

'You'd be more guilty of that than me. You can be very smug sometimes, Peter, to the point of being positively self-righteous.'

'Oh right, I'll have to watch myself then. I'll park in Pipe and Nook because of the bolts on the front door. The twins are bound to wake up. Can't help that. We'll take out only the essentials. I'm not up to unpacking properly at this time of night. In any case, we'll disturb the neighbours.'

The twins spent a very restless night, asking for drinks and crying for their mother. Caroline hardly slept at all. Twice Peter got up to them to give her a chance to rest, but they cried for their mother and refused to allow him to help them.

Caroline got up for good at six o'clock.

'Look, my darling girl. You stay up till I get back from prayers. I won't go for a run today, I can't find the energy. You settle them back into bed again and you go to bed too and I'll stay on duty while you sleep.'

'Wonderful. Right, come along you two, Mummy get you drinkies and some porridge. You always love porridge when you're not well, don't you? Lovely swirly syrup too. How about that?' Thumb in mouth Beth nodded, but Alex merely ignored what she said and demanded a cuddle.

Caroline had expected Peter back again by seven ready for his breakfast, but he hadn't come. At a quarter past seven the doorbell rang. 'Oh, he's forgotten his key. Coming, darling.' But it wasn't Peter it was Sylvia, worried because she'd seen the car parked in the lane and wondered what the matter was. Caroline explained.

'Oh no! Where are they? Alex, Beth, come to your Sylvie. Oh you poor sweethearts, oh my goodness me! Just look at your spots. Don't scratch, Beth. Don't they look dreadful? No wonder you had to come home.'

'I've been up and down to them most of the night, so when Peter gets back from prayers he's taking over. I shall put them back to bed and then I'll go too.'

'I'm so sorry about your holiday. What was the weather like?'

'Well, it was lovely all the week. Sun shining every day, but then by Thursday the children began to droop, and that spoilt it for us, of course. Anything of any note happen while we've been away?'

'No, nothing at all. Just the same sleepy village. You know what it's like, one week runs into the next. You look tired, I must say. How about I dash home for breakfast and then come back to give you a hand?'

'Certainly not, it's your holiday and I insist we shall manage.'

'If you're sure?'

'I am.' She held open the rectory door and invited Sylvia to leave. As Caroline was about to shut the door, Alex popped under her arm and out into the road. He set off after Sylvia, his pyjama legs flapping furiously as he ran. Caroline stepped out to catch him. 'Young man, you've had me up half the . . . night . . . and . . .' As she caught hold of him she glanced up the lane. Coming out of the lych-gate was someone she had thought she would never see again. Surely not? It couldn't be Suzy, could it? That silver-blonde hair of hers shining in the morning sun – there was no mistaking it. Oh, God! Caroline watched her pause for a moment, saw her turn back to face the church and give a slow gentle wave. There was obviously someone there returning her wave. Caroline snatched Alex back into the rectory, slammed the door shut and stood with her back pressed against it, breathing heavily. The shock of seeing Suzy again so unexpectedly made her heart pump frantically.

What was Suzy doing here? Hoping to see the twins? She wasn't. She wasn't seeing them. Over her dead body would she see them. They were hers, not Suzy's. She'd come to take Peter away from her and to get the twins – that was it. She'd come for Peter and therefore for the twins, they were theirs after all. Otherwise why was she here? What else was there for her to return to in the village, if not for the twins and Peter? God in heaven, *what was she to do*? Caroline felt crushed by the weight of her distress. In her agitation she clutched Alex against her chest and when he protested and struggled to get down she felt desolate, because his hatred of being squeezed felt like a rejection of her. Had he recognised his mother? Was he running to her and not to Sylvia? Had some sixth sense told him who she was? She mocked her own foolishness. Of course not, he didn't know her from Adam. She was being a stupid idiot. But Peter and Suzy had obviously met in the church. What had they said to each other?

He hadn't prayed at the main altar that morning but in the little side-chapel, converted to commemorate the men of the village killed in the First World War. Their surnames echoed those of the villagers of today.

Albert Biggs, William Biggs, Arnold Glover, Cecil Glover, Harold Glover, Sidney Glover, Fred Senior, Major Sir Bernard Templeton, 2nd Lieut. Ralph Templeton.

Dear Lord, what a loss. Four Glover boys. Four sons. How did their parents survive after that terrible blow? His own problems began to fade away, and he slipped into deep concentration and then to prayer.

He didn't hear Suzy's footsteps, and she didn't know he was there, hidden as he was by the oak screen carved in memory of so much horror. It was the sound of her accidentally sending a hymn-book spinning to the floor which disturbed Peter's absorption. He stood up and found himself looking at her through the screen. His heart missed a beat. Convinced he must be dreaming, he watched her walking about the church. What on earth was she doing here? Her lovely round cheeks were thinner than he remembered, but they still had that innocent glow to them; her splendid blue eyes were just as beautiful, and her hair, that lovely silvery-blonde hair, gleamed in the shaft of sunlight coming through the window above the altar. She hadn't changed much except she looked at peace now and not haunted.

He'd feel a fool if she came into the chapel and caught him hiding, so he stepped out from behind the screen and stood by the pulpit. She caught sight of him and he heard the swift intake of her breath. They looked intensely at each other, spanning the years with their memories. It was Suzy who spoke first.

'I'm so sorry, Peter. So sorry. I was told you were away from home. I was surprised to find the door open. I should have known. I've come to say goodbye to Turnham Malpas. You see, Michael's cooking our breakfast. If I'd known, I wouldn't have . . .'

'That's all right, we've had to come home because of illness.' He took a deep breath and making a huge effort to remember his duties as priest said, 'How are you, Suzy? You're looking very well.'

'I'm fine, Peter, thank you. How are you?' She reached out her hand but he ignored it. She put her hands behind her back. 'You're looking well. Everything is fine with me, is it with you?'

'Yes, thank you.' Peter paused for a moment and then said, 'Caroline and I are forever in your debt.'

There was a tremor in her voice as she said, 'No, you're not, not ever. The gift was freely given. I only gave you what was yours. I don't know why two old friends should be so solemn. I'll cheer you up. Michael Palmer and I are getting married in the summer. He's a lovely man, I feel so secure with him. I can depend on him – rely on him, you know.'

'Yes, I can understand that. Married? That's good. Wonderful news. I am glad.'

'This is goodbye then. I shan't be coming here again. I'm driving home this morning straight after breakfast. Don't tell Caroline you've seen me. I don't want her to be upset.'

Peter hesitated for a moment and then said abruptly, 'The children have chickenpox – that's why we've come home. They're covered in spots, and not at all well. She's been up most of the night with them.'

'I see, I'm sorry. Children can be a trial.'

'But worth it, worth it, you know. They are delightful.' He regretted those words the moment they were out of his mouth. What a fool he was to have said that.

Suzy's whole demeanour altered when Peter said how delightful they were. She became agitated. She twisted her hands together, then she put them to her mouth and almost gnawed on her knuckles. Then with her arms by her sides and her hands clenched tightly in her cardigan pockets she said, 'Delightful? Are they really? Are they . . . do they look like . . . like . . . me . . . or you?'

Peter felt himself to be reaching dangerous ground. 'They're both . . . that is, Alex . . . is like me but Beth is simply Beth.'

Suzy half-turned away from him and said quietly, 'Alex and Beth. They sound lovely. What I wouldn't give just for a goodbye peep. Just to say goodbye for ever.' Suzy faced him again. 'I wouldn't trouble you again, honestly I wouldn't and it wouldn't have occurred to me if you hadn't had to come home and been here when I . . . Please, Peter, please let me see them. It would kind of lay a ghost to rest if you would let me. Surely Caroline would . . . She knows I can't take them when they're yours, she knows they're safe. Please, just a peep.'

'No, no, no.' Peter backed away. 'Don't ask me, please don't ask me. Caroline is so deeply attached to them, almost more than if they were her own, if that's possible. The damage it would cause would be immeasurable. You really can't ask it of her. Your seeing them would distress her terribly.'

'But she has them for the rest of her life. I've lost them for ever.'

'You and I have caused her more than a lifetime of agony. It would be cruel, downright cruel of us to ask that of her. I'm sorry but no. Definitely no.'

Suzy came close to Peter and laid her hand on his arm. She looked intently up at him. He recalled the last time she'd laid her hand on his arm, when he'd been totally captivated by her gentle beauty. His innards turned to pulp. She tugged at his sleeve. 'Please.'

Peter brusquely pushed her away from him. 'I'm sorry, Suzy, but the answer is no. I can't let you down gently, I've got to be firm. No, absolutely no, both for her sake and yours. You've never seen them and that's the best way. If you do see them you'll never be free from heartache. This way at least you haven't got a picture of them in your heart for the rest of your life. It's best, believe me.'

He made the sign of the cross on her forehead, took her hand and slowly led her from the church. Her feet stumbled a little as the two of them walked down the aisle, and he sensed her struggle to control the sobs coming from deep within her. By the time they reached the church door, she had mastered her grief.

She turned to him and said sadly, 'Tomorrow, perhaps, I shall know you're right, but today I feel you've been very hard. I would have loved to have them, even if only a glimpse. Give them each a kiss from me, will you? Promise?' Peter nodded. 'I'll leave you then to finish your prayers.' When they reached the porch Suzy held out her hand. 'Goodbye, Peter. Be happy.' Peter shook hands, and then impulsively bent his head and kissed her, just one gentle kiss on her forehead, and for a moment he held her close.

'God bless you, Suzy. From the bottom of my heart I sincerely hope that your life with Michael will be tremendously rewarding, full of happiness and a great joy for you both.'

'I'm sure it will. Stay there and wave to me when I reach the gate, just this one last time. Just for me?'

He watched her walking slowly down the path to the gate. Michael was a lucky man. As she stepped out into the lane she turned and raised her hand to him. He raised his in blessing and then went back inside.

Caroline's prayer book was on the shelf in the rectory pew.

He read the words he'd written on the morning of their wedding day and knew how true they were. She was his and he was hers, '*from this day unto eternity*'. No one could part them. Suzy's ghost was at last laid to rest. He sat for a while and then realised that someone had entered the church. It was Willie, come to get ready for early service.

'Oh, good morning, Rector. Sorry you've had to come home. Right surprised we were when we opened the curtains and saw your car there. Sylvia popped in to see if she could give a hand but Dr Harris said you'd manage.' Willie peered closely at Peter's face. 'You not feeling too good, sir? You look peaky to me.'

'Put it down to a bad night with the children, Willie. I'll be off then. Don't want to upset things with my stand-in. I'll ring him later today – perhaps I could do Evensong.'

'No such thing. You keep out of the way, sir. It is your holiday after all. Looks to me as if you could do with some sleep. I'll see to everything, don't you fret.'

At home the twins were in their beds, eyes beginning to close. He found a place on Alex's face which was free from spots and kissed him. He took hold of Beth's hand and raised it to his lips. Caroline was already in bed. Now he'd have to find the right words.

16

Peter took off his shoes and laid himself down quietly beside her and tried to think how best to tell her what had happened. Once before he'd not told the truth; this time he had to tell her everything, no matter how much it hurt them both. But at least now he could say that he'd seen Suzy and he knew she didn't matter one jot to him because it was she, Caroline, whom he loved beyond all and . . .

'I'm taking the twins up home tomorrow.'

Peter half-sat up, resting his body weight on his elbow. He leaned over her and said, 'Up home? What for?'

'Because I need time to myself.'

'Why?' She didn't answer him. 'They're too ill to travel all that way.'

'They'll survive.'

'You're going to see your mother and father?'

'They should be leaving hospital tomorrow. They need me. You can tell everyone that's why I've gone.'

'But, darling, what help will you be to them with two small children to care for? They are such hard work, the pair of them. Leave them here. I'm off all this week – I can care for them.' Caroline didn't reply. He touched her arm and realised she was incredibly tense. What on earth was the matter with her? 'Look at me.'

'No, I shan't.'

'*Please* look at me.'

Caroline turned over to look at him and the pain in her eyes choked him. In a voice which was scarcely audible she said, 'I saw *her*. She was waving to *you*, wasn't she?'

'Dear God, Caroline, I'd no idea you'd seen her. That must have been the most tremendous shock. Why didn't you tell me straight away? I didn't speak because I thought you were asleep. I'm so deeply sorry that you've been suffering such pain. Please, my darling, believe me when I say I've been lying here trying to decide how to tell you, but I didn't know how. I was searching for the right words.'

'Oh, were you? I think you were hoping I wouldn't know, but Alex ran out into the road after Sylvia, and I went out to catch him and saw her wave.'

'It was goodbye. Before God, I didn't know she was here. Neither did she. Know we were here, I mean.'

'Yes, but you weren't going to tell me, were you?'

'I was. Believe me, I was.'

'It's always her who makes you not be truthful to me. The fact still remains that I'm going home tomorrow. You can tell the parish whatever you like, but that's what I'm doing. I'm terribly afraid and all mixed-up. I can't keep going any longer, so I'm going away. I'm leaving you. I'm leaving Turnham Malpas. I'm leaving the parish. Everything. I'm leaving it all.'

'As God is my witness we only said goodbye.'

'So you say. But I'm going. Going home.'

'Can I tell you what we said?'

Caroline's body jerked with anguish. '*No, you can't*. I don't want to hear. Not *one* word.'

The two of them were silent for a while and then Caroline, her voice strangely tight and jerky, said: 'Did she ask to see them? Because she isn't.'

'She did, but she isn't. I told her quite positively.'

'I would have killed her first.'

'My darling girl, I think maybe you're overwrought through sheer lack of sleep and too much worry, don't you?'

'Overwrought! What do you think I am? Some brainless idiot with nothing better to do than find wrongs to magnify and dwell upon? Peter! You know me better than that. You're reducing a deeply-felt anguish to a petty triviality. You must think me unbalanced. For God's sake!'

Alex, who'd been quietly crying for some time, began screaming.

Peter swung his legs over the edge of the bed. 'You stay there, darling, I'll go.'

'He won't let you see to him. *I'll* go.'

She got out of bed and climbed in with Alex and hugged him close. From sheer exhaustion she fell asleep and so did he. Secure in her arms.

'For one last time, I'm begging you not to go.'

'I am.'

'You're much too tired.'

'I'm not.'

'It's far too far for you to drive with the children by yourself. I'll take you. Please let me take you, and I'll leave you there with the car and come back on the train. If you don't want me there, that is.'

'I don't. Please, Peter, let me go. Just let me *go*.' Caroline grew angry and was within a hair's breadth of losing control. Her white face and clenched fists warned him how close she was to breaking down.

'Very well. But for my sake, ring me when you get there, so I know you're safe.' He reached out intending to kiss her goodbye, but as though his touch would be the last straw, she sprang away from him and jumped in the car.

He stood watching her turn the ignition key, fasten her safety belt; his arms and his heart aching with love for her. The children, still covered in spots and looking flushed and uncomfortable, waved their small hands to him and Beth blew him a kiss. He couldn't bear to see them go and quickly walked back into the rectory before the car moved off. He shut the study door, and stayed in there alone until Sylvia brought him his coffee.

'Here you are. I'll put it on the table for you, shall I? It's nice and hot.' She got no reply. 'There isn't much for me to do today. It looks as if Dr Harris did most of the washing and ironing yesterday. I've dusted round and got some shopping in, so I'll go if there's nothing else. Rector?'

'Thank you. Thank you for all you do. There was no need to come in this morning. You're more than kind.'

'I'll pop by tomorrow as well. Don't worry if you go out, I've got my key.' Sylvia looked at him and sighed. He was sitting so scrunched-up in the easy chair that he looked as though he'd shrunk. He'd shaved, she wouldn't have expected anything other, but his skin had a grey tinge. He looked more like forty-eight than thirty-eight.

'Don't take on so. They'll be back.'

Staring into space, Peter said, 'Her parents still live in the house they had when the girls were all at home. There's plenty of room for them, you see. They've a huge garden, and a dog. The children will be very happy there. So will she. She loves the wildness of Northumberland, especially the sea coast.'

'She'll be back. Trust me. Give her a few days.'

Peter looked at her for the first time. 'May God help me if she isn't.'

'Ron! Ron! Are you there?'

'In the bedroom.' Sheila ran up the stairs as fast as she could, her shopping still in her hand. She closed the bedroom door after her. 'Ron, you won't believe this but Caroline's left Peter.'

'Sheila, for goodness sake! You're spreading rumours again.'

'I'm not, it's true! They all know, they've just been talking about it outside the Store. Apparently Sylvia and Willie know the whole story but, of course, they won't tell. I bet even the Gestapo couldn't get it out of *them*.' Sheila sat down on the bed; in a stage whisper she asked, 'What about Louise?'

Ron looked at her through the mirror as he tied his tie. 'God only knows. More trouble, I expect. When is she blasted well going to get a job? If only she'd move away.'

'I'd better tell her not to go and see him.'

'Don't. She'll do the opposite. Say nothing.'

'All right then. I'm so sorry about it all.' She took her handkerchief from her pocket and wiped away a tear.

'Come on, old girl, they'll sort it out. Storm in a teacup.'

There came a tap on the bedroom door and Louise came in. 'I'm just off to sort out the choir music. I promised I would and I've done nothing about it. It might take all day. I'll come back for a sandwich, but don't make anything for me just in case.'

'Dad and I are going out, so we shan't be here. There's plenty in the fridge.'

'You sound odd. What's the matter?'

'Nothing's the matter. Off you go.'

Louise stopped at the Store to buy some chocolate to see her through the morning. By the till, elbows resting on the ledge in front of it, was a customer gossiping with Jimbo.

'I'm telling you, Mr Charter-Plackett, I saw it with my own eyes. Just out with the dog and I saw her leaving in that big car of theirs. Loaded up as if she's going for a lifetime. Pushchair, the lot. You don't need me to tell yer why, do yer?'

'Don't I?'

'Mean to say you 'aven't 'eard? Yer slipping, you are. Where've yer been this weekend?'

'We've all been away to a wedding. Got back late last night. What's happened then?'

'Well . . .' The customer regaled Jimbo with the whole story, embellished by her own conclusions, but nevertheless the essence of it rang true. 'Sly beggar, is that Mr Palmer. Still, quiet waters always run deep, don't they? So we're all concluding there's been a rupture at the rectory because of 'er coming for the weekend.'

'Rupture?'

'Well, it's certainly not rapture at the rectory, is it, let's put it that way. How much do I owe?'

'Oh right. Better pull myself together. Let's see.' He tried hard not to show how stunned he was by the news of Caroline's departure. He'd been wondering what they'd all been talking about outside on the seat, now he knew. No, he kept telling himself, it was all hugely gigantic supposition on the part of the village. They were prone to that if gossip was a bit thin on the ground. All she'd done was go home because her parents were coming out of hospital. Still, taking two small children with her, with chicken-pox . . . ?

Louise quietly chose a bar of fruit and nut, paying Jimbo the exact money so she wouldn't be delayed at the till and find herself betrayed by her boiling emotions. Safely out of the Store, she went swiftly over to the church. Caroline had gone! For whatever reason, she'd gone! Best of all, it wasn't her fault but Suzy's that she'd gone. That put her, Louise, in the best possible light; because she wasn't to blame, she could rightly sympathise. Right now his nerves would be raw. Absolutely raw. He would need a salve for his wounds. He would need understanding and – dare she say it? – comfort. She, who loved him, would have to serve that need.

In the choir vestry Louise took her big Oxford notepad out of her briefcase, two pens, sticky tape and scissors, some coloured stickers, a high-lighting pen and her fruit and nut. Where to begin? When your heart is thumping with joy it's difficult to assemble your thoughts. *She'd gone! She'd left him!* Best way to tackle it was to make piles, give each pile a title and then sort each pile individually, check all the pages were there, mend torn ones, throw away sheets beyond repair, but make a note in case Gilbert wanted to buy replacements. *She'd gone! She'd left him!* When she'd got it all written down on paper then she could put it into the computer, and he'd have a complete schedule of the music. *She'd gone! She'd left him!*

Gradually her heart slowed to a normal beat and she became absorbed in the music. At eleven o'clock Louise went to sit in the church to eat her chocolate, because every chair and every bit of floorspace in the vestry was covered with music. She was hot and sticky with clambering over the piles of music, so she chose a pew where she could rest her shoulder against the cool stone of a pillar. There was only one square of her chocolate left when the heavy church door opened and, caught by an unexpected gust of wind, slammed shut with an earth chattering clang. Louise peered round the pillar to see who had come in.

Oh God, it was him! She shrank back behind the pillar; she couldn't face him. She looked such a mess. You didn't have meaningful, crucial meetings with the man in your life, when your skin was hot and sticky, and your hair tousled and wringing with sweat, and your teeth gooey with chocolate. She ran her tongue round her teeth to clear them but what she really needed was a drink of water to get them clean. She hid behind the pillar and waited to see where he would go. Peter walked slowly towards the altar. He was wearing jeans and a blue shirt; his red-blond hair was in disarray. He looked like a small boy who'd been severely reprimanded, and was at a loss to know how to recover his self-esteem. Indeed, he did look smaller than usual. How could he? That was ridiculous. But he did. He'd shrunk. He looked defeated. He stood before the altar, hands by his side, head bent, motionless.

She couldn't get up and creep away; the slightest movement would be heard in the deep silence of the church. Louise, rigid with tension, her trembling hands clasping the chocolate wrapper tightly, daring it to rustle, longed for him to go. But he didn't. He knelt to pray on the altar steps, his head thrown back, his arms outstretched for a while and then his hands clasped to his chest, his head bowed. Louise asked herself how could Caroline do this to him? How could she hurt him like this, reduce him to this? When someone loved you like he must love her, you didn't leave them, no matter what they'd done. Caroline was destroying him. It seemed an eternity that she waited. She watched him cross himself and then he stood up and went to leave the church.

Louise was horrified by the expression on his face. She almost cried out with the pain of seeing him so consumed by his anguish. Never in a million years would she have the capacity to suffer as he was suffering at this moment.

She held on to her tears until he'd closed the door behind him, then they began to roll down her cheeks. Hot scalding tears – tears for his agony, tears for the love she finally realised he would never be able to return, tears for the unfairness of life in not endowing her with the ability to love as deeply as he. Bitter tears for her own foolishness in thinking she could ever win him for herself with her organisation and her lists and her highlighting pen. What a total idiot she'd been; she'd had absolutely no conception of how deep and enduring passionate love like his could be. There were tears for lots of things . . .

So noisy were her sobs that she didn't hear the church door open for a second time. It was Muriel, come to search for her umbrella. She'd lost it times without number, but it had a charmed life and always seemed to turn up again in the must unexpected places. Hopefully it might be in church; it had a habit of appearing there and Willie was so good with lost property – she knew it would be in the vestry if he'd found it. She heard the weeping as soon as she closed the door, but couldn't see anyone there. As she crossed in front of the pulpit, she spotted Louise, crouched by a pillar, hidden from view, her head bent almost to her knees.

'Louise, my dear.' Muriel went to sit beside her. She placed her hand on her arm and gently shook her. But sympathy made Louise cry even louder. Muriel dug in her pocket for a fresh tissue.

'Here you are, my dear, use this.' She sat stroking Louise's hand, waiting for the tears to stop.

Louise howled like a stricken animal. 'I can't bear it! I can't bear it!'

'Gently now, gently now. If you want to talk I'm willing to listen. When you're ready, that is.'

Louise's red eyes peered at her over the tissue. 'How can I? I can't tell anyone.' Fresh storms began and Muriel sat quietly waiting. Ralph would be wondering where she was, but dear Ralph would have to wait: Louise needed her more than he.

'I'm the soul of discretion, I truly am. I'm top of the class where keeping secrets is concerned. I shan't tell.'

'You won't, will you?'

'No, of course not, my dear. But perhaps your mother would be the best person . . .'

'Oh no, not her. She wouldn't understand.'

'I think maybe mothers are more understanding than daughters realise.'

'Mine isn't.' Louise made up her mind. 'It's Peter, you see. It's Peter.'

'Ahhh, right, I thought perhaps it might be. He needs all the love and prayers he can get right now.'

'So do I. So do I.'

'Surely not as much as he.'

The whole story came out, burbling and tumbling over itself, like a stream in full spate, here deep and bottomless, there shallow and swift, swirling along, hurrying here, idling there, and Muriel listened to it all in silence. Finally the stream of words fell still and Louise sat drained, awaiting the comfort of Muriel's words.

Muriel stroked her hand while she searched for words of wisdom. Before she married her dear Ralph she wouldn't have been able to understand even one jot of how Louise must be feeling, but marriage and love had given her an insight into feelings she never dreamed existed before she met Ralph.

'My dear Louise. Peter and Caroline are two very privileged people. They've found the one person in the world who means everything to them. They could no more be separated than . . . than . . . well, I can't think of it now, but they're welded together. It brings tremendous joy but also tremendous heartbreak sometimes. You've got to realise that you having Peter is impossible, no it's no good going down that route either in your thoughts or in what you do.'

Louise cried, 'I know that now.'

'Of course you do, you're not a fool, my dear. Now you've got to take yourself in hand, make a new life for yourself. Get a job, search out things to keep busy with, and build on the pain to make yourself a better person. Don't, whatever you do, become *bitter*. Not bitter. That's the worst thing to have happen. Bitterness twists everything. Now's the time to step forward bravely and take hold of life. Don't look back at the past, but ahead to the future because the future is yours. Don't waste your life grieving over someone you know you cannot have.'

'Oh, but I *am* grieving – for me it's as though Peter has died. I've lost him, you see. Though if I think rationally I never really had him in the first place, did I?'

'No, I think perhaps you didn't. He and Caroline belong, you know. One day you'll find someone like that and then you'll be privileged too. You've to put all this behind you and get on with life. Perhaps what's happened will make you more understanding, more sympathetic. *Build* on this experience, use it as a foundation of something new, don't let it destroy you. I'm quite sure you've plenty of courage. You'll do it if you try hard enough. There, I've talked for far too long.' Muriel stood up, giving Louise's shoulder a last comforting pat. 'Now I've got to find my umbrella. I expect Willie's put it in the vestry – I'll just go and look.'

It was half-past two before Louise had finished cataloguing all the music and storing it away again in the cupboard. She was beginning to feel hungry. She'd had a drink of water from the tap in the vestry wash-basin; it tasted bitter and flat, but she didn't mind – it was all part of her punishment. There was still lots more to do; neat packages of some kind were needed to keep all the copies of one sort together, but the essentials were done. When she got home she'd get on the computer and make her lists for Gilbert.

The air was cooler now, and she enjoyed the walk across the Green. Some tourists were taking photographs by the stocks. They looked expectantly at her, so she went across and let them explain the workings of their camera to her and she spent a few minutes taking snaps for them and chatting about the village. Some children from the school were out sketching by the old oak tree and she smiled and waved.

She pushed open the cottage door, glad to be home. It wasn't such a bad place really. 'Hello-o-o! I'm home!' Ron and Sheila looked at each other in amazement, rapidly straightening their faces when she came in. 'I'm back. Just making myself a sandwich and then I'm typing up this stuff I've done for Gilbert. Had a good morning?'

Sheila was surprised, as she'd fully expected to be asked to make lunch for Louise. 'Yes, thanks,' she said. 'Have you?'

'Yes, thanks. Excellent. Would you like a cup of tea?'

Ron said he would and so did Sheila; it was hard to disguise the fact they were in shock. Sheila listened for sounds of Louise in the kitchen and when she heard the kettle being filled, she whispered, 'Does she know, do you think?'

'I can't tell.'

'There's something fishy going on.'

'Let's keep quiet and make hay while the sun shines.'

'You don't think she's been to see him and they've . . . you know. Got an understanding?'

'Sheila, for heaven's sake! With the best will in the world you couldn't think for one minute he'd be interested in her.'

The disdainful tone in Ron's voice cut Sheila to the quick; after all, she was their daughter. 'Sometimes you're very unkind. She's not a beauty, I know, but she's attractive in her own way. It's just her *attitude*.'

The telephone rang. It was Mr Fitch for Louise.

17

Louise made the coffee at the next committee meeting, having arranged to do so with Caroline before she went to Devon. How on earth she was going to tell them what had happened that very day up at the Big House, she didn't know. These last four days had been hectic for her. The phone call Mr Fitch had made on what she now called her 'Revelation Monday' had changed her life. Of course, it was only supposed to be a temporary job but between themselves they knew it would be permanent because Fenella, his receptionist, sadly had terminal cancer. Louise was therefore in an admirable position for being the first to hear about the new development. The conclusion she'd arrived at was that they might as well cancel the entire Show.

Jimbo, Michael and Linda arrived together.

'Isn't it exciting, Mr Palmer, you moving away. And such a big school too.'

'I don't know about exciting, Linda. Certainly it's challenging.'

'Where will you live?'

'I'm going to rent somewhere to begin with, till I've had a chance to look round and find somewhere I like. I've never been a homeowner before.'

'Alan and I are moving in to Hipkin Gardens next week. It'll be so lovely, having somewhere with a bit of space. Alan's got all sorts of ideas for the garden. The cottage is a bit big for just the two of us but,' she giggled, 'hopefully we shan't be there on our own for long!'

'Seems I'm not the only one with a challenge then.'

Jimbo thanked Louise for his coffee. 'Two months and this Show will be over. Let's drink to its success. Old Fitch will have something to say if it isn't. If he could order the weather he would. No stone unturned is his motto.'

Louise didn't join in the general enthusiasm. She'd wait until they were all there to break the news. Barry came next, disappointed that Jimbo had taken his seat on the committee again; still, he was seeing Pat afterwards, and he'd brought her a present from London too. He tapped his pocket to make sure it was still there. Then came Bryn and Jeremy together, and her mother arrived last. Louise hadn't told her; if she had, Sheila would have been round to the store in a jiffy spreading alarm. She'd have been right too; it *was* alarming.

Louise tapped her spoon on her cup. 'Right, ladies and gentlemen. Can we be seated, please?' When they were settled she drew in a deep breath and said, 'I'm afraid I have some disquieting news.'

Barry interrupted, 'Don't tell me, bet I know: the sewers won't be finished in time. Been doing a job up in Mr Fitch's London flat. Only got back this afternoon – didn't look like much progress to me. They'd all stopped working.'

'Actually, yes, you're right – they *had* stopped working. This afternoon,' she cleared her throat, 'they found what looks like Roman remains.'

Sheila said, 'You didn't tell me! Do you mean bodies?'

'No, I don't. I mean remains of a building. Well, there might be bodies, but I don't think so.'

Jimbo was aghast. 'I can't believe it! This Show is destined not to happen. First sewers and now this. I thought they'd taken all possible precautions to make sure they *didn't* disturb anything.' He shook his head in disbelief.

Bryn twirled his moustache and said, 'Is there anything else fate could throw at us? It's just not possible.'

Sheila, affronted that all her well-constructed plans might come to nought, said matter-of-factly: 'Why the blazes can't they just pretend they haven't found anything? Lay the sewer-pipes and fill it all in. No one will be any the wiser. We can have the Show and the building or whatever it is can stay there. Who wants blessed Roman remains anyway? Just a few old stones. If they've been there for centuries let's leave 'em in peace. It won't make any difference to them, will it? This Show's a lot more important.'

Linda said, 'Oh, you can't do that. I know someone in Culworth whose house is close to Chantry Gate and they were digging to make a pond in their garden and found funny pottery an' that, and before they knew it the place was full of archaeologists and nearly the whole garden got dug up. Weeks, it took.'

Jimbo slapped his forehead with the flat of his hand. 'Thank you, Linda, for that contribution.' He asked Louise whereabouts the remains were.

'Under the front lawn beyond where he had the gravel laid for the car parking, just where we'd planned to have all the stalls. It's been a lawn since the year dot, so it's never been disturbed, literally for centuries. The trouble is, they don't know how large an area it might cover. It could be a terribly important find, or very minor and not worth bothering about. It's not on any of the maps, you see; so they didn't know it was there. The sewer people refuse to ingore it – more than their job's worth, they say. Right brouhaha there was the last time this happened and they tried to cover it up and say nothing. Some busybody leaked the news and there were questions in the House, they said. With working there this week, I had the job of ringing Mr Fitch to let him know. I don't mind telling you there was an awfully long silence. I swear the phone grew hot.' Louise grew uncomfortable at the memory. 'His language! He can't decide whether to be thrilled to bits or completely devastated.'

Barry said in a disgusted tone of voice, 'They'll be digging for months.' He ran his fingers through his hair and stared at the floor. 'All that wood and all that work I've done with the stalls. It can't be true.'

'Well, it is.'

'What about Gilbert?' Michael asked.

Puzzled, Louise echoed: 'What about Gilbert?'

'Well, he's an archaeologist.'

'Is he? I didn't know.'

'Well, he is. He'll probably be called in. He's only home at weekends at the moment. He's doing a dig out Salisbury way. He finishes this week, he said, and then the engineers are covering it over and getting on with the road. It's been delayed eight weeks to give them a chance to rescue what they can. Peter's been standing in for choir practice.'

Linda, latching on to something they were all bursting to talk about but hadn't, said, 'Isn't it a pity about Dr Harris? So sad. He looks like a lost soul. They say he's back at work, as you might say, on Monday but how he'll manage no one knows. Poor thing.'

Jimbo, seeing a gossip session in the offing, said firmly, 'Let's get on with deciding what we shall do about the Show.'

Sheila said, 'If *they* can shovel it under tons of earth, why can't we do the same with this one? No one will know if we don't say anything.' Jimbo and Bryn looked at her sceptically; the thought of Sheila not saying anything was almost laughable.

Jimbo said, 'Look, Louise, you're up there at the hub, you keep your ear to the ground as you might say, and let us know. We'll keep everything on hold until a decision's been made. Everything's organised thanks to you, so we can accelerate our plans at the last minute, surely?'

'Yes, but . . .'

'It's all right saying that . . .'

'How about if . . .'

Jeremy protested, 'But we've ordered the marquees, and the deposit's paid.'

'The printer has to be paid, too.'

'I can't bear to think about all the work we've done . . .'

'Neither can I.'

'It's in the Red Cross schedule as well. Mrs Redfern hates her schedules being mixed up.' This from Linda who had been looking forward to sporting her new uniform in front of all the people she knew.

Louise took the lead. 'Look, there's nothing we can do tonight, that's a fact. I'll keep you well-informed. We've just got to sit tight and hope. The one plus tonight is that the sewer people are working fast, or at least they were. I'm seeing Gilbert on Saturday morning about the choir music I've been cataloguing for him so I'll have a word with him, see what he has to say. We'll tentatively arrange an emergency meeting for next Thursday and I'll let you know.' Diaries came out, the date was written in and they left in a babble of speculation.

Barry said before he left, 'I think I'll stop work on the stalls for the moment. Just wait and see. What do you think, Louise?'

'Might be an idea. I'm sure Mr Fitch would let you have time to make a final burst with them in the last week, don't you?'

'I'm sure he would. What's it like, working in the Big House then?'

'Well, of course I'm still finding my feet. It's not really my kind of work but I didn't mind stepping in, in the circumstances. Poor Fenella, such a lovely person – it's really tragic. I'm just sorry it's her illness which has meant I've got the job.'

Barry nodded in agreement. 'Very attractive girl, Fenella was – *is* I mean. Very attractive. I'm off. See yer.'

Barry climbed into his van, kicked a couple of pieces of chipboard out from under his feet, started it up and drove hell for leather up to the Garden House. He slewed to a stop, narrowly missing Dean's bike which he'd left laid on the concrete by the estate mower. Barry went to stand it up for him. Poor old Dean. Exams, that's what it was – exams. He didn't know what he was doing.

He knocked on the back door and opened it wide, shouting, 'It's me, I'm back!'

Pat came into the kitchen. 'Oh, it's you. Hello, long time no see.' She grinned at him, unsure about how enthusiastic she should be. Maybe he'd changed his mind since he'd been up in London and seen all those smart women.

Then he opened his arms wide and she went into them and they hugged each other. 'By Jove, Pat, it's good to be back. I've brought you a present.'

'You shouldn't have. What is it?'

'Give me a kiss first.'

'You and yer kisses. Sex-mad you are!'

'Naughty but nice though, isn't it?'

'Go on then. But for real.'

'Well, well, getting choosy are we now? This makes a change. What's happened to the Pat who thought kissing meant a peck like in them nineteen-thirties' films?'

'You won't get one at all if you don't hurry up. Four days I've been without a kiss.'

'I've a mind to make you wait.'

'You won't, 'cos you can't wait to give me that present that's digging into my ribs.'

He laughed and slapped her bottom for her and she wriggled away. 'Not that, Barry, not that.'

'Not what?'

'Using yer 'and to me. I'm not having that.'

'I was only having fun. I didn't hurt you, did I?'

'No, it didn't hurt, but I'm not 'aving it.'

Barry looked hard at her and comprehension dawned. 'You mean your Doug used to hit you?'

Pat's eyes shut tight and she nodded her head.

'The sod! As God is my judge I have never and will never hit a woman, and more especially you whom I respect. You need have no fear of that from me. Honest to God'.

'I'm sorry, I know you won't. I'm sorry I spoke.' Pat swallowed hard and to divert his mind from his anger she tapped his pocket and asked, 'Well, what is it then?'

'I was going down Oxford Street and there was this chap with a suitcase open on the pavement and he was selling watches, five pounds with a free pen thrown in. He was having a shutting-down sale, so I got one. I think you'll like it.'

He took the box from his pocket and watched her face as she opened it. He knew she'd tried to cover her disappointment when he'd told her the tale about the suitcase and he couldn't wait for her to realise he was pulling her leg.

'Barry! Oh Barry, you daft 'aporth. This came from a proper jewellers. It's beautiful, really beautiful. My watch broke months ago and it wasn't worth paying for it to be mended. How did you know I needed one?'

'You looked at my watch a while back and I realised you hadn't got one of your own, and I thought, one day I'll buy her one she'll be proud of. Here, let me put it on for you.' He fastened it securely on her wrist and stood back to admire it. 'There, what do you think to that? Perfect.'

'It is, it's lovely. Just lovely.' She put the watch to her ear and listened to it. 'It's got a lovely tick. You shouldn't have.' Then to lighten things she began thumping him playfully. 'Telling me it was from a man with a suitcase, you cheeky devil you.' He twisted and turned, shouting his protests till she had him cornered by the kitchen door. Then he grabbed her and kissed her like she'd wanted in the first place.

'Cor, Pat, you smell great. It's real come-and-get-me perfume.'

'It's our Michelle, she bought it for me. Determined, she is.'

'What about?'

'You and me.'

'Keen then, is she?'

'Oh yes, she is. I don't know about me though. Not yet.'

Barry kissed her and said, 'Not another word. Wait till you've had that week away with me and we'll see how we feel then.'

'Cup o' tea?' Barry nodded. 'How did the meeting go?' She was admiring her watch while she said it. 'You're very generous, Barry. I've never bought you a thing.'

'No matter. I'm glad you like it.' He watched her fill the kettle. She was getting the milk out of the fridge when they heard footsteps. The door opened and it was Dean in his pyjamas.

'Hi, how's the exams going?'

'Hello, Barry. Not bad, thanks. Can't sleep for worrying though. Is there a cup of tea going?'

'Yes, love. Won't be a minute. Look what Barry's given me.' Pat held out her arm. The watch gleamed in the fluorescent light.

Dean whistled. 'Wow, Barry, that's great.'

'Bought it from a fella with a suitcase in Oxford Street.' His eyes twinkled at Dean.

'You never did. That cost a bomb. It's lovely, Mum.' He talked about his exams for a while and then decided to take his tea to bed. Dean grinned and said, 'Wouldn't want to cramp your style, you two.' As he was closing the door he added, 'It's like our Michelle says, and as the man of the house I agree with her for once. You two were made for each other.'

Pat went red and shouted, 'Get off to bed, yer cheeky little devil!' He hastily shut the door and they could hear him laughing as he went up the stairs.

'I suppose I should be grateful your children want me here. Some chaps would meet nothing but resentment.'

'Says a lot for you, I suppose.'

'If we . . . er . . . you know . . . I wouldn't want any more children. Yours will do for me.'

'If we . . . er . . . yer know . . .' she laughed, 'I wouldn't want any more either.'

'That's settled then.'

'So what did 'appen at the meeting?'

18

Rumours were rife in the village about the Roman ruins. In the Store on the Friday morning, Jimbo had the story *ad nauseum*. Most were of the opinion that the Show would have to be cancelled, others that Mr Fitch would cash in on the discovery and they'd be having coach parties coming to view the ruins and a reception centre built with a display and tea rooms, and public lavatories all over the place and . . .

'Hold on a minute!' Jimbo protested. 'They were only discovered yesterday. Could be they're so insignificant that they rescue some bits, put them on a shelf in a storeroom at Culworth Museum, fill in the hole and we hear no more about it, and all it'll be is a dot on a map at County Hall. In any case, a few more tourists would be a good idea.'

'Oh yes, and we all knows why. Why don't you build some public lavatories just outside 'ere and then tempt 'em in 'ere and make even more money. The only one to do well out of it would be Mr Charter-Plackett.'

'I say, that's a bit under the belt.' Jimbo was beginning to get angry. 'What have I done to deserve that?'

'Well, nothing really, but it just seems that at every turn, that chap up there and you is making money.'

'I see. Well, there you are then. Two of the biggest employers in the district and still we're at fault. It takes some understanding. Now, what can I get for you? Anything else? No? Right then, we'll add up.'

When the irate customer had gone, the next customer in the queue said, 'Take no notice, Mr Charter-Plackett. She's only mad because her daughter wanted that receptionist's job up at the Big House, but Louise Bissett got there first. It's not you really.'

'Thank goodness for that, I don't like being *persona non grata*.'

'Well, whatever that is, you're not it. You're lovely and we all love shopping in here. Brought life back into this village, you have and no mistake. How we'd manage without this shop . . .'

'Store, please.'

'This Store, I don't know. Two pounds of best steak, lean as poss.'

'Having a party?'

'My daughter's prospective in-laws are coming. Got to make a good impression.'

'Well, you will with two pounds of best. As a token of thanks for your compliments, could I give you a box of after-dinner mints?'

'Oh thanks, thanks very much – that'd be lovely. A right finale that'll be.'

'All part of the service.' Jimbo raised his boater and bowed to his customers. They gave him a round of applause and good humour was re-established.

Sylvia came in during the morning. Jimbo waited until she was his only customer and then he said, 'Sylvia, can I have a word?' He invited her into his storeroom and sat her on his stool, put his boater on top of a case of strawberry jam, folded his arms and said, 'Well?'

'She's not back yet. This is the fifth day. I'm worried sick.'

'How is he?'

'In a terrible state. He's supposed to be back in harness on Monday, but at the rate he's going he'll end up in hospital.'

'Bad as that, is it?'

'It is. I don't know what to do. I keep thinking I should ring her, but Willie says no.'

'No, I don't think that would be right.' He stood gazing out of the window deep in thought.

'He won't eat except bits and pieces when I insist. I'm not supposed to be working this week, but someone's got to do something. I can't just leave him, can I? I can understand her being hurt, but she knows, deep down she knows, there's nothing in it.'

'I wonder if I went to have a word?'

'I don't think he'll see anyone. He won't even answer the phone. Not that she's rung, not while I've been there anyway. I asked him this morning if she'd rung last night and he just shook his head. He won't ring her, you see; they seem to have this arrangement whereby they don't trespass on each other's ground. She's made this decision so it's her he has to wait for. Seems daft to me. They tell each other they're both free to make their own decisions, but they're not really; they're like two halves of the same thing. You'd have a shock if you saw him.'

'Hell's bells. I'm beginning to feel quite angry with Caroline, letting him get like this.'

'Well, I don't feel that, but I do feel helpless. He's such a dear man, such strong faith, devoted to the church, but without Dr Harris there he's like a ship without a rudder. I think it's guilt you know, for what happened. You know what I mean. And it's the children, too. He's missing them and so am I.' Sylvia took a handkerchief from her pocket and wiped her eyes. 'Anyway, I'll finish his shopping and get back.'

'If things get desperate, let me know. I might be able to say something which will give him a boost. Such a delicate matter though, isn't it?'

'It is.'

Jimbo looked at her severely. 'I sincerely hope Louise Bissett hasn't been round.'

'Oh no, she hasn't, much to my surprise, but then she has stepped in up at the Big House. So sad about that receptionist, isn't it?'

'Dreadful. Beautiful, beautiful girl. I sometimes have great difficulty in understanding this world. However, by the sound of it I've got customers. Don't forget – if you get in a fix, let me know and I'll come across. Any time, can't stand by and see him sink.'

Sylvia stood up. 'Thanks for listening to my troubles. You're most kind. I'll get back to him.'

Around midnight on Sunday night, Peter, unable to sleep, went out into the garden. Caroline's cats followed him out, tails up, twisting and turning around his legs, pestering for attention. He bent down to stroke them.

'It's no good, you won't find her out here. You miss her too, don't you?' By the light coming through the kitchen window he could just see well enough to wander about the garden touching her plants, admiring the pots of bright pink geraniums she'd bought this year, loving the deep blue delphiniums she'd planted their first summer. 'No country garden is complete without them, in any case I love them,' she'd said. He went to inspect the low wall which she'd filled with nasturtiums, laughing to himself when he remembered her daily battle against an unexpected plague of caterpillars. God, how he longed for her to be home. *Caroline, please come home.*

Out of nowhere a decision burst into his thoughts. He no longer cared for all these ideas about not trespassing – hell, it was his marriage, his life, his children that were at stake! The parish would manage. He'd burn his boats and go. If he went he laid himself open to rejection but if he didn't . . . if he didn't he might lose everything. Maybe that was what she needed to see, that she was more than life itself to him. Yes, that was it. Intelligence and logic and agreements didn't come into it any more. No, dammit! He would go up there, see for himself. He wouldn't even tell her he was coming. He'd simply go. It couldn't make matters worse; they couldn't *be* any worse.

The practicalities of his decision raced round his mind. He'd have to let people know he wouldn't be here, couldn't just depart when he was officially back. Say he had a family emergency, which in truth he had. Heavens above, what was losing your wife, the only one he would ever have on this earth, and your children, other than an emergency? Contact the vicar in Culworth, let Willie know, rearrange the two evening meetings he had for this coming week, and the Friday morning school prayers. He could be away by lunchtime at the latest. He'd have to go by train. Then, God willing, he could drive them all back.

Peter went straight back into the house, showered, and set the alarm for six-fifteen. He slept soundly for the first time since she'd left.

Sylvia, who'd come in at eight as she usually did when she was working, was delighted at his decision.

'You start making your phone calls, I'll pack you a bag and I'll take you into Culworth if you like. My car's just been serviced so it's not likely to break down.'

Peter couldn't resist teasing her. 'That'll make a change.'

'Rector! I love that car.'

'I know, I'm sorry.'

'I'm not, not if it's made you laugh.' She flapped her hands at him, grinning. 'Go on, get things organised.'

Despite his energetic endeavours he had the greatest difficulty in contacting the people he needed to speak to before he left. He seemed thwarted at every turn. By eleven-thirty he'd made his last phone call.

Sylvia insisted he had something to eat before he left. 'You've had next to no breakfast and a bite to eat now will stand you in good stead. A big chap like you needs good solid food.' He began to protest, he wanted to be off. 'I insist, never mind those wretched sandwiches British Rail serve, all clammy and sweating in those plastic packets. Sit down, it's all ready. And you've to let me know when you're coming back and I'll have everything ready for you all.'

His face changed and she saw him withdraw back into his anguish again. She could have bitten her tongue out. He pushed his plate away and stood up. 'You eat this, I can't.' The phone rang. 'I'll answer that, it might be—' He hurried to the study.

Someone in the parish had died. Finally, at half-past twelve, Sylvia left to get her car while he went to the bathroom to check his shaving kit and put it in his bag. The cats were watching him, as though they knew they were going to be deserted. They mewed and padded about after him, getting under his feet as he moved between bathroom and bedroom. Suddenly they left. He went to the top of the stairs carrying his bag and saw them race to the front door. It opened and there stood Beth and Alex, and behind them Caroline.

'Dada! Spots going. Beth better now.' She pulled up her T-shirt so he could see her chest. 'Look!'

'Dada, Dada, look Granda buy Alex boat, look Dada.'

Caroline and Peter looked gravely at each other, he from the top of the stairs, she from the hall. In the soft light they couldn't quite read one another's thoughts but their eyes devoured each other, measuring, weighing up, estimating the ravages of the last week. She was alarmed by his appearance; he was drenched with relief by hers.

To cover his shock he spoke to the children first.

'Hello, darlings, have you had a good holiday? Daddy is pleased to have you back.' When he reached the floor of the hall he put down his bag and hugged the two of them, kissing them and admiring Beth's receding spots and Alex's boat. They rushed off to look for Sylvia, leaving him and Caroline to greet each other.

'Are you going somewhere?'

'Actually I decided in the night I would go up to Northumberland, but I got delayed. Someone chose to die, and things . . . and . . .'

'I'm glad they did. We'd have looked pretty silly, you up there and me down here.'

'Yes, we would. Very silly. You've come back then.'

'Of course. I made up my mind in the night. I thought, There he is, that darling man of mine, and he's wanting me and I'm wanting him and I'm going to him. I could see you, for some daft reason, in the garden by the nasturtiums laughing about the caterpillars. Stupid, aren't I? And I wondered how my garden was and . . . and whether you were well and that . . . that sort of thing.'

'Whatever time did you leave?'

'I got up at five and packed like a maniac and the children wake early anyway, so we set off. We're dying for something to—' The door opened and in came Sylvia, her face alight with relief.

'You're back!' Sylvia, who'd always maintained a certain reserve in her relationship with Caroline, opened her arms wide and went to hug her. 'I'm so glad, so very glad you're back.'

Caroline embraced her and said, 'So am I.'

'Would you like a cup of tea, something to eat?'

'Oh yes, please, you're my saviour. Thank you.'

Sylvia went to the kitchen to greet the children. Caroline stood close to Peter. For the moment she couldn't kiss him or hug him; their estrangement had been so severe, they'd have to come to that later that night when they were alone, but she touched his face with her fingers. 'What have I done to you? My beloved darling.'

'Nothing your being here won't heal.'

Her eyes intently searched his face, looking warily for his reactions. She said, 'Mother told me off – called me a fool. She was right. Said I didn't deserve a man like you. Said it was only idiots who ran away from love. Said you are her bestest son-in-law to date, and if I ever do this again she'll turn me straight round and send me back.'

'I've always approved of your mother's common sense. How is she?'

'Frustrated by inactivity but bossing us all around as ever. They've brought help in so they're going to be all right. Dad isn't too perky; Mother won't let him rest, she will make him do things that he's not really up to yet. But they'll have to sort themselves out.' Caroline grinned at him. 'When Mother heard me packing in the night she shouted from her bedroom, "And not before time".'

Peter laughed. 'Only she could have survived such a serious accident so brilliantly.'

'Yes.' She smiled and made as though to kiss him, but changed her mind. Her voice shook as she said, 'I'll go and give Sylvia a hand.' He followed her into the kitchen, where the children were already seated at the table drinking from their Bunnikin cups, waiting for Sylvia to finish making their lunch. The sun had come out again and was shining into the kitchen, welcoming them all back. Sylvia looked at the two of them as they went in. She turned back to the worktop to finish putting the sandwiches on a plate and said, 'Can I invite the children to tea this afternoon? I've bought some things at the Red Cross sale they might like to play with. Make a change for them, wouldn't it?' She looked at Caroline. 'I could take them straight after they've finished lunch.'

'Thank you, Sylvia, that would be a lovely idea.'

'Bring them back about six after their tea?'

'Thank you, yes, thank you.' Peter recognised the unspoken message between them. Without it being mentioned, the two of them had arranged time for him and Caroline to be alone.

The children were eager to see what Sylvia had bought for them and they rushed off hand-in-hand with her, without so much as a backward glance.

'Be good, the two of you, be good.' Caroline closed the door and stood with her back to it. She was glad to have time alone with Peter, but it would have been a relief to have been able to postpone their reconciliation until her tiredness had lifted. She could hear Peter clearing the lunch away. She'd make a fresh pot of tea, just to have something to do to stop herself from clutching hold of him and never letting go. They must sort things out before that happened. 'I'm making myself more tea, would you like some?'

'Yes, please. They've found Roman ruins up at the Big House, by the way. The Show is in jeopardy yet again, I'm afraid.'

'Oh no! I don't believe it. What has . . . Louise . . . to say?'

'My darling girl, I have no idea, I haven't seen her. She's replacing someone up at the Big House so she's very busy. This Roman ruin caper has certainly upset the apple cart. There's an emergency meeting this Thursday, Sylvia says. You'll find out then, I expect.'

'Yes, I expect I will. Mr Fitch must be going mad.'

'I imagine so. I haven't seen anyone to ask.'

'I see. Here's your tea.'

'Let's go into the sitting room, the chairs are more comfortable.'

'Right.' Caroline led the way, Peter carried the tray in and placed it on the coffee table. They sat together on the sofa. When it had brewed he poured them each a cup.

Together they both said, 'Darling . . .'

'Sorry. You first.'

'No, you first.'

Peter put his cup down and began, 'I'm going to tell you what we said that morning. Every word. And you've to listen and then I'll listen to you. OK?'

'Yes.'

He told her word for word as best he could remember, even the kiss and the cross he made on her forehead and her sadness at not being able to see the twins, and how she'd sobbed and that she was marrying Michael and how he'd given her his blessing as she left, and how she meant nothing to him now.

Caroline told him about her fear. Fear that, seeing Suzy, he would want her and they'd take the children and go away and how it would crucify her if they did. After all, seeing her again he might realise it was Suzy he wanted more than her, but she couldn't live without him and his children. And did he think that now might be the best time to tell them because they'd *know* without *understanding*; the understanding would come in time but wouldn't, hopefully, hurt so much if they already *knew*. 'I feel as if we have to put things straight and then they'll stay straight for the rest of our lives. I went away partly because I was so distraught and partly because I wanted to get the children away from you both so you couldn't take them from me. I may not have given birth to them, but they are mine, believe me they are mine. This problem with Louise, too. I felt so threatened and like a fool I ran away instead of standing and fighting for what was ours.'

'You had nothing to fear. Nothing at all. There is never any question of that. Please believe me. You're right about telling the children. We'll tell them together when the right moment comes, I don't know how we'll put it to them, but we will somehow. Then we shall be straight, as you say, for the rest of our lives. God bless you for coming back.'

She rested her head against his shoulder and closed her eyes. He began to touch her, remembering her anew. He stroked her hand, kissed her hair which smelt of sea and sand, he ran a finger down her bare brown arm, he kissed her fingers. Trying not to disturb her head he turned himself gently towards her, and put an arm across the front of her, around her waist. He savoured the living life of her, the beat of her pulse, the smell of her flesh, perfumed and sweet. His hand touched her breast and he rubbed his fingers back and forth, enjoying the warm firmness of it. She took that hand in hers and with eyes still closed she kissed the palm, and then put it back.

He raised her up and put an arm around her shoulders so she rested half on his shoulder, half on his chest. He held her like that while she slept.

19

'Well, Mr Fitch, I had a word with Gilbert Johns, he's our tame archae-ologist around here, and he said nothing must be done till a team can get here to investigate.'

'You told him?'

'Well, of course I did. We need this solving.'

'I never gave you permission to do that! There is one thing you must understand, no, not understand, *accept!* I decide what happens around here, not you. Right?' Louise nodded, gritting her teeth at his male arrogance. 'I came back here last night with the intention of persauding,' he indicated inverted commas with his fingers, 'the men to lay the pipes and cover it all up and mum's the word.' Mr Fitch rubbed his forefinger and thumb together as though he was feeling twenty-pound notes. 'You know?'

Louise did know, but she couldn't let him do it.

'Yes, but . . .'

'Yes, but nothing. I'm going out there now and just watch me get my own way.'

She watched him march out of the office door and across the hall. Masterful he might be, but she'd a nasty feeling that it would be Gilbert out there. He'd said as much on Saturday morning when she'd showed him his well-organised music cupboard.

'My dear Louise, I shall be grateful to you to my dying day. What a miracle! If I'd done it, it wouldn't have been half so well organised as this. I just meant to make piles and leave it at that. But these wonderful plastic folders and the list. Amazing. I didn't know we had half this stuff. How can I ever thank you. It's a wonderful gift you've given me, it really is.'

Louise had blushed. 'It was nothing, really – not once I'd worked out how best to do it. Have you seen the handwritten anthems? I don't know enough to identify them, but you will. Look, here they are.' She'd checked the catalogue she'd made and then found the right shelf and pulled them out for him to inspect.

Gilbert had sat down to study them and she'd stood by awaiting his comments. He was so scruffy. No, not scruffy, kind of untidy in a scholarly way. Despite the chilly morning all he wore was a pair of old cotton trousers and a bright burnt-sienna shirt open almost to his navel, which meant she had glimpses of a seriously hairy chest. The sleeves were rolled up, showing dark brown sinewy arms. All that digging, she thought. On his bare feet were a pair of sandals, scarcely more than a couple of leather straps fastened to a thick hard-wearing sole. She noticed his toenails were scrupulously clean and neatly cut. Her nostrils kept catching a trace of his earthy scent as she stood waiting for his verdict; it stirred her inside in a strange kind of way. His face was striking. He wasn't handsome like . . . Peter, but the hollows of his cheeks, and the prominent cheek-bones and the piercing brown eyes were intriguing.

She noticed his hands were trembling. He looked up at her. 'What a find, listen.' Gilbert hummed a few bars. 'No, that's not right, no. Look, bear with me, we'll go and try them on the organ.'

She followed him into the church, unable to appreciate how someone could grow so excited over a few handwritten crotchets and quavers. He swung his legs over the organ seat and switched on. Gilbert then looked at her with glowing eyes. 'You never know, you could have found something of real value. Unknown, never performed. What a triumph!'

Louise began to catch his excitement. 'Really?'

'Oh yes. Now here we go.' Gilbert could only play the organ as he would a piano, but the melody was enchanting. 'Here are the words. You sing your part, I'll sing mine.'

The two of them had tried it. They'd had several stops and starts before they got it right and in parts Gilbert had difficulty reading the notes because they were so faded, but together they worked it out.

'It's wonderful! By the style, it's late eighteenth- or early nineteenth-century, I should think. Wait till I tell people about this. No composer's name though, what a pity.' Gilbert turned off the organ. 'With a bit of work on it I could use this in church. Clever girl, clever girl. What a find.'

She was warmed by his enthusiasm. 'That's not the only bit of news.'

'No? What other treasures are you about to unearth?'

'That's a highly appropriate way of saying it, actually.'

'Yes?' He put his head on one side, reminding her of a heron she'd seen once, watching for fish by the beck on the spare land.

'There's been what we think are Roman ruins found under the lawn up at the Big House.'

She almost jumped back with shock at his response. He appeared to have been electrified. 'At the Big House?'

'Yes. They were digging to put in these new sewers, and they found interesting bits and the men won't go any further. They've had trouble before, you see.'

Gilbert paced about the aisle with excitement. 'I want to see. Not been to the office for my messages. Got back too late. Don't know anything about it. This could be a major find. Oh yes. I don't suppose we could . . . No, of course not.'

'Could what?'

'Go and take a peep. Just a little peep, don't you know.' He'd begged with the innocence of a child wanting to peep at a birthday present before the day.

'I work up there now, for a while anyway, so perhaps . . . I know exactly where it is.'

He eyed her speculatively. 'Let's, shall we?'

'There's only a skeleton staff with it being the weekend, so no one of any importance will see us.'

'Let's go.'

Louise had noticed Gilbert blanch when he saw the diggers. 'Oh my God! They've got to be stopped.'

'Don't worry, they have stopped. It's a question of whether Mr Fitch will permit anyone to investigate. He wants everything finished because of the Show. It's to be his grand gesture in his Lord of the Manor campaign.'

Gilbert waved his hand in disdain. 'That! That's nothing, nothing at all. Trivial at best.'

'What is, his ambition or the Show?'

'Both.'

'Both?' Louise was horrified by his attitude, and for a moment rendered speechless. She stuttered and gasped and eventually came out with, 'But I've put an awful lot of work into the Show, and everyone's looking forward to it. We've got Morris Dancers . . .'

He waved his hand dismissively. 'I know about them.'

'Hot-air balloon, children's fancy dress, tug-of-war, you name it. So many people are involved, so much work. We *can't* cancel it.'

'If this proves important, nothing can be done till we've fully excavated it. Come on, jump down, let's see what we can find.' Louise had looked down into the trench. She could see bits of mosaic here and there and what appeared to be something earthenware poking out of the side.

Fascinated, despite her dislike of dirt and mess, she'd allowed him to grip her hand and help her in.

Her mother had been at home when she got back.

'Louise! What on earth have you done? Where *have* you been, you're filthy! Good heavens. Take your shoes off – don't put them on the carpet. I'll get a newspaper. Mind your skirt on the wall. Better just take your dress off and give it to me. Oh dear.' Louise didn't get a chance to explain until she'd showered and put on fresh clothes.

'Come on, then,' Sheila Bissett demanded. 'What's all this about?'

'If you laugh I shall never forgive you.'

'I won't.'

'I've been up at the Big House with Gilbert Johns looking at the Roman stuff in the trench.'

'You've been digging?'

'Well, not digging exactly, but he found one of those trowel things in his pocket and we had a bit of a poke around.'

'Bit! You look as if you've been laying the sewers singlehanded.'

'Not quite, Mother.'

'Not far off. So what does he say?'

'They mustn't lay any more pipes till he's had a chance to investigate properly. Gilbert being Gilbert says the Show is a minor consideration. I could have slaughtered him for that.'

'Did he indeed! Minor consideration! What about all my ladies and their flower arrangements? One of them's been all the way to Wales to get a piece of slate exactly the right shape for her display. I can hardly tell *her* it's all off.'

'We'll have to see. Mr Fitch will sort it out.'

From her position behind the reception desk she could see Mr Fitch striding back. Perhaps she was getting fanciful but she thought she could see smoke coming out of his ears.

'Do you know this bloody Gilbert?'

Feeling like a traitor she said, 'Vaguely. Seen him in church on Sundays.'

'Thinks he's got power — well, he's seen nothing yet. Get my MP on the phone pronto.'

'The one in London or the one here?'

Mr Fitch snorted. 'Both!' He stalked into his office and shut the door.

All week Mr Fitch struggled to make some common sense out of the situation. To Louise's dismay, it was Gilbert who came with a team of people to start the dig. Every morning Mr Fitch stood at the window nearest the reception desk watching and waiting.

'I'll get the measure of this chap before the week is out. Bloody man. Never argues, never shouts. I could deal with him if he did. Just gets on as if I haven't spoken. Never been ignored like this in all my life. He's a menace or a maniac, I don't know which. Married, is he?'

'No.'

'Thought not. Divorced?'

'No, never married at all.'

'Oh I see, he's one of those.'

'He most certainly isn't.'

'How do you know?'

'Well,' Louise thought quickly but couldn't come up with anything more decisive than, 'he isn't, that's all.' Then she blushed. Mr Fitch eyed her curiously.

'Where's he live?'

'Just outside Little Derehams, I think.'

'Rented?'

'No idea. I've said I don't know him that well. I'm sorry.'

'Choirmaster?'

'Yes.'

'I'll get him somehow. I know – do the boys need new surplices?'

'Sir Ralph bought them some a while back.'

Mr Fitch impatiently turned away from the window. 'He would! Is there anything else they need? Anything I could buy to put pressure on him to do as I say? Organ need repairing, updating – you know the sort of thing. I'll buy this or that if you'll . . .'

'Not that I know of. I could always ask.'

Mr Fitch looked speculatively at her and made a decision. 'You do that.' He approached her and, staring her straight in the eye, barked out: 'But remember whose side you are on. *Mine!*'

Louise quailed a little at his threat. It wasn't often she was intimidated by a man, but Mr Fitch could do just that. She made up her mind that in her coffee break she'd go and have a word with Gilbert.

'Here! Take a look at this.' Louise looked down into the trench where he was working. He'd cleared an area about three feet square, and exposed an almost intact piece of mosaic flooring. 'Brilliant, eh?'

'Definitely!' The colours weren't distinct because the soil was only partially cleared away, but she could see heavenly rusty red and a kind of grey-white colour in the pattern.

'Gilbert.'

He looked vaguely up at her and said, 'Yes?'

'Mr Fitch wants to know if there's anything you need for the choir. Like new robes or music or anything, or the organ updating.'

He stopped his gentle scraping of the mosaic, wiped his hands on his trousers and gazed at her. 'I hope he doesn't imagine he's dealing with a fool.'

'Oh no, nothing like that, but that's the message. He asked me to enquire.'

'There's nothing, thanks all the same.' He called an instruction to one of his team working just beyond him in the trench, then said to her, 'There's no way he can stop this work going ahead, you know.'

'Yes, but when will it be finished? We need to know. *I* need to know, not just Mr Fitch. All our plans are on hold, you see.'

'Have your Show next year instead then.'

'Gilbert, that's no answer!'

'It is. I've said postpone till next year. This,' he pointed to the exposed floor, 'could be of national importance.'

'If it's just this little bit, we could fence it off and make a detour with the pipes and then the men could finish the sewers and you could have your bit of fun too.'

'*Bit of fun?* And there was I, thinking I'd found someone with a soul.' Gilbert shook his head and sadly turned his back on her and began working again.

'Oh, you have, but you're not being fair. I was only trying to work something out to everyone's benefit.'

'I have no idea at this moment of the extent of this site. It could be just this bit or it could cover acres.'

'Acres? Mr Fitch won't have that.'

'Oh, won't he? You just wait and see.'

In The Royal Oak the Roman ruins were discussed with fervour. Vera decided that Mr Fitch would want to cover everything up.

'He'll do like they do when there's a preservation order on old trees. It was in the paper a while back. Builder wanted to cut some old oaks down, Council said not on your Nellie, so he felled 'em about five o'clock one Bank Holiday Monday morning. Daft Council said they couldn't understand him doing it at a time when no one was about to stop him. I sometimes wonder about these councillors.'

Jimmy asked what on earth trees had to do with Roman ruins.

'Same thing but different. He'll get some other company to come, at the weekend of course, and get it all filled in and then look us straight in the face and say, "What Roman ruins? Where are they?" There'll be no answer to that because they won't be there no more and the Romans haven't left an address book have they, to let us all know?'

'Gilbert Johns is digging up there,' Willie said.

'Well, he's about as much use as a yard of pump-water. My cousin Dottie cleans for 'im. She's not allowed to move a thing. There's old rubbish all over the place. As soon as one lot goes another lot takes its place. Drives her mad, it does. And books, they're everywhere. If she says should she sort some out to go to a jumble sale he nearly lies down and dies. "Dottie," he says in that sad voice of his, "these are my children, my life's blood. How can I thrust them out into an uncaring world?" Still, he pays well and never complains if she has one of her turns and can only flick 'er duster.'

Jimmy shook his head. 'Seems funny to me. How can yer make a living poking about with bits of old stone and that? Beats me. It's not like a man's job, is it?'

'Takes all sorts, Jimmy.' Willie shook his head. 'Talking of which, what's Louise doing about the Show?'

'Latest is they're still waiting to see what's happening about the ruins. They say old Fitch is nearly blowing a gasket. Blazing, he is. Told her off for telling Gilbert. Asked her who exactly it is she's working for.'

'Yer start to lose interest in growing stuff, when yer don't even know if there's going to be any Show.'

Jimmy shook his head sympathetically. 'Don't worry, Mr Fitch'll sort something out. Ridiculous state of affairs, you can't please yerself on yer own land now. Things is coming to a pretty pitch. When my grandad was a boy you were master of yer own destiny and what you owned you owned. Not nowadays, nowadays, it's . . .'

Vera shuffled about impatiently. 'You two going to put the world to rights, because if you are, I'm off. It's not the same since Pat stopped coming in.'

Jimmy felt annoyed by Vera's uncharitable attitude. 'You should be glad she's found someone.'

'Oh, I am, but . . .'

'Well?'

'I am, I said!'

'There's more to it than that. I can tell.'

'No, there isn't.'

'There is. Go on, tell us, we've a right to know, Willie and me. We've looked after 'er interests all these years.'

Vera hesitated only for a moment. It wasn't often she knew the gossip before these two did, and it really was a juicy piece of news. 'Well, they do say there's someone in Little Derehams after him for money.'

'You mean he owes 'em some?'

'No, I mean . . .' With her hand Vera draw a large arc around the area of her stomach and nodded knowingly.

'You don't mean . . .'

'I do. That's what she says. You'd think she was 'aving quads she's that big, so they say, and it's early days yet apparently. I don't know whether to tell Pat or not.'

Jimmy leaned across the table and pointed his finger at Vera. 'You keep well out of it, understand? Don't interfere. It could all be a tale. She could be naming him 'cos of his reputation; maybe she daren't name who it really is.'

'OK! So what if it's true?'

'Say nothing, please. Right? Just this once mind your own business.'

Willie, curiosity getting the better of him, asked, 'Who is it anyways?'

Vera looked warily at Jimmy and then whispered, 'Simone Paradise.'

Willie, amazed, shouted in a stage whisper: 'Simone Par—'

Jimmy nudged him. 'Shut up, keep yer voice down.'

'I don't believe it, I really don't. Her and him have nothing in common.'

'Well, they have now, or so she says!' Vera chuckled and then tapped Jimmy's arm, adding, 'Pat'll know soon enough, but *I* shan't tell 'er. I'm off. Don's bringing fish and chips home tonight, we're warming 'em in the microwave when he gets back. Wish we had a fish and chip van here. Be grand, that would. Toodle-oo. We don't get far but we do see life, don't we?' And she left the bar laughing.

Sure enough, Vera didn't get the chance to tell Pat. She found out for herself the next morning.

20

Pat went into the Store to have a quick check with Jimbo about when she would be required for his next list of functions. It was a busy morning and Jimbo and his assistant were having a hard time keeping up with the flow of customers. While she waited to speak to him, Pat wandered along the shelves trying to think of a little treat for Dean, seeing as he'd finished his exams. Chocolates? He liked them special ones in the gold boxes, but they were too expensive; he'd have the box finished inside five minutes. No, they wouldn't do. What on earth could she buy for him? She'd reached the stationery shelves, and was thinking of a nice new pen when she bumped into Barry's mother. They'd had an uneasy truce since Pat had informed her that she and Barry weren't sharing a room on their holidays.

'Morning, Pat.'

'Morning, Mrs Jones. How's things?'

'Fine, thanks. I'm thinking of entering the shortbread competition – any chance I might win?' She smiled a kind of crooked smile, half-teasing, half-serious.

'With me on a winning streak, perhaps not.' They both laughed. Then they fell to discussing the weather, the Roman ruins, the . . .

'Hello, Grandma!' A neighbour nudged Barry's mother and chuckled.

'Who are you calling Grandma?'

'Not me, that's for certain!' Pat joked.

'You,' she nodded in Barry's mother's direction. 'It's you I'm meaning. Thought you'd have been the first to know.'

Mrs Jones drew herself up to her full height and asked for an explanation.

'Oh dear, things is more serious than I thought. Not like you not to be in the know. It's your Barry got her in the club, she says.'

Mrs Jones turned and looked piercingly at Pat, who replied by raising her eyebrows and shrugging her shoulders. Mrs Jones asked her sharply. 'Do you know who she means?'

'Don't ask me, haven't a clue.'

The neighbour nudged Mrs Jones again. 'Yer know, Simone Paradise. It's 'er – she says your Barry's to blame.'

Pat went white as a sheet. Mrs Jones hit her neighbour a smart stinging slap across the face, followed by a swipe with her handbag, which sent the other woman's basket spinning out of her hand and the contents all over the floor. A bottle of tonic water smashed and spewed its contents over Mrs Jones's tights.

As she leaped back out of the way, Mrs Jones shouted, 'Don't you dare make disgusting accusations like that! Simone Paradise is a tart and my Barry would never go with a tart. My Barry's a good boy. Whatever she says isn't true. D'yer hear me? *Not true!*'

'Ask him then. She swears it's him. No good coming all indignant with me, the evidence is there for all to see. It'll be number five. Course I'm not saying they're *all* his, but . . .'

Mrs Jones almost boiled with anger. 'None of 'em's my Barry's. Believe me.'

'Little white hen that never laid away, is he? Come off it, Mrs Jones, we all know what your Barry's like, and your Kenny,' she paused for dramatic effect, '*and* your Terry.' The whole store was listening and the air was filled with sniggers at this last statement.

Pat, who'd been standing white and shaking during this argument, turned on her heel at this and left. Jimbo called after her but she ignored him. He then went to sort out the row.

'Now, ladies, shall we finish our shopping and then leave. I don't like to have this kind of confrontation in here; it upsets the other customers.'

Someone waiting at the meat counter shouted, 'Yer wrong there, this is why we come in 'ere. Good bit of nice clean fun it is, better than the telly any day.' There was a gale of laughter at this remark and Jimbo could feel things were definitely getting out of hand.

The neighbour said indignantly, 'And who's going to pay for this broken bottle? Not me, that's for certain. Put it on Mrs Jones's bill, will yer, Mr Charter-Plackett?' She gave a triumphant smile in the direction of Mrs Jones, who writhed with indignation.

'This is on me. No one pays for it. Just step out of the way and mind your shoes on the glass. Thank you, ladies.'

The assistant came to clear up the mess, and Jimbo returned to the till. Mrs Jones went home with her shopping only partly done; half her heart was feeling sorry for Pat, the other half for herself. She'd kill that neighbour of hers! No, she wouldn't – she'd kill the neighbour's pea plants instead. That would hurt her a lot more, watching her peas dying inch by inch, oh yes . . . a slow torturous death. Coming on lovely they were, be just right for the Show, 'cept she'd do for 'em once and for all. Saying that about her Barry. Weedkiller she'd put on 'em, all over 'em – the leaves, the stalks, every inch. She'd plenty in the shed, and she'd use it double strength. That'd sort her out.

Pat collected her bike from the school cycle shed and stormed home. Halfway up the drive she began to cry. That woman had punched a hole clean through her future. How could she have been such a fool as to think for one moment that he could have the slightest serious interest in her and her children? He'd been fooling her all this time. She'd been a complete and utter idiot. All the signs, everything she'd ever known about him she'd simply pushed to the back of her mind, ignored them, scorned them.

She'd believed all his talk about it being different with her, which come to think of it, it was. It really was. He'd never tried anything on. Always been restrained, even sometimes when she'd been tempted he'd said no. So what was he playing at? What's more, what was Simone Paradise playing at? It was that French grandmother of hers who was to blame. The Paradises had always been a queer lot, but the French blood had made them even odder.

She was beautiful though, was Simone. That long dark hair, almost to her waist when she'd not taken the time to roll it up into that great plaited bun at the back. The slow swinging walk, with her layers of beads jingling at every step, the roll of her hips, the gaggle of little children at her long swaying skirts. Always dreamy, relaxed, come day go day. The children she dressed at Oxfam; Pat's had been too, but Dean and Michelle didn't manage to look like Simone's kids, all peasant and gypsy-like. They said she and the children lived on pasta and beans. There were bins of them in the kitchen and great swathes of herbs hanging up to dry. Funny woman she was and not half.

In front of the mirror when she got home, Pat studied herself. OK, she was short, slimmer now since she'd dieted, though Barry said he liked something to get hold of so he didn't want her to get too thin, brown hair cut short – in a thousand years hers would never grow as long as Simone's – skin mediocre, nice straight nose, her mouth could be a bit more generous. Simone's was rich and soft and moist and ruby red without the aid of lipstick, but he wouldn't want that great gaggle of kids, would he? Oh no, Simone Paradise wouldn't be a marriage proposition. He didn't like pasta anyway – he'd told her as much. And that cottage was crammed to the thatch with kids, all of them in two bedrooms. Oh no! Pat Duckett was a better proposition from the point of view of comfort. Nice four-bed-roomed house, all mod cons, two children soon off her hands, money in the bank. Oh yes, she could see right through it all now. He was coming for tea tonight . . . well, she'd show him!

She wore the long skirt she'd bought years ago and never had the brass cheek to wear, topped with a long baggy brown blouse from Oxfam – no, it was from Cancer Research. She put on four necklaces, the biggest, heaviest ones she could find, then carefully applied eye-liner and eye-shadow, leaving her skin smooth and shining. She put on every ring she could find, including some of Michelle's, and then she boiled a great pan of pasta and emptied a large jar of tomato stuff onto the mince and added almost a whole tube of tomato purée. That'd show 'im.

When he came he politely made no comment at her appearance. She flung her arms round him and kissed him in front of the children and her dad. He returned her kiss, somewhat surprised because she was usually very circumspect about touching him in front of the family.

When they sat down to eat Michelle noticed her rings. 'Mum! You've got my rings on!'

'Only borrowed 'em, that's all. Like pasta do yer, Barry?'

'Er . . . yes thanks. I'm not keen on it usually, but this is good. Very tasty.'

'Well, yer'll be used to it, I daresay. They tell me she cooks a lot of it.'

'Who does?' He began to grow wary.

Grandad looked at the two of them. 'What's up?'

'Nothing,' Pat said as she shovelled pasta into her mouth, pretty certain it was going to work itself into a clump which she wouldn't be able to swallow.

Barry stoically struggled with his food. He had a nasty feeling that Pat knew about the rumours. She hadn't given him a chance to explain. He couldn't in front of the kids, didn't want them to lose faith in him.

'Finished, Dad?'

'Yes, thanks. Very nice that was – bit heavy on the tomato, but very nice.'

'Well, now.' Pat cleared away the plates leaving Barry's because he hadn't finished. 'Lemon meringue pie?' She looked round the table and Grandad, Dean and Michelle nodded their heads. 'And what about you, Barry? Perhaps some goat's cheese and oat biscuits with fresh fruit would be more to your liking – more natural-like?'

'Mum!' Michelle protested. She sensed things were wrong but couldn't understand what.

Now Barry definitely knew she'd heard the rumours. But this new Pat had jammed up his ability to talk. He wasn't on her wavelength at all. She came to stand beside him. His plate of pasta and mince was still not finished. He looked up at her. 'Now, Pat, what's up?'

'What's up? This is what's up!' She picked up his plate and emptied the contents on his head. Barry sat there, with tagliatelle and tomato sauce and meat sliding down his face.

'Now get out.'

'Mum! Mum! Don't! Poor Barry! I'll clean you up, Barry. She didn't mean it, did yer, Mum?'

Pat ignored Michelle's pleas. 'Out, and don't come back for the next thousand years.' She leaped towards the back door and opened it wide. 'Go on out. You lying, cheating sod. I can't believe I was such a fool as to believe yer.'

Barry stood up. He'd made no attempt to get the pasta and tomato sauce off himself, so it slid uncomfortably around his collar and down his shirt-front.

He slipped on a splodge of tomato sauce and almost fell, but Dean put a hand out to catch him. 'Barry, don't go.'

'Don't you dare stop 'im.'

Michelle began to cry. 'Barry! Mum! Grandad, stop her, please!'

'It's nothing to do with me.'

'It is! I want him for a dad.'

When Barry had left, Pat slammed the door after him, sat down and burst into tears.

Dean was angry. 'Well, what made you do that?'

Through her tears Pat said, 'You wouldn't understand.' She dragged all the rings off her fingers and the beads from her neck. She scrubbed her eyes, smearing the eye make-up, then hauled Michelle's flipflops from her feet and stood up and said, 'You lot can clear this up. I'm off to bed.'

'Mum, what have you turned him out for? What's Barry done?'

'Been spreading it around . . .'

Her father shouted, 'Pat!'

Contrite, Pat sat down again. 'I'm sorry. I thought I was the only one, but I've found out I'm not – he's got someone else. I know you like Barry and want him for a dad but there's things happened . . . and I'm not having it.'

Michelle wailed her disappointment. 'I'll never get a dad now. I want a dad. I want a dad. I want . . .'

'Come and sit on your Grandad's knee. Perhaps I'll do for now.'

Michelle snuffled a little longer into her handkerchief and then decided to sit on his knee.

Dean argued she'd been too hard. 'It was a nasty trick you played, Mum.'

'What kind of a trick do you call what he's been doing?'

'But what's he done? Or is it that you've listened to all those gossips in the Store that you talk about?'

Pat instantly realised the common sense of what Dean had said. But she brushed it aside because she was so angry. 'Never you mind.'

Michelle gave a horrified shriek. 'Our holidays! It's all spoilt now because of you! I hate you, Mum! I hate you! I want Barry back!'

Up earlier than usual the following morning because she hadn't slept properly, Pat was thoroughly at odds with herself. Michelle had fallen out with her over the holiday, and because of it she hated herself. She'd thrown away the best chance of a holiday they'd ever had. She'd been stupid playing that daft trick on him, with the pasta and that and her clothes and the rings and things. In retrospect she wished she'd behaved with more dignity. Pat opened the back door to let in some fresh air. It was going to be hot today. Make a change.

On the doormat in the porch was an envelope addressed to her. The handwriting seemed familiar. The letter read:

Dear Pat,

I was planning to tell you about the rumours going round but I realised last night you'd already heard.

I want you to understand, they are only rumours. That baby is not mine. I'm not saying I haven't, you know, but I haven't lately and the baby is nothing to do with me. I'm going to see her today, and ask her to stop telling these daft lies. I'm really sorry about all this. I don't want you hurt.

You know I'm fixed on you, and since we've been going out I haven't been with anyone else. Please believe me. Am I forgiven? Let me know how you feel.

Love and kisses. Barry. XXXXXXXXXXXXXXXXXXXXX

She tore the letter into tiny pieces and threw them in the bin. The whole village would be laughing at her, and brightness had gone from her life – all because she'd been jealous and stupid and listened to gossip. And she'd never given him a chance to explain. Serve you right, Pat Duckett, she thought, just serves you right. She'd thrown away the best chance she'd had in years. Pat Duckett was a fool.

21

The whole village had noticed the difference in Louise since she went to work up at the Big House. She was slimmer, she was livelier, she was kinder and more sympathetic, and above all she didn't look down on everyone as she used to when she first came back to Turnham Malpas. The change in her had been sudden and nothing short of miraculous. Malcolm the milkman even swore he'd seen her out running early one morning, but they'd all dismissed that as fantasy.

In the rectory they put it down to the accessibility of the pool and the fitness rooms at the Big House. In the Store they attributed it to her having a lover; it must have been quite five minutes before anyone was capable of speech, they'd laughed till tears were running down their cheeks. Sheila put it down to the voluntary work Louise had recently taken up with the homeless in Culworth. Though Sheila had to confess she didn't know where the homeless *were* in Culworth, because it didn't seem quite that kind of place. But coming home in the early hours after taking the soup and bread rolls round was certainly exhausting. Louise always slept late on those mornings. Once she'd helped out on a weekday night and Sheila had had a terrible time getting her up in time for the office. With Mr Fitch still on the rampage about the Show and its possible cancellation, that would be the last thing he'd need, his receptionist turning up late for work.

But at least, thought Sheila, she wasn't bothering with the rectory any more, and Caroline had found a nice retired secretary who was willing to come in, as and when for a few hours, and help out with the parish typing. So that little problem was solved, and working up at the Big House seemed to have turned out rather well. Louise was earning good money and enjoying the job, and she'd been out the previous Saturday and bought some lovely flattering clothes too. Best of all, she was much happier and easier to get on with. Sheila wasn't quite sure why she'd mellowed, but whatever the reason she was glad. Altogether life was much improved.

That was how Louise felt too. Life had taken a definite upturn. She lay in bed one morning in the middle of June smoothing her hands over her hips and right down her thighs thinking about Gilbert doing just that. He always ran his hands over her body, fingering her hip-bone, moulding his palm over the bone in her shoulder, smoothing his fingers over her elbows, running his hand down her spine. When he'd counted her vertebrae then she knew the real foreplay was about to begin and the anticipation of what was to come excited her more than she had ever imagined. You could read about it in books, see it on film and television, but actually experiencing it was something out of this world. The more often they made love the more her pleasure increased.

Gilbert had this strange earthy scent to him which she found incredibly stimulating. The first time she'd noticed it was when they'd been in the church trying out the handwritten music she'd discovered, but it was in the close proximity of his house when she'd called with a letter from Mr Fitch, that it had really hit her. He'd invited her in and his body aroma had made her crave his touch.

He'd recognised the look on her face and he'd unhesitatingly planted a soft response-seeking kiss on her lips. Her body had reeled with the shock of the intimacy she so powerfully desired, and he'd caught her elbow as she staggered. From that moment there was no going back. She was undressed and in his bed almost before she knew it. It was all so tremendously beautiful, her need for love so great, his approach so teasing and amusing that she was carried on the crest of a wave into a world of exquisite experiences the like of which she had never known before. When they'd finished, she'd lain beside this total stranger with her eyes closed, still shuddering with pleasure, thrilled by her daring, a slave to his sex drive.

She'd quickly learned the ways of love and desperately hoped, though never asked, that she satisfied him as he satisfied her. But there never was a post mortem for Gilbert, no analysis. It had happened and that was it. She knew that her appetite for him would always be insatiable.

Sitting in church the first Sunday morning after they'd become lovers, she'd watched Gilbert come in with the choirboys, his white surplice immaculate, his eyes downcast, his hair falling over his forehead as it always did. Who would have imagined, she thought, that he could be this wonderful lover of hers; that he could make taking off her dress into an act of worship? There was no hint of his sinewy strength nor his passion. Louise had looked round the congregation and said to herself, 'No one here knows the real Gilbert Johns, only me.' She then looked at Peter as he stood on the altar steps, waiting to speak. She was startled by the fact that she could look at him and feel only a small sadness, nothing devastating, just quiet regret. But when she gazed on Gilbert, her insides heaved and she longed for him to meet her eyes. But Gilbert didn't glance in her direction; he behaved as he always did when he was choirmaster – quiet, unassuming, absorbed in his music . . . a watchful eye on his boys, and his long, sensitive fingers conducting with such style.

Suddenly Louise recognised the music they were singing. It was the piece she'd found in the music cupboard on Revelation Monday and which had thrilled Gilbert so wonderfully. As the incredibly beautiful sounds reached the rafters of the church on their way to Heaven, Louise flushed with excitement. She was seized by the idea that Gilbert must have chosen to sing that particular piece, on this particular Sunday, as an offering to her. What more glorious tribute could he give her! Louise wept quietly for joy.

One Monday morning, Mr Fitch had said, 'This Gilbert Johns . . .'

Louise jumped at the mention of his name.

'Miss Bissett?'

'Yes, Mr Fitch.'

'I said Gilbert Johns is on the point of calling it a day.'

'Calling it a day?'

'Yes.'

'Oh! Is he?'

'About the Roman ruins.'

'Oh, the Roman ruins. Ah, right! Oh, is he? I didn't know.'

Mr Fitch smiled wryly. 'Seeing as you don't know him very well, I don't expect you do.'

'No, that's right. So, right. The Show. We can carry on then?'

'He says it's definitely a very minor find. He's rescued everything and the items are being catalogued or whatever they do with these things and they'll be sent to Culworth Museum. Heaven alone knows what kind of a mess he'd have made of our lawns if it had been a major find – he's dug trenches all over the place as it is. However, it's all turned out for the best. Thank goodness. The sewer people have promised to work night and day to finish laying the pipes and then the work in the house and surrounds can carry on and it won't affect the Show at all. So we've got the go-ahead: there's nothing to stop us now.'

'I'm so glad. I'll get a piece in the *Culworth Gazette* – let everybody know it's definitely on.'

'Yes, good idea. I want this Show to be the best ever. It's more than fifty years since the last proper Show at the Big House, and that wasn't anything like the size of this one. It's just got to be the best. I know I can rely on you, Louise.'

'You can, Mr Fitch, certainly. I'm so pleased. We've all done so much work and everyone's so involved with growing things and everything . . . what a relief. Thank goodness. It's all organised right down to the last detail. We just have to press the "Go" button.'

'Good. That's how I like things to be – in smooth running order. Have we invited the rector to sit on the platform? I think it would only be courtesy to do so.'

Louise found that her heart didn't even blip at the sound of Peter's name and the prospect of close contact on the platform. 'We haven't, but we can if you wish.'

'See to it, please. A courteous invitation – we must observe the niceties of village life.' Unusually for him, he smiled at her. 'You and I will get on very well together. Shall we agree between ourselves that this is a permanent job! Would you be willing to accept it?'

Thinking of Gilbert she said, 'Oh yes, of course I would.'

'You can get a letter done to that effect then, there must be a sample contract somewhere in the files. I'm afraid Fenella hasn't long to go now. Very sad.'

'It is.'

'However, life goes on. How are you finding village life, Louise? Not very exciting, eh?'

'I don't know about that. There's always something happening. For instance,' she lowered her voice, 'someone's had weedkiller poured on the peas they were growing for the competitions.'

'No! Really?'

'Oh yes. There's been a terrible upset about it. It happened in the middle of the night and they got caught. The police were called.'

'The police?'

'Yes, because there was a fight. Barry's mother, you know Barry the carpenter,' Mr Fitch nodded, 'and her neighbour Carrie Evans were fighting. Apparently they were both in their nightdresses in the alleyway between their houses. Barry came out, and one of his brothers, and the neighbour's husband and there was a real dust-up. Mrs Jones flatly denies she poured weedkiller on the plants but they were wilting unto death, *and* she was caught with the watering can in her hand.' Louise was laughing so much she had to wipe her eyes.

Mr Fitch was appalled. 'I didn't know these things were taken so seriously.'

'Oh yes. These competitions bring out the worst in people. Heaven alone knows what the neighbour will do to Mrs Jones's flowers in retaliation. She goes in for the cut-flowers class, you see. Been winning prizes at the Culworth Flower Show for years with her cut flowers.'

There came the sound of a gentle step in the doorway, and Gilbert entered carrying an outsize cardboard box. This morning he was wearing a vivid red shirt, open almost to his navel as usual, with the sleeves rolled up above his elbows. On his head was a stiff-brimmed Australian bush hat without the corks. To Louise he looked so vital, so vibrant, that Mr Fitch's dynamism faded into insignificance.

'Good morning. Good morning.' He nodded briefly to Louise. 'Brought some things for you to look at, Mr Fitch.' He put the box down on Louise's reception desk.

'Just a few, there are more, but these are some of the best pieces. This here is a very nearly complete wine jar.'

'Complete?' Mr Fitch queried the odd collection of bits Gilbert held in a small box.

'I know it looks nothing now but it will be when we've finished with it. The mosaic we found is in a crate, too heavy to carry in. Very pleased about that. Now here in this box waiting to be cleaned up are these . . .' he tenderly lifted some knobbly almost unrecognisable items and laid two of them on Louise's hand and two on Mr Fitch's. 'Those in your hand, Mr Fitch, are hairpins, and those you have, Louise, are rings – women's rings. Gold, I suspect. I think there'll be a carving on that larger one; we'll see when it gets cleaned up. Aren't they beautiful? Not seen the light of day for something like possibly sixteen or seventeen hundred years.'

'We're very privileged then.'

'You are indeed, Mr Fitch. And so am I, to have a job like this. Here's a brooch, this here is part of a spoon, and this, and this spoon is virtually complete. All quality stuff which, with the mosaic flooring we've found, makes me know it's the corner of a small villa, and not a peasant's house. Pity it's not complete, but there we are. Once the Romans had gone home the villas were looted for their stone and anything the owners had left behind, and over the years they were ploughed up and that kind of thing. So this appears to be all we're left with. There's lots of other bits and pieces I haven't brought in. County Hall have established the exact position on the map and so now the diggers have got the 'all clear'. I've had a word with the site manager and they're getting ready to restart tomorrow.'

He smiled at Mr Fitch. 'The Museum is going to make a special exhibition of all this, once we get it sorted. They'll be buying new display material to exhibit it. I don't suppose . . . ?' He looked at Mr Fitch with that curious 'heron' look Louise had noticed before; she almost expected him to be standing on one foot.

'You mean would I contribute to it?'

'Well, I was thinking of it being called the Turnham Malpas Fitch Collection.'

Mr Fitch couldn't conceal his delight. His face lit up and he beamed at Gilbert. 'Really? I hadn't thought of that. What a splendid idea! Really put Turnham Malpas on the map, eh?' He chuckled. 'I say. Never thought my name would finish up in a museum! The Fitch Collection. Marvellous. No expense to be spared. Remember, send me the bill. Well, well.'

Mr Fitch turned away and walked towards his study as nonchalantly as he could. He didn't need to think twice about it; he'd pay – oh yes, he'd pay! No matter what it cost. He was delighted beyond belief. It would give him more pleasure than all the big deals he'd brought off over the years. What was it about this village that had so captivated him, and got him so excited about a few broken remains found on land he owned. Ah! that was it. *Land he owned.* He now had three cottages of his own in the village – Pat Duckett's and the two weekender cottages. Soon, soon, he'd have the lot. Well, almost.

Gilbert waited until the door was safely shut. Louise was standing leaning against her desk. He looked at her from his deepset eyes, pushed his hair back from his forehead and came to stand beside her – close, so close. Louise's heart began thumping thunderously; he really shouldn't, not here at work. No one knew, and she didn't want them to know, and how long she could go on deceiving her mother about the homeless of Culworth she couldn't tell, but they mustn't find out about him, not yet at least. It was all too precious, too fragile to be shared. For a moment she leaned away from him but then she couldn't resist his touch. He kissed her without any preliminaries, a heart-stopping, blood-pounding kiss. She slipped her hands inside his open shirt and relished the slight sweat on his skin: something which, with anyone else, would have repulsed her, but with Gilbert it added to his attraction.

The door from one of the lecture rooms burst open and out came some of the students, laughing and joking on their way to lunch. Louise couldn't believe that they didn't know what earth-shattering things were happening to her. She was on such a high she was convinced there must be visible beams of passion radiating out from her. But the students were quite oblivious.

'Gilbert, you must go.'

'See you later then? Hmmmmm?'

'About eight?'

'Bye for now.' And he sauntered out with his cardboard box, apparently unaware of the turmoil of emotions he'd left bubbling in Louise.

22

The news that the Show would definitely be going ahead was round the village like wildfire. Willie Biggs, who'd been giving Caroline a hand to dig out a rosebush which had succumbed to some dread disease, said, 'Now the Show's back on, why don't you enter the cut-flower class? You've got some lovely blooms here.'

Caroline laughed. 'I'm not up to that standard, Willie. Heavens above! They would laugh themselves silly at my flowers.'

'No, they wouldn't. It's time that Mrs Jones had some real competition. You've got them lovely delphiniums – they'd be good for a start. Another week and they'll be at their peak. Think about it.'

'Well, I'm really flattered and it would be fun. Shall I?'

Willie chuckled. 'Go on, give it a whirl.'

'I will then. Yes, I will. I shall be so nervous. I've never done anything like it before.'

'I've got a spare schedule, I'll pop it through the door.' He lifted the bush into his wheelbarrow. 'There we are then. I'm 'aving a bonfire tomorrow with churchyard rubbish. I'll put this on it, got to burn it else whatever it's got will spread.'

'Thank you, Willie. You're most kind.'

'Not at all. Glad to 'elp.' He looked at her as though deciding whether or not to say something else. Then he made up his mind. 'My Sylvia loves working for you. Them children's like her own grandchildren. Forever telling me stories about the tricks they get up to, she is. I just hopes yer here for a long time.'

'Oh, I hope so too. I've been asked to do some morning surgeries at a practice in Culworth while someone's on maternity leave. It'll be after Christmas when the children go to playgroup. Under no circumstances can I ask Peter to take and collect the children, he's too busy and it's just not on – but do you think Sylvia would mind? I haven't spoken to her yet.'

'Believe me, whatever you do will be all right by her. She just loves working here.'

Caroline thanked him and then said, 'I wouldn't have survived without her.'

Willie knew she meant things other than housework. He bent to take hold of the wheelbarrow handles, to hide the fact there were tears in his eyes. 'All the village love you both, the rector's made such a difference to us all. Even those who don't go to church of a Sunday, think the world of yer. There's something about 'im that brings out the best in people. It's that look he 'as. Yer can't tell fibs to 'im. Remember what I said about the flowers.' Willie set off to walk round by Pipe and Nook Lane.

'Don't do that, Willie. Let's wipe the wheel and then you can take it through the house. It's a ridiculously long way round otherwise.'

'I'd carry it round, 'cept I don't want to dump all the soil. It's best to get rid of everything all round the roots, just in case.'

After he'd gone, Caroline put her idea of covering the surgeries to Sylvia.

'It would be three mornings and the twins would be going to playgroup three mornings to start with, so I'd have to leave before they went and wouldn't be back till roughly half-past one. What do you think?'

'That's fine. I'd have nearly three hours to get done in, wouldn't I? 'Cept in the holidays, that would be more difficult.'

'Yes, I realise that. Think about it?'

'Of course. You like the idea then?'

'Once a doctor always a doctor, it's in the blood!' Caroline went back into the garden to study over Willie's idea. She might, just might, do what he said. After all, it wasn't the Royal Horticultural Society, was it? Only a village Show. Even so, she wouldn't want to enter something which would make her look a fool. Yes, why not, she'd enter. What fun. She decided to go to the Store and announce her intentions; best find out the opposition.

Alex and Beth clamoured to go with her, so they wandered across the Green, hand-in-hand and into the Store.

Harriet was in there, behind the till and Linda was coping with a long queue at the post-office counter.

'Cut flowers? You're being ambitious, aren't you?'

'Harriet! Don't put a damper on my enthusiasm!'

'Sorry, but the competition's stiff in the cut-flower department. Believe me.' She leaned across the till and whispered, 'Mrs Jones always wins.' She nodded her head in the direction of the queue and Caroline saw that her main rival was next to be served.

'Oh right. Got to give her some competition then.' The two of them laughed and then Caroline's attention was taken by the twins who were busy filling one of Jimbo's wire baskets with all manner of sweets.

Beth's voice could be heard saying, 'Beth like choccy.'

'Maybe, but we can't possibly buy all these, we'll have to put some back. Now, which shall we choose?' But Caroline's placatory approach didn't please Beth, who promptly stamped her feet, and when Caroline attempted to put back some of the sweets, she flung herself down on the floor screaming, 'No! No! No!'

Alex kicked at her thrashing legs to stop her screaming, which made her yell louder still. Sadie came out from the mail-order office to see what the commotion was, and everyone in the post-office queue craned their necks to see this magnificent display of temper. Caroline, unable to quieten Beth, picked her up and gripping her firmly under her arm marched out, with Alex holding her spare hand. Beth's arms and legs were pumping vigorously as Caroline squeezed out through the door. The people in the queue could hear her screams fading away in the distance.

'Well, really, and them the rector's children!'

'Never heard such a row.'

'What an exhibition!'

'You'd think she'd manage 'em better than that. Spoiled to death, they are.'

Barry's mother turned contemptuously on her scandalised compatriots. 'Never 'ad none of your children throw a paddy, then? Always been quiet and well-behaved, 'ave they? I like to see a bit of spirit. She handled it right, she did. She's doing a good job there.'

'Well, she does love them children, I'll give yer that.'

'Of course she loves 'em. Who couldn't, they're that lovely. And I reckon she did right by the rector. Must 'ave been hard but there we are. She's a true Christian, she is; that's what being a Christian is. I admire her.'

'Yer mightn't be so keen if she wins the cut flowers. I've just heard her saying she's entering. That right, Mrs Charter-Plackett?'

Harriet agreed it was.

'I see. Well, all's fair in love and war. May the best man win. My pension, Linda, please and this parcel to post, while yer at it.'

As she weighed the parcel Linda said, 'How's Barry nowadays?'

'All right. Why?'

'I heard he'd blotted his copy book with Pat and they weren't seeing each other.'

'There's a sight too much gossip in this village. They've all got nothing better to do.'

The person behind her in the queue said, 'Hark who's talking!'

'And you can keep yer trap shut. I've heard about the trick you're getting up to with yer pot-plant entry.'

'And what do you mean by that?'

'You were seen sneaking round that new Garden Centre out on the by-pass last Sunday, eyeing their best begonias. We all know yer going to enter the pot-plant class.'

'So, what if I am?'

'You're going to buy one from the Garden Centre and enter it as yer own – pretend you've grown it. I wasn't born yesterday, even if the judges were.'

'Well, I never! What an accusation! That's libel!'

'I shall be watching out, believe me. I'll have my eye on them pot-plant classes.'

'What about you putting weedkiller on them prize peas then, eh? What about that?'

'I never.'

'You did.'

'I never.'

'Oh no! I bet!'

'Thanks, Linda. I'm off. Leave you to sort 'em all out.'

Barry's mother sauntered out with as much dignity as she could muster. They were all a sickening lot and she was fed up with 'em. She'd go home, have a nice cup of tea and sit where she could see her flowers and contemplate which ones she'd enter. That was it, yes. Do her nerves a power of good. As she passed the new houses Sir Ralph had built, and had inspected the front gardens that the tenants were now licking into shape, Pat came out from Jacks Lane on her way to the Store. Mrs Jones waved. 'Hello, Pat.'

'Hello.'

'Have you time for a word?'

Pat got off her bike and stood waiting.

'Our Barry's right upset, yer know.'

'I daresay.'

'He's off his food.'

'Oh dear.'

'He can't sleep.'

'Oh dear.'

'I don't know what to say to him next.'

'Neither do I.'

'He says it isn't his.'

'Does he.'

'Yes. 'Ow about it Pat?'

'How about what?'

'Letting bygones be bygones.'

'No. I've enough on without asking for trouble.'

'He's different about you, yer know.'

'So they say.'

'I'd have liked some grandchildren.'

'Well, there's always your other two. They might turn up trumps sometime.'

'I've been too good to 'em. Made life too comfortable. Barry's me favourite, yer know.'

'Is he?'

'Yes. Always has been. He can twist me round his little finger.'

'Well, there's one thing for certain. He isn't twisting *me* round his little finger.'

In a pleading tone Mrs Jones said, 'All men who are men have a little fling now and then.'

'There's flings and flings. I'll be off then.'

'They say your Dean's very clever, that the school says he'll be doing ten GCSEs, and two of 'em a year early.'

'Yes, that's right.'

'Nice that, having a clever boy. None of mine were interested. Couldn't wait to leave and get a job.'

'Your Barry's done all right.'

'Oh yes, but the other two are a waste of time.'

'I'm off then. I've a lot to do.'

'Think about him will yer, Pat? He hardly ever goes out now. Stuck in mooning about. Miserable, he is.'

'Can't help that.'

Pat felt a certain degree of satisfaction that Barry was taking her rejection of him so hard. Serves him right. But at the same time, deep in her heart, she regretted the lost opportunity. She could have easily been persuaded to marry him, very easily, but there was no way she was marrying someone who could beetle off and be getting his rations with someone else when he was supposed to be courting her. Then she remembered his beautiful teeth and that kind of antiseptic smell they always had. His thick dark hair and his laughing eyes. His strong legs and his powerful workmanlike hands. Hands that could be so gentle and inviting. She'd better stop this before she began seriously to regret her decision.

Michelle had not forgiven her yet, nor Dean. Pesky state of affairs when your children wanted you to marry someone that you didn't. Still, she'd sorted the holiday. Nice cottage by the sea. Bit off the beaten track, but never mind. They'd have a good time without him. Then she remembered he'd promised to take Dean fishing, and she recollected the comfort of his arm around her shoulders and she weakened. Maybe she *had* been too hard . . . Next time she saw him she might, just might, speak to him. After all he *and* his mother had said that Simone was telling lies. Maybe she was.

23

It was the Thursday before the Show, and Louise sat checking and rechecking her lists, determined that nothing and she meant *nothing*, could possibly have been overlooked. The telephone at the Big House had been in use nonstop almost all day. Mr Fitch had kept coming out of his office with yet another thought he'd had, and she'd had to check it all over again.

It was taking care of all the silly little things, like who was responsible for putting out the chairs on the platform and around the arena, which made for success. Had the Morris Dancers got the time right? Had Jeremy remembered he was in charge of collecting the money and putting it in the safe at regular intervals? Couldn't leave it till the end of the Show, that was asking for trouble leaving money lying about. Where would they put the bouquets for presenting to Mr Fitch's guests? Had they allocated sufficient parking space? With all the advertising Mr Fitch had insisted on, they'd probably have the entire county there. Small matters in themselves but so important on the day.

She let her mind drift off to eight o'clock that night. Her mother had already said she was an idiot to be going round with the soup and rolls so close to the Show. 'You'll need all the sleep you can get, you'll be so busy on the day.' But Louise had pooh-poohed the idea. She needed Gilbert just as much as Gilbert apparently needed her. She sucked the end of her pen and gazed out over the garden. Through her open window she could see her father watering the roses, and hear her mother supervising and criticising; an angry gesture here, hands-on-hips despair there. She wondered what made her father stay with her. What feeling they had left for each other . . . or didn't it matter when you got older? Was it all habit? Or when love mellowed, maybe you each couldn't live your life without the other. Or was it because there was nowhere else to go? Maybe that was it. You stayed simply because there was no choice.

And she and Gilbert? What had they got between them? Passion? Lust? Love? She decided yes to the first two questions, but no to the third. It wasn't love like Jimbo and Harriet had. Their love was tough – a firm anchorage, a belt and braces love affair. It wasn't love like Caroline and Peter's; that was all-adoring, all-giving, all-enduring. Not one of them could leave each other and walk away for ever, they'd no choice but to stay. She still had choice. Choice to stay, choice to go and be glad. Muriel Templeton had said . . . what was it she'd said? 'Find out who you truly are.' Perhaps that was what she had to do, despite her hunger for Gilbert. And it was a hunger and no mistake. She craved him. Poor Muriel – her face when she'd confessed to her about Gilbert. They'd met outside the church one midweek morning. There'd been only herself and Muriel around and they'd sat side by side on a gravestone and talked.

Muriel had been appalled at first, then she'd wiped her face clean of shock and become sympathetic. 'I have to tell you I can see the need. Before I married, I couldn't have done. I would have thought you sinful, but somehow marriage and . . . and . . . love have adjusted my thinking. But it really isn't right for it to be just . . . well, just wanting a man. It ought really to be for love. That's the best.'

'I know it is.'

'Gilbert's a lovely man. He deserves more than just wanting.'

'Yes, he does. You see, the trouble is I don't know what I am any more. This business with . . . Peter completely threw me. I thought I knew where I was going, but now I'm aware that I didn't. One half of me is eager to organise things, pleased to be praised for my success at it, but somehow there's another person emerging and I don't know really what she is.'

Muriel stood up to go. 'Then you need to sort her out, this new person you talk of, my dear. Think about finding who you truly are.'

Muriel was right. Perhaps she'd take her advice. She seemed so un-worldly did Muriel, but somehow she'd hit the nail on the head. Louise felt quite exhilarated with the thought of finding out who she really was. The Show would be her one last brilliant administrative success, her swansong. She'd be relieved when it was over. Lists and highlighting pens and coloured stickers didn't hold quite the fascination for her as before; Gilbert had changed all that. Now when she looked at the sky it was bluer than she'd ever realised, the flowers bloomed brighter, the crystal-clear water of the beck sparkled more enticingly, the houses round the Green looked more beautiful than she could have believed possible. She was even tempted to buy a pair of the dreaded green wellingtons and walk over the fields . . .

Louise rested her elbows on the windowsill and breathed in the country air. She recalled the thick smell of the air in the city when she'd worked at the bank. You didn't open windows there, the fumes would have con-stituted a serious health hazard, but here in Turnham Malpas, opening a window was sheer joy.

A ladybird crawled busily along the sill. Before Gilbert she would have angrily flicked it off and to hell with it, but now, with her finger she eased it towards a stem of the climbing rose framing her window, and watched it meandering up till it went out of sight. This philosophising wouldn't do. She'd check her lists one last time and then she'd get ready to go to Gilbert. Already in her nostrils she could smell his strange earthy scent; her insides churned with longing.

Sheila had begun to get cold feet. Decorating a church for a flower festival or organising a flower-arranging competition, she'd done that before, but this was scary. She'd begun to lose sleep over it. What she dreaded most was everything going wrong and having to face Mr Fitch and explain. She knew he was intimidating, in fact he must be because there were times when even Louise had been wary of him; she needed no more proof than that. The biggest worry was, did she have enough space for everyone who had entered? She'd just got home with the last of the entries when she heard Louise using the shower ready for going on the round with the soup and rolls. She found her reading glasses and sat down to try to make sense of it all. Why had she refused help from Caroline? She'd offered to help sort it all out, but Sheila had been too proud, and what's more too embarrassed because of Louise's behaviour, to accept.

She spread the entry forms out on the table and began to look through them. There were far more than she had anticipated. Mr Fitch's advertising campaign might well backfire if they got more people than they'd catered for. She had finally got everything into piles and was beginning to count the number of entries in the Victoria sponge section, when Louise came in to say she was off.

'I must say I wouldn't be wearing that if I was going out to help the homeless. It's so flimsy.'

Louise looked down at her dress and realised she'd made a bloomer. 'Well, we have to cheer them up, you know. It's no good wearing old things. It looks insulting, as if they're not worth bothering for.'

Sheila put down her pen. 'Look here, Louise, I'm not stupid. You're not going to see the homeless. If I didn't know any better, I'd think you were going out with a man.' She laughed at her little joke. Louise blushed bright red and glanced away from her mother's scrutiny. 'You're not? You are! I can tell by your face, you are!'

'What if I am? Don't sound so surprised, it's not very flattering.'

'I'm sorry. Who is it – anyone I know?'

Louise debated what to do. Tell her and the entire village would know by Saturday night. Not tell her and she'd be hurt, especially if she found out from someone else. She would be hurt anyway, not to say appalled, if she, Louise, told her exactly what it was she was really doing.

'Look, it's very delicate. You know how these things are, at the beginning. Do you mind very much if I don't tell you? Just till I'm more sure.'

'So you haven't been helping the homeless. You've been going out with someone.'

'You could say that.'

Sheila stood up and went across to Louise. Their physical displays of affection were very limited but tonight Sheila put her arm round Louise and gave her a kiss. 'I'm really pleased for you. Really pleased.'

'Thanks. I'll be off then.'

Sheila went to the door to watch her leave. She waved and smiled as Louise's little car disappeared in the direction of Penny Fawcett . . . Now, who could it be? Who lived in Penny Fawcett . . . ? In fact, Louise was going the long way round to Little Derehams. There was, after all, no point in telling her mother too much. She might be dim, but not *that* dim. And Mother must be pleased at her news; she didn't often earn a kiss and a hug.

Sheila finished sorting the entries and decided that it was going to be a success after all. What's more, her competitions would be the biggest attraction – yes, she'd bring the people in and no mistake. Mr Fitch would definitely be pleased with her. Fancy Louise having a boyfriend! She'd tell Ron when he got back from Newcastle; he'd be pleased too. Who on earth could it be? She'd find out soon enough. Perhaps he might be at the Show.

Barry was putting the finishing touches to the last of the stalls. They'd have them all erected tomorrow. Hope to God it didn't rain. Twenty stalls he'd made. The cost was astronomical but Mr Fitch had said if a job's worth doing . . . so he'd done a good job. Up at six o'clock tomorrow. His mum had cut all the crêpe paper for the stalls, he'd bought all the drawing pins and sticky tape, and he couldn't wait to see how good they looked. Barry took another mint imperial out of the bag in his pocket, propped his shoulder against the doorjamb of the estate workshop and stood looking out across the yard thinking about Saturday.

There wasn't going to be a lot for him to do on the actual day; he'd done his bit already. All he'd have to do was enjoy himself. Huh! Fat chance. He'd been round to see Simone and she'd laughed and said all right then, she'd deny it was his and leave everybody to guess. He knew she had no idea who the father really was. Well, for him those days were over. He wanted Pat. Pat Duckett and stability, and a family and a permanent relationship. No, that was the wrong word to use; it meant all kinds of things to all kinds of people nowadays. He wanted marriage. Marriage to Pat and a son and a daughter and even, he had to admit, a father-in-law.

This Saturday would see a turn-round. He wasn't going on like this any longer. She'd refused to see him, but this Saturday he'd sit in the refreshment tent from two o'clock till they closed up. He'd speak to her, if it was the last thing he did. He'd make her see sense. They were made for each other, and he couldn't think why he hadn't realised it years ago. But maybe the time wasn't ripe and maybe they'd neither of them been ready before now.

He was determined the kids shouldn't miss out on a holiday. He'd get them on his side. Michelle liked him and so did Dean. He'd bumped into Michelle once or twice this last week or so, and she'd been really glad to see him – and Dean had been such a help with the stalls since he'd finished his exams. A nice bright chap he was. A son to be proud of. Having made his decision, Barry locked the workshop door, jumped into his old van, kicked the bits of stuff laid on the floor out of his way, and made for home, more light-hearted than he'd been for some weeks.

Caroline was in the garden making her final decision about which flowers to use for her entry.

'I must be mad entering this blessed Show, Peter. Totally crackers. My flowers won't be a patch on Mrs Jones's and all I'll get will be understanding glances and I shall want to crawl away. Will you go in the marquee for me and see if I've won anything? I shan't dare go. It'll be so embarrassing if I get sympathetic looks.'

'My darling girl, it's only a village thing, not Chelsea.'

'I know, but it feels terribly important, and it is to everyone in the village.'

'Even more so to Mr Fitch!'

'You're right there. He's all of a dither, apparently. He's a funny man, so dynamic, so rich, with so much power over people's lives and yet pathetically eager that this Show should be a success.'

'He's quite a decent chap underneath all that authority. I'm sorry he never sees his sons. That must be dreadful.'

'What do you think to this one? It isn't blemished in any way, is it?'

'Can't see anything wrong with it. You know I'm on the platform, don't you?'

'I do. I think I'll chain the children to me, it's the only way. They're murder in a crowd.'

Peter took hold of her shoulders and turned her around. He kissed her and said, 'Love you.'

'I love you too.'

'I hope this clinic business won't be too much.'

'It's only for a few months. It'll be all right, you'll see. I promise you faithfully if the children show signs of objecting I shall stop immediately.'

'I know you will.'

'You would never ask me to stop, I know that, Peter, but if you really,

really feel you'd rather I didn't, I won't. But I do want to do it. Pathology got rather tedious, you see, and I'd like to try general practice again. It's such a golden opportunity to try my hand at it, isn't it?'

'Absolutely.'

'I have to stage my exhibit some time between nine and eleven on Saturday morning. Will you make sure you're free then? I shan't be able to do it if the children are with me.'

'Of course.'

'I'm so looking forward to this Show. I wonder if he'll hold it every year?'

'Probably. Especially now with Louise working for him.'

'Of course. So convenient. She's done a brilliant job, you know. Nothing can go wrong, I'm sure.'

'That's her talent, isn't it? Organisation.'

Pat had made one batch of shortbread the night before the Show, then decided to get up really early and make another lot before breakfast and see which she thought was the best.

She'd have to take her entry in by nine o'clock because she'd need to be in the refreshment marquee in good time. Her nerves were playing up something dreadful; she'd hardly slept. It was the first time she'd been truly in charge of an event and the responsibility was weighing heavily on her mind. Jimbo was lending her a mobile so she would be in constant touch with him, so that was a relief. Hopefully she'd only need to make contact if she began running out of supplies. She switched on the oven and got out her scales, and began. Last night's was in a tin so before she started weighing the ingredients she peeped inside it to see how it had fared through the night. Oh, it looked good, very good. Yes, she was pleased with that.

Butter, nothing less, caster sugar, plain flour – four ounces, two ounces, six ounces, pinch of salt. It was just going in the oven when Michelle came down to inspect, for the umpteenth time, the necklace she'd made of sweets. 'Wasn't it lovely of Grandad to find this jewellery box to display my necklace in? He says it had a necklace in he bought Grandma when they got married, so it's very old. It looks real, doesn't it, my necklace? Do you think I'll win?'

'You can only hope, but I reckon it should. It's lovely. Grandad up?'

'Yes, he must be, I can't get in the bathroom. He's sure to win something, isn't he?'

'He'd better, or Mr Fitch will want to know the reason why.'

'He's all right, is Mr Fitch. I like him.'

'Well, I wouldn't touch 'im with a barge-pole.'

'Mum, if Barry's there I'm going to talk to him.'

'If yer want.'

'Will you?'

'Might and then again I might not.'

'I did want him for a dad.'

Pat hugged her on the way to the fridge. 'I know you did. I'm sorry. Start yer breakfast.'

'I know what they say he did, but he didn't.'

Pat was appalled. Children nowadays! 'Michelle!'

'Well, he didn't, honestly he didn't. I asked him.' She swallowed a spoonful of cereal and grinned.

Pat was scandalised. 'You *asked* him?' Michelle shuffled her feet in her slippers and wouldn't look up. 'You'd no business discussing things like that.'

'Someone's got to talk to him about it. I mean, wouldn't it be nice if he was coming down to breakfast now? Him and you and me and Grandad and our Dean if he ever gets up. The shortbread's smelling.'

'Oh Gawd!' Pat swiftly opened the oven door. 'I've put the oven too high, it's already too brown on top and it's not even cooked. Blast it. Oh well, I'll have to use the one I made last night. Serves me right for trying to be too clever. I'll be too busy today to see to you, so stick with our Dean or Grandad. Isn't it maddening ruining it like this? What a waste.' She scraped the burnt shortbread into the pedal bin.

'I shall stick with Barry.'

Pat sighed. It really was aggravating that Michelle liked Barry so much. Dean too. And Dad. He came downstairs in his working clothes.

'Hurry up, Pat. I've a lot to do to get my plants ready. Old Fitch thinks he's going to laud it round the marquee showing his guests all the prizes he's won, so I must put my best foot forward today. Barry's done a grand job with the stalls. You'll be surprised when you see 'em.'

'Shan't have any time for going round, I'll be too busy. Still, I'm getting well paid. I'm just going to ring round and check none of my waitresses is crying off. Get yer breakfast.'

Grandad raised his cup to Michelle and she raised hers to his and they clicked cups and winked and he said, 'Here's to us, the champions!'

24

By half-past one, the crowds were already beginning to arrive. With the opening ceremony at two o'clock it looked promising. Louise had been working since half-past seven. Rushing here and rushing there, checking and organising. At half-past twelve she had gone home to shower and change and grab a bite to eat before returning to sit looking cool and calm on the platform to hear Mr Fitch give his opening speech. She rather felt she'd never feel cool and calm all the rest of the day. No way would she ever take on such a task again. What it would have been like if she wasn't a well-organised person, she didn't know. As it was, the chap listed for putting out the chairs round the arena hadn't turned up and she'd press-ganged Rhett Wright, odd sort of a boy, along with some of his friends to do the job for her. The one good thing was that the sky was a brilliant blue and there wasn't a cloud to be seen. Culworth's Summer Bonanza the previous Saturday had been a complete write-off. It had rained both on the day and the day before, so the site was a quagmire and the crowds almost non-existent.

Louise slipped on her dress and went to look at herself in the mirror. She'd lost almost a stone since she'd come to the village last November. She had a fine-boned jawline now, and when she turned sideways her bottom was no longer her dominant feature. Even her legs had slimmed down and her ankles were slender too. Altogether there'd been a vast improvement. Not only outside, but inside also. Gilbert had awakened a sensitivity in her, which was flowering wildly, and radically changing her outlook. There was no longer any true satisfaction, not deep-down satisfaction, in being an efficient administrator. It had felt good to be appreciated for it, but the real satisfaction came from the way her soul had been opened up by the first worthwhile illuminating relationship she had had with another human being.

She really wasn't going to wear the hat her mother had persuaded her to buy. She thrust the hat-box to the back of the wardrobe, put on her sandals, collected her handbag, picked up her file – couldn't go without that – and shouting to her mother that she was leaving, slammed the front door behind her.

The entire park and Home Farm field were looking magnificent. The stalls Barry had made were perfectly splendid. She'd doubted his idea about uniformity but he'd been right. Mr Fitch had organised a long series of flags of different countries lining the path to the square of stalls. They were blowing briskly atop their tall poles and drawing everyone's attention. The grass in front of the platform had been filled by Greenwood Stubbs with huge pots of vivid flowers, and the bunting which Barry had put up jerked and jumped in the summer breeze. Such a satisfying sight. The car park was already filling up and Louise smiled at the sight of the Scouts with their official red armbands and caps, provided by Mr Fitch to give them prestige, directing the cars.

She could see at the corner of the car park that some of the Morris Dancers from Penny Fawcett had already arrived, and faintly across the grass came the sound of their bell-pads jingling as they tied them to their legs. Thank God they'd arrived. That was one less problem. The marquees were sparkling white against the emerald green of the grass, and the pennants on their topmost points fluttered briskly. Louise could see the waitresses gathered in the open doorway of the refreshment marquee, watching the crowds arriving. Obviously Pat had got things in hand there. She just hoped the table for the VIPs' tea was looking good. Maybe she ought . . . No, Jimbo knew what he was doing, it would be OK.

She parked close to the Big House and went inside to meet Mr Fitch's guests. He'd provided long cool drinks for everyone and Jeremy was busy, with Venetia's help, handing round silver trays with tiny finger buffet delights on them. Louise shook her head; she thought she might just throw up if she ate anything now. Right in the middle of a conversation with a cousin of Mr Fitch, a dreadful cold feeling scrunched her stomach. Oh God, the loudspeaker system. She'd forgotten to . . .

'Excuse me for a moment, would you?' She sped out through the front door and across the lawns towards the platform. Mercifully there was Barry about to say 'one two three' into the microphone. 'Barry! Everything OK, is it?' He gave her the thumbs-up. 'Thank heavens. I'd forgotten all about it. You're an angel.'

'No problem.' He leaped down from the platform. 'It's all going to be fine. Don't worry.'

'I do hope so. I'm feeling so nervous.'

'Don't be. We all know what to do. If you need me I'll be in the refreshment marquee all afternoon.'

'Are you helping there then?'

'No. Not exactly.' He stuck his hands in his pockets, gazed at the sky for a moment and then said, 'It's Pat.' Barry rattled the small change in his trouser pocket. 'She won't speak to me so I'm going to wear her down by sitting there all afternoon.' He laughed ruefully at Louise.

She looked thoughtful and said, 'You do that, Barry. I've come to the conclusion that there comes a time when you've to take life by the scruff and *make* things happen. Good luck!'

When Louise returned to the Big House her mother was chatting to Mr Fitch. Louise's heart sank. She'd have to own up to the fact that she was her mother, but oh, help! Sheila was wearing a claret-coloured lace dress with long sleeves and a low, low neckline, which exposed her crinkled cleavage. On her head was a matching straw hat with a huge brim, decorated with claret-coloured lace and an enormous pink cabbage rose. Ron stood beside her twisting the stem of his glass in his fingers and trying to look as though he wasn't really there. Would Sheila never learn? At least she hadn't bought the matching parasol which she'd told Louise she was tempted to buy.

At that moment Peter came in. He was wearing light-grey trousers with a short-sleeved grey shirt and his clerical collar. Both his height and his looks with his fair skin and his red-blond hair drew everyone's attention. Louise took the bull by the horns and went to welcome him.

'Good afternoon, Peter. Aren't we lucky to have such a lovely day?'

He shook her hand, looked deeply into her eyes with that penetrating stare of his, smiled his kindly loving smile, and said, 'We are lucky indeed. It's a privilege to be alive today, isn't it? So many good friends having a great time. All thanks to you.' Catching Mr Fitch's eye he said, 'Ah, Mr Fitch . . .' The way he'd told her, 'All thanks to you' left Louise feeling completely forgiven for the trouble she'd caused him, and she knew she had his blessing.

Mr Fitch looked at his watch, cleared his throat and announced, 'The platform, ladies and gentlemen – shall we proceed? Will you lead the way, Louise? Lady Bissett?' He crooked his arm and invited Sheila to accompany him to the platform. She hid her nervousness behind a beaming smile, desperate not to put a foot wrong.

Mr Fitch suggested a tour of the competition marquee as soon as the opening ceremony was concluded. Sheila, flustered by the heat of the glaring sun and the tightness of her dress, nodded enthusiastically but with a sinking heart. All she really wanted was to sit down with a cup of tea, with plenty of sugar in it, and to kick off her blessed shoes. She'd been here at the Show since half-past eight, organising this and that, answering questions, smoothing the ruffled feathers of the competitors as they put their entries on display. Much of the aggravation was caused by people taking more space than they'd been allocated, and others complaining their entry was in a corner and could they move it out, please? She'd had no idea how irritating people could be. She'd used a whole roll of sticky tape and a complete box of pins and her stapler had run out and . . . She vowed she'd never do this again. Behind her she could hear Mr Fitch telling his elderly aunt that he'd be running this every year from now on. Oh yes? thought Sheila cynically. He really means we will, Louise and me. We've done all the work.

Mr Fitch's elegant cousin had taken a liking to her and was glued to Sheila's side as they toured the marquee. Sheila pointed out her own arrangement with its seaside theme. She forebore to mention that she'd won First Prize.

'Lady Bissett – this is your arrangement? How wonderful! I love those muted oranges and yellows, and the sand. What a good idea! The shells are fabulous, surely not from an English beach?'

'No, I got those when Sir Ronald and I were touring in the States.'

'What does it say on the card?' The cousin put her reading glasses on and read the judges' card. 'Oh, what a pity! They've said "Excellent try, but . . ." I think it's by far and away the best.'

' "Excellent try but . . . ?" ' Sheila shrieked. She recollected herself and said in restrained tones, 'I think you've read it wrongly. I won First Prize.' She fumbled in her bag for her own reading glasses and perched them on her nose. 'Someone's changed the cards round. This says "Mrs Carrie Evans". Just a minute.' She bustled further down the trestle table and found her own card in front of what she would have described as a pathetic attempt at throwing flowers into a vase and missing it. She swiftly changed the cards back again, swearing vengeance on Carrie Evans at the next flower arrangers' meeting, oh yes! She'd have her drummed out, just see if she didn't. Honour restored she smiled at Mr Fitch's cousin and they progressed around the rest of the entries.

Sheila called out, 'You've done well, Mr Fitch. That's the second First-Prize card I've seen with your name on.'

His cousin claimed he'd always had green fingers. This was said in the hearing of Greenwood Stubbs, Head Gardener at Turnham House, who winked at Sheila; she had the gravest difficulty in resisting winking back. How could Mr Fitch stand there and take all the credit? At that moment he went down in Sheila's estimation.

But then he came and took her arm and said, 'A cup of Charter-Plackett's excellent tea, I think, for this charming lady who's worked so hard to make this whole thing,' he waved his arm in a great swoop, encompassing the entire marquee, 'such a blinding success. If it wasn't for your competitions we wouldn't have nearly so many people here, would we, Sheila, my dear?' He squeezed her arm and bending down to reach under the brim of her hat, he planted a kiss on her cheek. 'It's ladies like you, Sheila, who make village life so rich and so rewarding.'

His cousin and his elderly aunt clapped their hands in appreciation and a few of those around also joined in. Sheila blushed and her cabbage rose bobbed as she acknowledged the clapping. 'Really, Mr Fitch, you're too kind. I shall be ready and willing next year, should the need arise.' She laughed graciously and followed Mr Fitch out of the marquee into the blazing sun. At last she'd finally arrived. She'd been recognised, in public, as an essential part of village life.

As Jimmy was pushing through the crowds at the entrance to the competition marquee, he bumped into Willie and Sylvia. He raised his tweed cap to Sylvia and then asked, ''As my eggs won, Willie?'

'By Jove they 'ave, and no mistake. Certificate of Merit as well!'

'Never! Well, I don't know. Certificate of Merit. Well, I never. I've got to see this. Certificate of Merit! 'Ave you won anything?'

'I 'ave so. First with me raspberries, me beans, and the vegetable selection. And to top it off I've won the Largest Potato! My Sylvia reckons I must be in line for the Templeton Cup. I'm that delighted I'm like a dog with two tails.'

'Who's won His Nib's cup for the flowers?'

'Looks as if it might be Sadie Beauchamp. She's swept the board with her roses. Beautiful they are. Mine's not in the same street. And she's won a sweet-peas class as well. Reckon it'll be 'er and no questions asked.'

'Wonderful! What a day, what a day. See yer tonight in the bar. We'll have a celebratory drink. You as well, Sylvia.' Jimmy pushed his way through the crowd and disappeared in the direction of the produce displays.

Willie Biggs, flushed with delight at his success in the competitions, pointed out to Sylvia that the hot-air balloon was just returning to earth.

'What do yer think, my Sylvia?'

'It looks lovely. They make the balloon bit so colourful, don't they?'

'My prize money easily covers the cost, and we'll have some over for a slap-up cream tea after.'

'Cost of what?'

'A ride.'

'A ride! Oh Willie, I don't know about that. A ride up there?'

'Go on, let's live dangerously.'

'Commit suicide, you mean.'

'Don't be silly. Yer'll be all right, yer with me. How about it, eh?' He squeezed her hand to encourage her. 'Go on, Sylvia love.'

'Oh Willie, I don't know. I like terra firma. Floating about up there . . .' She pressed an anxious hand to her diaphragm.

'You've been in a plane.'

'I know, but that was different. It had an engine and I'd taken my travel-sickness tablets.' Sylvia looked into his face. He had the eager, longing look of a small boy. He reminded her of Alex when he was trying to persuade her to let him do something she didn't want him to. Bless him. She couldn't deny him his pleasure. 'All right then. I'll give it a whirl. Come on.'

It was the powerful tugging motion as the balloon took off that she didn't like, but once they were up there floating, floating, floating, she couldn't believe how wonderful the world looked, how strong the colours, how blue the sky. Willie held her hand tightly and she loved him for it. His face! She wished she had a camera to capture his delight. He looked like he'd done on their wedding day when he turned to take her hand as she arrived at the altar. Filled to the brim with joy, no room for anything else.

Sylvia peered over the edge at the Show down below. Hundreds of people! And all the cars . . . like myriads of multicoloured ladybirds from where she was. The arena was a clear emerald-green square, and there right in the middle, the tug-of-war teams were busy straining. She knew The Royal Oak team were wearing red T-shirts, and The Jug and Bottle had chosen bright blue; it was the bright blues who were flat on their backs, legs waving. One up to The Royal Oak then. She cheered – '*Hurrah!*' Willie put his arm around her shoulders and laughed. It wasn't possible to be any happier than he was at that moment.

In the refreshment marquee the customers had been coming in even before the opening ceremony. Pat had gained confidence after a pep-talk from Jimbo and was actually beginning to enjoy being in charge. Nothing had been left to chance and she couldn't think why on earth she'd been so worried. The only fly in the ointment was Barry. He'd come in just as the opening ceremony had finished. Now he was sitting at the table nearest to the cash desk with a cup of tea and a cake, neither of which he'd touched for the last ten minutes. All he did was look at her. At first she was indignant, after half an hour she was furious but too busy to deal with him. There was a healthy sound to the consistent *ping!* of the till and she was feeling thrilled with her success.

'Tables to clear, Moira, if you please. Trace, more clean cups please, we're nearly out.'

Barry liked the sound of authority in her voice. This was his Pat finding her niche, and he loved it. Who'd have thought she'd be so good? Next she'd be giving up the school and just doing this for Jimbo. He got rather a kick out of the outfit she wore too. That frilly bow just above her backside added a certain something. He grinned at her, but she ignored him.

A crowd of women came in, and damn and blast, there was Simone with all the kids. Despite her long, loosely flowing dress it was obvious she was pregnant. He kept his head down, not wanting her to come across. He ate a piece of his cake and sipped his tea to make his presence more authentic. When next he looked up, Pat was talking to Simone at her table. The kids were all deep into cream cakes and making a thorough mess which didn't bother Simone one jot. He knew it wouldn't, she was like that. Pat was looking annoyed and then she smiled and then she looked serious. He watched her glance momentarily at him and then she shook her head and walked off. Blast it! What was it Simone had said? He wasn't leaving, he wasn't giving in. No way! He was staying to the bitter end.

His mother came in. She looked round, spotted him at his table near the cash desk and came across.

'We've got to celebrate, my lad. I've won the Victoria sponge! There were ten entries and I've come top.'

'Oh great, Mum, that's great.'

'Get us a cup of tea then, eh?'

'I'm really pleased. What about the cut flowers?'

'Second. Dr Harris won First Prize and though I say it myself, she deserved it. Lovely they are. Have you been in the Show tent?'

'No.'

'Been here all the time, have yer?'

'Yes.'

'Hoping she'll speak to yer?' Barry nodded. 'Leave it to me, I'll have a word with that Pat.' She half-rose to go but Barry pulled her back down again.

'No, don't. Please don't. Anybody says anything it's me. I'll get that tea. Cake as well?'

'Yes, if you like.'

Pat saw them talking but she was too busy to bother. He could sit there all day if he wanted, she wasn't giving in. Sending Simone to plead his case. Huh!

'One in the eye for Sadie Beauchamp for all her special seed from that grower. She only won one sweet-pea class; Mr Charter-Plackett won the other. Just goes to show.'

'What?'

'That it's the technique that counts. You'll never guess who's won the raspberries. Willie! And he's won the beans too. I reckon he might win the cup.'

'Really?'

'Are you listening to me?'

'Yes.'

'No you're not, you can't take yer eyes off Pat. Time you got her out of your system.'

Barry looked at her. 'Honest I can't. It's her or no one.'

'Hmmm. I see Mademoiselle Simone's here. How she's got the bare-faced cheek I don't know. Oh look! There's Michelle. Over 'ere, Michelle love.' She shouted and waved her arms, so Michelle, glad to see Barry, came across. 'Sit next to Barry and tell him what yer want, he'll get it for yer.'

Michelle, her face alight with triumph, said: 'Barry, yer'll never guess, I've won the necklace competition. And a Certificate of Merit!'

'Well, that calls for a celebration and not half. Does yer mum know?'

'Yes. I'll have an orange juice and a slice of cream cake please, Barry.'

'Your wish is my command.' He bowed from the waist, winked and went to join the queue. When his turn came it was Pat serving.

'Tea and a slice of cream cake for Mum and an orange juice and a slice of the cream cake, please, for Michelle. Hasn't she done well?'

Pat looked at him and said, 'Yes, she has. I'm really pleased for her. That'll be one pound eighty-five, please.'

'Thanks Pat, keep the change.'

'I don't need your tips, thank you very much. Here, fifteen pence change.'

'*Pat, please.*'

'It's neither the time nor the place.' And she turned to serve the next person in the queue.

Barry took the tray back to the table and found his mother and Michelle deep in conversation.

'And yer Mum's won the shortcake, I am pleased.'

'She is as well. And Mr Fitch has won some prizes too. Well, it's Mr Fitch on the card but it's my Grandad really, you know. I'm going to be a gardener when I grow up. I'm going to plan gardens with lots of lovely trees, and big gorgeous flowers in brilliant colours that make people think they're in Africa, but really it's good old England.'

'Are you now. You're a bit young at eleven for thinking about your career.'

'I know, but I am. I've got green fingers Grandad says, and he should know. Barry, is Mum talking to you yet?'

'No.'

'I don't know what we're going to do about her. She's that pig-headed . . .'

It was when Louise saw Gilbert disappearing in front of her at a great rate of knots, wearing Morris Dancing clothes and carrying a melodion, that she realised something might have gone awfully wrong. He was scarcely recognisable. She knew him more by his gait than anything. He was wearing an old jacket, to which, for some reason she couldn't quite comprehend, he'd fastened gaily-coloured strips of material, almost obliterating the black cloth of the jacket. On his head was a bowler hat covered with brightly coloured feathers and badges.

'Gilbert?'

He heard her shout and turned round. 'Hello, there.'

'I can't believe it's you! Your face is black! Why have you done that to your face?'

'All part of my costume. Tradition, you see. Where've you been?'

'Sorting out the Portaloos, for my sins. I didn't know you actually danced?'

Behind the Portaloos there was no one about and he greeted her with a long sensuous mouth-massaging kiss which made her feel as though her toenails were curling up. His hat got in the way, and his melodion dug into her ribs.

'Not in broad daylight in full public view, Gilbert! My face will be all black. Is it?' He gently wiped her mouth clean, making a lover's gesture of it.

'Thanks. Back to business.' She fanned her face with her file.

'Made your heart flutter, did I?'

'More than my heart. So-o-o-o, you've never said you were a Morris Dancer.'

'I don't tell my lover everything, got to keep some mystery. I am and have been for years. I love it. Medieval and pagan and all that.'

'So you're with the Penny Fawcett side?'

'Certainly not. They're mixed; we're the Culworth Sceptre side and we're traditional. Men only.'

A panic-stricken voice boomed out, 'GILBERT!' and he rushed off before Louise could clear her thoughts. If he was not in the Penny Fawcett side then who . . . Oh good Lord, the ones she'd seen in the distance in the car park were wearing red waistcoats and yes, there'd been two women there too, and they hadn't black faces. When her thumping heart had calmed, she thought, Oh well, it'll make for a better display. The two sides can dance together – even better.

Her watch said it was almost four o'clock. In that case the dancing would be about to start. She hurried out from the back of the Portaloos and headed straight for the arena. She found a space amongst the crowd and watched as the two sides came into the arena from different ends. Whether it was the burning sun, or the dazzle of the colourful clothes the dancers were wearing, or the noise of their bells jingling, or something ominous in the shouts of the crowd . . . Louise had a sudden dreadful premonition that things would not work out as she had hoped.

Gilbert headed straight for the other team. There was a heated discussion, made worse by the fact that they were all carrying sticks in preparation for their first dances. The crowd shouted encouragement as they watched the confrontation. She'd never seen Gilbert so angry.

'Excuse me, please.' She squeezed through the crowd and lifted the rope and stepped into the arena. There was a loud cheer as she walked towards the Morris Dancers.

'Please . . . there's been a dreadful mistake, I don't know how it happened, but—'

'There's no way we are dancing with a mixed side.'

'But couldn't you dance here and the other side over there and do the same dances?'

'*Same dances?* We're Border tradition, love – they're Cotswold. How could we do the same dances? In any case, we're all male, and they're mixed.'

'Well, obviously I can see that, but is it important?'

A woman from the Penny Fawcett side said, 'Look, we don't mind, let's take turns. Give us a chance for a rest in this heat at the very least.'

'Well, now,' said Louise. 'They can't say fairer than that can they?'

She turned to Gilbert's team and waited for an answer. They stood there, sticks at the ready, belligerent and almost begging for trouble, the black on their English faces seeming to emphasise their anger. The men all shook their heads. The tallest one with the recorder in his hand said, 'Sorry, we don't recognise them.'

'Oh, I know them all – I'll introduce them if you like,' Louise offered. 'They're lovely people.'

Gilbert sighed. 'He means we don't recognise them as real Morris Dancers.'

'How can they be anything else? They're all dressed up and ready to go.'

The crowd began to boo. Mr Fitch came marching across the arena. 'What exactly is the holdup?'

Louise explained. Mr Fitch rapidly came to the boil. 'I have never heard such arrogant nonsense in all my life. You're *all* Morris Dancers, so bloody well get on with it and sort something out. The crowd is getting restless.'

'We're getting more than restless. We've been booked for months. It really is only right that we should dance.' This was the Penny Fawcett side.

Gilbert said, 'And so have we, Mr Fitch.'

'LOUISE! How did this come about?'

'I only booked the Penny Fawcett side. I don't know why Gilbert thought I'd booked them . . . him . . . er, them. Look, please, just dance and we'll sort it out later.'

One of Gilbert's dancers stepped forward, stick in hand, and repeated: 'I'm sorry, not with them.'

Before Louise knew where she was, she and Mr Fitch were in the midst of an angry crowd of would-be dancers. All of them, sticks raised, were shouting. The crowd began to cheer. Bells were a-jingling, voices were raised, feet stamped and Mr Fitch, swearing loudly, came within an ace of being struck by a stick.

Suddenly Gilbert raised his voice. 'This won't do. Most uncivilised. My side will retire and leave the field clear for the Penny Fawcett team. There's obviously been a serious misunderstanding. I'll see you later, Louise.' He gathered them all together and marched his side off the field to the cheers and boos of the crowd. Louise and Mr Fitch followed in their wake, after they'd reassured themselves that the Penny Fawcett side would dance. The crowd clapped and cheered and the dancing began.

'My office, if you please.'

Louise, with broken heart, followed in Mr Fitch's footsteps all the way from the arena to the Big House.

When they got inside his office, he burst out laughing; peal after peal of hysterical laughter. Louise, who'd been expecting a dressing down, was stunned. All her planning, all her notes, everything in ruins and all he could do was laugh. Between his bursts of mirth he gasped, 'Never shall I forget this!! Never!! Oh God!!' He sat down in his chair, holding his side. 'I don't know when I've laughed so much! Oh Louise, I really thought we would have a fight. What on earth are they talking about – won't dance with each other? And I was so looking forward to it. I thought it a really interesting, colourful, heart-of-the-village touch. Brilliant idea of yours. Oh yes. Go and look outside – see if it's all right now. I'll pour us a drink.'

Louise went to look at the arena from the front door. The crowd had settled down and the dancers were dancing, and the music was playing, and it looked all English and medieval with the stalls and the crowds, and the flags; oh my word, the setting was absolutely right. Her heart repaired itself and she began to smile. How could they have made love all those times, and never mentioned Morris Dancing? Such a blasted stupid mistake. She'd have to apologise.

'Well, Louise, all right is it now?'

'Oh yes, come and look.' He did and he was pleased, so very pleased. 'How absolutely fitting, Morris Dancing at a village Show. I wonder how many years that's been going on?'

'Hundreds – right from the dawn of time, some say.'

'You can't get more English than that, can you? And tell that Gilbert to get himself better organised. Oh, of course, you don't know him, do you?' He winked and handed her a gin and tonic. 'You deserve that, my dear.' He smiled and they stood together in the doorway listening to the music and watching the ribbons flying, the sticks crashing, the feet prancing, and above their heads the hot-air balloon swaying steadily up into the bright blue sky, its red and yellow and orange stripes echoing the colours of the Morris Dancers on the grass below.

A group of young men who'd spent too much time in Bryn's beer-tent came in looking for trouble. Pat cast an anxious eye in their direction and decided to treat them politely and hope it would calm them down and they wouldn't cause trouble.

'Hello, my darling! Three teas, two lemonades, and what shall we have to eat, boys? Almond slice, cream cakes, butterfly buns, sandwiches? What will it be?'

They argued and then decided on sandwiches and an almond slice for each of them. When Pat told them how much they owed they were flabbergasted. 'Ten pounds? You've added up wrong, love. It's never ten pounds.'

'It is. One pound each for the sandwiches, fifty pence each for the drinks, and fifty pence each for the cake.'

'Cor, that Charter-Plackett fella must be making a packet. You overcharging and putting something in your own pocket?'

Pat began to grow cold. 'No, I'm certainly not. That's the charge, it's here on the blackboard. You can see for yourself.' Two of the men had already begun to carry the trays to a table, and two of the others followed. 'Just a minute. I want paying first,' she said firmly.

'All in good time, my darling. 'Ere you two, lend us some money – I ain't got enough.' He poked his finger amongst a collection of coins in the palm of his hand. ''Ere you are, seven pounds and seventy-two pence, and that's all I've got. Come on, you two, give us some more.'

'Shut yer face, it'll do.' Pat was about to acquiesce and let them have it to save more trouble, but the one left standing at the till shouted, 'Come on, let's be having yer, cough up.'

The smallest of the five men shouted a reply. 'Shut yer face, Fatty, and sit down.'

'Don't you call me Fatty, you little sod.'

'Little sod, is it? Right!' He stood up, pushed back his chair with a crash and lunged towards the man at the till. Pat hastily got her mobile out and dialled for Jimbo. Michelle, who'd been watching the argument from her perch on Barry's knee, said, 'Barry!'

He tipped her off onto the grass and quietly stood up. The fighting began with the big man punching the smaller one in the face. He reeled around for a moment trying to regain his balance, and then fell helter-skelter onto the trestle table laden with the clean cups and saucers. The table collapsed under the shock of his weight and there was a tremendous crash as the cups and the saucers and the man fell to the ground.

The heat had been almost unbearable before the fight, but now Pat felt as though the marquee was on fire. The customers began shouting, and some started to hustle their children and old grannies out before things got any worse. Pat shouted, 'This won't do, please stop it!'

This was when Barry decided to take charge. He strode forward and took hold of the T-shirt of the big man by the till. 'Out, you. Out!' He marched him towards the exit and then came back for the man laid unconscious on the ground. He pointed to the other three men. 'You lot, get him to the first-aid tent, pronto.' None of them made a move.

'Did you hear me? First-aid tent. NOW!'

As the three of them approached Barry threateningly, Pat came out tiptoeing her way between the broken crockery. Determined she wasn't going to let Barry rescue her, she shouted, 'Look here, just get out and we'll say no more about it. Go on – HOP IT!'

One of the men roared with laughter. ''Ark at 'er! Come 'ere, love, and give us a kiss. I like a woman with spirit.' He grabbed her by the arms and tried to kiss her. Pat brought her knee up hard into his groin and he loosened his grip and swore. His hand came back to strike her. Barry saw her cringe and begin to back away, and Michelle screamed, 'Mum!' Barry leaped forward and deflected the blow with his arm. From nowhere, it seemed, Jimbo arrived with the two men who'd been taking the money at the gate. Between them, they each took hold of one of the men and marched them out. The one who was unconscious on the ground began to come round, moaning and wincing as he gingerly touched his mouth, feeling the place where his lip had been split.

Michelle flung her arms round her mother and cried, 'Oh Mum, oh Mum.'

Pat rubbed her back and stroked her hair. 'That's all right, love, I'm OK. Don't worry.' She looked at Barry and mouthed, 'Thanks.'

Jimbo returned. 'Pat, you all right? Sorry about this.' He looked down at the man sitting on the floor. 'You can get up and go. The first-aid tent is just past the stalls. And don't come back, right? Here, Pat, have a nip of this.' He took a silver flask from his back pocket. 'Brandy, do you good, sit down here. Trace, Moira, Denise, look after things, will you? Anne, you be on the till. Chop! Chop! Business as usual. I'll get someone else to clear this lot up. Don't touch it, you'll only cut your hands. Thanks, Barry, glad you were on the spot.'

'That's OK. They'd had too much to drink, that's all.'

'Mmmm. One of life's hazards, I suppose. Look after Pat. I'll get someone with a shovel and some cardboard boxes.' He stabbed a finger at the broken crockery. 'That's a large slice of the profit gone, dammit.'

Pat tried to apologise. 'I'm sorry, Jimbo, I just didn't handle it right.'

Barry protested. 'She did, she did it absolutely right.'

'I'm sure she did. Worth her weight in gold. Time you recognised that.' He gave a brief nod in Barry's direction and strode out.

Pat blushed, Barry grinned and Michelle looked at them both. 'You two speaking again then?'

Pat said, 'Might be.'

'Yes, we are,' Barry told her. 'Aren't we?'

Pat thought for a moment and said, 'We could be.'

'The holiday's on again then?' Michelle asked excitedly.

Barry raised his eyebrows at Pat. She gave a nod and all three of them hugged each other. When Dean came in with a shovel and a cardboard box, a pair of gardener's gloves on his hands, he grinned at them all and said, 'Better get your fishing rods out, Barry. Looks as if I shall be needing some lessons before we go on holiday.'

They all four laughed, Pat the loudest of all. She screwed the top back on Jimbo's flask, stood up quickly but the brandy had affected her head and she almost keeled over. Barry caught her and planted a kiss on her cheek and said, 'With Jimbo's recommendation I've no alternative but to ask you to marry me.'

Michelle jumped up and down. 'Say yes, say yes.'

'All right then. Yes, I will.'

'I'm going to have a dad!' She danced out of the marquee to tell the world.

Mrs Jones, having removed herself with her tea and cake to a table in the furthest corner as soon as the trouble began, sipped her tea and smiled. She'd get her box of patterns out tonight and look out one for a jumper for Michelle. She'd plenty of time to finish it before the winter set in. Perhaps she'd even do one for Dean. One day in the future she'd be able to say 'my grandson at University', and 'my granddaughter, the one who designs gardens'. Now that was something to be proud of.

An army of boys, enticed by Mr Fitch's promise of great rewards and equipped by him with bin bags and plastic gloves, had begun clearing up the lawns and Home Farm field. The tractor had made dozens of journeys pulling the trailer stacked high with trestles and tables and chairs. The crêpe paper had been torn from the stalls, the pots of flowers returned to the greenhouses, the platform with its banners and flags dismantled, the marquees emptied, ready for taking down and carrying away by the hirers. Mr Fitch and Louise with his guests were toasting their success.

'To Louise! Many many thanks for all your hard work!' There were murmurs of agreement. 'Excellent! Wonderful day! Splendid!'

'Thank you. I can't make a speech because I've nearly lost my voice, sorry.'

'And no wonder. Brilliant feat of organisation. I'm lucky to have you working for me. Keep all your notes, ready for next year!' He raised his glass in recognition of her talent. Louise smiled and excused herself.

She went to her car. Sitting in the front seat was Gilbert. Louise got in and put her key in the ignition. In a husky whisper she said, 'I'm so tired, Gilbert, and my voice has all but gone.' She laid her head back against the seat and closed her eyes.

Gilbert took hold of her hand. 'Sorry about that damn foolish mistake over the Morris Dancing. I don't really know how I managed to make such a gigantic mistake. After all, you didn't definitely fix it with me, and knowing your propensity for having everything totally organised I should have known to query it. It was all my fault. Didn't really intend to cock it all up.'

'I'm sorry we never spoke about it properly.'

'Too busy doing other things.' He chuckled and she had to open her eyes and smile at him. 'You know, Louise, there's a whole bright shining wonderful person inside you . . .'

She placed her finger on his lips and whispered, 'It's thanks to you she's there at all. You discovered her.'

'That was my privilege. You only needed someone to unlock the door.'

'You've changed me, completely. I'm a new person.'

Gilbert looked steadily at her, his head on one side, his eyes studying her face. 'You're going to let her out onto the sunlit slopes then?'

'I think maybe this whole new person can already feel the sun on her face.'

'Wonderful! I rather thought so. There are moments in life which, when you look back on them, you know, yes *know* that they were completely special and terribly important to the rest of your life.' He kissed her fingers and then laying her hand on his knee and holding it there he said, 'I'm sorry I refused to have you in the choir. It's this all-male thing with choirs, you know how it goes. But I can't bear to hurt people's feelings.'

'It doesn't matter any more.'

'Good. I was going to suggest that tonight we go to my cottage, and you allow me to cook for you. I've something rather special in mind.'

'I didn't know you could cook.'

'My dear Louise, you don't know everything about me, not yet.'

Tentatively Louise said, 'Question is, do I . . .'

'Yes?'

'Oh, never mind.'

'You sit and relax whilst I cook and then we'll spend what's left of the evening reading or something, and go to bed early. To sleep, right? I think that's what you need most of all, isn't it? A good night's sleep.'

'You're absolutely right there. Oh yes. That's what I long for.'

'Do you . . . that is, would you . . .'

'Yes?'

'Could you ever get round to thinking long-term about me? *Very* long-term about me? Like . . . for always long-term about me?'

Louise didn't answer immediately. She stared straight ahead through the windscreen at the Big House and at Mr Fitch standing outside on the gravel saying goodbye to his guests. Then she turned to look at Gilbert. 'I think that might be a distinct possibility. In time, you know, in time. With you . . . yes, I might. Quite definitely.'

'I know Keeper's Cottage isn't exactly top of the shop where design is concerned nor convenience for that matter, but there's a lot of love going spare and that's what life's about, isn't it? Love.'

'You've taught me that, Gilbert. I'll go home and get my things.'

'Don't bother. I'll lend you my Father Christmas nightshirt with the matching nightcap, and you can borrow my toothbrush.'

Louise laughed. 'Better give Mother a ring or she'll worry.'

'You can do that from my house.' Gilbert kissed her full on the lips, leaped out of the car and went to find his own. Louise watched him walking away. Who'd have thought she would find a lover here in this village which she used to so despise. She'd only come back out of desperation – no job, nowhere to live, broken-hearted, home to Mother like a wounded child.

There was something undeniably captivating about Turnham Malpas. In her mind she could see the old oak tree still stout and hearty after what – five, six hundred years? The cottages equally as old, the stocks, the pond. The Store where she'd had that hint of the villagers' collective anger, the church where she'd experienced Revelation Monday, and the rectory where she'd loved and lost. There was something uncannily magnetic about this village; it drew people unto itself and enfolded them for ever. Something strong and comforting and healing – yes, that was the word, healing.

Gilbert tooted his horn as he reached the drive and Louise started up her engine and made to follow him. Yes, she'd stay because there was quite simply nowhere else in the world she wanted to live.

Turnham Malpas Show

Turnham House,
Home Farm Field
July 10th
commencing 2 p.m.

MAYPOLE DANCING
HOT-AIR BALLOON RIDES
CHILDREN'S FANCY DRESS
MOTORCYCLE DISPLAY
CHILDREN'S RACES
PUB TUG OF WAR
MORRIS DANCING
STALLS

REFRESHMENT MARQUEE ICE-CREAM STALL BEER-TENT
PRIZEGIVING FOR ALL COMPETITIONS AT
5.30 p.m. ON THE PLATFORM
(see schedule)

FREE CAR PARKING

Entrance 50p Adults
Children and OAPs free

ARENA EVENTS

2.15   Opening Ceremony
2.30   Children's Fancy-Dress
       Parade
3.00   Tug of War between
       Turnham Malpas and
       Penny Fawcett
3.30   School Display
4.00   Morris Dancing
4.30   Demonstration by the Police
       Motorcycle Display Team
5.00   Children's Races
5.30   Prizegiving from the platform

During the afternoon there will be an opportunity to take rides in a hot-air balloon. The charge will be £5 per adult and £3 for OAPs and for children under fourteen years. All proceeds to charity.

REMEMBER!! VISIT THE STALLS AND SUPPORT YOUR FAVOURITE CHARITIES

SCHEDULE FOR
COMPETITION CLASSES

A certificate of merit for best exhibit in
  each group of classes.
The Templeton Cup for the most points
  in the vegetable classes.
The Fitch Flowers Cup for the most points
  in the flower classes.

All judges' decisions are final.

Entries   by 7 p.m. Thursday 8th July
Staging   9.00–11.00 a.m. on day of show
Judging   11.00 a.m.
Show opens   2.00 p.m.
Prizegiving   5.30 p.m.

EXHIBITS MAY NOT BE REMOVED
BEFORE 4.30 p.m.

ALL EXHIBITS TO BE CLEARED
FROM THE COMPETITION
MARQUEE BY 5.30 p.m.

COMPETITION CLASSES

Large Flowered (HT Type) Roses
1. One vase of one bloom.
2. One vase of three blooms.
3. One vase of six blooms.

Cluster Flowers (Floribunda) Roses
4. One vase of three stems.
5. One vase of five stems.
6. One bowl of roses (any type) three stems.

General Floral
7. Three vases of cut flowers, three distinct types.
8. One vase of cut flowers, mixed, up to fifteen stems.
9. One vase sweet peas, same colour, up to six stems.
10. One vase sweet peas, mixed, up to twelve stems.
11. One pot plant, flowering.
12. One pot plant, foliage.
13. Hanging basket.

Fruit
14. Twelve raspberries, one variety.
15. Twelve gooseberries, one variety.
16. Twelve strawberries, one variety.
17. Six bunches blackcurrants, one variety.
18. Bowl of any three varieties of soft fruit.

Floral Art

19. Seaside.
20. The Royal Albert Hall.
21. Notting Hill Carnival.
22. Japanese Garden.

Children's Classes

UNDER 12 YEARS

23. Four scones, arranged on a plate.
24. Four gingerbread men arranged on a plate.
25. A necklace made from sweets.
26. A vase of flowers from a country garden.
27. Miniature garden.

12–16 YEARS

28. Four butterfly buns.
29. Four rock cakes.
30. Pot plant grown by exhibitor.
31. Greeting card.

Vegetables

32. Six kidney beans (French).
33. Six potatoes, matched for size, one variety.
34. Largest potato (judged by weight).
35. Smallest potato (judged by weight).
36. Six pods peas.
37. Selection of vegetables displayed on a dish (Maximum six varieties).

ADDITIONAL CLASSES TO THE ORIGINAL SCHEDULE

Eggs
38. Six matched brown eggs.
39. Largest egg (judged by weight).
40. Brownest egg.
41. Six matched bantam eggs (one variety).

Cakes
42. Victoria sponge with jam filling.
43. Single round of shortbread.
44. Six fruit scones arranged on a decorative plate.
45. Six sausage rolls arranged on a decorative dish.
46. Fruit cake (undecorated) no larger than eight inches across.

———————————

SAME COMPETITION
RULES APPLY

Village Secrets

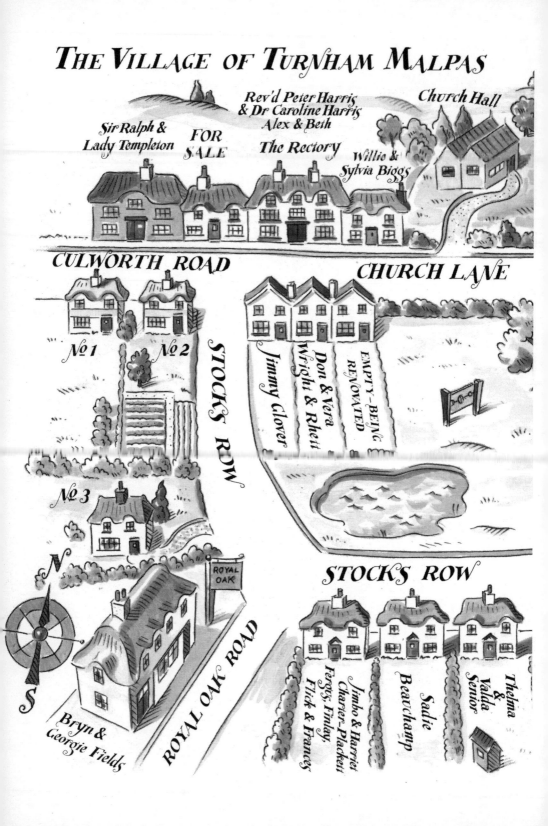

THE VILLAGE OF TURNHAM MALPAS

INHABITANTS OF TURNHAM MALPAS

Sadie Beauchamp	Retired widow and mother of Harriet Charter-Plackett.
Willie Biggs	Verger at St Thomas à Becket.
Sylvia Biggs	His wife and housekeeper at the rectory.
Sir Ronald Bissett	Retired trades union leader.
Lady Sheila Bissett	His wife.
Louise Bissett	Their daughter and Secretary at Turnham House.
James (Jimbo) Charter-Plackett	Owner of the Village Store.
Harriet Charter-Plackett	His wife.
Fergus, Finlay, Flick and Fran	Their children.
Alan Crimble	Barman at The Royal Oak.
Linda Crimble	Runs the post office at the Village Store.
Pat Duckett	Village school caretaker.
Dean and Michelle	Her children.
Bryn Fields	Licensee of The Royal Oak.
Georgia Fields	His wife.
Craddock Fitch	Owner of Turnham House.
Jimmy Glover	Taxi driver.
Revd. Peter Harris MA (Oxon)	Rector of the parish.
Dr Caroline Harris	His wife.
Alex and Beth	Their children.
Barry Jones	Estate carpenter.
Mrs Jones	His mother.
Jeremy Mayer	Manager at Turnham House.
Venetia Mayer	His wife.
Liz Neal	Playgroup leader.
Kate Pascoe	New head teacher.
Sergeant	Village policeman.
Ellie	His wife.
Greenwood Stubbs	Head gardener at Turnham House.
Sir Ralph Templeton	Retired from the diplomatic service.
Lady Muriel Templeton	His wife.
Dicky Tutt	Scout leader.
Bel Tutt	Assistant in the village store.
Vera Wright	Cleaner at the nursing home in Penny Fawcett.
Don Wright	Her husband.
Rhett Wright	Their grandson.

1

'She's here, Jimbo – Miss Pascoe! We've seen her car. It's just pulled up outside the school-house. She's got here earlier than we expected. Where's that box of stuff? Hurry up, we're waiting!'

Jimbo was at the till taking money. He broke off to pick up a cardboard box from behind the counter. 'Give her my regards. Here it is. Put the carrier bag in the drinks fridge in with it, will you? There's milk and butter and things in there, didn't want it going off.'

Pat Duckett eagerly took charge of the box and the carrier bag and Hetty Hardaker held open the door while she squeezed through.

'You know, Pat, Jimbo really is very generous. I just hope she appreciates it. Here, let me take the carrier bag.'

'Right, thanks. Well, you'll have her to deal with more than me, being a teacher – I'm only the caretaker. I don't mind telling you it'll be a breath of fresh air, it will. Nothing wrong with old Mr Palmer, but he did need a kick in the pants as you might say didn't he? A shaking-up like.'

'He did, but he was still a good teacher. I shall miss him.'

'Too right, so shall I.' Across the road, Pat saw a young woman dressed in black struggling to get a huge cat basket out of the boot of her car. 'There she is! Good morning, Miss Pascoe! Welcome to the school.'

Hetty Hardaker's greeting was rather more reserved than Pat's but just as sincere. 'Welcome, Miss Pascoe.'

Kate put the basket down beside the car and held out her hand. 'Kate, if you please, and it's Ms Pascoe to the children. Nice to see you again, Hetty. Looking forward to working with you. You've been here such a long time, I shall look to you for advice.' She turned to Pat. 'And you must be the caretaker. You were away when I visited the school.'

'Not away, no such luck, but blinking ill with one of them bugs you get nowadays.'

'Oh, that's right. I remember the rector telling me.'

Hetty indicated the box Pat was carrying. 'This is a "welcome to Turnham Malpas gift" from Jimbo Charter-Plackett at the Store. There's bread and tins and things, and in here' – she held up the carrier bag – 'is some milk and butter and cheese too, just to help you along.'

'The fridge is switched on, I did that yesterday,' Pat said eagerly.

'That's very kind. You wouldn't get that in a city school, would you?'

Hetty agreed. 'I don't think you would. Look, we'll put these inside for you and leave you to get settled in.'

Pat hitched the box a little higher, for it was beginning to slip from her grasp. 'The door's open, I left the keys on the windowsill in case I wasn't here in time.'

She followed Ms Pascoe inside. Somehow, despite having given the house a good clean, Pat felt the house wasn't 'right' for Ms Pascoe. Didn't suit her personality. Too faded, too masculine. Still, that was up to her. She was a modern young thing – well, not that young – thirty perhaps. She'd make some changes and not half. Time would tell. Pat hoped she wouldn't make too many changes too soon. New broom and all that.

'I don't think you could have chosen a colder day. Still no snow yet, thank goodness. I hear you've been teaching in Africa. Bit of a change, coming here in winter.'

'Well, I've been back in England for six months now, so I'm getting acclimatised, thanks. You've been more than kind. I won't hold you up.'

Seeing it as a dismissal Hetty began to leave followed by Pat, who in reality would have loved to stay for a chat. She made a stab at prolonging the conversation. 'Hope you get settled in all right, Ms Pascoe. If you've any problems, give me a bell. The phone's connected like you asked and I've put my number by it – just in case.'

'Why, thank you, that's very kind. Thank you too, Hetty, for taking the time to welcome me. See you soon. Bye bye.'

The two of them walked across the school playground without speaking. They turned to wave and Kate waved back.

When they were well out of earshot in Jacks Lane, Pat said, 'Dad'll be home for lunch soon, I must be off. She seems OK.'

'She does, although I'll reserve my judgement yet awhile. Bye Pat, thanks for coming, I'm sure she appreciated it.'

Kate Pascoe dumped the heavy basket beside the schoolhouse door and, full of anticipation, looked up at the stone lintel above her head. A.D. 1855. Like Pat had said, the keys had been left for her inside on the windowsill. Huge old keys – good grief, they could belong to a prison! Now, alone, she could take time to savour the place. There came a faint musty smell to her nostrils. She let Cat out of her basket and watched her step swiftly down the narrow passage to the first room. Kate followed more slowly.

The room had windows looking out to the side of the playground, curious old arched windows giving a kind of churchified feeling to the place

– to remind the head teacher that this was a Church of England school and that he or she must act accordingly? Kate mused.

The walls were a boring beige – a typical old-fashioned bachelor choice. The fireplace was a kind of 1930s tiled affair, a neat fan of newspaper concealing the grate. When she pushed open the kitchen door she had the distinct feeling that it really *was* 1855. A huge butler sink, bleached a scorching white, with a wooden draining board stood in one corner, the brass taps above the sink burnished bright. Beside what had been a fireplace, but which was now covered by a sheet of plywood, was a large cupboard, majestic in its proportions. Everywhere was clean but that was the nicest thing one could say about it. Someone had made an effort. The kitchen was large enough to have a table in, she'd do that. There was, thank heavens, plumbing for a washing machine and an outlet for a dryer, and several power points. Next to the sink stood an old and stately cooker. It worked! The gas flame flared busily blue when she turned it on. It had been cleaned, too. How many teachers had cooked a lonely supper on it? Kate wondered.

She emptied the carrier bag Jimbo had sent and was storing the contents away in the fridge, though she wouldn't be able to eat most of it, when there came a knock at the front door.

Standing outside, well-wrapped up against the cold, was a well-dressed lady holding a plastic cake box.

'Good day to you, Miss Pascoe. Welcome to Turnham Malpas and to the school. My name's Muriel Templeton.'

'Good day to you too, Miss Templeton. Do come in. It's too cold to stand outside.'

'I'm not staying, not when you're so busy. I've just called with a cake for you. Home-made – chocolate. Mr Palmer had a sweet tooth; I thought perhaps you might have, too.'

Kate studied her visitor's delicate features and white hair. There was a shy quality about her but at the same time a kind of strength. The light-blue eyes looked kind.

'Well, Miss Templeton, you really are nice. You're my second lot of visitors and I haven't been here more than about fifteen minutes!'

Muriel beamed with pleasure. 'Oh well, you see, we're a very friendly village and we're so glad to have fresh blood in the school. I do hope you like living here, though I don't know how you possibly couldn't. It's so lovely hereabouts. My husband suggested I called . . .'

'Oh, I beg your pardon, you're *Mrs* Templeton.'

'Truth to tell, I'm Lady Templeton though I'm still not used to it myself.'

'I see. Well, Lady Templeton, thank you so much for the cake. It sounds absolutely delicious.'

'Has the rector called yet?'

'No, not yet, but he promised he would.'

'Well, he will then. He always keeps his word. Right, I'll leave you to get on. We live along Church Lane – come to call anytime if you're in need of help. Keep the church on your right and we're the fourth house along.'

'Thank you. I'll remember if I'm in need of help.'

'Bye bye then. See you in church!' Muriel waved as she left the school playground.

Kate put the cake box on the kitchen worktop and carried on with her familiarisation tour of the house. The bathroom was downstairs. Brass taps, high-sided cast-iron bath, a washbasin large enough to bath a baby in, and a lavatory boasting a high cistern and chain for flushing. Upstairs, the one huge bedroom was again masculine in taste, with bare stained boards, a single curtain rail at each of the two windows. There were no clean patches on the wall to show where pictures had hung. Whoever had cleaned it for her had done a thorough job. It might be old-fashioned, but it was scrupulously clean.

Cat had investigated the entire house by now and given her approval by sitting down in front of the empty grate and washing her face. There was an hour to go before the van arrived with their furniture. Kate went out to the car again, and began lugging in boxes and bags – some for the bedroom, some for the kitchen, some for the living room. It had character, had this place, oh yes – a feeling of years long gone and plenty of atmosphere. Cat liked it and that was good. Never lived in England before and yet she'd taken to it as if she'd lived there all her life.

When she'd emptied the car, Kate went to take a look at the school from the outside. The windows were high and only by standing on tiptoes could she see anything at all. There were four classrooms: one for the playgroup, one for the Infants and two for the Juniors. She could just manage to see into the kitchen, which appeared clean and quite modern. A spotless roller towel awaited the beginning of term. The windows to the hall were even higher and she couldn't see anything at all.

Back at the house she wandered around the ground floor, then explored the upstairs again. It would take her one day to get straight, she decided, and then she'd decorate room by room. Rich dark colours, bright curtains, and that awkward corner in the bedroom where the ceiling sloped and one couldn't quite stand would be just right for . . . The sound of voices brought her back to earth.

'Hello, any one at 'ome?'

Kate made the removal men a mug of tea each and supervised where she wanted her furniture placing. Her books would have to stay in their cardboard boxes till she bought some bookshelves. Some, her special ones, would go upstairs in that awkward corner.

Cat observed all the activity from her position on the living-room windowsill. After their experience with the animal when they'd been loading the van, the men walked by her with respect. The excuse for her attacking them was that Cat was nervous, having just come out of quarantine, but the scratch on Bert's leg was deep enough, nervous or not. His trouser leg kept sticking to the blood as he walked. He quite fancied going to the hospital for a tetanus; you never could tell nowadays, specially when the damn creature had been in Africa. Yes, he decided: he'd finish this job and off he'd go.

There came a knock at the door. 'Hello, it's Peter Harris.'

One of the men called upstairs, 'Vicar's 'ere, Miss!'

Kate went downstairs to welcome him. 'How nice to see you again, Rector. Do come in.'

'I won't if you don't mind, just called to see if you found everything all right?'

'Oh yes, thank you. Bit hectic moving in, but everything's fine.'

'Here are flowers for you from my wife. She thought they might help to make the school-house more welcoming.'

'That is lovely of her – please give her my heartfelt thanks. They smell wonderful.'

'Good, glad you like them. Pat Duckett said she would clean the house for you, open a few windows and such for a while. It's been nearly six months since Michael Palmer left, so we felt it needed an airing despite the cold.'

'Couldn't be cleaner.'

'Heating working OK?'

'I haven't noticed!'

'Let me know if there's anything we can do for you, won't you? The rectory's two doors beyond the church.'

'Of course. Thanks for calling.' Kate stood at the door and watched him go. Well over six feet tall, broad-shouldered, good-looking, reddish-blond hair . . . he didn't look anything like the kind of rector she'd come to expect from books and films. It was his intense, all-seeing blue eyes of which she would have to be wary. She felt he could see deep inside her, and that would never do.

Kate stepped out of the door to look at the small patch of ground that was the school-house garden. Winter made it difficult to tell what grew there; she'd have to wait till the spring to find out. Of course, there were her special plants in plastic bags in the kitchen which she would have to get in quickly before they died.

For Cat's sake, she managed to get a cosy fire going in the living-room grate. She'd found wood neatly chopped and a supply of kindling in the small shed at the side of the back door, a large box of matches by the cooker. Someone wanted to make her welcome. She left Cat and, taking her set of keys, wandered slowly across in the dark to the main door of the school.

It was the largest key that opened it. The narrow passage which served as a cloakroom for some of the children's coats – obviously the infants for the pegs had nursery animal pictures beside each of them – gave off the usual school smell – a mixture of polish, disinfectant and that other, mysterious ingredient of which all English schools smelled. It excited her. What an opportunity to bring stimulus and excitement into the lives of these pliable young children. The sophistication of town children didn't lend itself to her kind of teaching. She needed fresh open young minds, untainted by city streets and scepticism. Innocence – that was it.

Kate had seen the head teacher's office when she'd visited the school, but she'd forgotten how small it was – scarcely more than a cupboard. There was a smaller key on the ring and she found it opened the filing cabinet squeezed between the washbasin and the hanging space the staff used for their coats.

The records were neatly written, indeed fastidiously written, with wry comments such as: '*just like his father*' or '*lazy like her two sisters*'. That must be satisfying, to have such a stable community. They'd said at the interview that Michael Palmer had been at the school for years and years. She could understand now she was here, why he'd taken so long to leave.

It felt cold in the school and Kate wished she'd put on her coat. She locked the main door with the huge key; it was a solid, heavy wooden door – obviously the original one. What vibes there'd be in this building! She could feel them already – the spirits of children long gone into the world. Kate wondered what kind of a success or otherwise they'd all made of their lives.

Back in the house she made herself a drink while Cat went out for a stroll. She knew Cat would be back. There was no running away, ever, for her. The two of them were kindred spirits.

Upstairs in the bedroom she had made a temporary altar in the awkward corner where she couldn't stand up. She sat before it, legs crossed, the backs of her hands resting on her thighs. The scent of the incense crept into every nook and cranny of the room. She lit a candle and meditated. Oh yes, this ancient village was just the right place for her.

2

'Mummy! Mummy!'

'Flick? I'm in the kitchen.' Harriet turned to look as her daughter raced in from the hall.

'Mummy! Ms Pascoe's got the most enormous cat!'

'What's she like?'

'She's black, black all over. She's got the greenest eyes you've ever seen – just the colour of your engagement ring. Green as green. And she comes to school, Ms Pascoe says, every day.'

'I should hope she does if she's a teacher.'

'Oh Mummy, I'm not talking about her, I'm talking about her *cat*.'

'Oh, I see.' Harriet chuckled. 'I really meant Miss Pascoe. What's she like?'

'It isn't Miss it's *Ms* Pascoe. Well, she's just like her cat. She's dressed all in black with the greenest eyes you've ever seen too. She's so slender!'

'Is that the cat or Miss Pascoe?'

'Oh Mummy, grow up! I liked Mr Palmer, but Ms Pascoe, she's going to be gorgeous. Daddy will love her.'

'Will he, indeed. There's your drink. Biscuit?'

'Yes, please.' Flick perched on a kitchen chair and blew a kiss to little Fran who had emptied the cupboard where Harriet kept her baking tins, and was sitting surrounded by them. She had a wooden spoon and was making a lot of noise pretending to mix a cake in the largest of the tins. 'I'm glad I'm in the top class, because I've got Ms Pascoe all the time. Her cat hasn't got a name.'

'Why not?' Harriet helped herself to a biscuit and sat down to talk with Flick, who tossed her long brown plaits over her shoulders out of her way and took a drink of her milk before answering.

'She says it's because she, that is Ms Pascoe, doesn't know what the cat's name is and she doesn't want to upset it by calling it a name which isn't it, if you see what I mean. So she just calls it Cat.'

'Oh, I see. What about your Hartley and Chivers then?'

'I hadn't thought of that!' Flick looked worried. 'Oh dear! Do you think I've been upsetting them all this time, calling them a name they aren't?'

'I doubt it. They know when they're on to a good thing. My guess is they've kept quiet about their names because they don't want to cause any upset. They seem quite happy, don't they?'

'I wouldn't want to give them split personalities. Just think if I'd called Hartley "Tiger" instead, when all the time he's a quiet cat and wouldn't say boo to a goose!' She finished the rest of her milk. 'Ms Pascoe's cat sleeps on the classroom windowsill. We're not supposed to touch her. She's an untouchable cat, says Ms Pascoe. Touching is *verboten*. But it's quite difficult because, as you know, I like cats. I have an affinity with them, Ms Pascoe says. Ms Pascoe says that cats *allow* us to look after *them*. We don't own them like ordinary people think we do. Ms Pascoe's cat is very intelligent, she says. I think I shall devise intelligence tests for my two and see how they score.'

'Apart from the cat, was school all right – first day back and all that?'

'Oh yes! Ms Pascoe says we're going to have a wonderful time at school, now she's come. I'm glad I'm not in Mrs Hardaker's class – she looks a bit grim. So does Mrs Duckett. She was quite snappy with me when I went to the kitchen to get a clean saucer for the cat's water – said she was the school caretaker and not a zoo-keeper. The twins started in the playgroup today. Beth cried, and cried. Come to think of it, she cried all morning.'

'Oh dear. Poor Beth.'

'Well, she is only just three.'

'I know, but she's always been the confident one.'

'Well, she isn't now. We could hear her all over the school. The rector came, because Mrs Neal couldn't do a thing with her. Her face was all blotchy when he took her home. He had to carry her under his arm because she wouldn't walk, and her legs were kicking and she was screaming. Good thing he's big and strong, isn't it?'

'Oh dear. Still, it won't last long – she'll soon get used to it.' Harriet asked Flick to play with little Fran for a while. 'She's missed you, and so have I, you being away all day, first day of term.'

'OK. Come on, Fran, we'll play with the doll's house,' and Fran trotted off after Flick. Harriet tidied the tins away, and began to make the evening meal.

She glanced at the clock. Four o'clock. Jimbo would be back soon. Harriet looked out of the kitchen window. She never liked the garden in winter. No snow yet though, thank goodness. It was already almost dark. This was Jimbo's worst time of the year. Somehow the dark months didn't suit his personality; besides which, December and January were his busiest time of the year for catering. By the time Christmas and the New Year were over he was exhausted.

The door banged. 'It's me. Boys home yet?'

'No, not yet.'

'Darling!' Wrapping his arms around her waist, Jimbo kissed the back of Harriet's neck and said, 'Mmmmmm. My darling. Where are the girls?'

'Playing with the doll's house.'

'Flick OK?'

'She's fallen in love.'

'Good God! Not yet, surely. She's only ten.'

'No, stupid. With her new teacher and the teacher's cat.'

'Ah! So how is this Miss What's-er-name?'

'*Ms* Pascoe, if you please. Well, Flick says you'll love her.'

'Will I, indeed. My word.' Looking in the kitchen mirror, he stroked his bald head, straightened his bow tie, and grinned at himself.

'Jimbo!'

'Only joking. She's Ms then?'

'She is. Busy day?'

'Very busy. Truth to tell, Harriet, the Store's turning into a gold mine. I envisaged it as a front for our other activities and never really expected to do more than break even, but not any more. It stands in its own right now – so does the mail order. Your mother is in her seventh heaven; she was positively skipping round the mail-order office this afternoon. Christmas, with the new mincemeat and the new chutney and your idea of a hamper-for-one, broke all previous records. "Sadie," I said, "you're a pearl without price!" I've invited her for supper tonight. All right?'

'Yes, that's fine.'

'We'll have wine, I think. Do the old girl good.'

'Not so much of the old. She was only eighteen when I was born, you know.'

Jimbo laughed. 'We'll be able to run her a good long while yet, then.'

'Ruthless you are! Completely ruthless.'

'I've decided, this year, come hell or high water, the whole family is going to have a holiday together. You, me, the children . . .' He heard the front door open. 'That's the boys home. Feed the brutes, quick.'

Harriet put a plate of biscuits and glasses of Coke on the table. 'Come and get it!' Fergus and Finlay strolled in. The two of them, though not twins, were the same height. Fergus had inherited his father's heavy build, while Finlay was slightly built like Harriet and with his mother's dark hair; they had Jimbo's round head and face, with determined chins like their father's.

They sat down. 'Where's the girls?'

'Playing with the doll's house.'

'Thank God! Give us a bit of peace.'

'Yes, your mother *has* had a busy day and hello to you both.'

'Sorry, Dad. First day back and that.' Fergus helped himself to a second biscuit. 'I worked out today I've got five more years and two terms, counting this one, to do at school. I don't think I shall last that long.'

'Pity you can't come running with me in the morning. Gets the old adrenalin flowing, makes a good start to the day.' Jimbo threw a mock punch or two at Fergus' head.

'Thanks, but I much prefer slumping on the old school-bus, Dad. It's a drag back and forth to Culworth, day in day out.' Finlay stretched his legs out and by mistake kicked the table. Coke splashed everywhere. 'God, what a mess!'

'Calm down, calm down.' Harriet mopped up the sticky pool.

'What's the new Head like? Can't believe old Palmer's gone for ever.'

'*Mr* Palmer to you.' Harriet chuckled. 'She's called Ms Pascoe, and Flick says Daddy will love her.'

'Watch out, Mum. I can see the headlines now: *Turnham Malpas entrepreneur disappears with delectable new headmistress.*'

Jimbo aimed another playful cuff at Fergus' head. 'Grandmother is coming to supper tonight, so please, homework done, pronto pronto, then you can entertain her.'

'Oh good, she's teaching us poker. Have you any money, Finlay? You know she likes to play for high stakes.'

'Harriet! Your mother is teaching your sons bad ways. Gambling at their age indeed!'

'Funny how they're *my* sons when they're up to no good. Clear off, boys, and get your work done.' Harriet was chopping carrots furiously. 'Poor little Beth screamed the school down this morning apparently. Liz Neal sent for Peter and he had to take her home.'

'Poor little mite. She's usually so bouncy. How can we possibly know what terrors they are experiencing?'

'True. I'm wondering if it's Caroline going back to doctoring that's caused it.'

'Ah, hadn't thought of that. She can scream when she wants to, that child. I bet they could hear her all over the school.'

They could hear her all over the school on Wednesday, too. Peter took her and Alex in good time to give Beth a chance to settle before the others arrived. He stayed for half an hour and then tried creeping out while she was busy, but as he reached the door Beth realised what he was doing and began screaming again.

Liz Neal took hold of her and told Peter to go, so he did, but Beth would not be pacified. There was a knock at the door and in came Ms Pascoe. She shouted above the din Beth was making: 'This won't do, you know. We can hear her even with the doors shut. What's her name?'

'Beth Harris. She's the rector's little girl.'

'Spoilt only child, is she?'

'Oh no. Her twin's here too. That's him over there playing in the sand – the one with the reddish hair. Beth, darling, hush hush.'

'I would have thought the rector would have brought them up better than this. Send for him or her mother. Where's she?'

'Dr Harris is taking a surgery this morning.'

'I see. Well, we can't go on like this. Either someone stays with her or she goes home. You'll have them all crying if this continues. She didn't cry yesterday, did she?'

'She wasn't here; she only comes Monday, Wednesday and Friday.'

'I see. Well, that's more than enough – but do something, *please*. OK?' Ms Pascoe patted Beth's leg but Beth tried to kick her and Ms Pascoe had to jump aside. 'My word. What a hellcat she is.'

'She is not. This behaviour is most unlike her.' Liz struggled to contain Beth, who was trying to kick Ms Pascoe again. 'She's normally a very social being.'

'Well, you must sort it out somehow. I'm teaching my class to meditate and this isn't helping.'

Meditate? thought Liz. 'Can I borrow your phone, please?' she said aloud.

'Of course. Gladly.' And Kate Pascoe swept back to her class. There were twenty of them aged nine to eleven. Nine boys, eleven girls. Eager. Bright. Perfectly splendid material.

From her window where Cat lay sleeping, she saw the rector carrying Beth Harris home. She was still screaming and her sturdy little legs were still kicking out. Peter Harris' face was briefly visible as he turned to check for traffic before crossing the road. His expression was a strange mixture of anger and distress.

Jimbo was in the Store on Friday busy serving his customers. His boater, short-sleeved white shirt and red bow tie, combined with the red-and-white striped butcher's apron he wore, gave him a certain panache. This morning he sported a brilliant scarlet and acid yellow ribbon around his beloved boater. Jimbo's particular brand of repartee delighted his customers, and there was plenty of it today; he was feeling particularly bouncy, having completed the year-end figures and found them so very satisfactory. He raised his boater in greeting to Pat Duckett.

'Good morning, Mrs Duckett. How's school this term?'

'Mrs Duckett?'

'Well, Pat then.'

'Bring back Mr Palmer, is all I can say. The sooner the better.'

'Oh dear – like that, is it? I was told your new Head was gorgeous.'

'I don't know who told you that, but from where I'm standing I wouldn't 'ave said so. Still, early days yet. Things might settle down – new broom and all that.'

Jimbo leant forward and whispered in her ear, 'If things are really bad, why not give your notice in and work for me permanently?'

Pat gave him a surprised look. 'Really?'

'Well, you'll soon be married, so you won't need the daily grind, will you, not to quite the same extent? And you proved yourself at the Show. Organised the refreshment marquee like a dream, you did.'

'Did I?'

'You know you did. I could find lots of work for you. I've so many requests coming in for catering that I shan't be serving in the shop before long.'

'You mustn't give that up. You're the reason people come in. They like your style – does 'em good. Oh dearie me, look, you have a visitor.'

Jimbo turned to see where Pat was pointing. Sitting on the chair by the customers' coffee machine was Beth Harris. Her sturdy little legs were swinging back and forth, her thumb was in her mouth and her face was streaked by dried tears. She'd taken out of her pocket the piece of old cot blanket she called her 'lover' and was rubbing it intently back and forth across the end of her nose.

'Heavens above.' Jimbo strode gently across to Beth. 'Good morning, my love. Come to see your Uncle Bimbo?' Beth nodded. 'Well, that's lovely. Your Uncle Bimbo is pleased to see you. Come with me and we'll find Flick's Grandma Sadie and we'll see what she's got for you.' He held out his hand. She slipped off the chair and confidently put her hand in his. They disappeared into the back of the Store to find Sadie in her mail-order office. She was packing some jars of Country Cousin Marmalade into one of Jimbo's fancy boxes.

Jimbo caught Sadie's eye and winked. 'Now, Grandma Sadie, have you got something a hungry little girl could eat while her Uncle Bimbo makes a phone call?'

'Of course. Sit here with me, darling, and we'll find something for you.' Jimbo slipped away to use the phone in his office.

Beth took the little box of Smarties Sadie gave her and said, 'Thank you.' Then: 'I want my mummy.' Tears began to trickle down her face.

Sadie looked at Beth's lovely rounded cheeks, her startlingly bright blue eyes, the soft ash-blonde hair, and her heart went out to her. What a sweet dear beautiful child she was. Each and every tear was painful to watch. 'Beth, Mummy's not far away and she'll be back for lunch, you know.'

'I want my mummy.' The words were blurred by her constricted throat and the tears which began coming too fast to count.

Sadie bent down to put her arms around her. 'I know, dear, I know. But you're getting a big girl now and big girls do some things by themselves, don't they? Alex does, doesn't he? Alex is being a big boy. You've to be a big girl. Is Alex still at school?'

Beth nodded.

'Shall your Grandma Sadie take you back to him then?'

'NO! I want my mummy!' The wails began to grow louder. The box of Smarties was dropped on the floor and she wept.

Sadie felt quite unable to cope with Beth's overwhelming sadness and longed to be rescued.

The rescue came in the form of Peter.

He ducked his head as he came into Sadie's office. 'Beth, my darling child. Come here.' He bent down and picked her up off the chair and held her close.

'I want my mummy.'

'I know, darling, I know. But see here, Beth, Mummy has not gone away for ever. Mummy will be back for her lunch and that isn't very long, is it? Now, Daddy's going to take you back to school. Mrs Neal will be worried, so we'll go and tell her where you are. Right now – OK?'

'NO! I'm not going back there! I'm not! I'm not!'

'I shall be with you, promise.'

'All the time.'

'All the time, I promise. Thank you, Sadie. Thank you.'

'All part of a day's work! Any time. Bye bye, darling. Chin up!'

Beth wouldn't smile. She merely looked down at her over Peter's shoulder and allowed herself to be carried away.

Pat watched the two of them leave the Store.

'Poor little mite. She's got a good pair of lungs, I'll give 'er that. I'll think over what you said about . . .' Pat nodded significantly to Jimbo because they couldn't exchange confidences as the Store had filled up again with customers, '. . . yer know, and talk it over with my intended.'

Jimbo nodded from behind the till and gave her the thumbs-up. 'Don't be too long about it.'

School playtime was just beginning when Peter crossed Jacks Lane and took Beth back to school. Kate Pascoe was in the hall.

'Good morning, Rector. Hello, Beth. All right now?'

'Good morning, Ms Pascoe. Sorry about all this trouble we're having. It must be very upsetting. I'll take her through to the playgroup and see Liz Neal and then I'll have a quick word, if I may.'

'Of course. See you in a moment. We're just having coffee. Like one?'

'Yes, please.'

The staff drank their morning coffee in the hall because the Head's room was too small to accommodate them. Hetty Hardaker and Margaret Booth, a pretty, energetic, fair-haired girl whom the whole of the infant class adored on sight, were sitting in the hall with Kate Pascoe when Peter returned with Beth in his arms. Hetty had worked at the school for ten years, and had hoped for the headship. Margaret had replaced 'poor' Toria Clark, as everyone always called her. They were both eyeing Kate Pascoe warily. The atmosphere was less than cordial.

Peter stood Beth down on the floor and she stood, quietly sobbing, gripping his cassock. 'Good morning, Hetty, Margaret. Sorry this daughter of mine is causing so much trouble. It's really very unlike her. She's the one with all the bounce and confidence. This has come as a great surprise.' He turned to Kate. 'I'm sorry she ran away, but concerned that no one had realised.'

'Oh, but we did, and we'd been searching for her. Jimbo rang just as we were about to phone you to see if she'd gone home.'

'I beg your pardon. I think I'll take her home for the rest of the morning.'

'Taking her home will solve nothing. You'll have to be firm. She's got to learn.'

Hetty Hardaker intervened. 'She'll learn nothing by being left to cry herself to exhaustion, *Miss* Pascoe. The rector's quite right to take her home. There's something very disturbing for Beth here, I don't know what, but there is.' She placed her coffee mug on the top of the piano and glared at Kate.

Kate ignored her. 'Well, Rector. Either she stops crying or she stays at home – the choice is yours. It's too disrupting for the other children. Our meditation time was quite ruined again today.'

'I'll take Beth back home for now. I'll phone you later, Ms Pascoe, if I may.'

'Kate, please.'

'Kate, then. Sorry again about all this.'

'So, Caroline, I've asked Kate Pascoe over for coffee tonight. Firstly as an apology about Beth's behaviour and secondly to find out more about her.'

'You sound as though you suspect her of something quite dreadful.'

'No, not dreadful – but meditation? For ten-year-olds?'

'I see what you mean. I shall look forward to this – it could be a very interesting evening.' She didn't notice Peter looking at her, surprised at her apparent lack of concern about Beth. 'If you've finished lunch, we'll clear away. Sylvia's got plans for turning out the children's room this afternoon. She'll be back any minute.'

They heard the front door open and in a moment Sylvia came into the kitchen. 'I've had a thought,' she told them both. 'Shall I stay with Beth at playgroup on Monday? It might help.'

Peter said he and Ms Pascoe were going to discuss it this evening and he'd let her know. When she got shut out like Peter had shut her out just now, Sylvia knew there was trouble brewing. Sighing, she snapped open the dishwasher. Please God not more trouble. They'd had enough last year for a lifetime and then some.

Peter was on the telephone so it was Caroline who opened the door to Kate.

'Good evening, Kate. Do come in. I'm Caroline, the rector's wife. How do you do?'

Kate shook hands and approved of Caroline. She appreciated her businesslike approach and she was so up-to-speed for a rector's wife. 'Not a very nice night, is it?'

'No, it isn't, but at least it isn't snowing. This time last year we had thick snow for weeks. Most unusual. We're in the sitting room – do go through and take a pew, the coffee's almost ready.'

As she carried the tray from the kitchen across the hall Peter came out of his study. 'That was Dicky Tutt, giving me the date for the Scout jumble sale – March the twentieth. Make a note and then we can have a clearout. Kate here?' He pushed the sitting-room door open a little wider to

accommodate Caroline's tray. 'Good evening, Kate. I don't need to introduce my wife, do I? Obviously you've already met. Firstly, I'm so sorry
about Beth. She's gone from being a perfectly happy sociable little being to
this hysterical monster, and we're not sure how to tackle it. My inclination
is to take her each morning and stay with her for say ten minutes, then
bring her home. Gradually lengthen the time she stays.'

Kate listened to his proposition. She noticed Caroline was saying
nothing. She was the child's mother, for God's sake.

'How do you feel, Caroline?'

'Coffee? Milk? Sugar?'

'Black, please. No sugar.'

Caroline sat down beside Peter and took a sip of her coffee. 'Frankly, I'm
completely at a loss. Although they are twins I prefer to treat them as
completely separate individuals.' Kate nodded in agreement. 'If Alex is fine
then he goes all morning. If Beth is finding it difficult then we adapt things
to suit her. I think Peter's idea is a good one. Sylvia could always stay with
her if he is busy.'

'Sylvia is employed as housekeeper, darling, primarily.'

'You have a housekeeper?'

Caroline raised an eyebrow. 'Yes, do you have a problem with that?'

'No, no. I'm just surprised, that's all. I'm all for throwing them in at the
deep end. It's surprising how resilient small children can be when once they
see you mean business. However, basically it's not for me to say, is it? Liz
Neal is the one who takes the brunt of it. What I deplore is the disturbance
it causes to the children whose school it actually is. Meditation is impossible with all that racket.'

Peter said, 'I wondered about that.'

'The disturbance?'

'No, the meditation.'

'It's the modern equivalent to assembly.'

'I see. It always was called prayers, or assembly.'

'I dare say, but nowadays we have to cater for all religions, not just
Christianity.'

'May I point out that all the children are white and Christian.'

'Just because they are white, it does not mean they are Christian.'

'At Turnham Malpas School they all are. All, except the two Paradise
children, go to our Junior Church or the Methodist Church in Little
Derehams. The school is a C. of E. foundation and the parents expect
prayers and religious teaching. You took the post on that understanding.'

'I did. But are you saying there is no room for silence and private
thought?'

'No, certainly not. Of course there's room for it, but there must be the
other side too. In Michael Palmer's time we had Friday-morning prayers in

the church. Hetty and Margaret were quite happy to go along with that. If you prefer, I could take prayers on Fridays in the school instead, but I should be disappointed.'

Kate looked to Caroline for support but got none. 'Then I shall have to adapt, shall I not? If Hetty Hardaker is willing to take prayers then she can. I shall conduct the silent thinking, afterwards.'

Caroline held up the coffee pot. 'More coffee?'

'Yes, please.' Kate saw two of Caroline's cats standing in the doorway. 'Oh, what lovely creatures! Come, puss, puss, puss.' Tonga and Chang fluffed their tails and arched their backs; Tonga spat and then they fled.

To cover his embarrassment at the weird attitude of their normally attention-seeking cats, Peter plunged in with, 'Then we shall for the moment compromise, but it must be clearly understood, Miss . . . *Ms* Pascoe, that there must be religious teaching even if you don't do it yourself. It is your responsibility to attend to that, however much you prefer not to. Hetty Hardaker did it all last term whilst we had no head teacher, so I'm sure she and Margaret will be quite happy to continue. We'll review the situation at half-term.'

'Very well. I shall do as you say, Rector.'

Caroline wanted to know more about Kate herself. 'Settling in at the school-house, Kate?'

'Yes, thanks. It's terribly dowdy, though. I'm brightening it up. When it's done, will you come for supper one evening? Or perhaps you won't have a babysitter.'

'Sylvia does it for us, so yes, we'd love to come. In fact, I've never been inside the school-house and we've lived here almost four years, so it will be interesting for us, won't it, Peter?'

'Yes, it will.' He looked at Kate. 'Now – about May the first.'

'Yes?'

'On that day, Michael always had Maypole dancing on the Green. All the parents are invited, there are cups of tea and a May Queen. Do you do Maypole dancing?'

'Ye olde phallic symbol? Village maidens dancing round in homage – rites of spring and all that jazz. Of course! Delighted to take part. Must go, want to do some more decorating before bed. Thanks for the coffee. Hope Beth settles down soon. Won't be long before you get my invitation. I'm a tigress once I get started.'

Caroline saw her out and went back into the sitting room to find Peter had gone. He was in his study, searching along his bookshelves.

'What are you looking for?'

'Maypole dancing. An innocent colourful pursuit, I thought, until tonight. I'd no idea that was what it represented. Phallic symbol, indeed! Is nothing sacred any more?'

Caroline laughed. 'Oh, Peter! She makes a change from strait-laced Michael Palmer anyway. He was a bit too solemn, wasn't he?'

'It's no laughing matter, my darling girl. We've got problems there and no mistake. I dread to think what will happen next.'

4

Jimbo met Kate the following morning. She came into the Store carrying a large shopping bag. He raised his boater to her and said, 'You must be Kate Pascoe from the school. Good morning to you!'

She put down her bag and reached out to shake hands with him. 'Indeed I am. And you must be Flick's father. She said you owned the Store. She was going to launch herself into a long story about how well you were doing, end-of-year accounts and that kind of thing, but I cut that short! But I do see what she means. It certainly is a wonderland. And I thought all village stores were on their last legs.' She looked appreciatively around the Store. 'I think perhaps I haven't thanked you for sending me that starter pack for my pantry? I really did appreciate your kindness. I've got to stock up my cupboards now.'

'We'll deliver for you if you wish.'

'No, that won't be necessary, thank you. There's only one of me. Soya milk?'

'Ah! We do have some but I don't get a great call for it – just one other customer who has a daughter allergic to cow's milk. Check the dairy cabinet, I think you'll find some.'

Kate wandered away, leaving Jimbo to carry on replenishing the fresh fruit display. The doorbell jangled and Kate heard Jimbo welcoming another customer. 'Ralph, this is a pleasure! Don't often see you in here.'

'Hello, Jimbo. Milk is what we need for the moment. We used the last drop at breakfast-time and Muriel's wanting her coffee.'

'Indeed and why not. I'll get it for you.'

'No, no, don't trouble yourself, I can get it. I'm going up tomorrow to see old Fitch about the cricket pitch. Care to come with me?'

'Much as I would like to, I'm afraid business calls. I'm quite sure you can manage without me!'

'Got to get it on a business footing, you see. No loose ends. Knowing his propensity for deviousness I want things quite clear-cut. Any more news about team members?'

'Indeed. Ah, Ms Pascoe. May I introduce our new head teacher, Sir Ralph? Kate Pascoe, this is Sir Ralph Templeton. He and his wife Lady Muriel Templeton live in the village.' Ralph extended a welcoming hand. Kate shook it with a half-smile on her face. He was certainly distinguished-looking – thin, tanned, with thick white hair, an aristocratic beaked nose, and the wearer of an extremely expensive overcoat.

'How do you do, young lady. Very pleased to meet you. My wife's already made your acquaintance; she said how charming you were and she was right. We needed new blood in the school. May I wish you every success?'

'Thank you, Ralph.' Kate didn't notice Jimbo flinch when she omitted Ralph's title. 'That's very kind of you. Did I hear you mentioning a cricket team?'

'You did. We've spent last summer and this winter resurrecting the old cricket pitch. It's a vast improvement on what it was but still not as good as Lord's – not yet.'

'I played cricket with my brothers when I was at home. Fabulous game.' Ralph raised an eyebrow at the use of the word 'fabulous'. 'I wouldn't expect to play in the team, but I'm a good hand at cricket teas. Would I be of any use? Or maybe you've got all that side of it organised already.'

Jimbo declared they hadn't and he'd be glad of help. 'I'm having nothing to do with the catering side. It's all voluntary, you see, so I'm sure Muriel and Caroline – you've met Caroline – ' Kate nodded ' – would be delighted by your offer.'

'I'm certain they would. Thank you very much.' Ralph smiled at her and went to collect the fresh milk.

'I've found some soya milk, Jimbo. I'm a vegan – I don't suppose you have many of those in the village.'

'Ah! First time I've met one in the flesh, so to speak. Is there anything at all which you specially favour? If so, I'll make sure we get it in. Can't have you starving to death!' Jimbo couldn't help remembering all the food he'd sent her. Privately he wondered where it had all gone.

Kate heaved her overflowing basket onto the shelf by the till. 'Today I'm OK. Thanks though, I'll let you know. Don't forget about the cricket teas, will you? I really mean what I say.'

'Certainly shan't. I shall pass on your offer to the appropriate quarter. There's your change – thank you very much.'

'What superb carrier bags! Much too nice for recycling as pedal-bin bags!' Kate grinned at him and went out.

'Well, Ralph, there's one thing for certain – I shan't be able to retire on what Kate spends in here. A vegan – God help us! Hope she doesn't start a new trend!'

'About the team . . .'

'Oh yes. I've got a list. Here it is.' He removed a piece of paper from a clipboard, and handed it to Ralph who put on his reading glasses and stood to one side while Jimbo continued dealing with customers.

Ralph read the list out in an undertone. 'Dicky Tutt . . . he should be good behind a bat but can he run, that's the question. Jimbo . . . Gilbert – oh that's a surprise. Surely Little Derehams will have something to say about us poaching one of their star players?'

'Well, it's Gilbert's decision. He asked me, not the other way round. Apparently he's sick of having to kowtow to their Captain who's high-handed and not the slightest bit democratic, and Gilbert says he's not a child and won't be treated like one.'

'Oh well, then, we'll have him! If I remember rightly he's an excellent batsman.'

'He is. Score average last season twenty-one.'

'Excellent!' Ralph returned silently to considering the list. Barry Jones . . . yes, Peter . . . yes, Neville . . . the slimy toad, Malcolm . . . the milkman, the Sergeant . . . Dean Duckett . . . Kenny and Terry Jones and Rhett Wright. An odd collection but some good may come of them; we've got to start somewhere. He flicked the list with the back of his hand and said aloud: 'Well, Jimbo, I must say you've done well. A good start. Right, I'll be off. Here's the money for the milk. I'll let you know how I get on. Strange girl, that Kate.'

'Rather gorgeous, I thought! Those green eyes . . . Nice of her to help with the teas.'

'Hmm.' Ralph shut the door and went off home looking forward to his coffee just as Muriel was. As he walked round the village green, Ralph admired the houses and the church. Home, Turnham Malpas, that was where he really belonged. His heart was here, where he'd spent his first years. It didn't matter a damn that he wasn't in the Big House any more. He could cheerfully leave that to old Fitch, because he, Ralph, had what Fitch hadn't – a loving passionate wife. Never mind all that hooey that passion belonged only to the young; he and Muriel had proved them wrong. As Ralph crossed Church Lane he said to himself, I just hope my damned ticker holds out and we have many years of fun before us.

'Muriel, my dear, here's the milk. I've just been introduced to Ms Pascoe from the school. Curious sort of girl – well, woman. Just hope she doesn't let the village down with newfangled ideas.'

Muriel opened the carton of milk and poured some into the tiny china jug on the tray. She checked that she had everything – Ralph's sweeteners, the coffee, teaspoons, cups, saucers. She was using the ones she'd brought from her own house when they'd married. She was so glad she had someone to share her nice china with. Dear Ralph!

'There we are, I've got everything. Come and tell me what you think of her.'

'All black – she's dressed in black. One thing in her favour, though, she's willing to lend a hand with the cricket teas.'

'Oh excellent! She can't be all bad then.'

'No, she can't, can she?' Ralph chuckled. 'I've that appointment with Fitch tomorrow. They'll be starting on the pavilion as soon as the weather improves – won't that be grand? We've fifty years of neglect to put right. I can just remember seeing my father batting. It was a hot summer day. My sunhat made my forehead sticky so I pushed it off; Mama wiped my face with cologne and put it back on again. That's something I remember about her – she always smelt beautifully. God! I'm sounding like a very sentimental old trout. Got to stop.'

'There's nothing the matter with memories, Ralph, nothing at all. Especially lovely ones.'

'No, you're right. Thank you for the coffee, my dear. I'm going to my study to open the post and to plan my meeting with Fitch. He'll be handing out money like there's no tomorrow, so long as it bolsters his campaign.'

'Campaign?'

'He's wanting to be president of the club.'

'But a Templeton is always president!' Muriel was scandalised. 'It'll have to be you.'

'I rather hope it might. Tradition and all that . . . but times have changed and money speaks loudest now.'

'I shall tell him,' Muriel said fiercely. 'If you have any trouble with him, let me know and I shall go up there and put him straight. President of the cricket club . . . Whatever next!'

Ralph smiled at her. 'I do believe you would.'

As he pulled up on the gravel at the front of the Big House the following day, Ralph couldn't help his heart lurching slightly. The place always had that effect on him. It really was time he let the past rest in peace.

To his surprise, Craddock Fitch's secretary Louise was working.

'Good afternoon, Louise. I hadn't expected to find you here on a Saturday.'

'Good afternoon, Sir Ralph. I've been having a few days holiday while Mr Fitch was away so I thought I would catch up while the House was quiet.'

'Did you go anywhere exciting?'

'To Paris.'

'Oh, wonderful! What a coincidence,' Ralph said suddenly, struck. 'Gilbert Johns has just been to Paris, too. Did you bump into him, by any chance? We had a chat about a recital he was going to in Notre Dame. He was so looking forward to it. Don't suppose you went, too?'

Ralph noticed that Louise was blushing. 'We didn't bump into each other. Mr Fitch is ready for you.'

'Thank you.' Ralph headed towards the library.

'Er . . . excuse me, Sir Ralph, Mr Fitch isn't in his office, he's in his private flat. Do you know where that is?'

'Oh yes, I do.' This was the hardest bit, walking up the stairs and along the corridors. Memories flooded his mind, but he mustn't let himself be disarmed by them; he needed to be on his mettle. The thought entered his head that old Fitch had decided to have the meeting in the flat deliberately, to disconcert him.

The door of the flat was open so Ralph tapped with his signet ring on one of the carved panels and called out, 'Craddock? Ralph Templeton.'

He heard quick positive footsteps. 'Ralph! Do come in.' Ralph wryly noted that Mr Fitch's country tweeds were so entirely co-ordinated that he looked as though he'd stepped straight out of the window of a Savile Row tailor, then grimly recollected the man himself was no tailor's dummy.

'Craddock! Good afternoon.'

'I've had tea organised for us. Is that satisfactory, or would you prefer something stronger?'

'Tea will be fine.' Ralph seated himself in a huge armchair, a patriarchal kind of chair; its twin was the other side of the fireplace and Mr Fitch went to sit in it.

Sadie Beauchamp carried in the tea tray. Ralph and, belatedly, Mr Fitch, stood up.

'Good afternoon, Sadie. How nice to see you.'

'Hello, Ralph. You're back. Had a good holiday? I'll catch up on your news with Muriel next week. Must dash. Everything's there, Craddock, I'll be off now.' She put down the tray on the big round coffee table standing in front of the fire between their chairs, and beamed at them both. She and Mr Fitch kissed each other's cheeks and she left.

Mr Fitch explained she'd been having lunch with him and had volunteered to make the tea before she left. Ralph replied, 'I see. Lovely woman, Sadie. Sharp mind, even sharper tongue!' Mr Fitch smiled his agreement.

They talked idly about this and that, and in particular about the international situation, and each in their turn prophesied the outcome, and then Mr Fitch put down his cup, dabbed his mouth with his napkin, and fired his opening shot.

'If I'm putting money into this cricket team I shall expect to be president.'

'Ah! I see. I thought perhaps you might.'

'Oh yes. There's no point in beating about the bush. I'm allowing the use of Rector's Meadow, paying for the renovations – or more accurately, the complete rebuilding of the pavilion – buying and supplying the equipment, too, and that's what I want in return.'

'It's completely against tradition.'

'Is it?'

'Templetons have been presidents since the cricket club was first started by my great-great-grandfather.'

'Well, it's more than fifty years since the last Templeton, your late lamented father, was president, plus no cricket team for fifty years, so I think we could safely say there's been a break with tradition, don't you?'

'The village won't like it.'

'Come off it, Ralph. God! There's hardly a soul living who remembers all that stuff. No, move with the times, I say. Money counts. Where else would you get it from if not from me?'

Bitingly Ralph replied, 'It would be pleasant if you could be a little more gracious about it.'

'*Gracious*? What's there to be gracious about? Facts are facts.'

'The village won't like it,' Ralph said again.

'They'll have to take a deep breath and swallow hard then.'

'Don't forget you've come up against their wrath once before.'

Mr Fitch gave Ralph a piercing look. 'About the church silver, you mean?' He flicked some ash from his cigar into the flames and paused for a moment. 'It was only the effigy they made, hanging from the tree.'

'And all the things going wrong here. The heating being off for three days in the dead of winter, your tyres let down, the strike of the kitchen staff and the   '

'You mean all that was engineered?'

'Of course. Hadn't you realised that?'

Unwilling to admit in front of Ralph that it had never occurred to him that the opposition from the village could be so vicious, he paused before replying. 'Well, it had crossed my mind, naturally; it all did seem rather odd, but I didn't take it seriously.' He sat silently watching the flames leaping up his chimney. The devil they did.

Ralph said, 'You'd have to be here fifty years at least before they accepted you, and unfortunately you've not got that much time left.'

Mr Fitch's head came up with a jerk. 'Neither have you.'

'True, true, but then I'm one step ahead. I'm already accepted and have been for centuries.'

'So they'll take my money but not me?'

'In a nutshell.'

'Damn them!!'

'That's just it.'

'What is?'

'Your attitude.'

Craddock Fitch strode about the room, puffing furiously on his cigar, his brown gleaming shoes rapping sharply on the polished floor. He came to a halt on the huge round rug in front of the fire. As he stubbed out his cigar in the ash-tray on the coffee table he said, 'You're saying if I insist on being president I shall lose what little kudos I might have already gained?'

'Something like that.'

'Who are these people who think they can dictate to me?'

'It is their village, their cricket team, not yours, not mine.'

'At this rate there'll be no progress.'

'Not much.'

'Well, I'm damned.' Mr Fitch stabbed his well manicured hand in Ralph's direction. 'All right then, you be president, but my name goes above the pavilion door. *The Henry Craddock Fitch Pavilion* – that'll sort 'em. No doubt who's paid for it then, eh? And my company logo on the gear I buy – you know, "sponsored by et cetera". Right?'

'Done!' They shook hands on the deal. Ralph glanced up at Mr Fitch, taking care to veil the twinkle in his eyes. 'And you can donate a cup, if you like.'

'Two! One to the batsman with the highest score in the season, and one to the bowler with the best average.'

'Done! I'll have another cup of tea, if I may. Now let's get down to business. Finance first. Shall you want rent for the pavilion? I rather hope not, for the first year at least.'

Mr Fitch raised his eyebrows at Ralph's outspokenness. 'I don't know how you got so high in the Diplomatic Service. There's not much diplomacy about your dealings!'

5

'Kiss, kiss, my darling children. Mummy's off to make poorly people better, isn't she? Now Beth, Mummy won't be long. Sylvia's going to take you and stay for a while aren't you, Sylvia?'

'Of course. Will you show me where the sand is, Beth? I love playing in the sand.'

Alex said, 'Me will, Sylvie, me will. Me knows where the sand is. Beth doesn't.'

Beth stamped her foot. 'Beth does.'

'Beth doesn't 'cos you won't play.'

'I will.'

'You won't.'

'That will do, children. *Please*. Now I'm going. Be good, and Mummy will have a present for you when she comes back.'

'Beth not going.' She sat down on the hall floor.

'Sylvia! I really must go or I shall be late.' Caroline kissed the two of them on the tops of their heads, and fled with her medical bag to her car.

Sylvia cheerfully went to get the children's coats from the hall cupboard. 'Now Alex, aren't you going to have a lovely time in playgroup today? I wonder if they'll have the sand out today for your Sylvie to play in. Or shall I play with the water? Do they have water to play with, Beth?'

Beth ignored her. She looked up when she saw her father's feet appear beside her. He bent down and stood her up. 'Coat on, Beth.' She allowed him to dress her, then she took hold of Sylvia's hand and set off without another word. Sylvia was greatly relieved. But the relief was shortlived. Within five minutes of arriving, Beth had disappeared. The playgroup door had been open for only a moment as another of the children arrived and Beth had slipped out. The moment she realised what had happened, Sylvia ran out of school but there was no sign of Beth.

Jimbo found her sitting on the same chair, sucking her thumb and rubbing her nose with her lover, but this time there were no tears, only deep sadness.

'Well now, Beth. Hello. Come to see Uncle Bimbo again? You left your Smarties last time. Shall we go get them?' Beth ignored him. 'Come with Uncle Bimbo, eh?' It was as if he hadn't spoken. He looked round the Store and asked a customer to keep an eye on her while he phoned Peter and the school.

Peter took her back to the classroom. Sylvia was out searching the playground, Liz Neal was distraught and Kate Pascoe was seething.

'Really, Rector, again!'

'Yes – again. I might add that my daughter is here under your protection. I can hardly be pleased with the way you're carrying out your duties.'

'I didn't qualify in containing Houdinis – what teacher has? The only way to keep Beth in is to lock all the doors – which I resolutely refuse to do. This is *not* a prison. In any case, the playgroup is not strictly under my authority. Although I do everything I can to help, the actual responsibility is Mrs Neal's. But the responsibility for your daughter's personal safety is getting too much.'

Liz apologised. 'I'm terribly sorry, Peter. I've never had this before. How about if we give her a break? Perhaps Alex going home and saying how much he enjoys himself might have a beneficial effect on her attitude. Or else it is that she's just not quite ready. Not all children take to it as easily as Alex has.'

'I think maybe you could be right. We'll keep her at home this week and try to find out what the problem is. Thank you. I'm sorry for all the trouble.'

'That's all right. We can't expect to run a playgroup without some hiccups.'

Kate returned to her class. Peter and Sylvia took Beth home. She ran through the door shouting, 'Mummy! Mummy!' When she couldn't find Caroline she went to Sylvia, clutched hold of her skirt and never left her side all morning.

'Beth is staying at home for the rest of the week.'

Caroline swallowed her last drop of coffee and said, 'You've decided to keep her at home this week? Without consulting me?'

'Yes.'

'Peter!'

'Her heart – her tender, loving heart is broken.'

'She'll soon get over it. Children can be like that – they don't like change.'

'I said her heart is broken.'

'I heard.'

'The pain is unbearable for her.'

'Nonsense.'

'I won't have my decision altered. She is not going on either Wednesday or Friday.'

'Just a moment. We are both of us her parents; decisions are joint ones.'

'In this case, I'm sorry, but my decision is final. I cannot remember when I felt the need to assert my authority so positively, but that is what I'm doing now. She is not going this week. She is putting her life at risk to tell us she is unhappy. Do you realise that? *Her life at risk.* She has twice crossed Jacks Lane *on her own*, when she is far too young and far too distraught to have any road sense. It only needs Barry Jones to come hurtling round the corner like he frequently does and . . . and it will all be too late.'

'This is arrogant interference in my domain.'

'Broken hearts *are* my business.'

'You're being very dramatic.'

'You didn't see her face when she couldn't find you when we got home.'

'This is ridiculous. She loves Sylvia, she'll be all right with her.'

'It was I who made her go this morning, and I shouldn't have done so. Look, Caroline, I don't wish to discuss it any further. I shall be in my study if I'm needed.' Peter stood up and pushed his chair under the table.

'That's right, hide in your study – you've had your say, trespassed where you shouldn't, so off you go to avoid any further discussion.' Peter looked down at her. It was her eyes which eventually avoided his. He turned on his heel and left the dining room.

Caroline began clearing the table. She caught the sound of Beth screaming as she crossed the hall. By the time she'd reached the bedroom, Beth was hysterical. Caroline hugged her tight, talking to her and trying to calm her fears. 'Have you had a nasty dream? Never mind then, Mummy's here, hush, hush, darling. There, there.' Caroline rocked her back and forth, back and forth and gradually the cries subsided. When she'd wiped her tears away for her, Caroline asked what the matter was. 'Can you tell Mummy what frightened you? Tell me, darling, please?'

'Mrs Neal, it was Mrs Neal.'

'She's a lovely lady, a friend of Mummy's.'

'Mrs Neal gave me a present.'

'Oh, how nice! That was a lovely dream, not a nasty one, surely.'

'She gave me lots of . . .' Beth sobbed. 'She gave me lots of worms, wiggly worms, all wiggly in my ha-a-nn-nd.'

'Oh darling, I'm so sorry. But it was only a dream, you know. There aren't any worms here really, are there? Look, see, open your eyes. No worms. Just a dream. Mummy will lie down on the bed and wait till you go back to sleep. How's that?' Beth clutched hold of her and closed her eyes. 'No worms, Mummy?'

'No worms, darling.' It was ten minutes before Beth relaxed enough to go back to sleep.

Peter left Caroline with all the dishes to clear and stack, an activity which, if he hadn't got an evening meeting, they usually did together. When she'd finished, she went in the sitting room to watch television. It was more than an hour before she heard Peter come out of the study. He didn't come immediately into the sitting room but went to the kitchen. She could hear him putting on the kettle and getting out cups. This was his way, she knew, of making amends for his outburst. Well, he wasn't going to get around her that way. Other women had careers and children! Why on earth shouldn't she? She'd make it work. Beth would just have to get used to the idea that her mother had other things in her life besides children. Much as she loved her, she loved general practice too. She'd had to give it up when she and Peter got married and he'd moved parish; hospital work had been the easier option at the time. Though she'd liked the hospital, it wasn't quite her métier. She was really enjoying general practice and *nothing* was going to stop her. Why shouldn't she have two lives? They could well afford Sylvia . . .

'Coffee, darling?'

'Yes, please.'

Peter put down the tray in front of her, and sat a moment in silence before he poured it. 'Instant, couldn't be bothered with the other. You don't mind?'

'No, not at all.'

'Ralph tells me he's been up to the Big House and persuaded Mr Fitch not to be president of the cricket club. But he's giving two cups and his name's going above the pavilion.'

'Oh, good – Mr Fitch will love that. Says something for Ralph's expertise in diplomacy, don't you think?'

'Exactly. I'm looking forward to the summer. I always liked cricket. Here's your coffee – is that all right?'

'Yes, thank you. You'll have to get back into your stride; you haven't played a stroke since we've known each other.'

'You're right – I shall have to get my eye in again. My best score was forty-five against Magdalen way back in . . . Can't remember.'

'It's no good, Peter.'

'What isn't?'

'Trying to talk as though nothing has happened. It has, and I'm very annoyed.'

Peter put his cup back on the coffee table and, fidgeting with his wedding ring, sat waiting for her to speak again.

'Why can't I have the best of both worlds? Other women do. Other women are back at work after six weeks at home with a new baby. They have nannies organised or au pairs organised, and everything goes with a swing.'

'Does it?'

'Oh yes.'

'On what do you base your assumption? Someone you know?'

Caroline sipped her coffee. 'Well, no one specific but you do hear about them.'

'In newspaper articles on the women's page?'

'Don't sneer, Peter, it's beneath you.'

'You putting the needs of your child second is beneath you.'

'So I'm to give up, am I? Let people down? Stay at home, play the role of Mummy ad infinitum? When shall I be allowed my life? When she's gone to university?'

'Now you're being ridiculous.'

'Ah! You're not?'

'No. Next time she makes it out of school, she may not go to Jimbo's.'

'Well, they'll have to take proper care of her, won't they? I'll have a word with Liz Neal. She'll sort it for me.'

'You are her anchor, you see. She loves you dearly; she relies on you for her security. Not Sylvia, not me. *You.*'

'Well, this job is only for six months.'

'I know.'

'You've put your sad expression on.'

'I haven't put it on. I look sad because I *am* sad. But there we are. I would marry an intelligent, highly motivated, passionate woman . . .'

'I married that kind of a man too.'

'You did, indeed. My own way this week?'

Caroline hesitated and then gave in. 'Very well.'

At five minutes to nine the following Monday, Hetty Hardaker rang the school-bell to call the children in. Margaret Booth came out to collect her infants.

'Rector's coming this morning – look.'

'So he is. Let's hope he has better success than he had last Monday, or else Madam will be fuming again.'

'You don't like her, Hetty, do you?'

'Kate Pascoe is a totally different ball-game from Michael Palmer and I don't . . . That will do, boys. In line, if you please. Flick, your shoelace is undone. That's lovely, Stacey – I'll look properly when we get inside. Brian, you've dropped your reading book. Pick it up quickly before it gets trodden on. Come along then, children, in we go.'

Peter waited until the main rush of children had gone in. He held Beth's hand tightly. Alex ran in without even a backward glance. Beth had her lover in her other hand, and under her arm her old rabbit from her baby days. With one ear missing it didn't look the least bit respectable, but she didn't care. Peter took her into the playgroup room and tried to make himself as inconspicuous as possible. Beth stood beside him, thumb in mouth. Nothing could tempt her to join in. Kate Pascoe popped her head round the door at playtime.

'Still here, Rector? All's quiet this morning. Coffee?'

'Yes, please.' Beth consented to having her drink and biscuit seated beside Alex at a little table, so Peter left her and went into the hall to join the three teachers.

'I've decided I don't want to continue having prayers in the church,' Kate began. 'I'd much rather have it in here, in school. Takes less time, for one thing . . .'

Hetty Hardaker indignantly interrupted. 'You have not consulted me about that, nor Margaret. I think it should be decided between us, don't you, Margaret?'

'Well, I enjoyed going into church. The rector does such good services for children; they all loved it and I think—'

Kate held up her hand for silence. 'Well, I think the rector could do just as good services here too. What do you think, Peter?'

'I prefer the church but then the school is yours so we must do as you wish.'

'Thank you. We'll see you Friday then, in here at nine o'clock.'

Hetty objected. 'It seems to me that, bit by bit, you are abdicating your responsibility for the religious teaching in this school. I'm to take prayers, you take meditation; whatever it is children of this age have to meditate on, I don't know – possibly who won the FA Cup or who's got the most Cub badges or something, or praying Dad will win the lottery this week and what they'll do with the money. Now we're told we can't go into church which we all know the rector prefers.'

'Hetty, may I remind you that I am Head here.' Kate's voice was hard.

'I don't need you to remind me. I *know*, only too well. I don't agree to this move at all, I'm sorry.'

Peter intervened. 'It isn't as if the children are not getting any religious instruction, Hetty, is it?'

'No, Rector, but it's being diluted.'

'I'm sure Kate doesn't—'

Kate interrupted Peter with a brusque, 'We have to move with the times.'

Hetty's face flushed with anger. 'That is the classic excuse for not keeping up standards. Mr Palmer would never have agreed . . .'

'Mr Palmer isn't Head here, *I am*. And I shall run the school as I see fit.'

Hetty Hardaker stood up, her voice heavy with sarcasm as she said, 'Time for the bell. May I ring it, or shall you as it is *your* school?'

Before Kate could answer, Liz Neal rushed into the hall. 'Anyone seen Beth come this way? She's disappeared again.'

Beth had missed Peter and gone to look for him. She'd tried the rectory door but couldn't reach the bell, and Sylvia, who was upstairs, hadn't heard her knocking. So now she had nobody, nobody at all. Finding Muriel's door open, she went in.

Ralph found her in his study, sitting on a chair in the window rocking backwards and forwards sucking her thumb, sobbing.

He shut the front door and locked it to keep her safe while he went in search of Muriel. She was on her knees in front of her china cabinet, giving it a good clear-out.

'Muriel, my dear, we have a problem.'

'What's that?'

'Beth is sitting in my study, crying.'

'Oh dear. Ring the school, they'll be looking for her.' She got up from her knees and headed for the study. Over her shoulder she said, 'Ring the rectory, too. On the upstairs phone, then she won't hear. I'll sit with her.'

Muriel's heart bled when she recognised the utter desolation Beth was feeling. 'Oh, my dear. Will you let Moo sit you on her knee?'

'Moo, Moo, where's my mummy?'

When Muriel had got her safely seated on her lap she answered, 'Well, Beth, before your mummy got you, she was a doctor, you know.'

'I know.'

'And she was a very good doctor, too. Everybody loved her.'

'Mummy love me?'

'She does, darling, yes, she does. Very much. You and Alex.'

'And Daddy?'

'Oh yes, and Daddy too. Well, now your mummy has the chance to help poorly people again. You'd like that, wouldn't you, for Mummy to help poorly people?'

'Little girls too, Moo Moo?'

'Oh yes. She gives medicine to little girls and little boys to make them better. So that's good, isn't it?'

'I need medicine. I've got a tummy ache.'

'Oh dear.'

'A really truly bad tummy ache.'

Ralph, meanwhile, had heard the bell and opened the door to Peter. 'She's in my study with Muriel,' he said, reassuringly.

'Very sorry about this. Thank you so much for taking her in.'

'She came in by herself. I'd left the door open for a moment and in she popped.'

'Thanks anyway. It's terribly worrying.'

'Daddy, got a truly bad tummy ache, need Mummy's medicine.'

'Well, I've got some at home.'

'All right then.'

She slipped down from Muriel's knee and, taking Peter's hand, pulled him towards the door.

'Aren't you going to say something to Muriel?'

'Thank you, Moo Moo. Come on, Daddy. Go home.'

Peter half-smiled a goodbye to Muriel, but his eyes were grim with both temper and despair.

6

Muriel called on Caroline that same afternoon. She was anxious and had decided to take the bull by the horns. She would tackle Caroline – something she was not accustomed to doing, but she was so moved by Beth's distress that she felt compelled to interfere. No, not interfere, just *talk*. She'd been worried by the thin line of Peter's lips as he'd left the house, and she knew by instinct that things were not well at the rectory.

'Muriel, how lovely! Do come in.'

'Are you free to talk for a moment?'

'Yes, of course.'

'Is Peter in?'

'No – why? Is it him you've come to see?'

'No, it's you actually.'

'Thank you very much indeed for taking pity on Beth this morning. I really do not know what we're going to do about her. I thought she'd be so happy to go to playgroup.'

'Well, she isn't, is she?'

Caroline's shoulders slumped. 'No, you're right there. Come in the sitting room, please. Do sit down. Sylvia's just taken the twins to see Harriet and Fran so we've got a while before they'll be back. You're quite right, of course. I just don't know what to do next.'

'You must be very worried.'

'I am. Peter is angry but of course he won't say it's because I'm working – yet I know that's what he thinks it is. I can see that it might be true, but I don't know how to solve it. Beth pretended to have a bad tummy and said she couldn't eat anything, but as soon as I got home she ate an enormous lunch. The two things don't add up.'

'I can remember when I was a little girl first starting school, I got tummy ache too, and my mother had to come all the way from the Garden House to collect me. Within five minutes of getting home I was playing with my dolls as happy as a lark. I remember the stomach ache felt very genuine.'

'You were fretting?'

'Of course. It took a couple of weeks for my father to see through this and then he put his foot down and made me stay at school. In those days, you see, they weren't quite so understanding as we are nowadays. But at least I knew my mother was at hand if I needed her.'

'So what are you telling me?'

'I think Beth is feeling deserted. All of a sudden she is expected to go to playgroup and settle down, while at the same time her mother has apparently begun disappearing. And where has she gone? You know – I know – Peter knows – but *Beth doesn't*. For all she can tell, you could have gone to the moon, and might never be coming back.'

'Would it be better if I gave it up?'

'Not yet. You've a brain, Caroline, and I can quite see you need to use it.'

'I do. I've loved being at home all this time, but suddenly it isn't quite enough. Solve it for me, Muriel.'

'I've been thinking, how about taking her to see where you work? You could go to the surgery and show her your desk and such-like. Perhaps if she has a picture of where you are in her mind, she will settle better.'

'Oh, Muriel!' Caroline stood up and grasping Muriel's shoulders, gave her a kiss on each cheek. 'Where would I be without you? Of course, it's worth a try. And, yes, you're quite right. I've done too much at all once – I see that now. But the chance came up and I took it without thinking of the consequences; it all seemed to fit in so nicely. It was asking too much of her, wasn't it?'

'I think perhaps so. Alex, you see, has taken it in his stride, but not all children are the same, are they? I must go. Ralph is wanting me to view the improvement in the cricket pitch – since yesterday, would you believe! I'm glad you and I are doing the cricket teas, and we've got Kate Pascoe to help too. Isn't that lovely?'

'It is indeed. Though I'm not in her good books, I'm afraid, because of Beth.'

'Never mind, we'll solve it.' Muriel turned back to add, 'You see, you can't let Peter take sole responsibility for her; he's got his own job to do. If he was off into Culworth every day to an office you couldn't rely on him, could you?'

'Certainly not. Thank you, Muriel, for helping me to see daylight.'

'Peter is very upset.'

'I know, and I haven't helped.'

'He's a dear, wonderful man. He's achieved so much since he came here. We hadn't – well, *I* hadn't – realised just how bad things had become; we needed him to revitalise us. In this day and age he has mountains to move in his work, you know; there's so much apathy towards the church. Well, I'd best be off. Bye bye, my dear. It will all work out, you'll see.'

*

'Tomorrow morning I'm taking the children to the surgery in Culworth.'

'Are you concerned about Beth's stomach? Is she worse?' Peter looked up from his book. He shut it with a snap as he waited for Caroline's reply.

'No, not at all. I'm taking them both to see where I go to work. Then they've got a picture of where I am when I disappear.'

'Ah, I see! That your idea?'

'Well, truth to tell it was Muriel's.'

'Muriel's?'

'Yes, she came round to see me. She'd pointed out I've done too much all at once and that's why Beth is so upset. It might work. We'll see.'

'If it does, I shall be relieved. She could be right.'

'I think she could. I owe you a thank you, Peter, for not pointing out to me that you never wanted me to work in the first place, and that it was all my fault.'

'You're right, I didn't want you to work. But at the same time I can see why you want to.'

'Are we friends again then?'

'Never been anything else but friends. It was just something we disagreed about. I love you, you see.'

'I love you, too. I'm sorry about all this.' Caroline ran her fingers through her hair.

'If it doesn't come right?'

'Ah! Well, I made a promise to you that if the children were upset then I would stop and I shall. But can I give it one more chance?'

'Of course. Take a toy or something of Beth's and put it on your desk – let her choose it. Then she'll feel there's something of her with you and you give her something to put in her pocket that belongs to you.'

'Peter, you are an angel! Of course, what a good idea.' She placed her hand on his cheek and bent to kiss him. His understanding of her and his willingness not to blame her for Beth's problem brought to the fore all her passionate love for him. Caroline knelt down in front of him between his knees. Peter put down his book and gathered her to him. He hugged her close, enjoying the scent of her, the lovely familiar feel of her warmth against his. He began moving his hands over her body, appreciating the slimness of her, the roundness of her hips, and then he took her head in his hands and kissed her lips. With his fingers he began smoothing her hair, tracing the curve of her ears, his eyes feasting on the shape of her face, her jaw, her eyebrows. Then taking her head between his hands again, he looked into her eyes. 'When shall I ever stop finding you so inviting?'

'Never, I hope, because I find *you* overwhelmingly exciting. We shall probably be still at it in our nineties!'

'Darling! You'll be such a gracious old lady.'

'Thanks very much! I don't feel like an old lady at the moment, but I am getting cramp in my foot. Ouch!' She slipped from his grasp and sat down to rub her foot. Peter pulled off her shoe and massaged her foot.

'Oh, that's better. Thanks.'

'Let's go to bed.'

'Let's. It's only half-past nine, but let's. I was going to do some jobs ready for tomorrow.'

'Let tomorrow take care of itself. Come on.' Peter pulled her to her feet and with his arm round her waist set off towards the stairs.

'We haven't locked up! I'll check the back door and the cat flap. You do the front bolts.'

Chang and Tonga were already in bed. 'Peter! Mimi's not in yet.'

'Never mind, she's always the last in, and it is early.'

'I shall worry.'

'Don't, she'll be all right. Hurry up!'

7

Before he pinned it up, Jimbo read the postcard Sylvia had brought for his Village Voice noticeboard.

'Mimi gone missing? Caroline will be upset.'

'She is. We waited all day yesterday for her to come home but she hasn't, and Dr Harris is very upset. Mimi was the first cat she had, you see, and she's quite old now – for a cat, that is.'

'Poor old thing.'

'I think she'll be back. She's the one who brings all the mice home and one day a young rat, heaven help us!'

'Oh God! Where did she put it?'

'Well, we caught her trying to struggle through the cat flap with it in her mouth, but she couldn't quite make it through and had to leave it outside.'

'Thank God for that!'

'Exactly.'

'I assume it was dead?'

'Oh no, she brings them home alive and gives them to Dr Harris.'

'What a delightful habit.'

'As you can imagine I'm not best friends with Mimi but I don't like to think of her as being missing. We're conducting a hunt in Rector's Meadow this afternoon – that's her favourite hunting ground, you see.'

'I'll put the card up right now. I'll mention it around, see if anyone's spotted her.'

'Thank you.'

'How's Beth this morning?'

'Well, she'd gone to playgroup with one of Dr Harris' scarves tied round her neck and an old handbag of hers with some treasures in it, and Dr Harris has taken BooBoo, an old toy rabbit of Beth's, with her. Fingers crossed, it seems to have worked. I've been playing with her for nearly an hour and suddenly she said I could go. So I went. But I'm going back to sneak a look in school before I go home. Dr Harris took them both to see the surgery yesterday and Beth seems more resigned now. If you find her on your chair again, please ring me, won't you?'

'Of course I shall. Straight away. Damned worrying, her floating about the village like that. Damned worrying.'

'I'll get my shopping done then. Thank you, Mr Charter-Plackett.'

'Hope the dreaded Mimi turns up.'

When Sylvia went back to the school at a quarter to twelve to collect the children she walked into a full-scale row.

Pat Duckett was standing in the hall, floormop in one hand, mop bucket by her side indignantly protesting to Kate Pascoe that the floor was clean by anyone's standards and she—

'I'm sorry Pat, but it isn't. The children laid down to do their floor exercises and every one of them was dusty and grimy when they stood up.'

'They'll 'ave to dust themselves off then, won't they? Stands to reason when the floor's been walked on all morning and it raining too! Every time someone steps outside a classroom they 'as to walk on the hall floor. Small wonder the floor gets dusty, at the very least, by the end of the morning.'

'It simply won't do – and then to eat their food in here with all that dust.'

'Well, I'm sorry *Ms* Pascoe but it isn't on my list of things to do, mopping the floor before I gets the tables out. There isn't time.'

'Time there will have to be. I can't think what the office would say if they came and saw the floor in this state.'

'And while we're putting our cards on the table, what about that cat?'

'What about it?'

'I don't never remember anyone bringing a cat to school, 'cept those days when Mr Palmer had an animal day and everybody brought something. A cat reg'lar isn't the thing in a school. Heaven knows what germs it might be bringing. Oh hello, Sylvia. What do *you* think about a cat in school?'

'To be honest, I don't know. Is there something in the regulations or anywhere?'

Kate Pascoe pointed to the floor. 'I've my class to get back to. Please see that this floor is clean before the tables are put out.' She turned on her heel and went back to her class.

Pat screwed the mop dry and began mopping. Then she leant on the mop handle and said, 'You don't want a job as school-caretaker, do yer, Sylvia?'

'No, thanks.'

'I thought not. I'm about at the end of my tether with her. And that cat. It spits if yer get too close. It 'as claws like a tiger's. I reckon it's related to a panther. Black as night, evil it is. It's got all-seeing eyes. Does my nerves no good at all.'

'You'd better leave.'

'I've half a mind to. I reckon it can put the evil eye on yer – yer know, like yer read in books. If cats start disappearing it'll be 'er that's spiriting 'em away.'

Mindful of Mimi, Sylvia went off to collect Alex and Beth, thinking over what Pat had said. It was all ridiculous of course but . . . 'There you are, come along then, you two. Had a nice morning?' Beth held up a picture for her to see.

'Oh Beth, that *is* lovely, Mummy will be pleased. What have you made, Alex? A car. That's splendid. Let's get home. We've got everything, I think. Come along then. Bye bye, Mrs Neal.' Beth's thumb was in her mouth, her lover tickling her nose, the scarf still round her neck, her handbag hanging from her arm. Alex skipped blithely along, his sister walked quietly, as though weighed down by care. Sylvia glanced down at her; at least she hadn't run off. Thank goodness.

Caroline put the children's boots on and then her own. 'Come along, children. Ready, Sylvia?'

'I am. Have you seen my gloves?'

'Here they are on the table.'

'Oh, right, so they are.'

They crossed Pipe and Nook Lane and climbed over the wall into Rector's Meadow. The children ran along in front kicking a ball while Caroline and Sylvia walked behind looking in the grass as they went and calling. The wind was keen and Caroline pulled her scarf more closely round her neck.

'Mimi! Mimi! Really, I suppose it's pointless calling. If she sees us she'll come, won't she?'

'Yes. Have you seen Kate Pascoe's cat?'

'No, but we shall tonight. That's where we're going when you sit in.'

'Oh, I hadn't realised. Pat says it's related to a panther. She doesn't like its eyes.'

'Oh, honestly!'

'That's what I thought.'

'We could try the old barn, couldn't we?' Caroline pointed to the stone barn alongside the wall adjoining the Big House estate. 'She might have got in there and can't find her way out.'

'That's an idea. Yes, we'll do that.'

They wandered all the way round the edge of the field calling for Mimi and looking in the long grass, but there was no sign of her. When they reached the barn Sylvia said, 'The door isn't locked. Never is. And look – there are places at the bottom of the door where she could have got in. It's rotting away.' She took hold of the bracket where the padlock once was and pulled the door open. It opened about a foot and then jammed and they all squeezed in.

Once a barn for holding winter-feedstuff for cattle, it still had bale upon bale of hay stacked against the walls. The thick stone walls had withstood a couple of centuries of weather and were still as strong as the day it was built. The roof, a sturdy construction of timber and tiles, was intact; the only light came from two square openings high up at the apex of the opposite shorter walls. The hay was dry and old and long past its usefulness.

Caroline called, 'Mimi! Mimi!' but there was no answering mew, only a scuffling amongst the bales. 'This place is huge. It would make a fantastic house, wouldn't it?'

Sylvia said, 'I heard something then.'

'Did you? I didn't. Do you think it's Mimi?' Alex and Beth were climbing onto a bale and jumping off with great shrieks of delight. 'Mind! Careful, you two.'

Sylvia's eyes widened when she heard the rustling noises again. She mouthed rather than said, 'Rats?' Caroline looked at her in silent horror.

'I've always had a dread of . . .'

'So have I.'

'Come along, children, Mimi's not here. Let's go home. Mummy's feeling cold. A hot drink, I think, when we get back. Time to go, darlings, come along. We're wasting our time. I'd rather find her dead than not *know*. That's the hardest part, not knowing.' Despairingly she called again: 'Mimi! Mimi! No, it's no good. Let's go. Don't forget your ball, Alex. I wonder if she's gone into Sykes Wood? I'll try there tomorrow perhaps, as a last resort.'

'Peter, I've just had a thought. If Kate is a vegan, what on earth shall we have to eat?'

'I'd forgotten that. I can see I shall be having a bacon sandwich when I get home to fill me up.'

'I can't think what vegans make for a dinner, can you?'

'You'll soon find out.'

'Ready?'

The lights were on at every window in the schoolhouse when they got there. Caroline was full of anticipation. She loved seeing other people's houses; it gave one such a brilliant clue as to what made them tick.

Peter rang the bell and they heard footsteps approaching the door. 'Do come in. Isn't it cold tonight?' Kate was in black, a kind of evening dress with long sleeves and bugle bead decoration on the bodice. Caroline had come in a smart winter dress and felt she'd made an error of judgement, but it was too late now. Kate's long black hair was plaited and the end of the plait fastened up on top of her head with a wide velvet ribbon. It left her long thin neck quite bare; around her throat was a selection of thin silver necklaces with pendants of one kind or another hanging from each one.

Tonight she wore make-up – a magenta lipstick with magenta eyeshadow between her eyebrow and eyelashes and a black line all around her eye. Peter found her rather alarming; Caroline was amused. What kind of statement was she making here? She was like something out of a nightmare. Her long pointed nails – the kind which made Caroline wonder however the owner managed to achieve even the simplest task without the nails getting in the way, were painted to match her lipstick. Somehow Caroline didn't fancy food prepared by hands which looked like that. But then she shrugged her shoulders; she was being quite ridiculous. What on earth had long nails to do with the food she ate?

What really took her breath away was the decoration of the narrow entrance hall. Where she, Caroline, would have used light colours to give the passage width, Kate had used dark navy. The ceiling was light blue with silver stars of different sizes stuck to the ceiling. The same treatment had been given to the tiny sitting room – dark walls and a light blue ceiling, but this time golden suns with rays coming from them were stuck all over the ceiling. God! If Michael Palmer could see this!

Peter said, 'I love your decorations – they are so unusual. You must have worked awfully hard to get all this done in such a short time.'

'I have. At the weekend I stayed up all night to get finished. I'm glad you like it. I know it's not to everyone's taste, but I've tired of magnolia and all that dratted stippling effect and stencilling everyone's been doing for years. Thought I'd have a change.'

Caroline seated herself on a sofa draped with Indian throw-overs. She sank almost to the floor, the sofa was so soft. Peter sat in a chair more suited to a tiny elderly aunt than a man of six feet five. He dwarfed it and it looked in serious danger of collapsing under his weight.

'A drink?' Kate suggested. 'The meal's almost ready.' They both nodded. 'I have orange juice or elderflower wine. Or dandelion if you prefer.'

'Well, I've never tried either so I'll plump for the elderflower, thanks.'

'So will I.' Peter raised an eyebrow as Kate left to get the glasses. He mouthed 'Help' and went to sit on the sofa beside Caroline. She kept her face straight and looked round the room. The pictures were of wild stark landscapes and one was of sea crashing onto dark, forbidding rocks. There was a kind of threatening effect to the pictures which quite unnerved Caroline. How could Kate be so pleasant and yet like – actually choose to buy – such forbidding prints?

'This elderflower is very refreshing, Kate, very pleasant.' Caroline lifted her glass in a toast to Kate.

'It is, isn't it? The dandelion is very potent, so you can try some before you go home. At least you don't have to drive!'

'Do you make the wines yourself?'

'I do but not this one; a friend gave me this.'

'Can I help with the dinner at all?'

'Oh no. Well, you could carry things in. I'll just check the potatoes and then I'll give you a shout.'

Peter sipped his elderflower wine and silently gazed at the decor and the furnishings. It really was quite amazing. He felt something brush his leg and he jumped. He looked down to see what had touched him, and found himself staring into a pair of the greenest eyes he had ever seen. 'Good grief, it's a massive cat.'

'Shush!' Caroline looked towards the kitchen door, and hoped Kate hadn't heard him.

'It's a monster! I thought Tonga was big but this is ridiculous. Hello, puss.' Cat spat and Peter hastily pulled back his hand.

Kate called from the kitchen, 'Ready, Caroline!'

'I'm coming.'

Between them they carried in a huge selection of salads. The protein was provided by what looked like meatloaf. There were thick slices of French bread and a dish with what looked like butter in it, but couldn't be. She brought in hot new potatoes in a covered dish and invited them to sit down.

Peter admitted that out of ignorance he thought vegans lived on the odd lettuce leaf and a bowl of rice. 'Obviously I'm very wrong. This looks like a feast fit for a king!'

Kate nodded her head in acknowledgement. 'Certainly not, Rector, that really does show abysmal ignorance.'

'I do beg your pardon.' He bent his head to say a silent grace.

'This is a nutloaf I made myself to an old Turkish recipe. The salads are self explanatory. The spread is not butter but made from soya beans.'

They began to help themselves and Kate whilst filling her plate said, 'Beth seems to have had a better morning, Caroline.'

'Yes, she does. I'm hoping we've turned a corner. It just needed a bit of careful thought and we think we've found the solution.'

Peter helped himself to a pile of new potatoes and said, 'Tell me, Kate, are you settling in OK?'

'Oh yes, thank you. Bit of a blip this afternoon, though, I'm afraid.'

'Oh? Anything I can help you with?'

'Pat Duckett has given in her notice.'

'I'm sorry to hear that. She's been at the school a long time.'

Kate rolled her eyes heavenwards. 'So she frequently tells me.'

'Does she give a reason?'

'Yes – me.'

'You?'

'Yes. I won't have things slipshod, you know. It won't do. She's got very lax.'

'I see. I'm surprised. Then we shall have to find someone quick. Still, we have a whole month, don't we? She'll have given a month's notice.'

'Well, no, she hasn't. She's leaving on Friday. Says she's not bothered about her pay.'

'Oh? That's most unlike Pat. She's been so reliable. The office will want an explanation of such a hurried departure.'

'I know. I wondered if there were any mothers who come to mind who might be interested.'

Caroline was enjoying the food beyond her wildest expectations. It was so spicy and aromatic, she had to give credit where it was due. 'This food is delicious,' she enthused. 'I'd love to try a few of your recipes. How about Bel Tutt?'

Kate looked puzzled. 'I don't know that dish. Is it good?'

'No, it's not a recipe! It's a person. She might be interested in the job.'

'Oh, I see.'

'Dicky Tutt is the Scout Leader and Bel helps. Any nonsense and Bel wades in. They've all learned to respect her!'

'If you'll give me her number, I'll give her a ring.'

Peter offered his help. 'Better still, I've some paperwork for Dicky which I'm dropping into his house tomorrow. I'll have a word with Bel myself if you like. Explain the situation.'

'Thank you, Rector, please do that. If she's interested I'll see her any time out of school hours.'

Next morning, Peter had a real hangover. 'This must be the result of that second glass of dandelion wine. I feel terrible, what about you?'

'Ghastly! I'm so glad I haven't got surgery today. I've a dreadful pain in my head.'

'Same here. Quite weird, actually. I keep thinking ridiculous thoughts.'

'She did warn us it was potent. I shall stick to water if we go again.'

'So shall I. I'm not going running this morning – I just can't. I'll dash off and say my prayers and then come home. Jimbo will laugh. He always declares he's much fitter than me, and boasts he could do double the distance if he had the time. The children are still asleep.'

'They're tired from playgroup.'

'You stay in bed till they wake up.'

'I shall. I wonder if Mimi will come home today? I'm going walking in Sykes Wood this morning, see if I can find her.'

'Not by yourself?'

'No, Sylvia said she would come too. Even though she has never liked Mimi.'

'I'm not surprised.'

'Peter!' He grinned. Caroline snuggled down; he went to the bathroom and groaned when he saw his reflection in the mirror. He looked appalling and felt it.

Peter was in his study when he heard the doorbell ring. Shortly afterwards, Sylvia tapped on his door.

'Rector, have you time for a word with Pat Duckett?'

'Of course. Come in, Pat.'

'Thank you, Rector.'

'Here, sit down, make yourself comfortable. Is it too early for coffee, Sylvia?'

'Seeing as it's you sir, no, it's not. Milk and sugar, Pat?'

'Just milk, please.'

When she'd left the room, Peter turned to his visitor. 'Now, Pat, what can I do for you?'

Pat peered closely at him. 'Aren't you well, Rector?'

'I'm fine, thank you.'

'Oh, but you don't look it. Anyways, Rector, I've come to tell you that I've made a right mess of things. Given in my notice.'

'Kate Pascoe told me so last night when we went to her house for dinner.' Pat tut-tutted at this. 'I'm very sorry indeed. You've always done such a good job, come hail or shine. Seven, eight years is it now?'

'Thereabouts. I got on really well with Mr Palmer. We 'ad our ups and downs but it was mostly ups. But . . . well, I can't see eye to eye with *Ms* Pascoe. I'm not saying she's in the wrong, it's just that we're not on the same wavelength, if you get me. We had a flaming row. She wanted this doing and that doing, all extras and some quite unnecessary, I think, and it's sending me timings all wrong and I'm nearly dizzy with it. Anyway, when I got home and cooled down I thought, You fool, Pat Duckett, giving yer notice in just when yer need the money. So I 'aven't actually written it, only *said* it – so do you think you could put in a good word for me and get me job back? I wouldn't ask but we all know how persuasive you can be.' Head on one side she grinned at him. 'Would you?'

'I very likely could, if that's what you want. I mean, why can't you get on with her?'

'I don't really know – can't put me finger on it. It's just that I'm worried, like – don't know whether I'm coming or going. Barry says I'm imagining it. Anyway, I've decided I'm being daft and I'd like to carry on and I shall try to adapt.'

Sylvia came in with the coffee. They chatted for a while as they drank it but Peter came no nearer to finding a clue as to why Pat was upset with school. It was as she said: she just didn't feel right.

'Not long now, Pat.'

Pat raised her eyebrows. 'I don't know what you mean. Oh, the wedding! Our Michelle's that excited.'

'Aren't you?'

'He's a lovely man, is Barry. Honest, hardworking, good at his job – and he really likes the children and they like him.'

'That isn't what I asked.'

Pat put down her empty mug. 'I can't quite believe it's happening to me, you see, Rector. I've had years of struggle, and never expected to be happy again. Truth to tell, I wasn't that happy with me first. Now and then I get a glimmer of how happy I'm going to be, but I'm not going to get too excited.' Pat fidgeted with her beads. 'You never know, I might be making a big mistake.'

'Well, you *are* going to be happy again – I'm sure you are. I've had a long chat with Barry and I'm positive everything will be fine. Believe me. You deserve it. Barry's a great chap.'

'He's wicked, he is.' She grinned at him. 'I won't take any more of your time, I'll be off. When that Ms Pascoe said she'd be glad for me to leave, she meant it, she really did. You could have a difficult job on your hands. If you don't succeed don't worry, it *is* my fault. After all, it might make me take the plunge and do more jobs with Jimbo. I don't quite believe in myself enough you see, to do that.'

'Jimbo's a very astute businessman. He wouldn't be asking you if he didn't believe in your capabilities.' Peter stood up and saw her to the door. 'I'll give you a ring when I've seen her. I'll do my best. Good morning, Pat. God bless you.'

'Thank you, Rector, thank you.'

8

Beth watched her mother getting her boots out from the hall cupboard, then Alex's and then her own. 'Mummy, no playgroup morning?'

'No, darling. We're going for a walk in Sykes Wood to see if we can spot Mimi.'

'Sylvie coming?'

'She is.'

'Don't like playgroup. Don't like Pascoe.'

'*Ms* Pascoe, Beth. Why?'

'Funny.'

'Oh, come on, she's nice. Here, lift your foot. That's it. You can do the other one yourself, can't you? Show Mummy.'

'Can't.'

'You can.'

'Can't.'

'*Won't*, more like. I'll do it then. Here's your coat, put it on.'

'Can't. Mummy do it.'

'Alex has got himself ready except for his buttons.'

'Beth can't.' She stuck her thumb in her mouth and took her lover from her pocket. Caroline kissed her and dressed her herself. If dressing Beth was what it took to make her happy then she'd dress her.

'Not going to playgroup 'morrow.'

'We'll see. Ready, Sylvia?'

'Coming.'

The four of them left the rectory and walked along Church Lane. The world and his wife seemed to be out and they exchanged greetings with two of the weekenders who were spending a holiday week redecorating and were off to get food at the Store, then with the gardener sweeping the drive of Glebe House. When they passed the gate to the Big House, they read its smartly painted notice telling them it was TURNHAM HOUSE and in small letters underneath *Fitch plc London and Brussels.* They climbed the stile into Sykes Wood and followed the well-worn path which led right through the middle of the woods. Alex rushed along ahead of them with Beth following slowly in his wake.

'Jimmy Glover buried his dog Sykes here, do you remember?'

'I certainly do, Dr Harris.'

'Along with all his snares; he said he buried them really deep so the foxes couldn't dig them up. Mimi! Mimi! Shout for Mimi, darlings.'

Alex and Beth shouted until they were hoarse, but Mimi didn't appear. They came to a clearing and Alex pounced on a burnt stick. Right in the middle of the clearing was a large circle of ashes and burnt branches and twigs.

'Look, Mummy, bonfire.'

'So there is.' She felt the ash. 'It's cold. Fancy having a fire in the woods in the middle of winter.'

Sylvia looked down at the ash, and poked it about with her boot. 'Could have been in the summer. It's difficult to tell when it was.'

Alex rushed to Caroline. 'There's a glove – look, Mummy. Man lost a glove.' It was a large, thick black woollen glove with a big hole in the thumb, a kind of burnt hole as though the owner had been wearing it while tending the fire. But it wasn't wet or dirty or going rotten. It had been left quite recently.

'Throw it down, Alex, there's a good boy. How odd!' Caroline shivered with the cold.

Sylvia persuaded herself she knew the answer. 'It'll be the Scouts on one of their midnight hikes. Cooking sausages and things, you know what they're like.'

'Of course, you're quite right. It will have been them. Beth, what have you found? What is it?'

'A stick, a big stick.' She dragged the stick along the ground. The end was burnt as though it had been used for poking the fire. As she dragged it along, some rags from just under the surface of the ground became entangled with it. There'd been a half-hearted attempt to bury them.

'Curiouser and curiouser!' Caroline bent down to look at the rags, which turned out to consist of an old shirt and a woman's blouse, dirty and wet.

Sylvia, still poking about with her boot in the soft loamy soil close to the ashes, suddenly glanced at Caroline to make sure she wasn't looking, and bent down to pick up something and put it in her pocket. She said, 'Let's go. It's nothing to do with us. Come on, Dr Harris, let's leave it be. I don't like it here. We shouldn't go any further. Let's turn back.'

'Very well. Come along, children, we'll go home. Mummy's cold and I'm sure you must be too. We'll have to forget looking for Mimi today.'

Sylvia was shuddering. 'There's something unpleasant here and no mistake. Hurry up, children, please. Come on, Dr Harris, let's get away from this place!'

'Why, you're shaking!'

'I am. There's things here not for the likes of us.'

'You mean it wasn't the Scouts?'

'I hope not. Baden Powell will be spinning in his grave if it was.'

'Are you psychic or something?'

'No, but there's a funny feeling here I don't like.'

'Now I'm frightened. Two grown women getting the wind up, this is ridiculous.' Nevertheless Caroline took the hands of Alex and Beth and hastened them along. Both she and Sylvia breathed a sigh of relief when they had climbed the stile and were standing out in the road. Then, they both burst out laughing.

'We are stupid, really we are!' Caroline kept tight hold of the children as Barry Jones hurtled by in his van. He waved, slammed on his brakes, came to a screeching halt, and then reversed dangerously up to them.

'Morning! What's up?'

'Oh, nothing. We just talked ourselves into being frightened in the wood back there. Sylvia reckons there's something there not for the likes of us. We're searching for my cat Mimi – she's been missing for three days now, and she's the smallest of my Siamese, so I'm worried. Don't suppose you've seen her on your travels?'

'Sorry, no I haven't. I'll keep a look out for her though. Bye, Dr Harris, keep smiling. Bye, Sylvia, bye kids!'

'There's no two ways about it. I'm going to have to accept that my Mimi is gone for ever. It's one whole week today since I last saw her.'

Jimbo offered his sympathy. 'I'm really sorry. It's downright awful not knowing, isn't it?'

'It is. Leave the card on the Village Voice noticeboard a little longer will you, Jimbo, please? Just in case. I've been round Rector's Meadow twice and once into Sykes Wood but no luck. You never know, someone might have found her though and given her a home. They might even see the card.'

'She was quite old?'

'Twelve – no, thirteen. However, there we are. No Mimi.'

'Shall you get another?'

'No, I shan't. Your two cats are all right, are they?'

'Yes, why do you ask?'

'Just wondered if we had a phantom cat-stealer, that's all. Silly of me really, but you do wonder.'

Jimbo began adding up Caroline's purchases. 'Beth's getting better at playgroup?'

'Yes, thank you – a little. Alex is perfectly all right, that's what's so odd. You'd think they'd react the same, wouldn't you?'

'That'll be ten pounds ninety-seven pence, please.'

'Thanks. Flick liking her new teacher?'

'Oh yes. Thinks she's lovely.'

'Good, I'm glad. I'll be off then.'

Caroline carried home the shopping, put it away in the fridge and the cupboards. Having decided that Mimi was a closed chapter in her life she was feeling in need of sympathy, and Peter being the only one who could satisfy her need, she went to find him. But he'd left a note on his desk to say he'd *gone to Penny Fawcett, back for lunch*.

Caroline sat down in the easy chair in his study and thought about her cat. She'd been sweet and gentle in the house, but a holy terror where hunting was concerned. Chang and Tonga had always accepted that she was the senior cat and, if she so chose, they allowed her to push them aside and finish off their food. Now, as if in answer to her thoughts, the two of them stalked into the study.

'Come on then, come up.' She patted her knee and they both jumped up onto her lap. She stroked them each in turn, enjoying their companionship. She thought about Mimi when she'd first got her, a small creamy-coloured tiny thing, soft and warm. The tears began to fall and she had to fumble in her pocket for her handkerchief. Sylvia came in.

'There's a letter come through the door for the rector. I'll— Why, whatever's the matter?'

Caroline sniffed. 'I'm being silly. I'm thinking about Mimi and how I shall miss her. But she's only a cat. I've got to keep things in perspective, haven't I?'

'Yes, but I can understand.'

'She was my first cat before I met Peter, you see, and it was lovely to come home to my flat and find Mimi waiting; it made all the difference. It's not knowing the end that's the worst. I *know* she wouldn't have gone off to live with someone else. Anyway, at least I've got these two.'

'Indeed you have.'

The children came bursting in through the door.

'And these two!!'

'Mummy, play tiddlywinks. Come on.'

Caroline pushed the cats onto the floor and stood up. 'I certainly shall. What else are mummies for? Come on.' She grinned through her tears at Sylvia and said, 'Sorry for being such a fool.'

'Not at all. I can quite understand.'

9

'Far be it from me, Ms Pascoe, to criticise your methods. Taking the children here there and everywhere is lovely, but when the end result is that it shortens the time the children spend on the three Rs, then it is *not* at all beneficial. In fact, I think it's a retrograde step.'

'Hetty! There's more to life for children of this age than pen and paper. What on earth can they find to write about if their experiences are so narrow? If they lived in a city they'd be doing all sorts of exciting things, but country children's horizons are so limited.'

'But think of the money. I know it's lovely to walk on the walls in Culworth and learn about the Romans firsthand as you might say, but that will be the second outing your children have had this term.'

'So, what's wrong with that? You can take *your* children whenever you like.'

'I know that, but you see a lot of the children round here are not very well off. Two outings in the first half of the term is a lot for their parents.'

'Nonsense! No parent minds providing money when it's to the children's advantage.'

'What if they're unemployed like the Watsons? They've got two in your class.'

'Then we shall use school funds if they can't afford it.'

'We only used to have an outing in the summer term when Mr Palmer was here.'

'Mr Palmer *isn't* here, is he? I am. And I shall be obliged if you don't keep telling me about what *used* to happen, Hetty! Now is now.'

Hetty turned to Margaret. 'What do you think, Margaret?'

'Well, I . . .'

But Hetty interrupted her. 'This business of the children coming straight into school the moment they arrive in the mornings. We've never allowed it before.'

Kate grew impatient. 'There you go again, Hetty. In the past. It won't do.'

'I'm thinking about our responsibilities. I was here at quarter past eight on Tuesday morning and there were already three children in the school. It's not right.'

'Pat Duckett is here.'

'She is not legally responsible, as well you know.'

'Oh really! What harm can come to them?'

'Once the parents realise that the children can come straight into school they'll be sending them at some ungodly hour, just to get them out of the way so they can get off to work. Speaking of ungodly, I took real exception to you talking about Hinduism in that manner yesterday. None of us are Hindu and the children must be very puzzled. They never see a coloured person from one week to the next.'

'All the more reason why they should learn about them then.'

'I disagree. What do you think, Margaret?'

'Well, I . . .'

'The rector won't be at all pleased.'

Kate smiled. 'Don't tell him then. It *is* my school.'

Hetty encouraged Margaret to support her. 'Say something, Margaret.'

'I think—'

'I have been employed as Head, and as far as I can, within the bounds of the national curriculum, I shall teach as I see fit, and if going on an expedition helps them to understand the world better, then on an expedition we shall go.'

'My children will be complaining. It makes me look mean.'

'You arrange an outing for them, then. Broaden their outlook, encompass the world if you can. Isn't that so, Margaret?'

'Oh! Yes, I supp—'

Realising she was fighting a losing battle, Hetty asked Margaret: 'Whose side are you on?'

'I don't—'

Kate got up to go. 'Time I was off. Got people coming for a meal. I'll love you and leave you.'

Hetty Hardaker waited till she was out of earshot then said bitterly, 'Well, some support I got from you, I must say.'

'You didn't give me a chance to speak.'

'I asked your opinion.'

'I know, but you interrupted or Kate did.'

'It's not right. I *know* it's not right.'

'Where shall you take your class then?'

'Heaven alone knows; I'll have to think of somewhere. I hate school outings, it's the worry of losing someone.'

Margaret gathered her things together. 'I'm off. She's only trying to do her best and she does have a point.'

'About what?'

'About the children's limited experiences.'

'You could be right.'

'I am. She's like a breath of fresh air.'

'Hmm.'

'Mr Palmer was not at all flexible, you know.'

'Yes, but the children were well-taught. We shan't be getting anyone into Prince Henry's or Lady Wortley's if we do as she says. We've three children sitting the entrance exams next week; there's not a word about that, is there?'

'There's more to life than academic success.'

'You try telling the parents that!'

'Harriet? Kate Pascoe here. Hello. Would it be possible to pop into school to see me this week? Round about four when the children have gone?'

'Why, yes, of course. Is there a problem with Flick?'

'Nothing serious, just wanted a chat.'

'I'll come today then. About four?'

'Lovely, thanks. Be seeing you!'

Harriet replaced the receiver and stood watching Fran who was glued to the children's TV. What on earth did Kate want to see her about? Flick hadn't said anything.

She dialled Jimbo's mobile phone number. 'Hello, Jimbo? Could you come home early today? Well, Kate Pascoe from the school has rung and wants me to go and see her this afternoon about four. I don't know what for, but she does. You don't have a clue, do you? No, I haven't either. Be home just before four, darling? OK, bye.'

When Flick got home Harriet asked her if she'd done anything naughty at school.

'No, of course not, Mummy. As if I would.'

'Well, no, of course I know you wouldn't, but do you have any idea why Miss Pascoe wants to see me?'

'Ms Pascoe? No, I haven't. It's my entrance exam next week – maybe it's something to do with that.'

'Oh, yes. That'll be it. Of course.'

Harriet left Jimbo with instructions about Fran and wended her way to the school.

Kate offered her a coffee but Harriet declined. 'You have one if you wish. Don't let me stop you.'

'I will, if that's all right. Hard work, teaching.'

'I'm sure it is. Do we have a problem? Is that why you've asked to see me?'

'Not a problem as such.' She stirred her coffee while she found the right words. 'I do worry about Flick, do you?'

'Not particularly.'

'I see. She's very uptight, isn't she?'

'I wouldn't have said so.'

'That's how she comes across in school. Always a bundle of energy, first with her hand up, eager to please. Very competitive.'

'She comes from a competitive family.'

Kate smiled. 'Of course. But I think she needs to relax a little and let the world go by, don't you know.'

'She does, at home. Reads books by the score, laid on her bed.'

'That's it, you see. Reading . . . not very relaxing, is it?'

'What do you suggest?'

'My suggestion is,' Kate paused and eyed Harriet carefully as though debating the wisdom of what she was going to say next, 'she doesn't go ahead with the entrance exam.'

Harriet was startled. 'Not go ahead! What can you possibly mean?'

'I mean she should go to a school where, unlike Lady Wortley's, there will be less pressure to succeed. I'm pretty sure she'll find the stress of a high-flying school too much and she could have serious problems.'

'Just a moment. You are basing your opinions on, what is it, three weeks experience of her? You know she's very bright, and Lady Wortley's is where she needs to be to reach her potential.'

'Harriet, there are other ways of reaching one's potential without stretching oneself to breaking point.'

Harriet frowned. 'Breaking point? What on earth are you talking about? Are you having this same conversation with the other parents?'

'Oh yes, I am. I think it's terribly important that the children have an all-round experience in school, and I honestly think Prince Henry's and Lady Wortley's are very one-sided.'

'Well, Kate Pascoe, I'm afraid Flick will have to put up with a one-sided life if she gets in, and let's hope she does, because *she* can't wait to get there. I'm sorry, but we have no intention of withdrawing her from the exam, and I should imagine you will find the same attitude with the other parents. I'm amazed, I truly am.'

'You'd rather put your prestige before the well-being of your daughter?'

'My prestige?' Harriet suddenly began to feel very angry.

'You know – "Oh, my daughter is at Lady Wortley's. She'll meet all the right people . . ." et cetera, et cetera.'

'I think you've overstepped the mark, Kate. Your opinions about class have no place here. You can take it from me that my daughter is sitting the exam, full stop. I'll leave you now, the boys will be home shortly – from Prince Henry's I might add – and they're in need of TLC when they get in.'

'There you are, you see. It's the pressure.'

'Pressure, my foot!'

'Please don't be upset with me, I'm only thinking of Flick's welfare.'

'I'm sorry. Yes, of course you are. Thanks for talking with me anyway. I'll speak to Jimbo about what you've said, but I already know his answer.'

'Thanks for coming. I'm just sorry I haven't persuaded you.'

'You won't, I'm afraid. Good afternoon.'

'Bye.'

'So what do you think? Are we being too pushy? I was so wild I gave her a real mouthful, I'm afraid. I could have bitten my tongue out afterwards.'

Jimbo shifted his arm from under Harriet's shoulder and rubbed the pins and needles away. 'My dear Harriet, I love Kate Pascoe. She fills the eye every time she comes in the Store, but – and I mean but – she has odd ideas and I think this must be her oddest.'

'But what if she's right? I mean, look at Alex. Goes to playgroup as happy as Larry, yet Beth can hardly bear to walk through the door. Two children from the same mould and their reactions so different. Perhaps like they say an onlooker sees most of the game. Maybe Flick isn't like the boys; maybe she couldn't stand the pressure. She did have that fearful accident.'

'I know she did, but she's got guts. Even the specialist Archie what's-his-name said so. No, I think we're doing the right thing. She's got to be given her chance just like the boys. If she doesn't get in, then all well and good – it's meant to be.' He paused. 'But she will!'

'Jimbo! No wonder she's so competitive.' Harriet turned on her side and looked into his eyes from three inches away. 'Do you really find Kate attractive?'

'Of course, what man wouldn't?'

'Really. I can't see it, you see.'

'Well, you're a woman.'

'I can see Simone Paradise is attractive.'

'God, that woman and Kate make a pair. Rice this and nut that, soya milk and pasta that. How they survive I don't know.'

'They were talking outside the Store the other day. Simone's children were running wild as usual and she took not a blind bit of notice of them. They were very engrossed. Maybe they were swopping recipes!'

'There is a kind of recognisable affinity between them, isn't there?'

'They don't dress alike though, and they've got totally different lifestyles.'

'I know, but there is some indefinable something or other. However, give me a solid well-fed woman like yourself any day.'

'I know I've put weight on since I had Fran, but really.'

'Come here to your Jimbo. God, I love you.'

'I'm glad. Will you talk to Flick or shall I?'

'I shall. I shall tell her we'll love her just the same whatever happens. Too competitive indeed!'

10

Ralph received a letter from Mr Fitch outlining the financial arrangements for the cricket club. He was halfway through reading it when he broke off to admire the headed notepaper, which had *Turnham Malpas Cricket Club* at the top. The words were printed in old-fashioned type, a little like the Ye Olde Teashoppe signs painted above so many pretentious cafés. In smaller type below it said *President: H. Craddock Fitch.*

'H. Craddock Fitch? Muriel?'

'Coming.' She appeared in the doorway dressed for going out.

'Muriel! That man up there – is there no end to his conniving? He's put his name on the cricket club notepaper as president.'

'Ralph! No, he can't have done. He promised.'

'I know, but he damn well has, after he agreed. Right, that's it. The knives are out.'

'What shall you do?'

'I'm not sure. Confrontation? He'll only laugh.'

'Is he at the Big House at the moment?'

'Possibly – he has signed the letter personally. But his terms are very, very reasonable. No rent to pay on the pavilion for two years – which is far longer than I had hoped. We shall be on a sound financial footing by then. He's providing all the equipment, we can't grumble at that, though how we can take ourselves seriously with *Fitch plc* emblazoned across our chests I don't know.'

Muriel sat down and began to laugh. 'Oh really, you do take this cricket business far too much to heart. It's only a game.'

'Only a game!' Ralph was appalled. 'My dear, I have played cricket all over the world. It is not a game to be treated lightly. A piece of home, no matter the temperature or the altitude, a game which cuts a swathe through race, creed and colour. I remember once in Venezuela . . .'

'Ralph, I have no time for cricket stories. I have to be off – Celia Prior will be here any moment now. We're having lunch together, I told you yesterday.'

'In Culworth?'

'Yes, she's taking me in her car. I've left you some lunch out in the kitchen.'

'Thank you, my dear. You enjoy yourself. She's very nice.'

'She is.'

'Arthur is going to be our official score-keeper.'

'Oh, how lovely. There's Celia's car. Bye bye, dear.' She kissed his cheek, and left in a flurry of lost gloves and a handbag she'd put down somewhere but couldn't remember where.

Ralph stood watching Muriel get into Celia's little Rover. Well, he'd better find out if old Fitch was in residence, and if he was, he'd have to sort him out. The damned fellow didn't behave according to the rules of a gentleman. He could deal with him if he did. He and old Fitch didn't . . . what was it Muriel said the other day? Oh, that was it: he and old Fitch 'didn't sing from the same hymn-sheet'.

'I changed my mind.' Craddock Fitch tapped the ash from his cigar into the cut-glass ash-tray on his desk.

'Changed your mind?'

'Yes. I thought, damn it, I'm rebuilding the pavilion, I'm providing all the gear – why *shouldn't* I be president?'

'I thought we'd agreed.'

'We had.'

'This is a bit infra dig.'

'Don't quote your Latin tags at me, Ralph Templeton, just to impress me with your education. Take it or leave it – Craddock Fitch is President. Now, I have another meeting in five minutes. Is there anything else?'

'No, nothing else. But you disappoint me.'

Mr Fitch said he was sorry, but the tone of his voice implied he didn't care a fig about disappointing anyone.

'Good morning.' Ralph stood and left the library seething.

Needing to let off steam to someone who understood his mood he went to the Store.

'Morning, Jimbo. Got a minute?'

'For you, yes.' He called to his assistant to attend the till and then invited Ralph into the storeroom at the back.

He took off his boater and laid it on a shelf and invited Ralph to sit on his stool.

'Well? I can see you're very annoyed.'

'I am. Fitch has changed his mind.'

'About the pavilion?'

'Oh no, not about that. He loves the idea of his name above the door too much. No, it's not that.' Ralph paused, then: 'He's decided to be president.'

'The devil he has! I thought you said he'd agreed for it to be you?'

'He did.'

'Everyone's going to be very upset,' Jimbo predicted. 'He'll poke his interfering nose into everything we do. He won't be a president in name only, you can bet your life on that.'

'Exactly. But you be careful, Jimbo. I know how much you have at stake with him businesswise, so don't do anything silly, will you? You see, not being a gentleman he doesn't play by the same rules as you and me.'

'There's no way we can find the money to rebuild the pavilion on our own. Look at the first estimate we got – what was it, thirty-five thousand pounds? You'd think we were repairing Buckingham Palace!'

'Much as I should like to step in and pay for it, I really can't. Got to see Muriel's well provided for.' Ralph paused for a moment. 'And, of course, I've sunk a great deal of money into the houses in Hipkin Gardens.'

'But what a gesture. You've brought eight families into Turnham Malpas who wouldn't have had a cat in hell's chance of being here otherwise. It's going to make such a difference to the school. That's worth something by anyone's standards.'

Ralph stood up. 'Thank you. I've taken up enough of your time, so I'll be off. I shall take this blow like a true gentleman, and say not another thing to him about it!' Ralph smiled wryly at Jimbo, shook hands and left.

The bar in The Royal Oak simmered with the news of Mr Fitch deciding to be president.

'Who told you, Willie?' Jimmy asked.

'Malcolm, when he left the milk.'

'How does he know?'

'How does he know anything? He hears all his news from all the housewives he chats up on his round.'

Jimmy drained the last of his ale, slapped his tankard down on the table and said, 'Well, I for one feel right upset. We all know it should be Ralph. But then old Fitch is paying for the pavilion and that. I bet the bats will be the best money can buy.'

'Yes, and then you know what?'

'What?'

'He'll expect the team to be top every season.'

'That's his trouble yer see, always 'as to be best.' Jimmy scowled. 'Nothing about the game. Now Ralph would see it as how good a game yer played and that, but not his nibs, oh no. I don't know for certain but I bet he's giving a cup.'

'Two!'

Jimmy laughed joyously, and thumped the table with his fist. 'I knew it! I knew it!'

The other drinkers glanced up and smiled.

'Tell us the joke, Jimmy,' someone shouted.

'Old Fitch is giving two cups for the cricket.'

They all laughed uproariously.

'Typical.'

'Show-off.'

'He's like a great big kid.'

'Thinks he can buy his way in – well, he can't.'

'Not likely. The laugh is he doesn't realise we know what he's up to. Thinks we're daft.'

'Still, we can take the benefits and laugh like drains when we gets home.'

'Yer right there! What else can we screw out of him, eh?'

'Nice smart chairs for us to sit on instead of lolling about on the grass?'

'China cups for us tea!'

'Waitress service!'

'Champagne when we win!'

'The list is endless!'

They all fantasised a while longer about Mr Fitch and his generosity and then one group in particular put their heads together and became conspiratorial.

Jimmy nodded his head in their direction. 'Wonder what they're up to? No good, by the looks of it.'

Willie twirled his glass round on its little mat, and then casually remarked: 'Heard anything odd about Sykes Wood lately?'

'No. Why?'

'My Sylvia and Dr Harris found an old bonfire in there in that clearing where the old charcoal-burners used to be. Remember?'

'Bit before my time.'

Willie was annoyed by his flippancy. 'You know what I mean. I'm serious. 'Ave yer?'

'No. Nothing funny about 'aving a bonfire, is there?'

'No, but Sylvia got really frightened. They'd gone to look for Dr Harris' cat. It's gone missing, yer know. Mimi, it's called. Well, she . . .'

'Yes?'

'If I tell you something, can I have yer absolute promise not to tell anyone?'

'Hope to die.' Jimmy drew his finger across his throat and bent his head closer.

'Sylvia found something.'

'What? Like a skellington or something?'

'No.' Willie drew closer. 'She found Mimi's collar.'

'No!'

'Right close by the bonfire – not in it but near it.'

'What did Dr Harris say?'

'Sylvia never told her. Bent down and popped it in 'er pocket and didn't let on.'

'Collar, yer say?'

'Yes.'

'Funny, that.'

'Exactly. Then Sylvia got this strange feeling and begged Dr Harris to go home. She felt all shaky. Unfastened it was, the collar, and the buckle quite stiff, so it weren't no accident it came off. It hadn't got pulled off while Mimi was climbing a tree or anything; it had been *taken* off. Found the collar but not the cat.'

'Strange. But 'ow did she know it was Mimi's collar?'

'Her collar's brown to match the markings on her face, and it 'as a little identification thing on it. So she knows.'

'But she hasn't told Dr Harris?'

'Well, she was going to later, like, but she didn't know how she was going to tell her and she kept putting it off and then one day she found her crying about the cat, and didn't like to say anything, in case she made matters worse. So I've said she's to tell the rector and see what he thinks.'

'That's best. I'll 'ave a wander round there, see if I find anything. I knows them woods like the back of my 'and.'

'Thanks, Jimmy. I 'oped yer would. If anyone should know them woods it'll be you, considering 'ow much poaching yer did in there. But not a word. Dr Harris mustn't find out from anyone except the rector.' Willie tapped the side of his nose and Jimmy winked in agreement.

Sykes Wood, eh? He knew just where Willie meant. The charcoal-burners' cottages had long since disappeared, most of the stones carted away for building other houses years and years ago, but the clearing was still there. Odd that. He'd have a look tomorrow before he went to work.

11

'Mummy! Mummy!' Flick slammed the front door and raced through to the kitchen. 'Mummy, we've been on a walk.'

'Where to?'

'Sykes Wood. We've been communing with nature.'

Harriet folded up the ironing board and went to the fridge to get Flick her drink. 'What does one do to commune with nature?'

'Well, one of the things we did was to hug a tree.'

'Hug a tree? Whatever next.'

'It's all to do with listening to what the tree says to you.'

'And what did yours say to you? Here's the biscuit tin. Want one?'

Flick chose a Bourbon and bit a huge piece off it so her mouth was too full to answer. Harriet said, 'I would have thought that with your exam tomorrow, a bit of hard work would have been more appropriate.'

Flick sipped her milk and then began, 'Well, Kate said that—'

' "Kate said"? Ms Pascoe, surely.'

'She says that as we are in our last year we can call her Kate.'

'Well, I don't approve at all.'

'Get up to speed, Mummy. You're so old-fashioned. Though Mrs Hardaker did say *she* didn't like us calling Ms Pascoe Kate, and *she* thought we should be working but Ms Pascoe said "Nonsense" and Mrs Hardaker's lips went all straight like they do when she gets cross. She said, "Miss Pascoe, I really think—" But Ms Pascoe just tossed her head and said, "Come along, Class Three, away from these four walls out into the world, for another brilliant experience" so we did.'

'So what did you hear when you hugged your tree?'

'Well, I didn't hear anything actually, because there were creepy-crawlies all in the cracks in the bark and I couldn't concentrate in case they got in my hair.'

'So you didn't have a brilliant experience.'

'No, it was a bit disappointing. Kate says trees scream when they get a branch chopped off or get cut down. She says when the world was young we would have been able to hear them but not now. That's dreadful, isn't it? I never thought they could feel hurt. I shall worry now. Shall I go and rest ready for tomorrow?'

Harriet laughed. 'That's your way of saying you'll go and join Fran watching television, is it?'

'Yes.'

'Well, it's not for long. She's getting square eyes, absolutely hypnotised she is and doesn't understand one tenth of what she watches, so you must get her to play in a while.'

'OK.'

Flick came back from the day of examinations exhausted. Harriet had collected her in the car at three o'clock and when she saw how weary Flick looked she began to have reservations about her angry retort to Kate.

'How did it go? Everything all right?'

'Mummy, I'm so tired. It was quite exciting though. Two girls burst into tears, another one fainted, and one went out to be sick. The lunch was lovely, and the teachers! They were so kind.'

'And the exam?'

'Oh, that. Quite easy, actually.'

Harriet's heart sank. Quite easy? Oh dear. That could mean she hadn't understood what was required of her. 'Well, I'm glad. We'll just have to wait and see. You won't have to be too disappointed if you don't get in. Daddy and I, Grandma Sadie and the boys and Fran will all love you just the same, you know.'

'I know. Daddy's already told me that about five times.'

'Sorry, but it's true.'

'I know.' Flick looked out of the car window. Parents! She knew she would get in. It was where she was destined to be and she couldn't wait to play lacrosse – such a distinguished game. She'd seen some of the girls going out to the playing-fields from the window of the examination room, and longed to join them. The uniform! Oh, roll on, September! 'When I get home I shall give Fran a big hug and tell her all about it,' she declared, 'then she'll know for when it's her turn, and I shall want a cup of tea and a piece of cake.'

'OK, fine. You can go in the Store and choose a fancy cream one if you like.'

'Great! Shall I have to pay? I've no money on me.'

'You know Daddy's rules.'

'Yes.' Flick sighed.

Harriet dropped her off outside the Store with a pound coin in her hand. 'Don't be long. I'll put the kettle on.'

Flick decided to wander around the Store for a moment; it seemed a long time since she'd been in there and it was only right she should know what was going on. She'd have to tell Daddy that the greetings card shelves were not quite as full as they could be, and that his new assistant was spending too much time chatting instead of taking the money quickly when there was a queue. People hated waiting. Ms Pascoe came in.

'Hello, Kate! I had a lovely time at the exam, I've just got back. Did you miss me?'

'Of course I did. Everything all right?'

'Oh yes, thanks. It's lovely, I hope I get in.'

'If that's what you want, so do I.'

'I do. I'm buying a cream cake for a treat.'

'Some fresh fruit would do you more good.'

Flick laughed and tossed her head. 'But I'm having a cream cake, sorry!'

She lingered by the video-lending shelf and pondered whether or not to ask Mummy if she could borrow one. Being short she couldn't be seen over the top of the stand and quite by mistake she overheard two women talking. One of them was Kate Pascoe. 'Ten o'clock. Tonight.'

The other voice said 'Righteo. We'll be there.' Flick slipped quietly to the end of the shelving and peeped round the corner. It was Simone Paradise who had answered.

She bought her cream cake and went home, and told Fran all about the exam, and watched television and fell asleep for a short while dreaming of playing lacrosse wearing that wonderful purple sweater she'd seen on the girls that very afternoon.

'Harriet! This damned tie won't behave itself. Help! Rescue me, please, I'm running late.'

'You never have been able to do these ties. Why don't you buy one of those made-up ones?'

'I have bowed to modern technology in all corners of my life but I will not bow to a made-up tie. That is definitely sartorially *verboten*.'

'OK, OK. There we are. You look good. Much better in that suit now you've lost weight.'

'Thank you – I do, don't I? More youthful, don't you know.'

'Hurry up!'

Flick was reading Fran a bedtime story and she shouted through the bedroom door. 'Why isn't Mummy going?'

'It's all men tonight, my dear child.'

'I thought Ms Pascoe and Mrs Paradise were going.'

'Certainly not, though I mightn't mind Ms Pascoe, she's a cracker.'

Harriet, standing in the doorway, said, 'Why did you think they were going?'

'I heard them saying they were meeting at ten o'clock. So I thought they must be going where Daddy's going.'

'Ten o'clock? You must have misheard. They would have said seven o'clock.'

'I'm not daft, Mummy.'

Harriet shrugged her shoulders and went in to kiss Fran good night. 'Good night, my sweetheart.'

Fran lay on her side, snuggled up to the cuddliest teddy bear her grandmother had been able to find. Her long dark lashes fluttered as she began dropping asleep, one hand tucked under a rosy cheek. 'Ni', ni'.'

'Time for your bath, Flick, you must be tired. Thanks for reading the story.'

Jimbo shrugged on his overcoat and gave Harriet a hug. She straightened his silk scarf and kissed his cheek.

'Have a good time.'

'I will. Be all right?'

'Of course. I won't wait up.'

Harriet stood at the door watching him start up the car and waved as he turned up Stocks Row. As she locked the door the thought crossed her mind, what on earth had Simone Paradise and Kate Pascoe got in common? Not a blind thing as far as she could see.

Harriet had decided to spend the evening while Jimbo was out, going over the accounts on the computer in the study. She'd just switched on and was checking through in her mind which aspect she would take a look at first when she heard the front door being unlocked.

'Jimbo? Is that you? Hello-o-o?'

'Only me, darling.'

'Mother!' Harriet went into the hall. 'I didn't expect you tonight.'

'Thought I'd keep you company. Where are the boys?'

'Scouts. Coffee or something stronger?'

'Stronger. You'd better get one for yourself. You might need it.'

'Why, what's the matter?'

'I need your advice.'

'*My* advice – since when?'

'Since last night. I'll sit down.'

'Of course. Whisky?'

'And water.'

They sat in the study, Harriet patiently waiting to hear what she was supposed to be advising about.

Sadie swirled the whisky glass round and round in her hand. She was elegantly dressed as always, her long slim legs in fine nylon tights and smart high-heeled shoes, her outfit a straight black skirt, silver-grey long-sleeved silk shirt, and a scarf loosely tied around her throat. Harriet admired her as she sat deep in thought sipping her whisky. 'Well, I'm waiting?'

'I'm thinking of getting married.'

'I beg your pardon?'

'Like I said, I'm thinking of getting married.'

'To whom?'

'Craddock Fitch.'

Harriet was stunned. She couldn't believe she'd heard correctly. 'You? Marriage to Craddock Fitch? Are you pulling my leg?'

'As if I would. He's asked me and I'm almost ready to say yes.'

'I see. Well, you did know him when he was a strip of a lad. I was aware you were seeing a lot of him, but *marriage* . . . Are you sure?'

'Are you asking that as a fully mature adult or as a child of mine?'

'Ah! At times like this the two are very mixed. It's difficult to know which I am at the moment.'

'Exactly. I don't know which I am, either. Am I a grown woman and a grandmother – heaven help us! – or have I gone back to being a seventeen-year-old like I was when I first refused him. Maybe I've taken leave of my senses.'

'Why *did* you refuse him?'

'I've always been independent right from the cradle, and some sixth sense told me that being married to Craddock – well, Henry as he was then – would be suffocating. He would have expected complete loyalty, complete absorption in his business affairs, because it was obvious even then that he was going to be a businessman, and I baulked at the idea of being so completely taken over. I engineered a row and that was that. He hated the idea that anyone owned him, you see, so I deliberately said something, whatever it was I can't remember exactly, to annoy him and he blew his top.'

'And now?'

'Now he's different. He respects me, which he didn't before. I can answer back without him freezing me out with his stony silences. We can discuss and argue and he listens to my opinion. And what's more, I still find him fascinating. He's not the chilly person he appears to be. Oh no! He wants to be a warm loving man, and he's trying very hard.'

'Look, Mother, if you love him, for heaven's sake marry the man. Whyever not?'

'You may be right, but . . .'

'Yes?'

'This mail-order business. I've built that up myself. Agreed, it stemmed from an idea of yours, but the work and the success has been mine – agreed? I've felt fulfilled making a success of it. I love Harriet's Country Cousin marmalades and jams, and the labels! I get a thrill every time I look at them. And the Christmas hampers are bliss! It's about the only thing apart from you that I can look back on as an achievement which is wholly mine.' Harriet nodded. 'I can hardly bear the thought of giving it all up, which I would have to do.'

'I can't stand the idea either. I'd have to get someone else to do it.'

'Obviously I'd give you my shares.'

'Well, thank you. I shall miss you and so will Jimbo.'

'I haven't said yes yet.'

'No, but I think you will. At the very least you'd keep a rein on his more blatant excesses.'

Sadie looked annoyed. 'What on earth do you mean?'

'You know, buying himself a position here in the village.'

'Oh that. They all know what he's up to, so why not if the village benefits?'

'Why not indeed!'

Sadie sat for a while staring at the carpet. She finished the last of her whisky and then said, 'I might say yes. I could very well say yes. You must understand that my will leaves everything to you and the children, so I wouldn't want you to worry about that. Craddock has quite enough. He doesn't need my money, neither do you really, but it's all yours.'

Harriet got up and went to give her mother a kiss. 'Your money is the last thought in my head. If you do decide to go for it I hope you'll be very happy. I hold no brief for my father so I certainly shan't get in the way if it's what you want. Mr Fitch would definitely be able to keep you in the style to which you would like to become accustomed!'

Sadie grinned. 'I shan't let him take my grandchildren over, though. Definitely not – they're mine. I do hope it won't make a difference to Jimbo's business relationship with him.'

'I shouldn't think so.'

Sadie stood to go. 'Harriet, before I leave you in peace, I should tell you that there was a scene in the Store today.'

'Really?'

'Jimbo's new assistant was serving and I could hear a lot of noise and shouting, so I went to take a look. Simone Paradise was in there with that crowd of little louts she calls her sweeties. They were causing mayhem. Pulling the greetings cards off the shelves and throwing them down. Picking up chocolate and sweets and trying to open the packets up. One took a bite out of an apple . . . I can't remember all they did. I protested and told her to get them all out. She hitched the baby up in that ridiculous sling thing she makes from her shawl and said in that slow drawling way she has, "Sweeties, come on we're leaving now." I was furious. I asked her what about the cards they'd stamped on and we can't sell, and the apple they'd bitten a piece out of? To say nothing of the sweets. She said she couldn't afford to pay for them and it was our fault for having the goods displayed where the children could get hold of them. I'm afraid I saw red.

Did my Dame Edith Evans bit, you know the kind of thing. Told her in my most superior manner that she needn't come back in the Store again with her horde of brats because her kind of business we could well do without. Time she got them under control. Et cetera. Et cetera. Simone fixed me with what can only be described as the evil eye. I'm shuddering now when I think about it. I'm not an imaginative person but I felt as though time had stood still. Then it jerked back into rhythm again and there were the children standing beside her angelic and quite still.' Sadie visibly pulled herself together. 'However, what I was going to say was, do watch out for her. She really is odd. Night, night, my dear, take care.'

'I will. I'll tell Jimbo. Good night, Mother. Thanks for talking to me about it. The decision is yours in the end, you know.'

'Yes, but it's nice to know you would approve if I said yes, which I probably shall. I love you for it, my dear. I hope to be as lucky as you. I adored your Jimbo from the first moment I saw him; you did well there, my love, very well. And thank you for all my grandchildren, too. I'm so proud of them all.' She leant forward and kissed Harriet and patted her arm. 'Good night, Harriet. See you tomorrow.'

Harriet closed the door after her mother and decided she couldn't go back to concentrating on accounts and in any case the boys would soon be home. She switched off the computer and sat for a while in Jimbo's armchair – his 'thinking chair' he called it. If her mother could be as happy as she was with Jimbo then she should go right ahead. Sadie had endured years of loneliness, somewhat alleviated by coming to live in the village just after she and Jimbo bought the Store, but even that wasn't quite the same as sharing one's house and one's bed. A stepfather. Wow!

Harriet felt glad to have been consulted. It wasn't often her mother let down her guard and spoke of herself and her feelings; it had indeed been a rare moment between the two of them.

12

The news that Sadie had died in her sleep that night shocked the entire village. More than one of them had been on the receiving end of Sadie's forthright opinions, and she had in the short time she'd lived in Turnham Malpas become something in the way of a legend. But Sadie *dead*? Her strong life-force, cut down at one stroke? No one could remember ever having seen her looking anything but at her best, always full of pep and get-upand-go. And so stylish. They'd envied her style. It wasn't that she spent loads of money on clothes, just that she knew what would flatter her and she'd worn it well. Chic was what she was. Every customer spoke of their horror at the suddenness of her going, or savoured over and over again the times when they'd clashed with her. And no chance to say goodbye even – that was sad, real sad. But then Sadie would have hated any kind of sloppy sentimentality so maybe it was best she went the way she did. All the same. So suddenly . . .

On the day of her funeral the church was packed with mourners. Not a few noticed that Mr Fitch, grim-faced and silent, was there sitting with the family. But then he would be grim-faced, wouldn't he? He'd no heart. But what was he doing, sitting with the Charter-Placketts? That he was a close business associate of Jimbo's they all knew but in the front with family mourners . . . ?

It was the three grandchildren for whom the villagers felt the most compassion. They were devastated and quite uncomprehending of this terrible blow, for Sadie must have been a real fun grandma to have. The two boys wore their Sunday suits and little Flick, bless her, that new coat she was so proud of with its fur collar. They remembered how distressed Sadie had been when Flick had her accident. But it was Sadie now they were mourning.

When the service was finished and Sadie had been laid in her grave, they all noticed that Harriet went to speak to Mr Fitch. Funny that; she'd drawn him to one side so they couldn't be overheard. Pity – would have been nice to know what they had to say to each other.

'Craddock, thank you so much for coming,' Harriet said gently. 'I do appreciate it. The night before my mother . . . died, she told me about your proposal.'

'Did she? Did she?' Mr Fitch blew his nose and turned away his face and looked across the churchyard towards the yew tree, so she could only see his profile. 'What did she say about me?'

'That she found you fascinating.'

He turned back to face her. 'Was that all?' The longing in his face overrode anything Harriet might have decided to say and she impulsively said 'She told me she was going to say yes.' No one but she knew Sadie hadn't absolutely made up her mind, but the grief in Craddock's face was unbearable, and if she could give him some comfort, why not?

'Really! I'm so glad. When we were young I loved her very much. My word, she was a spirited young thing. Still is. Was, I mean. If we'd married then, we'd have had some rare old fights. But now it would have been very rich, but without the fights. I think. Maybe not! I'm very sorry for you, Harriet, but it was a lovely way for her to go. She would have hated being less than herself – you know, crippled or senile. This was the best for her, but not for you and me. Thank you for telling me that.'

He clasped both her hands in his and then raised them to his lips and kissed them. 'Thank you, my dear. You would have made a lovely stepdaughter. I should have been proud. So proud.'

Harriet kissed his cheek, Mr Fitch turned away and left the graveyard. Then Jimbo gathered the children and Harriet, and took them home, so the other mourners never did find out what they'd said, but then they remembered that Sadie and old Fitch had known each other years ago. That's right. That'd be why.

'I'll pick up Fran and we'll take off these black things and put on something jolly. It's what she would have wanted, Harriet.'

'We ought really to be having a big party with lots of drink and fun. She always loved parties.'

'I know, but we both agreed it would be too hard on the children. They wouldn't understand.'

'No, perhaps you're right. Oh Jimbo!' Harriet laid her head against his shoulder and wept the first tears since her mother's death. Jimbo hugged her tightly until the tears slowed. 'There, there, darling, you'll feel better for that. It's no good thinking we shall all be over it in no time at all; it's going to take an age, but she wouldn't have wanted us to be miserable, she'd rather we were brave and carried on. She's left such lovely memories for us all.'

'I know, but I shall miss her. She was so young to die. I thought she'd be a grand old lady for years and years.'

'So did I. I had the distinct feeling she'd outlive us all, but there we are.'

'I'm so glad she came to see me the night before. We had the closest conversation we've had in years. Do you think she had a premonition?'

'Bit too practical a chap I am to know about those kind of things. Just be grateful she did come and you did talk.'

'I can hardly bring myself to speak about it, but you know the post mortem? Well, it wasn't really conclusive, was it? They couldn't really find out why her heart had stopped, could they?'

'No. All very odd. Felt sorry for old Fitch.' Jimbo wiped Harriet's face for her. 'All that happiness snatched away.'

'I told him she'd definitely been going to say yes.'

'That was a bit of a fib, darling.'

'Only a teeny weeny bit of a fib, but it did bring him comfort.'

Flick appeared in the hall. 'There, look, I'm wearing the dress Grandma bought me in the summer. She loved it and so do I. It still fits me, look. Mummy, Fran won't remember Grandma, will she?'

'No, darling, she won't.'

'Don't cry any more, Mummy, please. I'm going to get lots of photos and put them in an album and call it Grandma's and then we can show it to Fran when she gets older, and we'll tell her about playing cards for big money, and all the naughty things Grandma did, like having her hair dyed, although you'd never have guessed if you didn't know, would you, and such.'

'Thank you, Flick, that will be lovely. I think you'd better put a cardigan on, darling, or you'll be cold.'

'All right, I will, Daddy, who will do the mail-order now?'

'I haven't worked that one out yet. Do you have any ideas?'

'If I was older it could be me.'

'You'd do a very good job, I'm sure. I shall have to put my studying cap on.'

'It'll have to be someone good. Grandma wouldn't like it all to fail, would she?'

'No, she wouldn't.'

Suddenly Harriet was crying again and she fled upstairs and shut the bedroom door with a slam.

'Daddy, shall I . . . ?'

'No, I'll go and collect Fran from the rectory then we'll make a cup of tea and take it up to her in a little while, that'll be best.' Jimbo patted Flick's shoulder and strode away to the rectory. Little Fran screamed when she saw her Daddy had come to collect her. She wanted to stay with the twins and she wasn't going home. No! No! No! But Jimbo insisted. He knew that cuddling Fran would be a great comfort to Harriet right now.

'Thank you, Sylvia, thank you very much. Hope she's not been too much trouble.'

'Certainly not. Good as gold.'

Trying to get the mail orders off in between all his other activities was too much for Jimbo. He knew Sadie had liked to send orders off by return if it was at all possible, and he was failing dismally on that score.

The morning after the funeral, Barry Jones' mother came in and asked him how he was coping.

'Not too good. One never really appreciates how much work people do until they're not there any more. The mail orders are piling up and Sadie would be angry if she knew.' He took off his boater and rubbed his bald head in agitation. 'Now, what can I do for you?'

'What can I do for you, more like. If it's just a question of reading an order, picking the items out and packing them up in them lovely boxes you 'ave and addressing a few labels, I could do that temporary like till you find someone. Wouldn't be any good with accounts or anything, but the rest is a question of common sense, isn't it, really?'

'Do you mean that?'

'Wouldn't say it if I didn't. You and I, Mr Charter-Plackett, have not always seen eye to eye, but I don't mind 'elping someone in trouble. A bit of extra money towards our Barry's wedding would be very useful too, but we'll discuss that later when we see if you're satisfied with what I've done. What do you say?'

'I could run the money side and pass the orders to you, couldn't I?'

'You could. And I haven't got far to go to post the parcels, 'ave I?' Mrs Jones twinkled her fingers at Linda behind the post-office counter.

'You're on. Temporary.'

'Right, I'll get my sleeves rolled up. I'll just ring Vince, if that's all right and tell him where I am, otherwise he'll worry, I don't think.'

'Be my guest.'

'I always liked Mrs Beauchamp – bit like me, spoke 'er mind when necessary. I was in 'ere when she 'ad that row with Simone Paradise. Nasty, that was. Yer could feel it in the atmosphere. Charged it was, like they say in books. That Simone is cracked, yer know. Got friendly with that Kate from the school. Right! Show me where to start. I shall enjoy this.'

And Jimbo's newest assistant attacked her job with zeal.

13

'Hetty! We've met the most marvellous man at the museum this morning. He's promised to come and give the children a talk. He's one of the senior archaeologists! Aren't we lucky? I'm sure your class would enjoy it too, wouldn't they?'

'I'm sure they would. When's he coming?'

'Tomorrow. It was either tomorrow or not for four weeks, and that's too long for my class to wait. We shall have moved on from the Romans before then.'

'What's his name?'

'Gilbert Johns.'

Hetty stopped marking exercise books and looked up at Kate. 'I'm surprised you don't know him already. He's our church choir-master.'

'Really! I didn't realise.'

'Not having been to church you wouldn't, would you?'

'Now, Hetty, don't get me into trouble, please. He's giving the talk at half-past nine, and bringing lots of artefacts for the children to handle. Nothing like "hands on" is there?'

'He's a very sweet man.'

'He is – a soul-mate, I think.'

Hetty was amused. 'I don't know about that.' She returned to marking the books. 'There were Roman remains found in the grounds of the Big House last year.'

'Can we see them?'

'No. Gilbert rescued what he could and they were taken to the museum for display, but it's not finished yet.' Hetty slapped the last of her exercise books on to a pile and, clasping them to her chest, stood up to go. 'There, that's that lot finished. In your classroom or mine?'

'Oh, mine I think. We have all the pictures and things up so it'll be more appropriate. Does Gilbert live in the village?'

'No. Down the lane from me in Little Derehams – Keepers Cottage. I called there once collecting for Christian Aid, and it was so untidy! Mr Fitch's secretary Louise seems to be a very frequent visitor.'

'Oh, I see.'

'Don't think the rector won't have noticed.'

'What?'

'That you're not going to church; he misses nothing. It is expected in your position.'

'Yes, well. I'm not breaking a *rule*.'

'No, not a rule as such, but it won't be in your favour.'

'I shall come to it all in good time.'

'Yes?' Hetty raised a sceptical eyebrow and returned to her classroom. Kate watched her leave. Hetty had a point. The job had been offered to her partly because of her having worked in the mission school in Kenya, the assumption being that she was a communicant member of the church, which in fact she had been. But now . . .

Kate had expected Gilbert to arrive a few minutes before half-past nine. In fact, he was there before nine.

'Too early, am I? Car won't start so I've begged a lift.'

'Not at all. We're all bright-eyed and bushy-tailed quite early here, so please feel free.'

'Where?'

'Oh right! In this classroom, please.' With a wide gesture of her hand, Kate indicated the classroom walls for his closer inspection. 'Well, what say you?'

'Oh, very good. I like this. Very good indeed. What clever children you must have and what a clever teacher to get all this from them.' Gilbert turned to smile at her. What a sweet smile he had. Nothing sexual or patronising, just a genuine smile of praise. She liked him for it.

'Here, are we?'

Gilbert turned to face the door. 'Ah! This is Louise. She gave me the lift. Yes, here please, by the table. Mind – that's quite heavy.'

'I can manage, don't worry.' Louise put down the box and went to shake hands with Kate. 'Hello, we've not met before. I'm Louise Bissett, secretary up at the Big House. You must be Kate.'

'Yes, I am. Pleased to meet you.' Kate was surprised that Louise, well-dressed and businesslike, could attract such a sweet gentle man as Gilbert Johns. She would have imagined he'd go for someone in long swirling skirts and lots of beads and long braided hair. However, each to his own – they obviously thought a lot about each other. Louise and Gilbert brought in two more boxes and then Louise wanted to hurry away to work. 'Got to dash. New lot of students today. Busy. Busy. Can I pick this lot up after work, Kate, please, if Gilbert's car isn't repaired?'

'Of course. Give me a knock on my door.'

'Fine. Bye, Gilbert.'

They were the same height. Gilbert kissed her, on the mouth, and Kate couldn't miss the quick flushing of Louise's face as he did so. Two of the children watched from the doorway. Kate coughed. Eventually they broke apart and Louise fled. Gilbert winked at Kate, wiped some beads of sweat from his forehead with the back of his wrist, and began unpacking the boxes.

Gilbert attended prayers sitting quietly on a small chair at the back, his bony knees almost to his chin, joining in the hymns with his powerful tenor voice. The children began to giggle and Hetty had to still them with a piercing look from her eagle eye. When Kate took over for meditation Gilbert sat with bowed head, quite motionless. As she gave her short speech to help the children direct their thoughts she was intensely aware of him. Of his red shirt unbuttoned almost to his trouser belt, of the brown sinewy arms revealed because he'd rolled up his sleeves. The dark hair dropping forward over his forehead. The well-tanned face, the hollowed cheeks, the dark dreamy eyes. She shook herself mentally. This wasn't what meditation time should be used for.

'Thank you, children. Our five minutes of tranquillity is over. Stand quietly and go to your classrooms. I'll see Class Two in my room at half-past, Mrs Hardaker.' Kate stood up.

The children left the hall. Gilbert returned to the classroom to finish sorting his boxes.

They all had the most wonderful hour and a half listening to Gilbert, looking at what he'd brought, handling the combs, the spoons, the jewellery, the toys. Acting out little happenings for him and generally getting the feel of being a Roman. For that was how he'd presented his talk. Encouraging them to imagine they were Roman children, getting up, washing, eating, working, learning, playing, helping in the house. Every-thing a Roman child might do. He brought it all so vividly to life.

At the end, the children ran out to play leaving Hetty to make the coffee and Kate to help clear up.

'I can't thank you enough for what you've done today. You were absolutely brilliant.'

'Louise's idea actually. A day in the life of et cetera. Worked well, didn't it?'

'Indeed.'

'This meditation business – what's it all about?'

'A New Age approach.'

'Does Peter know?'

'Yes. He doesn't object.'

'How do you know he doesn't?'

'He hasn't said anything.'

'That's Peter all over.'

'It *is* my school.'

'Don't develop it any further.' Gilbert stored the last of his things and glanced around to make sure he'd not forgotten anything.

'It's none of your business.'

'No. But don't develop it any further. Not with the children.'

'I shall do as I please.'

'Not with other people's lives, especially children's. You're not at liberty to do that.'

'You don't know what you're talking about.'

'Maybe not. But despite being male, I am very sensitive to the fact that things are not quite as they should be.'

'Pity you haven't used your sensitivity where Louise is concerned. Not your kind at all.'

Gilbert's sweet expression changed alarmingly quickly. He almost snarled his reply to her. 'Louise is my concern and no one else's.'

'My affairs are my concern.'

'Not when it affects the children.'

'Sitting silently is a crime, is it?'

'No, but I suspect you're leading them on to your own agenda, which has no place here in this school.'

'What a pity you've spoiled such a wonderful morning.'

'What a pity you can't or won't take on board your proper responsibility for these children. They are in trust to you, they are not yours to do with as you will. They're not guinea pigs. Where shall I leave these? They must not be touched.'

'Here, in this corner, where I can keep my eye on them.'

'Right. Sorry for speaking out, but it had to be said. Any time, I'll come any time.'

Kate preceded him into the hall. 'Coffee?'

'No, thanks, someone to see and then I must catch the noon bus into Culworth. Bye, Hetty. See you Sunday about ten, Margaret. That OK?'

'Yes, I've got everything ready. Louise coming too?'

'Yes, she'll be there.'

'Good. We'll need her organising ability.'

'We will indeed. Goodbye, Kate Pascoe.'

'Thank you again.'

'Not at all. Any time, like I said.'

It was Peter he called to see before he caught the bus. He was in, and led Gilbert to his study.

'Just a quick word, Peter.'

'Sit down, please. Not had a chance to talk to you for a while apart from hymn numbers and tunes and things!'

'No, that's right. Been very busy.'

'How's life treating you?'

'Very well, thanks. And you?'

'Ditto, thanks. If you've come to see me about Sunday, I've been through—'

'I know you will have. No, it's not about Sunday. It's about Kate Pascoe.'

'Why Kate?'

'I'm not sure. I'm uneasy, that's all. Can't put my finger on it but I've told her this morning – been doing a Roman Times thing for the older pupils – that the children are not guinea pigs and she's not to have her own agenda for them. Sounds stupid, when I say it in broad daylight, but I was there and I saw and I felt. You should drop in some time, unexpected. You are allowed to do that, surely?'

'Yes, I expect I am but I don't.'

'Wish you would. Please?'

'Very well, I will. Although I'm sure you're wrong.'

'Maybe. But keep an eye out, OK?'

'OK. Will do.'

'It's the children I'm concerned about.'

'Of course.'

'Good grief! Is that the time? I shall miss the bus. He never waits a moment after departure time – in fact, I swear he goes early sometimes on purpose! Still, he has to have some excitement, doesn't he? Who'd want to drive a bus all day?'

'Goodbye. I'll bear in mind what you say.'

14

The following Saturday night the bar of The Royal Oak was exceedingly busy. Every table was occupied and the dining room constantly full. The low-ceilinged room was hot, for massive logs were burning in the ingle-nook fireplace and great waves of heat poured out across the room. The customers were grateful, for the night was cold. It had taken three years for the villagers to come anywhere near accepting Bryn and Georgie Fields, the licensees, into their lives. Three years wasn't long enough though for the couple to have been initiated into the centuries-old undertow of prejudice and bias which coloured present-day arguments. Cricket was the subject under discussion at the small table beside the fire.

'My grandfather played in the cricket team before the Second World War, and his father before him played as well. They had some grand times in here after they'd won a match. Drunk as lords they were, singing and dancing. By jove, my grandad said the beer flowed and not half. Him' – the speaker jerked a derisive thumb in the direction of the Big House – 'up there's no business to be president. Should be Sir Ralph. Tradition counts. They always had a party up at the Big House to celebrate the end of the cricket season. My grandad said they used to eat till they could hardly stand. Wonderful cook they had up there. None of this daft French busi-ness with a couple of peas on your plate and hardly a mouthful of meat but plenty of fancy sauce. Great piles of food they had. Delicious. They didn't eat for a week after. And the ale and cider never stopped coming. They was gentlemen, was the Templetons. Everything given with a good heart. Him' – he jerked his thumb again – 'him, he likes *gratitude*.'

Vera Wright laughed. 'You're right there, he does.'

'Sir Ralph's a real gentleman, yer see. Can mix with anyone, high and low. Grand chap.'

'You're only saying that because he came in here the other night and bought you a couple of drinks. Sat here an hour or more you were with him, raking over old times.' Vera glanced up as the door opened and in came Willie and Sylvia. 'I shall have to go, me friends have just come in.'

'I'm off, they can sit here if you like.'

'Oh, thanks.' Vera waved to Sylvia and she came across.

'Isn't it busy? Bryn and Georgie must be making a bomb tonight. Doing really well out of it.'

'Yes, they must be. Everybody seems to be doing well except me, good old Vera Wright. There's Pat marrying the best pair of thighs in Turnham Malpas, and she's got that wonderful Garden House 'cos of her Dad's job, there's that awful Alan Crimble grinning his head off behind the bar, got married and got a lovely house as well. Mr Charter-Plackett's like a dog with two tails, his business is doing so well. Though I shouldn't say that, not since Sadie died. Unnerving, that was. Even so, everybody seems to be doing well but me.'

Sylvia watched Willie threading his way between the tables carrying their drinks. 'Come on, Vera, things can't be that bad.'

Willie put down the drinks. 'Evening Vera. There's your drink, my Sylvia.' He leant over and kissed her as he handed her the drink.

'See what I mean? You two's happy as sandboys as well.'

'Look, life's what you make it. You've got a lovely steady husband, couldn't be steadier, and a nice grandson.'

'Nice grandson? I don't think. Out all hours, he is. Must have been three o'clock this morning before he got in. At least tonight we'll be able to get to sleep. He's gone to stay with a friend top of Ladygate in Culworth. So we'll have two nights of peace at least.'

Willie proffered the idea that maybe he'd got a girlfriend.

'Come on, Willie, he's only sixteen, he's got no girl. Having said that, in the paper last Sunday there was this story about a boy of twelve, put in care he was because . . .'

Their three heads came close together in conference as Vera revealed the details of the story. But they were interrupted by the bar door crashing open so hard that it swung back and smacked into a chair which fell over with a resounding clatter. Everyone looked up to see who was coming in. It was Jimmy. He staggered in, looking as if his legs would give way at any moment, and headed straight for the bar counter. Leaning on it he heaved in several deep breaths and feebly requested a double whisky, which he proceeded to swallow in one gulp.

Jimmy – a double whisky? He hadn't had one of those since the night he won the pools. Surely he couldn't have won again, could he?

But Jimmy's face, not as tanned as it used to be when he was an idle good-for-nothing who spent most of his waking hours in the woods and fields poaching, was ashen. He tremblingly placed his empty glass on the bar counter and dragged the words 'another double' out of his throat.

Bryn said, 'Now look, you're not used to drinking whisky. Let this one settle first and then I'll serve you another.'

But Jimmy would have none of it. He gestured pleadingly at Bryn, so he was served another double.

Sylvia said to Willie, 'I really think you should go to him, you know. I can see him shaking from here. Go and find out what the matter is.'

Someone had put a bar stool under Jimmy's bottom and he'd sunk gratefully on to it as he downed his second whisky.

The colour was beginning to creep back into his cheeks when Willie said, 'Now then, what's the matter, seen a ghost?' Jimmy's colour receded again and he clutched Willie by his lapels and whispered in a voice which sounded as though he was being strangled, '*Sykes.*'

Willie, thoroughly startled, whispered back 'Have you seen something horrible in Sykes Wood, is that it?'

'No, no.'

'Well, what is it then? Tell me.'

Jimmy shook his head and the trembling grew worse. He took out a handkerchief and wiped the sweat from his face.

'It was 'im. It was 'im.'

'Who?'

Jimmy struggled to speak and eventually came out with, 'I treated him like a son, I did. Loved him like a son. And now this.' Tears began to roll down his cheeks. Willie had never seen him cry, not even when his wife and baby died. He stood in front of him to shield him from the other customers; he didn't want all the world to see Jimmy's tears.

'I can't help yer if I don't know what yer talking about,' he said gently.

'It's Sykes. I saw Sykes.' The tears continued to rain down his cheeks.

Willie was so surprised he said loudly, 'Saw Sykes?'

Someone said, 'Sykes? Who's that?'

'His dog. Died three maybe four years ago.'

'What's he on about then if he's dead?'

Jimmy asked for another whisky.

Bryn shook his head. 'No, I'm sorry, no.'

Jimmy was by now too distressed to protest. 'It's punishment, you know.' He gestured to the ceiling with a thin shaking hand. 'Him, Almighty God, He's punishing me for what I did. For the way that poor dog of mine died. It was all my fault.'

'No, it wasn't. Of course, it wasn't. You weren't to have known.'

Jimmy's lips trembled as he said, 'It was my rabbit snares that killed him – let's face it. Best Jack Russell terrier any human being could have.'

'But how can yer have seen him when, he's, yer know, when he's as you might say, dead . . . like?'

Jimmy raised his voice to convince Willie. 'I 'ave, I tell yer I 'ave. Out in Church Lane.'

'It's dark, it'd be a cat.'

'It barked.'

Willie, taken aback but reluctant to believe Jimmy, protested, 'Yer can't 'ave. There's no such thing as ghosts.'

'Sez who? You've seen ghosts. What about that tomb in the church you say is haunted.'

Willie agreed, but then ghosts near tombs in churches were only right and reasonable, not like a dog out in Church Lane.

Sudenly there was a commotion at the table where Jimmy and Willie and Vera and Sylvia usually sat. One of the customers had stood up and said, 'There's a dog under here.'

'Don't be daft.'

'There is – I can smell it. That wet warm woolly smell yer get when they've been out in the rain and they're drying off. It's brushed past my leg. Get the damn thing out. It'll be ruining my new trousers.'

They all looked under the table but there was no dog there.

'But there *was* a dog, I felt it!'

Willie and Jimmy were electrified. Jimmy pointed towards the table with a shaking hand, and proclaimed in a loud voice filled with fear: 'See? He's followed me in here. He's there where he usually sat. Remember, I allus put me glass down there and he'd have a drink. Come back to haunt me, he has. Come back to haunt me. Divine retribution. That's what.'

The group finished their drinks and left in haste, unnerved by Jimmy's assertion that they'd felt a ghost. The chatter in the bar rose to a crescendo and more than one was visibly shaken by the idea of Sykes revisiting his old haunts. Not a few ordered more drinks to calm their nerves.

Bryn laughed. 'It'll be good for trade, then. A haunted pub.'

Georgie, furious, nudged him sharply and said, 'Shut up!' Patting Jimmy's arm she said comfortingly, 'Look, love, go home, Willie will take you, and you get to bed with a couple of headache tablets. You'll feel better in the morning.'

Resolutely Jimmy shook his head. 'Can't do that, he might follow me 'ome.'

Sylvia stood up. 'Now look here, this is all getting absolutely ridiculous. We'll all go – Willie, Vera, Jimmy and me – and we'll sit at our usual table and you can put a glass of ale down where you used to, Jimmy, and we'll all sit there and prove there's no smell of a wet dog and the ale won't be touched and we'll know it's all imagination. It's worth trying it out as an experiment, isn't it? Jimmy can't stay here all night, can he? We'll settle our minds once and for all. Come on, bring yer drinks.'

Rather hesitantly the three of them drifted across to the table where Sylvia had already plumped herself down on a chair. Bryn carried across the glass of ale and Jimmy placed it just where he always had done when Sykes was alive.

At a loss for conversation while the experiment took place, Sylvia began talking about the shoes Willie had bought that afternoon in Culworth. She was just describing how rude one of the shop assistants had been to her when all she'd said was 'these same shoes are two pounds cheaper down the road', when they distinctly heard the sound of a dog lapping. Everything stopped. Conversation. Drinking. Laughing. The entire bar froze. The only noise was the lapping which sounded almost indecently eager for a ghost. Sylvia looked at the three of them to see which one of them was going to dare to look under the table. But Willie and Jimmy and Vera were paralysed. Their only movement was their eyes, swivelling from side to side in terror. So it was she who bent down to have a look. Everyone heard the sound of breath being rapidly drawn in through tightly clenched teeth, then, energised by some unknown force, Sylvia's head shot up from under the table, she leapt up onto the seat of her chair, clutched her skirt around her knees and screamed, 'It's 'im! It's 'im!'

Someone muttered a heartfelt, 'Bloody hell.'

Vera slid off her chair in a dead faint.

'So there I was, Rector, up on the chair screaming my head off! Bryn came and enticed it out from under the table with a biscuit. I was still standing on the chair, my heart was absolutely pounding. The relief was unbeliev-able. It's a nice little dog and the absolute spitting image of Sykes. Same size, same colouring, even to the placing of the black patch round his left eye. Just like Sykes it is. 'Cept perhaps the black isn't quite as black as Sykes' patch but, as someone said, what else could you expect when he'd been buried in the wood for three years? Jimmy didn't take kindly to that remark, I can tell you!! It hadn't a collar on, so we still don't know whose it is.'

'Where is he now?'

'Well, Saturday night what could Jimmy do but take it home with him. He tried turning it out on Sunday morning and it went straight to church. Like you saw him when you went to Matins at eight. Then when the ten o'clock service was over it went back to Jimmy's and it's been there ever since. Anyway, Willie saw Jimmy first thing this morning. He was off to see the Sergeant, ask him if anyone had reported a dog missing, and the dog was trotting behind him for all the world like Sykes used to do. I've half a mind to think he'll keep it if the real owners don't turn up.'

'I wish I could have seen your faces!'

'I'm glad you didn't. I felt such a fool afterwards. I don't mind telling you we were scared and not half! But you know, there is something very odd about that dog. First it had a liking for ale which Sykes did – he loved it, would've been drunk as a lord every night if he'd been allowed. Then when Jimmy got it home it knew exactly where to go to look for a drink, the exact place where he always kept Sykes' water bowl, and when it was time for bed it went to stand where Sykes' bed had been, but Jimmy's got a little table there now so it couldn't lie down. Anyway, Jimmy moved the table and the dog laid down on the carpet with its back against the skirting board in exactly the same position as Sykes. So Jimmy got an old blanket out Sykes had used and put it down and he settled on it as if he'd been sleeping there for years. I don't mind telling you it's put Jimmy's thinking cap on and no mistake. He's not the man he was. What do you think, sir?'

'It does all seem very odd, Sylvia. I mean, the dog appearing is not so peculiar; obviously it's lost and happened quite by chance to appear in Turnham Malpas, but what you say about it knowing where Sykes slept and where to look for his water bowl is certainly more than a bit disconcerting. I don't know much about dogs really; maybe they have a sixth sense of where the best place is for sleeping and such. I just don't know.'

'There's something else I've got to tell you, nothing to do with the dog. Have you got a minute?'

'Yes.'

Sylvia told Peter about finding Mimi's collar. 'So I've still got it here in my bag. I'll give it to you and perhaps you can decide what's best. It's been weighing on my conscience and it's time I did something about it. I couldn't tell Dr Harris, just couldn't find the words. Don't you think, sir, that there's a strange series of coincidences nowadays. First Mimi missing, then poor Sadie Beauchamp dying so sudden and now this blessed dog.'

'All perfectly explainable.'

'I know, but together all very odd. Here's the collar. Make sure you hide it; can't have her coming across it by mistake. Shall you tell her?'

Peter fastened the collar and tried to pull it open with a crooked finger. But he couldn't. 'Unfastened, you say?'

'Oh yes, and half kind of buried in the soil.'

'I'll think about what to say. Thanks.' Peter smiled. 'Vera came round all right, did she?'

Sylvia chuckled. 'Well, it took a double brandy to bring her round properly, but then we had had a terrible fright!'

15

Many of the children at school that morning had been in church on the Sunday when the little Jack Russell had been found sitting for all the world like a regular worshipper on top of the tomb Willie claimed was haunted. They were full of the story and could talk of nothing else.

'What do you think, Ms Pascoe?'

Tight-lipped and dismissive she snapped, 'Just a stray dog from somewhere, just happened to be like Mr Glover's.' Then, to avoid the children's questions, Kate went to her office.

'My mum says it's just like Sykes was.'

'It is. That black patch that makes him look like a pirate.'

'That's right and they say he knows Mr Glover's house like the back of his hand, er paw.'

'Pissed as a newt he . . .'

Hetty Hardaker interrupted. 'Brian, that will do! You know better words than those with which to describe the condition he was in.'

'He was just like Mr Glover then!' The children burst into hysterical laughter at Brian's joke.

'Children, time for prayers, now come along.'

'My dad says old Jimmy was as white as a sheet. Shaking, he was.'

'I 'opes nobody claims 'im. Be nice for Mr Glover to have a dog again. Perhaps he'll dig up his snares in Sykes Wood and start poaching again.'

'I hopes not. There'll be Sykes' skellington there. Ugh!' Stacey shuddered.

'No, there won't 'cos he's been spirited to life. That's what my mum says. Brought back to life! She's certain it's the real Sykes, she is. She was there when they found him.'

'Something funny going on, my dad says. Lights in Sykes Wood at dead of night. He's seen 'um.' Stacey rolled her eyes, enjoying the sensation she was creating.

Brian asked what Stacey's dad was doing in Sykes Wood at dead of night?

Stacey tapped the side of her nose. 'Ask no questions, get told no lies.'

Hetty Hardaker said, 'I think it best you don't ask what Stacey's father

281

was doing in Sykes Wood at night, Brian. Now, you can be leader and take us into prayers. Stand tall and lead the way. Miss Booth is already playing the "settling down" music. Come along, Class Two. Chop chop! Nice straight lines, nice straight backs. Lead on Brian, quietly, and *don't* stamp your feet, please. We're not on Horse Guards Parade, and there's definitely no need to salute.'

As they settled down for prayers Peter came in from the playgroup room. The children all turned and without prompting chorused, 'Good morning, Rector!'

'Good morning, children. May I join you for prayers this morning, Ms Pascoe? Mrs Hardaker?'

Kate said, 'Certainly. Can someone fetch a chair for the rector?' A flurry of hands shot up. 'You Flick, get my chair from our classroom. The rector needs a grown-up's chair.'

'I'll sit at the back.'

One of Ms Pascoe's children gave him a hymn book and he seated himself on the chair Flick brought for him.

It was a dull dark morning but the children's enthusiasm for life seemed to Peter to fill the room with light. Mrs Hardaker announced the first hymn. Those who could, found the number for themselves and then helped those who couldn't.

Miss Booth played the first line and the children began to sing '*If I were a butterfly*'. Peter joined in and the children had to restrain their giggles for he sounded like Mr Johns except his voice was deeper and louder even though he was trying to sing quietly.

When Hetty Hardaker asked the children if they had anything they needed to thank God for this morning, Brian suggested, 'Sykes. Let's thank God for bringing Sykes back.'

Several of the children agreed. 'Yes, that's a good idea!'

'I don't think that Sykes has actually come back, Brian. Not really Sykes, just a dog who *looks* like Sykes.'

There came a strong murmur of dissension from the floor of the hall. 'How come he knowed where Sykes' bowl was then?'

'Yes, and he knowed Mr Glover. Stuck to him like glue he did.'

Mrs Hardaker began to flounder. 'Perhaps we should pray that the real owners will come to claim him. After all, they must be very sad to have lost their dog. I expect they love him very much.'

'How can they, when he's Mr Glover's Sykes?'

'Let's pray for all pets, that they are all as well cared for as your animals are. Hands together, eyes closed.'

By the time Mrs Hardaker's part of prayers was over Peter could see she was more than glad to hand over to Kate Pascoe.

Kate stayed sitting on her chair to the side of the children. She looked around at them all to catch their undivided attention before she began to speak. 'Some days ago, Class Three went with me into the woods on a nature walk. Because it is winter most of the trees were bare of leaves, but we could see the beautiful symmetry of the twigs and branches reaching skywards high up above our heads. The trees were sleeping – no growing, no leaves rustling in the wind. They were biding their time, waiting for the sun to shine, the earth to warm up, for longer days and shorter nights so they can begin to stir to life. It won't be long now before that happens; we call it Spring. Let us think about those trees and plants in the wood, waiting quietly through the cold months for the whole wonderful miracle, which comes every year, without fail. Imagine yourself like a tree, able to feel pain and hurt if you get damaged or chopped down, silently waiting like all nature is, for the right moment to wake up. Imagine yourself feeling the first stirrings of life.'

The children sat for fully five minutes quietly but not necessarily meditating on Kate's theme. Peter sat quietly too. Mentally he checked his diary for the day – yes, he did have a spare hour around four if he cut short his usual Monday-morning visit to Penny Fawcett and thus got back from hospital-visiting early. And it didn't matter what Ms Pascoe had in mind for after school, she was seeing him. Trees feeling pain, indeed! Whatever next!

Peter got to the school just as the children began to leave for home. Hetty Hardaker was running across the playground calling out to one of them:

'Craig! Craig! Your stamps; you've forgotten your stamps! Catch him for me, Flick. Why hello, Rector, twice in one day, we are honoured! There you are, Craig, I've put the album in this plastic bag then you won't lose anything out on the way home. Mind how you go. See you tomorrow. Come to see Miss Pascoe?' She went back into school followed by Peter.

'Yes, I have.'

'She has a parent with her at the moment, but she won't be long. Do I know what it's about?'

'Very likely.'

'If you need my opinion which you don't but I'm saying it just the same, it's not right. Believe me it's not right. Well-meaning, I think, but misguided.'

Peter nodded his head and gave a noncommittal 'Hmm.'

Kate offered him a cup of tea, but he refused it. She felt that he filled the small room not just because of his size but with the strength of his persona. She was really into this business of aura and she could feel his almost touching hers.

Kate looked into his face and saw he was troubled. 'Is there something I can help you with, Rector?'

'There certainly is.'

She placed her empty cup on the desk and, having offered Peter the one and only chair, she perched herself on the edge of the washbasin and waited.

'While I am well aware that the church does not have quite the same influence on the education of the children in its schools as once was the case, I really feel that I must speak up. During your short speech directing the children's thoughts to a subject for meditation, you never once mentioned the One to Whom we should give thanks for the beautiful world in which we live. Nothing was attributed to Him and I should like to know why in such a context God's name was never mentioned.'

Kate didn't answer immediately and Peter, as so many of his parishioners knew to their cost, didn't fill the silence for her.

'That's a sticky one.'

'It was meant to be.' Peter waited patiently.

Kate turned her face from his scrutiny and looked out of the window. Her view was of the school dustbins and the cycle shed. She heard the slip slap of Pat Duckett's old shoes and watched her come into view to empty waste paper into the recycling bin. She wished she lived Pat Duckett's uncomplicated life. With Peter present, she had been a fool not to have mentioned the Deity. Now what? Abject apology was called for. 'You're quite right, I should have. It won't happen again.'

'Good. Talking about trees feeling pain, that is ridiculous, and has no place being presented to these impressionable children by someone whose word they see as absolute truth. They have to believe what you say, otherwise they can't learn. If you say two and two make four then that's the truth to them. If you say trees feel pain then, in just the same way, they believe you. It's a most tremendous responsibility. And hugging trees? Come, come!'

Kate opened her mouth to protest but Peter held up his hand and silenced her.

'There is another matter I need to speak about. At one time the absence of the head teacher from Communion and indeed from any service in the church would have been a matter for stern admonition. Not nowadays, however, but you're never there *at all*. Is there a reason for this?'

'None. I've just not got round to it.'

'You've an example to set. Your behaviour doesn't go unnoticed in such a small community.'

Kate swung round from staring out of the window, and looked him full in the face. 'What do you mean by that?'

'Nothing sinister, I assure you. But straight from a mission school to nothing? It doesn't add up. Well, I'll be on my way. Won't take up any more of your time. No offence meant, only the very best of intentions. I know you'll think over what I've said.' Peter stood up. 'I expect you'll be pleased Beth has settled better. We do have the occasional dodgy morning, but mostly she comes quite happily. If there's one thing you learn about children it's that they are full of surprises.' He smiled. 'God bless you, Kate.' He left and so didn't see her shudder.

Peter got home late from a meeting that night, to find Caroline already in bed. He called upstairs, 'All right, darling? I'm just making a drink – want one?'

'Yes, please, don't mind what. You're late.'

'I know, lot to discuss. Won't be long.'

He glanced appreciatively at her as he took the tea into the bedroom. She was sitting up in her dressing gown on top of the duvet reading a book. He placed her cup on her table and bent to kiss her. 'You feel damp and deliciously perfumed.' Peter bent still further and kissed the hollow at the base of her throat. His tongue trailed up her neck, up her chin as far as her mouth and he kissed her again, tasting the toothpaste. 'Love you.'

'Love you. You look tired.'

'I am. Long day. Looking back on it I'm having doubts if I should have reproved Kate the way I did. Perhaps I came down a bit too heavily.' He sat beside Caroline and sipped his tea. 'What do you think?'

'Not heavily enough in my opinion. I don't want our offspring learning to hug trees and things.'

'Neither do I. There are rumblings from the parents, too.'

'Hardly surprising.' Caroline put her cup down and leant forward to kiss him. 'Don't worry, it'll all come out in the wash. Believe me!' She kissed him again and tasted the hot tea in his mouth. 'Isn't it odd, there's no other person in the whole world I would want to kiss like that but you.'

'Thank heavens for that! I'd have a lot to say if there was.'

'Never. You'd take it patiently and wait, and leave the decision with me.'

While Peter thought over what she'd said he held her hand to his cheek. Kissing it, he said, 'I wouldn't stand by in circumstances like that. I'd be in there hauling my woman back to my cave!'

Caroline laughed. 'And you a pacifist!'

'Darling girl!' He relished the taste of her toothpaste again and was thinking of stripping off his clothes and stretching out on the bed beside her when the phone rang. 'Blast.' He climbed over her to pick up the receiver on his side of the bed.

'The rectory. Peter Harris speaking.'

'That you, Rector? It's Vera. Vera Wright. Can yer come? I know it's late but it's our Rhett. He's out of his mind and we don't know what to do. Please, come, please tell us what to do. He's going mad.'

'I'll come, though it sounds as if you need a doctor rather than me.'

'If we get a doctor they'll cart 'im off. *Please*, Rector!'

'I'm on my way.' He put down the receiver and stood up to straighten his cassock.

'What's the matter?'

'Rhett Wright appears to be going out of his mind. Sorry, I've got to go. I'll try not to wake you when I get back.'

'I could be unprofessional and give him a jab if things are difficult – I've got my case with me. If you ring for a night-call it could be hours before anyone comes.'

'Thanks. Let's hope it doesn't come to that. Is Rhett on drugs, do you think?'

'Not that I know of, but then we don't see much of him.'

Don Wright let Peter in. 'Thank God you've come, Rector. I didn't want Vera to ring but it's just that we don't know what to do. He's gone stark raving crackers.'

'Tell me, Don. Have you ever thought he might be on drugs?'

Don looked embarrassed. 'Well, a while back I might have said yes, but not these last months now. Got in with a different crowd.' From upstairs the sound of howling drifted down to the hall.

'Come on, then. Show me the way.'

Vera was in Rhett's bedroom on her hands and knees, peering round the door of the built-in cupboard.

'Thank God you've come. He's in here.' She pointed to the bottom of the cupboard and moved aside so Peter could see him. The howling was spine-chilling.

Rhett was crouched in the bottom of the wardrobe amongst the shoes and boots; he'd made his body as small as he could. On his head he'd rammed a sports bag and with his arms through the handles his head was completely hidden. His hands were gripped around his shins. Although his howls were muffled by the bag they were still loud enough to wake the dead, as Vera observed.

Peter shouted above the howling. 'Hello, Rhett, Peter here from the rectory. Come to see if I can help at all. Is there anything I can do?'

There was a violent shaking of his head, but no dislodging of the bag.

Peter retreated from the cupboard and asked Vera how long he'd been like this?

'Been to a friend's to stay, got home about five, went out in the garden for a drag, beggin' yer pardon Rector, but I won't have him smoke in the house, and next news he's deathly white, shaking from head to foot, and can't speak. He raced in and hid in 'ere and he's never moved since. Just howled.'

'Did he seem odd when he came home or do you think he saw something while he was outside, or perhaps he spoke to someone? Did someone threaten him, perhaps?'

'Only Jimmy spoke to 'im. I was outside there getting some coal in and Jimmy called over the fence.'

'What did Jimmy say?'

Vera tried to remember the exact words. 'He said "Now, Rhett, how about that then? What d'yer think, eh?" Then he laughed and pointed at that dratted dog he's found. Rhett peered over the fence and was took bad immediate like. That's all.' Vera wrung her hands. 'Oh God, Rector, I'm at my wits' end. He hasn't eaten or drunk anything and not been to the you-know-what for nearly six hours. What shall we do?'

'He must be thirsty. Get him a drink – whatever he favours.' Peter bent down inside the cupboard. 'Rhett, we're just getting you a drink; you must be ready for one after all this time. Your grandmother is very worried about you, Rhett, so how about coming out and sitting on the bed? I'm a very good listener; I've heard some rare tales in my time. You can tell me absolutely anything and it will be entirely confidential.'

Rhett's howls grew louder and he began thrashing about inside the wardrobe, hammering with his fists against the back and slamming his feet at the end panel. Still with the sports bag over his head he said, 'Go away, the devil'll get you. Get away.'

With absolute conviction Peter said, 'He can't get me, because I'm wearing my cross. I believe the devil always runs from absolute goodness and that is what Christ is – total goodness. Here, you hold it.' Peter unhooked the cross from his belt, took the chain from around his neck and reaching inside the cupboard touched one of Rhett's hands with it. He clawed it into his grasp. Almost imperceptibly the howling began to lessen.

Vera came up with a glass of shandy. She whispered, 'He's a bit quieter. Thank Gawd for that.'

'Indeed. Here we are, Rhett, your grandmother's brought you a drink.' There was a violent jerking of Rhett's whole body and the glass of shandy spun out of the cupboard, spilling its contents over Peter and the carpet.

'Oh sir, I am sorry.' She shrieked at the cupboard: 'Rhett, you stupid ungrateful boy! Look what you've done!'

Peter put his finger to his lips and waved her away. Vera went to stand by the bedroom door. She heard Peter telling Rhett that he wanted him to bring the cross out into the open into the light, and he'd be quite safe while he did it.

'Come on now, come out, Rhett. Slowly. Slowly.' Peter opened the door, shielding Rhett. 'Let your hands go. That's it. Hold the cross. That's right. I'll lift the bag off. Slowly. Yes, yes, I'll do it very slowly. That's great. Now your legs, one at a time. Don't hurry. That's it. Slowly. Grip my arm.'

'Lights, is the light on? Mustn't be dark. I want the light.'

'If you open your eyes you'll see it is.'

Inch by inch, Peter extricated Rhett from the cupboard. When he was finally standing on the carpet he raced for the bed and shot head-first under the duvet, his dirty trainers resting on the pillow.

'Oh thank Gawd.' Vera shouted downstairs, 'Don, he's come out! What is it, love? Tell your old gran.'

Peter said, 'Let's leave him for the moment. I'd love a cup of tea, Vera. I'd just poured one out when you rang.'

'Of course, Rector. Cup of tea coming up.' Vera scurried away downstairs, leaving Peter alone with Rhett.

'Now we've got your grandmother occupied, can you come out?'

'No.'

'You've got the cross. No harm will come to you. Remember, you can tell me anything and I shan't tell a soul unless you want me to. I've heard it all; there's nothing can shock me.'

Very slowly, Rhett began to emerge from the bottom end of the duvet like a mole testing the night air. Peter's cross was gripped in one hand and his eyes were covered by the other. Peter felt compassion for him. He was a typical teenager, lean and gangling, three rings in each ear, close-cropped hair, smooth-skinned but with a spotty chin.

Rhett opened his fingers slightly and peered at Peter through the gaps. 'Can't go to sleep. Daren't go to sleep.'

'If you could let me know what's troubling you, then perhaps I could help to make you feel better.'

'Can't tell you, sir. Oh no, not you.' Quietly he began howling again, rocking from side to side.

'Look, Dr Harris — my wife — could give you something to help you to sleep. Then we could talk in the morning when you've rested. We'll ask your grandfather to help you undress and get you into bed, and then she could come across.'

Rhett nodded his assent and whispered, 'Can I keep your cross? Till tomorrer?'

'Of course. I'll come back and we'll talk. Right?'

'Right.'

16

'It's that blasted dog, Mr Charter-Plackett. The thing's damned, that's what.' Mrs Jones snipped the parcel tape on her twelfth package of the afternoon and neatly pressed the gummed address label onto it. 'Poor Rhett's clean out of his mind and now it's affected the sergeant's wife.'

'Really, I hadn't heard that?'

'Oh yes. Jimmy went round to ask if anyone had reported a dog missing, took the blasted thing with him, and the sergeant's wife was doing her bit of dusting and that in the office – when lo and behold she collapsed against the counter and they had to get her to bed. Incoherent, she was. Drip white. Her eyes rolling all over the place. They say her hair stood on end, like she'd been electrocuted, but I think that's a bit of an exaggeration. Still in bed and won't talk. The sergeant did think of sending for the rector but when he mentioned it he thought she was going to strangle him.'

'Really?'

'Oh yes.' Mrs Jones selected another jar of Harriet's Country Cousin Apricot Chutney from the shelves. 'This is going well; we'll soon be needing some more. Will I ring her that makes it, or will you?'

'You can.'

Mrs Jones nodded her agreement. 'So, she won't hear of the rector going to see her, hysterics she 'as if his name's even mentioned. Rhett's started sitting in the church which is a first for him, I don't mind telling you, and Vera's gone out and bought him a cross of his own so the rector can have his back again. Said she felt a complete fool buying a cross, but it seemed the only way to give Rhett peace of mind. I tell you, Mr Charter-Plackett, there's more in this than meets the eye.'

'Such as?' Jimbo took a huge bite out of his lunchtime pork pie, and looked up expectantly at her.

Mrs Jones settled herself on Sadie's old chair, pushed a strand of hair back into place and told Jimbo what she thought. He hadn't imagined when he'd taken her on all of three weeks ago that he would find such satisfaction in talking to her. She was a window on the village in a way that Sadie could never have been. She had her finger on the pulse.

'Well, Rhett won't tell the rector why he's so upset. Refuses point blank. The rector's tried and no mistake but to no avail. But whatever it is, the sergeant's wife is affected the same way, isn't she? One sighting of that blasted dog and they're off their heads. Nothing could be more out of character than Rhett Wright going about with a cross round his neck and sitting in church. I mean, all this because of that dog. Now, where has it come from, eh? Answer me that.'

'A stray, that's all, just a coincidence.'

Mrs Jones glanced around the mail-order office as though expecting someone who shouldn't to appear from behind the boxes. 'Well, there's more than me think it's from the devil. Why should a dog cause such an upset otherwise?'

'I've seen it, you've seen it and we're not behaving oddly.'

'No, you've a point there, but couple it with lights in Sykes Wood in the night and what have you got?'

'Badger-watchers?'

'No! Badger-watchers?' Mrs Jones snorted derisively. 'No way. No, this is something more sinister.'

'Such as?'

'Sykes the dog, Sykes Wood – there's the connection, you see. He was buried there, wasn't he?'

'Mr Charter-Plackett! Can you come, please? The rep's here you were expecting.' It was Linda calling from the Store.

Jimbo left Mrs Jones to her parcels. There were times when the villagers' logic completely baffled him and this was one of them.

Peter had already called to see the sergeant's wife but she had adamantly refused to meet him. The sergeant had leaned his elbow on the station counter and confided in him.

'You see the thing is, Rector, I know you won't take this any further,' Peter had agreed he wouldn't; of course not. 'I thought, well, I thought she'd got another man. She suddenly started going out late at night, 'bout once a week, like. At first she told me it was the drama society. Well, I knew different. I mean, who'd want my Ellie on a stage? There weren't no rehearsals, neither. And you don't rehearse for a play at midnight, do yer?'

'Indeed not.'

'I asked her straight out one night. I said, "Ellie, what you doin' coming 'ome this time o' the mornin'? Have you got yourself another man?" "What if I have. You mind yer own business," she said. "I've slaved for you all these years and now I'm having a bit of life of my own." I tried all ways – police techniques and that I learned at Hendon once when I went on a course, but to no avail. Now she's bedridden. Can't speak, and near throttles me if I mention getting help. Women! There's no weighing 'em up is there, sir?'

'It can be difficult. The dog upset her then?'

'Oh yes. Didn't bite her nor nothing. She just took one look and she hasn't spoken since.'

'Has anyone laid claim to it?'

'No, and there ain't going to *be* nobody coming to claim it. Had a fax from Culworth yesterday. Turns out it was in a car what was involved in that massive smash-up on the by-pass that Saturday tea-time. It escaped completely unhurt, which considering its owners were squashed to a pulp is nothing short of a miracle. Vicar and his wife from up North travelling back off their 'olidays, perhaps that accounts for 'is liking of going into the church. Anyways no one noticed it running off, and the relatives never gave it a thought, they was that upset yer see, then they remembered it but they don't want it, and they're glad it 'as a good 'ome. But it ain't no good me telling our Ellie that. She says she knows whose it is, it's Jimmy's Sykes and there ain't no one who can persuade her different. So now we know where it came from, but it's still frightening. Seems too much of a coincidence, both dogs being so alike.'

Peter didn't take him up on this idea; everyone was quite superstitious enough without him encouraging them. 'Is Ellie eating?'

'Well, she is now. Spends most of her time moaning under the bed-clothes, but she will eat so long as it's under the covers like. Won't have the light turned off at night, though. I can't go on like this. Hospital it is, if there's no improvement.'

'If she decides she wants to see me, ring me any time – night or day.'

'Well, that's very generous of you, Rector. I'll do what you say. This isn't like my Ellie at all. Not at all.' He lifted up the flap on the counter and came out to see Peter to the door. 'Be retiring soon. Police house goes with the job. Be moving away.'

'That's a pity.'

'Might be for the best, all things considered.'

Peter had waved and driven away, puzzling about the whole situation. The village was getting very twitchy about Jimmy's dog. Everyone appeared affected by its arrival. Yet the dog seemed harmless enough. Nice little thing, very friendly. Quiet as a mouse in church on Sunday. Bit unorthodox allowing him to stay. But poor Ellie! Poor Rhett! Being jobless at sixteen couldn't be much fun. Peter had wondered who might possibly employ him. As he'd turned up Pipe and Nook Lane to put the car in the garage he thought of the Big House and the grounds. Surely *they* might be able to find him work, even if it was only part-time. He did a U-turn immediately and drove straight up to the Big House.

As he'd expected, Louise was at the reception desk.

'Good morning, Louise.'

'Good morning, Rector.' There was no longer a hint of the constraint in her voice which had been present ever since her misguided predilection for him. 'What a lovely surprise! What can I do for you?'

'I'm looking for Jeremy.'

'He's here, I'll give him a buzz. Do sit down if you wish. He won't be long.'

While Louise tracked Jeremy Mayer down, Peter went to look out of the hall windows. The lawn, now restored to its former glory after the disastrous episode with the new sewers, was a joy to behold. Peter caught a sense for a brief moment of how hard Ralph must find it to come up here and see his old home. Especially now it was in the hands of an insensitive entrepreneur like Craddock Fitch; though since Sadie's death the man had been a little less assertive than before. He felt as much as heard the heavy ponderous step of Jeremy Mayer.

'Good morning, Rector. Pleasure to see you.' Peter turned and shook the outstretched hand. Jeremy was not getting any thinner. His upper arms resembled large hams, and his feet looked ridiculously small at the end of his necessarily wide trouser legs. Peter surreptitiously wiped his palm dry on the handkerchief in his cassock pocket.

'And to see you. I've come on a begging mission.'

'Donation is it, to some worthy cause?'

Peter quelled his indignation at Jeremy's assumption and said, 'No. I'm speaking to you in your capacity as estate manager. I wonder, are there any vacancies at the moment, or likely to be in the near future, for unskilled teenagers? Anything would do – kitchens, gardens, handyman, anything. I have a particularly needy case in mind.'

'I don't think we have. I wish I could help.'

Peter was disappointed.

Then Louise pushed a piece of paper across her desk. 'You've come on the right day, Rector. There's this advertisement I've just written out for a garden labourer.'

Jeremy, angry with himself for appearing out of touch, said: 'Ah yes, I'd forgotten about that. Gardening any good?'

'Anything at all.' Peter flashed a grateful glance in Louise's direction. 'Before you put it in the paper, could I be given the chance to speak to this young chap?'

'Someone in the village?' Louise asked.

'Yes, Rhett Wright.'

Jeremy laughed. 'Poor chap needs all the help he can get with a name like that. That's the one who's gone off his rocker, isn't it?'

'I wouldn't quite put it like that.'

'Whole village seems to be jumpy. All over a dog. Amazing!' Jeremy's mountainous body shook with laughter.

'Worrying, actually. I just wish I knew what it was all about. Neither Rhett nor the sergeant's wife will tell me why they're so terrified. I'll be in touch, Louise, about the job as soon as possible. OK?'

'Fine.'

'Bye, Jeremy. Thanks for the chance. I'll return the favour one day.'

In The Royal Oak that night Vera expressed her eternal gratitude. 'The drinks are on me and if the rector was in 'ere tonight I'd be buying him one as well. Gawd! Am I grateful. Rhett's been up there meek as a lamb and Greenwood Stubbs, head gardener though he might be, 'as been that lovely with him. Told him there's a career waiting for him if he puts his mind to it. Promised to teach him all about the greenhouses, growing them grapes and peaches and whatnot as soon as he proves himself diligent-like. And he's promised him a day a week at college if he shows interest! Can yer imagine our Rhett at college? Never thought I'd live to see the day.'

'Wouldn't have thought your Rhett would know one end of a spade from the other,' Jimmy wryly observed.

'He doesn't, but he soon will. I've promised him a nice packed lunch each day and I'm keeping my fingers crossed.'

'Better now, is he?' Willie asked.

'Much improved. But it's unnerving, this business of 'im sitting in the church such a lot.'

Willie became indignant. ''Armless enough occupation. Might do 'im a bit o' good. Better than sniffing drugs. Saw him in there this morning when I was clearing up. He isn't praying. Just sits there or walks about reading the memorial tablets and the like. This job could be the making of 'im.'

'I 'ope so. Teenagers need money in their pockets nowadays; it'll be grand for 'im. Here's to the rector and Greenwood Stubbs and our Rhett. Let's 'ope he sticks with it.'

Willie and Jimmy raised their glasses and joined in the toast.

Jimmy wiped his lips, put down his glass and said, 'What d'yer reckon made him go crackers then?'

Vera looked shiftily at Jimmy and chose her words carefully. 'To be honest, Jimmy, and I 'ope you won't take offence, but he went funny after he'd seen that dog of yours.'

'Sykes?'

'Have you called him Sykes?'

'I have. I'd no alternative and no one's reported him missing as yet, so I'm keeping 'im.'

'Really?' Suddenly afraid, Vera asked, 'Is he under the table now?'

'Yes.'

'Oh Gawd!' She leapt up and made to leave.

'He's pulling your leg, Vera. He's not here.' Willie laughed. 'It's all daft, this being frightened. I mean, he's only a stray.'

Jimmy shook his head. 'Don't you be too sure about that, Willie Biggs. He's far too wise just to be a stray. Mark my words.'

'If it's Sykes, who was it brought him back to life, then? Answer me that.'

Vera whispered, 'The devil? Our Rhett's frightened of the devil getting him, that's what he says. That's why he's so scared.'

'For heaven's sake, don't let the rector hear you talking like that.'

'There's lights in Sykes Wood at night. I reckon there *is* someone dabbling with the devil.'

'Let's hope they have a long spoon then if they're supping with *him*.'

'Ms Pascoe's cat's been seen late at night in the woods.'

'That's nothing to go by. Dr Harris' Mimi used to go huntin' there. Rector's Meadow, Sykes Wood – you name it.'

'Yes, and look what happened to her. She's never been seen since.'

Willie saw he was on dangerous ground and, fearful of betraying what Sylvia had found in the wood, he tried to change the subject. 'Pat's still at the school then.'

'That's another thing. Ms Pascoe, what's she up to?'

'Teaching if she's any sense,' Willie replied.

'And some. I reckon she's up to something funny with them kids. The rector's been and given her a telling off.'

'How do you know?'

'Pat told me. They left the office door ajar and she was dusting in the hall, quite by chance.'

Jimmy and Willie both said, 'Of course.'

'She couldn't hear everything but she did hear him tell her she'd no business teaching the children about bloody trees feeling pain.'

'That's not evidence she's doing deals with the devil, is it?'

'I haven't finished.' She leant towards the two of them and said softly, 'Last night my Don was coming back 'ome later than usual after one of his late shifts, two o'clock in the morning it was, and he passed Ms Pascoe walking along towards the village, with that cat of hers. *From the direction of Sykes Wood.*'

'Is this true or have you made it up?'

'True as I'm 'ere – ask him if you like. You know Don don't exaggerate, and he 'adn't been drinking 'cos as you well know he doesn't. So what's she doing that time o' night walking home from Sykes Wood, eh?'

17

It was not only Don Wright who'd seen Kate walking home in the night. Ralph and Muriel had been to dinner with an old Diplomatic Service colleague of Ralph's and the two men had been reminiscing with such enjoyment that Muriel had not wished to spoil their pleasure by reminding them how late it was getting, with the result that they hadn't left his house until a quarter past one. Muriel was very tired and dozed for most of the way home.

Ralph had woken her when they were about five minutes away from Turnham Malpas. 'My dear, time to wake up. Five minutes and we shall be there.'

Muriel stretched. 'I wasn't really sleeping, just dozing. I'm glad you had such a wonderful evening, Ralph.'

'We rather neglected you, I'm afraid.'

'No, you didn't, I enjoyed hearing about your exploits. He seems to have been great fun.' In the beam of the car headlights Muriel spotted someone walking by the side of the road. 'Oh look, Ralph! Be careful, there's someone there. Look!'

'So there is. Who on earth can it be?'

As they passed, Muriel saw it was Kate Pascoe with Cat.

'What is Kate doing out at this time of night? Quick! Do stop and give her a lift.'

'No.'

'Ralph! Perhaps her car has broken down. Do stop.'

'I don't want that cat in my car.'

'I think that's most unkind, and not at all like you.'

'She's nearly home anyway. I don't like cats, Muriel. Particularly ones the size of a young panther.'

'You're not succumbing to this village superstition thing, are you?'

'Of course not.'

'You don't sound very sure.' She turned her head to look into his face. There was a half-smile on his lips and she said, 'You are, just a little bit, aren't you?'

'I was born and bred here, so perhaps I am in tune with the spirit of the village.'

'Well, really, I'm ashamed of you. I truly am. I was born here too, but I don't feel like that. It's nonsense.'

'There's an atmosphere in the village at the moment that I don't like – a kind of wary atmosphere – and people are finding it difficult to meet one's eye. Have you noticed that? But then there have been some strange happenings recently, haven't there?'

'Ralph – you're as bad as everyone else! Sadie dies in her sleep, which I'm very sorry about because I envied her her *joie de vivre* and I shall miss her, one cat goes missing and a stray dog turns up. No connection at all.'

'Two people, one quite young, are both quietly going out of their minds. You've forgotten that.'

Muriel shivered. 'You're right.'

'I am. Somewhere there's evil about. Someone is toying with the devil.'

As Ralph was putting the car away in the garage, Muriel remarked, 'I overheard in the Store that there's been lights seen in Sykes Wood at night.'

'Ah!'

'Why "Ah!"?'

'We've just seen Kate Pascoe, with a torch, walking along in the early hours of the morning, haven't we?'

'We have. Ralph, how about if *we* go and take a look one night? Very late.'

'Muriel!!'

'Why not?'

They walked down the back garden path full of their idea, and Muriel fell fast asleep with an image of Enid Blyton's Secret Seven in her mind. She'd so enjoyed those books when she was a girl, and she and Ralph setting off to investigate a mystery made her feel like a schoolgirl again.

A week after seeing Kate coming home in the early hours Ralph made up his mind to do something about it. He had to find out for himself what it was that the village was so upset about. That evening, he made one of his rare appearances in the bar of The Royal Oak. It was nine o'clock. Being midweek the bar was only half-full but the two people he was hoping to see were there. He ordered his whisky, exchanged views with Georgie and Bryn about the long winter they were experiencing, and then took his drink across to the table where Willie and Jimmy were conferring.

They both looked up as his shadow crossed the table. 'Hello, Ralph.'

'Hello, Jimmy, Willie. Can I join you or are you expecting someone?'

Jimmy moved further up the settle. 'Sit here. There's just the two of us. Sylvia's sitting in at the rectory and Vera's having to fill in on the late shift at the nursing home.'

'Thank you, I will then. How's Sykes?'

Jimmy put his finger to his lips. 'Sssh – he's under the table, but don't let on; it only upsets everyone. I can't leave him by himself at home all evenin'.'

'Saw you taking him out the other morning. He's indistinguishable from the old Sykes, isn't he?'

'Yes, and a grand dog he is, too. We're becoming real friends. He's good company.'

'Capital. There's something a bit special about dogs, something extra in their companionship which you don't get with a cat.'

'Exactly.'

'I keep wondering if Muriel should get another dog, but she can't forget Pericles.'

'When you've 'ad a good dog, yer can't replace 'em easily. I've taken to 'im,' Jimmy pointed under the table, 'only 'cos he's so like old Sykes in looks and that.'

'And that?' Ralph queried.

'Habits an' that. Uncanny it is sometimes.'

'Uncanny?'

Willie interrupted. 'This is leading somewhere, Ralph?'

'You've both finished your drinks – will you allow me to get you another?'

Willie pushed his glass across the table. 'Thanks very much. Same again, please.'

'And me,' echoed Jimmy. Ralph took their glasses to the bar. 'He's got something on his mind, he 'as.'

Willie agreed.

Ralph settled down again at their table and when they'd thanked him for their refills, he said heavily, 'Sykes Wood.'

'Yes?' Jimmy said. 'What about it?'

Willie looked away, tried to pretend he hadn't heard. Jimmy lifted his glass and having taken a long drink, wiped his mouth on the back of his hand.

'You've been there, haven't you, to take a look?' Ralph asked.

'I 'ave, yes, but I saw nothing unusual at all, 'cept for a dead bonfire.'

'I think there's something untoward happening there. Do you?'

Jimmy put down his glass, and fiddled with the beer mat, making it straight and placing his glass right in the centre of it.

'Per'aps.'

Willie looked anxiously at Ralph. 'What do yer mean?'

Ralph leaned towards them both. 'I think it's witchcraft or black magic. Something of that ilk.'

Jimmy nodded. 'Some years since we 'ad any of that round these parts.'

Ralph glanced about and then asked quietly, 'Remember what happened then at the time?'

'Must have been twenty years ago – no, maybe twenty-five. Tell yer who was involved,' he counted them off on his fingers, 'the Senior sisters, Simone Paradise's French grandmother, Gwen Baxter's mother and a woman who'd been evacuated 'ere during the war and stayed on – forget her name. Used the old cricket pavilion for services or whatever they called 'em. Right uproar there was. Old Reverend Furbank, not so old then o' course, was at his wits' end. Thelma and Valda's mother finished up running screaming through the village in the night in her night-dress, got herself so frightened she 'ad. Blamed it on a black cat of Valda's, said it was Valda's familiar or some such. Looked damned ordin-ary to me.'

Willie joined in. 'I remember that. They held a meeting in the church-yard one night – Hallowe'en it was. I 'ad a grave dug ready for the next day, and one of 'em fell in it and nearly died of fright. She dislodged a lot of soil and, before we could use it, I 'ad to get down in it and clear it out a bit and I found a dead cat. Horrible it was. But yer don't have that kind of thing in this day and age. Heavens above. Course not.' Willie shuddered.

Jimmy disagreed. 'Don't you be too sure, there's a sight lot more going on in this village at the moment than meets the eye. There's something nasty and I reckon Ralph's suggested the very place where it's all 'appening. And you know more than you're saying, Willie Biggs.'

'I don't.' Willie shook his head emphatically and tried to signal to Jimmy not to say any more.

'You do.'

'Care to investigate?' Ralph said this very casually.

The hairs on the back of Willie's neck stood up. 'Investigate?'

Ralph raised a questioning eyebrow and said softly, 'Tonight?'

Willie shook his head. 'Rector and Dr Harris are out very late tonight. Gone to a party at the George. When I've finished here, I've promised to go and keep Sylvia company, seeing as she's staying so late.' The relief on his face was noticeable.

'Very well – can't be helped. I need you, Jimmy, because you know the woods so well. I have a powerful torch I keep in the car in case of a breakdown, so we'll take that. Anything else we need?'

'I'll bring Sykes.'

'Good – he might give us early warning if there's anything wrong. Midnight, at my house, right?' Ralph downed his whisky and said good night.

Jimmy surreptitiously put his glass down under the table for Sykes to drink the remains of his ale. 'Well, well,' he said slowly. 'Who d'yer reckon we'll find?'

Willie answered Jimmy's question with a shake of his head. 'You'll see nobody. Not a bloomin' soul.'

The church clock was striking midnight as Jimmy knocked at Ralph's door. It was a cold night so he was well wrapped-up. He'd unearthed his old poaching jacket and Ralph answered the door wearing his Barbour jacket with a corduroy cap Muriel never liked him to wear in daylight.

'You carry the torch, Ralph.' Muriel appeared and handed it to him. Ralph looked at her in astonishment. She was dressed for going out, wearing that jaunty wool hat she loved, a thick winter coat and wellingtons.

'My dear, you're not coming.'

'I am. I'm all dressed ready to go.'

'I can't possibly allow you—'

'I'm sorry, Ralph, three heads are better than two and I'm coming.'

'Absolutely not. It could be dangerous.'

'Phooey! Dangerous? This is Turnham Malpas, not downtown New York.'

'Jimmy! Say she mustn't come.'

'I'm having nothing to do with it. I'm not coming between married folk. But make up yer minds, please. It's cold standing 'ere.'

Disappointed at not getting immediate support from Jimmy, Ralph sighed. 'Very well, my dear, but at the first hint of—'

'Ralph! Don't mollycoddle!'

They climbed the stile into the woods and Ralph led the way followed by Muriel and then Jimmy. Somewhere close an owl hooted. Muriel jumped. The deep silence in the wood, to say nothing of the very deep blackness of it, unnerved her, though she would have died rather than admit to it. She'd lived in the country the first fourteen years of her life, but had never been what could be called a countrywoman. Now, take Jimmy, he was a countryman right to the tips of his toes. So too was Ralph. They actually enjoyed field sports – but not Muriel. The fields and woods gave her pleasure and they gave her space to breathe and she wouldn't have wanted to live anywhere else, but . . . she tripped over a tree root.

'Mind out,' Jimmy whispered hoarsely. 'Be careful, watch where you're going.'

'Sorry!' Muriel stumbled on. They'd be there all too soon at this pace. Ralph wasn't half determined once he'd made up his mind – just like he'd been as a boy at the village school. A twig flicked against Muriel's cheek and startled her. Anyway it was more than likely they'd find nothing, absolutely nothing. She wished she'd brought a torch for herself; Ralph's torch going on ahead wasn't much use to her walking behind him, but the path was too narrow to walk alongside each other. Sykes ran back to check on Jimmy, and Muriel had to pause for a moment to avoid tripping over him.

It was Sykes' low rumbling growl which upset Muriel; there was a menacing note in it which boded ill.

'Quiet, Sykes! Shut up!' Jimmy snarled, but the dog wouldn't be hushed. 'Wait, Ralph. Listen.' The three of them stood quite still straining to hear what Sykes had already detected. Ralph had switched off his torch so that darkness was even deeper. The owl hooted again, fraying Muriel's nerves once more. An unexpected gust of wind rustled the trees.

Jimmy whispered, 'There's a while to go yet before we reach the clearing. Can't hear a thing, can you?'

Ralph said he couldn't either. 'Let's press on.'

Muriel followed feeling more alarmed than ever. Why ever had she said she'd come? She was always doing this, getting involved and then fervently wishing she hadn't. As for Sykes . . . Dogs knew things human beings didn't and she'd an idea that Sykes knew more than most. She guessed they'd chosen the right night, because . . . Out of the corner of her eye, she spotted a pair of gleaming green eyes, low down amongst the undergrowth. It was only for a fleeting second but very frightening. Oh dear Lord, if she'd been a woman who crossed herself she'd have done it then and there. She poked Ralph in the back, and pointed but Ralph only shrugged: he could see nothing. Then there they were again, the eyes, watching them. Sykes, who was keeping close to Jimmy, renewed his rumbling growl. Muriel poked Ralph again and pointed but, as Ralph's torch flicked the other way, the eyes could no longer be seen. Muriel didn't really know whether she wanted to watch out for them again or whether she wanted to stare straight ahead and ignore them.

Jimmy cannoned into her as Ralph halted unexpectedly. The torch went out and they were in utter blackness again. That owl! It chilled her spine. They sounded so lovely at night when she was safely tucked up beside Ralph, but not out here in the dark. Then she smelt woodsmoke, and through the trees she could just detect a blaze. Oh God in heaven! There they were. Faintly she could hear strange chanting, like in church but different. Sykes' ears were on alert, his head twitching from side to side as though detecting the direction of a sound he'd heard close by. Muriel thought about the green eyes, and her flesh began to creep. Had they got a wild panther in the woods? Was that what had got Mimi?

Jimmy's shoulder was touching hers as they stood listening; he tugged at her sleeve and she felt rather than saw him turning off the path and going between the trees following Ralph. *Towards the green eyes.* Oh heavens above! She couldn't see a thing. She stumbled amongst the closely packed trees, catching her arms, her face, her elbows, her feet on twigs and stones and low-lying branches. Once her coat caught on a branch and by the time she'd unhooked herself she couldn't see Ralph ahead.

A hand reached out and grabbed her arm. It was Jimmy. They moved on stealthily until the chanting grew louder, the light from the fire brighter. Then Ralph stopped and crouched down. He waved his hand behind him to signal that they should do the same.

Between the bushes, they could see there were five of them dancing round the fire, black figures silhouetted by the flames. You couldn't identify anyone, except to say one was short, one was tall, two were thin, one was fat. Then after the chanting had reached a climax and the frenzied dancing had slowed, one of the figures reached towards the fire and then walked towards a pile of stones. They were carrying something they had lit from the fire. Muriel saw they were lighting candles at the top of the pile of stones. The figures stood in a circle around the stones and then one lone voice began a chant. The only sound was the voice. Unchurchlike and yet churchlike. Worshipping and yet not. Fascinating but yet repellent.

The spell was broken by Sykes, who suddenly flung himself out of Jimmy's grasp and hurtled towards the clearing. Muriel saw the green eyes again: Sykes was heading straight for them. Though the two animals were fighting in the light of the bonfire, it was impossible to see what was happening for they were fastened into a tight ball of snarling, spitting, scratching and yowling. Rolling over and over, never letting go. Occasionally Sykes yelped but mostly he snarled. The fight seemed to last an age; the effect it had was startling. The five figures simultaneously snuffed the candle-flames, picked up belongings from around the fire, and fled in five different directions.

Only the cat and dog remained, still fighting as though to the death. Jimmy raced towards them, shouting. Ralph shone his torch between the trees attempting to catch a glimpse of the figures fleeing into the darkness, but he was too late. They had gone. The cat and dog rolled too close to the fire and the cat's shrill shriek as it rolled on the glowing ash at the edge of the bonfire cut Muriel's fragile courage from under her. She screamed. The cat fled. The fight was over.

Sykes stood up panting, laughing in his doglike way at Jimmy, waiting for praise for his efforts. With one arm gripping Muriel tightly, Ralph shone the torch on Sykes. There was a long bleeding gash from his right eye down the side of his face to the corner of his mouth, and a tear down his left flank. But he was triumphant; no one could deny him his victory.

Ralph asked, 'Did either of you catch a glimpse of who they were?'

Both Muriel and Jimmy shook their heads.

'Neither did I. What a pity. No doubt in my mind that cat was Kate Pascoe's.'

'Nor mine. Must have been, 'cos they were of a size. Come here, old lad. Good dog, good dog. Jimmy'll see to them scratches when we get home.' Jimmy patted Sykes where he could without touching his wounds and Sykes wagged his tail. A job well done, he seemed to be saying.

Fired up by the fight and the flight of the participants, Jimmy wanted to find out more. 'Let's look around, see what we can find.'

They found that the candles were black. Muriel shrieked. 'I read about that in a novel once. Oh dear! Oh dear!'

'What did you read, my dear?'

'They had the black candles.'

'Who did?'

'The witches!'

'So we are right, it's just as I thought.' Ralph shuddered. 'Let's be gone from this evil place.'

He held Muriel's arm in a tight reassuring grip. She was shaking with fear. Looking round the clearing, a place she had once thought was lovely, and indeed a place where as a girl she had often picnicked with the Guides, Muriel felt nothing but horror. To think it was people from her own village who were doing these dreadful things. Perhaps dreadful things to Mimi. And whatever it was that had frightened Rhett and the sergeant's wife. Maybe they really *had* reincarnated Sykes. She shook herself. Pull yourself together, Muriel, she thought. You would come on this adventure, it's all your own fault. 'Let's go, Ralph. Come on, Jimmy.'

Jimmy kicked a lot of earth onto the bonfire to damp it down. Ralph pulled one of the candles free from the altar, pinched the wick to make sure it was completely out and stuffed it in his pocket. 'Evidence.' Then he proceeded to kick down the column of stones, till it was just a heap, and the remaining black candles crushed into pieces.

As they left the clearing there was a massive clap of thunder directly above their heads, and huge spots of rain began to drop. By the time they'd reached the stile there was a full-scale thunder and lightning storm raging. Huge flashes of sheet lightning were spreading across the sky and Muriel was wishing she was safely at home in bed with Ralph; she wished she'd been there all night and had never encouraged him to come on this adventure. They'd found out more than they'd bargained for and she was frightened.

When they reached Jimmy's cottage, Ralph cautioned him: 'Not a word about what we've seen, Jimmy – to anyone. I shall speak to the rector first thing in the morning. I'm going to him because I don't know what else to do. I'll let you know developments. Good night, and thank you for coming with us, Jimmy. Someone had to find out. We shall have to put a stop to it, but I'm not sure how, when we don't know who it was.'

'But we do. It was Kate Pascoe's cat, sure as eggs,' Jimmy argued.

'Yes, I'm certain you're right on that score. Good night to you.'

Ralph and Muriel went to their own house and Ralph unlocked the door for Muriel but, before he followed her in, he stood in the road looking round at the sleeping village. Well, well. What next? But they'd withstand this crisis. The village had withstood heaven knew what for centuries – a bit of black magic wasn't going to destroy it. Civil war, world wars, plagues, kings and queens . . . all had come and gone, but here it still was, and here it would be for all time. The canker would have to be plucked out of its heart. He, Ralph Templeton, would see to that. He wasn't going to allow some pathetic people with twisted minds to destroy the peace of mind of this beloved place.

18

Hetty Hardaker rang the school-bell at five minutes to nine, as she always did. The children made their neat lines, Margaret Booth came to collect her infants and there was the usual hubbub of happy young voices, eager for the school day to begin. She couldn't help smiling. Where else would she find such satisfaction?

'Sophie, use your handkerchief dear, please. You haven't got one? Go and get a tissue from the box in my room.'

'Mrs Hardaker, it's my birthday today.'

'I know, Brian, I've got the candles all ready. I've put five out – that's right, isn't it?' She laughed at her joke. The children chuckled.

Brian protested. 'Eight!'

'Of course. I know. Just testing! Right, Miss Booth?'

'Right, Mrs Hardaker. Come along, Class One. Gently now.'

The only cloud on the horizon this morning was that Kate Pascoe was late. Hetty looked across at the school-house. The curtains were still drawn. Odd.

'Miss Booth, could you take prayers? When I've done the register I'm going across to the school-house to see what's happened to Miss Pascoe.'

'Will do.'

Hetty slipped on her top coat and strode across the school playground. She kept thinking Spring was on its way but this morning she knew she was mistaken. The wind blowing across the open space between the school and the house was cruelly cold. She knocked on the front door. She knocked again. She tried the knob, but the door was locked.

Only the curtains in the kitchen were open. Shading her eyes she peered in. Everything appeared to be quite normal. Neat, tidy, nothing out of place. Typical Miss Pascoe. But acid green kitchen walls? Hetty shrugged her shoulders. She stood below the bedroom window and shouted, 'Kate! Kate! Are you all right?'

Hetty returned to school. The head teacher's absence made a complete hash of the school timetable. She'd better inform the Education Department in Culworth to see if they could send a teacher to help out. At the back of her mind there was a nagging feeling. This was so unlike Kate. Hetty wished wholeheartedly that Mr Palmer was still here. Those were the days. Still, she couldn't deny him the happiness he'd found at last. His wedding to Suzy Meadows had been so beautiful . . . Maybe Kate was ill, Hetty thought suddenly. That was it! Too ill to get help. Oh dear. She hadn't got a key, so she couldn't get in.

Pat Duckett was just finishing in the kitchen when Hetty hurried back into school. 'No message from Miss Pascoe is there, Pat?'

'No, nothing. Funny she's not here. You'd think she'd have let us know.'

'Exactly. I think she must be ill and *can't* let us know. If I had a key I'd go and find out.'

'Look no further. I've still got one. Mr Palmer always let me keep one for him in case he lost his. Been meaning to give it to Ms Pascoe and never got round to it.'

'Where is it?'

'Safe at home. Too 'eavy to carry around.'

'I must go and see to the children. Is it asking too much to suggest you go home and bring it back here?'

'No sooner said than done.'

By the time Pat had cycled up to the Garden House and back again she was tired, but her curiosity urged her on to suggest Mrs Hardaker oughtn't to go into the house by herself just in case.

'You come with me then. It's better if there's two of us, just in case as you say.'

The decorations inside the school-house appalled Pat. It felt decadent. It *was* decadent. Give her a nice light emulsion and some chintzy curtains any time. This was a nightmare. There'd been two deaths on school premises, Toria Clark's and Mr Palmer's wife before that. Was this to be the third? She shuddered.

There was nothing and no one downstairs so Hetty called up: 'Kate! *Kate!*' Still no reply.

Nervously, she climbed the stairs with Pat close behind. The bed in the little bedroom hadn't been slept in. There was no sign of habitation except for a pair of black velvet slippers under the bedside table, and a book laid on the bedspread, which was dyed the deepest purple Pat had ever seen. Good grief! She'd never sleep a wink under that thing.

Then Hetty looked in that awkward corner under the eaves. There was an object shrouded beneath a black cloth. Two black candles stood sentinel either side. She whisked the cloth off and found a crystal ball.

Pat blanched. 'Lord help us! She's a witch.'

Hetty snapped her reply. 'Don't be ridiculous, Pat.' Despite her anger at

Pat's remark she covered the ball with the cloth and went down the stairs much faster than she had gone up them.

They stood at the bottom of the staircase looking at each other.

Hetty said, 'It's not a criminal offence.'

Pat trembled. 'The cat – where's the blasted cat?'

'I've always hated that cat.'

'Unnatural it is. I don't fancy finding it.'

'Neither do I. Where is she though?'

'I've just had a thought.' Pat raced outside. 'Look – her car's not here.'

Classes Two and Three had just gone out for their morning play when Kate's car drove into the school playground. Hetty ushered the children to one side whilst Kate parked it beside the school-house.

'Miss Pascoe! Thank goodness you're all right. Where have you been? We've been so worried.'

In answer to Hetty's questions Kate reached into the car and carefully lifted out a wire cat-carrier. Cat was inside. The animal had a wide bandage all the way round her middle, and looked much the worse for wear.

'Oh dear, I am sorry. Whatever happened?'

'A coal flew out of the fire and burnt Cat before she could get out of the way. It's a terrible burn and I had to take her to the vet's in Culworth. I've been so upset.' And indeed, the head teacher looked strained and hollow-eyed. 'They took ages attending to her. I'm sorry I didn't let you know but it's been terrible. I've been up all night with her. They wanted to keep her in but I insisted on bringing her home.'

The children pressed round to see the horrific injuries and were quite disappointed that the bandage prevented it.

'Oh! Ms Pascoe!'

'Ohhhh! How awful!'

'Awww. The poor thing!'

'It must hurt!'

Kate unlocked her door and said, 'Mrs Hardaker, I'll be in school by the end of playtime. I'll just grab something to eat and then I'll come.'

'Are you sure?'

'Of course I am. I can't leave you holding the fort.'

Hetty had to admire her, but at the same time . . . Crystal balls? What was the teaching profession coming to! At dinnertime when Pat came back she'd have to warn her not to let Kate know that they'd been in the house. At all costs Kate must never find out. It would put their working relationship, already somewhat tetchy, on such a precarious footing if Kate knew she'd seen the . . . well, not to put too fine a point on it . . . *the altar.*

*

Ralph had rung Peter at nine o'clock that morning to ask if he would be free to see him.

'Of course, if you come in about half an hour. After that I have various appointments which I can't ditch.'

'That will be absolutely fine, Peter.'

'Good, see you then.'

They settled down to talk in the study. Peter said, 'Before you tell me what you've come to discuss, can I say the builders have given me the quote for pointing the church tower and replacing any necessary masonry. When it's been agreed, they'll go ahead as soon as the weather improves.'

'Good – not before time. Can't have the tower falling down. Stitch in time et cetera.'

Ralph mentioned the cricket club and his hopes for the summer, and that the first match in the League was on the first Bank Holiday in May; they would be playing against Little Derehams. What did he think?

'Brilliant!' Peter, a born athlete and keen cricketer, was pleased. 'I understand they're a very good team.'

'They are. They are,' Ralph beamed.

'The pavilion will be finished then?'

'Oh yes! Have you not been to take a look?'

'No. I keep meaning to find the time. It's not lack of interest.'

'It is going to be excellent,' Ralph enthused. 'All modern conveniences in every sense of the word, plus a marvellous wide verandah right across the front – old Fitch's idea, and give him credit it's a good one. Best pavilion in the county when it's finished – but then that's typical of the man.'

Peter looked at Ralph with a reproving expression on his face. Ralph apologised immediately. 'Sorry! I truly am grateful for what he's done but it does rather stick in the craw. However, we shall have a superb summer cricket-wise, I'm sure of that, and the pitch is coming on a treat.'

'Is it cricket you came to see me about then?'

Ralph sat forward and rested his hands on his knees as he always did when he was searching for the right words. Looking up at Peter he said, 'It was nearly half-past one last night before I got to bed.'

'Oh, I'm sorry. What was the problem? Muriel not well?'

'No, no, nothing like that. I was in Sykes Wood with Jimmy and Muriel.'

'Ah. Yes?' Peter's expression changed.

Ralph told him what had happened in the wood and asked his opinion.

'I am completely bewildered. Who on earth can these five people have been?

'The cat Sykes had the fight with was Kate Pascoe's.'

'Oh good Lord, I don't believe it.'

'It got badly burnt. It actually rolled on the glowing embers with Sykes on top of it. It's bound to have burns. That will be proof of a kind.'

'I can hardly ask to see her cat can I? What excuse could I give?'

'None. But I won't have black magic or whatever it is they're doing, in this village. People are being affected by it, and it must stop.'

Unable to believe what was happening, Peter said, 'They'll not meet there again, will they, now they've been seen.'

'Exactly. I didn't mean to let them know we were there but Sykes thought differently.'

'I wonder who else is involved?'

Ralph retorted. 'No idea.'

'Hardly a police matter is it? But there's no doubt it is a church matter. They've done nothing criminally wrong, have they?'

Ralph shook his head saying 'No, but morally wrong.'

'Indeed. This calls for intervention on my part. I shall have to act, and quickly.'

'Quite. A sight of the cat is most important. Evidence, you see. And here's the other bit of evidence – one of the black candles.'

He took the candle from his pocket, and put it on Peter's desk. Peter picked it up. 'Oh, my goodness. That is ominous.'

'It is, isn't it? I must go, Muriel will be wondering where I am. She's very upset after last night, but she would insist on coming with us. She can be quite headstrong sometimes.'

'Thank you for telling me, Ralph. Action is called for, definitely, but I'm not yet quite sure what to do.'

'Neither am I. If I get any more information I'll let you know.'

'Very well, and I you.'

When Ralph had left, Peter moved one of his appointments to the afternoon so that he would be free to collect the children from playgroup.

'I *want* to go, Sylvia, I have a particular reason for going, OK?'

'Very well, Rector, but don't let Beth forget her wool hat. Dr Harris and I are taking them both to Bickerby Rocks this afternoon. Wear them out a bit, we hope!'

Peter laughed. 'Got to go, but I will collect them, don't worry.'

When he got to school at five minutes to twelve he went straight to the playgroup room and picked up the twins.

'Just need to see Ms Pascoe for a moment, children. Come with me.'

'Daddy.'

'Yes, Alex?'

'Cat's got a big, big bandage round her tummy and she's in her cage and she's poorly, and you can't see her eyes, she won't open them.'

Beth, not to be outdone, said, 'Ms Pascoe's been crying. Truly crying.'

Peter's heart sank. As he crossed the hall Kate, looking quite dreadful, came out of her classroom.

'Hello, Ms Pascoe. The children tell me your cat's been in the wars.' He felt very two-faced saying this but couldn't see any other way round it. He could hardly tell her outright that he knew the cause.

Kate didn't answer immediately. When she did it was in a low voice. 'A coal shot out of the fire and tangled in her fur and burnt her before I could get it out. She's really quite unwell.'

'I'm so sorry. She'll need good care.'

'Of course, and she'll get it. Cat's a dear friend.'

Peter smiled and said goodbye.

'Peter! I'm amazed you didn't realise yourself it was all lies,' Caroline said that evening when they were sitting by their own fire. 'I told you she'd bought a load of logs from Greenwood Stubbs. You remember, they cut down those trees and he'd advertised the logs for sale on the Village Voice board? I heard her in the Store ordering them from Pat, and giving her the money. So she's a liar to boot.'

'Maybe last night she burnt coal instead.'

Caroline sighed. 'Come on, Peter. I saw Sykes this morning. Chang and Tonga couldn't inflict wounds of that size and depth on Sykes, they're not big enough nor strong enough. But *her* cat could. Sorry, but you've got a witch for a head teacher.' Caroline burst out laughing. 'That must be a first!'

'It's all very well you laughing, Caroline Harris, but I've got a monumental problem. It doesn't just concern the school: it's affecting the whole of my parish. It's got to stop.'

'Well, don't ask *me* for advice! I haven't the faintest idea what to do with a witch.'

'Darling, in the light of what has happened, I can't avoid telling you something that I've kept putting off and putting off till now I can't delay any longer.'

Caroline turned swiftly to look into his face. She asked sharply: 'What have you got to tell me?'

'It's about Mimi.'

'Mimi!'

He paused, then looked Caroline full in the eyes. 'Have you accepted the fact that she might be dead?' he asked gently.

'Of course.'

Caroline waited for him to go on. She noticed he was twisting his wedding ring round and round, a sure sign he didn't like what he was going to have to say. 'Her collar's been found,' Peter said at last.

'Her collar? Where?'

'In Sykes Wood, near the bonfire you saw.'

'Oh God! You don't think they used her for—'

'I doubt it. It could just be chance.'

'Who found it?'

'Sylvia, but she didn't dare tell you. She was so frightened, and she didn't want you upset.'

Caroline took out her handkerchief and wiped her eyes. 'I can't bear to think of those dreadful people having poor Mimi in their power. When did she ever do anything unkind to anyone at all?'

'Never. Come here.' Caroline laid her head against his chest and wept quietly. Peter encircled her with his arms and wished he could say something of comfort but there wasn't anything that could alleviate her distress.

Caroline finally put her hands on his chest and pushed him away from her. 'I shall personally strangle the woman,' she said in a quivering voice. 'I shall go round to the school tomorrow and *do it*.'

'Darling, we have no evidence that she is involved – none at all. It's all pure conjecture.'

'No evidence? Of course we have!'

'What evidence? Tell me that.'

'The cat fighting Sykes.'

'But the cat could have been there quite by chance.'

'Why will you go round this world believing the best of everybody? I bet if you'd been on the jury at the Yorkshire Ripper trial you'd have found a reason for letting him off! It won't do, Peter. It won't do.'

'It's the way I'm made.'

'Poor Mimi! I shall make sure that Kate gets her comeuppance. She's got her cat, but I haven't got mine because of her evil ways.'

'Caroline!'

'Don't say "Caroline" in that tone of voice. She'll have to go.'

'I can't sack her! There are no grounds for me to do that.'

At that moment, Chang and Tonga flicked through the cat flap. They'd come in to go to bed. Caroline rushed towards them and hugged them close. 'We shall have to have litter trays and they won't be able to go out ever again.'

'Oh no! That was something we knew we couldn't have once we got the children. You agreed on that. No more litter trays. I never liked them in the first place and we are not having cats doing their business in this house. I forbid it.'

'You *forbid* it?' The ringing challenging note in Caroline's voice made Peter's heart sink. He forced himself to speak calmly.

'You have got to be rational about this. Much as I love the cats, the children's health and well-being come first. As a doctor, you know I'm right. Besides, it's cruelty of the first order to forbid the cats their freedom. I can't bear such cruelty.'

'But if it's to save their lives?'

'Even to save their lives. I refuse to have an argument about it. No litter tray and the cats have their freedom. One year of freedom is better than ten years locked in a house. I won't have it.'

'They're my cats.'

'They're your children.'

There was a split second of stunned silence and then she rounded on him and, in a controlled, ominously quiet voice, she said, 'The cats are *not* my children. I'm not some idiotic sentimental fool.'

Peter was furious that she should think that he knew so little of her as to make such a mistake. He retorted angrily, 'I know you better than to think that of you. I didn't mean the *cats*, I meant Alex and Beth are your children.'

Caroline opened her mouth to protest and then changed her mind. He was right: the children did come before the cats. Peter watched her gather herself together.

Caroline swallowed hard. 'I'm so sorry. Of course you're right. I do beg your pardon. I got everything out of proportion with being so upset. Yes, the cats shall have their freedom, no matter what. But Kate Pascoe is another matter. I shall go to see her tomorrow, and you mustn't try to stop me.'

'No, Caroline. Please, leave it to me.'

'Someone has to confront her with it.'

'I know, but I need time to think how to go about it.' He took both her hands in his and raised them to his lips. 'My darling girl, I'm so sorry about Mimi; so very sorry. I wouldn't have you hurt for the world.'

'Peter, where's her collar now? I'd like to see it.'

'Are you sure?'

'Yes.'

'Wait there.'

When he came back with it in his hand, Caroline smiled sadly. She cradled it against her face, looked up at him and said, 'You know, I used to confide in her about you. When I got back to the flat after being out with you, I told her what you'd said and the things we'd done, and where we'd been. Told her how lovely you were and how much I loved you. Silly, wasn't I?'

'Of course not. I love you for it.'

'Do you think she suffered?'

'I don't honestly know. I just hope not.'

'And so do I. So do I. But Kate Pascoe will have to go.'

19

Kate surveyed the paintings Class Three had done that afternoon. They were most unsatisfactory. Almost all of the children had become obsessed with black. There were black cats, black hats, black trees, black people, black clouds and two of them had a dreadful black interpretation of the devil. What on earth had happened to them all?

'Weird, ain't it?' Kate jumped. It was Pat Duckett coming in to clean the classroom. 'Downright spooky. Our Michelle didn't do paintings like that when Mr Palmer was 'ere. He wouldn't have allowed it.'

'But then Mr Palmer didn't know how to encourage children's talent.'

'Well, if that's talent give me mediocre any day. I don't know about him not encouraging them – all three of the kids who've applied for Prince Henry's and Lady Wortley's this year have had interviews. They'll be hearing any day now. So he must have taught 'em something.'

'Indeed he must, but that was the three Rs; this is creative talent.'

'Is it? I wouldn't have known if you hadn't told me. What about Liz Neal's boys? Guy's turning out real talented at painting at Prince Henry's. Liz says—'

'All right, Pat, there's an exception to every rule.'

Pat began to sweep. 'I'll say this for you, you keep a lovely tidy classroom. No bits to pick up at all and every cupboard top as clean as a whistle. No Brownie points though for the paintings. That one of the devil is the rector really.'

'I beg your pardon?'

'Well, when it's Stocks Day in June the rector dresses as the devil, horns and the lot, but underneath he has his white wedding cassock on and he flings off the devil's costume, blesses the stocks and everything's all right for another year. Something to do with the time when the Black Death came to the village, and we always celebrate it every year or else things worse than the Black Death might 'appen. So that's 'im. Strikes me he'll have to be doing some of that exorcising that a man of the church like 'im can do. There's another one of 'im there, look, with great big horns. You can just spot the white of his cassock at the bottom – see? These kids knows a thing or two, they do.'

'Nonsense!'

'Everybody's scared to death. Talking of death, look at Sadie Beauchamp – alive and kicking one day and dead as a dodo the next. Never ailed a thing. And why's Rhett and the sergeant's wife frightened out of their skins? Answer me that.'

Kate dismissed the ideas as quite ridiculous. 'They are all a load of rubbish, these scaremongering tales. And it's time you got on with your work, Pat.'

'Thanks very much. Only offering a bit of advice.'

Kate swept out of the room ahead of Pat's broom. She went to her little office, and stood looking out at the bins. Cat came in and, sensing the disturbance of Kate's mind, jumped up on the desk and rubbed her head against Kate's hip asking for attention. Cat's huge bald patch caused by her burn was beginning to grow new fur, and she was feeling and behaving more like her old self.

'Hello, Cat. Time to go home, is it?' Kate fondled Cat's ears and tickled her chin. Outside, Pat came round the corner to empty a wastepaper basket. Kate watched her. The paper cascaded into the recycling bin, except for one piece which blew upwards in a sudden gust of wind. She watched Pat reach out to catch it. Pat was right. The children *were* being affected, that was obvious from their paintings. In their own ways, they were suggesting that Peter did something about it for them. Kate shook herself. She was becoming even dafter than Pat, reading such ludicrous things into paintings the children would have forgotten about by now. Exorcism! Whatever next? All of it was pure coincidence, wasn't it? Cat purred. Pure coincidence.

'Tea and toasted teacake, I think, Cat. What about you?' Cat purred louder still; Kate's finger was scratching her in just the right places. Life was good here in Turnham Malpas. Everything had fallen into place. Soulmates, yes indeed, there were soulmates here. Cat jumped down ready for going home. When Pat came in to clean the staff washbasin, Cat, back arched, tail fluffed, spat at her.

Kate usually drank her afternoon cup of tea at the kitchen table, but today she took it into the living room and put a match to the fire. Her technique for lighting fires had improved by leaps and bounds and it was crackling healthily in no time at all. Cat had learned nothing since her accident and was sitting as close as she possibly could to the flames, busy washing herself and licking the bald patch as though to speed the growth of the fur there. Kate watched her dreamily.

She'd definitely done the right thing by leaving Africa and coming home to England. The climate suited her better and suited Cat better too. And here in Turnham Malpas there were such possibilities. The school for one offered her a tremendous opportunity to educate as she saw fit. The tight lines within which Michael Palmer had operated were not for her. All-round education, that was what these children needed, and the next thing she would do on that score was to buy computers. It was nothing short of scandalous that there were none in the school. One wouldn't be enough, not by any means. Kate had just put her mind to how she would fund her computer project when the front door burst open and the sound of children invaded the house.

Cat sprang up and ran to see who'd come, but Kate already knew. It was Simone with her brood.

'Hi! It's me. As if you didn't know.'

'Hello! Come in!'

'We are.'

The children spread like a plague of locusts around the little living room. Simone had the baby enveloped in the huge shawl she used as her baby carrier. Only wisps of dark curly hair showed above the shawl. Simone hitched the baby higher and sat down on the futon.

'Well?'

Kate raised an eyebrow. 'Well?'

'What about it then?' Cat leapt onto her knee, purring gleefully and begging to be stroked. 'What are we going to do?'

'Do?' Kate echoed again.

'Don't be stupid, Kate. You know what I mean.' The fact that the children were playing with just about every moveable object in the room, some of which were in imminent danger of being broken, didn't intrude on Simone's consciousness at all. It made Kate edgy.

'Do I?'

Simone pushed her long black hair away from the baby who was entangling her fingers in it. She stared at Kate with her large dark intense eyes. 'You do. The venue.'

'Tea?'

'Thanks.'

Kate went to the kitchen for another cup and some biscuits for the children. She hadn't any unbreakable cups and she wouldn't risk Simone's children getting their hands on her china.

She returned with the cup of tea for Simone, put it down on the table beside the futon and handed her the biscuits. 'These are for the children.'

The children began to argue and fight over an ornament. Simone stood up, took it from them without a word, put it high up on the mantelshelf, and passed round their biscuits.

'You haven't answered.'

'No.' Kate took a sip of tea. 'It's getting too much.'

'Oh! Is it? Just when we're getting successful.' Simone tickled Cat behind her ears and Cat reached her face upwards to encourage Simone to continue. She kneaded her claws into Simone's leg, the pleasure of being caressed by her almost too much to bear. Kate felt a stab of jealousy. Cat was *her* pet.

'Don't you call it success?' Simone pursued.

'No, I don't. You've been too successful.'

'Can one be *too* successful?'

'You can. It's getting in too deep for me.'

'What's "deep"?'

Kate moved one of the children away from the fire. 'I've no proper fireguard, not having children myself. Can you ask them to keep away?'

Simone ignored her and pressed home her question. 'What's "deep"?'

'I prefer not to do harm.'

'Harm? What harm have we done?'

'You don't need me to spell it out.'

'Only their just deserts.'

'No, not their just deserts. Punishment.'

'Going moral, are we?'

'Yes, if you like to call it that. I've a job to do here and I don't want to jeopardise it.'

'It won't.'

'It will if these last weeks are anything to go by.'

Simone accused her of backing out.

'Perhaps.'

'I'll take Cat then.'

'No, not Cat.'

'I shall. I can.'

'Simone! Leave Cat here with me.'

'On loan.'

'No, not even on loan.'

Simone smiled that slow, deep smile of hers. It was an all-knowing, threatening, wait-and-see smile and Kate didn't like it.

Simone slid Cat off her knee and stood up. 'I'll leave then. I'll let you know when and where. I've a place in mind.'

'I shan't come.'

'You will, or I'll have Cat.'

Kate stood up to emphasise her protest. 'Not Cat; she won't come.'

'Won't she?' Simone raised an eyebrow at Kate and then stared deliberately into Cat's bright green eyes. Cat was looking up at her adoringly.

The children followed their mother out of the house. She didn't tell them she was going, didn't gather them together ready to leave; they were simply expected to follow. Kate watched her crossing the playground. Cat scratched at the outside door wanting to be let out, but Kate ignored her. She had a strong feeling that Cat really would go with Simone and she wasn't having that.

But, later that evening, Cat just had to go out.

'Mummy! Mummy!' Harriet heard the front door slam and the thud of eager footsteps into the kitchen. Why did her children always assume she was in the kitchen? It said something about her that she didn't quite enjoy.

'Flick! I'm upstairs changing Fran.'

The footsteps pounded up the stairs and she heard Flick saying breathlessly as she reached the landing, 'Cat's missing!'

'They're not – they're in the house somewhere.'

'No!' Flick appeared in the bedroom, flung herself down on the bed next to Fran and gasped, 'I mean *Cat*, Ms Pascoe's cat.'

'Oh dear!'

'She's said we must all keep our eyes open and check our sheds and things just in case she's locked in somewhere. Have you checked our shed?'

'No, I didn't know to check it, did I? That's it, Fran, there you are. Off you go.' Fran sat up and began searching Flick's pockets to see if she had brought any treasures home from school. Harriet sighed. 'Can't wait for the day she's trained. Roll on the glorious day!'

'She won't be a baby sister any more then, will she?'

'Not a baby, no. So, about the cat. How long has she been missing?'

'Since last night. We've searched everywhere. Ms Pascoe's so upset she doesn't know what she's doing today, but she did say she's going to get us computers for school. Though I shall have left by then, won't I?'

'You will. Lady Wortley's here you come!'

'I'm glad I got in. Celebration night tonight, isn't it? I wish Grandma could have been here. She would have been so pleased for me, wouldn't she?'

'She would indeed, darling. I'm sorry too.'

Flick changed the subject quickly; she didn't want Mummy crying again. 'Can I go round to the Store with my pocket money?'

'Yes. Mind when you cross Shepherd's Hill. Have your drink when you get back, eh?'

Flick marched purposefully to the store, her pound coin held tightly. As she pushed open the door she listened for the ping of the bell, a sound her daddy said he loved, which she knew meant he loved the idea that customers were coming in to spend; it really wasn't just the *sound*. It being going-home-from-school time the Store was crowded. She loved it crowded. It felt like the shops she went to with Grandmama Charter-Plackett when she stayed with her in London in the holidays. It was good going out with her, but she still liked Grandma Sadie best. She was fun! *Had been* fun.

Flick pushed her way to the sweet counter. The Paradise children were there and she saw Dickon Paradise sneak a tube of Love Hearts into his pocket. 'Dickon! I shall tell your mummy. You've to pay for that.'

In reply Dickon kicked her ankle hard, little Valentine added another for good measure, and so did Hansel. Flick hopped about complaining, 'That hurt! Mrs Paradise, Dickon's got sweets in his pocket. He's nicking them!'

Simone gave Dickon a hard look and he pulled the sweets from his pocket and gave them to her. She put them back on the display.

Dickon poked his tongue out at Flick as far as it would go. She put hers out too and they stood within a hair's breadth of each other grimacing fiercely. Flick pulled her very nastiest face at him and turned away.

Then she saw Ms Pascoe. 'Ms Pascoe! Isn't it busy in here?'

'It certainly is. This is quite the wrong time to come, isn't it? What are you here for?'

'Spending my pocket money.'

Simone passed close by. Flick heard Ms Pascoe say quietly, 'Well, where is she?'

Simone Paradise paused and, pretending to be choosing corned beef, said innocently to a tin from Brazil, 'Who?'

'Cat.'

'I don't know where your cat is. I know where *mine* is.'

'You've enticed her away. She wouldn't leave me otherwise.'

'No?'

'You've locked her up.'

'Me? Do that to a defenceless animal? Tut tut!'

Flick stood looking up at the two of them, unable to understand. She could feel the sparks between them though. Almost touch them. How funny, feeling that. Mrs Paradise must have stolen Cat. She hadn't got a cat, she knew that for a fact. Dickon longed for one and his mother said 'no'. Another mouth to feed, she always said and she was right; she had six people to feed already and no daddy working for them. Flick wondered where their daddy was, though there'd be no room for one more in that tiny cottage; they must have to sleep head to toe already.

Ms Pascoe said, her lips tight with anger, 'Let her go!'

'At the next meeting.'

'I'm not coming.'

'You are. I'll tell you when.' Simone sailed to the till, the children struggling to keep up, and queued to pay.

Flick looked up at Ms Pascoe's face. She wished she hadn't. Ms Pascoe was sad and angry and fearful all at once. She bought herself some chocolate and went home, puzzled by the adult world and glad to get back to Mummy and Fran who made sense. Poor Cat. Perhaps Mrs Paradise was only teasing. That would be it, she was teasing and Ms Pascoe didn't realise she was. She'd tell her in the morning.

But there was Cat asleep as usual on Ms Pascoe's classroom windowsill when Flick got to school the next morning.

'Oh, Ms Pascoe! Cat's back again. I knew Mrs Paradise was teasing. Did she come back all by herself?'

'Last night.'

'I expect you'll be relieved.'

'I am.'

Kate found it hard to lie outright. Cat had indeed come back last night, but only because Kate had gone to get her. She'd waited until half-past eleven and then driven to Little Derehams and parked her car just before she came to the first house in the village. Her torch had flashed onto the name on the first gate. *Keepers Cottage.* Who lived there? Oh, that was it, Gilbert Johns. There was a car parked outside – a little Fiesta. Visitors at this time of night, Gilbert? The village would be talking.

Unlike Turnham Malpas, Little Derehams was one of those spread-out villages. The cottages were dotted here and there along the entire length of what was known as the High Street. The shops and the smithy and the little school and the inn had all been converted into bijou residences and the village lay quietly sleeping, just as it did during the day. Here and there a light shone from a bedroom window but that was the only sign of life.

Kate, having checked the address in the school records, had easily recognised Simone's cottage. The front garden, instead of having lawn and flowers like everyone else's, had a children's swing in one corner and the rest was given over to vegetables. It couldn't be anyone else's but hers. There were no lights showing at Simone's windows, so she could perhaps safely assume they were all in bed, but even so not wishing to risk the gate squeaking Kate had climbed over the collapsing wire fence. She followed the little earth path which ran down the side of the cottage and found the shed. She was sure that was where Cat would be, locked in the shed. There was a padlock, but the door and the shed itself were so worn and rickety that she pulled the padlock off with the bracket with scarcely any effort at all. In a loud whisper she called, 'Cat! Cat!' But Cat wasn't there. Simone must have shut her in the house. Unless she'd k—. Kate shuddered. No, she wouldn't have, because then she'd have no further hold over her. No, Cat must be in the house.

Typical of Simone's relaxed attitude to life, the back door was shut but unlocked. Kate very, very gently turned the knob and slowly opened it. Her heart was pounding and her hands were shaking. She stepped in and shone her torch round the room. At some time the two rooms of the cottage had been converted into one, so the room now ran from the back to the front of the cottage; it was long and narrow and so dreadfully disorganised and untidy that Kate shivered. She recognised that with five children in the house it would be difficult to keep tidy, but this! Heavens above. What a mess! Dried herbs interspersed with small garments belonging to the children hung to dry from a long pole suspended from the ceiling by old rope tied to each end. Dishes stood unattended in the sink. Shoes and socks and clothes lay on the threadbare carpet; discarded toys all over the table, along with a half-full milk bottle and the remains of a loaf of bread, roughly hewn as though one of the children had cut the last slice. Dust and clutter were everywhere.

Kate shuddered again. Cat living in this mess. There was a scratching sound. Kate panicked, someone was coming! Hang on – she knew that scratching sound. She opened the door which concealed the staircase. And there was Cat waiting on the bottom step. Kate picked her up and Cat purred intensely. Terrified that someone upstairs might hear the loud purring, Kate hugged Cat to her and headed for the back door. Just as she reached it she heard noises from the far end of the room. She swung round searching for the source of the noise and her torch shone on Dickon. The poor child must have been sleeping on the sofa. Now he was standing up on it wearing only a short, badly-torn vest, clutching a blanket in his hand. When he caught sight of her face in the beam of the torch he shouted, 'Simone! It's Ms Pascoe. She's pinching Cat. Simone!'

But Kate was gone. Clutching Cat to her she fled down the earth path, stumbled over the wire fencing and set off down the High Street for the safety of her car. Quick! Quick! She wouldn't put it past Simone to come racing after her in her nightgown – that was, if she ever wore anything so normal as a nightgown. There was a long gap between the last cottage and the one belonging to Gilbert Johns, and by the time Kate was nearing the latter she was gasping for breath; it was so awkward walking rapidly with a heavy cat in her arms. The beam of her torch shone directly onto Gilbert Johns. He was standing on the footpath close to the Fiesta, kissing Louise from the Big House. Then Kate tripped and couldn't save herself. Cat leapt out of her arms, and Kate measured her length on the path. 'Damn and blast! Cat! Cat! Come here.'

Gilbert's clutter was almost as bad as Simone's but his, caused as it was by books and archaeological artefacts, was more acceptable. Louise made her a hot drink, found an old dish and gave Cat some milk, while Gilbert bathed Kate's knees, and tried to scrape the grit from a cut on her hand with a wet tissue.

'My dear Kate, what on earth are you doing in Little Derehams at this time of night with your cat? Nice though it is to see you, it does seem a rather late hour to be about, does it not?'

Kate sipped her tea. To hell with it having cow's milk in it. 'What am I doing here? Searching for Cat, and finding her.'

'Where was she?'

'That doesn't matter.'

'Huge cat,' Louise said. 'Some people say it's descended from a panther.'

'Some people are daft.'

'Sorry!'

'Didn't mean you! But she isn't, she's just grown big that's all. Ouch!'

'Sorry, trying to be gentle. It's a nasty cut. Can you find the first-aid box, darling? I think it's in the boot with the spades and whatnot.'

Kate almost smiled. Somehow the word 'darling' coming from Gilbert's lips seemed out of place, but he obviously thought a great deal of Louise. Lucky girl to have someone like Gilbert. Such a nice man. Louise reappeared carrying an enormous bright green first-aid box.

Kate was amused. 'Overegging the pudding rather?'

Gilbert laughed. 'It's the one I take on digs. Can't be too careful.'

He cleansed her grazes with antiseptic wipes and then put dressings on both knees and on her hand. 'There we are, all done. You can finish your tea in peace. Louise would you give Kate a lift when she's ready?'

Kate answered for her. 'No need, my car's just down the road a bit.'

'I smell a smattering of skulduggery here. Can I give you some advice?'

'About my cuts?'

'No, about the company you keep. Just watch it. You've too much going for you to let it be spoilt by dabbling . . . Well, you know what I mean. Think on it, OK now?'

Kate stood up. 'Come on, Cat. Let's go home. Thanks. Thanks for the tea and the plasters and the advice.'

'Not at all, any time.'

20

Kate got the message about the next meeting in a note given her by Simone's daughter, Florentina. Both Dickon and she were in Miss Booth's class. Florentina knocked on her office door just before school began. 'Note from Simone.' She was a child of few words like her brother.

Kate waited until Florentina had left and then she opened the note. It was scribbled on the back of a leaflet advertising the start of a mobile hairdressing service visiting the villages. On the blank side, Simone had written *'Eleven p.m. tonight. Rendezvous to be advised. Come.'*

Well, she wouldn't. Not any more. Gilbert was right: she'd too much going for her. Kate tore the message into little pieces and dropped it in her waste bin. This afternoon after school she was going fund-raising and the first person she was trying was Mr Fitch. The appointment was for four o'clock and she would be going up there full of charm and persuasion. She'd get him to buy the computers if it was the last thing she did. She'd wear her most demure dress because she felt that was what would impress him, being the kind of man he was. Oh yes! Craddock Fitch, here I come! The bell rang so she went out into the hall ready to start the school day.

Louise welcomed her and asked her to take a seat. 'Mr Fitch has someone with him and they're over-running their time, but I'm sure he won't be long. All your injuries doing well?'

'Yes, thanks.'

'Lovely day! Spring is sprung as they say.'

'Quite! Gilbert's nice.'

Louise blushed. 'He is.'

'You should marry him.'

'Didn't think you'd recommend that. Not your style.' The telephone rang and she had to break off. When she'd replaced the receiver and made a note of the caller, Louise finished by saying, 'I might at that.'

'Why not. Men like him are hard to find. He seems besotted.'

'He is. I don't know why.'

Kate nearly said, 'Neither do I' but changed it to, 'Don't do yourself down.'

Mr Fitch's caller suddenly emerged from the library and stormed out through the front door without so much as a good afternoon.

'Whoops! Better watch it. That didn't go too well, did it? Best of luck!'

Louise showed her into the library. Kate loved the room immediately she entered it. It was large and although oak-panelled, wasn't a dark room because of the almost floor-to-ceiling windows. Mr Fitch stood up to greet her. There was a spill-over of anger from his last appointment; his thin lips were pinched into a straight line and his eyes sparking angrily which didn't bode well for Kate, but she ploughed on just the same.

'Good afternoon, Mr Fitch. I'm pleased to meet you. I've heard so much about you.'

'Not all of it good, I've no doubt.'

'Not so. I've heard about you paying for the central heating at the church and rebuilding the cricket pavilion. Both excellent contributions to village life.'

'Thank you. Tea?'

'That would be nice. My voice needs lubricating after a day teaching; a cup of tea would be wonderful.'

Mr Fitch called Louise and asked her for tea. 'Now, young lady, what can I do for you? Not wanting a job, I assume?' He smiled when he said that and she felt warmed by his attitude.

'I'm here in my capacity as head teacher in the school. I may as well come straight to the point: the office won't or can't provide us with computers. Too small a school to make the expenditure worthwhile et cetera, et cetera. But these children need them. They'll go to the comprehensive in Culworth at eleven and they'll have them there and our children will be seriously disadvantaged. I don't like to think of them missing out on modern technology, it's just not right. I'm aiming, you see, to give the children an all-round education. Not just the three Rs, though they are necessary as they are the tools with which they learn about the world and everything in it. So I wondered with your expertise in marketing if you could think up a way of me raising the money to purchase them. I know a computer auction place where I could buy second-hand ones relatively cheaply, so I could probably buy two for the price of one new one if you get my drift.'

Louise brought in the tea and poured out for them. She handed Mr Fitch his cup for which he simply nodded his head and gave Kate hers. 'Thank you. That's lovely.'

'How many were you thinking of buying?'

'Ten.'

'Ten?'

'Oh yes. There's nothing more frustrating than waiting a whole lesson for a turn and the bell going and that's your chance out of the window for that day. Ten definitely. Well, that's my aim to start with.'

'Who'd do the teaching? I mean, I can't see that old biddy Hetty Hardaker having much nous about computers.'

'Me.'

'I see. You've it all worked out then.'

'Yes.'

He sipped his tea and looked speculatively at her over the rim of his cup. He put it down on the saucer without saying a word and fiddled instead with his gold pen on a piece of paper, making calculations.

He clipped the top back on his pen and said, 'In August, while we have no students here, this place is being stripped out and re-equipped with the very latest in computers. As I expect you are aware, as fast as you install computers there are new developments which make yours out of date almost by the time the staff have mastered the use of them. We're having state-of-the-art systems put in – the whole shebang. If you wait till then, I'll let you have fifteen computers and some printers for an absolute song. They're worth next to nothing on the market; they were old hat when they came here, but for what you want them for, they will be ideal. It would be a start, wouldn't it? What do you say?'

Kate was overwhelmed with gratitude. She stood up, then sat down again, hardly able to contain herself.

'I can't believe it. I am so grateful – you've no idea. I only came to pick your brains for some fund-raising ideas! Wait till I tell the children. They'll be thrilled. I am too – absolutely thrilled. Thank you very much indeed. Such generosity.'

Mr Fitch was obviously very well-suited with her response. 'Not at all. Got to help the children along. Couldn't talk to that stuffy dyed-in-the-wool Mr Palmer, but you're different.' He stood up and wandered over to the windows, his hands in his pockets. 'I've been meaning to set up an educational trust. The kind of trust which would help bright children to get the best from life. The sort of thing I have in mind is paying for someone to go to Prince Henry's or the girls' one, Lady whatever . . .'

'Wortley's.'

'That's right, Lady Wortley's – someone who's clever enough to go but can't afford the fees. What do you think?'

'I have to be honest with you. I don't agree with private education.'

'Why the blazes not? What's wrong with children being clever?'

'They can be clever at the comprehensive.'

'Well, I'm disappointed. Very disappointed. Maybe I misjudged Mr Palmer. He would have jumped at the chance, him being an old stick in the mud.' Kate couldn't see his smile nor the twinkle in his eyes as he said this.

Kate felt lashed by the assumption that Mr Palmer would have been more open to new ideas than she. Perhaps Mr Fitch was right. Why shouldn't children from poorer homes have the benefits? 'Could I give this my consideration and get back to you?' she asked. 'We've three children going in September, but all their parents can pay, no problem. I'll think about the children who'll be leaving in July next year. I'll let you know.'

'It would be called the Beauchamp Educational Trust.'

For a moment Kate couldn't think what the Beauchamp bit was, and then she remembered Flick's grandmother. 'Right. I see. Yes. Well, Mr Fitch, I mustn't take up any more of your time, but I will say this – I can never thank you enough for your promise of the computers. Never. I shall be indebted to you for ever. As for your idea of the Trust, I shall put my mind to it forthwith. This village should appreciate all you do for them. The cricket club especially, this year. I'm so excited. I'm a fanatical cricket fan.'

'Do you play?'

'I did with my brothers, but I'm in the tea-making department this year. The pavilion is looking marvellous.'

'You've been to see it?'

'I have. Thank you again. I shall be in touch.' She shook hands with Mr Fitch and went out. Louise looked speculatively at her as she shut the library door. 'Your interview went well by the looks of it.'

'It did. All due to the Pascoe charm. He's promised to let me have the old computers he's throwing out in the summer for the school! I just can't believe my good luck.'

'Wow! You must have made an impression! He's had a really bad day today, poor man. I wonder he didn't bite your head off.' Kate winked at Louise and left, her heart full to bursting with pleasure. Fifteen computers for virtually nothing. She couldn't believe it. All she had to do now was sever her connections with Simone as carefully as possible. That part would have to be stopped. She had never meant it to go so far.

When she got back to school Hetty Hardaker's car was still there.

Kate put her head round Hetty's classroom door. 'Hello, Hetty, still here? Everything all right?'

'It is. I can't stand these walls any longer so I've ripped everything off and I'm making a fresh start. New notices, new pictures, new charts.'

'Spring must have got to you!'

'Indeed it has.'

Not relishing Hetty's response to her computer idea, Kate said speculatively, 'I've got good news.'

Hetty paused. 'Yes?'

'In the summer Mr Fitch is having his computers replaced and he's promised us the old ones for the school.'

'I don't believe it. Great minds think alike!'

'What do you mean?'

'I've been thinking about computers and wondering how we could lay our hands on some, and there you've come up with the answer. Brilliant!'

'Brilliant?'

'Oh, yes. We need them so badly.'

'Do we?'

'Oh, yes. I wanted Mr Palmer to get some but he wouldn't. The dear man was such a love but he could be quite narrow-minded.' Hetty rolled her eyes heavenwards.

Kate was amazed. 'I didn't think you would agree. Are you at home with computers then?'

'Oh yes! Theo and I spend many a merry hour with our computer. It's Theo's hobby.'

'So you would be able to teach the children then?'

'Oh yes, I'm sure I could.'

'Well, that's wonderful. I thought you wouldn't want them.'

'I most certainly do.' Hetty rolled up a heap of old paintings and stuffed them into a bin bag. 'I'm sure Theo would give a hand to set them up, if you like. Right – I'll just get rid of these and then I'll be off. We'll have to persuade Margaret, she's not computer friendly at all, but leave her to me.'

And Hetty bustled off to the bins leaving Kate nonplussed. How surprising people could be. She'd have laid a bet on Hetty being antagonistic to modern technology and here she was, probably more knowledgeable than herself. Kate raised her clenched fist and shook it at nothing in particular. Great! At last Hetty was coming over to her side.

The following morning Pat Duckett was banging on Kate's door by five minutes past eight. Kate was already dressed and hurried to the door, toast in hand.

'Ms Pascoe, you'll have to come – the school's been vandalised! Such a mess you never did see.'

Kate stood for a moment trying to take in what Pat was saying. 'Vandalised? What do you mean?'

'Everywhere's had paint thrown over it, the piano music's been torn to shreds, the books in the library corner 'ave all been torn up, and . . . Oh, it's terrible – it's as if a bomb's dropped on it. They got in through the kitchen window – all the glass is in the sink. I'm so upset.' Pat got her handkerchief out and blew her nose. 'I've never seen such a mess in all my born days. If I'd known they were going to do it, I wouldn't have wasted my time cleaning last night. I'll call the police, shall I?'

'Not yet. Let me see it first. I'll just get my things.'

Pat waited for her and the two of them crossed the playground together and went in through the main door. One of the children had left his coat the previous night; the sleeves had been cut off and they lay on the floor of the passage.

The library corner was devastated. Some of the books had been thrown right the way to the other end of the hall, some had been dropped where they'd been torn up. The Maypole ribbons had been cut close to the top and what was left of them hung in silent condemnation. Chairs were overturned, and the piano stool had had its lid almost wrenched off; its contents were in shreds, strewn all over the floor. And over everything were huge splashes of the paint the children used for their artwork. Red. Blue. Green. Yellow. Black. Orange. Purple. Great vivid streaks of it thrown at random straight from the jars. The jars themselves had been smashed against the wall between the doors to Classes One and Two.

The glass window in Kate's office door had been broken as though punched by a great fist. Kate stepped carefully through, broken glass littered the floor. Her filing cabinets hadn't been touched, thank goodness. All those school records!

She came back out into the hall again to speak to Pat. 'Don't touch anything. I'll ring the sergeant, though what he can do about it I don't know. They haven't exactly left their calling card, have they?'

Then, for some reason she didn't know, Kate looked up at one of the hall windows. The windows were set so high that the children and the teachers could only see the tops of the trees at the edge of the playground. Whoever had painted on the window must have had a ladder or managed to climb up on top of the piano and reached from there. In each pane of glass except for the topmost ones, there was a crucifix, painted in black. But each and every one was upside down.

Pat drew in a deep breath which was audible all over the hall. 'Oh, Good Lord! Ms Pascoe, what does that mean?'

Kate tried hard to disguise the fact that she was trembling. She cleared her throat. 'We won't call the police, I think. Better not.'

'Oh, but we must! If you don't, I shall. These children need protecting. Whatever would the parents say if we didn't? There might be something here the police can detect that we can't. Well? Shall I or will you?'

'I think the thing to do is for us to clear up as best we can, and say nothing at all.'

'The office won't like that. What about the insurance? They can't replace all this stuff without the insurance knowing the police have been. No, I'm phoning them now and then we'll get in touch with the office when it opens. Better make it ten past nine as they won't be there dead on time, I don't expect – the lazy, idle beggars. Do 'em good to be at the sharp end for a while, then they'd know what life's about. Come on, Ms Pascoe, don't take on so. Once the police have been we'll soon get this lot cleared up.' Pat put her arm round Kate and gave her a hug. Kate was white and shaking and unable to speak. She seemed rooted to the spot staring up at the upturned crosses.

'I'm right, yer know, we've got to phone the sergeant.'

Kate nodded and Pat tiptoed amongst the broken glass in the office to look up the village policeman's number in Mr Palmer's old address book.

The sergeant was there within ten minutes. 'Now then, what have we here?' He was as appalled as Pat and Kate had been.

'Well, this is a first, and not half. I've been 'ere fifteen years and this has never happened before. *Never*. They get it in Culworth but not here. That right, Pat?'

Pat nodded. She heard the sound of children's voices. 'Ms Pascoe, the children are arriving, and it's raining now. What shall we do?'

Kate visibly pulled herself together. 'I haven't looked in the classrooms. Are they all right, Pat?'

'Seem to be. Shall I put the first ones in your classroom then?'

'Yes, please.' Pat went off to see to the children.

'Anything missing, Miss Pascoe?'

'Difficult to tell, but I don't think so. It's just pure vandalism. Children, I expect.'

'Them crosses upside down on the window – that's not kids. No, them's ominous they are.'

21

'Just what is going on, Ms Pascoe? The welfare of these children and of the school is of the deepest concern to me. I want answers, please. Now what have you to say?'

Peter was sitting in the head teacher's chair and Kate was perched on the edge of the washbasin. He folded his arms and waited. She hadn't noticed before just how penetrating his eyes could be – a rich blue, not an icy Scandinavian blue, and they were looking straight into her soul, or so she felt. Kate had intended having the crosses washed off the windows before he saw them or, better still, before the news leaked out all round the village, but the pressure of keeping the children under restraint while Pat and she made everything safe had prevented her from climbing up to wipe them off. So now he'd seen them and he was utterly determined to find out what she knew.

Did she know, or was it only surmise? She knew all right. But just how little could she get away with telling him?

'I really have no idea who's done this. Just mindless vandalism, and it happened by chance to be our school.'

Peter looked reproachfully at her. 'Please don't take me for a pathetic nincompoop just because I wear a clerical collar. The two are not synonymous, believe me. It is not vandalism quite by chance at all. You know as well as I do that what has happened is *significant*. Crosses upside down have a special symbolic meaning, don't they?'

'Do they?'

'Whoever did this has connections with black magic or witchcraft, or alternatively is trying to give that impression.'

Kate didn't reply.

'I am well aware you know far more than you are willing to tell me, Kate. I'm sorry, but you've made me very disappointed in you. As you are not willing to tell the truth, then I can only assume you are implicated in some way and I shall have to take steps. Quite what I don't know, but something will be done about it, and don't think I shall brush it all under the carpet and play a wait-and-see policy because I shan't. Now get me a bucket of warm soapy water and a cloth and I'll climb up and clean off the crosses. Being tall, I can easily do it from the top of the piano.'

Peter stripped off his cassock and, wearing only his shirt and trousers, climbed onto the piano with the bucket and cloth. The children leaving their classrooms to go out to play giggled when they saw him.

'Give us a tune, Rector!' Brian couldn't resist saying.

'Oooh, mind out, Rector. Don't fall off!'

'*When I'm cleaning winders.*' Stacey thrummed an imaginary banjo.

Peter grinned down at them and pretended to flick water on them out of the bucket, then he grimly carried on wiping. Fortunately it was only the school water paint the vandals had used, so with only a small amount of energetic rubbing the windows quickly came clean.

Pat called up. 'You shouldn't be doing that, Rector. I was going to get Barry to do it in his lunch-hour.'

'Don't you worry about that. Have you some window-cleaning stuff, Pat, then I can give them a good polish while I'm up here?'

'That's not for you to do, sir. The window cleaner's due next week.'

'I'd like to do it.'

'Very well then, hold on a minute.'

By the time he'd got down from the top of the piano, the children were coming back into school from the playground. Kate was standing in the hall holding a mug of coffee for him. Peter took the mug from her and just before he drank from it, he said, 'Well?'

'Will you give me forty-eight hours?'

'Then you'll have something to say to me?'

Kate nodded. 'Yes.'

'Very well. In the meantime I shall make my own enquiries.'

'Thank you.' Kate half-turned away and then turned back and said quietly, 'Be careful.'

Peter raised his eyebrows at her but she had gone.

'So there he is up on top of the piano cleaning the windows.' Pat took another sip of her drink and then nudged Vera. 'Tell yer what, he strips well. Can't see nothing under that cassock he wears, but by jove, yer should have seen 'im! He looked great, he did. Muscles the size of cannon balls he has and such a broad back. Must be all that squash he plays.'

Willie disapproved. 'That's enough. It's not decent to speak of the rector like that.'

'Come on, Willie. He's a man isn't he, as he has well proved.' Pat winked at Vera.

Vera giggled and gave Pat a dig in the ribs. 'Shut up, Pat, show some respect!'

'I 'ave a lot o' respect for him. Can't think of a worse job for a man to be doing. You 'ave to be devoted and not 'alf, to do what he has to do. He's a wonderful chap, and I'd be the first to say so. He was lovely when Barry and me went to see him about fixing the wedding date. All I was saying was he looks great when he isn't togged up.'

'Tell us what happened then.'

'Well . . .' Pat launched herself on a description of the hall as she'd found it that morning. Vera and Willie were appalled. 'But the worst was, the crosses were upside down. Before she saw that, she was all set for phoning for the sergeant, then she claps 'er eyes on them crosses and Bob's yer uncle she changed her mind. Now why, I ask yer? Why should that be?'

Willie said, 'I reckon she knows a thing or two and she's protecting someone.'

Pat leaned forward across the table, pushed her glass aside and said in a low voice, 'No, yer wrong there. Not *protecting* someone, *frightened* of someone 'd be nearer the mark.'

'Frightened?' Vera said loudly.

Pat gave her another sharp nudge. 'Don't shout. All the bar'll know.'

'It must mean something nasty-like, putting 'em upside down.'

Willie nodded sagely. 'Something evil, I'll be bound.'

They all three turned to look at the bar counter when they heard Ralph's deep voice. 'Good evening, Bryn. A double whisky if you please.'

'Good evening, Sir Ralph. Still keeps cold, doesn't it?'

'It certainly does.'

'Lady Templeton well?'

'Yes, thank you, very well. She's gone into Culworth with Celia Prior to an exhibition of quilting so I thought I'd come in here and catch up with the gossip.'

Bryn smiled and nodded his head in the direction of Pat's table. 'I'd sit over there then, if I were you. Pat's in the thick of it about the vandalism at the school last night.'

Ralph paid for his drink and acknowledging Bryn's advice, went across to join them.

'Good evening. May I join you or would it be an intrusion?'

Willie moved along the settle and patted the seat next to him. 'Sit 'ere, you're more than welcome.'

'Good evening, Vera, good evening, Pat.' They both chorused together, 'Good evening, Sir Ralph.'

His presence put rather a damper on Pat's story and she found it difficult to carry on.

'Your very good health.' Ralph drank from his glass and then prompted her to expand on her story. 'Bad news about the school today. I'm sorry.'

'So was I. Took us two hours to clear up and all the children there and everything. All the piano music will have to go in the bin when the insurance has seen it, and most of the books in the library corner. Her on the mobile library 'll have something say, I've no doubt. She swops our books over for us from time to time, yer see. It'll have right depleted her stocks.'

'Any idea who it was?'

'No, none at all. The rector's very upset. He cleaned the windows for us. Do you know what it means, Sir Ralph – crosses upside down?'

'Work of the devil, I should think.'

Vera eagerly took him up on this. 'Well, our Rhett said just the same. It's upset him, it has. Thought he was going to start being all funny again, but he's managed to master it.'

'He thought so too, did he? Ever get to the bottom of what it was that upset him?'

'No, all he'll say is that it was the devil after him. He still keeps the cross round his neck that I bought him and he's been real quiet since it all happened, not going out and that. Mind you, he's that jiggered when he gets home after working outside and that in the gardens, he's no energy for anything. Eating like a horse he is now. He'll eat anything at all. Best day's work the rector did, getting him that job. Doing him no end of good.'

'Would Rhett talk to me?'

Vera fidgeted with her glass for a moment and then said, 'Well, I don't rightly know. He can be a bit odd if yer try to talk to him about it. Shuts up, like.'

'I can be very persuasive. Is he in now?'

'Well, yes, he is. Don's at work and I just came across for an hour.'

'Drink up and we'll go across together, but you'll have to leave us to talk. He probably wouldn't open up if his grandmother was there.'

Vera eyed him speculatively. 'Are you thinking he can throw some light on this trouble at the school?'

'Yes, I am.'

'He didn't do it, Sir Ralph. It really wasn't him, he's not like that.'

'Not for one moment was I thinking on those lines. No, no, not at all. I simply want to talk to him about his experiences. Now, will you let me?' He smiled that famous Templeton smile, the one Muriel always found so irresistible, and it worked the same magic on Vera.

'Well, of course. Yes, of course.' Rapidly she ran through in her mind just how tidy she had left her living room. She hadn't expected to be taking aristocracy home with her when she'd set out.

'Finished then? No time like the present.'

'Oh yes, of course, yes.' She got up to go. Vera gave Pat a nervous smile and went ahead of Ralph who had stood waiting for her to go in front of him. He held open the door for her and she scuttled out.

As Vera put her key in the latch they heard footsteps behind them and, while she struggled with the door which was stiff after the rain, she heard Ralph saying, 'Oh good evening, Peter.' And there he was, dressed in jeans and a thick bright pullover.

'Ah! Good evening. I've come hoping to see Rhett. I didn't know you had company, Vera. I'll come another evening, shall I?'

Ralph asked Vera if she would mind being invaded by not one but two visitors. Vera swallowed hard. 'No, not at all. That's quite all right, I'll go in the kitchen and keep out of the way. Rhett's in 'ere.'

He was laid full-length on the sofa watching television, his boots resting on one arm, his hands behind his head on the other, an empty beer can lay on its side on a table by his elbow. Vera said loudly, 'Our Rhett, you've got visitors.' Ralph blinked when he saw the picture on the screen. Rhett shot into a sitting position; his finger went straight on the video remote control and the screen went blank, for which Ralph was grateful. Never in all his days . . .

But Peter was speaking. 'Quite by chance, Rhett, you've got two visitors and I have an idea we're both here on the same errand. Would you have some time to spare to talk to us?'

By this time Rhett was on his feet. 'Yes, yes of course.'

Without waiting to be asked Ralph chose a chair and sat in it. Peter went to sit on the sofa and Rhett stood on the hearth-rug.

'As you were the first on the doorstep, Ralph, would you like to begin?'

'Very well. I know this is a very delicate subject for you, Rhett, and you've been quite ill with the worry of it all, but it's reached a time when we've got to talk. By the way, I should have asked you first how's the job going.'

'All right, thanks. I like working with Mr Stubbs. He's good. Says I can go on a day-release course at the horticultural college if I show I'm taking an interest.'

'And are you?'

'What?'

'Taking an interest.'

'Oh yes. It's great. Can't wait to get going in them greenhouses. You should see what Mr Stubbs grows in there.'

'I know, it's quite wonderful, isn't it?'

'Yes, it is. Them greenhouses is over a hundred and fifty years old. Growing grapes for one hundred and fifty years – can you imagine that?'

'Well, yes I can.'

Rhett flushed and looked embarrassed. 'Oh, of course. I'd forgotten.'

'That's all right. Let's get down to business. Now you're feeling so much better, can you tell us why it was you were so frightened by seeing this dog Jimmy's adopted?'

Rhett's hand went inside the neck of his shirt and out came the cross his grandma had bought; he wrapped his fingers tightly around it. He looked at Peter, then back to Ralph. He stared at the floor, he gazed at the blank screen and then eventually muttered, 'I thought I'd seen a ghost.'

'There was more to it than that, wasn't there?'

Rhett stared at Ralph. 'The devil. I could see the devil in him.'

'He's a harmless, bright little dog. Got lost and happened by pure chance to turn up here.'

'Not chance.'

'No?'

Peter said, 'If it wasn't chance, then what was it?'

Rhett hesitated and then gazing anywhere but at the two of them, he said, 'He'd been called up.'

Ralph, making military connections with the words Rhett had used, was puzzled. 'Called up?'

'By . . .'

Peter prompted him. 'Yes?'

'The devil.'

Wishing to clarify things and move the story on, Peter said, 'You believe Sykes was brought back to life by the devil?'

Rhett nodded. 'We was in the wood doing these incantation things and . . . they said they knew Sykes was buried there and we'd practise on him. Prove just how powerful we were. Like an experiment what wouldn't harm nobody and we'd see if we could do it.' Rhett had difficulty continuing. He took in a deep breath and started again. 'Course, I thought it was daft but then it seemed to get serious and what with the dark and the fire and the candles and that, and all these strange words and them speaking like being in church kind of – I began to believe we could do it. Then next morning in daylight-like, I thought how daft can you get? He's dead and buried like, isn't he? Dead as a doornail. Then I saw him in Jimmy's garden and . . .' Rhett shuddered at the thought of that terrible encounter.

Peter, looking straight into Rhett's eyes, said, 'You mean you really believe this new Sykes *is* the old Sykes?'

'Well, I did at the time. Absolutely convinced, I was. Now I'm not so sure – not after I'd talked to you. But it does make yer think, doesn't it?'

Peter reassured him. 'Well, it isn't the real Sykes, I can assure you of that. You mention other people. Who leads this "meeting"? We need to know.'

Rhett shut up like a clam.

Ralph tried another tack. 'After you'd been taken ill I went to investigate for myself and I saw five people in the wood, with the altar and the black candles, but they all ran away before I could identify them. Who were they?'

Rhett began pacing up and down the room. Finally, he appeared to come to a decision and stood in front of Peter. 'I won't give any names,' he blurted out. 'Definitely daren't give names. I've never been again, not since that night. I was too scared of what we were doing.'

Peter said, 'You weren't successful, though it must have looked like that to you at the time. It was coincidence that the dog turned up when he did.'

'Are you sure? Just a great big coincidence?'

'I'm sure.'

'Thank God for that. Beg yer pardon, Rector.'

'No need to beg my pardon, I'm glad you've got it sorted out once and for all. Thank you for telling us that, Rhett. All this damage at the school is connected with it, too. It's got to be stopped.' As an afterthought he asked, 'You're not being threatened, are you?'

'No, not really.'

'I want you to know that if you need help, you can ring me or come to see me at the rectory any time, day or night. We can't have people like you and the sergeant's wife,' Rhett looked uncomfortable and cast shifty glances at Ralph and Peter, 'scared out of their wits. These things can escalate and cause terrible trouble, which indeed they already have. If you feel one day that you are able to name names to me or to Sir Ralph, your information will be treated in the strictest confidence. We shall never and I mean *never* divulge who told us. You're not a fool, Rhett, you've a good job with prospects and you can't let wicked, evil people ruin your life. I forbid it. So you and I together will conquer this. Right?'

Rhett looked pleased that he had an ally. 'Yes, sir. Right.'

'I must know who else is involved. If you can't speak the unspeakable then put a note through my letterbox. I shan't know who's put it there, shall I, when you haven't signed it?'

Rhett managed a slight smile. 'I'm not going any more. I daren't. But I might write that note.'

Ralph stood up. 'I won't have the life of this village torn apart. People can't look each other in the eye any longer. It's never been like that before. You and the rector and I shall put a stop to it.' Ralph changed the tone of his voice. 'By the way, I see you're down for the cricket team, Rhett. Delighted. We need young chaps like you, and with all that hard work up at the Big House you'll be building good muscle. We'll make a batsman out of you yet!'

'Bowling's my thing.' He imitated a bowling action and Ralph was impressed.

'By jove! Very good. Yes. Mr Fitch is providing us with practice nets and I shall be interested to see how you develop. We'll be off now.'

Peter said as he left, 'Good night, Rhett.' He shook Rhett's hand and smiled encouragingly. 'Thank you for all your help. You're a grand chap with a lot going for you. Remember, I'm on your side in this. God bless you. Sleep well.'

Ralph and Peter crossed the road together and stood talking in the light of the lamp above Ralph's door. 'So now we know why the sergeant's wife has gone so peculiar. She was obviously there that night too. That's two names anyway.'

Ralph nodded. 'Let's hope he takes the hint and gives us the other names.'

'He's been dreadfully frightened. The shock of seeing the dog! No wonder he went berserk.'

'Is there any wonder that he snatched at some kind of excitement? Things aren't what they were when I was a boy, are they? I feel sorry for teenagers nowadays. When they're too young to have their own transport what on earth do they do every night stuck here?'

'Watch appalling videos?' Peter asked.

Ralph groaned. 'My goodness me. No wonder his mind worked over-time, no wonder at all. Any more ideas yourself about who's involved?'

'Might have. Good night.'

22

The forty-eight hours were up and Peter had heard nothing from Kate, so when he took the twins to playgroup he made his way to Kate's little office and tapped on the door.

'No good knocking there, Rector. Ms Pascoe's not in this morning. She's in bed with a sore throat. We've a supply teacher coming any minute.' Pat folded the duster she'd been using to get the early-morning dust from the piano keys and shook her head. 'Oh yes, sore throat it is. She sounded really ill – could hardly speak. I've offered to go in and get her anything she needs but she said no, thanks.'

'Oh dear, I am sorry.'

'Hopes to be back in tomorrow, though I can't see that, 'cos she sounded so dreadful. Didn't seem quite right in the head, yer know. Her mind was wandering, kind of. If it's urgent you could pop a note through her door. I know where she keeps her scrap paper.'

'It's not urgent, it can wait. Only six weeks to go to your wedding, Pat. Got everything organised?'

'We have. We've not invited loads of guests, only from Barry's side. Dad and me's not got many relatives. I'm glad you and Dr Harris and the twins have accepted. Jimbo's doing the food, so we know that'll be good.'

'Barry got the honeymoon arranged? He seemed very secretive about it when I spoke to him last.'

'All I know is, it involves an aeroplane and hot weather and I've to pack a swimsuit and some suntan lotion and I've to have smart dresses for the evening. That's why we've had such a long engagement – well, ten months – he's been saving up for it. Says he wants the honeymoon of a lifetime as he won't be going on another.'

Peter was about to relate to her the story of his own honeymoon when Hetty Hardaker brought her class in ready for prayers. Pat dashed off towards the kitchen.

'Mrs Hardaker, would you like me to take prayers as Ms Pascoe is ill?' Peter offered.

'I would indeed, Rector, that would be a help. I'll leave it to you and Miss Booth then, if I may.'

When prayers were finished, Peter went to stand in the school playground and look at the school-house. The bedroom curtains were drawn, and there were no signs of life at all, apart from the living-room windowsill where Cat lay sleeping.

As he set off back to the rectory he glanced towards the Store, and by chance sitting outside on the seat so thoughtfully provided by Jimbo, was someone with whom he wanted to have a word.

'Good morning, Ellie.'

The sergeant's wife looked up, startled, her lacklustre brown eyes showing no recognition. Her hair, never more than an orderly bird's nest, was now quite awry, and her face, paler than ever, gave the impression the blood had been drained out of her. Her squashy nose sat like a lump of blanched dough on her face. Ellie could never have claimed to dress in the height of fashion, and she certainly wasn't dressed in it now. Her coat was buttoned up wrongly, leaving the top edge on one side rubbing against her chin. Her tights were wrinkled, her shoes grubby and she had odd gloves on.

So that his height did not intimidate her, Peter sat down on the seat. It held four comfortably so he didn't overcrowd her.

'I haven't seen you for a while. How are you?'

Ellie finally recognised who he was. 'Don't you 'ave nothin' to do with me, Rector. You buzz orf. I ain't your kind.'

'Why's that?'

'I be evil, I be.'

'Anyone less evil than you, Ellie, I couldn't imagine.'

'Oh, yes, I be.'

'Why? What have you done? Robbed a bank?'

She looked puzzled. 'Robbed a bank? That'd be nothin', no, nothin' that'd be.'

Peter sat silently waiting. Ellie eyed him furtively. She fidgeted with her gloves and looked at them with surprise as though realising for the first time that they were odd. She shuffled around in a coat pocket and came out with what was obviously one of her husband's handkerchiefs. She blew her nose, wiped her eyes and then said, 'If I went to church, would that get me out of it?'

'Very likely.'

'It gets a hold, yer see. Gets a hold. I'm frightened to sleep.'

'Nightmares?'

She seemed relieved he'd got to the root of her problem. Her head nodded vigorously. 'That's right.' Ellie shuddered. 'Terrible.'

Peter sat companionably beside her.

Two people, one of them Mrs Jones, Pat's future mother-in-law, came by the seat.

'Good morning, Rector. Nice fresh day.' She looked at Ellie then at Peter and strode inside eager to get on with her work, for the temporary takeover of Sadie's mail-order business had changed to permanent and she loved it.

Ellie sat lost in thought. Jimbo came out with two coffees.

'Chilly sitting out here. Mrs Jones thought a coffee might be welcome.' He winked at Peter and went back inside to deal with his customers.

Ellie found the coffee too hot. 'There's no sugar in it either.' Peter didn't offer to go inside to get her any. He had the distinct feeling that if he left she would disappear. Then she gave a huge sigh. 'I can't go on no longer. Got to talk.'

'I'm listening.'

She stared into the distance watching Jimmy's geese chasing a dog away from their pond. 'Life gets terrible boring living hereabouts. I'm a town girl myself, you know. Hustle and bustle I likes, really. That's me. Markets and people and cinemas and things. Can't stand all this quiet. Stood it fifteen years, then this happened and it pepped things up no end – at first. Really looked forward to it. Like a whole new world, it was. But, Rector, things is bad. That bad, I don't knows which way to turn, I don't.' Tears straggled untidily down her cheeks and settled in the grooves beside her mouth.

'Fun it was, exciting. 'Tain't exciting being married to the sergeant. He's that predictable. Nothin' different, always the same. Black treacle on his porridge summer and winter. He even stirs it just the same way every mornin'. Always says, "Isn't this grand? Why don't you 'ave some?" Every blessed mornin'. But the bonfire and the chantin', like. Now that was thrillin'. But now I'm terrified.'

'You don't have to stay terrified.'

'Don't I?' For the first time she stared directly into his eyes. 'Look at what 'appens to them that defy her.'

'What?'

'School gets done over, don't it?'

'You mean Ms Pascoe defied her?'

Ellie nodded. 'We 'as to attend, yer see. She's got a grip. Be makin' a doll like Ms Pascoe, she will, sticking pins in it. Oh yes, it'll be the end of her.'

'Who'll be making the doll?' As soon as he'd asked the question he knew he'd gone on ahead too far, too fast. Ellie leapt up from the seat, the coffee in its paper cup spewing out all over her coat. To delay her, Peter took out his handkerchief and, gripping her arm, sympathised over the spill and began to wipe it away. 'There we are, Ellie, got you all clean and smart again. Now, where were we?'

Ellie sat down again. She gave the village green a full inspection and answered, 'I don't know where you are, Rector, but I'm in hell. Hell on earth.'

'Look Ellie, tell me everything, get it off your chest so to speak. I shan't tell *her* what you tell me. Believe me. As God is my judge, I shan't say a word.'

She looked at him, assessing his trustworthiness. '*She's* a witch, there's no two ways about it. *She* put the evil eye on Mrs Beauchamp and she died. Then *she* had a go at bringing Sykes back to life, and she did. It was then I knew she really had killed Sadie Beauchamp. We couldn't stop. Now *she's* going to get rid of anyone who crosses her. Full of power now, yer see. Evil that's what she be, and her with all them kiddies. Success has gone to her head. You've got to stop it, Rector. Something's got to be done.'

'I find it hard to believe that this mysterious "she" could actually kill someone.'

'Oh, but *she* did. Oh yes. There weren't no proper verdict, were there? Not heart attack nor nothing. It be very peculiar. We're all joined to her in sisterhood, so we's all guilty of murder.' Ellie clutched his hand. 'Help me, Rector.'

'I can't help unless I know who's the witch.'

Ellie stood up. 'If I tell you I'll be dead in the mornin'. That's the threat – death. I sometimes think it would be for the best.' She looked vaguely about her and then said, 'The sergeant wants steak for his dinner. I'll have to go and see to that.' And Ellie trailed off into the Store leaving Peter studying the geese.

So it wasn't Kate. Unwittingly Ellie had told him who the witch was – Simone Paradise. She always had been strange. Her lifestyle told one that, even if one didn't know about the evil eye and such-like. Kate had said 'be careful'. Even though he never acknowledged it to Caroline, for the logical part of his brain denied the truth of it, he still felt shudders down his spine when he recalled the two near-brushes with death he'd had over the church charity fund a while back. And now this, too, was evil and menacing.

Witchcraft. *Was* it witchcraft or someone pretending it was? Whatever, people were believing it. What he had to do was witness what went on. But now he didn't know where they met. And there was this business of making a doll . . . and Kate *was* ill. He shot to his feet. Caroline was the answer. As soon as she came back from the surgery he'd get her on to it.

He got home about half-past one, hoping that she would be able to have a late lunch with him. 'Caroline! Caroline!'

She came running down the stairs. She'd changed from her surgery suit and was wearing a hyacinth-blue jumper with black trousers and she looked lovely. He desired her, but that would have to wait.

He bent down and kissed her lips. 'I'm late. Had lunch?'

'No. Waited for you.'

'Good. Need a word.'

Sylvia had made their lunch for them and it was waiting under wraps on the kitchen table.

'Thank you, Sylvia. We need a quiet moment, if you don't mind.'

'Not at all, Rector. Coffee's ready in the pot. I'll go and sit with the children. It's *Sesame Street* time.'

As Sylvia closed the door behind her, Caroline said, 'What's so private that Sylvia can't hear?'

'I want you to go across to the school-house and see if Kate is ill.'

Caroline raised an eyebrow. 'What are you up to, Peter?'

Peter explained his conversation with Ellie.

With her sandwich halfway to her mouth, Caroline said, 'Oh my God! Really!'

'That's why she was so frightened when Sykes turned up – well, not Sykes, as you know, but she thought it was. She thought then she knew that Simone really had done Sadie in.'

'Oh my God! I can't believe this.'

'Exactly.'

'But it can't be *proved*, can it?'

'Well, she didn't do it really, did she? Now come on, darling, you know it's not possible.'

Caroline looked doubtful. 'Isn't it?'

'No, definitely not. It's all in the mind.'

'Yes, it is. But it's like witch doctors in Africa – they can have a powerful influence on the mind.'

'For heaven's sake, Caroline, you're a scientist, a person with a trained mind. You are not allowed to believe it.'

'No, of course not, but . . .'

'So will you go? Pretend you're concerned and can you help in your capacity as—'

'A nosy-parker?'

Peter laughed. 'If you like.'

She finished her sandwich, took a long drink of her coffee, and said, 'I'm off then. To do the rector's dirty work.'

'I can hardly go myself, can I?'

'Certainly not. Don't eat my fruit pie. I'll have it when I get back.'

Caroline knocked on the front door of the school-house knowing she wouldn't get an answer, but she had to knock first. She went round the side and looked in through the kitchen window. There was a mug and a plate on the drainer by the sink, but nothing else. So presumably Kate had had something to eat at some time. As Caroline peered in, Cat came into the kitchen. She jumped up onto the draining board and licked the plate, jumped down again and prowled about and cried.

Caroline went to stand below the bedroom window. 'Kate! Kate! It's Caroline Harris. Let me in.' There was no reply. Caroline could hear the children having a singing lesson. She checked that Kate's car was there. It was, so she must be either in school or in the house.

In school there was no sign of Kate. A teacher Caroline didn't recognise was taking the singing. She went to tap on Hetty Hardaker's door. 'Ms Pascoe not here?'

'No, Dr Harris. She's in bed with a sore throat. Sorry.'

Caroline acknowledged the information by nodding her head and smiling. So she was in the house.

Pat was leaving after clearing up from school lunch. 'Hello, Dr Harris. Long time no see.'

'It is. How are things, Pat?'

'Fine, thanks.'

'Not long now.'

'No, that's right.'

'Got your suntan lotion ready?'

'So you know about it too.'

'Oh yes, but my lips are sealed! I wish I could get into the school-house. I'm worried about Kate.'

Pat went to a drawer below the kitchen draining board. She pushed her hand right to the back, behind the tea towels she kept in there, and came out with a huge key. 'Here we are. Spare key she doesn't know I've got.'

'But how shall I explain that?'

'If she's dead you won't have to.'

'Dead?!'

'You don't know these days, do yer, with all these strange things going on hereabouts. Anything could have 'appened.'

'Now I really am feeling spooky. Come with me?'

'Sorry, no. Not again.'

'You've been in before then?' Pat nodded. 'What have you seen that makes you not want to go again?'

Pat shook her head. 'Nothing. Time I was off. Good luck.'

'Won't you wait to see?'

'I'll know soon enough. Sorry.'

The key turned readily in the lock. 'Kate! Kate!' Caroline called. There was no reply.

Caroline went cautiously up the stairs. She was being ridiculous. She'd seen plenty of dead people before now – had dissected them, in fact. But she really didn't want to see Kate dead, still less contemplate all the conclusions the village would draw if she were.

She wasn't dead. But she was dreadfully ill. Caroline could immediately see that she had a raging temperature and was quite oblivious to her surroundings. She'd thrown off her duvet at some stage and lay haphazardly on the mattress like a doll carelessly flung down in a temper. Sweat poured from her face, and her body glistened with it. Her nightgown, which Caroline couldn't help noticing was deep purple satin, was soaking. Her long dark hair lay like damp ropes on the pillow and around her shoulders.

'Kate? Kate?' But she couldn't be wakened.

Caroline ran downstairs and dialled Emergency. 'This is Dr Harris speaking. I need an ambulance.'

Caroline went with Kate to the hospital and gave the duty officer in Casualty as much information as she could. When the doctors heard Kate had worked in Africa for several years they said that might be a possible area to look at when diagnosing what the matter was.

Caroline went to see her each day, but it wasn't until the fourth day that she was able to speak.

'Kate – at last! I thought you would never wake up. How do you feel?'

'Terrible!' Her voice was slight and very husky.

'Better than when I first found you, anyway. You've been getting the full treatment. Everyone's been so worried about you.'

'Sorry.'

'I've been worried that there might be someone I should have contacted, but I didn't know who.'

'There isn't anyone really. My brothers are all abroad. I have an uncle but he wouldn't come to see me anyway.' A tear slid from the corner of her eye.

'I've brought flowers from the children at school.'

'How lovely. They are great, my children are.' Her voice croaked as she asked, 'Could you possibly help me to a drink of water?'

'Of course. Gladly.'

Caroline settled her back onto the pillows again and said, 'You must be exhausted. Shall I leave you to sleep now?'

'Yes, please,' Kate whispered. 'There really isn't any need to come to see me again. I know how busy you are.' Another tear slid down her cheek.

'It's Peter's hospital day tomorrow so he'll come if that's all right.'

Kate turned her head away. 'Peter gave me forty-eight hours.'

'Did he?

'You don't know, do you?'

'A bit. He doesn't tell me everything.'

'I've been such a fool.'

'It's never too late.'

'It nearly was. If it hadn't been for you . . . How did you get into the house?'

Caroline couldn't lie. 'Pat has a spare key she's been meaning to give you. Mr Palmer gave it to her in case he lost his.'

'I see. Well, there we are then. Saved by Mr Palmer.'

'Sleep yourself better. Peter will be in tomorrow. I'll ring the day after and see what the position is.'

Kate gave a half-smile and her eyes began to close. 'The trouble with Peter is you can't withhold the truth from him for long, can you?'

'I know who's at the bottom of all this. Altogether, I have four names now.'

Kate eyed him warily. 'You do?'

'Inadvertently, someone gave the game away. If you're feeling well enough you can fill in the rest of the story, starting with Simone.'

'The one thing I dread doing is anything which will leave those children without their mother. There are five of them – all dear children, but hopeless in school. Too tired, undernourished, badly clothed, badly housed . . . I mean, have you ever been inside their cottage? It's terrible. Just awful. I wouldn't allow Cat to live in the conditions those children have to endure. Poor Dickon sleeps under a blanket on the sofa and his night-clothes are a torn vest. But they adore their mother, and she them in her own way.'

'Well, perhaps I can do something about that. You tell me your story.'

Kate reached for the glass of water on her locker. She sipped it slowly, using it as a delay while she assembled her thoughts. She put down the glass, drew in a deep breath and said, 'I've been thinking long and hard since I became conscious.'

'What has been the matter, by the way?'

'The tests aren't completed yet but they think it's one of these recurring things I picked up in Africa. Gradually, let's hope, the attacks will become less frequent.'

'I'm glad about that. Everyone thought Simone had stuck pins in a doll and your illness was the result.'

Kate gave a small smile. 'It could very well be. She was very angry because I'd decided not to attend any more meetings. Saw me as a kindred spirit, you see. She thought the others only came for the excitement – which they probably did. I was the real convert, she thought.'

'Which to a certain extent you were.'

Kate looked straight at him. It was now or never. She had to decide. Did she tell the truth or mask it in generalities? She studied his face, his red-blond thatch of hair, the startlingly blue eyes emphasised by the contrast of the deep black of his cassock. His silver chain on which his cross hung, tucked as always into his leather belt. An ancient garb which didn't manage to disguise the astute, up-to-the-minute man beneath. Confronted by Peter there was no place to hide.

'When I was in Africa, I met a modern version of a witch-doctor while I was visiting a mission school in the hills. I came under his spell. I couldn't stay away. That particular school came in for a great deal of my attention. He taught me such a lot.'

'About *what*, though?'

'Herbal medicines, spells, witchcraft. About the language to use – everything. He gave me Cat. Said she was my familiar. I fell in love with him. "Obsessed" is the only word to describe my state of mind. In his own way he loved me too, though I knew it was partly pride that his knowledge was superior to mine – I was the pupil and he the teacher. I had it all worked out. I was going to stay in Africa for ever and live with him. Then one day there was one of those sudden inexplicable risings which are a feature of a country where a tinpot despot, with the army in his pocket, rules supreme. Jacob unwittingly came across a group of the terrorists and . . . well, I hope they killed him quickly. I knew nothing for days, had no news at all. Then some refugees from one of the schools I visited, recognised me and told me what they'd found in the bush.'

Kate paused for a moment to control her tears. 'It doesn't bear talking about. Africa held no more fascination for me after that. I had a slight bout of this illness, though medicine being what it is in remote parts of Africa no one knew what I had, and I made that my excuse for leaving. Said my health couldn't stand the climate, et cetera.'

At last Kate wept. Peter handed her a tissue from the box in her locker. He held her hand whilst the storm raged. A nurse smiled round the door and quietly pulled it shut. The clatter of the busy ward next door was shut away and the two of them were left together in the silence.

Slowly Kate's tears subsided. 'I'm so sorry.'

'Not at all. It will have done you good.'

'How embarrassing.'

'Don't fret. I've watched healing tears many times before.'

'I expect you have. But I'm sorry for breaking down like that. It's this dratted illness, it's left me feeling so weak.'

'Look, if you feel you've said enough for today . . .'

'No, don't go. I must tell you everything. Right now. You need to know. The people involved are Ellie, Valda and Thelma Senior, Venetia Mayer from the Big House – you know, Jeremy's wife . . .'

'Venetia Mayer? I don't believe it!'

'Oh yes, she's a fervent participant. Simone, of course, Rhett Wright but he refused to come after the dog turned up, and that's about it. Two of the weekenders came a couple of times but then they stopped.'

'About this business of Sadie Beauchamp . . .'

'We had nothing to do with that at all. That was Simone and only Simone.'

'The way you say that, you seem to really believe she could be responsible for someone's death.'

'Do I? That's stupid of me. She can't, of course.' But Kate didn't speak convincingly.

'And Simone – how about her?'

'Somehow she guessed the very first time she saw me with Cat how things were. Foolishly, I acknowledged she was right. I got embroiled but drew the line when things got too deep. She behaves like, and considers herself to be, some kind of witch. There is no doubt in my mind about that. She happens to be evil, unfortunately. I'm sorry. I'm so tired now.' Kate lay back against the pillows and closed her eyes.

'I'll leave. May I say a prayer?'

Kate nodded. Peter held her hand, asked for God's blessing on her, and made the sign of the cross on her forehead with his thumb. This time she didn't shudder.

As he left she said, 'Take care. Please, take care. Never underestimate her power. She's so full of her success she is on the verge of being evil just for the sake of it.'

23

That night the twins had feverish colds and Caroline knew when she put them to bed that she was in for a bad time. Alex couldn't stop coughing and Beth had a vicious sore throat and a runny nose which, despite Caroline's anxious care, had already made her nose bright red.

'It's no good, Peter, I'm going to put the camp bed up in the children's bedroom and sleep in there. Otherwise I shall be back and forth all night, and you'll not get any sleep either.'

'Let me help.'

'Certainly not. I've no surgery tomorrow and you have a day's work to do. I insist.'

'Well, if you're sure, but do wake me up if things get serious, won't you?'

'Of course.'

'I'll get the last out and make it up for you — it's the least I can do.' He turned to go then came back into the kitchen. 'They are going to be all right, aren't they?'

Caroline studied his face. 'It's this witchcraft thing, isn't it?'

'Kind of.'

'Of course they are. They've both got a cold, that's all. Children do get them all the time.'

'I suppose they do. It's Kate, you see. She's an intelligent woman and yet . . .'

'And yet?'

'And yet she's quite alarmed about Simone Paradise. She doesn't believe Simone killed Sadie, but at the same time . . .'

'Yes?'

'At the same time she's terribly wary of what Simone will do next. She warned me to be careful.'

'I think you should do something tomorrow, before it's too late. I'll give it some thought in the dark hours of the night when I'm awake with our best beloved.' She shooed him out of the kitchen and made up a flask of cold orange juice to take upstairs for when the children woke.

Before she left the kitchen, Caroline stood looking out at the garden. A strong wind was getting up, the bushes at the bottom by the boundary wall were already swaying back and forth, and the wind seemed to be rustling through the thatch in an insidious kind of way. She was glad she lived in a solid well-built old house and not some flibberty-gibbet jerry-built construction. As she watched, the rain began – heavy slow blobs which dripped steadily onto the terrace. What should have been a moonlit night was dark and foreboding. A huge flash of lightning lit the garden and thunder cracked loudly right overhead.

'Mummy!'

Caroline picked up the flask and ran upstairs. 'All right, darlings, Mummy's coming.'

The storm was the worst in living memory. When the villagers opened their curtains the next morning and saw the damage, there were quite a few who trembled. Indeed, they'd trembled during the night too, for the storm had raged for three hours, whistling down chimneys, slamming doors, and waking children who'd rushed to huddle in their parents' beds. Jimmy's chickens had squawked and screeched until he'd been driven into going outside to check on them. Sykes, well aware it was forbidden, had crept into Jimmy's bed and when Jimmy got back in, they'd clung to each other through the worst of it. Cats had fled into wardrobes, dogs had howled and debris blowing about had smashed a window at the Store.

But what really struck terror into their hearts was the sight of a huge branch of the royal oak tree lying on the ground. Almost one third of the tree had crashed down. Old villagers and newcomers alike knew the legend – when the oak tree dies, so will the village.

Peter had gone to the church at half-past six to pray. He'd been awake a large part of the night despite Caroline's solicitude; no one could have slept through that storm. So much water had run away down the church path that his trainers squelched as he walked. Before unlocking the door he'd decided he would walk round the building to inspect it for damage just in case. There might be tiles off the roof or hanging dangerously. He'd found that lightning had struck the church tower. The spire was fine but the square tower, where the lightning conductor should have saved it, had a long blackened streak down one side and several stones had been dislodged.

Willie appeared with his raincoat on over his pyjamas. 'Well now, Rector, this is a pretty kettle of fish. What a night! See what's happened? That daft builder's taken down the conductor while he pointed them stones and never put it back. Look, yer can see.'

'I can. Never noticed that when I came round to inspect it yesterday.'

'Better get on to 'im then, the lazy idle . . .'

'He wasn't to know we were going to have the storm of the century, was he?'

'No, I guess you're right, but he'll have to bring his scaffolding back and start again. You can see there's been a long line of stones dislodged right from the top. Any damage to the rectory, sir?'

'No. You all right?'

'Yes, we's fine thanks. Couldn't sleep mind, but who could? Mr Charter-Plackett's hammering some wood onto his window, can yer hear him! Be ages before he gets a glass firm to come right out here. They'll be too busy in Culworth.'

The window was in fact replaced before lunchtime. The men from the glass firm were enjoying a coffee from the customers' machine when Peter, in response to a telephone call from Jimbo, went into the Store to speak to him.

The two men touched their caps to him. 'Morning, Reverend. Bad night last night you 'ad 'ere.'

'It was, indeed. I'm surprised you're here. Thought there'd have been more than enough work for you in Culworth.'

'No, not there, Reverend. It's bin windy an' tha', but no broken windows. Seems Turnham Malpas caught the worst of it. The eye of the storm, I think they calls it. Well, we'll be off now. Thanks for the coffee, Mr Charter-P. Would you sign for us, please?'

Jimbo did as he was asked and when they'd left he looked at Peter and nodded his head in the direction of his storeroom. Peter followed him in. Jimbo took off his boater, smoothed his bald head, folded his arms and said, 'Well?'

'Well?'

'What about it?'

'I'm sorry?'

'Isn't it time something was done?'

'I've got the men coming this afternoon. They're putting the scaffolding up again and then—'

'I'm talking about this witchcraft thing.'

There was a tap at the door. It was Linda. 'Excuse me, Mr Charter-Plackett, sorry to disturb, but Sir Ralph's wanting a word.'

'Show him through here, if you please.' They paused for a moment awaiting Ralph's arrival.

'Good morning, Ralph.'

'Good morning, Peter, Jimbo. Top-level conference, what?' Ralph smiled at the two of them.

'Sort of.' Jimbo looked at Peter again. 'Well?'

'If either of you is going to stand here and tell me that the storm last night was anything at all to do with witchcraft . . .'

Ralph retorted, 'We're not, but—'

'*But*,' said Jimbo, 'the whole village is frightened. They've been coming in here this morning exchanging news about the damage that's been done and uppermost in their minds is the damage to the church – where else would the devil aim for, they say – and the damage to the royal oak. Some of them have blenched when they've seen the old tree. They are truly scared. There's nothing in it, I know, but it is all getting very sinister.'

'I know all their names.'

Ralph looked surprised; his bushy white eyebrows shot up. 'You do? Excellent! Give them to me and I'll pay them all a visit. Tell them where to get off. I'm not afraid.'

'Neither am I, but what does one say? "Please stop consorting with the devil?" Or: "I shall report you to the police?" And: "Was it you who brought this storm down on us?" The more we say, the more credibility we are giving them. But somehow it must be stopped because I, as a man of the church, will not allow it to go on. I can feel evil in the air. But how?'

'Tell them to damn-well give it all up; they're endangering their immortal souls. How about that?'

Peter nodded his head. 'They are, but they won't listen to that. On the other hand, I think I may have found out where they're holding their meetings now.'

Ralph's head came up with a jerk. 'Where?'

'Caroline was up with the children most of the night, as they've got heavy colds. They sleep in the bedroom overlooking Rector's Meadow and before the storm really got going she saw lights in the old hay barn.'

'Right! I shall watch every night from our bedroom window and when I see lights again I shall telephone you and we'll surprise them, the three of us – agreed?'

Peter and Jimbo looked at each other and then they both said, 'Very well.'

On Sunday morning when Peter went into St Thomas à Becket's for the ten o'clock service he found that almost every seat was taken. The congregation had been growing steadily since he'd first come to Turnham Malpas, but for an ordinary morning service the numbers were phenomenal. He knew enough not to congratulate himself on making a breakthrough. These people were in church because they were scared; it was a clustering together for mutual support. As he took his place and was about to say his opening prayer, his eye caught Ralph's.

Peter was surprised to find himself recognising a Lord of the Manor look in Ralph's eyes. A look which said, 'This morning you will preach the sermon these people, *my* people, need.' The incumbent, long ago at the mercy of the Templeton family to be dictated to as they wished, was under no obligation to the Templetons any longer, but Peter felt compelled to acknowledge Ralph's request. As they sang the first hymn, he battled with himself. Ralph had no authority to be instructing him in what he should say from his own pulpit, none at all. But he was right. Peter's theme of 'Go out into all the world and preach the Gospel' had no place here this morning. The congregation needed a strengthening sermon with a message of comfort – and that was what they would get.

After the service, Ralph came to stand beside Peter as he shook hands with his flock. 'Mind if I shake hands, too? I'll stand further down the path.'

'Not at all. Of course you may.'

Many of the congregation thanked him for his sermon; many of them also looked to Ralph for support.

That night, Ralph keeping watch yet again from his upstairs window, saw the lights and telephoned Peter and Jimbo.

24

Muriel was scared. Going by chance to seek out the witches' coven had been exciting, but the enterprise Ralph had initiated tonight was quite another matter.

Ralph kissed her cheek. 'My dear, please don't worry yourself. Three grown men going to rout out some silly women with turnips for heads is nothing for you to get scared about. Now go to bed—'

'Go to bed – how can I? I shan't sleep a wink.'

'Of course you will.' He kissed her cheek again, his face full of excitement.

'I think I'll come with you. I shall be dressed in a trice.'

'Absolutely not, my dear. I cannot allow it.'

Reluctantly, Muriel acquiesced. 'Very well then, but take care, Ralph, you're all I've got.'

'Muriel! But someone has to get rid of these people, haven't they – and who better than me?'

'No one better than you.' They heard a knock at the door. 'Off you go.'

'I'll try not to wake you when I get back.'

Muriel couldn't help smiling. How on earth did he think she was going to sleep with all this going on? As he left to go downstairs to answer the door she called over the banister, 'And they haven't got turnips for heads! Remember!'

Ralph chuckled as he opened the front door to Peter and Jimbo.

The three of them walked through Ralph's house into the garden and then via his back gate into Pipe and Nook Lane. They climbed over the stone wall and stood quietly conferring.

'There's no cover at all. I think the best thing is to walk round the perimeter anti-clockwise, don't you?' whispered Jimbo.

'And come up on the lee-side of the door, so to speak? Yes, I agree. Let's keep well into the hedge.' Ralph led the way. He had his walking stick with him and he noticed Jimbo had one too. Peter had come unarmed.

The sky, still sombre and looming after the storm, afforded little light for their walk. Ralph set a steady pace and Peter remembered his heart attack and wondered whether it was wise for Ralph to have come. But there was no stopping him once he'd made up his mind. Above the heads of Jimbo and Ralph he could see the barn. There was a glimmer of light through the opening at the top of the roof. They must surely be there then. In his heart, Peter was dreading the confrontation. Who would they find? A few women in need of excitement like Ellie had said, or an evil woman set on devilry? A few sad teenagers lulled into believing like Rhett had been, or serious opposition? Real danger from a handful of fanatics, or two illicit lovers having found a safe place to meet? Then they really *would* feel foolish.

They arrived at the barn rather sooner than Peter would have wished. Listening below the opening at the apex of the roof they could hear very little: the murmur of voices, rustling of feet, nothing more.

Ralph went quietly round the end of the barn to the huge door set midway in the long wall. He couldn't get it open. The three of them stood holding their breath but no one inside appeared to have noticed they were trying to get in. The door was made to open outwards and it took all Peter's strength to budge it. He did it slowly, slowly, daring it to creak. He slipped inside first, followed by Ralph and then Jimbo.

At the far end, an altar had been made from an upended bale of hay. Glowing black candles were balanced precariously on it. On top of the bales which were stacked two and three high against the walls, about twenty more candles had been lit to illuminate the great barn. Six people, all dressed in black, were standing within a circle drawn on the floor of the barn. In the light of the candle-flames Peter could recognise Simone, Venetia, Valda and Thelma Senior, Ellie and . . . *he couldn't believe it* . . . Kate. He wiped the sweat from his top lip and glanced at Ralph and then at Jimbo. They were quite motionless. Eyes wide. Staring.

The candles cast wavering shadows on the walls of the barn and on the bales of hay. The air was filled by the smell of the burning wax and, overlaying that, the reek of old dry-as-dust hay. The combined stench was suffocating. Peter shuddered. The group was chanting. There was a strange feeling in the air – a menacing atmosphere by which a man of his calibre and outlook should not be affected. But he couldn't help it. It was like being in church yet not, just as Rhett had said. The hairs on the back of his neck stood up and Peter could feel his spine begin to tingle. He and Jimbo and Ralph were still undetected. The figures in black were too intensely involved in their chanting, to be aware of the three men standing in the shadows by the door.

There was a movement just beyond him on his left. Instinctively, he flicked his head to see what the threat was. There was Cat crouching high up on a bale. Her tail wagged furiously from side to side, the movement of it playing a sinister dancing pattern on the wall behind her. Suddenly Cat leapt down to the earth floor, and covered the distance between herself and Peter in less time than he believed possible. She sprang and yowled at the same moment. Her claws, like a dozen fine needles, sank into his leg. He bit his lip to stop himself from shouting out and alerting the worshippers, but it wouldn't have mattered. Cat's spiteful howl had broken the absorption of the group swaying in the circle. It took them a moment to focus, for their minds were so completely out of this world, that they couldn't take in what had happened. When they did, their reaction was like that of Cat's.

None of the three men had fought with a woman before but they were doing it now. Only Kate stood back; the other five were clawing, biting, kicking, clutching, grabbing, screeching. As they struggled and fought, they cannoned into the bales of hay and the candles wobbled dangerously. Some fell to the floor. Small fires began here and there but no one noticed.

'Stop it! Stop it!' Kate screamed. She rushed forward to try to pull the women away, first one and then another. But her meagre strength could do nothing with these maniacal figures. Ralph in desperation began hitting out with his walking stick, threatening rather than striking. Cat clawed and bit whenever the opportunity arose, and the pain of that, combined with the utter surprise of these wild women attacking them, almost overwhelmed the men.

Jimbo, who was nearest to the door, managed to push it open again and get out into the field. 'Come on! Come on!' he shouted.

The rush of cold air sharpened Peter's wits. 'THAT WILL DO! STOP IT THIS INSTANT,' he bellowed.

He gained a moment's respite and he used it to say again: 'THAT WILL DO. STOP NOW!'

But Simone wouldn't stop. She was the one least influenced by him. Howling like a banshee, she went behind the altar with the candles still burning on it, came out with a knife in her hand and lunged straight towards Peter, her eyes wild with hate.

Kate saw her intention and darted at Simone. She pushed her back; Simone ricocheted against the altar and more candles fell over. In a second the loose hay scattered on the floor flared up.

Ralph, looking round and realising that the fire was catching hold, saw their danger. 'Get out, everyone! Get out!' he shouted. But the foot-wide gap afforded by the open door impeded their escape.

Jimbo tried to open it further from the outside but couldn't. One by one, the women struggled out. Then Ralph. Then last of all Peter. They stood gasping for air, their struggle forgotten in the fear of being burned alive. Peter was standing bent over, his hands gripping his thighs trying to get his breath back so he could speak.

'Who's missing?' Ralph shouted. 'There's someone missing!'

No one answered him, for just then a column of rats streaked through the gap of the door and squeezed out through the rotting places at the bottom, young and old, large and small, tumbling over each other in their rush to escape. The women screamed and they all hastily leapt about to avoid the rats running over their feet. They could hear the scrabbling of their feet and the rush of their bodies through the grass as they fled certain death.

When their panic had subsided, Ralph looked around. 'Simone's not here,' he said.

Peter rapidly counted heads. 'You're right. Stay there – I'll go in!' Jimbo went ahead of him but neither of them could see anything at all. The barn was filled with acrid smoke and scorching flames.

'We can't leave her.'

'We can't see.' Jimbo began coughing.

'She was by the altar.'

Jimbo grabbed Peter's arm. 'Get out, come on – *out!*'

The smoke made Peter's eyes stream with tears. 'We can't leave her,' he said again.

'Get out! And that's an order!' he grabbed Peter's arm and hauled him through the door. 'Ralph – tell him he's not going back in!'

Kate was weeping. Venetia cried too, thick rivulets of mascara running down her cheeks. Valda and Thelma stood rigid with shock. Ellie was retching into the long grass. Of Cat there was no sign. The flames were leaping at the barn door and licking at the openings at each end. It was an inferno. No one could be alive in there now.

'The fire brigade!' Peter shouted. 'We need the fire brigade!' Jimbo dragged his mobile phone out of his pocket and was punching in 999 when they heard shouting.

Across the field from the direction of the Big House they could see someone. It was Jeremy, lumbering along as fast as he could.

'Are you all right?' he called out. 'What on earth's happened? Have you seen Venetia?'

Jimbo waved his mobile phone. 'She's over there. I'm just phoning the fire brigade.'

'God! What the hell is going on? How did it start?' Venetia ran into Jeremy's arms. 'Steady on, old girl. I say, steady on. You're all right now.' He clumsily rubbed her back as he comforted her.

Venetia moaned, 'Take me home, take me home.'

Peter was too distraught at the thought of Simone's death to take Jeremy aside and explain. He had to leave that to Ralph.

Jeremy shuddered. 'Simone? Oh no! Can't we get her out? Surely we can.'

Jimbo told him hoarsely: 'We can't get in, it's a wall of fire in there. Believe me, we've tried.'

They stood stricken as the flames roared. The huge wooden beams of the roof withstood the heat for a while but there was a sudden deafening roar and the roof began collapsing. Instinctively they retreated and helplessly watched Simone's funeral pyre.

Peter caught Jeremy's eye and looked questioningly at him, but the other man, shamefaced, avoided his eyes. Peter guessed he'd known all the time what Venetia was doing.

'I'll go and open the field gate for the engine,' Peter said and sprinted across the field towards the gate which was further down Pipe and Nook Lane beyond the rectory. As he rushed past, he saw Caroline standing at the end of their garden. He waved and shouted, 'Don't worry, we're all fine! Just opening the gate for the fire brigade.' The gate was held shut by a complication of chains but thankfully no padlock. On his way back, Peter stopped to speak to her. 'We can't do anything – the fire engine's going to be far too late. The roof's already going. Can't stop.' He embraced her briefly.

'Peter, for God's sake be careful,' she pleaded.

'Of course!'

Five minutes afterwards the engine carefully negotiated the open gate and humped and bumped its way across the field, the large crowd which had gathered in the last few minutes separating to make way for it.

'Heaven help us, whatever next!'

'Thank God nobody's inside!'

'But Sir Ralph said . . .'

'Simone? No!!'

'Them poor kids!'

'Oooh! They'll be all on their own. Poor little devils!'

Peter was devastated. If they hadn't interfered, Simone would be alive still, and some harmless tampering with the devil would have, in all likelihood, soon fizzled out. Jeremy had taken Venetia home. Valda and Thelma still stood in silent shock. Ellie was clinging to the sergeant's arm and impeding his activities. Kate stood watching alone. He went across to speak with her.

It was difficult to talk. The noise of the fire-engine pump, the shouts of the men and the sound of the water pulsating onto the flames made conversation almost impossible. They'd put up the ladder from the engine now and were pumping water into the barn through one of the openings. Peter drew her to one side away from the noise and the ears of the crowd.

'Kate!' His reproachful tone brought tears to her eyes. She looked up at him, her face illuminated by the searchlight on the engine.

'I came to ask her to stop, but somehow . . .'

'Well, she's gone now, God rest her soul, so it can all stop. For good.'

'I've been punished for it, haven't I?'

'You have?'

'Cat's not come out.'

'Ah! Cat.' Peter rubbed his leg where Cat's claws had struck. 'I deeply regret what's happened tonight, but it does put an end to Simone's bizarre influence, doesn't it? If the sergeant's finished with you, I'll see you home. I've already spoken with him. He'll be taking proper statements in the morning when they've . . . you know.'

Kate's face looked girm. 'Found the body, you mean.' Something occurred to her. 'Peter! The children! She left them on their own when she came to the meetings.'

Before he could answer, Caroline was at his elbow. Startled to find her there, his immediate thought was for his own children. 'The twins – what have you done with them?' he asked brusquely.

'Calm down, calm down, Sylvia's with them. I just had to come. Kate, you OK?'

'Yes, thanks.'

Caroline looked devastated. 'Dreadful thing to have happened, really dreadful.'

Peter said, 'Kate's just reminded me of Simone's children. She left them in the cottage on their own.'

'I'll go to Little Derehams straight away and check on the poor things. I'll just fetch the car.'

'We'll come too. You mustn't go by yourself – heaven alone knows what you might find. Come on, Kate. Sergeant! We're going to see to Simone's children. Will you take Mr Pascoe's statement tomorrow?'

'Certainly, sir. We can do no more here tonight.'

Peter drove the car to Little Derehams, Caroline beside him, Kate in the back. He caught the occasional sound of her weeping but he didn't comment. She had more than enough to weep about, and he blamed her for a lot of what had happened. His leg was stinging and he'd be glad to get a chance to look at.it. But first things first.

The back door was shut but unlocked. Kate went in first and her fingers searched the wall for the light switch. When she pressed it, no light came on.

'The electricity's been cut off!'

Caroline went back to the car for a torch. The beam showed them the utter chaos of the cottage. Caroline was speechless. She shone the torch along the walls to find another switch and picked her way carefully towards it. But nothing happened when she turned it on. 'You're right, there's no power. How could they do it when there's five small children in the house? It's unbelievable.'

At this moment Dickon piped up: 'Simone? Simone?'

Kate said 'It's all right, Dickon, it's only me. Ms Pascoe from the school.'

He stood up on the sofa cushions, his blanket in his hand. Tonight he didn't even have a vest to wear.

Kate went towards him. 'Where's the light, Dickon? We can't see.'

'Oil-lamp. Got no matches.'

Caroline ran her fingers despairingly through her hair. 'Dear Lord. What are we going to do?'

As they stood motionless trying to take in the deprivations the children had been forced to tolerate, they heard a hesitant fumbling on the staircase. Caroline turned the beam of the torch towards the sound.

Florentina, Valentine and Hansel were creeping quietly down. They were dressed in an odd assortment of clothes – not quite nightclothes and not quite dayclothes. The moment Valentine saw them he began screaming. He struggled down the last three steps, stumbled his way over to Dickon and, pulling him down from the sofa, flung his arms around him and howled.

Florentina, rubbing her eyes, said, 'Go away.'

'The baby. Where's the baby?'

She nodded her head in the direction of the bedroom. Caroline found the baby sound asleep in a large drawer on the floor; it smelt as though its nappy hadn't been changed all day. The bedroom stank of unwashed bodies, of bed-wetting and sheer neglect. Caroline retched.

'They've found her body. She and Cat were together. We think she stayed behind to rescue Cat and then—'

'Peter, *please*! I can't bear it. We're all to blame – us, the school, social services. Every manjack of us.'

'We weren't to blame for this witchcraft business. That was her decision entirely. That's when everything began to go wrong.'

'They never appeared desperately neglected before all this, did they? They *used* to be clean and reasonably well fed, but as Kate said, this last few months Dickon and Florentina were useless where school was concerned. Too tired, too hungry, never there. Where are they now?'

'A temporary foster home has been found for them all in Culworth. At least they'll be clean and well-fed and cared for there.'

'And Kate – what was her explanation for being at the barn?'

'She'd gone to ask Simone to stop, and then kind of couldn't resist her influence.'

'I shouldn't say this, but we're well rid of her *and* that bloody cat.'

'Caroline!'

'It's true. Not even you could have brought her to her senses.'

Peter drew back the curtains and looked out at the fading light. 'What a night! What a day!'

'It was hell this morning in the surgery. I don't mind telling you, if I made a correct diagnosis it was only by sheer chance. I *felt* and I'm told *looked* dreadful.'

'You were brave to go. I've had a dreadful day too, full of recrimination and despair.'

He was totally drained, his inner resources leached from him by the flood of people seeking his comfort and reassurance wherever he went.

His early-morning prayers in church had been interrupted by a remorseful Venetia. She had come in and knelt beside him in the war memorial chapel and wept bitter tears. 'Can I come to confession? Do you do that sort of thing?'

'No. You have a direct line to God, Venetia. You don't need me like some kind of holy telephone exchange.'

'Well, will you listen and sort me out? Please, Peter?'

'Of course.' And he had. And he'd listened sadly to her promises to come to church every Sunday, now she had reformed. And he'd wished he could believe her, and had pretended he did.

His regular Monday visit to Penny Fawcett had been delayed an hour by Valda and Thelma Senior begging forgiveness and wanting to take communion, something they hadn't done in years. He'd put them off, said they needed to think some more before they did that. Ralph and Jimbo had both come to see him, to seek assurance in their own way. Ralph had said he was sorry about Simone, but Peter knew full well that underneath Ralph was glad the whole matter had been resolved and if it took a death to do it, so what? The village had been saved from destruction and that was what counted. Peter had visited Kate in school to check on how she was coping, and of course the children were eager to embellish the story of the fire, and request his version of it.

Brian wanted to know where had Mrs Paradise stabbed him?

Flick asked about Cat and had she gone to heaven like her poor old Orlando? Stacey had said, 'My dad says good riddance to bad rubbish.'

A comment Peter felt compelled to explore for his own sake as much as hers.

Altogether he felt trampled. It wasn't just Simone's death, it was the ramifications of it which he found so difficult. And those children. Fatherless all their lives and now motherless. At least the baby, Opal, was too young to know the pain of grief.

He felt Caroline beside him. She put her hand in his and said, 'You've got to hold on in there. You've so much to achieve, so much waiting to be done which can only be done by you. If it's any help, you are my best beloved. I adore you, and I adore your children; they're like my own flesh and blood. They *are* mine, I think, sometimes.'

Peter gripped her hand tightly. 'Thank you. Two such inadequate words, but believe me they are from my heart. Without you I couldn't carry on.'

25

Kate had gone to bed early the night after Simone's death. She'd hoped to sleep for hours, she was so exhausted. Up all night and then school all day with the children hyped-up by the night's events, her nerves and her body were strung to breaking point, but she couldn't get to sleep. Kate half-remembered that line from *Macbeth*: '*Sleep that knits up the ravell'd sleave of care.*' If only!

She got up and went to the window. The sky was clear, the village at rest. The moon came out from behind a cloud and lit the houses with a caressing silvery light. English nights weren't like African nights. English nights were gentle and comforting. African nights, dramatic and challenging; there were times when the blood ran cold at the triumphant howl of an animal or the death screams of tortured prey. Turnham Malpas nights were mild, reassuring, and tranquil by comparison. Kate shook herself. *Tranquil?* Anything but, of late.

She should have gone in herself to rescue Simone, but the heat! The flames – and Cat! Simone . . . Jacob . . . Africa! All in ashes. Her head spun. Well, she'd have to allow the flames to cleanse her of everything evil. She'd been possessed. Absolutely possessed! She'd have to go to Peter soon and tell him how she felt and what she was going to do, now it was all over. What *was* she going to do?

Her fingers trailed a pattern on the windowsill. Around the carving of a black child, around a ceremonial knife, around a carved wooden necklace Jacob had given her. Part of the cleansing would be getting rid of anything and everything which reminded her of Africa. Cat had gone – she paused for a moment and grieved – now all the things which hitherto had been such precious mementos must go, too.

Kate resolutely swept the carvings from the windowsill, then rushed to that awkward corner under the eaves and swung angrily at the crystal ball and the candles. The ball fell with an enormous crash, the candles rolled silently across the carpet. She put her slippers on and stamped on the candles, breaking them into a hundred pieces and grinding them into the carpet. She dragged the picture from the wall above the altar and tore it to shreds.

From her wardrobe she took every item of black clothing she could find and stuffed them all into binbags. What she'd wear tomorrow for school she didn't know, but they had to go.

In the kitchen she took her cook's scissors and chopped great lengths from her hair. Then she ran a bath and scrubbed herself, every inch of her body until her flesh stung.

At two o'clock she fell into bed and slept.

'Mummy! Mummy! You'll never guess what! Not in a million years will you guess.'

'Tell me then,' Harriet called out.

'Ms Pascoe's cut her hair. It's so short you wouldn't believe. We didn't recognise her.' Flick held her finger and thumb three centimetres away from each other and said, 'That long, that's all. And you'll never guess something else.'

'What?'

'She was wearing a funny old red shirt and a blue skirt. They didn't match at all, but it did make a change. She's not wearing black any more, she says. She's going into Culworth this minute to buy clothes, she says.'

'Well, well.'

'And,' Flick took a deep breath, 'and she's going to have two of Mrs Biggs' kittens.'

'No!'

'Yes, she is, *and* . . .' Flick paused for dramatic effect.

'Yes?'

'And she's calling them Beano and Dandy!'

'What sensible names.'

'I told her they'd have to have names or they'd have an identity crisis, being two of them. You couldn't call both of them Cat, could you?'

'Certainly not.'

'And she's organising a holiday for anyone who wants to go – a five-day geography field trip.'

'Really?'

'Yes, it's only for the leavers, though. Not absolutely everyone.'

'Of course not, they're not old enough.'

'Exactly. Mummy, can I go?'

'We'll ask Daddy about it.'

'Daddy will say yes. He always does for me. That's because I'm going to work in the Store when I've qualified.'

'Qualified?'

'Got a degree in something, and I shall work up from the bottom in the business in the holidays.'

'Is that really what you want to do?'

'Well, the boys aren't interested, are they? And I am, so I shall. We shall have lots of Stores when I'm helping Daddy, and you can be rich and do nothing all day like you do now.'

'Thanks. I shall look forward to that.'

'I'm to be Queen of the May. You've to go and see Ms Pascoe about my dress, please, she says.' Flick sat herself down at the kitchen table.

'Darling, how lovely.' Harriet kissed the top of her head. 'You've kept the best till last. Daddy will be thrilled.'

'Where's my biscuit? Oh, home-made – lovely!'

'That's just one of the thousand things I've done today. I shall go and see Ms Pascoe tomorrow about your dress. How exciting. That's wonderful!'

'And my milk, please. Where's Fran? Thanks.'

'Playing with the twins.'

'I wish she wouldn't. I like her to be at home when I get in. She *is* my sister. She likes the twins too much.'

'Well, they are more her age, aren't they? And they are good fun. It gets lonely for her here on her own when you're at school. They love looking after her.'

Flick sipped her milk thoughtfully and then, not looking at her mother, said, 'I shall be glad to leave school. You outgrow things, don't you? Sometimes they seem to talk such nonsense. It happens and you don't know it till they say something and you think that was stupid.'

'I know just what you mean. Geography field trips can be very uncomfortable – tents and things. Are you sure you'd like that?'

'Oh, we wouldn't be in tents. We'd be in a big house. I'd like that.' Flick stopped at the door for a moment. 'Ms Pascoe's quite different today. She took prayers herself, and we didn't meditate.'

'I am glad.'

'So am I. It was a bit silly, wasn't it?' Flick trailed away upstairs leaving Harriet feeling that her little girl had suddenly grown up overnight. Thank God Kate had decided to join the rest of the human race, and not before time.

Kate rang the rectory bell at eight o'clock that night. She'd come to talk to Peter. Make a clean breast of everything and tell him she'd done with voodoo and black magic. All it had brought was tragedy – to Jacob, to Cat, to Simone. It was a moment before her ring was answered. When the door opened, it was Caroline standing there.

'Why, Kate! How lovely to see you. You look so different – it's your hair. Do come in.'

'Thank you. Is Peter in?'

'Out, I'm afraid. Can I help?'

'Oh well, I'll leave it then, come another night.'

'Please don't. I'm all by myself, the children are in bed and I'd enjoy some company.' She didn't want Kate to leave; this could be her chance to find out.

Kate stepped back out again on to the stone step. 'No – no, thanks.'

'Please!' Caroline pleaded with her.

Kate smiled. 'Very well then. Yes, I will – why not?'

'Good. I'll take your coat.' She held out her hands for it and then gasped when she saw what Kate had on underneath. 'Oh, what a lovely suit, such a gorgeous red. I've only seen you in black before. And your hair – turn round, let me see. Oh, it really suits you.'

Kate looked embarrassed. 'I've been into Culworth and put all my black clothes in the bin.'

Caroline studied her face. 'New start?'

'Something like that.'

'Good, I'm glad.' Caroline showed her into their sitting room. 'Do sit down.'

Kate took an easy chair. 'I think I said this the last time I was in this room, but I'll say it again. I do like it very much.' She looked round appreciatively.

'You should have seen it when we moved in. Foolishly Peter said we would take it as it stood, furniture and all.' She raised her eyes to the ceiling. 'It was dreadful.'

'Well, it's beautiful now.'

'Thank you. Getting organised for May Day?'

'Oh yes, indeed! Flick Charter-Plackett is to be Queen of the May and we've chosen her attendants; now we're practising the dances. I've got a group of mothers in charge of the refreshments, and I've organised the muscle required for bringing the piano onto the Green and carrying out the Maypole. So, all we need now is the weather.'

'I understand there's only been one year when it rained so much they had to hold it in the school, and that was 1902! So, with luck . . .' Caroline crossed her fingers and laughed.

'Don't you think that's wonderful, this kind of ongoing memory?' Kate enthused. 'It gives such stability, such a sense of history. We're all so lucky to be living here, aren't we?'

'We certainly are. You know the village has this superstition that when the royal oak tree dies, the one on the Green' – Kate nodded – 'then the village will die too. They all felt we came pretty close in the recent storm. They considered it was brought on by – well, witchcraft. You've had a narrow escape, Kate. The village can be very vindictive if something doesn't suit.'

There was an uncomfortable pause and Caroline decided to come straight out with it. She'd a right to know.

'My cat.'

'Yes?'

'My cat Mimi.'

'I'm sorry?'

Unexpectedly Caroline's throat was choked with emotion, and she couldn't continue.

Kate said, 'I'm sorry, you were saying . . . ?'

'Her collar was found by the fire in Sykes Wood.'

Kate flushed as comprehension dawned. 'I see. I didn't know the cat was yours.'

'What happened? I've a right to know. It was you, wasn't it?'

Kate chose her words with care. 'I was there, yes. She came upon us that night quite by chance. She must have been hunting or something.' Caroline nodded. 'Simone said, and Thelma and Valda agreed with her, "Here's our chance to experiment." I said, "No, we mustn't. It's not right," but they wouldn't listen. Venetia wasn't too sure, and Rhett and Ellie and the weekenders were nervous. "What? Do what?" they said. Simone raised her voice, stretched her arms towards the heavens and said dramatically, "Sacrifice her!" '

Kate wasn't looking at Caroline when she said that; she was staring into the fire, recalling the horror of it all. If she'd looked at Caroline, she wouldn't have continued or, at the very least, would have softened certain aspects of the story, but she felt as though she were in the confessional, and her own need drove her on regardless of Caroline's feelings.

'Simone said—'

Caroline snapped: 'Simone! Always Simone! Didn't you have a mind of your own?'

Kate looked shocked. She didn't answer for a moment and then she said, 'I suppose that's right. At that moment I didn't. But afterwards I did, and protested.'

'When it was too late for my Mimi.'

'I'm sorry, yes. When it was too late.'

'Did she suffer?'

'No – well, I don't think so.'

'You must know whether she suffered!'

'You see, Simone mesmerised her. Spoke to her, hypnotised her, I suppose, so she didn't feel the knife.'

Caroline leapt to her feet. 'The knife! What knife?'

'Simone's.'

'Simone had a knife ready?' Caroline sat down again. 'How . . . how do you know she didn't feel it?'

363

'Because she didn't fight back.' Kate stared into the fire again, reliving the moment. 'Just lay there motionless, and let herself be sacrificed.'

'Sacrificed? Oh, God! I can't believe I'm talking to a human being. How could you, an intelligent, educated person, allow such a thing to happen? My dear cat, whose only crime was happening upon you at that moment – how could you do it to her?'

'I only watched.'

'Only watched!' Caroline's voice rang with sarcasm. 'Oh well then, that exonerates you, doesn't it?'

Kate shook her head. 'No, it doesn't. I know that now. I'm so sorry.'

'What then?'

In a voice scarcely above a whisper Kate said, 'Then we laid her on the altar as an offering.'

Caroline's voice was dry and throaty as she asked, 'By then, she was properly dead, I hope.'

Kate nodded. The silence between them lengthened while Caroline came to terms with what she'd heard and Kate tried to come to terms with herself.

Peter walked in at that moment. Neither of them had heard his key in the door. He stood just inside the room, looking first at one and then the other, puzzled by the pent-up emotions he could feel.

Kate was the first to notice he was there. She smiled briefly, apologetically at him.

As he put down his sports bag, Peter said, 'Lovely to see you, Kate. I'm just back from playing squash, as you see, I'm going to take a shower and then perhaps—'

'Kate's just leaving.'

'Oh, I'm sorry. I was going to suggest—'

'I said, she's leaving.'

Kate faced Caroline. 'I'm so sorry. If I'd known it was your cat . . .'

'Any cat, any cat at all, not just mine. The guilt is the same. Has it all stopped now with Simone gone?'

'Oh yes.'

'So I should think. Not before time. Such evil. I can't believe it.'

'It has stopped. Definitely. I shall never forgive myself for coming under her influence in such a way. It all stemmed from my experiences in Africa and my grief at losing Jacob. It seemed a comfort at the time; it assuaged my grief a little. But I admit I've been totally wrong.'

'Such evil, in this lovely place. The others were just foolish and misguided and afraid – but you, you *actively* agreed with it all. You knew and understood the thinking behind it. You deserve some kind of punishment for what you've done; what you've encouraged by your lack of protest.'

'I've been punished.'

'Oh – how?'

'I've lost my cat too, in horrific circumstances.'

'No more horrific than my poor Mimi's. Just go – leave my house. Perhaps one day when I feel you are truly repentant I might be able to forgive you, but not right now. Peter's much better than me at that kind of thing.'

Kate left the two of them, took her coat from the chair in the hall and let herself out.

'Whatever you do, *don't* sympathise nor ask me what she's just told me. *Please.*'

'I won't.'

'I need a drink.'

'By the look on your face a brandy might fit the bill.'

Her hands were shaking as she took the glass from him. 'Go and have your shower.'

'I thought I'd delay that for a while, till you look better.'

'I need to be alone.'

He bent over intending to kiss the top of her head, not knowing how else to express his anxiety, but Caroline pulled her head away. 'No! No sympathy, or I shall fold completely.'

When Peter came back downstairs after his shower, she was still sitting where he'd left her. The colour had come back into her face, and the brandy glass was empty. She glanced up at him as he stood before her.

'Sorry for being snappy.'

'That's all right, my darling, I understand.'

'You're too forgiving of me. I wish I could be the same to her.'

'You will one day. You're too generous not to be.'

'It doesn't pay to love too much, does it? Love brings so much heartbreak with it.'

'You mean Mimi?'

'People too, really, not just animals.'

'To get things in proportion, let's thank God it's not one of the children you're grieving for tonight.'

'Oh Peter, what a perfectly dreadful thing to say!' Caroline burst into tears and sobbed as though her heart would break.

Peter knelt down in front of her and took her in his arms. 'Darling! My darling!' He stroked her hair, while he waited for her tears to subside. 'Please, please don't distress yourself so; I should never have said that. I'm so sorry, so sorry.' He lifted her head from his shoulder and tried to look into her face, but she wouldn't let him. 'Whatever happens, remember it's always, always worth loving to the utmost; nothing less is neither right nor good. You can't hold back on love.'

Caroline's sobs began to lessen. She wiped her eyes. 'I . . .'

'Yes?'

'I'm so sorry. I'm not so much grieving for Mimi as for what Mimi meant to me when I was alone.' She gave a great shuddering sigh. 'Of course, you're quite right. Thank God I'm not grieving for one of the children. That's too frightening even to contemplate. I love them so. And I've caused Beth such pain. I'm so sorry.'

'Not at all. I've realised this parenthood business is something we have to learn as we go along.'

Caroline smiled. 'I suppose so. I'm all tuckered out, as the Australians say. I'll just get a few things ready for tomorrow and then I'm going to bed.'

'Thank you for being such a lovely mother. And wife.'

Caroline dried the last of her tears, and gave him a faint grin. She faked a punch at his jaw. 'Don't let's get all sentimental, for heaven's sake. Life has to go on. But that Kate! I can't forgive her.'

'Neither can she.'

26

'So, Gilbert, I wondered if you could possibly bring your Morris dancers that afternoon.'

'May the first?'

'That's right.' Kate moved the receiver to her left ear so she could check her diary. 'It's a Thursday. I know it's short notice, but it suddenly came to me in the night what a highly suitable activity it was for May Day. How about it?'

'The last time I was asked about my Morris dancers, there was a mix-up; two teams turned up and we had an argument. My team's been a bit chary of Turnham Malpas ever since. They were very upset, you see. They'll take some persuading, and of course most of them work.'

'Look, it won't happen here. I don't even *know* another team to invite, I promise. Please – I want to make it a kind of traditional village afternoon. I've got a Punch and Judy man coming and a chap who has a kind of mobile children's roundabout – you know, the old-fashioned kind. I'm desperate to make a success of it. I know that all it's been before is a parade and the crowning and the Maypole dancing and then the tea, but this time I want to make it more worthwhile for people to come. Not to make money or anything – just to provide a thoroughly good afternoon.'

Gilbert didn't answer straight away. He guessed she wanted to make a success of the afternoon to atone for the trouble she'd caused. She'd come within an ace of being on the receiving end of the villagers' wrath; how she'd escaped, he didn't know. Possibly because she was making such a success of the school, *and* because Peter had backed her.

'They'll have already been up before dawn because we always dance at dawn on May Day – perhaps you didn't know that. We go to Bickerby Rocks, the great hill on the other side of the by-pass. It's all very symbolic. Look, leave it with me,' he said, beginning to relent. 'It's short notice, but I'll do my best. I'll let you know by tomorrow night.'

'Thank you, thank you very much indeed. I do appreciate your co-operation.'

Kate replaced the receiver, put her diary back in its place in the top drawer of her desk and gazed out at the bins. She clenched her fist and struck the palm of her left hand. She'd make this May Day a success if she never did another thing. It was ironic that May Day was also an important festival for . . . No, she'd done with all that.

She'd had her talk with Peter. The day after the disastrous evening with Caroline he'd called in when school was finished and everyone except Pat had gone, and they'd sat in her classroom – he on her chair and she perched on a desk with her feet resting on one of the children's chairs. Peter hadn't criticised her, found her guilty, or remonstrated with her. He'd simply sat there and let her ramble on, all the guilt coming out, the fears, the reasons. Her disgust at the turn Simone's activities had taken, her lack of protest. 'That's what I feel so guilty about. If I'd protested louder and more vehemently, all this might have been avoided. It's like Caroline said – by watching and knowing and doing nothing, I was implicated; I can't escape that. But I have put it all behind me and I shan't allow myself to become influenced again, never! I shall make this school so successful they'll be coming from miles around to get their children's names down before they've even been conceived!'

Peter had laughed. 'Good! That's wonderful. You've so much to give – you're a born teacher.'

'Thank you for backing me – I don't deserve such loyalty. I am indebted to you.'

'You're not indebted. My support was freely given. Anything else? I see Pat loitering by the door wanting to get in to clean.'

Kate had slipped off the desk ready to leave and then turned back to say, 'I'd like to have prayers in church again, if that's all right with you, starting this Friday? I couldn't before; my conscience wouldn't let me.'

'But of course. Delighted.'

'Thank you.'

She'd gone straight from school into the church, the first time since she'd arrived in the village. The heavy door had needed all her strength to open it. Inside, the air was chill. She'd chosen a pew at the back just in front of the ancient Templeton tomb with the carved marble knight laid on the top, and sat looking round. There was a scitter-scatter in the aisle and there stood Sykes. His bright eyes looked eagerly at her, his short stumpy tail wagging.

'Hi there, Sykes. What are you doing here?' She could have sworn he'd grinned at her and then he'd leapt up onto the seat beside her and from there up onto the flat smooth surface at the end of the tomb at her shoulder. He'd curled up and settled down to sleep, his back against the knight's ankle and right beside the dog standing by the knight's feet. What a strange little dog, spending his time in church. Perhaps there was more to Sykes than one ever guessed.

She'd relaxed in his companionship and begun looking around at the huge stained-glass window above the altar, the ancient banners rotting away on their poles high up above the pillars, the shining brass on the altar table and the flowers below the pulpit. It was all so beautiful, so peaceful and . . . The door had opened and Muriel had come in.

'Good afternoon, Lady Templeton.'

'Why, good afternoon, Kate. I hope you don't mind but I've got very late with my brass polishing this week. It's my week, you see. Will I trouble you if I polish while you meditate?'

'Can I help?'

'That would be wonderful. I need to be quick because we're going out to dinner tonight, and I always take ages to get ready. I do so like to do Ralph credit and I hate to be late. Of course I never *am*. Ralph tells me I couldn't be late if I set out to be – it isn't in my nature. I always worry I shall be though. Have done all my life. Silly, isn't it? I'll just get the cloths out. They're all clean, as I gave them a good wash last week.' Sorting through the wooden box which housed her polishing materials, Muriel had taken out a couple of well-washed cloths and a tin of brass polish and said, 'Now, I usually start with the big cross.'

'I'll climb up and do that, shall I?'

'How lovely! I always use one of the altar chairs to stand on. Spread this cloth over it first before you climb up, it seems irreverent to stand on the tapestry seat without a cover. Here's your Brasso and this one's the putting-on cloth. I'll make a start on the lectern.'

Together they had rubbed and polished and buffed until all the brass-work gleamed. When they'd finished they sat together in the front pew to admire their handiwork.

'It all looks so beautiful,' Muriel sighed. 'You know, we have some wonderful old silver things for the altar on high days and holy days. They're kept locked away in the safe when they're not in use; they're too valuable to be on display every day. But I'd miss cleaning the brass if the silver was out all the time. So satisfying, isn't it, when it's all shining?'

'It is. It looks lovely.'

'I'm always reminded of that penniless acrobat who in desperation went to seek shelter in a monastery. I can't remember where I heard the story, maybe it was in a sermon? The monks fed him and gave him a bed and he stayed for a few days. When he knew it was time to move on he didn't know how to thank God for their loving care. He'd no money to give, he couldn't sing like they did, he hadn't the first idea about how to pray, but he could turn cartwheels and things. So he did. Right in front of the altar. He gave the performance of his life. It was the only thing he could do, you see, to thank God. I'm sure God must have smiled on him, don't you think? So, I keep hoping He smiles on me for doing the polishing, for I haven't much more to offer than that. I haven't skills like you have, for teaching and such. I'm not terribly clever, you see. Whereas you, you've so much to offer. There, I'll be off.' Muriel had stood up and looked down at her. 'Thank you for your help, my dear. I'm glad you've got things sorted out. We all of us need to be at peace with ourselves.' Muriel had kissed her cheek and left with her polishing box under her arm.

Kate had felt very humbled. She'd sat a while longer after Muriel had left, pondering on how foolish she had been. She'd been within an ace of being killed in her desperation to rescue Cat, but Peter had grabbed her arm and forcibly dragged her to the door: the other women had been too intent on saving their own skins to bother about her and Cat – so much for the sisterhood. A bond wrought by fear wasn't the strongest, after all. All that was left of all that business was Simone's remains, laid to rest in the churchyard. She knew Peter had had a struggle with his conscience about that, but in the end he'd agreed. She'd no one but herself to blame for being taken in by Simone. She'd wept silent tears for Jacob, for Simone, and for Simone's children.

She'd been to see them. Though they'd cried when they saw her because she reminded them of their mother, she could see how much better they were all looking. She was sure Dickon had grown; he'd certainly put on weight. Florentina was wearing a delightful outfit and her hair was well-washed and brushed and tied in bunches with matching ribbons. She'd even smiled a little. Hansel and Valentine were bright-eyed and energetic as all little boys should be. But Opal! The biggest change was in her. She'd blossomed from a thin, listless scrap of baby with enormous dark eyes in a pale luminous face, to being bouncy and giggly and quite adorable.

Their foster-mother was a large, comfortable woman who obviously enjoyed having them. When Kate had thanked her, she'd laughed. 'Don't be silly, I'm loving it. Couldn't believe my ears when they rang me and said "It's an emergency, we've got five for you!" We've only just started fostering, you see. The kiddies have transformed our lives. In fact, my hubby and I have talked about asking to adopt them all. We've got this big house and garden going to waste. It's hard work, mind, 'cos they've got problems, as you can imagine – tantrums and bad temper and the like, and the four older ones need training in more ways than one. Sometimes when I go to bed, I am so tired I feel like sending them all back! But I'm hoping good food, and a routine and love, most of all love, will solve everything. It'll all come right, given time.'

'I'm sure it will. I'll keep in touch.'

'I'd be glad if you would. You'll be like family you see, for them.'

'Of course.'

And she would keep in touch. She owed them that; it was the least she could do. No, that wasn't absolutely true. She *wanted* to see them again.

She couldn't take them on herself; the school meant too much to her for that. She'd be no good as a mother anyway. But she'd remember their birthdays and take them out.

Well, she'd been given her chance to start afresh and that was what she would do. School was her first priority now. She still had the opportunity to develop it along the lines she wanted; that at least hadn't been taken from her.

Her reverie was brought to a halt by the sight of Brian creeping round to the recycling bin. He lifted the lid and began throwing handfuls of the paper up into the air, scattering it to the four winds, gleefully watching it spiralling away. She rapped briskly on the window. He looked up startled, grinned, and reluctantly began collecting what he could and putting it back into the bin.

The bell rang for afternoon school. She rubbed her hands together in anticipation.

After school Kate went into the Store. Another decision she'd taken that day was that she'd stop being a vegan; she'd be a vegetarian instead. There was a limit to the number of hair-shirts she could tolerate and being a vegan was, she'd realised, one too many.

Jimbo was nowhere to be seen; only Bel Tutt and Linda were there.

Linda called across, 'Hello, Ms Pascoe. Nice day!'

'It certainly is. How are you, Linda? Someone was saying you hadn't been well.'

Linda blushed. 'Well, no, I haven't but I'm much better at the moment.'

'Stomach upset, they said.'

'That's right.' Linda leaned as close to the post office grille as she could get and whispered, 'Well, actually, it wasn't really a stomach upset. I'm expecting.'

'No! Are you pleased?'

She blushed even redder. 'Oh yes. And Alan's thrilled to bits.'

'I am glad. Congratulations!'

'Thanks.' She was about to launch herself on the story of her pregnancy when they heard Jimbo's voice booming out from his office at the back.

'Mother! This I do not believe!' There was a silence and then they heard him say, 'Very well. Of course I'm not saying I don't want . . .' The rest they missed as he had lowered his voice, then they heard the slam of the receiver and he stormed through into the Store. He'd left his boater somewhere, his bow tie was askew and as he marched thunderously up and down between the shelves muttering to himself, he constantly ran a hand over his bald head.

Linda kept her head down and busied herself with her accounts. Bel Tutt, to escape his wrath, plodded away into the storeroom for further supplies for her shelf-filling. Jimbo almost ran Kate down by the ice-cream freezer.

'So sorry.' He went to raise his boater and found to his amazement it wasn't on his head. 'I do beg your pardon. Running the customers over isn't quite the thing, is it? So sorry.'

'Is there something the matter, Jimbo? You seem very agitated.'

He seemed surprised. 'Do I?' He considered this for a moment. 'Well, I am. Very. What Harriet is going to say I do not know. May God have mercy on my soul because I'm going to need it.'

'Is it something I can help you with?'

He gazed distractedly at her and then said, 'Would that you could! Linda, I'm going home. I could be back in ten minutes, on the other hand if I'm not, you'd better order flowers; sprays preferably, I don't like wreaths.'

He rushed out of the Store and Kate watched him dash down Stocks Row. Suddenly his footsteps slowed and he stopped, undecided. He turned back, changed his mind, and walked slowly in the direction of home.

Kate said, 'I wonder what on earth is the matter.'

'Well, he did say "Mother", didn't he?'

'Yes, he did.'

'See – his mother's a right you-know-what. "Old cow" comes to mind. Been to stay a few times, she has. Mrs Charter-Plackett can't bear her. They have stand-up rows. Trouble brewing, by the sound of it.'

Kate laughed. 'Well, well, I've never seen Jimbo so upset. Didn't think anything could ruffle *him*.'

'Not! You should have seen him when . . .' But Linda had a customer who was in a hurry and wouldn't wait. What was the matter with everyone today? They usually liked a gossip. It was always so much more interesting if the customers lingered a while. Sometimes it took her an hour to tell Alan all the news she'd garnered.

Kate took home her luxury ice cream, and her cheese and her eggs and all the things she'd denied herself for so long, put them away in the fridge and the cupboards and then sat at the kitchen table and ate a whole tub of pecan and toffee ice cream and felt sick. But somehow, released.

27

'Mummy? Mummy?'

Jimbo snapped. 'Be quiet, Flick, please.'

'Daddy!'

'I mean it. Just go away and watch TV or something, but don't bother Mummy right now.' Jimbo stood looking out of the window. Harriet sat on the sofa. In reality, the actual distance between them was small but it felt like a million miles. When Jimbo had broken the news about his mother, Harriet had stared at him in disbelief.

'I shan't. Just tell her I shan't.'

'I know, but she's already sold her own.'

'I don't care. As far as I am concerned, she can sleep in a cardboard box in a shop doorway in the Strand. She can be a bag lady. That's right – a bag lady. Serve her right.'

'Now, Harriet.'

'And don't look so reproachfully at me. You don't want her either.'

'I never said that!'

'You didn't need to. Well, I shan't sell Mother's house to her. Definitely not. My mother wouldn't rest easy *ever*, with her in the house.'

'That is ridiculous.'

'No, it's not. Ring her – no, I'll ring her. I'll tell her she's not buying my mother's house. It *is* mine so I can choose who buys it.'

'Now, Harriet.'

' "Now, Harriet" nothing! Watch my lips: I shall say this only once. *Your mother is not living in my mother's house. I won't sell it to her.*'

'Now, Harriet.'

'If you say that once more . . .'

'All right, all right. But she is an old lady and getting very frail.'

'Frail – your mother? God, that's a laugh! Frail – huh!'

'Now, Harriet!'

'Right, that's it. You're not listening to what I'm saying. Sitting on the fence you are and waiting to see which way to jump. Well, I'm not having it.' She got up from the sofa and went to get her coat from the hall cupboard. 'The meal's all ready in the oven. I'll leave you to it.'

'Harriet, please! I haven't agreed anything, you know.'

'No, but you soon will. She'll steamroller you like she always does.'

'She doesn't!'

Harriet looked sadly at him. 'Jimbo, she does. It's not fair. I was so looking forward to Flick being May Queen. Now I shan't enjoy one minute of it, thinking about her coming to live here. It's all ruined. Ruined!' Her eyes brimmed with tears and threatened to spill over onto her cheeks. She shrugged on her coat, picked up her handbag and stormed out of the front door. Flick and Fran were crying and so too, almost, was Jimbo.

He heard the car rev up, watched her drive away, and sent up a silent prayer for her safety. Jimbo scooped up Fran and took hold of Flick's hand. 'We'll get the boys their drink and biscuits out, come on.' He looked down at Flick and her grief-stricken face broke his heart. For her sake he had to stop his voice shaking when he reassured her. 'Don't worry, she'll be back. Mummy's just a bit cross, that's all. She'll have to come back, 'cos she hasn't got her toothbrush with her.'

Flick smiled through her tears and squeezed Jimbo's hand. 'Of course, she'll have to come back. She's so particular about her teeth, isn't she?'

Jimbo discovered Harriet cleaning her teeth when he went to their bathroom. He had been sitting in Fergus' bedroom talking with him man to man about women and the problems they could cause men.

'When all's said and done, Dad, are they worth all the trouble?'

'Definitely. Oh yes. Can't manage without 'em. Bless their hearts.'

'Well, with the problems you've got with Gran and now with Mum.'

'Ah, well. There you are.'

Fergus settled down to sleep and asked as Jimbo was switching off the light, 'She will be back, won't she?'

'Of course.'

Jimbo stood in the bathroom doorway enjoying the sight of Harriet bent over the washbasin. As she rinsed her mouth for the last time she brought up her head and saw him in the mirror. They looked at each other for a moment and he broke the silence.

'You're back.'

'I am.'

'The best I can say is that she can't buy your mother's house, but if she really wants to come and live here, she can buy another house when one becomes empty. How about that?'

'I'll think about it.'

'Thank you.' He paused. 'Where've you been – if I can ask, that is.'

'At the rectory with Caroline.'

'All this time?'

'A lot of it.'

'I see.'

'Do you?' Harriet turned to face him as she spoke.

'I try.'

'I'm going to give the children a goodnight kiss.' Harriet tucked Fran in more tightly and smoothed Flick's hair away from her face and, in the half-light, saw the sleepy smile on her face as she felt her mother's kiss. She took some books off Finlay's bed and straightened his duvet for him, and kissed Fergus who gave her a hug and said, 'Glad you're back, Mum. It's Dad who's been really upset.' Then she too went to bed.

When Jimbo emerged from the bathroom she was sitting up making a list. 'This is my list for Thursday.'

'What's happening on Thursday?'

'May Day.'

'Of course. I'm thrilled Flick's going to be Queen. Who's doing the crowning bit?'

'Muriel.'

'Oh great! It's a lovely thing for Flick and she'll do it superbly. Just like her mother, everything she does, she does well.'

'Jimbo! Flattery will get you nowhere with me.'

'It's true! I shall record the whole event on the old camcorder.'

'Oh, of course! What a good idea. Mother would have gloried in her being Queen. Oh, I do miss her.'

'Of course you do. We all do.' He sat silent on the edge of the bed for a while and then said, 'She was a pearl of great price.'

'She adored you.'

'Did she? I didn't know.'

'I'm sure she'd have married you if you'd have had her.'

Jimbo laughed. 'No! I'm glad I married her daughter.'

'So am I.'

'Forgiven?'

'Almost. But I must let it be known now this minute and then I shall never refer to it again, that I do not get on with your mother. Never have done, never will. But I do appreciate that she isn't getting any younger and needs family about her, but I can't, I *won't* sell her my mother's house. In any case, it's far too big for someone your mother's age.'

'Thank you. I'll warn her off, right? I can't brook her interference either. She's keeping out of the Store, which I know she'd love to reorganise for me, and she's to be kept out of our family affairs. I won't have the boys upset by her constant criticism. And she's not having a key to our house like your mother did, that's definite. Mother did suggest she took over the mail-order now we've no longer got Sadie, but Mrs Jones is doing such a good job, way beyond anything I'd expected, that there's no way I'm putting Mother in charge. So that's the agreement.'

'Right, it's a deal. Oh Jimbo, why didn't you have brothers and sisters, then they could have taken their turn?'

'Having me nearly killed her, she says. Couldn't believe childbirth could be so appalling and so *uncivilised*. So that was that. My father was extremely disappointed.'

Harriet rolled her eyes. 'Some men do have a lot to put up with, don't they?'

Jimbo turned off his bedside light and sighed. 'Indeed they do. Look at me for instance. Slaving from dawn to dusk. Money to find for two sons at Prince Henry's, and soon even more for a daughter at Lady Wortley's *and* she's being May Queen so there's the dress to pay for, a incredibly pretty small daughter to feed and clothe,' he paused, 'and sadly, truth to tell, the biggest fly in the ointment is the wife. I can see there's going to be no end to my troubles . . . ever.' In the darkness at his side of the bed he grinned, thumped his pillow and laid down. Harriet kicked him.

'Ow!! That hurt.'

'I'm glad.'

There was a silence while Jimbo rubbed his leg. 'The children were very upset.'

'I'm sorry. I was just so angry and you didn't seem to be listening.'

'I was and I am. I'm torn, you see.'

'I know. But if I can be assured you're on my side, then that's all right.'

'I am.'

'Good. I'll finish this list and then . . .'

'Right.'

Harriet wasn't the only one with a list. Kate had one, too. Thursday was proving a hectic day. She'd worked all week with the children – cajoling, inspiring, organising. There wasn't a stone left unturned. Hetty Hardaker had to admit that for organisation Kate couldn't be bettered. 'I thought Mr Palmer had everything at his fingertips, but you . . .'

'Thanks, Hetty. Thanks for all your help, too. Without you we couldn't have managed.'

Hetty flushed with pleasure. 'I'm sorry I was so awkward to begin with. But some of it was justified, wasn't it?'

Kate smiled. 'Yes, it was. But I think now we've come to an understanding.'

'You've changed since you came. All the witchcraft business, it wasn't right. It felt so lovely going into church on Friday for prayers. You have to admit Peter is good with children.'

'He is. Very good.'

'Now, back to basics. Margaret wants to know how she will know when to commence playing the piano when she's out on the Green and can't see for all the parents. We could do with a couple of mobile phones.' They walked away together discussing the whys and wherefores. With only two hours to go there was still a lot to do.

Mercifully the sun had decided to shine. Occasionally a cloud came over but it remained dry which was as well because the piano, and the maypole, and the children's chairs awaiting the parents and friends were already out on the grass. Someone, somewhere must be smiling on them, Kate thought.

Mr Fitch had given permission for a couple of his estate-workers who were parents to give a hand, and as Kate and Hetty went back into the hall they were heaving the large wooden boxes which, fixed together, would create a dais for the Queen and her attendants to sit on for the crowning and where Flick would sit to preside over the dancing.

'I've got a gorgeous bright red Indian cloth for covering the dais – I'll bring it out in a moment. The Queen's chair is here, look, already decorated.'

'Thanks, Ms Pascoe, we'll just get these sorted first. All right, Bill. Your end first.' They staggered out with two of the boxes, down the narrow passage to the main door. Kate watched them squeeze out and as they left, in came Greenwood Stubbs. He touched his cap to Kate and said, 'Mr Fitch has asked me to bring you some plants to decorate the platform for the Queen.'

'Oh, Mr Stubbs, how kind! Why, they're magnificent.'

'This is just two of them – there's a vanload outside. Barry Jones has brought them down for me. Come out and tell me where to put them all.'

'A vanload? This I don't believe.'

She rushed outside and was stunned by how beautiful they looked.

'How's that then?' Barry laughed at her delight. 'Brilliant, eh?'

'Yes – brilliant!'

'We've to put them all out for you and then we'll collect them at the end. Except you've to choose the one you like best and keep it. It's a present from Mr Fitch. He's coming, he says, if that's all right.'

'Of course it is. Right – they need to be banked round the dais when Bill and Ben have put it together.'

Barry gave a mock salute. 'As you say, Ms Pascoe. Where's the Queen? Just need a glimpse of her, can't stay to watch.'

'She's inside already dressed. Go and take a look.'

He found Flick seated on Ms Pascoe's chair, the skirt of her white dress spread carefully out so as not to crease it. On her head she had a small circlet of fresh flowers, her long plaits had been undone and her hair was hanging down her back shining and bright. Her eyes were alive with pleasure.

'Why, Flick! You look gorgeous, absolutely terrific! Has Pat seen yer yet?'

Flick was blushing. Barry always made her feel like that. 'Thank you, Barry. No, she hasn't.'

'I'll tell her to come and take a look. Best May Queen in years.' He bowed like some eighteenth-century courtier, gave a flourishing wave at the door and disappeared.

Harriet, too, couldn't believe how pretty Flick looked. It was Fran who had the beauty in their family but today, somehow, it was Flick's turn. Flick waggled her white satin pumps in the air and said, 'Aren't they just beautiful, Mummy? I could be a bridesmaid in these, couldn't I?'

'You could. Fran – no, don't pull them off.'

'Let her. You try one on, Fran.' Fran did so. Flick always let her have her own way with everything.

The classroom was full of mothers dressing the attendants, changing the Maypole dancers into their outfits, teachers rushing in and out with messages, Pat collecting the last of the home-made refreshments everyone had volunteered, children getting underfoot, teachers disciplining the wayward ones.

The temperature and the tempers began to rise. With only half an hour to go, Kate was beginning to fray. 'Yes, that's right, they all sit on the left. No, not the Maypole dancers. They stay with me – right! OK?'

The questions were unending, the children excited, the parents almost beyond control and there sat Flick enjoying every minute of her reign.

In the midst of it all, Muriel arrived. 'Should I be here or out there?'

'Lady Templeton! There you are. We've borrowed chairs from the church hall and you and Sir Ralph are to sit on the front row of them in the middle. There are names on the seats. There's a quarter of an hour to go.'

'I must be in your way. I'll leave you to it, you're obviously busy. And the crown?'

'Ah! Sebastian Prior has the crown. He'll present it to you on a velvet cushion at the appropriate moment.'

'I've prepared a short speech – just a couple of lines.'

'Lovely!'

'Oh Flick, my dear. How pretty you look!' Muriel's eyes filled with tears. She bent down and kissed her on either cheek. 'You make a wonderful May Queen!'

Muriel smiled at Harriet, and Harriet smiled back.

Gilbert came in then. 'Ms Pascoe, we're here!'

Kate turned to look at him – a transformed Gilbert. A Gilbert with a blackened face and a bowler hat covered with bright feathers and badges, and a black jacket to which he'd fastened gaily-coloured strips of material. On his feet were boots, and on his ankles bells which jingled at every step he took. 'As promised!'

'Wonderful! I could give you a kiss!'

'Past experience tells me you'll have a black face if you do! Just reporting in. We're sitting on the grown-ups' chairs awaiting our turn. Is that all right?'

'Of course – here's the programme of events. Keep that. Flick will call upon you to perform.'

'At your service, Your Majesty!' Gilbert grinned at Flick and left.

Seated alongside Muriel and Ralph and in front of the Morris dancers were Mr Fitch and Louise.

Gilbert had given her one of his special smiles when he'd come to take his place. Mr Fitch, arms folded, leant towards her and whispered out of the corner of his mouth, 'When are you going to marry that man?'

Louise blushed. 'Shortly.'

'Good. Not before time, from what I hear.'

Louise blushed even redder. The cheek of the man. Really! And she thought no one but her mother knew. You couldn't do a thing in this village.

On the other side of Mr Fitch sat Muriel. She'd been waiting for her chance and now it had come. While Ralph went to help Margaret Booth readjust the piano stool and devise a method of keeping her music from blowing away while she played, Muriel took the bull by the horns.

'Mr Fitch.'

'Craddock please, Muriel.'

'Craddock then. You know I've beeen very disappointed with you of late.'

He looked startled. 'Disappointed, with me? What about?'

'About lacking understanding.'

'If I've been tactless about something, please put me right.'

'Sometimes one does more good, you know, by *not* doing something than by doing it.'

'You're speaking in riddles, Muriel. I don't understand.' He followed her gaze and realised she was looking at Ralph.

'It's about cricket. The whole village are grateful for what you've done with the pavilion and the equipment, believe me they are, but they don't like . . .'

'Yes?'

'They don't like you trying to lord it over them.'

Mr Fitch began to boil. Lord it over them? Not him! Ralph did that – he was an expert at it. He himself did nothing but good. *Nothing but good.*

Muriel, staring into the distance, said, 'It's tradition, you see, that's what counts. The village likes to keep its traditions. Like today. Like Stocks Day and the Village Show.' She turned towards him and smiled at him in such a genuinely kindly way that he felt uncomfortable, and knew she was going to get him to do something he didn't want to. 'And the cricket team comes under the same heading, you see,' she went on gently. 'They want things to remain as they were. There's a place for tradition and a place for progress, we need them both. So for your sake, *not* Ralph's, you need to let him be president of the cricket club.'

The village green was bustling with life. Mothers and the dads who could spare the time from work were squatting on the school chairs; the throne for the Queen was ready; the flowers arranged around the dais giving it glorious colour; the Punch and Judy man was waiting his turn beside his red-and-white striped booth; the horses on the merry-go-round were poised to spring into action. Now, round the corner of the Village Store trotted a procession of the playgroup children coming to take their places, led by Beth and Alex walking hand-in-hand. The Maypole was waiting, the dancers self-conscious in their costumes sitting around its foot. Muriel watched Ralph talking to some of the parents on his way back to his seat, and she thought how much she loved him. Her love for him gave her courage.

'Well, Craddock?'

'You've a very persuasive way with you, Muriel Templeton. Very persuasive. But I don't see what I shall gain if I step down.'

'You won't gain anything visible or tangible, but you will march to the same drum as them if you do.'

'March to the same drum?'

'Think about it.' The piano burst into life. 'Oh, they're about to begin, and I've forgotten to look at my speech, and here comes Ralph. Oh dear, and now I can't find my speech – where did I put it?' Mr Fitch bent down and picked up a piece of paper from under Muriel's chair.

'This it?'

'Oh, thank you.'

There came a breathless hush as Muriel waited for one of the attendants to remove Flick's circlet of flowers. Then she held the crown high above Flick's head and said in ringing tones, 'On this wonderful gloriously happy day, I have the great honour to crown Felicity Jane Charter-Plackett Queen of the May. Long may she reign! Long live Queen Felicity!!'

Peter stood up and called for three cheers for the Queen. *Hip Hip Hurray! Hip Hip Hurray! Hip Hip Hurray!!*

Queen Felicity stood up, her crown, plain gold-coloured metal with ten points around the top, each with a large pearl attached, its red velvet edge nicely placed along the top of her forehead, and said in a loud clear voice: 'I thank you all for coming to my crowning today. I hope you will all enjoy yourselves. My subjects will now perform the traditional Maypole dancing, for your delight.'

The crowd sat down again, ready to be entertained. Margaret Booth at the piano performed miracles and the dancers were inspired. Their final dance, the 'Spider's Web' was the most complicated, and when they finished the intricate weaving and unravelling of the ribbons, the crowd got to its feet as one and clapped and cheered.

'Brilliant!'

'Wonderful!'

'Well done!'

They watched the Punch and Judy Show, jeering and hissing and clapping at all the right moments, and when Flick announced the Morris Dancers there was a cheer of delight. Chairs were moved to make a bigger space in front of the Queen. Gilbert played a lively tune on his melodeon and the dancing began.

Kate was beside herself. She was standing at the back watching everyone. It was all going perfectly splendidly. She couldn't have asked for a more worthwhile and rewarding afternoon. Gilbert was giving it all he'd got, playing with gusto while his dancers nimbly entertained the crowds. It seemed impossible that in his working life Gilbert was a serious academic. At this moment, he was a medieval man celebrating the First of May like villagers had been doing for centuries. The crowd began clapping and an impromptu group near Kate got up from their chairs and began dancing too. She laughed. What fun! Someone dragged hold of her hand and pulled her in and made her dance. She didn't know what was expected of her but she joined in just the same. It didn't seem to matter. Nothing did except total happiness.

When the applause for the Morris dancers had died down, Queen Felicity announced from her throne that tea was being served and the merry-go-round would begin shortly.

There was no need for Kate to help with the refreshments for Pat had got that under her control. There was obviously more to Pat than she had realised and Kate felt quite disappointed that Pat would be leaving the school when she got married. Apparently she was going to work for Jimbo in his catering business. Well, she would be well qualified for that, judging by this afternoon. Then Kate felt a small hand slip into hers. She looked down and saw it was Beth's.

'Hello, Beth, isn't this lovely?'

'Yes. I'd like to be Queen when I'm big.'

'Would you?'

'Can I wear a crown like Flick's?'

'Of course. I'll remember.'

Beth looked up at her and smiled. 'I like playgroup at your school.'

'I'm glad.'

'It's nice.' She looked up again. '*You're* nice.'

'Thank you. And so are you.'

'I like you next best after my mummy.'

'That's only right. Your mummy comes first. Here she is – look.'

Caroline was walking towards them, hand-in-hand with Alex. 'Oh there you are, Beth! I've been looking for you. Do you want squash or tea?'

'Squash, please. Mummy, Miss Pascoe says I can be Queen when I'm big. Isn't she nice?'

Caroline looked at Kate, and Kate looked at her.

It was Caroline who smiled first. 'Wonderful afternoon, Kate. I've had a lovely time. You must feel delighted with yourself.'

'Good, I'm glad you've enjoyed it. Thank you.'

'Come along then and we'll get you your squash.' Caroline walked away with the two children leaving Kate feeling grateful that things had thawed a little between the two of them.

'Kate!' It was Harriet bringing her a cup of tea. 'I've come to say thank you for giving Flick such a wonderful afternoon. She's loved it.'

'Oh! Tea – just what I need! Thank *you* for having such a smashing daughter. She's done well, really well. I'm proud of her. She'll be in her element at Lady Wortley's, I'm sure.'

'You don't mind any more then?'

'No. Why shouldn't she have the chance?'

'Thanks. I didn't want to remain at loggerheads about it. After all, I've got Fran coming along!'

'I expect I shall be here still. This place gets into your bones, doesn't it?'

'It certainly does. I'm glad you've come here – the school did need a shake-up, though I won't have a bad word said about Mr Palmer'.

'Certainly not.'

'Hold it, you two, keep talking!' It was Jimbo with his camcorder. 'I've filmed just about everyone else so I mustn't miss the chief organiser of the event, must I?' He filmed busily whilst Kate and Harriet chatted.

Kate interrupted him. 'There's Hetty signalling. Must go. Sorry, Jimbo!' She dashed away.

'All right, darling, you can take a break.'

Jimbo switched off the camcorder and stayed to talk. 'Wasn't Flick lovely? I'm so proud of her.'

'So am I. I almost cried.'

'Hope the thought of Mother coming hasn't ruined the day for you?'

'No, but I'm not looking forward to it.'

'Perhaps she's run out of steam a bit now she's older.'

'I doubt it, Jimbo.'

He shifted the camcorder to his other hand and put an arm round Harriet's shoulder. 'I shan't let her upset you, honestly I won't. She's an old dragon and we shall have some tempestuous times while she settles in, but I shall keep her under control if I die in the attempt!' Flick came walking sedately towards them, remembering to hold her head carefully because of her crown. 'Here she comes, Queen for a day.'

'Mummy, do you think it wouldn't be queenly to take my crown off? I can't do a thing when I'm wearing it.'

'Take it off, and go and enjoy yourself. Even queens are allowed a bit of fun sometimes. Here, give it to me.'

Flick gave Harriet her posy of flowers too and ran off to queue for a ride on the merry-go-round.

Ralph was having a cup of tea. He'd lost Muriel somewhere; no doubt she was helping in one capacity or another. What a lovely afternoon he'd had. And the summer only just begun. What fun life could be. He spotted Mr Fitch threading his way across the green towards him. Oh no, not old Fitch today.

'Afternoon, Craddock,' he said affably. 'Surprised to see you here. Thought this wouldn't be quite your scene.'

'I provided the flowers for the dais, Ralph, so I had to come to make sure they looked good. Got to keep up standards, you know.' Mr Fitch cleared his throat. 'I've been thinking.'

'Yes?'

'This cricket business . . . I've been wondering if perhaps I've made a mistake. The way I see it, you and I each have our own role to play. I play the benefactor, you do the paternal bit. So I've given it my earnest consideration and the long and the short of it is, I really think it would be best if you were president of the club.'

'I see.'

'Tradition and all that, you know. All part and parcel of village life. Best if you're president. People will like that. Afternoons like this make one realise how important tradition is.'

'Well, I must say, Craddock, that's very generous of you. I shan't refuse. Tradition is it, that made you stand down?'

'That's right.'

Ralph followed the other man's gaze, which was focused on Muriel standing behind the huge teapot she'd borrowed from the church kitchen. 'I do appreciate your gesture,' he said, then added mischievously, 'I'm glad you came to your decision all by yourself.'

Mr Fitch looked hard at him. 'Oh yes, it was my decision, all right. I make all my own decisions – *after* I've weighed up the evidence.'

'Of course, just like me.' Ralph raised his cup in salutation to Muriel, and in acknowledgement of the smile she was giving him. 'Thanks anyway.'

'My pleasure. It doesn't affect the name over the pavilion though – that stays.'

'Naturally. Your generosity has to be acknowledged. I wouldn't want it any other way. All the arrangements for Saturday are well in hand. Opening ceremony at two forty-five. Game commences at three. Jimbo's doing the food for the inaugural match like we arranged.'

Mr Fitch said, 'Send me the bill.'

'Well, that's even more generous of you. We shall be in debt to you for years.'

Mr Fitch ignored Ralph's gratitude and nodding his head in Muriel's direction, he grunted, 'That wife of yours. Was she in the Diplomatic Service too?'

'No, she just has her own way of achieving her objectives.'

'A perfect lady, Ralph. Someone to be treasured. You're a very lucky man'.

'Indeed I am. We were childhood sweethearts and then got separated and met up again quite by chance. Well, maybe it wasn't chance. Perhaps it was meant to be.'

'Childhood sweethearts, eh? I wish, how I wish that Sadie . . .'

Ralph glanced at him and then looked away. Didn't want to embarrass the chap, don't you know. 'I'm sorry, so very sorry. Mrs Beauchamp was much loved.' His voice was gruff.

'She was. Different as cheese from chalk, your Muriel and her, but each quite splendid in their own way.' This time they both raised their cups to Muriel and she blushed bright red.

It was five o'clock by the time everything had been cleared up and the last of the children shooed off home. The Green had returned to its usual quiet self. Jimmy's geese, having at last got their grazing ground back again, were busily marching up and down re-establishing their ownership. Barry Jones' van was heading off to the Big House filled with the plants Mr Fitch had provided. In her hand Kate had the one she had chosen. In her other hand was a bag of cakes Pat had given her. 'Surplus to requirements, so you'd better take them. You've done a great job, Ms Pascoe. Best May Day we've had in years and I've seen my share, I can tell you! I'm glad you've come to Turnham Malpas, and I'm sorry to be leaving the school, but I can't turn down this offer of Mr Charter-Plackett's. It's too good to be true. Bel Tutt will do a good job, I know. Sleep well – I'm sure you will after the day you've had!'

Kate crossed the school playground and slotted her key in the door. She heard a mewing sound, it was Beano and Dandy greeting her return. They stood on her toes, chewed her sandals, jumped up to catch at her skirt with their claws.

'Now you two, in you go. I want a cup of tea. I know, yes I know, you want feeding too.'

That night before she went to bed, Kate sat by the open bedroom window in her nightgown, a peach silky affair, and looked out. The sky was still quite bright with small clouds sailing lazily across it. She could just see the new houses Sir Ralph had built, and the trees behind them. Tomorrow after school she'd put on her boots and go for a long walk by the beck. Blow her cobwebs away. She'd been here only four months and yet the place had wound itself round her heart. Their cheers at the end of the afternoon were something she didn't deserve. Truth to tell, she'd nearly brought the village to its knees, and retrieved it only just in time. They seemed to have overlooked that; how generous-hearted they must be. On Saturday she was taking the three older children of Simone's out for the day. She was looking forward to that. In fact, there was a lot to look forward to. Cricket teas. Computers. New children next term. Beano and Dandy. Church. The youth club she intended starting – a debt she had to repay if only for Rhett's sake.

The sun was slowly going down and the village was becoming rosy in the fading light. She could hear the laughter in The Royal Oak. What fun they must be having; a visit there from time to time would be a good idea. She needed other relationships besides those with her children. She drew the curtains and climbed into bed. The awkward corner by the eaves was just the right place for Mr Fitch's plant; after she'd turned out the light the white of the petals glowed in the half-darkness. As Kate closed her eyes, the scent of the flowers reached her and she smiled. She remembered an embroidered picture her grandmother had hanging over her bed. There was a little thatched cottage on it, with a tiny country garden in front, and embroidered underneath were the words: *Home is where the heart is.* As a child she'd never understood it, but now she did.

Scandal in the Village

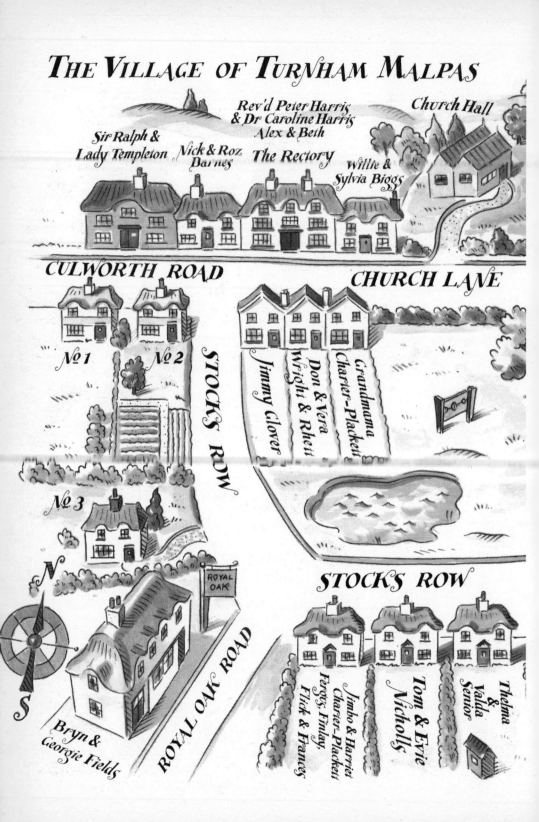

INHABITANTS OF TURNHAM MALPAS

Willie Biggs	Verger at St Thomas à Becket.
Sylvia Biggs	His wife and housekeeper at the rectory.
Sir Ronald Bissett	Retired trades union leader.
Lady Sheila Bissett	His wife.
James (Jimbo) Charter-Plackett	Owner of the Village Store.
Harriet Charter-Plackett	His wife.
Fergus, Finlay, Flick and Fran	Their children.
Katherine Charter-Plackett	Jimbo's mother.
Alan Crimble	Barman at the Royal Oak.
Linda Crimble	Runs the post office at the Village Store.
Bryn Fields	Licensee at the Royal Oak.
Georgie Fields	His wife.
H. Craddock Fitch	Owner of Turnham House.
Jimmy Glover	Taxi driver.
Mrs Jones	A village gossip.
Barry Jones	Her son and estate carpenter.
Pat Jones	His wife.
Dean and Michelle	Her children.
Revd Peter Harris MA (Oxon)	Rector of the parish.
Dr Caroline Harris	His wife.
Alex and Beth	Their children.
Jeremy Mayer	Manager at Turnham House.
Venetia Mayer	His wife.
Kate Pascoe	Village school head teacher.
Sir Ralph Templeton	Retired from the diplomatic service.
Lady Muriel Templeton	His wife.
Dicky Tutt	Scout leader.
Bel Tutt	School caretaker and assistant in the Village Store.
Don Wright	Maintenance engineer.
Vera Wright	Cleaner at the nursing home in Penny Fawcett.
Rhett Wright	Their grandson.

1

'Talk of the devil! Here he comes!' Georgie finished pulling the pint, handed it over to her customer and waved to Dicky.

Bryn snorted his disapproval. 'Dicky Tutt! You mean you've lined him up to launch it? What does he know about show business?'

'He doesn't need to, he's a natural. A born comic.'

Dicky came bounding across to the bar and ordered his drink. 'Good evening one and all! My usual, please. And how's my Georgie tonight? Blossoming bright and beautiful as always.'

'Flatterer!' She drew him his pint and as he paid her she felt him give her fingers a slight squeeze. Georgie rewarded him with one of her stunning smiles. 'You're on top form tonight.'

'Of course. Heard the one about the dog with two tails?'

Dicky launched himself into his story with extra verve, knowing full well Bryn was on the qui vive as far as he was concerned. He'd honed to perfection the art of taunting Bryn and felt guilty but also elated by the knowledge. As Dicky reached the climax of the story Bryn leant over the counter and waited for his chance to speak.

'Don't imagine for one moment that this is a dress rehearsal for a slot in this ridiculous showbiz scheme Georgie's come up with . . .'

Dicky pretended innocence. 'What ridiculous scheme?'

'This business of having entertainment on Fridays here in the bar. I've put my foot down about it. We're not. Right?'

'OK. OK. I'm either way. Doesn't bother me.'

'Well, don't come up with any more bright ideas for in here, ever again.'

'I didn't suggest it. It was Georgie's idea.'

Georgie intervened. 'It was, Bryn, honestly. It was me asked him. I think you're being daft. We could just try it once or twice and see what happens couldn't we?' She opened wide her lovely bright eyes and looked up at Bryn to plead her cause. 'Please, just once. Dicky would be a good one to start with. Dip our toes in the water, eh? How about it?'

Bryn twirled his Flying Officer Kite moustache and looked down into the pretty face of the woman he'd loved for twenty years. He wanted to please her, but something, he didn't know what, warned him to steer clear and he couldn't bring himself to agree. 'No. Sorry. It'd lower the tone.'

Dicky grinned up at Bryn. 'Eh! Come on, my jokes aren't mucky.'

'Not now they're not, but they might be once you get in your stride.'

'Oh no, they wouldn't be, I don't tell doubtful jokes. I've got all my Scouts to think of, got to keep their respect.'

'Anyway, it doesn't matter whether they're smutty or not 'cos you're not performing in here, in this pub, whilst ever my name is over the door. I'm the licensee. Subject now closed.'

Jimmy Glover, for once drinking alone called across, 'Come on, Bryn, liven the place up. Bring more trade in, surely you can't object to that?'

'It's not bringing in more trade that I'm objecting to, it's what it might lead to that worries me.'

Georgie and Dicky exchanged a quick glance. She hastily served a whisky to a customer and as she pinged the till she said, 'There's nothing for you to worry about, it's just an experiment and Dicky's willing to give it a whirl and he's not expecting getting paid either. You know how everyone loves his jokes. Come on, Bryn, let's give it a try. Mmmmm?'

'Absolutely not.' Bryn began drying some glasses and turned his back to her.

She glanced at Dicky, pursed her mouth and shook her head. Dicky took the hint. He stood with his back to the bar and looked round. Jimmy was still alone and there were only three other punters in the bar besides him and Jimmy. There was no doubt about it, the pub could do with some new attraction to liven it up.

The outside door opened and in came Sir Ronald and Lady Bissett with their little Pomeranian.

Dicky called out to them, 'Evening Sheila! Evening Ron. This round's on me. What would you like?'

Sheila beamed her approval. She liked Dicky, he might be beneath her in the social scale but she liked him nevertheless. 'Gin and tonic, please Dicky. How are you?'

'I'm fine thanks. Ron, what's yours?'

'A pint of that special of Bryn's, please.'

Dicky ordered their drinks from Georgie and the three of them stood at the bar discussing the weather. Sheila's dog Pompom had to be kept on a tight lead because in his old age he had developed an alarming habit of sinking his teeth into the ankle of anyone who happened to displease him, and Dicky was a frequent target. Dicky moved away a few more inches when he heard a low rumble in Pompom's chest.

Sheila bent down to pat him. 'Now, Pompom, now, now, it's only Dicky. I think it's because he can't see as well as he did, he mistakes feet for cats.'

Dicky chuckled. 'Does he indeed. I'll keep my distance then if you don't mind!'

Ron, becoming increasingly hot in his ginger tweed Sheila insisted made him look like an English country gentleman, unwittingly brought up a subject of conversation close to Dicky's heart. 'I was thinking about you the other day, Dicky. Read an article in the paper about how successful clubs are nowadays, working men's clubs and suchlike. They're becoming the place to be discovered by a talent scout. They have entertainers, weekends – the big clubs get the big names of course, but they say the smaller clubs are a very good place to start. It named a few comics, and singers, who've got their feet on the ladder to success in the smaller clubs. I thought about you with your jokes. You'd go down wonderfully well I'm sure. I'm still laughing over that one you told us about the . . .'

Bryn poked a sharp finger into Ron's shoulder-blade. 'I don't know if this is all part of a plot, but don't encourage him if you please. I'm not having it and there's an end to it.'

Sir Ronald, surprised at receiving such a body blow, asked what made Bryn so annoyed, all he'd done was mention . . . ?

Sheila, feeling that a wholesale row was brewing and knowing she could never rely on Ron to be as tactful as she always was, interrupted by saying, 'Let's hope this good weather holds for the Harvest Festival, all that effort we put in, it does so put people off from coming when the weather's bad.'

Dicky raised his glass to Sheila. 'I've nothing but admiration for you on that score, Sheila, every year I think the church can't look any better than it does this year and blow me next year it does. You've had some wonderful ideas in the past, and I've no doubt it'll be decorated even more brilliantly than last year.'

Sheila beamed with pleasure. 'Why, thank you. It's all team work really, my committee are very talented, believe me. You know, you really are the most charming man.' She tapped a lacquered fingernail on Dicky's sleeve. 'Most charming, your Bel did right to snap you up. In fact if you weren't spoken for I could . . .'

Ron like a terrier at a bone said, 'Bryn! Sorry! Didn't mean to give offence, though I don't know how I did, I was only . . .'

'Beg your pardon. It's just that Georgie here is wanting to start entertainment on Friday nights, and I won't have it. I thought you were encouraging her.'

Ron thumped the bar counter with delight. 'But there you are, there's his chance. Dicky here would be excellent. Just the man for the job! You'd do a turn wouldn't you?'

Deliberately Dicky pretended to be deaf to Ron's question. Pompom suspecting that Dicky's shoe was shuffling a little too near and the light tan of it was just the colour of that cat they called Chivers, lunged and snapped at Dicky's ankle. The lunge pulled Sheila's arm to its fullest extent and she overbalanced. Her glass, escaping her grasp, flew up before it fell down, and she tried to retrieve it as it passed her. Pompom took another snap at Dicky's ankle as he tried to avoid the gin pouring down his jacket, Sheila made another try to catch the glass, Pompom took another snap and down Sheila went. Her foot slipped between the brass footrest and the front of the bar and they all heard the crack of bone as she landed, awkwardly trapped by the rail on which only a moment before her foot had been resting. Dicky just managed to save himself from falling on top of her and Pompom howled as Sheila's bottom almost flattened him.

Ron tried to lift her up. Georgie dashed round to the front of the bar shouting. 'Don't move her! I'm sure she's broken something.'

Sheila racked by searing pain and in shock, wept. Pompom hid under the nearest table. Dicky knelt down beside Sheila and put his arm round her. 'There there, keep quite still. Just a bit longer, yes I know it's uncomfortable crouched like that, but stay still just a bit longer till you know how you feel, then we'll move you.'

'Oh Dicky! It's so painful you've no idea. Whatever am I going to do?'

'Nothing for the minute. Then Bryn and your Ron, 'cos they're bigger than me can lift you onto a chair. It's your leg I'm afraid. It sounded like a break.'

'It is, I'm sure. That's all I need. The week before the Harvest . . .'

'Now, Now, Don't you fret about that. That's the least of your worries right now. Bryn, come and give a hand here will yer?'

Bryn came round and pushed his way between the customers. He peered anxiously at Sheila, took hold of her under her armpits and, very very gently, hoisted her up and propped her against the bar. She was ashen and sweating with the pain but felt slightly less ridiculous than when she'd been crumpled on the floor. She supported her bad leg. The pain she was suffering caused sweat to run off the end of her chin.

'God, Ron! I feel terrible . . .' Sheila's voice trailed off and she fainted. Bryn caught her with Ron's help.

Bryn shouted, 'Someone go get Dr Harris, and quick.'

Jimmy volunteered to go. He knocked loudly on the rectory door. When it opened Peter was standing there looking down at him.

'Rector! Sorry to trouble you this time o' night but could your good lady wife come. Sheila Bissett's had a bad fall and we think she's broken her leg and now she's fainted.'

'Oh goodness. Yes, of course.' He turned away from the door and using his most powerful voice called out, 'Caroline! there's an emergency. Can you come?'

Caroline dashed through from the kitchen. 'Shush! You'll wake the children! Well, Jimmy, hello, what's the matter?'

Jimmy was always impressed by Caroline. Her cheerful competence and generous smile never failed to lift his spirits, and her short dark curly hair and pale skin reminded him of . . .

'I'll explain as we go along. I'll return her to you quick as a flash, Rector.'

By the time Caroline reached the bar Sheila had regained consciousness and was seated on a chair.

'Oh Dr Harris! It's so kind of you to come. They shouldn't have troubled you!'

'Of course they should. Now let me look.' Very, very gently Caroline explored Sheila's leg causing her to wince several times. 'I'm sorry to hurt you. Unless I'm much mistaken it's more than a sprain, there is definitely a break there. It's hospital for you, Sheila, I'm afraid.'

Sheila put a hand on Caroline's shoulder. 'I rather thought so. It's incredibly painful.' Two large tears fell down her plump cheeks. 'I'll have to be very brave, won't I?'

Caroline smiled and patted her arm. 'You will, but you are a brave person anyway, aren't you?' Caroline stood up. 'Sir Ronald, if we help her to your car could you . . . ? You'll get there quicker than waiting for an ambulance.'

'Yes, yes of course. I'll go right now and bring it round. I'll bring that old blanket for you, Sheila, keep you warm. Shock and that.'

Glaring meaningfully at him she said, 'You mean the car rug, don't you, Ron?'

Taking her meaning he said, 'Yes, of course, the car rug. The tartan one.'

'The Royal Stuart one,' Sheila called feebly after him as Ron hurried out. '. . . and my handbag . . .'

Pompom yelped from under the table. 'Oh, Ron's forgotten Pompom. I don't know what to do any more. It's all too much. Ohhh! the pain.'

'Don't worry, I'll take him home to the rectory with me. He can sleep in Mimi's old basket. Sir Ronald can collect him in the morning. No, change of plan, better still I'll bring him over to you and see how you are. Now you won't worry about him will you? I'll spoil him to death.'

Sheila's bottom lip trembled. 'It's at times like this that you learn who your friends are, isn't it? But I'll be in plaster for weeks and there's the Harvest, I can't let the Rector down.'

Looking down into Sheila's tear-streaked face Caroline forgot about all the times she had clashed with Sheila and felt nothing but pity for her. 'Don't you worry. You've made all the plans quite beautifully, and we'll carry them all out to the letter. Just think about yourself for now. There's the car. They'll give you painkillers and you'll be surprised how much better you'll feel when they've set it.'

Between them Ron and Bryn contrived to give Sheila a bosun's chair into the car whereupon she almost fainted again. Caroline bent down to speak to her. Tucking the car rug around her she said, 'Now, promise you won't worry about Pompom. I'll ring Casualty and tell them to expect you. God bless.'

Reluctantly Pompom allowed himself to be taken to the rectory, dragging his feet and protesting at every step.

'Now come along. Sheila's being brave and so must you be. I'm not putting up with any nonsense.' Hearing the firmness of her tone Pompom decided that he would have to give in and he followed her meekly back.

Caroline slipped her key in the door, briskly invited Pompom inside, locked it after her and called out, 'Peter! I've got Pompom, approach with caution please!'

He emerged from his study and made gentle clucking noises in an attempt to entice Pompom to restrain his vindictiveness.

'I'll keep him on his lead for a few minutes just in case.'

'Has Sheila broken her leg then?'

'Oh definitely. Ron's just taken her to hospital. It's quite a bad one I think. Poor thing.'

'You don't usually have sympathy for her.'

'Well, I have tonight. She's in awful pain. No, Pompom, behave yourself!'

Peter bent down and offered his hand, and Pompom sniffed it gently,

Triumphantly Caroline said, 'There you see, all he needs is firm handling. Now, young man, I'll get out the old cat bed and you can sleep in the kitchen, and no nonsense.'

By the time they'd settled the dog, reassured the cats, locked up and taken their cups of tea to bed it was half past eleven.

Peter was sitting up in bed reading when Caroline returned from the bathroom remarking 'I'm exhausted today.'

'Truth to tell you've not looked well for quite a while.' Peter closed his book and placed it on his bedside table. 'Do you think you're doing too much? Surgeries and such and Sylvia doing fewer hours?'

Caroline snapped at him, 'No, certainly not. I'm all right. Just too much to do at the moment.'

Peter apologised. 'I'm sorry, but you see what I mean, you don't usually snap at me.'

Contrite, Caroline said, 'You're right I don't. It's me who needs to apologise. Just had a bad week.' She climbed into bed and shuffled across into the safety of his arms. 'I do love you, but you really musn't mollycoddle me. I'm grown up now you know.' Putting her face close to his she ran the tip of her tongue around the edges of his lips. 'You're a beautiful man, do you know that? All six feet five, red-blond, blue-eyed, fresh complexioned bit of you. Every single bit.'

'Thanks,' he said modestly.

'Far more handsome than you've any right to be.'

'Thanks again' he said, even more modestly.

Caroline laughed. 'Well?'

'Well, what?'

'What are you going to say about me?'

'That you're beautiful in body, mind and spirit and suit me to the enth degree. I wouldn't swop you, not for anything.'

'That's not very romantic!'

'I didn't think you were in a romantic mood and you haven't been for several weeks. I have begun to wonder why.'

Caroline turned away from him, drew the duvet up around her neck and said, 'I'm going to sleep now, so I'll say good night.'

'Good night, then, my darling girl.' He paused and then continued with, 'If you've gone off me I'd like to know.'

'Not really, just tired like I said.'

Thoughtfully, Peter leant over her and kissed her cheek. 'God bless you.'

'And you.'

Peter turned away from her and they lay back to back quite quietly for a while, so he never saw the tears which welled around her eyes and then slid silently onto her pillow. She brushed them angrily away but they wouldn't stop coming. Finally when there were no more tears left to cry she said, 'I love you, you know that don't you? For always and for ever no matter what. You love me, don't you? Really love me?'

'Absolutely. I tell you that every day of my life and mean it. Good night, my love.'

'Good night, darling. I'll go see Sheila straight after taking the children to school. I expect she'll be feeling very sorry for herself.'

'Indeed. Poor thing. It's no joke breaking a leg at her age.'

'You're right. It isn't.'

By some kind of intuitive telegraph most of the mothers at the school gate knew about Sheila's fall, and asked Caroline how she was.

'She was in an awful lot of pain last night, but I haven't heard anything this morning. I'm going right now to find out.'

'Give her our love. She might be an old bat, and bossy with it, but you can't help but feel sorry for her can you?'

Caroline laughed and agreed. 'She won't be a lot of use for the Harvest, so we'll all have to pull our weight on her behalf.'

'We all will, just give us the word.'

'Lovely, thanks.'

With Pompom in tow Caroline knocked on Sheila's door.

Ron opened it and invited her in, Pompom completely forgetting how Caroline had lavished loving care upon him in his hour of need, leapt about filled with excitement at his return and rushed to find Sheila.

She was sitting in an armchair still in her négligé and matching night-gown, with the broken leg, now in plaster, sticking straight out in front of her resting on a tapestry footstool. Pompom bounded about leaping up to reach Sheila's face to give it a welcoming lick.

'Down, Pompom, down, I say. Oh Ron, I can't bear him, take him away. Don't let him touch my le-e-g-g-g. Ohhhh!'

When Ron had safely shut Pompom in the kitchen Caroline asked how she had got on at the hospital.

'It was horrendous, they did their best though, we got home about one and I haven't had much sleep, however, I must say, I am feeling a little better this morning, thank you.'

'I thought you'd be in bed.'

'I can't stand lying in bed. So boring. No television, nothing to see. I thought I'd be more cheerful downstairs.'

'Of course you will. I told you last night you were brave and you are, you see.'

'I could soon cry. The slightest little thing.'

'Naturally.'

'I got the VIP treatment with you phoning up. Thank you ever so much.'

'Not at all. The least I could do. You're not to worry about a thing. Give me any messages and I'll attend to them and then Sir Ronald can spend his time looking after you.'

'That's most kind. We've been talking about the Harvest Festival decorations. I just don't know what to say. I don't see how I can help.' Tears began to fill Sheila's eyes. 'It's not fair it happening right now, of all the times to choose. One of my most crucial times of the year.'

'Say no more. I shall rally everyone and we'll all manage perfectly. You've got the file haven't you?'

'Oh yes, but I don't . . .'

'I know, you don't like other people to have it, that's quite under-standable. On the Saturday you shall sit with it in your lap and give us our instructions and we'll do all the work. They'll all rally round, you'll see. I haven't got a surgery today so I shall get Willie to go into the church hall loft and get me the boxes of things out and tomorrow night at the committee meeting we'll have a good dust of everything and get fully sorted, repair anything that needs it . . .'

'I doubt I shall get there, Ron's speaking at a training session of trades union representatives in Birmingham tomorrow afternoon so . . .'

'You can't possibly manage on your own shall I . . . ?'

'No, please, you have enough on your plate and you've been too kind already, no, the children . . . well, I mean Louise and dear Gilbert, are coming and making my meal and settling me down for the evening. Ron will be back before bedtime, it's an early-evening meeting.'

'Are you sure? Because I can . . .'

'Absolutely. There were two corn dollies which needed refurbishing and I never got them done and you remember we used . . .'

They heard the doorbell and listened to Ron answering it. Through the open lounge door the commanding tones of Grandmama Charter-Plackett could be heard enquiring if she could help.

Sheila visibly shrank into the chair. Caroline raised her eyebrows in despair.

Ron tried to put her off from coming into the house but she wouldn't hear of it. 'I must come in, I know how conscientious Sheila is, and I've come to relieve her of her worries. Is she in bed?' Without waiting for an answer she swept towards the staircase.

In a shaky voice Sheila cried, 'I'm in here, first on the right.'

Grandmama stood in the doorway, and surveyed the scene in the lounge. A proud autocratic woman in her seventies, dressed with her usual pin neat smartness and attention to detail, her hair rigidly set in waves and curls she nodded her head at each of them in greeting. 'Good morning, Caroline. Sheila. Now, how are things? I was so sorry to hear about your fall. I heard it was both legs and an arm. Obviously it's not.'

Sheila answered in a trembling voice. 'Oh no. Just this leg.'

'Is it agony, my dear? Of course it must be. Never had a broken limb myself, but I'm sure it must be excruciatingly painful. I've come to offer my services. She's not to worry about a thing, is she Caroline?' Before Caroline could answer Grandmama pushed on with her offer of help. 'Coffee! Yes, coffee. The kitchen, I'll do it.' She flapped her hands at Ronald. 'No, no, you've quite enough on with the dog and the house and the shopping. I'll do this for us all. You won't be staying, Caroline, will you? I expect you've a lot to do. Has the dog been out yet, Sir Ronald?'

He had only time to shake his head before Grandmama said, 'Well, in that case you take the dog while I'm here and then Sheila won't be left on her own. Sugar, Sheila?'

'Yes, please.'

Ronald scuttled out with Pompom thankful to have a reason to get out of her way. Caroline pulled a face at Sheila and then said loudly, 'I'll be off then.' Bending over Sheila's chair she whispered, 'Don't worry about tomorrow night, we'll attend to everything. You stay here and rest, OK?'

'Are you sure?'

'I am.' As she reached the door Caroline called out 'Bye-bye then. I'll call in tomorrow. I'm going, Mrs Charter-Plackett.'

'Very well, leave everything to me, my regards to the Rector!'

2

Sheila's accident had been the main topic of conversation in the Store and Grandmama Charter-Plackett had determined as soon as she heard about it to step into the breach. If that common woman Sheila Bissett couldn't organise the Harvest Festival then she would. After all, it was only a bit of flower-arranging, any fool could do that. She'd taken her shopping home, put it away, remembered to check herself in the mirror in her tiny hall, wrapped the flowers Harriet had given her only two days ago in fresh paper and had sallied forth to Sheila's house.

On her way round the green she'd planned her strategy. The best approach would be sympathy to start with. Then she could move on to saying 'if', and 'but' and 'of course' and before she knew it she'd be in charge. Musn't appear too eager. The door chimes on Sheila's door had grated her nerves. Some people had no taste. Grandmama had followed Ron in, wincing at the decorations. Honestly, artificial flowers everywhere, whatever next. She bet her last shilling there'd be a lacy cover on the spare toilet roll in the downstairs lavatory. This wasn't going to prove much of a nut to crack, not for her anyway. She'd ease the way with a cup of coffee.

While the kettle boiled she found a vase and arranged the flowers with an imaginative flourish. Carrying them into the sitting-room she said to Sheila 'I've brought these, nothing like . . . fresh flowers is there?'

She held them close to Sheila and watched her sniff them. 'They smell gorgeous. Thank you so much. Most kind. Ron . . . Ronald isn't much good with flowers.'

'Well, there is a lot of skill in flower-arranging as you know. I'll put them here on this low table. The coffee won't be a minute now.' She twinkled her fingers at Sheila as she left for the kitchen. Mentally rubbing her hands she congratulated herself on the way things were going. Sheila was at her most vulnerable, she could tell that.

Grandmama carried in the coffee, placed it on the smallest of a nest of repro tables and when she'd settled herself back in her chair she chatted about this and that and gradually came round to how incapacitated Sheila would be for the next few weeks.

'They say I shall be in plaster for at least six weeks.'

'Oh dear. That will mean the end of October then at the earliest.'

'I'm afraid so. Such a nuisance. Ron . . . Ronald and I were hoping to go on Eurostar to Brussels in a fortnight, right after the Harvest Festival but we shall have to cancel. I couldn't manage that. At least with a bit of re-organisation I'll be able to manage the Harvest Festival arrangements though. It's so aggravating, it being one of the peaks of my flower year.'

'You don't mean you help with the Harvest Festival as well as all your other activities?'

'I'm the organiser!'

'Well! I'd no idea. But I should have realised, you being so involved with flowers at every turn. I wasn't here last year you see. Whatever will you do? How shall they manage without you?'

Sheila put down her cup and said 'Don't worry. I've got it all worked out. Louise, my married daughter you know . . .'

'No, I don't, I haven't had the pleasure.'

'You must have seen her about, she's married to the choir master Gilbert.'

'Oh, of course, that's your daughter. I hadn't realised.'

'Well, she put all the details on her computer for me last year, so she's printed it all out again and with one or two alterations I have everything at my fingertips. Ron can drive me round to the church and I shall supervise from the front pew.'

Grandmama shook her head in admiration. 'Well, I think that is most extraordinarily brave of you. That is a sacrifice above and beyond the call of duty.'

Sheila looked puzzled. 'Above and beyond . . . I don't understand.'

'It's people like you making those kind of sacrifices who are the back bone of village life.'

Sheila beamed her pleasure. 'Oh, I am, where flowers are concerned. I've organised the competition marquee for the last three Village Shows, this year's, last year's and the one before that which was the first and the hardest to do, and they've been a roaring success. Believe me, the Harvest Festival display will be nothing in comparison. No, nothing at all.'

Grandmama could see she was a harder nut to crack than had first appeared. 'A fall like you have had is a terrible shock to the system, you know. You do realise you're still in a state of shock.'

'Am I?'

'Oh yes, and it can be very dangerous to the nerves if you struggle on when really you should be resting. Breaking a bone is equally as serious as a major operation. And what would they be saying to you if you'd had a major operation? I can tell you. Rest, complete rest, no aggravation of any kind.' Grandmama nodded her head very wisely after delivering this salvo and Sheila began to be impressed. 'It's just the same as when you have the flu. Get up and about too soon and you're back in bed as soon as. These things take their toll.'

'I suppose they do. I have been feeling a little odd.'

Triumphantly Grandmama said, 'What did I tell you?'

'Perhaps I am trying to be too brave.'

'Exactly, but then you're that kind of person aren't you? You've the kind of grit we had to have in the War.'

'I don't remember much about the War, I was too young.'

A shade too hastily the reply came back, 'Oh well, of course, so was I, but my mother told me.'

There was a pause while Grandmama restructured her campaign. Sheila shifted uneasily in her chair, and her visitor gazed in admiration at the picture over the fireplace.

'What a wonderful picture. Who painted it?'

'I don't know who the artist was, it was a parting gift from the Union when Ron . . . ald retired. It's a very good likeness isn't it?'

'It is very good. They've captured his . . . *strength* haven't they? I admire strength in a man.' Frankly she thought it wooden and not one jot like the man himself but people like Sheila put such store by things like that. 'This list which . . . Louise was it? put together for you on her computer, do you think someone else should have a look at it too, you know, just in case you aren't able to cope as well as you would usually do? I'm not meaning to interfere but the show must go on as they say and it might be as well to have an understudy, mightn't it? What do you think? I'd be the last person to step in where I wasn't wanted, and of course your word is law, you've so much experience.'

Sheila, by now overwhelmed by Grandmama's arguments and not at all able to stand up for herself as she normally would have done, began to feel herself weakening. It would be good to have some help. Taking a look at the list wouldn't mean she was in charge would it?

'It's in the file in that drawer there at the bottom marked Harvest Festival.'

Grandmama was out of her chair and across the room almost before Sheila had finished speaking. She held up the file with a reverent air as though it was the prized acquisition of a major museum. 'Here we are. I'll wash up our cups, and then I'll leave you in peace to have a little sleep. Studying this file will be my first priority. Between us we'll get this sorted. Can't let the Rector down can we?'

As she left, Grandmama said, 'Now you're not to worry. I've met people like you before, working your fingers to the bone for everyone else with not a thought for yourself. Well, now someone is thinking about *you* for a change.' She patted Sheila's arm and continued, 'No, don't get up. There you go again, always thinking of other people. I'll let myself out. Have a good sleep.'

She spent the rest of the morning reading through Sheila's lists. There was no doubt about it, the woman was much better organised than she'd first imagined. Names, addresses, telephone numbers of her helpers. A plan of the church, with notes of who did what and where. A colour scheme carefully laid out with lists of fruits and vegetables and types of greenery necessary to achieve the right effect. One could be forgiven for thinking they were decorating Westminster Abbey for heaven's sake. Even a list of where and what they had stored in boxes for use from year to year. Plant holders, swathes, corn dollies, the list was endless.

She came to the conclusion this wasn't Sheila's plan. Behind this meticulous scheme there was a very different kind of brain from hers. Maybe it was that Louise. But the thought occurred to Grandmama that change was needed. It couldn't be the same as last year, not exactly the same. She'd have a word with the Rector. That was it. The Rector. She glanced at the clock. Twelve thirty. Time for lunch and then off to the rectory. No, she'd go now. Before lunch, try to catch him in.

'It's about the Harvest Festival. Is the Rector in, Sylvia?'

'The Rector's already got someone in his study right now, but I'll go give him a knock, if you'll wait here, Mrs Charter-Plackett.'

'Thank you.' Grandmama stood in the hall looking at the decorations. Much better taste here. Oh yes, the Rector and his wife were more her kind of people. She could hear Sylvia speaking to the Rector, then she came back into the hall.

'If it's about the Harvest Festival he says would you like to come through.'

Sitting in one of the easy chairs was Harriet with little Fran on her knee. Peter stood up to greet her.

'How nice, two Mrs Charter-Plackett's and a Miss Charter-Plackett all at the same time. What a pleasure. We're just discussing the Harvest Festival so you've come at the right moment.'

'Good afternoon, Rector.' Such a gorgeous man. Even a lady of her age found him . . . disturbing. 'Good afternoon, Harriet. Hello, Grandmama's favourite girl. What a coincidence.'

'Good afternoon, Mother-in-law. What brings you here?'

Grandmama tapped the file in her hand. 'I've got the master plan for the church here.'

Harriet registered shock. 'You have? How've you managed that? Sheila never lets it out of her sight.'

'My dear, she is desperate. This accident has completely thrown her, she's not at all well, she's just so grateful for my offer to step into the breach.'

'Sheila is? Is she? I'm amazed. Have you misunderstood?'

'Here is the evidence. I didn't steal it from her.'

Peter intervened. 'Does she not want to be in charge?'

'How can she? She can barely walk, and she's racked with pain. I've read through and made a few notes. The basic idea will be the same but I shall make a few minor changes, after all it will be boring if the same design is done year after year. I see you're down for the bread, Harriet. Usually a sheaf of corn design. Well, this time I think we'll have something more simple, I have in mind an extra large cottage loaf. More natural don't you think?'

'But I've always made a sheaf of corn.'

'My point exactly. Time for a change.'

Harriet, determined not to be steamrollered, said, 'I'd like to talk to Sheila about this. After all, she's the expert.'

Grandmama shook her head. 'Don't, when I left her she was going to have a sleep. She's not at all well. There's no need to worry her, believe me. This afternoon I shall telephone all the people who helped last year and tell them of my changes of plan. She can't be at the meeting tomorrow night, so I've promised to chair it for her.'

'I see. Well, Mother-in-law,' Harriet lifted Fran off her knee and stood up ready to leave, 'I'm not at all happy about this. There's still two weeks to go, plenty of time for Sheila to have made at least a partial recovery and I for one am not prepared to go ahead without a word from her.'

Peter stood up too. 'I think we should leave the telephoning for a couple of days, that way we'll have a better idea of how Sheila is coping. I'm very grateful to you Mrs Charter-Plackett for stepping into the breach, but I would feel happier if I could be given the chance to speak to Sheila before anything definite is done. It is her baby as you might say.'

'Of course, Rector, anything you say, but you'll see it's me she wants to have deal with everything. There's absolutely no need for you to worry. Everything will go swimmingly, believe me. I shan't let you down. I might just make a few preliminary calls, break the ice so to speak.'

Harriet swept out hand in hand with Fran. 'Thanks, Peter, see you soon.' As she passed him she gave him a sceptical look of which her mother-in-law was blithely unaware saying, as Harriet left, 'I must give credit where it's due, she has made very careful lists about everything, there'll be no problems I can assure you.'

'In a village we have to step very delicately, I have known major incidents arise from quite insignificant beginnings. One can never afford to give offence of any kind, the repercussions can be so far reaching.'

Grandmama picked up her handbag, and smiled up at him. The combination of his red-blond hair and those blue all-seeing eyes was quite stunning. She reminded herself she was seventy-five. 'Of course I quite understand, there'll be no repercussions with this matter, believe me. If we're both on the same side . . .' Her smile was conspiratorial.

Peter's heart sank. The confrontations he'd had with Sheila in the past loomed uneasily in his mind. No one had told him when he was ordained that diplomacy would need to be high on his list of skills.

That afternoon several villagers received phone calls which pleased them not at all.

3

The following morning Peter called in the Store for a few things he needed. Seeing Jimbo serving at the meat counter he called across, 'Good morning, Jimbo!'

'Morning, Peter! Nice day.'

'It is indeed. Lifts the spirits no end.'

There came a chorus of 'Good morning, Rector' and then the general hubbub recommenced. The Store was extremely busy for so early in the morning. There were three people waiting to pay at the till, a clutch of people taking advantage of the free coffee machine and gossiping by the ice-cream cabinet while they did so, and two people clustered around the post office grille listening intently to a story Linda was telling them from the other side.

He gladly embraced the sounds and smells of the Store, for not only was the weather uplifting this morning but coming in the Store was too. One was drawn in as though by a magnet to the warm welcoming atmosphere Jimbo had created: to the inviting displays, the bright lights, so clean, so smart, so enticing it was extremely difficult to leave without buying something. Jimbo might have been a merchant banker but he was a born shopkeeper too. From the vivid colours of the greengrocery to the smart businesslike post office counter it was all so appealing and best of all his prices were competitive too, even though it was the only place to shop in the village.

Drifts of the conversations came to him as he studied the selection of toothbrushes.

'I'm telling you, I know. I saw. Dicky and Georgie have gone away together.'

'Noooo! They can't have.'

'They have. Her and Bryn had that row in the bar the other night and apparently, after Lady Bissett'd broken her leg and gone orf to 'ospital, it went from bad to worse. It's not right all that rowing in the bar.'

''Tisn't. I agree. But going off together! That's a bit much. Poor Bryn. I'd no idea that was the way the wind was blowing.'

'Neither 'ad I and I wouldn't have known if it hadn't been for the baby waking early and I was standing at the window rocking him and I saw Georgie come out of the pub and Dicky pull up in his car and she got in. She only had a small case so they can't be going for long. All tarted up she was and no mistake. I tell yer there's advantages in living at number three!'

'And 'im the Scout leader! Disgusting I calls it. Perhaps he was only giving her a lift to the station.'

'Got yer rose coloured spectacles on then this morning! So why wasn't he at Scouts last night then?'

The coffee drinkers were discussing other news.

'I see Lady Templeton's back.'

'Well, she won't say a thing, you know how kindly she always speaks of everybody.'

'Not always, she has been known to have her say.'

'She won't like old Mrs Charter-Plackett telling her what to do though will she?'

'No, she won't. And I'll tell you who else won't like her taking liberties.' The speaker nodded her head in the direction of the door marked *Private*. 'Mrs Jones. How Mr Charter-Plackett manages to keep the peace with 'er lording it over the mail-order office I'll never know. Still adds a bit of spice to life, doesn't it? Where would we be without someone to talk about?'

Peter, trying hard not to listen to these snippets of news, finally settled on a toothbrush and began contemplating the razor blades, hoping he'd remember which kind he used. He heard Mrs Jones call from Jimbo's mail-order office.

'Mr Charter-Plackett! Was that the Rector came in a minute ago?'

'The man himself. Do you want a word?'

Mrs Jones came through into the Store. 'I do. Bit private. Is it all right if the Rector comes into the back? Would you mind, sir?'

Peter had a very good idea what she wanted to see him about. 'I'm in a hurry, Mrs Jones.'

'Won't take long.'

She asked him to sit on her stool and propped herself against the racks where she stored Harriet's Country Cousin jams and marmalades.

'I've never had a lot of time for Sheila Bissett. She's a bossy interfering person who likes all her own way, *but* I had a phone call yesterday from the Duchess, sorry, Mrs Charter-Plackett.'

'Ahhh!'

'You know then.'

'I did ask her not to do anything until I'd had a word with Sheila.'

'Well, she told me that I was moved from being in charge of the window-sills to doing the small display we always put in the choir vestry. I've done the window-sills for years. I have to admit that since Sheila took charge my window-sills have improved out of all recognition. I've liked what she's suggested and gone along with it. We've an understanding she and I. But I'm not being demoted to doing the choir vestry display. That's a kid's job.'

'I see. Did she give you a reason?'

'Something about the window-sills need to be coordinated with the rest of the church and it'll be better if the people doing the church itself do them. Meaning she's doing the church in place of Sheila, so she wants a bigger slice of the action. As you know, I don't like causing trouble,' mentally Peter raised his eyebrows at this remark, 'but I had to say something.'

'Leave it with me.'

'You'll have to move fast, she's rung I don't know how many people. They're all up in arms.'

'Oh dear.'

She nodded her head in the direction of the Store. 'You see it's a bit difficult for me working here and the Duchess being his mother, can't say too much can I?'

'I'm sure Jimbo knows his mother for what she is.'

'Maybe, but she is his mother after all. Got to press on, Rector. I'll wait to hear.'

'Right. I think she's only trying to help because of Sheila's accident.'

'No, Rector, she's taking charge. There's a difference.'

Peter paid for his shopping and went back to the rectory. He'd been in his study only a few minutes when Sylvia came in with his coffee.

'Thank you, Sylvia, here, look, I'll make a space.' He moved some papers further along his desk and she put down his cup.

'I expect they've all had a word have they, Rector?'

'About what?'

'About the Duchess going behind Sheila Bissett's back and reorganising all our arrangements?'

'Indeed they have. But I'm quite sure Sheila won't allow her to.'

'I think Sheila's too poorly to have any choice in the matter, she must be, she's let the Duchess have her precious file.'

'Well, Sylvia, I think we can just wait and see. I'm sure she means well.'

'She also went up to the Big House yesterday afternoon and sweet-talked them into letting her borrow lots of potted plants from the glasshouses so it's going to look more like a garden centre than anything. Also she's going to buy palms and rubber plants and charge them to the church. It's going to look ridiculous.'

'Charge them to the church?'

'Yes.'

'I did warn her to tread carefully.'

'Well, if that's the Duchess treading carefully, heaven alone knows what'll happen if she puts the boot in. And Lady Templeton has been compulsorily retired, too.'

Peter smiled at her. 'Leave it with me. Thanks for the coffee.'

After Sylvia had left Peter sipped his coffee while he thought up a way to soften Grandmama's overbearing scheming. He'd ask Caroline. Her commonsense approach to life most often produced an answer for him to questions of this kind. After all, she was on the committee and might resolve the problem for him. Grandmama was well meaning but so domineering. He glanced at the study clock. Eleven. Three hours before she got home. Somehow problems never seemed so bad when she was home.

But he had this niggling worry about Caroline. Nothing specific, but he knew things weren't right for her. They never had secrets, well only that one which he'd handled so badly he'd nearly lost Caroline, and the guilt had made him want to die. But not now. No secrets now, except . . . He picked up the photograph he kept on his desk. It was of her and the twins taken about two years ago. Alex so like himself and Beth dear little Beth . . . He shut his mind off from thinking about whom she was like, with her blonde hair and rosy rounded cheeks. With the best will in the world you couldn't say she resembled Caroline.

The phone rang.

'Turnham Malpas Rectory, Peter Harris speaking.'

'Peter, it's Harriet Charter-Plackett. Is Caroline there?'

'She's taking surgery this morning, she won't be back until about two-ish.'

'Ah! I need to speak to her about tonight, the Harvest Committee. Ask her to ring as soon as she gets in? It's urgent.'

'Sure. Are you cancelling it with Sheila not being there?'

There was a pause and then Harriet answered, 'Not exactly. But it's urgent.'

'Understood.'

Caroline returned Harriet's call from the telephone in the study and Peter couldn't understand the intrigue which was afoot. After she'd put down the handset he asked her what was going on.

Caroline tapped the side of her nose with her forefinger and said, 'It's a secret, the fewer people know the better.'

'Darling!'

'It's better you don't know. Has Sylvia left my lunch out?'

'She has. What's Harriet up to?'

'Will you have a drink with me, tea, juice, coffee?'

'No, thanks. Will Jimbo like this secret plan?'

In truth Jimbo didn't. At that very moment, just like Peter he was questioning *his* wife about her phone calls and Harriet was answering him with undisguised glee.

'We've all rung each other up and decided to boycott the meeting.'

'Why?'

'Because your mother thinks she is taking us over and we're not putting up with it.'

He'd looked at her in astonishment. 'You mean mother's going to be there at the meeting and no one else?'

'Exactly. Sheila told Caroline yesterday there was no way she would be able to cope with getting to the meeting so that's what we've decided, we're not going either. I wish I was a fly on the wall and could see your mother's face when she realises no one's turning up.'

'How could you do that to her, Harriet?'

'Very easily.'

'She's your mother-in-law.'

'You don't need to remind me. I know!'

'I think that is the unkindest thing I have ever known you do.'

'I beg your pardon.'

'You heard.'

'Whose side are you on?'

'Yours, of course. But . . .'

'You are siding with your mother, ergo you are *not* on my side.'

'But there are limits, and in this case . . .'

'Sorry, Jimbo, but none of us is going to the meeting and that's that. You'd do well to remember the promise you made to me before she came. You promised me you'd back me against your mother in any dispute.'

'I always do.'

Harriet pointed her finger at him. 'You're not. You pledged yourself to be on my side. I didn't want her to come to live here, we've never got on and we never will. She's an interfering, bossy, inconsiderate, overbearing, insensitive woman with no finer feelings *at all*. But, she's your mother and I agreed I wouldn't object to her coming to live near her only family in her . . . well, I was going to say in her declining years but I take that back because they're not declining, not one bit. But I warn you, you are skating on very, very thin ice here . . .'

Jimbo was shocked at the threat in Harriet's voice and decided to deflect his anger from her onto other members of the committee. 'I'm appalled at Caroline and Liz not going, the others perhaps but not them. Caroline especially.'

'You can be as appalled as you like because it won't make one jot of difference, we are not going to the meeting. Someone has to take a stand.'

'For a person who has in the past complained about Sheila Bissett's tactlessness and bossiness you amaze me.'

'Do I indeed? Well, being annoyed with her is something quite different from standing by and allowing the niche she has carved for herself to be dismantled piece by piece by your battleaxe of a mother.'

Harriet stood arms akimbo glaring at him.

'Does Sheila know about this?'

'No. We daren't tell her because she can't keep a secret as we all know to our cost.'

'Is Peter privy to it?'

'We've all taken a vow of silence, so I'm pretty certain Caroline won't have told him.'

'If he knew he'd be livid. He'll blame me. I've a good mind to ring him.'

'Don't even think of it. Because if you do . . .'

'Yes?'

'If you do . . . your life won't be worth living and I mean that. I have *never* been more serious in my life.'

On that Harriet left the sitting-room and went into the kitchen, crashing about in there as though she was demolishing it cupboard by cupboard. Jimbo knew that things were bad when she was like that. He did think of quietly going round to his mother's house and telling her what was afoot, but changed his mind when he recollected how much he loved his home to be a haven, not just for him, but for his children too. There was no doubt about it, this time for the sake of peace it was his mother who would have to be sacrificed.

Grandmama Charter-Plackett, fully expecting that Sheila would not come, as she was still in pain despite the tablets from the hospital, was looking forward with pleasure to chairing the Harvest committee meeting. It was her first opportunity to prove her metal since she'd moved into the village. This was something she could really get her teeth into.

It was being held in the small committee room in the church hall. She was there first and turned up the thermostat on the radiator. That Willie Biggs was very parsimonious with the heating. The church could well afford to keep the hall warm, after all she understood Mr Fitch had paid for it to be installed so they only had the running costs to contend with. She glanced at her watch, only five minutes to go, they were all running late. Still it was a weekday evening and everyone had things to do before they came out. How did Caroline manage to keep her job with all the other things she was involved in to say nothing of those two little shockers. She'd never known two such adorable but inventively naughty children in all her life. Thank God she hadn't had twins. Two at a time! Heavens above!

There came a shuffling at the door and a voice calling out. She went to see who it was. The last person she'd expected to see, nor indeed wanted to see, was Sheila, but there she was.

'Hold the door for me, Mrs Charter-Plackett, please. Thank you.'

Between them they got her through the door and onto a chair. Sheila, panting with exhaustion slumped onto the chair and heaved a sigh of relief. 'I'd no idea how far it was from our house to the church hall. I'm sure they must have moved it further away since I was last here!'

Her mind working overtime trying to adjust to this unwelcome surprise, Grandmama took Sheila's crutches and propped them against the wall. 'You really are extremely brave, Sheila. Considering the pain you're in. I . . . We never expected you here tonight. You shouldn't have come. No, you shouldn't.'

'Well, I have. Didn't want to let everyone down. Ron's not due back till late tonight, he's been delayed, and so when Gilbert and Louise left for home I thought, sitting here all by myself and that meeting going on, it's no good I've got to go. I thought I'll manage somehow. So here I am! But it's nearly killed me. Where's everyone else?'

'I don't know, they're all busy people, don't worry they'll be here shortly.' Grandmama was in a serious dilemma. Her idea of being in charge, which she admitted she was perfectly capable of being, was in serious jeopardy now Sheila had arrived.

'Oh, good! I see you've brought the file. I'll have it back. Thank you.' She held out her hand. Grandmama didn't have an answer to this, and short of saying 'absolutely not' which in the circumstances she couldn't justify, she had to hand it over. She made a last-ditch effort. 'Are you sure? Are you really well enough to cope?'

Immediately Sheila was struck by a lightning flash of understanding. 'Am I sure? Of course I'm sure. I sincerely hope you weren't expecting to take over? Were you?'

'Of course not! Simply trying to help a . . . friend in distress. Of course I wasn't.'

Sheila opened the file and the first thing she saw was a list in Grandmama's handwriting.

'What's this list?' Sheila took out her reading glasses, placed them on her nose and studied the list. She didn't speak, but she did flick through her computer lists. Here, there and everywhere were red ink notes and crossings out. She was in such a temper that the file, almost as though it had a life of its own flew into the air and fell on the floor at Grandmama's feet, who automatically bent down to pick it up.

Sheila shouted. 'Don't dare! Don't you dare pick it up! Not taking over! That was an absolute lie! You've changed everything.'

'No I haven't, just made a few notes here and there.'

'A few notes! You've massacred my plans. All your pretending to be helpful, you've ruined it. Have you told everyone you're in charge? Have you?'

'Not really, no.' She wasn't accustomed to opposition like this, but she'd no intention of allowing this situation to become her Waterloo. She'd have to regain the lost ground and quickly.

Despite her extreme discomfort or maybe because of it Sheila almost screamed, 'Not really! I don't believe that. I'm in charge! Do you hear. I will not be usu . . . usur . . . I will not have you taking over. This is my pigeon.'

'Well, really! I was only trying to help. I'm sure you would have made changes, you can't have it the same every year and . . .'

'It isn't the same every year! We develop it. Your trouble is you think you know better than everyone else. Well, you don't. You can't just come to this village and ride roughshod over everybody.'

'Let's face it, Sheila, they're not exactly at the leading edge all these people are they? They need a push here and a nudge there to bring them into the twentieth century never mind the twenty-first. Between us, you and I could make a real difference. You with your knowledge, me with my style. We'd be a stunning combination.'

Grandmama could be very persuasive when she chose and Sheila went silent. Having organised the big Village Show Competition marquee so successfully three times now, she'd grown in confidence and in the realisation that she had a real part to play in village life. There was no longer a need to stand her ground against stiff opposition as she had in the past. She'd arrived. Now the Duchess was undermining her all over again.

'No good being a stunning combination if we've no committee, is it?'

Grandmama looked round the room. 'You're quite right. Where is everybody!'

Sheila looked at her watch. 'We did say seven thirty. Or I did. Did you change it?'

'No, of course not.'

'There's no "of course" about it. You'd change anything you wanted if you'd a mind to it. It won't do. I'm not putting up with it. Pass me the file. Please.'

Grandmama picked it up and handed it to her. 'There you are.'

Now the papers had been reshuffled by the fall, the top most one was the one where Grandmama had reallocated the tasks. 'What's this? Lady Templeton always does the organ flowers. You can't reorganise her. She's aristocracy.'

'Oh come, come. She was only a solicitor's secretary, you really can't call her aristocracy.'

'Muriel *is* Lady Templeton whatever you might say and I'm not moving her without her consent.' Sheila glared at Grandmama. 'Has she said she doesn't want to do it?'

'Well, I haven't had a chance to speak to her, she's only just back from holiday.'

'Right that's it. I'm taking this file home and I'm getting Louise to print it all out once more and I'm starting from scratch, again. You're having nothing to do with it.' She took another look at the list. 'And, look, what it says here. Palms and things in front of the lectern. The Rector's wife always does the lectern arrangement from time immemorial. Dr Harris will be most offended. You're a stupid interfering old . . . old . . . old . . . *baggage.* Pass me my crutches.'

Grandmama's mouth twisted into something like a smile. She sat quite still. Sheila persisted. 'Please.'

'You'll have to wait for the rest of the committee. I'm not having some trumped up trades union leader's wife speaking to me as you have done, knighted or not. No one speaks to Katherine Charter-Plackett like that. No one. So you can sit there until tomorrow morning as far as I'm concerned. I'm going home now.'

Sheila suddenly realised the impossible position she was in. She couldn't get off the chair without help, and she couldn't reach her crutches from where she sat. She couldn't reach a phone to call for help either; the Duchess had her absolutely in her power. Then another thought intruded. Where was the committee? Her devoted committee who'd never let her down, ever. Had they abandoned her? They certainly hadn't come. Was everything she'd worked for in ruins? She glanced surreptitiously at her watch. Twenty minutes to eight. They weren't going to come now. They always had a nice coffee before they started and Caroline or Harriet brought cake and it was all friendly and gossipy and thoroughly pleasant.

'You wouldn't dare walk away and leave a sick helpless woman.'

'I would. You've spoken to me as I've never been spoken to in my life. You're a common little woman.'

That remark struck home. Sheila had known for years that she lacked good taste. But ever since Ron had put his foot down that time when it was the Flower Festival in the church and she'd gone out with him and bought that green suit which everyone had liked and she'd stopped peroxiding her hair, she really had tried. But she knew that every now and again that lack of taste manifested itself in some ridiculous buy she made and then regretted. It was a continuous battle that, keeping the common side of her under wraps, and now this terrible woman had unearthed it all over again.

'How dare you say that! Who do you think you are?'

Grandmama stood up. This distasteful conversation really must be brought to a close. 'Well, I know who I am, do you know who you are? I'm going home.'

'Righteo, Duchess. You go. It'll be all round the village tomorrow, what you've done to me. It'll be a really juicy piece of gossip for them all. Do you no end of good. I don't think. We've now no committee, all because of you, so the Harvest Festival will be in ruins and I can't face telling the Rector. I don't know what he'll say.'

'Duchess? Who calls me Duchess?'

The tone of her voice gave Sheila the idea she might, just might, be able to get back at her and really slap her down. Her lip, unaccustomed to curling, did so as she said, 'Everybody does, didn't you know?'

But the shot misfired. Grandmama drew herself up, picked up her crocodile handbag, bought in Harrods years ago but still as good as new, and said, 'Well, at least people do have respect for me then. I'd no idea.' She smiled and left.

4

'So, there she was waiting. 'Er leg too painful to stand on and she was too unbalanced with the weight of the plaster to hop. She'd been there an hour when I found her.'

Vera laughed till the tears were rolling down her cheeks. Willie knew it was funny but he didn't think it was that funny. He'd had to get his Sylvia to bring her car round and give Sheila a lift, because she'd been too distraught and exhausted to tackle the walk home. For once in his life he'd felt sorry for Sheila, really sorry.

Eventually Vera had calmed herself enough to speak again. 'But what I don't understand is where were the rest of the committee?'

'They'd agreed not to turn up, believing Sheila would never get there anyway, and that would leave the Duchess high and dry with no committee to boss around and it would serve her right.'

Vera picked up her glass to finish the last few drops of her shandy when a thought struck her like a thunder bolt. 'But Harriet Charter-Plackett's on the committee. Do you mean she dared do that to her own mother-in-law?'

'Yes, apparently she did, and her and Jimbo had a terrible row about it. He said she should go out of loyalty to 'is mother and she said she shouldn't out of loyalty to Sheila and the rest of the committee. Right bust-up I understand. Bel Tutt said they still weren't speaking this morning, so when Harriet went in to 'elp in the Store while little Fran was at playgroup, they passed messages to each other through her and Linda.'

'That must have been a laugh. Still it's not nice when yer in-laws come between yer. Jimbo and Harriet are really keen on each other, aren't they? I'm glad you mentioned Bel Tutt though.' She nodded her head in the direction of the bar counter. 'Is it true do you think about Georgie and Dicky?'

'Look, two people happen to go away for a couple of days at the same time. It doesn't mean they've gone together does it?'

'No, but Bel's 'is wife, why hasn't she gone? There's no reason is there?'

From where he sat Willie had a good view of the saloon door. He was about to answer Vera when he turned and, looking straight into her eye, he said, 'Don't look now, she's just come in. She's at the bar ordering a drink. Alan's serving 'er.'

'Bel?'

'Yes. She's coming over. Don't say a word.'

'Right.'

'Hello, Bel. Coming to join us?'

Bel estimated whether or not she could squeeze in next to Willie on the settle but decided the gap was too narrow and lowered herself onto the chair next to Vera, who, bursting to know the real truth of Dicky and Georgie's holiday situation, blurted out, 'Lonely on yer own with Dicky away?'

Bel studied Vera's face. 'You could say that.' She took a long draught of her shandy, put the glass down on the table and looked about her.

Not to be put off with such bland meaningless statements Vera asked, 'Gone somewhere nice has he?'

'You could say that.'

Willie became embarrassed, sometimes Vera could be just too inquisitive. 'I hear there's been trouble at the Store today.'

Bel's face lit up. 'You could say that. Linda and me, we've been at our wits' end. Was I glad when it got to half past eleven and I could nip off to the school. Mind you Mr Charter-P wasn't much better in the afternoon. He has got a point though, she should have supported his mother.'

Vera was enraged. 'Support the Duchess? I don't see why she should. She's an interfering old bag . . .'

'Vera!' Willie hissed between his teeth.

'Old basket then.'

Bel smiled for the first time. Bel's smiles were worth waiting for. They illuminated the whole of her large round face. Her smiles touched not only her lips which curved up at the corners most attractively but her cheeks lifted, her eyebrows and even her forehead rose up and a light burst forth from her eyes. Her smooth pink and white skin glowed with her delight.

'She's a right case is that mother of his. She comes in to the Store sometimes with a determined look on her face and you can see Mr Charter-P brace himself for a fight. She makes suggestions about him changing things round and if it was hers she'd do this and that. Quite often though you know she's right but he wouldn't admit it to her. When she's gone he'll prowl about for a bit and then change things about just like she's said, then he shrugs his shoulders and winks at me. Some of her ideas are good, but some well . . .'

Vera's thirst for knowledge still not having been assuaged she pressed on with her enquiries. 'The midnight hike. Our Rhett's all organised. You'll be taking it all on your own, with Dicky away?'

Bel looked at her. 'He's back tomorrow. Wouldn't miss a hike, not Dicky.'

'Oh I see I thought . . .'

'What?'

'Oh nothing.'

Willie mused. 'Curious name Bel, how did it come about?'

'Isobel actually, but I couldn't say it so I said Bel and it stuck.'

To encourage Bel to further revelations Vera commented 'There was that Belle Watling in *Gone with the Wind*. Our Brenda's favourite book, that's why she called our Rhett, Rhett. Poor kid. He doesn't half get teased.'

'He should change it. He could change it to Robert or Roland or Richard.'

'That's what your Dicky is isn't it, Richard.'

'You could say that.'

'Funny how Dicky is short for Richard, they don't seem to belong do they? Not like Les for Leslie?'

'You could say that.'

'Perhaps he couldn't say it either, just like you.'

'I suppose.'

Bel sipped her drink. Willie wondered what to say next and Vera remembered she had to get to bed in good time as she was on early turn.

'I'll say good night then. Nine thirty for the hike, Bel?'

Bel nodded. 'Outside the church hall. They can eat the food in their fingers, but tell him to bring a cup of some kind.'

'Will do. Night, Willie.' Vera wended her way out, speaking to a few people before she left. Bel watched her leave.

'Quiet for you is it without Dicky?'

'It is. Good company is Dicky. Georgie not in?'

'No. They had a row did her and Bryn and she's hopped off on holiday. Over your Dicky.'

'Over Dicky?'

'Didn't you know? She'd asked him to do a turn. A comic turn like. You know what Dicky's like with his jokes. She's wanting to start up having entertainment here in the bar and Bryn won't have it and she had Dicky lined up for the first turn.'

'I see.'

'Didn't he tell yer? Could have been the start of a showbiz career! Yer never know.'

Bel finished her drink, heaved her bulky body out of her chair, took her glass to the counter and left without another word.

Next morning in the Store Bel was very quiet. Jimbo noticed and put it down to missing Dicky. He'd quite enough on his plate though without worrying about other people's marital problems. He'd been in hell for over twenty-four hours now and hell didn't suit him. The children had become seriously fractious because of the atmosphere at home and little Fran had cried at having to go to playgroup. He hated her to cry. Couldn't bear it in fact, but what was worse was Harriet having shut him out.

Caroline came in. 'Morning, Jimbo. Morning, Linda.'

'Good morning, Dr Harris. How's things?'

'OK thanks. How's that little Lewis of yours?'

'He's doing fine. Alan's that delighted with him. He's such a sunny little boy. Your two OK at school?'

'Oh yes fine. Before I know it they'll be in Kate's class and ready for leaving! Just got these two letters to post. They're both going to India.'

'Put them on the scales then, please!'

'There we are.'

'Eighty pence each.'

'Thanks. Harriet about?'

Linda nodded. 'In the back in the kitchens. Treat with care!'

Caroline raised her eyebrows and Linda pointed to Jimbo and pulled a face.

To Linda's disappointment her next customer was the Duchess. She'd promised herself that she would treat her with the barest civility for what she'd done to Sheila Bissett. Leaving her all alone in that state, it simply wasn't right.

'Good morning, Linda. I have a registered parcel to post. How are you, my dear, today? Baby being good?'

'Yes, thank you. That'll be four pounds twenty-two.'

'Four pounds twenty-two? Are you sure?'

'Registering is very expensive.' Rather maliciously Linda added, 'If you can't afford it, proof of postage is cheaper.'

'There's no need to be insolent, my girl. Jimbo! Come here.' He came across. 'The cost of posting this parcel is outrageous. Can't you make it cheaper for me. I am family.'

'Not on the post office counter, Mother. Sorry.'

'Very well, though I don't see why not. Register it, please, it is rather important. Don't mistake me, I can afford it, it's just that it seems so disgracefully expensive for such a very small parcel.'

'It does weigh quite heavily though.'

Grandmama put her change in her purse and as she snapped it shut she asked, 'Is my daughter-in-law in?'

'Er . . . yes.'

'In the back?'

'Er . . . I think so.'

'Well, is she or isn't she?'

'Well, yes, she is . . . I think.'

Grandmama found Harriet propped against one of the huge freezers, talking to Caroline.

'Harriet! I've been waiting.'

'What for?'

'For an apology.'

'For what?'

'Your behaviour at the meeting.'

'I wasn't there.'

'I know, that's what I meant.'

Caroline began to excuse herself, but Harriet stopped her. 'No you stay, please. You can be a witness.'

'I don't think I . . .' Caroline tried to make her exit as gracefully as she could, but Harriet held her arm.

Grandmama directed her glance at Caroline. 'You owe me an apology too, Dr Harris.'

'Me? You will not get an apology from me!'

'You both do. You both thought that Bissett woman wouldn't be there and you deliberately refused to come to the meeting, obviously intending to make a fool of me.'

Jimbo's voice interrupted the confrontation. 'I'm very busy but I've broken off to remonstrate with you about last night. I was very upset about them boycotting the meeting but no longer upset when I heard what you'd done to Sheila. It was quite dreadful. I did hear correctly, did I?'

Fast losing control of what she had hoped would be a magnificent climb down on Harriet and Caroline's part, Grandmama turned to face Jimbo. She'd never seen him so angry. There didn't seem to be quite so much pleasure in her challenge as there had been up to now. Obviously Sheila's popularity, though she couldn't think why, was much greater than she'd realised.

Holding her chin a little higher than normal Grandmama said quite clearly, 'You did. All I was doing was giving a helping hand, assisting someone in dire need and what do I get in return? Insulted! Lady Bissett' – scathingly she repeated – 'Lady Bissett – I ask you! – called me an old . . .' – there was hesitation here, should she tell? Yes, she must. She had to justify her actions, she really had – 'an old *baggage*! She only got what she deserved.'

Harriet smothered a grin.

Jimbo's face never slipped. 'Mother, I am ashamed. Whatever everyone will think of you I cannot imagine.'

'Well, I've resigned, so I'm not in charge any more. Perhaps now, everyone will be satisfied.'

'They won't forget though and neither will I.'

His mother rounded on him. 'Jimbo! It was your wife who insulted me the most. She should have supported me and come to the meeting no matter what the others said. My own son's wife! My daughter-in-law!'

Jimbo, furious, came out in defence of Harriet. 'My dear wife is quite capable of making her own moral judgements, she doesn't need me to vet her actions. The way things turned out, it's my opinion she did the right thing.'

'How could you? I came to live here looking forward to your support.'

'And you'll have it, so long as you behave yourself. Now please, Mother, leave before any more damage is done.' Jimbo stood aside from the doorway and waited for her to leave. Grandmama opened her mouth to protest, changed her mind, gathered the remnants of her dignity together and prepared to leave.

She strode from the freezer room intending to find a way out other than going through the Store, but due to her fury she was too confused to find one. Rather than ask for help she marched between the customers who had gathered to eavesdrop on what was being said, and then on past the till. Someone slyly sang the *Dambuster's March* in time to her masterful stride. As she shut the door a cackle of hysterical laughter rose to a crescendo. But the laughter was hastily cut short when Jimbo came through from the back. He glared round at everyone, and they quailed at the anger in his face. Then, his sense of humour being restored by remembering that Harriet had said quietly as his mother left, 'Thank you, Jimbo, darling', he raised his boater and bowed to them all.

5

Caroline had gone straight back to the rectory after leaving the Store. She closed the door behind her and stood with her back to it, leaning on it. That woman would be the death of her. Hell's bells. She'd felt quite guilty enough not going to the meeting, because it did seem a nasty trick to play, but to be told she should apologise! That really was too much. They'd finally tamed Sheila into being more reasonable and now she'd been replaced in the aggravation stakes by Katherine Charter-Plackett. These things are sent to try us she thought. But I should never have answered her back like I did. As the wife of the rector, as the Duchess said, she shouldn't have. But of late her own worries seemed to override her innate good manners. The rectory was quiet. Peter was out, Sylvia was in Culworth at the dentist's and the children at school till half past three. Nearly five years old. Where had all the years gone? She'd have a quiet coffee all by herself and read the morning paper. Hopefully the telephone wouldn't ring.

The kitchen was warm. She adored this kitchen. She loved its bright walls, the pine table, the big Aga. She remembered what it had been like when they'd first moved in. Thirty years of a bachelor rector in residence had taken its toll. Peter had declared they'd never get the Aga into shape at all, old Mr Furbank must never have used it preferring the nasty little table-top gas cooker which they'd had removed, but some careful cleaning and a genius of a man who understood cookers had seen to that. Now it was her pride and joy. Though it was Sylvia who used it more than she. Thank heavens for Sylvia.

The coffee was jolly hot. She found the newspaper and carried it and her coffee into the sitting-room. Bliss! One peaceful morning all to herself. Though she loved general practice it was so draining, one always saw people when they were at their lowest ebb. Lowest ebb. The thought which had been pushing about in the back of her mind returned. She, a doctor, who'd said so many times as gently as she could 'it would have been so much more sensible to have come to me as soon as you realised, wouldn't it' and here she was doing just that. Ignoring it. It was telling Peter which was going to be so difficult. That was what she dreaded. She could face it, but Peter wouldn't be able to. She knew, even without his frequent affirmation of it, that without her he would be totally desolate. Love like his made hurting him horrifyingly easy.

Caroline picked up the newspaper and tried to concentrate, but every piece of news she read was full of doom and gloom. Was there nothing happening that was joyous? Apparently not. She laid the newspaper down again and tried to face up to her problem. Having been born with a badly deformed womb and now being more than sure that there was something insidious growing on her ovaries it seemed as though there would be nothing left in her to make her feel a woman. The phone rang.

'Darling! Peter here! Look, I've got held up here in Culworth. Seeing as you're having the day off why don't you come in and have lunch with me? We don't often get the chance do we?'

'Sylvia isn't back yet for a while.'

'Never mind. She won't be long, leave her a note and put the answer machine on till she gets back.'

'Shall I?'

'Yes, please!'

Caroline didn't feel like being happy. She simply wanted to hide and to be left alone. But the pleasure in Peter's voice! She really couldn't deny him. A café in Culworth wasn't exactly the right place for telling one's loved one about operations, so she could justifiably put off telling him.

'You're right! I'll come! One o'clock at Abbey Close?'

'Lovely!'

When she saw him coming, striding eagerly out of the Abbey Close towards her she wept inside. There was never going to be a right time to tell him. The smile of greeting on her face was genuine though. The very sight of him lifted her spirits. His vigour, his thick red-blond hair, the lovely glowing smile on his face which the sight of her had inspired. How could she break his heart?

'Darling!' Peter took hold of her elbows drew her close to him and kissed her full on the mouth. She kissed him back with a desperate fervour.

'Peter! I don't think rectors are supposed to kiss like that in public!'

'Why not? I'm not a saint! And I am married to you! Where shall we go?' He tucked her hand into the crook of his arm and smiled down at her.

'Not the George. Not at lunch time. They always take so long to serve.'

'Well, then. How about the Belfry Restaurant? Right here.'

'OK. The Belfry it is.'

The waitress suggested a table in the window, which someone had just vacated.

'Well, as I'm playing hookey I might as well be seen by everybody from the abbey.'

'No point in doing things by halves is there?' Caroline gave him her coat and he hung it up for her beside his cloak. She'd bought him the silver clasp for it when they'd first got married. He needed a new cloak now. She'd buy him one as a surprise, measure this one with her dressmaking tape. The cloak would have to be specially made because of his height.

'Miles away? I asked what you would like?'

'Sorry, darling.' Caroline looked at the menu and all she could see was lasagne. 'I'll have lasagne.'

'Are you sure? My treat?'

'Absolutely. Thanks. Just coffee. I won't have wine with driving straight back.'

'No, of course not. I think I'll have the steak and all the trimmings.'

'Good, you need something to fill that frame of yours!'

'You laugh, but for days now the laughter hasn't reached your eyes.'

Caroline pulled back from people watching and stared at him. She'd forgotten how perceptive he was. 'I've had an altercation with the Duchess this morning. She claimed I was without honour. And Harriet too! I'm afraid I gave her a mouthful and stormed out.'

'Oh dear! That's not my Caroline at all. Quite out of character. But that's today. What happened to all the other days when you haven't . . .'

The waitress came for the order and when she'd gone Caroline gave him a blow by blow account of the happenings in the Store kitchen. 'So to conclude Harriet and Jimbo have been restored to each other, so all's well with their world.'

'Might be all well with theirs but not with yours. Are you overtired? Look, you don't have to go to the practice. I'm sure there's plenty of eager young things only too willing to take your place. Have a rest for a while. You've been working, albeit part time, for a good while now and I would appreciate you being at home. Is that the problem do you think, that you're overtired?'

A short portly figure marched by the window. Caroline waved. 'Oh, look there's the Dean going past. Turn round and wave!'

'Hope he doesn't come in. Oh! he hasn't.'

'Nice man, the Dean. I like him.'

'Wet!'

'Peter!'

'Stop changing the subject.'

'I didn't make him walk by.'

'I wouldn't put it past you.'

He sat twisting his ring round and round and round. Caroline read the signs. He was worried about her but he didn't know why, his suggestion of being overtired was simply a stab in the dark to get the real truth from her. Well, she wasn't going to tell him, not today. Not till she knew for certain.

'I'm just tired I expect. It's quite hectic working and then having two four-year-olds when I get home and at the weekend. You're always so busy then you see.'

'Yes.' Peter looked across the restaurant. She obviously wasn't going to tell him. But he knew there was a problem. But what? Maybe she didn't know what it was either, just a general feeling of unsettledness. He was selfish. He'd brought her here, buried her in the countryside and it was all getting too much. Perhaps he should get out . . . for her sake. 'I've been thinking about a change.'

Caroline didn't answer until the waitress had finished serving them. 'Thank you. Parmesan? Yes. Thank you.' She brought her attention back to him. 'A change?'

'Yes, we've been here over five years, perhaps it's time . . .'

'Do you seriously fancy a move?'

'Do you?'

Caroline hadn't begun her lasagne. She'd picked up her fork intending to start but there was a strange tone in Peter's voice she was wary of. She put down the fork and sat back. He was scrutinising her face, watching for the slightest sign, anything at all that might give him a clue.

She answered him very quietly. 'The only reason we would move, my darling, is because *you* want to. That was the agreement we had. Your mission in life has a higher priority than mine. I can get a job anywhere I want to. That's our rule. OK?'

'But perhaps rules need changing?'

Very firmly Caroline answered 'Not this one.'

'So this sadness isn't . . .'

'Isn't anything. I've come out to enjoy your company. Isn't it great that Alex and Beth have settled so well at school. I was dreading Beth being difficult, when you remember how bad things were when she started playgroup. She loves her school dinners, I suggested packed lunches but she's refused them.'

Peter decided to cheer himself up for Caroline's sake. 'Yes, it is. It's a great relief.' Then another thought occurred to him. 'It's not the children starting school is it? Made you feel like a spare part?'

'A little teeny bit. But I can't keep them at home for ever can I? I grew up and so must they. Alex gets more like you every day.'

'He does, doesn't he?'

'Beth gets more like Suzy.' There came a silence when Caroline said that. She knew he found it hard when she mentioned the children's mother but there was no point in pretending Suzy had never existed. They only had to look at Beth to know she did.

'Yes, that's true.' Peter pushed his unfinished meal away from him, placed his knife and fork side by side, and sat back to look at her. 'So is that it? Is it this barren thing come back to haunt you?'

So near the truth. Maybe now was the moment, but there was a flurry of new arrivals and a man's cultured voice saying delightedly, 'Peter! Caroline! How lovely to see you. Not often you get away together for lunch! This is our first time here, we usually go to the George but they had a conference there today and it was far too busy for comfort. Muriel, my dear, look who's here.' Peter stood up as Muriel joined Ralph.

'How lovely! It must be good if the Rector and his wife are lunching here! What a nice surprise.'

Caroline, seeing a way out of her problem, began pulling out the chair beside her. 'Look, do join us.'

Muriel glanced at Peter, recognised a desperate kind of sadness, and shook her head. 'Certainly not! You both look to be enjoying being by yourselves for a change. We shan't intrude. Come, Ralph! Bye-bye! see you soon! Enjoy your lunch.'

Caroline caught the sound of Ralph protesting but Muriel was being quite firm with him.

Peter said, 'Well, that ruse didn't work did it? By the look on your face they were heaven-sent.'

'I did not come out to lunch to be psychoanalysed. You're my husband not my therapist. Finish your lunch! Eat up your greens! I'm sure your nanny must have said that to you many times!'

'She did! She was a tartar! Once I . . .' Caroline let him ramble on about his nanny, back on safe ground she thought thankfully. He took the hint and they chatted about everything under the sun including Dicky Tutt and Georgie Fields.

'Caroline, do you really think they've gone away together?'

'I shouldn't imagine so. You know what the village is like for inventing things on the slightest pretext! I saw Georgie crossing over to the Store when I was locking the door, whether Dicky is back as well I don't know. Everyone else thinks they have. Bryn apparently is like a bear with a sore head and Bel has gone silent and that's not Bel. She's as good as Jimbo for livening us all up!'

'He's the Scout leader you see. One has to be so careful even in this day and age.'

'But poor Bel! Poor Bryn!'

'It can't be very funny in a small community like Turnham Malpas, where we all know each other's business before we know it ourselves.'

'Apparently Jimmy nods his head very wisely but keeps his lips clamped and won't tell anyone what he knows.'

'Does he indeed? Honestly, it's always the same. I wonder what he knows? Help! I'm getting as bad as everyone else. One little hiccup and they have you dead and buried!'

Caroline didn't laugh. Neither did Peter when he looked at her face.

In bed that night Caroline watched Peter getting undressed. 'I don't think you've put an ounce of weight on since we married.'

He went to stand in front of the mirror. 'I don't think I have. In fact I know I haven't. Weighed myself a few weeks ago and I'm exactly what I was then.'

'Well, you do work hard at keeping fit. I admire your strength of character in going running in all weathers.'

'Habit. Jimbo doesn't come every morning like he used to, only about three times a week, says he doesn't have the time any more. I've warned him all the weight he's lost will slowly go back on again. But he claims he's so busy now with all his enterprises, he's on his feet all the time so he reckons he doesn't need it quite so much. Won't be long.'

He went to the bathroom. Caroline curled up on her side preparing to go to sleep. She'd tell him when . . . no she'd tell him tonight. No, she'd wait until she got a date. That was it.

Peter got into bed and drew her towards him and they lay, him with an arm under her neck and his other arm across her waist. He nuzzled his face into her hair and said 'Love you.'

'Love you too.' Caroline put an arm across his chest and hugged him.

'I'm sorry you're upset, would making love be any comfort to you?'

She released herself from his arms. She couldn't face that. 'No, I don't think so.'

Peter lay silent for a while, frighteningly puzzled by her refusal. 'That must be the first time ever you have refused.' Trying to put a lighter note in his voice he joked, 'Are you turning into one of those women who get convenient headaches? Ten years of marriage and you've had enough!' He turned to watch her face, but it gave nothing away.

'That was a cheap joke. Of course not!'

He hadn't switched the light off on his side and he reached over and moved the lamp slightly so that the light fell on Caroline's face. Peter saw the beginning of tears. One escaped and trickled down her cheek. He wiped it away with his thumb.

'My darling girl, whatever the matter is, there's nothing which cannot be said between the two of us. We don't have secrets, you and I. We are truthful with each other.' He moved to take hold of her again. 'You and I.'

She shrugged herself away from him. 'Not always, Peter, not always.'

Twice he opened his mouth to speak, and twice he silenced himself. Then he said, 'I was terrified of hurting you.'

'But I would have preferred to know.'

'Then if you would have preferred me to have confessed and cause you dreadful pain when it might not have been necessary, though in the end of course it was, why can you not be truthful to *me* now, if that's what *you* would have preferred then?'

'All I can promise at this moment is that I will tell you when I can.'

'That's the best you can do?'

'At this moment. Yes.'

He couldn't bear the closed up, shut off Caroline who lay curled tightly on the other side of the bed. 'I need to hold you close. Nothing more. Is that OK?'

She was across the bed and in his arms weeping almost before he'd said 'OK?'

'Darling! darling! There! There!' He held her close, soothing her as he did the children when they had nightmares. 'Gently! I've got hold of you. There's nothing can harm you. I won't let it!' When the tears subsided he found a tissue and wiped her face for her. 'Listen! There is nothing in this world we can't face together. Now, is there?'

'No.'

'Well, then. I won't ask you again. You tell me what's troubling you when you're good and ready. Good night, and God bless you.' He pushed her hair away from her face and gently kissed her forehead, the kiss was a token of his love for her; it lacked desire, it lacked lust, it lacked a lover's touch, it was quite simply his salute to her as the person to whom he was giving his total, all adoring, all encompassing support.

And she loved him for it.

6

The morning of the Harvest Festival dawned bright and sunny. There was a sharp autumn nip in the air but, as everyone declared when they opened their curtains first thing, 'Grand day for the Harvest. Sky's real clear.'

At a quarter to ten the ever burgeoning ranks of Scouts and Cubs, Guides and Brownies streamed up the church path carrying their harvest gifts. The church was already almost full and although Willie with Sylvia's help had filled in every available space with extra chairs from the Sunday School they were beginning to run out of seats. Eventually they had standing room only behind the font, and Willie thought one more person and we shall have to build an extension.

But what a feast met their eyes. Being a special day the church silver, for which they all had great affection after their fight to save it, gleamed on the altar and the great candlestick stood behind with its huge creamy white candle lit. Its flickering light shone on the festoons of flowers and greenery overflowing from the sill of the great altar window. Huge vases of flowers and foliage stood around on the floor. In front of the lectern was a vast arrangement of orange and yellow flowers with delicate grey-white eucalyptus leaves cascading from it. Caroline had spent a long time on Saturday morning getting it just right, and even someone who knew nothing of flowers would see it was special.

Each window-sill down the sides of the church was decorated with fruit and berries and greenery. Small trails of ivy trickled over the edges dropping down the stone walls beneath. Mrs Jones couldn't keep her eyes off them. She hated the thought of dismantling it all on Monday morning. Best do it tonight she thought, get it over with, though she'd be in the way of the people making up the parcels to go out to the children's home and the old people. Still she'd be quick. The stone pillars had swathes of yellow and white cactus chrysanthemums securely anchored to them, the trailing greenery softening the sandy coloured stone, apparently held there by magic.

Sheila, from her privileged position in the front pew where she sat to allow her to prop her broken leg on a kneeler, if she just craned her neck a little could admire most of the church excepting the arrangement in front of the organ seat. She was overwhelmingly well satisfied with how things had turned out. In fact, despite all her problems of not being mobile, of nearly losing control to the Duchess, of pain and anxiety at the restraints her broken leg put upon her, she was intensely proud.

All their planning had worked out beautifully, far far better than she could ever have hoped in the circumstances. They'd had such a jolly meeting at her house after that dreadful night when she'd thought her committee had abandoned her. Louise had printed out all the schedules for her again and they'd got together and cancelled all the Duchess's changes and restored the friendly atmosphere as though nothing had happened at all. Mrs Jones had her window-sills back and Lady Templeton her organ arrangement, Harriet had made a sheaf of corn as everyone loved her to do, and under persuasion from Dr Harris they'd agreed to allow the Duchess to arrange the flowers along the screen to the memorial chapel as a gesture towards good relations. Altogether the whole thing had become a major triumph for her, for the committee had demonstrated their loyalty to her beyond anything she'd any right to expect.

Grandmama Charter-Plackett arrived late. She had thought about not coming at all. That would show them! How she disapproved. But then it occurred to her that they wouldn't care anyway. Probably wouldn't even notice she wasn't there. So she'd planned to arrive at the last minute.

At the organ Mrs Peel, quite by coincidence, was playing a particularly triumphant piece when Grandmama entered. Without realising it she marched down the aisle in time to it, looking from side to side for a seat, but there were no seats to be had. She'd hoped to be able to squeeze into the Templeton pew right down there at the front but it was filled by Muriel and Ralph and that gaggle of four Prior girls, some poor relations of Ralph, she understood, though it seemed surprising that he should have poor relations with his background.

There was one small space in the rectory pew. Caroline caught her eye and shuffled the twins further up and Grandmama could just get in next to those two awful sisters, Valda and Thelma Senior. Why they should have a prominent seat at the front of the church just because they'd decided to attend every single service that ever was held after being scared out of their wits with that witchcraft business last year before she'd arrived, she really couldn't think. She just hoped they'd both remembered to wash properly before they came, they really were in very close proximity.

Caroline smiled a greeting when Grandmama got up from her knees. She was in church so she'd better be magnanimous so she smiled Caroline a greeting in return. She had to admit the church looked wonderful. Her own arrangement along the foot of the screen carved in memory of the fallen looked excellent. That was a prime site if ever there was one. Those blood-red blooms Mr Fitch had let her have mixed with the dark dark shiny green of the foliage and the red berries certainly were very fitting. Very appropriate. In fact everywhere looked very tasteful. Though the palms and rubber plants would have added that extra . . . no perhaps they wouldn't after all. She reluctantly had to agree that Sheila Bissett knew her stuff.

The Rector came in. He was a lovely young man. Pity Caroline was looking so thin. She was sure she'd aged ten years since that altercation in the Store kitchen. Though the twins must be very wearing. Alex was singing gobbledegook, out of tune, at the top of his voice and didn't know when to stop for the end of a verse, and Beth was trying to tie her shoe laces and Alex's together. Really! Caroline didn't even seem to notice. She had eyes for no one but the Rector. And no wonder. That snow-white surplice he was wearing, dripping with antique lace made him look . . . well just too utterly . . . Grandmama pulled her mind back to the service.

If it was the last day of September today then her hospital check-up must be on Wednesday. Ten thirty if she remembered rightly. Oh good! lunch at Jimbo's today. How nice. She could just see Fergus and Finlay in their Scout uniforms and down the other side just out of sight she knew Flick must be standing with the Guides. Fran she couldn't see, Jimbo and Harriet must have been very late, because she hadn't spotted them when she came in.

There was that Dicky Tutt! What cheek he had. Standing there bold as brass, the self-righteous little man. They all said he'd been away with Georgie, disgraceful. Hymn book in hand, singing his head off as though butter wouldn't melt in his mouth. Holding himself up as an example to all those boys. She'd tell Jimbo to remove her grandsons from such a disgusting influence. If she glanced just behind her to her left she could see Georgie Fields, at the end of the pew. Good thing, she was only tiny she wouldn't see a thing if she wasn't on the end. Such a pretty woman. No longer in the first flush of youth but very attractive still. Georgie was watching Dicky! She was. How dare she. People had no shame nowadays. What could she see in him? He was a runt of a man really. Not quite small enough to be a jockey but not far off. That Dicky Tutt was kneeling in prayer. She peeped at him from between her fingers. Crossing himself too! A wonder he wasn't struck by lightning. She'd have a word with the Rector. The kind of thing he was getting up to gave the Anglican Church a bad name, to say nothing of the Scout movement.

When prayers were finished and Dicky stood up to sing he looked across at Georgie. Oh! My goodness! Dicky had twinkled his fingers at her and winked! Georgie was blushing. At least she'd shame enough to blush anyway. Bryn, standing next to Georgie, tall and well able to see Dicky, went a dull red. Grandmama thought, he knows. He knows! There must be something in it then. He's fuming. Georgie in her confusion dropped her hymn book. Not a few heads turned to see. Bryn bent down to pick it up for her. From the corner of her eye Grandmama saw him, *positively* saw him make up his mind. Before she knew where she was Georgie's elbow had been gripped by Bryn and he was manhandling her down the aisle. Perhaps manhandling was too strong a word but she was speeding down the aisle, her feet scarcely touching the stones.

Willie, standing by the door, hastily opened it and let them out. The singing trailed to a standstill, leaving Mrs Peel playing to herself and then she stopped playing thinking she must have played one too many verses. Only Peter's voice carried on without a falter, though Grandmama knew he knew because she saw him watching. Mrs Peel caught up with him and the congregation rallied and attempted to continue singing.

Peter carried on as though nothing had happened, and gradually the congregation pulled itself together. Though Grandmama guessed that quite a few of them would beat a rapid retreat to the Royal Oak at the end of the service.

Just when everything had settled down and she was enjoying the children doing their little play and the parents were beaming with satisfaction at their unbelievably talented children, Caroline fainted. Not dramatically or noisily, she simply slid off her seat and fell into the side aisle. Because the church was so crowded no one noticed at first what had happened. Grandmama was the only one alert enough to take action. She squeezed past Thelma and Valda who were dumbstruck, and past the two children who were beginning to cry and didn't know what to do, and knelt down beside Caroline. She took off her fur jacket and propped Caroline's head on it. Sylvia miraculously appeared from behind her and said, 'I'll get a drink of water. You stay with her.' Grandmama fumbled in her handbag and found her smelling salts. Old-fashioned they might be but she was taking the only possible course of action.

Sylvia went into the choir vestry and by now there was a lot of attention being directed at their part of the church. The children carried on with their play and Peter sitting on a chair with his back to the congregation watching them didn't notice what had happened.

The smelling salts brought Caroline round in a moment. Grandmama whispered, 'No, don't get up, not yet. Lie quite still.'

Sylvia came back carrying an old cup. 'It's all I could find. Here we are, Dr Harris, have a sip. That's it. There we are. Sit up a bit. Lovely.'

Grandmama whispered, 'We'd better get her out into the air. You get the twins.'

Caroline struggled to pull herself together, fearful of disturbing Peter's service. 'I'm so sorry. It's the heat. I'll get up now.'

Grandmama who was supporting her agreed. 'We'll go outside where it's cooler. Come along.'

The congregation was clapping the children and it wasn't until Peter turned to address it that he saw Grandmama helping Caroline out, with Sylvia following behind with the children. Willie, after a consultation with Sylvia, crept down the aisle to whisper to Peter. He nodded his head and then continued to announce the next hymn.

As Mrs Peel launched herself into the first line Peter went down the aisle and into the porch. Supported by Grandmama, Caroline was standing just outside breathing deeply and beginning to revive.

'Peter! It was the heat in there and the smell of the flowers. Please darling, you go back in, I'll be all right . . .'

He took her hand and squeezed it. 'Darling! I'm so sorry you're not well. The fresh air's making you feel better is it? Thank you Mrs Charter-Plackett for helping. I'd no idea.'

'You get back inside. We can manage. I'll take her back to the rectory as soon as she feels able.' She let go of Caroline and wafted her hands at Peter. 'Go along now. Everything's under control.'

'Will you be all right if I go?'

'Of course. I'm much better now.' So he went but didn't know how he would get through the rest of the service. But it was like she said, the church was hot and the smell of the flowers too. Then he remembered their conversation in bed the other night. 'I will tell you when I can.'

The children were clinging to Caroline's skirt not knowing how else to show their concern. Sylvia said, 'Come along, children, you lead the way. We'll get the kettle on and you can give Mummy a lovely cup of tea. She'll like that won't she?' They scurried away each holding one of Sylvia's hands looking back all the time as they walked down the path. Caroline could hear Beth saying 'Is my Mummy *very* poorly, Sylvie?' Oh God, she was. She watched them walking away. She had to be strong, for their sakes. She had to fight.

Grandmama helped her home as soon as she felt able to walk. She didn't come in; left her at the door for Sylvia to take care of, and went back to the service.

Only by a supreme effort of will, apparent to everyone there, did Peter manage to see the service through to the end. As he stood shaking hands with everyone and accepting their concerns for Caroline the truth dawned on him. How selfish could a man be? Occupied with his own work, striving to be a good pastor to his flock, being a father and a husband, the one thing he should have noticed he hadn't. Caroline had been losing weight. In fact she looked quite ghastly. She'd been uncharacteristically short-tempered with him and irritable with the children and not the slightest bit interested in him as a man. Be blunt here, he thought, she hadn't wanted sex, and that had always been one of the mainstays of their marriage.

He was standing at the door nearly twenty minutes, longing to leave, but so many people to see. So many reassuring him that Caroline would be all right, no wonder she fainted. So hot. Lovely service. Thank you, Rector. Lovely as usual. Never better. Sheila came hobbling out on her crutches with Ron in attendance.

'Sheila! Many many thanks . . . The church looks wonderful, truly wonderful! Never better.'

Overcome by his gratitude she muttered her thanks.

'Will you thank your committee personally from me? I'm so grateful for all you do.'

'Of course I will, they are a brilliant team, they've really rallied round this year. And thank you, I'm glad you liked everything. It's time you went home to Dr Harris. See how she is.'

'I will shortly. Mind how you go.'

Finally he excused himself and left.

Sylvia had settled the children down with some toys and Caroline was sitting at the kitchen table sipping tea. The colour had come back into her cheeks and she greeted him with something like her usual enthusiasm.

'So sorry, Peter, for causing a sensation in the service. I really do apologise. I know how important it is to you.' She turned up her face for him to kiss. Peter bent down and kissed her cheek.

'Please don't apologise. I'm only too sorry I couldn't leave to bring you home myself. Sylvia, Willie has nearly finished. You go home and get him lunch. I can cope.'

Sylvia standing out of the line of Caroline's vision pointed her finger at Caroline and said, 'Are you sure?'

'Absolutely.'

Sylvia nodded her head in the direction of the hall. 'I'll leave then.'

He followed her out of the kitchen, closing the door behind him.

Sylvia didn't speak until they'd reached the front door. 'She hasn't confided in me, but you must get her to confide in you. I don't like the look of things, Rector. Not at all.'

'I've tried, but she won't. We've agreed she'll tell me when she's good and ready.'

'Then you'd better try your utmost. This business of you not trespassing on each other's ground is quite out of place now. That girl in there is either ill or there's something worrying her quite dreadfully. I'll be here first thing tomorrow.' With her hand on the front door latch Sylvia turned back and said, 'Remember, I shall want some answers tomorrow morning or else. I think a lot about Dr Harris, you know. It needs sorting.'

Peter stripped off his cassock and hung it in the hall cupboard, braced his shoulders and returned to the kitchen with the firm intention of finding out.

'Don't seem right coming straight in 'ere from church, but I'm dying to know what's going on.' Vera, accompanied most unusually by Don, settled herself down with Jimmy at his favourite table.

Don raised his glass of orange juice and said, 'Here's to you both.'

'And to you,' Jimmy answered. 'Nice to have some male company. Don't expect Willie will be in today, he doesn't on Sundays and not with Dr Harris being taken bad.'

'One time if yer fainted like that it meant one thing.'

'What?'

'Yer were in the club.'

'That's not likely is it. We knows they can't have children.'

Vera's theory having been dismissed she felt quite deflated and sighed. 'Yep! I expect we do. And we know it's not him at fault. He's proved that.'

'Well, then.' Jimmy glanced about him. 'Eh! Georgie's just come in. Got changed out o' that sparkly suit she wears on her rare excursions into church and she's smiling like there's no tomorrow. The cheek of it.'

'Bold as brass that Dicky waving and winkin' in church. Be different if they were kids and single.'

'Well, yer know when Cupid's arrow falls . . .'

'Cupid's arrow! They should 'ave caught it and sent it flying back. At their age, they ought to have more sense.'

Jimmy laughed. 'This wife of yours is very indignant, could she be just a bit jealous, Don? Did you see 'em?'

'No.'

Bryn was busy serving with a grim smile on his face. Even his Flying Officer Kite moustache appeared to be bristling with annoyance. Georgie was pulling pints too, but well down the other end of the bar.

Jimmy called out, 'Feeling better Georgie? It was hot in there wasn't it?'

Bryn scowled. Georgie said, 'It was very hot. I wonder no one else had to leave.'

Someone said, 'They did. Rector's wife left just after you. Went clean out on the floor. Terrible white she was.'

'Oh! So I wasn't the only one then. There we are, one pound eighty please.'

As the customer pocketed his change he said, 'Thought you looked flushed Georgie.'

'I said it was hot.'

Jimmy slyly remarked, 'Your Bryn sized up the situation in quick sticks, 'ad you out in a flash.'

Bryn glared at Jimmy and for a second Jimmy thought he would be coming across and thumping him but the moment passed and Jimmy took a hasty gulp of his ale.

Vera was scandalised. 'Honestly Jimmy! You'll be getting a black eye, you will.'

'Not me, but he might.' He nodded his head in the direction of the saloon door.

Vera and Don twisted round to look. Bel and Dicky had just come in. It was so rare for them both to come in together that everyone would have stared in any case but today, this lunchtime, they not only stared they were appalled. Dicky really was sticking his neck out coming in. Bryn could have a very short fuse on occasion, and as he was something like twice as big as Dicky things could get lively. Roast beef and Yorkshire pudding could wait, something more appetising was on the menu.

To everyone's intense disappointment Bryn's attention was taken by a problem in the dining-room so he had to leave Georgie and Alan behind the bar.

Vera shouted across. 'Good turn-out for the Scouts this morning, Dicky! They're a credit to yer!'

Dicky, who'd changed out of his Scout uniform and was looking quite the dandy in a rather startling bright red polo-necked sweater and black and white checked trousers, shouted 'Thanks Vera! They're a good set of boys, all of 'em! See you've dragged that husband of yours in. What are you getting up to nowadays, Don?'

Don lifted his glass in acknowledgement. He was known as a man of few words was Don but this time he excelled himself. 'More to the point, Dicky, everyone's asking what *you're* getting up to nowadays?'

An audible gasp went round the bar. Vera choked on her drink and had to search for a hanky to dab her chin. As for Jimmy, well there was no other word to use but to say he guffawed. The customers round the table by the fireplace burst into side splitting laughter, but Bel went bright red and looked at the floor and Georgie shook her head in warning which Dicky chose to ignore. 'Oh, this and that yer know,' he said. He raised his glass to Georgie and grinned. 'This and that. Eh! Georgie, have you heard the one about the husband who went home early from work one night and found his wife in bed with . . .'

Bel hit him very hard on the side of his head with the flat of her hand. If his head wasn't ringing with the blow everyone else's was. Then she hit him again on the other side with the other hand. He began backing off but she followed him right round the bar, giving him another good slap with every step she took.

'I'll teach you to show me up in public!' When she was opposite Georgie she stopped slapping and faced her over the bar. 'But for this counter between us I'd be slapping you too!' Bel grabbed hold of Dicky by the neck of his sweater and frogmarched him out. As the saloon door shut on them they could hear Dicky shouting 'Bel! Bel! I haven't finished me drink! Have a heart!'

The customers nearest the windows rushed to watch them go by.

'She still hasn't let go!'

'He's twisting and turning!'

'She's hit him again!'

'He's got away!'

'He's coming back!'

'No, he isn't.'

'Yes, he is!'

'He is! He is! Oh, my God!'

Bryn walked back into the bar from the dining-room at this moment and they all quickly sat down, but their excitement was trembling in the air. Bryn looked round for answers but there weren't any. Everyone was avoiding meeting his eye. He looked at Georgie but she found an urgent necessity for rooting about under the bar for a clean cloth to polish some glasses.

The door burst open and back in came Dicky. He was red faced and breathing fast but never one not to face up to a challenge, he'd come back in to finish his drink. He marched to the bar conscious that all eyes were on him, and as he loved the drama of it all he decided to play his audience to the utmost.

Picking up his drink he stood facing everyone and drank a toast to them all. First to one group and then to another. There were a few sniggers, then downright laughter and then loud applause. But he hadn't realised that Bryn was there watching his every move.

Dicky put his empty glass down on the bar, did a few tap dancing steps and then bowed. As he straightened up Bryn caught hold of his arm.

'Out, you little runt! Out! You're banned!!' Dicky was dragged across the floor for the second time in as many minutes. Bryn flung him out, not caring what happened to Dicky as he staggered down the two steps out onto the road, and when Bryn came back in he slammed the door shut with a loud bang.

'Alan! Where's Alan?'

'Here.' Alan lurching in from the cellar with a crate of bottled beer in his hands asked 'What's up?'

'Can you manage for ten minutes?'

'Yes, of course.' Bewildered he looked round for a clue as to what was going on. But there wasn't a single person looking in his direction, they were all watching Bryn who was glaring at Georgie. She was eyeing the distance between her and the door marked *Private*. Bryn went towards her, a menacing look on his face.

She started to retreat. With a beautifully filed and lacquered finger she prodded the air between her and Bryn. 'You lay one finger on me and I'm out the door and never coming back!'

'Never have done and don't intend to start now. In the office this minute.'

He opened the door into the back and stood aside for her to go through first. Before he shut the door on them they heard Bryn say, 'And now, madam, I want to know what's going on.'

Don finished the last of his orange juice and with a deadpan face, said to Vera, 'Having brought things to a head, I think it's time we went home and you made me my dinner.'

7

Grandmama had thought of asking Harriet to take her to the hospital for her check-up but in the event Harriet was too busy so she'd booked Jimmy to take her in. The bus was so smelly and the times so inconvenient that it was easier to go in with him. This was the first check-up she'd had since moving to Turnham Malpas. They said they'd transferred all her notes so it should just be a formality. She hated having to go, in fact this time she might suggest she never went again. After all, there'd been no recurrence in five years now, there was no more requirement for wasting their time.

She asked Jimmy to drop her off at the main entrance, she wasn't having him know she was going to the cancer treatment department, or else it would be all round the village in no time as she'd found to her cost with the Harvest debacle. The main entrance was obviously part of the original hospital but over the years it had quadrupled in size, and she couldn't find her way. She asked a nurse, she was brown but seemed to know what she was talking about, and set off to follow the directions.

The arrows on the direction signs appeared to point not only straightforward and left and right but, rather significantly, heavenwards too and Grandmama became confused. She pushed through some swing doors and found herself in the antenatal clinic. Really! She waited to find a nurse to ask where to go, but there was only a receptionist sitting at a desk on the far side, so she tripped across between the children and the toys and the mothers in various stages of pregnancy, so many in fact she wondered if they hadn't got television in Culworth yet, and went to ask. The receptionist was on the telephone so Grandmama had to wait. One of the doors marked with a newly painted sign saying *David R. Lloyd-Jones, Consultant* opened and out came Caroline Harris! Of all people! What a coincidence! A very distinguished looking man came out with her and they shook hands and she heard him say 'Good luck' and Caroline said 'Thanks for everything', checked her watch and hurried away.

Well, well. So she was right. It was a baby after all. Looking thin and preoccupied must be bad morning sickness, it took some people like that. Well, fancy! After all these years. A baby.

Grandmama realised the receptionist was addressing her. 'Excuse me! I said "Can I help you?"'

'I think I must be in the wrong department.'

'I would think so too.'

Grandmama's intense eyes gave the receptionist a bleak look and then asked directions. Having had them explained to her twice because she was so excited with what she'd just seen she couldn't take them in, she departed in haste, she was going to be late if she didn't hurry.

Peter couldn't concentrate, he was waiting for Caroline to ring, for today was the day she got the result of her scan. He'd offered to take her in to Culworth and wait with her but she wouldn't hear of it. Now he wished he'd insisted.

'I've a surgery straight afterwards, there isn't any point. I'll ring at lunchtime to let you know. It would mean going in two cars anyway. It's better this way.'

'Look, how about going private?'

'Certainly not. I'm a doctor, I can't take advantage of a privileged system when the majority of my patients can't. That wouldn't do.'

'Of course not, I see that.'

He went to the garage and got her car out for her and brought it round to the front of the rectory.

'Oh thanks, darling.'

'Least I can do. Caroline, I . . .'

She'd cut in to prevent him from saying something encouraging which might penetrate the wall she'd built round herself. 'When I've had my appointment I'm going to see David Lloyd-Jones, I don't need to refresh your memory about him do I?' She'd smiled wickedly at him.

'Of course not! Has he taken up his appointment already then?'

'Started on Monday. Want to congratulate him.'

'So long as that's all!'

'Peter! After all these years! You're not still jealous!'

'Not really. No.' He'd looked away.

'You are! Well, well. Must go or I'll be late.'

He'd kept the conversation as she wanted it. Ordinary. Unemotional. Brisk. If that was how she coped then he'd have to go along with it. 'Bye then! Don't forget to ring!' He'd longed to kiss her, hold her, hug her, longed to suffer it for her, anything but this.

He'd watched her drive away and then stepped into the house thinking about the Sunday when he'd walked back into the kitchen after Sylvia had gone and he'd found Beth sitting on Caroline's knee being cuddled. Her thumb was in her mouth and Caroline was rocking her. 'I do love you, Mummy. Are you better now?'

'Much better, darling. Much better.' Alex had got up from the floor and gone to stand beside her. He'd leaned against her legs, put an arm round her waist and said, 'You're a doctor, can you make yourself better?'

'Sometimes, but sometimes even doctors need help.'

Beth lifted her head from Caroline's shoulder and asked, 'Are you going to need help now?'

'Perhaps.'

Alex said, 'When I'm grown up I'm going to be a doctor.'

Beth wrinkled her nose. 'I'm not. It's nasty being a doctor. You have to stick needles into people like they did when we had our booster to go to school. That was horrid. It hurt.'

'My needles wouldn't hurt. I wouldn't let them. I could make you better couldn't I, Mummy?'

'Of course you could.'

Beth gave him a push. 'You couldn't, you're too little.'

'I'm not!'

'You are!'

'I'm not am I, Mummy? I'm bigger than Beth aren't I?'

Before Caroline could answer Beth sprang off her knee and shouted 'You're not, you're not, we were both born together, so you can't be.'

'I am, look!' They stood back to back and Peter had to confirm that Alex was indeed taller than Beth.

Beth moaned, 'It's not fair.'

'Men are always taller than their mummies. Look at Daddy.'

'They're not! Mr Tutt isn't. He's little and Mrs Tutt is big.' She stretched her arms as wide as they would go.

Caroline had to laugh. 'Go away you two. I want to set the table for lunch. It's been in the oven for ages and I can smell it's more than ready.'

After lunch the two children had gone to play on their bicycles in the back garden leaving Caroline and Peter to finish their coffee.

'Lovely service, Peter, and didn't the church look wonderful? Best ever I think. I was really chuffed with my arrangement. The eucalyptus leaves against the dark wood looked great, they almost lit it up.'

He didn't answer.

Caroline said, 'Hellooo! Anyone at home?'

'Oh yes.'

'Well?'

Not looking at her while he answered Peter said, 'How much longer are you going to leave me in the dark?'

Caroline looked out of the window and watched the children racing each other down the path. Beth's sturdy little legs were pedalling as fast as she could make them, yet Alex's long ones, pedalling far more leisurely, were pulling him ahead of her.

'Well? You haven't answered me. I treasure you, I cherish you above and beyond anyone else on this earth, and yet I am not to know.'

She poured him more coffee, passed him the sugar.

'My darling girl, *it is crucifying me.*'

'*And me.*'

Peter waited. The kitchen clock struck the quarter hour.

Caroline gave a huge sigh and said quietly, almost inaudibly and very very slowly, 'There's no kind way of saying this, no way of letting you down gently, so I might as well say it straight out. I've had a scan because they think . . . they think I might have a growth on my ovaries. I get the results on Wednesday.'

From outside came the excited laughter of their two children. Inside, the kitchen boiler burst into life and the clock ticked away the seconds. Long startling frightening seconds during which Peter almost suffocated with shock. For Caroline's sake he took a deep deep shuddering breath and then another. And then a third, before he had his voice under control. 'My darling! Why ever haven't you told me before? How long have you known?'

'A while.' She reached across the table and stroked his hand.

'What can I say which doesn't sound empty and trite? I am deeply sorry. You've been carrying this burden all alone. How can I possibly have failed you so much that you felt you couldn't share it with me? I am so, so, sorry that I've let you down.' He placed his free hand on top of hers. 'I shan't treat you like a fool and say are you sure, might there be some mistake, I know you too well for that.'

'There is no mistake, darling. And you haven't let me down. It's my fault, I couldn't bear to tell you. I didn't want to break your heart.'

'My heart! What's *my* heart got to do with it? It's you who has it to face.'

'You have it to face, too. Let's be frank. If it's worse than they think then . . . it may mean you coping on your own.'

'Dear God! Dear God!' Peter sat with his elbows resting on his knees and his head in his hands. He sat up again. The shock of what she'd said had drained all the colour from his face, it was deathly white. Just as slowly as she had spoken when she'd broken her news he said, 'Let's look on the bright side. We musn't assume the worst. It could be a matter of a simple operation and hey presto! it's all over and done with. Obviously you'd have to take care and perhaps only work a few hours, not try to do too much, but there's no reason why things couldn't be back to normal in no time at all. Is there?'

'None at all.' Caroline smiled bravely, and he recognised the bravery and held out his arms to her. She got up and went to sit on his knee. 'This is why you fainted is it? I can scarcely manage to ask this but, are you in a lot of pain?'

'Sometimes. But maybe it's all in the mind, fright you know. That's why I get snappy.'

'Snappy? I hadn't noticed! Wednesday. Three days. Will you go to the surgery just the same?'

'Yes, it's easier that way. Keep busy, you know. No time to dwell.'

Peter sat patting her arm, stroking her knee, rubbing his cheek against her hair. 'I've been so blind. I've been absolutely unforgivably blind.'

'I told you not to ask didn't I?'

'I shan't do as you say ever, ever, again. Never. If I want to question something I shall. This not trespassing is ridiculous.'

'No, it's not. It's agreeing that we are two intelligent human beings with rights to our own thoughts and decisions. What could you have done if you'd known? Nothing. No one can.'

'I could have been more considerate.'

'You are already far more considerate than is good for me. I haven't told anyone at all. No one knows and I don't want them to.'

'We shall have to tell Sylvia.'

'Why?'

'Because she told me as she left just now that I . . . that she wanted some answers on Monday or else.'

'I wonder what "or else" will be?'

'Caroline, you must tell her, or I will. It's only fair. We may need to rely on her.'

She held Peter's face between her two hands and studied him closely. With her fingers she traced his eyebrows, and then with her thumbs gently closed his eyelids and kissed them sweetly. 'You are my beloved. All the David Lloyd-Jones in the world can't hold a candle to you. And why I don't know. I wasn't really a church person at all you know, so it wasn't your dog collar that did it, but that morning when you walked into my surgery with your bad throat and your streaming nose and red watery eyes and that dreadful cough and your face all flushed . . .'

'Heavens above! I can't have looked very appealing!'

'You didn't. But you twanged my heart strings and they've never stopped twanging since.'

Peter grinned at her. 'I've often wondered what that curious noise was when I got close.'

'Oh that noise! That's my hormones clamouring!'

Peter began laughing but it changed to tears. She kissed his tears away. 'Stop or I'll be crying too.'

'You're being so brave. I've discovered I'm not brave at all.'

'You will be, just you wait and see.' She got off his knee. 'Let's clear up. The children are very quiet, just look out and see what they're doing.'

He blew his nose, ran his fingers through his hair, and then went to look out of the window. 'You're not going to like this.' He raced out of the back door leaving it wide open. Caroline hurried to see. Alex was balanced on top of the wall and was preparing to leap down into the back lane. Beth was coming back in through the gate hobbling, both her knees badly grazed and holding her hand as though it hurt. Great fat tears were beginning to roll down her lovely rounded cheeks. 'Oh heavens!'

They'd had them both to sort out as, before Peter could reach the wall, Alex had jumped. The drop was something like five feet and the surface of the ground uneven, so he'd hurt himself too.

After they'd settled them both in front of the television well bandaged and drinking hot sweet tea, which Alex declared doctors always said you needed for shock, Caroline had sighed and said 'Never a dull moment!'

So here he was waiting for the telephone to ring. He'd tried concentrating on some study he wanted to do in preparation for the following Sunday but he might as well have been reading the *Radio Times* for what good it did him. Peter's thoughts were interrupted by the phone ringing.

It was Caroline. It was only eleven o'clock. 'I'm coming home.'

'Oh, right!'

'Won't be long.'

'No, right. Drive carefully. Take care.'

Then she told him as soon as she got in. The growth was larger than they'd anticipated and they had to operate a.s.a.p. He hugged her tightly to him. 'Sort of in the next few weeks, when there's a bed, kind of thing?'

'No, this Friday. Gave me a day to get organised.'

'That must mean . . .' He stopped and changed tack. 'There's no organising to do.'

'There is. We have to tell the children, for one thing. I've two meetings next week, I shall send my apologies, say I've had a clash of appointments or something, anything, anything at all, but I don't want people to know.'

Very gently Peter said, 'We can't disguise the fact that you're going in to hospital. They'll have to be told something.'

Caroline slumped down into Peter's chair, laid her head on his desk and wept. She was inconsolable. Her sobbing tore at Peter's heart. In all their lives together he'd never seen her so deeply, so torturously distressed, and there seemed to be nothing he could do to reassure her, to give her comfort. He stood beside her helplessly hugging her shoulders. Gradually the sobbing slowed and she turned to him, put her arms around his waist, and pressed her head against his body.

'Oh Peter! I do need you. Please help me!'

8

Grandmama had been invited to take coffee with Muriel on the morning after her hospital appointment. Despite herself she couldn't but be flattered at the opportunity. Muriel might be a retired solicitor's secretary but she was still called Lady Templeton and had that lovely man Ralph for a husband. Grandmama paid meticulous attention to her toilet and emerged at eleven o'clock feeling on top of the world. As she turned the key in the lock and stood back to admire her cottage with something akin to love in her heart, some children from the school came past, walking in a neat crocodile. With them was that nice girl Kate.

'Good morning, children! Good morning, Miss Pascoe!'

'Good morning, Mrs Charter-Plackett. Isn't it lovely today?'

'It certainly is. Out for a walk?'

'We're going for a visit to Nightingale Farm.'

'How lovely! You've chosen the right day! Bye-bye, children.'

'Bye-bye, Mrs Charter-Plackett.' She distinctly heard at least two of them say 'Bye-bye, Duchess' but she didn't fix them with her most disdainful eye, they were only being complimentary.

Muriel answered the door when she rang. Muriel in smart checked trousers and a lovely rose silk blouse. Give her her due she could dress well, but considering the money they had she should look smart.

'Good day to you Muriel!'

'And to you Katherine. Do come in. Lovely day.'

'It is indeed.'

Ralph came from his study. 'Good morning, Katherine.'

'Dear Ralph! And how are you?'

'Well, thank you, yes, very well. I'm leaving you two ladies to your coffee, I've a business meeting. See you after lunch, my dear.' Ralph kissed Muriel on the lips, when Grandmama thought a kiss on her cheek would have sufficed. She hated it when sex came into a relationship between two people at their age. It amounted to obscenity.

Muriel patted his cheek. 'Take care, Ralph. No fast driving!'

'As if I would!' He laughed and Grandmama saw the young man he used to be and for a second was quite envious of Muriel, but she'd invited her into the sitting-room and the moment passed.

'The kettle's just boiled, I'll make the coffee.'

Grandmama placed herself in the chair, which from its size she guessed was Ralph's. Really this room did have charm. There were a lot of uncoordinated things in it which Ralph must have collected during his years abroad but somehow he and Muriel had made it all gel and the room was welcoming and attractive and it had warmth. The colours of the furnishings were pleasant to the eye too. Lovely mellow creams and soft browns, and a hint of peach which spiced the overall impression.

'Here we are!' Muriel placed her tray on a small table in front of the fire. Grandmama was very gratified to see that the family silver had been brought out in her honour. Coat of arms no less!

Muriel poured the coffee into a china cup so thin Grandmama thought she could see right through it. There was a matching plate and she put on it two of the homemade biscuits Muriel offered her.

'This is delightful. So civilised!'

'We are!' Muriel laughed.

'I didn't mean *you* weren't, but some of them around here are definitely not civilised.'

'It doesn't do to think that you know. They're all kind well-meaning people. Salt of the earth.'

'Well! After what happened on Sunday in the public house, I do wonder!'

'It all adds to life's rich tapestry.'

'I know something to add even more to life's rich tapestry as you call it. Oh yes. I had occasion to visit the hospital yesterday . . .' Muriel's instant concern for her made Grandmama have to reassure her. 'Only for a check-up, I shan't have to go again.' Muriel relaxed and Grandmama continued her story. 'I got lost, it has such a bewildering layout and I had to ask at reception in the antenatal clinic which way to go. Well, I was waiting while the receptionist finished a long-winded conversation about a changed appointment or something and who should I see! Guess!'

'I don't know. A patient you mean?'

'Yes, exactly that.'

'I don't know anyone expecting a baby in the village.'

'Well, there is someone. She fainted on Sunday.'

Muriel was nonplussed. 'Fainted on Sunday! Someone else fainted too then?'

'Only one, my dear Muriel, only one.'

'You can't mean Caroline.'

'The very one. Coming out of the consultant's room. He said "Good luck" and she said "Thanks for everything". I guessed when she fainted that that might be it, but I got confirmation didn't I? Otherwise what would she be doing in the antenatal clinic? She doesn't work at the hospital does she?'

'Not any more. No. But I understood . . .'

'So did we all, but there are things that can be done nowadays aren't there and she has been looking decidedly peaky of late. Morning sickness of course, but you won't know about that.'

'Well, no, I don't. I'm amazed though. Truly amazed, oh she will be pleased. So very pleased.' Muriel clapped her hands with delight. 'How absolutely lovely.' She sipped her coffee, took a bite of her biscuit and then said, 'But we'd better not say anything, you never know.'

'Why ever not?'

'Because . . . well, I don't know why but it would be indelicate and thoughtless to spread the news, just in case . . .'

'Indelicate in this day and age? When they're doing it, well *almost* doing it I hope, in full view on the television, I don't think we need to be coy about it!'

'Doing it? Doing what? Who is?'

'Really, Muriel, I sometimes wonder if you are in the real world at all. However to use your own words I will refrain from being indelicate and we'll close the subject.'

Muriel sat silently contemplating her guest, thinking about Caroline and Peter. They couldn't be. On the other hand Katherine did have a point, and she was very astute, it must have been Caroline she saw. A lovely glow filled her, she felt so warmed by the news. But she wouldn't say a word to anyone, well only to Ralph.

'If I might be so bold, Katherine, I think it would be best for them to tell us the news themselves. Perhaps it's early days and they're not quite sure, sometimes there are mishaps.'

'But everyone will be so pleased for them. I know, I am. Those twins might be Caroline's pride and joy but every time she looks at them she can't fail to remember how she came by them.'

Muriel was indignant. 'Well, really!'

'Who wouldn't want children to that gorgeous man. I think he's the most attractive man I've met in years. Were I but thirty years younger, well between you and me, forty years younger, I could set my cap at him.'

Muriel began to boil. 'I think you need to choose your words more carefully. "Set your cap" indeed. I've never heard such a thing.'

'Grow up, my dear. You can't mean to tell me you haven't noticed how attractive he is, the sheer delight of it is *he* isn't aware he is! I bet there's many a female heart fluttered madly when he's looked at them with those deep blue eyes of his. I should think he has to fight them off in droves! It must be a constant worry to Caroline, especially when he's strayed once and with such dire consequences!'

Muriel positively steamed. She got to her feet and proclaimed, 'I had looked forward very much to this morning but I'm rapidly beginning to regret inviting you. I don't know how you can have such thoughts running through your head.' She heaved in a great breath and continued fiercely, 'It's preposterous! Indeed outrageous!'

Grandmama's cup rattled in the saucer, she was so incensed. She placed it on the little side-table by her chair and stood up. Her cheeks were wobbling with fury. 'That's the last time I shall tell you any news Muriel Templeton! Preposterous indeed! Outrageous! I'm only speaking the truth, as you well know. What's wrong with the truth?'

'Sometimes it's best left unsaid.'

'Is it indeed. When I'm proved right about the baby I hope you will eat your words and apologise to me! I think it best if I leave now. Thank you for the coffee and good morning to you.' Grandmama left Muriel's sitting-room in a rage. She had to struggle to get the front door opened, and when she did she couldn't face the thought of going home and being in a rage all by herself, but didn't know where to go.

Then she decided, and stormed off in the direction of the Royal Oak having a real need of something to fortify herself after that little con-frontation. She pushed open the saloon door and marched in. It was the first time she'd been in there and she was agreeably surprised by the furnishings and the general pleasurable air of the place. Quite upmarket she thought. Georgie was behind the bar.

'A whisky, please. Make it a double.'

'Why, how nice to see you, Mrs Charter-Plackett.' Georgie served her and said, 'On the house, seeing as it's your first visit.'

'Why thank you.' She downed it in one go.

'My word, you look as though you needed that.'

'I did. There are times when Muriel Templeton's Goody-Two-Shoes attitude is distinctly trying. I'll have another.'

'Very well.'

She downed the second one and then proffered a ten-pound note. 'Take for two, I need another, but I'll drink that slowly with water. I don't like standing at the bar, would you care to sit down and join me, you're not busy.'

'For a while yes, I will.'

'Take for another drink for yourself then.'

'Thanks.'

Grandmama went to sit by the log fire in the huge inglenook fireplace. At least it's a genuine one she thought, not made with modern bricks trying to look ancient by being blackened with synthetic soot.

Georgie chose a stool and sat down beside her. 'A fire's comforting isn't it?'

'It is. I like my cottage for having an open fire. You can dream dreams.'

'Ah! Yes.' Georgie sat, drink untouched, staring into the fire.

'You look as though you have dreams to dream.'

Georgie sighed. 'Ah, well!'

'I heard about Dicky.'

'You did?'

'Listen to me, my dear, if you will. I know I don't know you very well, but perhaps I can offer some advice, you should *never* pass up a chance of happiness. Life doesn't present us with many bouquets and when it does, one should hold out one's hands and grasp it.'

'Think so?'

'I'm sure so. There's nothing worse than living with regret. Nothing. Believe me. I know.' She sipped her whisky and decided to change the subject. 'I know you won't have heard this, because I think I'm the only one to know, except for Muriel Templeton that is, but I believe we shall be hearing the patter of tiny feet at the rectory before long.'

Georgie's face changed from dejection to delight. 'Really! I'd no idea. Well, that's wonderful! Really wonderful. Dr Harris will be thrilled. Is it she who told you?'

'No, but quite by chance I met her in the antenatal clinic at the hospital. And after fainting on Sunday . . .'

'I didn't know that.'

'Well, you went out before it happened. That Dicky is certainly a card isn't he? Bold as brass.'

Georgie blushed. 'I do wonder what he'll do next.'

'Bryn angry?'

'Oh yes. He is. Poor Bryn. We've been married twenty years and each year that goes by I . . .'

'I know. Even the smallest habit annoys.'

Georgie looked at Grandmama, grateful for her insight. 'That's just it. All the magic's gone. Every single little bit. I sometimes think if he asks me once more to do a job for him, you know, order this, order that, wash this, wipe that, ring him, ring them, I'll murder him. He thinks because it's for the business I should find it fun. Well, I don't, not any more. The only conversations we have are about work.'

'Tell him.'

'I have but he can't understand what I'm talking about.'

'More fool him, try once more and then go in search of your own happiness.'

'Hop it you mean?'

'Yes, go. Is that what Dicky wants?'

'He's never said, not yet. He can't really, we've not reached that stage. And then there's Bel.'

'Of course. Poor Bel. It can't be fun for her.'

'It's not fun for any of us.' She got up to go, a customer had come in, and she left Grandmama sitting by the fire. Georgie's cheerful 'Hi there! What can I get for you?' sounded false, but the customer didn't appear to notice.

Grandmama finished her whisky and thought next stop the Store. There were a few things she needed and she was dying for Harriet to hear about the baby.

'Hello, Linda! Harriet in?'

'Just gone to collect Fran. Mr Charter-Plackett's in his office though.'

'Thank you, dear.' She marched into the back, nodded in passing to Mrs Jones, and headed for Jimbo.

'Hello, Mother. Here take a pew. Won't be a minute.' Without getting up he pulled a stool out for her from beside his filing cabinet and continued tapping away on his computer. Grandmama waited. She never thought of Jimbo as an organised person but here in his office he most certainly was. Everything filed away, labelled, standing straight, even his desk was uncluttered. He stopped typing and swung his chair round to face her.

'And what can I do for my dear mother today?'

'I'm forgiven then?'

'For what?'

'Making all that stir about the Harvest. I'd no idea it would cause so much trouble. They do get on their high horses don't they?'

'Well, you're a newcomer, it'll take you about fifty years to be accepted for what you are.'

'Too damn late for me then.'

'Almost too damn late for me!'

'Oh, I don't know, I think you're doing all right. Everyone always speaks well of you.'

'Till I offend their sensibilities and then it'll be curtains for Jimbo Charter-Plackett and Company.'

'Nonsense! It was really Harriet I intended to see. I've got wonderful news.'

Jimbo's love of gossip made him prick up his ears at the prospect. 'What? Tell me.'

'I do believe Caroline Harris is expecting a baby.'

Jimbo met this gem with total silence.

Rattled by his silence Grandmama demanded, 'Well? Aren't you pleased for them?'

'I don't know all the details of why she can't have children, obviously Caroline hasn't confided something so sensitive to either Harriet or me, but I think you're wrong. What makes you think she is?'

Grandmama told him. He shook his head. 'Look, she has all sorts of medical connections, both her parents are doctors, she knows all kinds of medics, it could just have been a visit to a family friend. Take my advice and say no more.'

'Don't be ridiculous. They'll want everyone to be pleased.'

'Not if it's not true they won't.' Jimbo stood up. 'Time I was relieving my help.'

'The trouble with everyone in this village is that they're all too good to be true. That Muriel Templeton is a pain, she was quite . . .'

'Have you told her?'

'Yes.'

'Well, at least she won't spread it around. Now do as I say and not another word.'

He got engrossed behind the till so it wasn't until he heard a customer relaying the news to a neighbour whom she'd bumped into while choosing a card for her dad, that he looked up and saw his mother outside on the seat with a tight knot of villagers around her and he realised too late she'd done exactly the opposite of his advice.

The village hummed with the news that night and those who hadn't been told in person heard it over the telephone. Delight broke out like a rash.

Not wanting to worry them for longer than there was any need, they'd broken the news to the children about Caroline going into hospital that afternoon, when Sylvia brought them home from school.

Both had understood immediately. 'You are very poorly then, Mummy!'

'Yes, I am. They're going to take away what it is that's making me have tummy ache.'

Alex looking relieved said, 'Oh, if it's only tummy ache take some of our tummy ache medicine, we don't mind sharing do we, Beth?'

Beth looked scornful. 'You are silly.' She walked away, took out the doll she liked the best and sat down and began to rock it, her thumb in her mouth.

Alex burst into tears and rushed to Peter for comfort. 'I don't want my Mummy to go into hospital. Tell her she's not to.'

'If you had tummy ache and needed to go to hospital I wouldn't stop you from going there to get better would I? So we mustn't stop Mummy. We want Mummy to get better don't we?'

'Yes, but there'll be no one to tuck me up at night and give me a kiss.'

'Well, you'll have to make do with me and your Sylvie, just for a while and you'll be able to talk to Mummy on the telephone too, won't he Mummy?'

'Of course. Every night.'

'Will it be weeks and weeks and weeks and weeks?'

Caroline answered 'No, of course not. Just a little while.' She looked to see how Beth was coping and saw the reason for her silence. She was rocking rapidly backwards and forwards and great rivers of tears were running down her cheeks. 'Beth, come to Mummy.' She shook her head. 'Please, darling, Mummy wants a cuddle.'

Beth dropped her doll and raced into Caroline's arms. With her chubby little arms wrapped tightly round Caroline's neck she cried, 'Oh, Mummy, I do love you.'

'I love you too, so very, very, much.' Then she too burst into tears. Alex struggled down out of Peter's arms and went to hug his mother.

Peter, his eyes brimming with tears said, 'This won't do. We've all got to cheer up. Mummy won't be away long and we've all to be glad she's going to get better. Now, come on, let's dry our tears. Each one of us. Poor Mummy is going to be sad if we all cry, and that's not fair. Come on you two, cheer up! We must all be brave.'

There came a knock at the sitting-room door. It was Sylvia. She'd been crying too. 'I'll be here eight at o'clock tomorrow as usual, Dr Harris, good night. Rector, there's just a message I have to give to you, could you come?'

She led the way into his study. 'Close the door, sir.'

'Couldn't it wait?'

'No. It couldn't I'm afraid. I don't know how to tell you this, but forewarned is forearmed, I'm glad it was me went to collect the children, and do you know why?' Peter shook his head. 'Because the news is all round the village that . . . I don't want to say this at this moment but there's no way I can get out of it, you've got to know . . . there's a rumour started that Dr Harris is . . . pregnant.'

'What?!'

'Shhh! It's true, there is. How or why it started I do not know, but there we are. And I said I didn't know what they were talking about and I was very upset, as if things aren't bad enough as it is.' Sylvia sat down on the nearest chair and sobbed.

Peter clenched his fists. The crushing weight of it all was unbearable. Just when they were needing support. That this should happen now. He stood silently for a minute and then said, 'Thank you, Sylvia, for letting me know. Nothing could be further from the truth, could it?'

Sylvia made a brave attempt to collect herself. 'Indeed not. I want you to know I shall do absolutely everything I possibly can to make things go smoothly. I shall do as many hours as need be and I shan't expect paying for it, in fact I shall be insulted if you offer it. If, though I don't suppose it will be necessary, you need to stay very late, like all night late at the hospital, Willie, that is if you don't mind him being here but I wouldn't want to be on my own with the children just in case, and I, we'll sleep in that room I used to use when I first came. I've already put sheets on the bed. So there's no need to worry.' She wiped her nose and said, 'I think the world of her you know. I can't hardly bear it.'

'Neither can I. But she's being so brave.'

'I wouldn't expect anything else. She's strong but that doesn't mean she isn't afraid. Shall we tell the truth then?'

'We can't avoid it. Just enough of the truth, not too much. She doesn't want a big fuss. Thank you, Sylvia.'

'Remember anything at all, any time. I shall come in every day, Saturdays and Sundays too. So don't worry about that. We shall probably have her home in no time at all, and then we can look after her ourselves and get her better, eh? I'll be off now. I'm sorry I had to tell you that, but I had to hadn't I? Couldn't have you being greeted with congratulations not having been forewarned.'

'That's right. Thanks.' Peter nodded not able to trust himself to say any more.

'I'll be off then. We'll be thinking about you both. Good night.'

Damn them! Damn them! How on earth had they got hold of such a heartbreaking idea. It wouldn't have been amusing at the best of times, but now! Thank God, he'd been worried about getting back in time and had asked Sylvia to pick up the children. If Caroline had gone! It didn't bear thinking about. If he'd gone he'd probably have hit whoever'd said it.

He heard Caroline calling, 'Peter? Is everything all right?'

Opening the study door, he checked there were no tears on his face, and called out brightly, 'Everything's fine. Just coming.'

9

It didn't take much imagination to guess who it was who'd climbed up the church tower and out onto the parapet to fasten the banner up there to the square bit of the tower below the spire. *Happy Birthday Georgie* it read, in bright pink letters on a white background. The letters ran in a line one below the other right to the bottom where it had been secured to the drain pipes either side of the tower door.

The stockman who'd rented one of Ralph's houses in Hipkin Gardens was the first to see it when he left for milking at Nightingale Farm at half past four. The next was Malcolm from the dairy coming specially early to do his round because his girlfriend was due any minute and he wanted to get back as soon as he could. There wasn't much Malcolm didn't know about the village and he chuckled to himself, wondering what their response would be when they woke to find that. They couldn't miss it. Definitely they couldn't!

The people in the queue waiting for the first bus into Culworth reeled with laughter.

'Oh God! It must be Dicky!'

'He's a right one.'

'And not half!'

'But poor Bryn.'

'Poor Bel.'

'Whatever next.'

'Wish my husband would think up something like that for my birthday, I'm lucky if I get a card when he gets home from work. Thinks he's done wonders "Well, yer've got it on the day 'aven't yer?" he goes. Huh!'

'I'd wring his neck if it was my wife!'

'Give over! You couldn't knock the skin off a rice pudding, you couldn't!'

Willie, unable to sleep because Sylvia had been tossing and turning all night worrying about Dr Harris, went out earlier than usual to set about his duties of putting the heating on and getting the children's hymn books out ready for the school Friday morning service, except Kate Pascoe would have to conduct it seeing as the Rector would be taking Dr Harris into Culworth as soon as they'd seen the twins off to school. He went through the lych-gate and took his regular long distance view of the church before he headed up the path. He couldn't believe his eyes when he spotted the banner. Not that it took much spotting it was so big, you couldn't avoid it. Blowing there, brazenly in the breeze! Just wait till he got his hands on that Dicky Tutt. Always supposing it was him. But it must be. Certainly wouldn't be Bryn. Nice chap but not very imaginative.

'The fool. The absolute fool. That Dicky needs his brains examining.'

Willie unlocked the church and went to switch on the heating. Rector didn't like the church to be cold. My, what changes he'd wrought since he came. Wasn't like the same place. Everything alive, bouncing with energy. Congregation bigger than it had ever been in his lifetime, and all of 'em people who *wanted* to be there, not coming just because it was the thing to do.

Halfway down the aisle Willie stopped in his tracks. This morning of all mornings he'd have to have a quick word with his Maker. He wasn't what could be called a praying person, due respect and all that, but not prayerful. But this morning he went to kneel in the little memorial chapel, where he knew Peter prayed every morning of his life except today, and said a prayer for Caroline. 'I may not be much cop Lord, at praying but, by Jove, I'm praying today. I 'aven't got words like the Rector has, no book learning yer see apart from the village school, but if yer can listen to a prayer from an ordinary man then this is it. Whatever you do don't call on Dr Harris to be one of your angels this week. Nor for that matter any day in the immediate future. The Rector needs her something bad and them children which, as you know Lord, she took under her wing under very difficult circum-stances, they don't half need her too. Matter of fact, we all do, she's such a good young woman and we all love her. So if it pleases you Lord, leave her with us. Amen. By the way, I shall be back tomorrow, expecting to thank you for bringing her through the operation. Amen.'

He got up from his knees and for extra measure crossed himself, then set off to get the big step ladder to see if he could reach the banner and drag it down.

When he got outside with the ladder he found Dicky standing on the church path with his camera, laughing fit to burst.

'Hey! Willie doesn't it look good. Won't she be pleased?'

'Pleased! See here, it won't do. Simply won't do. When the Rector sees it he'll be livid.'

'Livid? Whatever for?'

'The church isn't here to display your love messages, Dicky Tutt. It's disgusting!'

'Disgusting! What's disgusting about being in love?'

'You're both married or has that escaped your notice? You ought to know better.'

'You're a spoilsport you are. Move your ladder and buzz off and do whatever you're going to do and then you won't be the wiser. I want to take a photo.'

'I'll do no such thing. Hop it, go on, hop it.'

'Come on, Willie, you know what it's like when you're in love. Give us a chance. I want her to have a memento. Go on, just one teeny weeny photo. No one will know.'

'It'll be you having the memento if you don't move, and your memento'll be a black eye. Now get off home to Bel. You ought to be ashamed.'

A thought suddenly occurred to Dicky. 'What are you doing with that ladder? You're not thinking of taking Georgie's banner down?'

'I am.'

'You're not.'

'We've the school coming for morning prayers in an hour. I'm not having the evidence of your . . . your illegal amours 'anging 'ere for them to see.'

'But that means Georgie won't see it, she never gets up before nine with working late.'

'Hard cheese.'

'Just one photo, that's all I ask.'

'No, I'm not moving from this path.'

'Right then, I'll have you on the photo, and it'll look as if you helped me to put it up.'

Willie already angry almost exploded and he shouted, 'Don't you dare. Take your damned camera away.'

Dicky laughed, went much further down the path turned round and took several photographs. He guessed that Willie would be hardly recognisable because he had to stand so far away to get the whole of the banner in, but so long as Willie was left in doubt that was all that mattered.

'I'm having them developed this morning at a shop near work, I'll let you have a couple of prints!'

'Don't bother!' Willie propped the ladder against the church wall and set off down the path to see Dicky off church property. Dicky dashed away, still laughing, leaving Willie angrier than he could remember ever having been. He knew the Rector wouldn't see the banner before he left, it was out of sight from the rectory, but he didn't want him coming back from the hospital and finding it there.

But no matter how he tried he couldn't budge it. Now what could he do? There was no way he could climb up the tower steps. He hadn't done that for years, not since he was a boy when he'd been taken so ill climbing them on the annual saint's day. He'd managed to get to the top and then all but collapsed when he'd gone out and looked over the edge and seen how high up he was. So ill he was paralysed and they'd had to carry him down. Acrophobia they'd said it was and he'd never climbed the tower since. He'd have another go and then . . . but it wouldn't come down. Drat that Dicky. Drat him. He'd have to get Jimmy. He'd do it, he'd go knock him up right now. But Jimmy must have left early, because there was no reply.

Peter came home from the hospital, parked his car outside the rectory and went straight to Church to say his morning prayers. He saw the banner as soon as he went through the lych-gate. He guessed immediately that it must be Dicky's doing. Why on earth hadn't Willie got it down?

'I tried, sir, I did, but I couldn't budge it.'

'Not even from the top? What on earth has he fastened it with then?'

Willie looked uncomfortable. 'Well, not from the top, no.'

'Why ever not? I would have preferred the children not to see it.'

'So would I, sir.'

'Then why ever not?'

Willie shuffled his feet and then had to confess. 'You see, Rector, I never go up there.'

'Never go up there?'

'I've got acrophobia?'

'What's that?'

'Fear of heights.'

'Are you telling me that you've been the verger all these years, how many is it now?'

'Fifteen.'

'And you've never been up there?'

'I am.'

'Who does then? Who sweeps and things?'

'Jimmy. He does it for me.'

Despite his anxiety Peter had to laugh. 'Well, well.'

Willie had to ask. 'How's the Doctor, is she all right? When you left her, you know?'

Peter said, looking anywhere but at Willie, 'Being brave, not wanting to worry me. They said to ring about four, but I think I'll go rather than ring.'

'That'll be best. Yes. Now about this banner. I've knocked at Jimmy's door but he's not in.'

'I'll do it. Have you the key? How did Dicky get in?'

Willie scowled his annoyance. 'I don't know, but when he gets back from work I'll ask him. Taken a photo of it he has. I could strangle him.'

'I'm not too pleased with him myself.'

'You'd better take scissors or, I know, I've got my Stanley knife in my tool box in the boiler house, I'll get that.'

Peter began the long climb up the stone spiral staircase. It was narrow, and the steps too small for his large feet, it had been built for men much shorter than himself. Once he caught his knee on the rough stone walls, twice he caught an elbow. As he climbed he thought about the bells being rehung and them ringing out across the fields. That would be wonderful. He imagined the sounds of the bells calling people to worship again like they had done for hundreds of years. Thank you Mr Fitch. In fact thank you Mr Fitch for the central heating, for the newly repaired organ and now thank you Mr Fitch for the bells. Decent chap but he seemed to have been born without a heart, though he had been visibly moved by Sadie's death. Death. For now he wouldn't think about it. Not today. He climbed the rest of the stairs, pushed open the trap door and climbed out.

He'd been up before on All Saint's Day each year but then it was always so busy that there wasn't time to contemplate the view. He unfastened the Stanley knife, secured the blade in place and went to cut the ropes holding the banner. Dicky had certainly done a good job. He leaned over to shout to Willie, and saw Georgie standing on the path talking to him. Even from such a height he could see she was agitated, and when she saw him looking down at her, her face flushed red.

'OK, Willie! Here goes!' Peter sliced through the ropes and the banner fell fluttering to the ground. He watched Willie begin cutting through the bottom ropes and then turned his attention to the view. From this side he could see the village. As he walked round the parapet he could see the Big House, then Bickerby Rocks, the fast moving traffic on the bypass and, he thought he could just catch a glimpse of the great spires of Culworth Abbey something like eight miles away. Between Turnham Malpas and Culworth were rolling fields, some still stubble, some already ploughed for next year. Next year. Would there be a next year for him? If Caroline . . . But then there'd be the children. He'd have to keep going for their sakes. Prayer. He'd go say prayers.

By the time he got to the bottom of the tower Georgie had gone and Willie was still struggling to fold up the banner. 'Too blowy, sir, can't keep control of it.'

Between them they managed to roll it up and store it in the boiler house.

'Tell Dicky I want to see him. Not today, I've other things on my mind but I'll see him tomorrow some time. Georgie, what did she think?'

'Half embarrassed, half delighted. He'd rung her from work and told her to come out to have a look. He's a fool is Dicky.'

'More than a fool. Just going to say prayers. Here's the tower key.'

As Peter was leaving the church after his prayers he met the Duchess coming in with an armful of flowers.

'Good morning, Mrs Charter-Plackett! Lovely flowers.'

'I'm taking a turn at doing the altar flowers with Sheila Bissett being laid up. I would normally have done them Saturday morning but I'm going out with Harriet and the children so I thought I'd do them today. Aren't they lovely? Mr Fitch gave me them. Such a kind man.'

'Very generous.'

'He is. I can't let this chance go by, seeing as we're on our own. Will you allow me to say how pleased I am?'

'How pleased you are?'

'Yes, about the, well I know it's a secret, but about the baby. I saw Caroline in the hospital in the antenatal clinic. I suspected as much when she fainted in church, but when I saw her there I knew. You must be thrilled and I expect she is too.' She was so delighted with herself she didn't notice the change in Peter's expression.

'It's you then who spread this rumour?'

The Duchess was about to exonerate herself from being a rumour-monger when something in his tone of voice pulled her up short.

'Rumour?'

'Yes. In truth she's having an operation today. I took her to the hospital this morning. For cancer. Ovarian cancer.'

The Duchess was left standing completely devoid of speech. She watched Peter walk down the path, and disappear from sight as he passed Willie's cottage. The blood hammered in her head and she couldn't see properly. Whatever had she done? That poor man. He wouldn't have said that just to upset her, would he? Not something so serious as . . . cancer? She knew all about the fear that word instilled in one's soul. She'd known all about that, oh yes. But a young woman Caroline's age and with children to bring up. It didn't bear thinking about and here she'd been telling everyone . . . She'd never live it down. Fifty years Jimbo had said. It might as well be one hundred and fifty. Well, she hadn't meant to be malicious. Not at all. She was only going on the facts. Facts? People fainted for all sorts of reasons, as had Caroline. Obviously she *had* been seeing a friend in the antenatal department. It took her well over an hour to arrange the flowers. She'd so looked forward to doing it and now she couldn't make them look good for love nor money. Flowers! She never wanted to see another flower as long as she lived. Lived. What if Caroline . . . She'd better have a quick word of prayer before she left. In fact she'd better be on her knees all day. Contrite heart. That was what she'd better have. A contrite heart.

Unable to wait any longer and wanting to be out of the house before the children came home from school and begged to go with him, Peter left the rectory at half past two. He drove steadily because he knew his mind was elsewhere. Past the dreaded crossroads where he'd had that strange encounter with the tractor, and on into Culworth. It was always difficult to find a space in the hospital car park at any time of day, but he could take advantage of the fact he was an official hospital padre and he parked in the space specially reserved for them.

Being familiar with the hospital layout he was in the ward in no time at all. The nurses greeted him and assured him things were going fine, she was recovering nicely and yes of course he could see her.

She was laid flat on her back, fastened to a drip and what seemed to him a multiplicity of tubes and wires.

'Caroline! Darling! It's Peter.'

Her eyelids fluttered and then opened, she looked vaguely at him and a smile started on her mouth but she slid back into sleep before it had happened. He found a chair, put it beside the bed, sat down and took hold of her hand.

Helpless. Totally vulnerable, his Caroline was right now. Always so organised and energetic. So loving and kind and considerate. He didn't deserve her. This business of having to put others before his own, it was asking too much of anyone. A nurse came in to do routine checks.

'Good afternoon, Reverend. You're not to worry, you know, she's doing fine.' She patted Caroline's cheek and said, 'Dr Harris! Hello!' Caroline stirred and opened her eyes. 'All right?' There was no answer, Caroline was sleeping again.

'Everything seems OK. She won't be talking for a while yet. Why don't you go for a cup of tea or something? Another hour and she'll be coming round properly.'

'I do have another patient to see. I might do that and then come back.'

'Good idea.'

But he wasn't prepared for what he saw when he came back. He couldn't see her for the hospital staff filling the room.

'Stand away!' They all stepped back from whatever they were doing and he had a clear view of Caroline's body jerking with the electric shock. The monitor was displaying a straight line, no heartbeat at all. A nurse was counting and rhythmically pressing her hands on Caroline's chest and they were giving her oxygen and everything fell into a sort of chaotic madness and all Peter could do was call out 'Caroline? Caroline?'

Someone snapped 'Get him out!'

'Come along, sir, leave her to us.' He felt hands steering him towards the door. He didn't want to go out. His place was beside *her*. Peter turned to go back in. 'Better leave her to us. We're doing all we can.' He felt hands pushing him away again. The sounds of instructions, of haste, of a kind of controlled desperate energy came through the door. She couldn't be left alone not right now. He went back in. They were too busy to notice him. The line on the monitor was straight.

'Caroline! Caroline!' He called in his loudest voice. The sound ricocheted back off the walls, deafening in its intensity in that small room. There was a blip on the screen, and another and another, then the line went straight again and then restarted irregularly, and suddenly the blips were regular and the razor sharp alertness in the room reduced and with it the intensity of the last few minutes. There was an audible sigh of relief.

'Right. Thanks everyone, she's back.' The line on the screen had a reassuring steadiness about its blips. The doctor stood beside the bed, cautious, alert, checking the controls, watching her breathing, observing her colour.

The staff began putting away the equipment disappearing to other duties leaving Peter with Caroline and the doctor. He became aware of Peter standing the other side of the bed ashen and trembling and saying 'I'm not leaving. I'm staying here. No one is making me leave. Do you understand? I won't be turned out. I'm staying with her.'

'Of course. All night if you wish. My word, she gave us a few anxious moments there. Can't do to lose a good doctor can we?'

Peter's voice was shaky. 'Nor a good wife, come to that.'

'No, indeed. Definitely not. I'm so sorry. A doctor will be in and out and a nurse will be in very frequently to check her but should you have any anxiety just ring. We'll need to find out what caused that little hiccup, if we can.'

'Little hiccup! She died!'

The blips continued steadily.

'Her heart stopped momentarily.'

'Well then, she died. Don't try to pacify me with euphemisms, I'm not for pacifying. In any case it was longer than a moment.'

'I'm sorry, very sorry.'

The blips kept going on, beating away.

'What caused it?'

'Bad reaction to the anaesthetic possibly. We'll have to find out. Most unexpected. Anyway, things have settled down now. If you need anything you've only to ask. She should be making good progress from now on.'

Less ashen than he was and with the trembling under control Peter thanked him. He pulled forward his chair, which had been pushed out of the way in the emergency, and sat down again beside her. Her hand he took in his own and bent his head to kiss it. He felt a very slight squeeze of her fingers and he thought he saw a tiny almost imperceptible smile on her lips.

Then his reaction began. Sweat rolled down his face as though he'd been running a marathon in a scorching midday sun. His knees went to jelly and his hands were shaking so violently he had to release Caroline's for fear of upsetting her. A nurse came in to check the monitor, but didn't speak. Peter couldn't have answered her if she had; his throat had closed up and his teeth were clamped tightly together. The nurse noted his ashen complexion and the sweat running down his face.

'Everything's going to be fine, Mr Harris. Look.' She pointed to the blips. 'No need to worry. Not now.'

He nodded.

'I'll go put the kettle on, make you a cup of tea.'

The tea was in his shaking hands almost as she spoke. Time, somehow, had done a head over heels. He tried to get the cup to his mouth. But he shook so much it was spilling everywhere. The nurse took it from him and held it to his mouth herself. He was icy cold. The tea was burning hot.

'Go on, drink some more, it'll do you good.'

Slowly the shaking stopped and he took charge of the cup himself, with one eye on the screen he finished the tea right to the bottom of the cup where he could see grains of sugar undissolved.

The nurse held out her hand to take his cup. 'Another one?'

'Yes, please. I'm so thirsty.'

'You've had a bit of a shock, that's why.'

'You could say that.'

'Well, more than a *bit* of a shock. Won't be a minute.'

Briefly he went to the telephone to speak to Sylvia and explain he wouldn't be coming home just yet, possibly not until the early hours and he would be glad if she and Willie could stay and could he speak to the children and yes, Caroline was doing fine and thank you for everything. He reassured the children, yes, Mummy is doing very well. Yes, he was staying with her for a while and be good for Sylvia. Yes, he'd be home in the morning. Night, night, Beth. Night, night, Alex. Yes, he'd give Mummy a great big kiss. Night, night, sleep tight. God bless you both.

10

If he could, Jimbo avoided working in the Store on Saturdays but this Saturday it was unavoidable. Added to which Harriet was upset about Caroline, his mother was distraught at what she'd done and generally he sensed a black cloud over his life he could well have done without.

Life must go on though, he'd lined the morning papers up neatly on their shelf by the till, he'd tackled the meat counter, the vegetables were looking their sprightly best, the stationery racks were filled to bursting and it was October and Christmas would be upon him before he knew where he was. Last night had been a good night. If there was one thing he liked it was a good party and that twenty-first last night had been such good fun. He remembered he must ring Pat Jones and tell her how pleased he was with her efforts. People were a continuous surprise to Jimbo, who'd have thought Pat had such potential. Well, that was one thing he could give himself a pat on the back for, finding her potential and putting it to work to his advantage, and hers come to think of it.

The bell jingled and in came Peter. To Jimbo's eyes he looked terrible. Gaunt, exhausted, shredded with anxiety.

'Good morning, Peter. Well, what's the news?'

'When I left about three this morning she was beginning to shape up nicely. I've rung just now and she's continuing to improve, so I'm taking the children to see her this afternoon.'

'Thank God for that!'

'I have. Just got some shopping to do, I want to take something in for her, and Sylvia wants a few things too. I'll just take a look round.'

'Feel free. I'd be grateful if you'd take her some flowers from Harriet and me. With our love.'

'Thank you, thank you very much, she'll like that.' Peter took a wire basket and began to do his shopping. He'd just picked up the milk and a box of eggs when the doorbell rang, and in came Dicky. He saw Peter's red-blond hair over the top of the shelves and began to beat a quick retreat, but Peter straightening up saw him as he was making his escape. 'Dicky! I need a word!'

464

Reluctantly Dicky turned back and shut the door.

'Now look, Peter, it was a harmless . . .'

'See here, your personal life is your affair, but when it intrudes on the church then it becomes mine. What were you thinking of?'

Dicky looked down at his shoes, put his hands in his pockets and then looking up at Peter said, 'To be honest I don't know. I can't help myself. It's out of my control.'

'Is it?'

'You know this love business. Cupid strikes and everything goes up like a rocket.'

'I know all about this love business, but you're carrying it too far. I mean, a banner on the church, and the children coming for a service. Whatever they must have thought I don't know. And Bel. What about her?'

'She's mad as heck, but I can't stop it. I'm on a roller-coaster and where it leads I have to go.'

'But Dicky, think of Georgie . . .'

'Can't stop. She's gorgeous Georgie as far as I'm concerned.'

'She is very attractive I know . . .'

'Isn't she?' Dicky's face lit up. 'Very, very attractive. It's the combination of that blonde hair and those petite features . . . and she's just the right size for me! I can't think why I haven't realised it before now. Seen her day in day out when I've been in for a drink and then one day I looked at her and wham! bang! there I was head over heels. It was as if I'd never seen her before that day. I felt as though I'd been pole axed. She's the yeast in my bread, the sugar in my tea, the icing on my cake, the fizz in my drinks, the cream in my coffee, the sherry in my trifle, the . . .'

'Dicky! Please think of your position. You're the Scout leader. You've an example to set.'

Dicky's face fell. 'I know. I've been a Scout since I was eight. In my blood as it were and if I had to give it up well . . . it doesn't bear thinking about. But . . . what can you do when love takes you by the throat? You know the feeling?'

'Indeed I do.'

'We're twin souls then, you and me. I've just met Willie, he told me about Dr Harris, how's things this morning with her?'

'Coming on nicely. Came through the operation OK, just got to wait to find out how successful it's been.'

Dicky put a hand on his arm and gave it a squeeze. 'Lovely lady. It must be hard for you. I'm so sorry. Give her my regards won't you? Must press on.'

'Thank you, I will. Will you pay some heed to what I've said?'

'Of course.'

'There are four lives at risk not just yours, you know.'

Dicky nodded. 'I know. I won't use the church again for a banner or anything, but I can't promise any more than that.'

'Dicky!'

Dicky grinned. 'My best wishes to Dr Harris. Very fond of her I am.' His eyes twinkled and Peter had to laugh. Dicky handed Jimbo a loaf of bread. 'That's all this morning. Thanks. Be seeing yer! Bye!' He dashed out of the door laughing.

As Jimbo totalled up Peter's shopping he said, 'I'm very very sorry about that rumour my mother spread. I told her not to say a word but there was no stopping her. I'm so grateful that Caroline didn't hear it.' He looked up anxiously. 'She didn't, did she?'

'No. Mercifully. It was an understandable mistake.'

'You're too generous. She means well, just has this domineering streak you know. She's very upset at what she's done.'

'Well, then, perhaps she'll think twice next time.'

'We should be so lucky. I'm dreading what she might get her teeth into next. I've an idea it could be opposition to the bells ringing. If I could just channel all her energy in the right direction before she . . .'

'Don't worry, Jimbo. How much?'

'Twelve pounds ninety-seven.'

'Thanks.'

Jimbo wrapped Caroline's flowers. 'Don't forget the flowers! Here you are. Our love to her. She's a great lady.'

'Thank you, you and I, both of us have been very lucky.'

Jimbo couldn't resist saying. 'Well, looking at the two of us I should say they've been lucky too!'

Peter couldn't help grinning, and as he left he said, 'It always does me good coming in here, gets life in perspective, I don't know how you do it.'

Caroline opened her eyes to see who had come in to visit her. 'Darling! I hadn't expected you tonight as well as this afternoon! How lovely! Are you sure you can spare the time?'

'Of course I can. Saturday is my day off after all. These flowers are from Jimbo and Harriet with love, I forgot to bring them this afternoon.'

'Of course. I'd forgotten it was Saturday. They're lovely, how kind of them. I'll get someone to put them in water. Were the children all right when you took them home?'

'Absolutely.' He didn't tell her how they'd cried when it was bedtime, nor the way Alex had clung to him and asked when she'd be home, nor about Beth's tantrum at bathtime when she'd laid on the floor and screamed and drummed her heels because he'd forgotten to put the bath bubbles in, when it was she who didn't like them very much. Nor that Beth had gone to sleep with Caroline's favourite scarf hidden under her pillow which for her sake he pretended not to notice, nor indeed that Alex had got his baby beaker out from the cupboard and insisted on having his bedtime drink in it.

'Really?'

'Well . . . they wanted you, naturally, but we got over that bit. How are you tonight, my darling? If you want me to go because you're tired just say so.'

'I am tired but I don't want you to go. Sometimes I just fall asleep even when I'm talking to someone.' She gazed somewhere behind his head and then said, 'I've never had an operation before, you know.'

'I know, neither have I. I think you're being awfully brave.'

'Not really. Peter . . .'

'Yes?'

'Peter, there's nothing left of me now you know. Not the me that's *me*!'

'From where I'm sitting there seems to be all the bits left that I love, so what's the problem?' He reached out and lifted her hair at the front and pretended to inspect it. 'They haven't removed your brain too have they?'

'Don't make me laugh, it hurts!'

'Sorry! Well, they haven't have they? You're still my Caroline whom I adore.'

Caroline turned her head away from him and stared at the wall. 'But everything that makes me a woman has gone. I might as well be a hundred for what's left that's feminine. Whilst ever I had everything else intact there was, foolishly really, just a tiny bit of hope that I *could* possibly have your children even though my womb was tantamount to nonexistent. It was all very silly of me I know, because I couldn't have carried a baby in fact, but now absolutely all hope is gone.'

'As Rhett Butler would say "Frankly, my dear, I don't give a damn". You and I will continue having a wonderful married life together and no surgeon, whoever he is, is going to put a stop to that.'

Caroline shuffled painfully about in the bed trying to get herself more comfortable. She was silent for a while and Peter thought she must be falling asleep again but she said, 'What I'm so afraid of is that I feel less of a person than I was before. How can you possibly want me after this?'

'Caroline, I'm not going to stop loving you just because, as Sheila Bissett would say, you've had everything taken away. It won't make one jot of difference to me and we won't let it make one jot of difference to you either.'

'Do they all know?'

'I expect so by now.'

'I wish they didn't have to.'

'Unavoidable. By the way, your mother's been on the phone, four times. She's phoned the consultant twice and threatened what she'll do to him if anything goes wrong. Apparently they've realised he was in the same year as your father at medical school. She's coming down when you come out.'

'Oh right. I can understand her wanting to come, and I'm grateful that she is, but I wish she wouldn't, I shan't feel like being stirred up.' She fell silent and lay with her eyes closed. Without opening them she continued speaking. 'I felt you pray for me yesterday. Well, not pray but kind of call out to me. I can't remember when it was. Were you here when they brought me back from theatre?'

'A while after.'

'You said my name twice and I came back into the room to see what you wanted, it was really very odd.'

'Ah, right! I see my flowers have come.'

She smiled at him. 'They're beautiful. Thank Jimbo and Harriet for theirs for me will you?'

'Of course. Shall I sit with you until you sleep?'

'Yes, please. I'll go to sleep now.'

Peter rested his elbows on the edge of the mattress and held her hand close to his cheek and then kissed it. 'God bless you.'

'And you. Give my two little ones a kiss from me. I hope they're not being too difficult.'

'No, not at all. Good as gold. Between us Sylvia and I are managing very nicely, though we shall all be glad when you're back.'

'I do love them. So much. And you. I love you dearly.'

'I know, and I love you.'

Faintly he heard her say, 'We're so lucky aren't we, you and I.' She squeezed his hand and smiled and then fell asleep.

In church on Sunday when Peter was saying prayers he told the congregation about Caroline's operation, that it was for cancer and would they give thanks with him for her safe recovery.

No one prayed more fervently than Grandmama. She'd lived a thousand years since she'd met Peter on the Friday morning and he'd told her the real truth of the matter. Thank heavens she hadn't met Caroline and said something. That didn't bear thinking about. If only she'd listened to Jimbo and done as he'd said. But she hadn't and she'd blundered on in her usual bossy way. But she was right about some things. After all he often took notice of her ideas for the Store. He never said he would, but next time she went in he'd have done whatever she'd suggested. Not always, but a sufficient number of times to make her feel useful. But for now she'd pray. Between her fingers she could take a peep at the twins sitting with Sylvia because they'd made a commotion in Sunday School and had to be brought out. Dear, dear little things. Wriggling about a lot, but then who wouldn't at their age?

When the service was concluded Grandmama made her way to the twins and gave them each a pound coin. 'Now this is for you to spend in the Store when Sylvia gets a chance to take you after school. It's closed today but you can go in tomorrow, can't you? Something nice, remember?'

Through tight lips Sylvia forced herself to say 'What do you say children?'

'Thank you, Mrs Charter-Plackett.' The two of them studied the shiny coins for a moment and then stored them away in their pockets.

Having made sure the children had behaved politely Sylvia turned her attention to Grandmama. 'I can't disappoint the children when they're so upset about their mother, but if it was my decision I'd throw that money back at you. You can't buy favour with us, not with none of us.'

'How dare you!'

'I dare all right. I've found out it was you who started that rumour about Dr Harris being . . . you know. How could you? How could you?' Sylvia stamped her foot and a small crowd, beginning to gather in the aisle because they couldn't get past, were paying delighted attention to Grandmama getting told off.

'It wasn't done maliciously, I just put the facts together.'

'But they weren't facts were they?'

'They seemed like it.'

'Well, they weren't. Can you imagine how she would have felt if you'd met her and said that and her knowing what she was having to face? If we still had a ducking stool that's exactly where you'd be, in the pond and drowned for your wicked ways. It happened more than once in that pond in years gone by to nasty old gossips like you.'

Someone in the crowd contributed to the discussion with 'And for what she did to Sheila Bissett. That was cruel that was.'

'It was. Downright cruel.'

Grandmama began to feel in need of help, things were getting very ugly. To her relief Jimbo came to her rescue.

He declared rather more loudly than there was any need, 'Mother! There you are. Coming home for lunch?' He elbowed his way to the middle of the crowd and took her arm.

Sylvia found she had a lot of support. 'Sylvia's right. You tell her, Mr Charter-Plackett, you tell her to keep her meddling ways to herself. Nasty she's been, real nasty.'

'We all make mistakes. It wasn't done to be nasty,' Jimbo retorted sharply.

'Go on, get off home with your Jimbo, it's only because we all like him so much that we can excuse yer, but don't you try us too far. Else Sylvia'ull be right, they'll find yer floating in the pond.'

There was a bit of elbowing and nudging and Jimbo knew he had to get her out of the way before things got uglier still. 'Come along, Mother, right now.' She looked tempted to stay a moment and give them a piece of her mind from the security of Jimbo's arm, but he led her off and as they went down the aisle they could hear some of the congregation saying, 'Spreading such tales.'

'Disgusting.'

'Poor Dr Harris.'

In his usual forgiving way Peter shook hands with Grandmama and asked after her health but she couldn't face him and lowering her eyes, thanked him and went quietly away with Jimbo.

Sunday lunch at Jimbo and Harriet's was a boisterous meal but it gave Grandmama the opportunity for reflection. The children didn't appear to notice how quiet she was but Harriet did and when they'd reached the coffee stage and the two girls had left the table she enquired from Grandmama how she was feeling. 'Are you not well, you're very quiet.'

'I'm quite well, thank you.'

'Not like you, that's all.'

Fergus passed her the sugar and said 'It's all right, Grandmama, we all know what's up. I saw Sylvia giving you a drubbing. Didn't know she had such a temper.'

'Fergus!' Jimbo couldn't face another smoothing of Mother's ruffled feathers.

'Be quiet, Jimbo, he's quite right.'

Harriet raised her eyebrows and Finlay grinned, 'Your face was red!' Fergus began to laugh uproariously.

Under the table Jimbo kicked Fergus' ankle, but Grandmama gave a tight little smile and answered, 'It was very embarrassing. But she was quite right. I should never have said it. I should have waited to see.'

'Never mind, Mother, we have to be thankful Caroline's come through the operation OK.'

'Indeed. Now boys it will soon be half-term. Have you any plans? I've money going spare if you're fancying a day out somewhere or a visit to the cinema or something.'

They began discussing how best to spend their Grandmama's money and no one mentioned the matter of her rumour-mongering again, except Harriet and Jimbo in the kitchen after his mother had left.

'My word! That's a turn-up for the book! Your mother feeling apologetic! Don't forget the dishwasher powder. Here.'

'Well, perhaps this time she will have learned her lesson. I understand she also has had a tiff with Muriel, so she's got that to sort yet.'

'Do you think we might be sailing into calmer waters with your mother now?'

'Since when has she *ever* sailed in calm waters? That's just wishful thinking.'

Harriet sighed. 'You're right, but I do believe it's brought her up short. She's never been so apologetic.'

'Right that's it, everything's done. I don't know how seven people can use so many dishes and pans. I didn't even know we had so many.'

'So many children or so many pans?'

'Both. Do you ever fancy having another one? Make it five, eh? How about it?' He had pinned her against the dishwasher and, with both hands resting on the cupboard above, he kissed her soundly. When they'd finished she answered him. 'Definitely not.'

'Go on. Let's.'

'At your age? Or mine come to that. No, Jimbo, I've just got back into the swing of things and I'm not being tied to the house yet again. Four children is enough for anyone.' She pushed him away and went to see if anyone fancied going for a walk.

While they were out at Bickerby Rocks only Harriet saw Dicky and Georgie hand in hand disappearing out of sight down the hill towards the car park.

11

When Bel went over to the school at eight o'clock on Monday morning to open up and check the heating had come on she was unprepared for what she saw chalked in letters two feet high out in Jacks Lane. The words were strung in a line along the tarmac. 'I LOVE GEORGIE'. The letters were written in a kind of dancing, prancing, sprightly style which added to the potency of their message.

Her lovely open friendly country woman's face became flushed from her hairline right down to her throat. She'd kill him she would. There was a limit. She'd wondered why he hadn't been in the house when she got up, they usually left together, him for his newspaper and then work and her for the school. She'd scrub it off with the playground broom. But she'd have to do her own jobs first. No, she wouldn't. She'd scrub it off first and then see to the school.

Bel did check the heating before she collected the broom and bucket from her broom cupboard in the school kitchen and went out, the water in the bucket sending up swirls of steam into the early winter cold. She began with I and then progressed to LOVE . . .

'What's this then?'

Bel looked up to see who was speaking to her. It was the postman, Ted.

'You can read I'm sure, at least I hope you can.'

'Oh, I can. Don't need to see it all anyways. I've already read it.'

'You're early this morning then.'

'No, not really, it's outside the pub as well, saw it there first. Bryn done it has he?'

Bel seethed. 'Outside the pub as well?'

'Just seen it.'

She snapped, 'No, it isn't Bryn.'

'Who is it then? Who's daft enough?'

Bel pondered for a moment and then answered by denying all knowledge of who it could be.

Ted laughed. 'Whoever it is they're stupid to do it right outside the pub.

472

Bryn's like a bear with a sore head just lately, tore me off a strip just for delivering a letter of his to one of the weekender's cottages by mistake. Course they didn't come back for two weeks did they, so his letter was really late. Weren't my fault. Didn't do it on purpose. He can have a nasty temper and not half.'

Bel finished scrubbing off GEORGIE, picked up the bucket and left Ted to ruminate on his own. He delivered the school post, and two letters to Miss Pascoe and then went to the Store. There was quite a pile of post for Jimbo, he heaved it onto the counter and shouted into the back.

'Mr Charter-Plackett! I've left the post on the counter.'

Jimbo came through from the storeroom carrying a box of apples.

'Morning Ted. Thanks.' Ted reached into the box and chose an apple. He raised his eyebrows at Jimbo who nodded and Ted sunk his teeth into the reddest part of it. When he'd swallowed his first mouthful he said 'Someone's written "I love Georgie" on the road outside the school. In chalk. In big letters.'

Jimbo swung round to face him. 'Has Bel seen it yet?'

'Just scrubbing it off. Was her face red!'

'I'm not surprised.'

'Know who did it then, do yer?'

'I can give a good guess.'

Ted took another large bite of his apple. By the time he'd emptied his mouth sufficiently to be able to speak Jimbo had disappeared into the storeroom again. Ted saw the lovely Comice pears. He tested one for ripeness, checked Jimbo wasn't about to come back in and popped it in his mail bag, but only just in time.

Ted asked, 'Who is it then?'

'I expect you'll know soon enough. It'll be Dicky Tutt.'

Ted's jaw fell open. 'Dicky Tutt! Dicky Tutt! Never.'

'On your bike, Ted, I'm busy.'

'In yer van, yer mean. I'm mechanised now. Well, I never. Poor Bel.'

'Bye to you, Ted, and I'd have given you that pear if you'd asked.'

Ted blushed. 'Sorry.' He went to take it out of his bag.

'Don't bother, but don't do it again.'

Jimbo wasn't quite sure how to greet Bel when she came to work after finishing at the school. But she came in with her usual cheerful greeting and made it difficult to broach the subject.

'Morning all. Isn't it bright and sunny today? We'd better make the best of it while we can. What would you like me to start on this morning Mr Charter-P?'

Linda behind her post office grille felt full of pity for Bel. Such a nice person she was, blasted shame she was having to put up with all this from Dicky. She'd seen the message in the lane, couldn't help it, plain as day from their bedroom window it had been. She'd watched poor Bel start scrubbing away but then the baby had wanted attention and she'd had to press on. And here she was cheerful as ninepence, as if nothing had happened. She'd kill her Alan if he ever did anything so blatantly obvious. Come to think about it she'd kill him if he even so much as looked at another woman never mind advertised it. Linda called across, 'Good morning, Bel. My stationery shelves could do with filling up, there's quite a few gaps.'

Jimbo rounded on her. 'Those shelves are your responsibility, Linda, not Bel's, she has quite enough on her plate at the moment. You've no customers so kindly attend to them now if you please. Bel, start shelf filling in the groceries will you, I've an appointment in half an hour and I'll need you to be on the till while I'm out. OK?' Jimbo looked at Bel and studied her face for a moment but her guard never slipped, and he had to let the moment pass.

At a quarter to ten, only fifteen minutes after Bel had come to start work the door banged open and in came Bryn. His appearance in the Store was very unusual in itself for it was always Georgie who shopped, never Bryn. Linda was glad Jimbo hadn't left yet for she rather suspected that by the look of him Bryn might possibly be quite furious; his face was purple and there were beads of sweat on his forehead, and his fists were clenched, and he was positively *grinding* his teeth.

Straightening up from filling the gaps on the bottom shelf with packets of envelopes, she said the first thing that came into her head. 'Good morning, Mr Fields. Has something upset you, you don't look well.' He was towering over her and as a precaution Linda stepped back a little. 'Is there something I can get you?'

Through clenched teeth and in a tightly controlled voice he said, 'Bel Tutt in?'

'Could be.'

'Either she is or she isn't. Well?' As though on cue Bel came through from the back with a clip board in her hand. The moment she saw Bryn she began to retreat. 'I want a word with you! Come back here!'

Bel hovered in the doorway seemingly unable to make up her mind as to what she should do. In the background she could hear Jimbo on the telephone and Mrs Jones in the mail-order office furiously stapling things together as though there was no tomorrow. She could see Linda beside Bryn looking frightened and beginning to back off towards the outside door.

Bel took a deep breath. 'There's a little word you've forgotten.'

There was a moment's silence and then Bryn said 'Please.'

Slowly Bel moved forward and went to stand beside the till. She rested a hand on the counter as though for support and waited.

'Have you seen what's been chalked on the road outside my pub?'

'No.'

'I love Georgie. That's what. I . . . love . . . Georgie.'

'I didn't do it.'

'I don't suppose for one minute you did. But your Dicky did.'

'Did he?'

'You know damn well he did. I'm up to here.' Bryn stepped towards Bel and tapped the edge of his hand on his forehead 'up to here, with your Dicky. I've banned him from the pub but still he's getting at me. Tell him from me' – Bryn stabbed at his chest with his finger – 'if this tomfoolery doesn't stop I shall have him. God help me I will. I'll have him and I'll squeeze him till there's not a drop of breath left in his stunted little body. Right!' He wrung his hands together as though they were around Dicky's throat.

'I'll give him your message.'

'If you don't, I shall. He's to leave my Georgie alone. Alone! Right? Or else as God is my judge, I'll see there's an end to him.'

'Right.'

'You can also tell your Tom Thumb from me that's he's a pipsqueak, he's a stunted, undersized, blasted little squirt. A dwarf.' Bryn paused for breath searching for the most damaging thing he could say without committing a total breach of etiquette. 'A bloody evil little dwarf.'

By the time Bryn had finished this speech he had an audience of Mrs Jones, Jimbo, two assistants from the kitchens, Harriet, Linda and Grandmama. She'd come in halfway through the tirade and been standing listening open-mouthed to what he was saying. As he moved to leave she stepped forward and blocked his way out. In her most superior voice she upbraided him for his outburst.

'My man, have you given one moment's thought as to how Bel must be feeling? She too is an injured party, you know, just as much as you. Your behaviour is most reprehensible, you should be ashamed of yourself. Have you ever given a thought as to why Georgie appears to find Dicky so fascinating? Or indeed as to why Dicky finds Georgie so engaging? Have you given it your earnest consideration? Oh no! I don't expect you have. Foolish man. Go home and think about it. And don't march in here laying down the law ever again. These are business premises not a fairground boxing ring. Such language! Venting your spleen on Bel in this way. It's absolutely disgraceful! Now, get out!'

She opened the door and waited for him to leave. Which he did, but not without throwing a fevered glance at Bel as he left and saying to Grandmama, 'And you, Duchess, are an interfering old *hen*,' before he slammed the door behind him. There was a stunned silence as the Store reverberated with the sound of the door slamming.

The first to recover was Grandmama. She brushed her gloved hands together as though ridding herself of something thoroughly unpleasant and looking round at everyone she smiled. 'Well, now, is anyone serving in here this morning or not? I want notepaper and envelopes and a tub of single cream, for I've someone coming for coffee. Chop, chop! Bel go in the back and get Jimbo to give you a brandy out of his first aid box. You look as though you need it. Good morning, Harriet.'

'Good morning to you.'

Slowly everyone resumed their places, Mrs Jones went back to her mailorder office full of admiration for the dignified manner in which Grandmama had dealt with the situation, it took class it did to give a dressing down like that, class, nothing less. Linda went to the bottom stationery shelf for notepaper and envelopes, careful to choose the most expensive she could find. Bel, white and trembling, disappeared with Jimbo in her wake. Harriet went to the chilled shelves for the cream.

'My word, Mother-in-law, you certainly gave him what for. I have never in all the time he's been here known him explode like that. Things must be serious for him to behave like that.'

'They are, Harriet, they are.'

'You know?'

'I do. That's fine, Linda. Thank you. In very good taste, I must say. Tot it up for me, Harriet, I'm in a hurry. I've Muriel coming for coffee.'

'Indeed. I thought you two weren't exactly . . . you know . . . friends.'

Grandmama looked uncomfortable. 'There's been a slight hiccup which I intend to proper over today. That doesn't sound quite right but you know what I mean. Thank you, my dear. See you soon.'

Grandmama left feeling well satisfied with her morning's work. Now all she had to do was butter up Muriel and then all would be right with her world. There was nothing quite like a demonstration of power to make one feel . . . what was the phrase she was after? Cock of the dung heap? Oh dear no, that wasn't it. Ten years younger? On top of the world? She'd think it over while she got the coffee things out. Pity she'd no family silver to bring out, but there you couldn't have everything.

After taking coffee Muriel went home to lunch very amused by Grandmama's attempts to apologise for her loss of temper and for spreading the rumour about Caroline. She, Grandmama, was a very proud woman and it must have cost her a lot to apologise so profusely. Muriel's kind heart could do no other than accept graciously and they had parted the best of friends. At least on the surface, for Muriel was tempted to wait to see what other escapades Grandmama might get up to.

'Ralph, my dear, have you heard?'

'No, I don't expect so.'

'Oh there you are!' Muriel stood in the doorway of his study and admired Ralph, his snow white, well barbered hair, his fresh complexion, his alert brown eyes and, to her, his wonderful aristocratic nose. 'You grow more handsome each time I see you!'

'Thank you, my dear. Is that the news? That Ralph Templeton grows more handsome every day?'

She laughed. 'Of course not! That was an aside. No, Grandmama tells me that Bryn has been in the Store and told Bel off quite cruelly about Dicky, and I've just seen her crossing the road to school and said how sorry I was and that she was to ignore him and she said she was, but I said it must be very difficult and she said it was, so I said she'd have to put her foot down and she said you know Dicky so I said I do and he's a very naughty boy so she said that's just right that's what he is so I said would she like you to have a talk with him and she said . . .'

'Muriel!' Ralph raised a hand in protest. 'Muriel! I am not getting involved in someone else's marital affairs. Please.'

Muriel looked quite crestfallen. 'But, Ralph, he needs someone like you to . . .'

'No, he does not.'

She went to stand beside him and putting an arm around his shoulders she bent to kiss the top of his head. 'Please, my dear, someone has to do something and we can't expect Peter to with Caroline so ill.'

'I am not. Sorry. And kissing me won't make one jot of difference.'

'Oh Ralph! Please.'

'No.'

'Then I shall.'

'I expressly forbid you to say anything at all, Muriel. Let them sort themselves out.'

'Forbid me?'

'I beg your pardon. Of course I don't forbid, but please take my advice and keep out of it.'

'How can we, the whole village is agog.'

'Then agog they will have to be. It's becoming quite sordid and I don't want to have anything to do with it.'

'You must admit though, Ralph, if they weren't all married it would be a rather wonderful romance. Telling all the world about how your heart feels. So romantic, so . . . compelling. It's like a film. A nineteen fifties film like *Spring in Park Lane* with Anna Neagle, or *Brief Encounter* with Trevor Howard, when there was romance and not simply sex.' She sighed longingly.

'Muriel?' He put down his pen and resting his elbows on the desk studied her face. 'I do believe you like the idea of having messages left all over the village. Maybe I'm letting the romance in our marriage seep away through neglect. I shall have to think up something for you, maybe Dicky could give me some suggestions.'

Muriel blushed. 'Oh no! not something like that. That would be too embarrassing.'

'Then beware, my dear, if I discover you've been handing out advice to them all, I shall find a way of embarrassing you good and proper!' Ralph chuckled at the consternation in Muriel's face.

'That's blackmail!'

'Indeed it is. But I shall, you may take my word for it.'

'Ralph!' She sped away into the kitchen quite overcome by Ralph's teasing.

But the opportunity to speak to Dicky came the following evening and Muriel couldn't resist the chance. She'd been busy all day and it was dark before she got an opportunity to call at the rectory with a cake which she hoped in some small way might help Sylvia. It was she who came to the door when Muriel rang the bell.

'Good evening, Sylvia. I've brought a coconut cake, thought it might help.'

'Thank you very much indeed. I really appreciate that. Coconut, lovely!'

'What's the news today?'

'A big improvement. We're all feeling much happier. She's out of bed and she's beginning to be more like herself.'

'I'm so glad. He's with her tonight?'

'No, he's presenting the prizes at the Guides' annual whatever,' Sylvia turned as she heard the study door close. It was Dicky with an envelope in his hand. 'Got what you wanted?'

'Yes, thanks. He'd left it out for me, like he said. Tell the Rector I'll get it back to him before the end of the week. Oh, good evening, Lady Templeton.'

'Good evening, Dicky. I'll say good night then.'

'Thanks for the cake, save me baking tomorrow.'

'Good, I'm glad.'

Dicky and Muriel stepped out of the rectory together and the opportunity couldn't be missed. Before they left the pool of light cast by the lamp over the rectory door, Muriel cleared her throat and took the plunge.

'Could I have a word, Dicky?'

'Of course. Can't be long though, I've got Venture Scouts in ten minutes.'

'Oh, it won't take long. I had a word with Bel yesterday, I feel very upset for her.' Dicky, the same height as herself, looked straight into her eyes without answering. Muriel grew uncomfortable, and she wished she'd never begun the conversation at all, she really should have listened to

Ralph's advice. But she had to say it. Just had to. 'I can quite understand about you being captivated by Georgie, totally understand it, she's a very attractive person and I know it can be difficult when they're the light of your life and your feelings overwhelm you and you feel quite helpless and . . . I . . . I don't mean to interfere, but it's not right what you're doing.'

'Not right? Not right to be in love?'

'Well, no, I can't say it's not right to be in love, we shouldn't turn our faces against love at any time, but you shouldn't be should you? In love, well, not with Georgie.'

'Does love ask for your credentials before it strikes?'

'Oh no, of course not. No, it doesn't, but . . .'

' "But", exactly. I can't help it.'

'All the world doesn't need to know, though, does it? You don't have to advertise the fact do you?'

'What else can I do when it's bubbling out of me? I've been well and truly clobbered by her and I can't think of anything else.'

'But your reputation. Think of that.'

Dicky gazed up the road, thought for a moment and then said very quietly, 'I don't care one jot for my reputation, not one jot. I love her and that's all there is to it.'

'Then at the very least you could think of Bel, think how it must be for her. I felt truly sorry when I heard what Bryn said to her in the Store yesterday, she must be feeling it very deeply. Often, you see, the cheerful, happy people are the very ones who hurt the most. So it's Bel I feel the most concerned for, after all, she is *your legal wife*. You should think of her, first and foremost.'

Dicky didn't answer immediately, he first looked deep into her eyes. He appeared to be weighing up if whether what he was about to say would be a good idea or not. He patted her arm and said 'The word "legal" isn't in the equation at all, so there's no need for you to worry yourself about Bel. Good night to you, Lady Templeton.'

12

Peter had kept Caroline up to date with all the village news so when she came home ten days later there wasn't a great deal she didn't know. Except, of course, no one knew what had passed between Muriel and Dicky the previous Tuesday night. Sylvia went to collect the children from school and the first words they said to her were 'Is Mummy home?'

'She is.'

The two of them raced across the playground towards the gate.

'No! No! Mind the road!' Fortunately Miss Booth was by the gate and she stopped the two of them from leaving.

'Oh, thank you, Miss Booth. They're so excited, the Doctor came home this afternoon, you see, and they can't wait.'

'I know! They've talked of nothing else all day. I am pleased.' Miss Booth patted their heads. 'She will be happy to see you both.'

Beth nodded her head in agreement. 'We've been to see her in hospital but I didn't like that. I don't like hospitals. Come on, Sylvie, be quick!'

'We've got to cross the road properly, Beth, no matter what. Hold my hands. You as well Alex.'

Alex urged her to hurry.

They burst in through the rectory door shouting 'Mummy! Mummy!'

'In the sitting-room.' Alex rushed in and flung himself upon her and hugged her but Beth stood outside the door peeping round it watching Alex greet Caroline. 'Where's my Beth? I'm in here, darling.'

Very slowly Beth walked into the room and stood looking at her mother. Caroline spread her arms wide and said 'Come here, my darling.'

Beth unable to cope with the emotion she felt on seeing Caroline at home at last, fled to the kitchen to find Sylvia. But it was Peter who was making a drink for them all.

'Why, Beth darling, what is the matter?' he scooped her up into his arms and her chubby little arms squeezed his neck so tightly he could scarcely breathe. Her hot tears prickled onto his neck. He felt the cold of her cheeks and inhaled the fragrance of her hair, and hugged her close.

'Dearest child, Mummy's home now and quite safe. Come and say hello.'

'I can't, it hurts.'

'Where does it hurt?'

'I think it's in my heart, I think it's going to burst.'

'No, it isn't. What you need is Mummy to give you a hug, that will mend your heart. We'll go in there together.'

'Does your heart want to burst, Daddy?'

'Oh yes. It does.' He carried her through into the sitting-room and placed her on the sofa next to Caroline. 'There we are. You hug Mummy, that'll make it feel better.'

Caroline hugged her tightly and gradually Beth's fear subsided, and the horrid broken jigsaw of her life fell slowly into order and she felt her world had been put to rights.

'Mummy, Daddy needs a hug, his heart's ready to burst too.' So Caroline sat on the sofa with one arm round Alex, the other round Beth and Peter kneeling in front of her his head resting against her chest. Their tears dried up and when Sylvia came in with tea, which she'd finished making on Peter's behalf, she stood with the tray in her hands in the doorway and smiled, a huge great beaming smile the like of which she felt she hadn't done for days. At last everything was back to normal and she gave an enormous heartfelt sigh of relief.

'Tea anyone?'

Caroline had refused to go to bed while the children were up. She talked and joked and listened and played herself to complete exhaustion. Peter took them up to bed and when they were happily tucked up, Alex with his teddy and Beth, with her thumb in her mouth, clutching old Boo Boo rabbit he went downstairs to Caroline.

'Peter, I'm so tired.'

'I can see that. You should have gone to bed sooner than this.'

'I know but the children, they need to see me looking more normal, they need reassuring. You know?'

'Let me help you upstairs. Have a sleep, eh?'

'That would be lovely.'

He helped her undress and when she was safely laid in bed he suggested that he'd come up about ten with a hot drink, what did she fancy?

'Tea I think and a piece of Sylvia's cake, whatever she has on the go at the moment.'

'Good idea. You need to get some weight back on.'

'Don't put pressure on me, please, I'll get round to things in my own good time.'

'Sorry, just anxious, you know.' He hung her skirt and cardigan in the wardrobe, put her shirt and underthings in the linen basket and left her to sleep.

Peter sat for a long while in his study in the easy chair. He alternately thought and prayed, underscoring his gratitude for her coming through the operation with prayers of thanks to God. He had no living relatives, no one to turn to in times of need. Only Caroline and the children on earth. They were his whole world. This terrible threat to their happiness had heightened his awareness of how much he needed her to sustain him in his daily life, how much he needed her common sense, her humour, her strength. Caroline gave so much to so many people; to him, his children, her patients, her friends, her own family, the parish. They none of them could manage nearly as well without her.

On his desk were the pile of get well cards Caroline had brought back with her from hospital. He read through them one after the other, they were from parishioners, from family, from friends, many of them unknown to him. The last one right at the bottom was from David Lloyd-Jones. He didn't pose any threat but the man could still waken feelings of jealousy. Peter had to laugh at himself.

She wasn't out of the wood yet though, the specialist had said to him, but the prognosis was excellent. The hurdle of therapy still had to be faced, but he was determined to remain cheerful on that subject, yes definitely cheerful.

The little carriage clock on the study mantelpiece chimed ten o'clock. He went into the kitchen to put the kettle on, prepared a tray with an Indian cloth Caroline had brought back years ago, found the best teapot and cups and saucers and a matching plate and a lace doily for the cake.

When he entered the bedroom Peter laid the tray on his bedside table and looked to see if Caroline was awake. She was fast asleep, with Alex cuddled up on one side of her and Beth on the other. Peter debated what he should do, but decided to leave them where they were. The two of them would both heal quicker that way, sleeping close to her. He carried the tray into the children's room and went to sleep in Alex's bed, altogether envious of his children.

13

Grandmama burst through the front door calling, 'Harriet, my dear, where are you? Are you there? Hello, Fran, my darling!'

Jimbo came out of the sitting-room. 'Hello, Mother, what's the matter, is there a fire?'

'Not a fire, Jimbo, dear.' She held her face for him to kiss. 'I've got such news. You won't believe. Where's Harriet? What are you doing home at this time?'

'Half day, I do have one occasionally, I've a function tonight.'

Harriet had been washing her hair and came down the stairs rubbing it dry. 'Hello, Mother-in-law. What's the news then?'

Grandmama nodded her head in the direction of the kitchen. Jimbo and Harriet followed her in.

'Didn't want little Fran to hear, the children aren't home yet are they?'

'Another half an hour. Why?'

Grandmama seated herself at the kitchen table and digging into her handbag brought out a small plastic bag. 'In here is the piece I need for repairing my sewing machine. It's so old they've stopped stocking the spare parts for it now and I've searched all over and found a little man in Culworth who's managed to get it for me.'

'Is that it? Is that the news?' Jimbo was very disappointed, he'd expected a murder at least.

'Of course not. But you should be delighted for me, I've really missed not being able to use it. I'm going to make things for charity. I've a very good line in stuffed dolls, they are very stylish, of course, they're not some arty crafty rubbish masquerading as designer dolls. However, while he was finding out how much I owed him this chappie asked me if I lived in Culworth and I said no I lived in Turnham Malpas, so he said in that case then you'll know Dicky Tutt. He knows Dicky because it's where Dicky works in the office that the sewing machine man managed to get this piece from, so he knows Dicky very well, you see. Been dealing with Dicky's company for years and years. So we got talking about what a nice man he is and what fun, which he is, and I said his wife's lovely too, she's the village school caretaker and she works for my son.' Grandmama paused and looked at them both to make sure she had their complete attention. 'Then he said . . . You'll never believe this . . .'

Jimbo stood up. 'Now look, Mother, I'm not having you going round spreading rumours again. You'll please me if you keep this all to yourself, I really don't want to know. Your rumours have proved dangerous in the past, so you are stopping right there.'

Harriet intervened. 'Steady on, your mother's only telling us what he said, she hasn't made it up has she?'

'Thank you, Harriet, for springing to my defence. As Harriet said, I'm only repeating to you what he said to me.'

'I don't want to hear what some piffling sewing-machine repairer has to say about anything. Now please, Mother, say no more. If all you have to talk about is unreliable gossip then you can leave right now.'

'Jimbo! I think . . .'

'I don't care what you think! and if I hear that you've breathed one wrong word, and I say that again, *one wrong word* about Dicky Tutt then you'll have me to answer to. I mean that, Mother. Whatever this chappie claims, it in no way affects the brilliant job Dicky does with those boys.'

Grandmama stood up. 'I'll go before the children come home. If you don't want to hear my interesting news then so be it. But don't expect me to tell you anything at all, ever, in the future. Coming from someone who loves a tasty piece of gossip, I think you're being two-faced. Anyone else's gossip is all right but mine isn't.'

'No, it isn't, and you're not to repeat it to anyone. I had thought you'd learned your lesson. Apparently you haven't.'

Grandmama stormed from the house, Jimbo's 'I mean what I say' following her out.

Harriet went to put the towel to dry on the radiator. 'I'm afraid you came down a little too heavily there Jimbo.'

'Since when have you been on Mother's side?'

'I'm not, but even so I can be fair to her.'

'I've put the frighteners on her on purpose. Tough measures for a tough cookie. That's what.'

'She was only telling us what he said.'

'The thing is Mother's assuming this man in Culworth is right in whatever it is he's told her. He could be quite wrong.'

'I wonder what it was he said? You shut her up far too soon, I would have liked to have heard what it was.'

'Harriet! You're as bad as Mother.'

'OK. OK. I'm going over to see Caroline for five minutes. I won't stay long. Her mother's driving down tomorrow, so it's best if I go today. I'll just brush my hair.'

'Give her my love.'

'I will.'

The following morning Malcolm was late with the milk because the baby had been awake half the night, and Ted was early so they both arrived at the Royal Oak at the same time.

'Morning, Ted.'

'God you look awful.'

'It's the baby, yer long for 'em to come and then . . . He went to sleep just as it was time to get up and I dropped off by mistake. Eh! Look at this.'

He was examining the window boxes. There were three under the long window between the two entrances. Each one had been filled with winter pansies by Georgie and the ivy which had been burgeoning in the summer was hanging on by a thread now the cold weather had come. All the way along the front edge of each box were red roses, stuck into the soil. Each and every one had a small heart-shaped label attached with the word Georgie written on it with a red pen. They looked like very tall guardsmen on parade. There must have been three dozen Ted reckoned. 'He's at it again. There's no stopping him is there? The daft beggar.'

'Wouldn't like to be in his shoes when Bryn finds out. Blasted miserable sod he is nowadays.'

'Hardly surprising is it considering? Would you like it if your wife was being courted under your very nose?'

'I'm not daft, I ain't married.'

'Well, then. Leave yer milk and let's be off before he finds out.'

'He won't be up for a bit yet.' Malcolm left his regular crate of milk for the dining-room and went off. Ted put the letters through and checked he'd not forgotten any, not after the last time.

When finally they both got up, Georgie asked Bryn to bring in the milk as they hadn't sufficient for breakfast, so it was he who saw the roses first.

Bryn didn't know whether to laugh or cry. How could this man do this to him? How could he? He was being made a laughing stock. That was the part he resented the most; being made to look a fool. Georgie and he belonged to each other. When they'd married he'd lusted for her like nobody's business. So pretty, so petite, so lively, he couldn't resist her and they'd built such a good business, such a good following in the other pub and now here, the dining-room, the bar. They worked together so well. The hours were crippling agreed and he wasn't coping with them quite as easily as he used to, but there you are. Open all hours, what else could she expect.

Well, she damned well wasn't seeing these. He'd pull them out and get them in the wheelie bin before she saw them. Swiftly he raced along the boxes pulling out the roses as he went. The thorns scratched his fingers, tore at his hands, made his wrist bleed but he didn't care. When he'd got the last one out he glanced round to see if anyone was about and then raced round the outside to the wheelie bin in the car park, and back again in a trice.

'Bryn, where's that milk? I'm dying for a cup of tea.'

'Just coming.'

The morning went along as usual. Alan came to start work and Georgie disappeared to make the bed and to pretty herself up ready for opening for the lunchtime trade. The chef arrived to start work on the dining-room food, and his assistant, a brash blonde with more bounce than brains came too. Bryn began to congratulate himself on a successful outcome to his secret piece of sabotage.

By a quarter to one the regulars were in and a very good sprinkling of people who'd booked tables and were having a drink before sitting down to eat. Jimmy was in, it being his day off, and Willie and Sylvia too.

Jimmy wiped the froth from his top lip and asked why Willie and Sylvia were in at lunchtime?

'My day off and the Rector said Sylvia should take a day off too with working so much when the doctor was in hospital. So we're having a drink and then having lunch and then we're off into Culworth.'

'Lunch, eh?'

Sylvia saw immediately what he was hoping for. 'Care to join us?'

'I'd like that if you don't mind.'

'Not at all, do we, Willie?'

Willie shook his head. 'You're welcome.'

Jimmy smiled his thanks. 'Dr Harris all right, is she?'

'Getting better every day. We're right pleased with her. The Rector's smiling again, thank goodness.'

'Caught sight of him in Culworth one day when she was in hospital, he looked terrible he did, something terrible. Poor chap. It's hard when yer love like they do and . . .'

They'd all heard the phone ring but took no notice, it was probably a booking for the dining-room, but from the sound of Georgie's voice it wasn't a run of the mill conversation. She put the receiver on the bar counter and, lifting the flap, crossed to the outside door and went out. Bryn, who was collecting up empty glasses from the table by the fire watched her go. His heart began beating rather fast. He slipped across to the counter, picked up the receiver and shouted 'Get stuffed!' into it and quietly replaced it on its cradle.

Everyone was aware a drama was being played out and they eagerly awaited Georgie's return. By the time she came back in Bryn was pretending to straighten his collection of brass toasting forks hanging above the fireplace. She marched across to the phone and stood gazing in surprise at the receiver.

'Did you put this receiver back?'

'Receiver? No.' Bryn stopped to have a conversation with a customer, keeping a wary eye on her while he did so. She was standing looking at the telephone, then in an instant they could see she made up her mind. Georgie was round the counter and standing in front of Bryn before you could say Jack Robinson.

The customers jointly held their breath.

'It's you isn't it? You've taken the roses out of the window boxes?'

Roses in the window boxes in October? What did she mean?

'Roses? Me?'

'Bryn Fields, you're lying to me. It was you, I can see it written all over your face. You lying cheating so and so.'

'What do you expect me to do? Stand by and let that little runt of a man court you as though you were free to be courted? Well, you aren't and I shan't. The worm has turned. I pulled them out and stuffed them in the bin, and I shall do whatever is needed to stop that nasty little beggar from stealing you from me. We're a team you and me.' He gestured with his arm to the counter and the customers. 'We've built this up, we've made it what it is, him with his twopenny ha'penny office job couldn't keep you like I can, never in a million years.'

'What good does it do me having money in the bank? We never can enjoy it. We're always too busy. Too busy for fun. Always the bar, the bar, the bar, day after day. At least he is amusing and alive and he *cares* which is more than can be said for *you*! I'm sick of it, Bryn, sick of it. I'm going now to get the roses out of the bin and I shall find the loveliest vase I can and put them in it and stick it right here at the corner of the bar for all to see, and don't you ever dare put the receiver down on any call of mine ever again.'

Sylvia couldn't but admire Georgie's spirited defence of her lover. 'But she shouldn't say all that in front of everybody. Give Bryn his due he took her in the back when he wanted to protest.'

Jimmy disagreed. 'More fun though out in the open. What do they mean by the roses? He must have put some outside at the front. That Dicky! He's going to be in serious trouble he is.'

Willie said, 'He's daft he is, absolutely daft. Rector's not going to be pleased. It's no example for them boys, no example at all. He should behave right, he should. This is plain daft.'

At this point Georgie came back in carrying a huge cut glass vase filled with Dicky's red roses. Some were looking a bit worse for wear but most were still quite splendid. She placed the vase right where she said she would, where the counter curved round, no one could miss them.

Bryn who'd been swishing some glasses through the soapy water in the sink behind the counter watched her out of the corner of his eye. Dropping the pint tankard he was washing, which fell with a great sploosh back into the sink, he reached out and swept the vase clean off the counter. It smashed into a thousand pieces on the stone floor. Water and roses and shards of glass were everywhere. Georgie burst into angry tears and beat at Bryn with her fists, but he thrust her aside.

Two customers had to jump back to avoid the water and flying glass, two more walked out in disgust. Sylvia stood up and said, 'Get me a dustpan and brush, Georgie, I'll give you a hand.'

'You won't.' Bryn moved towards her as though daring her to interfere.

Sylvia held her hands, palms upwards in a conciliatory gesture. 'Very well, I won't.'

Willie moved to her side. 'Don't you dare threaten my wife.'

Belligerently Bryn replied, 'If you don't like what's going on then you can always leave.'

Willie drew himself up to his full height. 'I shall. This pub isn't what it was. I'm sick of witnessing your stupid quarrels, I swear they're turning the beer. We come in 'ere for a quiet drink with friends and what do we get? You smashing the place up, all because you aren't clever enough to hold on to your wife.'

Bryn moved towards him his face grim and his fists clenched, but Willie refused to be intimidated. 'Come on, Sylvia, we'll eat in Culworth, they tell me they do grand food at the Plaice by the River, I could just fancy a nice tasty piece of fish.' He took her arm and weaving their way between the tables they headed for the door. As he opened it for Sylvia to go through Willie turned and said, 'Before long you'll have no customers left and it'll serve you right. Coming with us, Jimmy?'

Jimmy got up from the table, 'Might as well, the drama seems to be over and my ale tastes rotten. They tell me the Jug and Bottle in Penny Fawcett serves some good beer. If this goes on much longer I might start going there.' As he reached the door Jimmy put on his cap and shouted, 'Good day to you all.'

14

While they were having lunch Willie had organised Jimmy to go up the tower and sweep the steps, check the light bulbs and generally give a tidy up in preparation for All Saints' Day. Since time immemorial parishioners, and anyone else who cared to pay for the privilege, could climb the church tower and spend time up there enjoying the view. When they came down there was tea and fatty cake to be had in the church hall. No one could remember when they had first begun serving cups of tea and still less could anyone remember when they'd begun serving fatty cake. Strangers furrowed their brows at the mention of fatty cake and the older inhabitants of Turnham Malpas nodded their heads knowingly but refused to divulge their secret recipes.

There were only certain people, with ancestors mentioned in the very oldest parish records, who by tradition made the fatty cakes for All Saints' Day. Lavender Gotobed who now lived in Little Derehams but whose family had resided in Turnham Malpas for centuries was one, Mrs Jones from the Store was another, Willie Biggs and Jimmy Glover, the Nightingales of Nightingale Farm, Thelma and Valda Senior and in charge of organising the cakes was the current Lady at the Big House. So as there were no longer any Templetons at the Big House it was Muriel who had to ring around and check that the fatty cakes would be made and delivered in time on the day.

Willie always had the door at the bottom of the tower unlocked at ten o'clock on the morning of November the first. This was the sixteenth time he'd done it and as he settled himself on a chair by the door, wearing every conceivable item of clothing he could think of as protection against the cold, he wondered just how many people would come.

He'd said to Sylvia only that morning, 'These old customs is all right, but they're bound to lose their excitement. There's so many other things folk can do nowadays. Watch TV, go shopping in them shopping malls, driving here and there, going to the coast, computer games and these winter sun holidays they go on and that, stands to reason they'll start losing interest in a simple thing like climbing a tower for a good view.'

'You wait and see, it's tradition and they like tradition round here. Leave these four fatty cakes in the church hall for me will you? Two from you and two from Jimmy. See, I've used the very best raisins and butter, they should taste good. Your mother's recipe I reckon is the best.'

Willie perked up at that. 'Always loved making 'em she did. Never made 'em any other time. Every year she kept one back and we had it with our tea, but she never let on and we didn't either. Bad luck or some such I think she thought, but she couldn't resist. I'll be off then. When are you coming?'

'About eleven, got your tin for the money?'

'I have, I've always liked this picture of Queen Victoria on the lid. Her Golden Jubilee tin it was. Been used every year since then for this very job.'

'You'll be late.'

'Give us a kiss.'

'Righteo, there you are.'

So he was sitting there waiting for customers. The first up the path was the Rector and the twins.

'Good morning, Rector.'

'Hello, Willie.'

'Mr Biggs, here's my money. Can we go up now?' Beth wearing her red wool hat which she'd had since the Christmas she was three and which she refused to be parted from, looked up at him with a lovely eager smile on her face.

'I reckon this is your first time.'

'It is. Mummy said we were too small before but now we're at school she says we can go.' Alex backed away and stared up at the top of the tower. 'It's a long way up.'

'It is. Yer'll need strong legs to get up there. Let's 'ave a feel at yer muscles.' Willie bent down and pretended to test Alex's leg muscles.

'And me, and me. I'm strong.' Beth offered her legs for testing too.

'Well, I reckon, Rector, with muscles like them they'll both make it.'

'So do I. They've been pestering to come since eight o'clock. Are we the first?'

'You are, sir. Mind how yer go.'

Willie's tin began filling up with the steady stream of twenty-pence pieces from the people eager to climb the tower. The weather was cold and there was an east wind which cut cruelly through the warmest coat. He couldn't imagine what it must be like up at the top.

Dicky Tutt came up the path. He stood talking to Willie but his mind was obviously not on the conversation for he kept glancing down the church path as though expecting someone. Then he abandoned Willie altogether when Georgie came hurrying up. Willie watched as Dicky visibly restrained himself from greeting her with a kiss.

Dicky dropped his money in the tin. 'Here you are then, forty pence.'

Georgie greeted Willie with 'Good morning, cold job for you sitting there.'

'It is, but it's all in a good cause.'

'What's the money going to then this year?'

'Save The Children.'

'You should make it fifty pence not twenty.'

'Well, it's twenty, makes it too much when you've a family to take up. You'll need something warmer than that on when you go up. I'm told the wind blows something terrible up there on days like this.'

Dicky pulled a wool hat out of his pocket. 'Here you are, Georgie, wear this.'

They disappeared into the tower hand in hand. Willie couldn't believe the boldness of it. They don't care that's it, they don't care who sees 'em. It's not right.

In the past when it got really busy Willie had had to form a queue outside on the path and wait for some people to come down before letting any more climb up. There were several passing places up the spiral staircase so it didn't matter too much if people were going both up and down at the same time but the space at the top being so limited he had to make sure there weren't too many up there at once. Didn't want no one falling over the edge in the crush.

Flick, Finlay and Fergus came next and then to his horror, hard on their heels came Bryn Fields. Willie hadn't been in the Royal Oak since that lunch time when Bryn had shoved Dicky's roses off the bar counter. He really hadn't expected Bryn to come and, oh God, Dicky was up there. He'd have to think of something quick.

'Hello, Bryn, I'm afraid you'll have to wait a while, there's getting to be too many people up there.'

'One more won't make any difference, I'm going up.'

'I'm sorry, but I've got to be quite firm about this. There's already enough people up there, I've got to ask you to wait.'

'I'm not.' He fumbled in his trouser pocket and brought out a pound coin. 'Here, there's a pound and worth every penny.'

Bryn flung the coin in Willie's tin and sped off towards the bottom of the steps.

Willie got up off his chair and entered the tower door. 'Bryn, come back down.' But Bryn had disappeared round the turn of the spiral staircase and Willie had to climb the first few steps to make himself heard. 'Bryn, do as I say, come back down.' All he could see was the heels of Bryn's shoes disappearing rapidly round the next bend. There was no way Willie was going up there so whatever drama was about to unfold he wouldn't witness it.

At the top Georgie stood with her back against the wall getting her breath back. 'That's a climb and not half. You must be fit, Dicky!'

'I am! Come and look!' He leaned as far as he could over the edge, only one of his well polished brogues was on terra firma.

'Be careful! You'll be over.'

'I won't, nine lives, I've got.'

Georgie went to stand beside him. 'Just do me a favour and keep both your feet on the ground, you're giving me the heebie jeebies.'

He tucked her hand in the crook of his arm and they both looked over the village. Dicky was pointing places out to her and they were in a world of their own.

'Hello Mr Tutt! I've never been up here before. Isn't it good?'

'Hello there, Beth, where's your dad, you're not on your own are you?'

'No, of course not, he's round the other side with Alex, looking at the cars on the bypass with Daddy's binoculars. Hello, Mrs Fields. Where's Mr Fields?'

'Working.'

'I expect he'll come later when he's not busy. You can see a long way can't you? I wish I was tall enough to look over the top, I can only see through the holes. I can put my leg right through them, look.' She waved her foot out through a gap between the stone uprights. They're just the right size for me.'

Dicky smiled down at her. 'Well, you'll grow soon enough. I'm not lifting you up to see, that's a fact. I can only just see over the top myself.'

'If you were tall like my Daddy you'd be able to see everything. He can see everything wherever he goes.'

'I would, you're right. Here he is, look. Bit breezy up here isn't it?'

Peter agreed. 'It certainly is. For the sake of my nerves, Beth, bring your leg back in. In! Thank you. How are you Georgie? Long time no see.'

The biting wind battered Georgie and she pulled Dicky's wool hat closer about her ears. 'Busy. You know how it is. Open all day.' She turned her back to him, she really couldn't withstand Peter's all-seeing eyes today. Nor the disappointment she could recognise in them.

There was a hustle and a bustle at the top of the steps and bending low under the door lintel Bryn appeared, breathing heavily. He didn't speak because he couldn't, he'd climbed the stairs far too fast. His lack of speech only served to fuel his anger. Dicky hadn't noticed he'd arrived and was still looking out over the village. Georgie nudged him. He turned to look at her and smiled, a loving, possessive kind of smile. An unmistakable smile to someone like Peter who knew all about loving and Peter's heart sank. He glanced at Bryn and realised he'd seen the look too. Bryn, uncontrollable fury in every line of his face, lurched forward and grabbed Dicky by his collar.

Gasping he snarled, 'I knew I'd find you up here. I just knew you two had planned to meet.'

'Bryn! Let go of him! Let go!' Georgie grabbed at Bryn's arm and tried to pull him away but he brushed her off.

Before anyone could say or do anything Bryn was heaving Dicky up by his collar and the seat of his trousers and was trying to lift him over the edge. Dicky was writhing, wriggling, struggling to escape but Bryn held him in a madman's grip.

'I warned you I'd do for you and I shall. You're not having her.' As he spoke he pursued his intention of heaving him over, but Dicky was hanging on to the stone balustrade and was proving far harder to heave over than Bryn had thought possible. Georgie, screaming and crying was trying to keep hold of Dicky, and Bryn was shouting, 'I'll do for you. So help me I will. Leave go, you bastard.' It all happened so quickly that it took Peter a moment to absorb what was really happening. He thrust the children behind him and stepped forward, stood behind Bryn and concentrated all his strength on gripping Bryn's arms and pinning him to his chest. There was a fierce struggle during which Peter could hear the children screaming and Willie shouting from the ground. 'What's goin' on up there?' Several people joined him in the fight to prevent Bryn from finally tipping Dicky over the edge. Gradually Peter, with their help, began to win and Bryn started to release his hold on Dicky and all of a sudden Bryn's maniacal strength left him and he let go completely.

Dicky ashen and breathing fast straightened his clothes. Georgie stood watching the collapse of Bryn. Bryn who'd always been a tower of strength, hard working, tenacious, ambitious and here he was leaning against the balustrade, looking a broken man. All because of her.

Peter, flushed and breathing hard realised that the children were terrified by seeing their father fighting and that he had to reassure them when he hardly felt capable of doing so because he was so shocked at the thought of Dicky being killed.

He gasped, 'Hush, hush, Daddy's all right. We're all safe. Steady now, you're not to worry.' Peter breathed deeply for a few seconds and managed to pull himself together. All the people at the top had gathered on the side overlooking the village green aghast at the possibility of Dicky crashing to the ground. Dicky's face was putty-coloured and he was sweating, Georgie and the twins were crying, and Bryn stood by the balustrade, his elbows resting on it and his hands covering his face in an attempt to disguise the fact that he was weeping.

Peter in his sternest voice said, 'Dear God man, you nearly killed him! What were you thinking of? Dicky, you and Georgie go down, get right out of the way. I'll come down with Bryn when he's composed himself.'

Mrs Jones offered to take the twins down with her. 'I'll go down the first and make sure they don't fall. We'll go for a piece of fatty cake shall we, perhaps your Daddy will join us when he's ready?'

Peter nodded his gratitude. Beth called out urgently, 'Don't fight Daddy will you, Mummy won't like you fighting. Please, don't fight Mr Fields again.'

'No, Beth, I shan't. I promise.'

Mrs Jones grabbed her hand and drew her towards the door. 'Don't you worry, I'll look after them. Come along, Alex. As for you, Dicky Tutt, you want your brains examining. This is all your fault!' She disappeared through the low door with the twins, and Peter heard Alex saying 'Isn't my Daddy brave?' They were followed by the people who'd witnessed the incident and who were quite glad to return to the ground. In any case it was a brilliant piece of news for the church hall. That'd make them sit up and stare and not half. Why they'd almost witnessed a murder! And all for twenty pence. If it hadn't been for the Rector they would have. Just think if he hadn't happened to be up there, would any of them have had the strength to stop Bryn? No, they wouldn't. He'd been like a man possessed. A maniac no less.

Grandmama was in charge of the teapot in the church hall. She'd already had her tea and fatty cake, even though she hadn't been up the tower. Climbing church towers wasn't quite sensible for a lady of her mature years, and besides someone had to be there when the first ones came in for their tea, and putting on a martyred air she'd volunteered to make a personal sacrifice by presiding over the teapot.

The first rush of customers were the ones who'd witnessed Dicky's close encounter with death. Grandmama listened to the story feeling absolutely shocked at the incident and Mrs Jones said, 'We really ought to go tell Bel, she should know.'

Kate Pascoe from the school volunteered to go to the Store to tell Bel. A few minutes after she'd gone Dicky came in and sat on a chair, while Georgie went to ask for two cups of tea.

As Grandmama poured out the tea she whispered. 'Georgie, I'm so sorry to hear about what has happened. How is Dicky?'

'In shock. I'm hoping the tea will revive him a bit. I don't know how I got him down the stairs, his legs are so shaky. He's been terribly sick in the church yard, retching something awful.' Grandmama offered the sugar and the fatty cake. 'Yes, he'll have sugar. Two please. But no fatty cake it might set him off again.'

'My dear, whatever are you going to do?'

'I don't know. I just don't know.'

'Well, if you need a roof over your head I can always make up the spare bed.'

Georgie looked at her with gratitude. 'Thanks, I may need to take you up on that.' She carried the tea over to where Dicky was sitting and stood over him while he took a drink of the tea. He'd drunk half the tea when in walked Bel.

The chattering stopped. Everyone secretly glanced at Dicky and Georgie. She was standing beside him with her arm around his shoulders, too busy comforting him to notice Bel's arrival.

Bel, arms akimbo, went to stand in front of the two of them. 'Satisfied are you now? Done everything you can to completely upset the apple cart? Caused enough trouble have you? The pair of you need your heads cracking together. You most of all Dicky Tutt. You ought to be ashamed of yourself. All through you, Bryn could have been up for murder. Come to think of it though, it's a pity he didn't tip you over, it's only what you deserve.' She turned her attention to Georgie. 'As for you, madam, the sooner you get yourself straightened out the better for everyone. You've already got a man of your own, what do you want another one for? I would have thought one was enough to be going on with. That poor Bryn, you've driven him to the absolute edge.'

'To say nothing of Dicky . . .' someone said rather too loudly and those around them laughed.

Bel swung round on them. 'Funny is it? Find it amusing do you? Bit of gossip for the weekend is it? It's blinking serious. Too serious for you to make a joke of. We could have been sending for the undertaker for him' – she jerked her thumb in Dicky's direction – 'right this very minute.' She turned back to Dicky. 'As for you, you're coming home with me *now*, where I can keep my eye on you. On your feet.'

'Now, Bel . . .'

'Now, Bel, nothing. You're coming home and you, madam' – Bel stabbed at Georgie's shoulder with a sharp finger which made her stagger slightly – 'can get back to doing what you do best, chatting up the punters from behind the bar.' Bel was about to drag Dicky to his feet and take him out when the outside door sprang open and Peter and Bryn came in. It is frequently observed in Turnham Malpas that they might not get far but they do see life. Never was it more true than now. All four of the protagonists under one roof and them all there to witness it. A deathly hush fell.

15

Dicky leapt to his feet, his face which had been close to recovering its natural healthy glow had gone drip white again at the sight of Bryn. He gave a slight hint of a whimper as Peter closed the door behind them and Bryn came right into the hall, and stopped within feet of where he stood.

Bryn was still very distressed. He appeared to be of two minds, he didn't know whether to have another go at eliminating Dicky or whether to weep again at the dreadful, fearful thing he'd attempted to do.

Peter spoke in a tense well-controlled voice. 'I should be glad Dicky and Bel if you would come to the rectory and we can have a try to sort this out. You too Georgie. This incident is extremely serious, and I am grievously distressed by it. Grievously distressed. It is so serious that if Dicky chose to he could press charges of attempted murder, which I should be honour bound to support. I sincerely hope we can avoid such an occurrence.'

'Why avoid it? Let's go for it. He's a mad man.' Dicky's voice held a hint of hysteria which aggravated Bryn. He clenched his fists again and moved threateningly towards Dicky. Dicky picked up a chair and prodded the legs in the direction of Bryn.

Bel stepped towards him and wrestled the chair from him. 'Don't be stupid, there's enough trouble already. Come on, let's be off to the rectory.'

'I'm not going to the rectory, I'm having nothing to do with him. He's dangerous, he nearly killed me.'

'And whose fault is that?'

Peter went to open the door. 'Come along Bryn, and you too, Dicky, I insist.'

'I'm sorry, Rector, but no. There's no way I'm being closeted with that maniac in your house. Who's to say he won't try again.' Dicky shook his head. 'No way.'

Peter tried again. 'Bryn has given me his solemn word that he won't try anything again. Now for the last time, come with me to the rectory, I will guarantee your safety.' Raising his voice and coming close to losing his temper with them all he shouted, 'All of you, this minute. Well? I'm waiting.' He stood with the door open.

Bel said 'If you don't go of your own accord, Dicky, I shall boot you all the way there. So it's up to you, go on. *Go!*'

Dicky weighed up the consequences of refusing to go of his own accord and decided walking there was better than being kicked there by Bel. Slowly he headed for the door skirting Bryn with as much caution as he would a raving lion. Bel, Bryn and Georgie followed and Peter shut the door behind him. There was an air of anticlimax in the church hall when they'd left. To their extreme disappointment the anticipated fracas had not materialised.

Mrs Jones shook her head. 'Poor Bel, it's her I feel sorry for. Fancy having your husband running after someone else in broad daylight, it's bad enough if they keep it quiet.' Mrs Jones stood up and took hold of the twins' hands. 'I do, I feel really sorry for her, the poor thing. The embarrassment. The shame.'

'She's got no claim on Dicky. He's free to do as he likes. They're not married,' Grandmama blurted out.

'Not married! Are you sure?' Mrs Jones sat down again abruptly.

'No, they're not. I have it on good authority.'

A general hubbub broke out all over the hall at this bombshell.

'Not married! I don't believe it.'

'Neither do I. Be careful, we've been conned with one of the Duchess's tales before.'

'Who'd have thought it.'

'Well, I never.'

'Whatever next?'

'So he's a free agent then . . .'

'Where did you learn this?' Mrs Jones enquired of Grandmama.

'I have my sources. It was someone who's known him for years who told me. This tea's getting cold, I'll go make another pot.'

In bed that night Peter sighed and Caroline asked him what caused him to sigh so.

'I intended spending some time polishing my sermon for tomorrow, some chance of that. I have never met four such obstinate people.'

'But you did get them to listen to reason eventually.'

'Eventually, as you say. Bryn is so incensed and no wonder. When I finally got them to agree to give themselves a week to sit back and *think* where all this is leading I was exhausted. Georgie's wanting to leave Bryn. Bryn's wanting to leave the village and make a new start with Georgie, some idea he's got about running a bar on a cruise liner, I ask you! Dicky's determined that Georgie is the one for him and Bel is the only reasonable one and she's the least guilty of them all. So with the whole situation on hold for a week I hope, hope mark you, we shall reach a reasonable solution.'

'I'm just so glad Dicky isn't pressing charges.'

'Exactly! I told him that if he really wanted to wash his dirty linen in public and ruin the reputations of both Bel and Georgie, to say nothing of Bryn and his business and Dicky himself, then that was the right way to go about it and would be no solution to anything at all.'

'But it will mean two divorces if Dicky has his way won't it? That is just so painful.'

'Not two, only one.'

Caroline sat up and looked at Peter. He was laid with both his hands locked behind his head staring at the ceiling.

'Only one? What do you mean?'

Peter turned his head slightly and looked seriously at her. 'If I tell you, there's not to be one word outside this bedroom! OK?' Caroline nodded. 'No one but those four and you and I know, you see. Bel and Dicky aren't married.'

Caroline fell back on the pillow and laughed till she had tears rolling down her cheeks. 'Not married! Oh Peter! Oh Peter! What a mess! They told you this today?'

'Hush! Don't make so much noise you'll wake the children! Yes, they did, though somehow I got the feeling it wasn't the whole truth somehow, there was something they were all four holding back. However, please don't breathe a word because if they knew they'll be spreading it around then saying Dicky isn't fit to be Scout leader and I'm not having that. He's brilliant. There's no one can compare and I'm not having the Scout troop jeopardised by some narrow-minded bigots.'

Caroline wiped her eyes and, with a straight face bent over him and looked Peter straight in the eye and said 'I can remember a time when you were very upset about Willie and Sylvia living together before they got married. Oh yes, you had a lot to say about that, to me at any rate. You've certainly changed your tune.'

'It's a question of priorities. If no one knows, the village won't be any wiser and everything can carry on as before. He's started the Scout band as you know and Gilbert Johns has volunteered to help and I thought I might . . .'

'Peter! You've given them a week. A week of comparative peace, but what if at the end of it Dicky and Georgie decide not to get together? The idea of them all still living in the village is fraught with problems.'

'Well, we'll cross that bridge when, and if, we come to it.'

'Yes, you're right. The story of this particular All Saints' Day will last for years! They'll still be talking about it in a hundred years' time! Come to think of it they nearly got another saint added to their number on a very appropriate day! Oh dear! I've got to go to sleep. I've suddenly gone very tired. Good night, Peter.'

'Good night, my darling. I love you.'

'I love you.'

'God bless you.'

'And you.'

'Caroline, are you feeling better? About us?'

There was a silence which Peter waited for her to fill. She knew he would leave the question in the air if she didn't reply and she knew she wouldn't sleep if she didn't answer him. She searched about under the duvet for his hand and having found it, she took it to her lips and kissed it. 'Thank you for being such a wonderfully understanding man. No, understanding *husband*. You've seemed to know instinctively how to go about making me feel whole, when I'm not and won't ever be. And I thank you for that from the bottom of my heart. Yes, I am feeling much better about us and when I've got the go ahead . . .'

'Which you sound confident of getting . . .'

'Which I am confident of getting, then I truly believe everything will be all right between us. When I first came home I'd gone off you terribly, it was quite horrifying, but I expect it was because I was feeling weak and very frightened or maybe that's how you feel when you've had my kind of an operation. I really could hardly bear you close to me which sounds a dreadful thing to say about someone one loves but it's true. But now I do believe I appreciate your maleness all over again.'

'Hallelujah!'

But 'Hallelujah!' wasn't the word Peter used on reading the letter which he found on the mat when he went downstairs on Monday morning.

'Damn and blast! Who the blazes has let the cat out of the bag?'

He read on . . . 'As a consequence of these events it has been brought to our notice . . . living with someone who is not his wife . . . even in these more relaxed times his position is untenable . . . and we the under-signed . . . are agreed that Dicky Tutt is no longer a suitable person to be in charge of the St Thomas à Becket Scouts . . .'

'Blast it!'

'Daddy! That was a very rude word.'

'Alex, you're quite right it was and I'm sorry.' He raced up the stairs. 'Caroline! Look at this.' He dropped the letter on her knee. 'Who's responsible for drafting this I wonder? They promised me they wouldn't say a word. Not a word. Now, apparently everyone knows.'

Caroline broke off from helping Beth to dress and scanned the letter. 'Oh dear! So they must. Here, Beth, put your tights on. No, the other way round, that's it. Just look at the signatures. Six! Six of them. How could they? Some haven't even got any connection with the Scouts. Look! Thelma Senior, she wouldn't know a Scout if she met one in the street. Venetia, Vince Jones but not Mrs Jones. This is awful. It simply isn't fair to Dicky. How dreadful of them!'

Over breakfast Peter and Caroline discussed the matter further and Peter decided for a day or two at least he wouldn't reply. Pressure of work he called it. Caroline called it avoiding the issue. They were both laughing about her comment when Sylvia came in to start work.

Caroline poured her a cup of tea as she said 'Good morning, Sylvia.'

Alex jumped off his chair to show Sylvia his new shoes. 'Look, Sylvie. Look at my new shoes.'

'They're lovely, Alex. What a good choice! They will keep your feet warm. I like the colour. Morning everyone. You're looking better this morning, Doctor, in fact much better.'

'Thank you, I'm feeling better, much better. I expect you've heard the latest news?'

'About Dicky's close encounter? I have of course. There's no other subject of conversation.'

'Peter got a petition this morning, asking for Dicky Tutt to be removed from being Scout leader. Someone's found out that . . .'

Peter cleared his throat. 'I didn't think we . . .'

'Sylvia will know soon enough, someone's let it out that Dicky and Bel are not . . .' – Caroline glanced at the children and continued by saying – 'are not living in wedlock.'

'Well, we all know who that was, don't we?'

Caroline raised an eyebrow. 'Do we?'

'I was in the church hall checking to see if they needed any help before I climbed the tower and I heard the Duchess tell everyone. Said someone who'd known Dicky for a long time had told her.'

'That blasted woman!'

'Peter! *Pas devant les enfants.*'

'Sorry.'

Alex said 'That's two times today, Daddy.'

'I beg your pardon. Could be four or even five before this day's out. This whole situation is developing into a major crisis when there's no need at all. If everyone had just kept still tongues in their heads it would have all blown over. However, it's Monday so it's Penny Fawcett first. Anything you want from their market Sylvia? Caroline?'

'Fresh vegetables, Rector, please, particularly potatoes.'

'Caroline?'

'Nothing thanks. I think I'll take the children to school this morning. The fresh air and a change of scene will do me good.'

'What a splendid idea. Yes, you do that. I'm off. Bye, children. Bye, darling.'

'Don't forget your cloak, it's cold.'

'OK.'

After Caroline had left the children at school she didn't feel like returning home straight away so she wandered into the Store hoping for a chat with anyone who happened to come in. She'd been feeling really cut off since her mother had gone back, and felt it was time she took steps to widen her horizons.

Jimbo welcomed her with open arms. 'Come for a hug have you? It's lovely to see you out. Here, sit on this chair and I shall serve you with a coffee if I may. Just made it, so it's absolutely fresh.'

'Oh yes, please. That would be lovely. How's things?' Jimbo handed her a cup and offered her sugar. 'Thanks I will. Don't usually but Peter says I must get some weight on, so I will.'

'You need to.'

The coffee was too hot to drink so Caroline put it down on the shelf nearest to her and asked Jimbo again if he had any news.

Before he could answer her Linda came in. 'Oh, Doctor Harris, how lovely to see you out. I am pleased. Life getting back to normal is it?'

'Well, not quite but nearly.'

'My word, your two little ones must have had a nasty shock on Saturday. I'm glad I wasn't there. Are they all right?'

'Thankfully I don't think they realised what was happening. They were so worried about their father fighting, that was what impressed them the most! Alex gave me a very graphic description when he got home. He was rather proud of Peter and couldn't or wouldn't understand that he wasn't really fighting.'

'Thank God for the Rector is all I can say. What a blessing he was there. Then when the Duch— Mrs Charter-Plackett let on that they weren't married. You should have seen everyone's faces, they couldn't believe it. They were gobsmacked I can tell you . . .' Linda propped her hip against a shelf and looked set for the morning. 'Mrs Jones said . . .'

Jimbo ever mindful of his business interrupted. 'Excuse me, Linda, but you were ten minutes late to begin with and I see you've someone tapping their foot by your counter. Could you get started, please. The customer is king in our set-up.'

'Sorry, I must say.' She hastened off and then had to come back for the key to open the post office till. Jimbo took it out of his pocket and she almost snatched it from him. He raised his eyebrows at Caroline. 'Come in the back. Bring your coffee.' Jimbo called out to Linda, 'If I'm needed I'm in my office. Bel shouldn't be long.'

He settled Caroline on his chair and perched on the stool.

'Peter is not best pleased at what your mother said in the church hall on Saturday. It has proved to be true, I know, but Peter had been hoping it could be kept secret.'

'I know, I know. She told me a week or so ago that she had some news about Dicky but I wouldn't let her tell me. I said she musn't say a word to anyone at all, keep mum, et cetera. But I expect the temptation proved too much.'

'The other thing is, Jimbo, you'll soon know so it won't matter if I tell you first, Peter had a petition put through the letterbox this morning, stating that Dicky should be sacked from the Scouts. It was in your mother's handwriting and her name was the first signature, I'm afraid.'

Jimbo groaned. 'Oh no! I don't believe this. After all I said to her. Obviously I didn't say enough. I wish to goodness she'd never come here. She's worse than a child. As soon as Bel comes I shall go pay her a visit. She really is the end. The absolute limit.'

'Who is?' Standing in the doorway was his mother. Dressed immaculately in black and white she was the epitome of the well-dressed older woman.

'Close that door.'

'I beg your pardon?'

'I said close that door.'

She did. 'Well? Who is?'

'You are, Mother. I asked you not to say a word about what the sewing-machine man told you. But what do you do? You blurt it out in front of half the village. As if that wasn't bad enough I hear you've signed a letter of protest about him. It simply will not do. What you do reflects on me. My position in this village is paramount to the success of my business. Are you determined to ruin it for me? Besides which it's most unkind of you, quite thoughtless, in fact, to be a party to that petition.'

'Don't speak to me in that tone of voice. I am your mother!'

'I do not need reminding.'

'In any case it was bound to come out in view of Saturday. Bound to. Sooner rather than later I say. And I meant what I said about him in that letter, my grandsons' moral rectitude is under threat and I won't tolerate it, even if you condone it.'

'I never said I condoned it, I said it was none of my business.'

'Fudging the issue, that's all that is. If you'd let me tell you at the time, you would know all the story. When I said Dicky was married the man in the shop said, "Dicky Tutt married! Not Dicky, he isn't the marrying kind. Likes to play the field does Dicky, he wouldn't let himself get trapped into marriage." So I said, "Well, he is married now." He said, "Well, I know for a fact he isn't." I said, "Well, he is." And he asked me her name and of course I said "Bel". His whole demeanour changed then, you could have thought I'd said a dirty word, he gave me a funny look, handed me my change and shut up like a clam. When I thanked him for saving my life with the spare part for my beloved machine he turned his back on me and didn't even say goodbye. So it's not just that Dicky isn't married it seems to me there's something else as well!'

'Mother! You're at it again! I warned you you'd have me to reckon with and . . .'

Caroline could see that Jimbo was working himself up into a colossal temper, his normally pallid skin was flushed deep red and his hands were clenching and unclenching at a furious pace, so she interrupted him. 'Mrs Charter-Plackett, out of Christian charity I think it would be a good idea to let this suspicion go no further than these four walls. What on earth the significance is of the man behaving so oddly when you said his wife's name was Bel I really cannot guess, but for everyone's sakes, please don't repeat it.'

'As if I would. I must apologise for my son's bad temper, he got that from his father not from me.' Grandmama smiled at Caroline and in a completely different tone said, 'Now, my dear, I am glad to see you out and about. You are looking well.'

Linda called out, 'Mr Charter-Plackett! Can you come, they're queueing at the till and Bel's not here yet.'

'Right ho! I'll love you and leave you. Stay as long as you want, Caroline.' Jimbo pushed past his mother and left.

Caroline watched him go. 'I'm going too. It's the first time I've been out, I don't want to overdo it.'

'Of course not. Any time you're fancying a little walk, call and see me, I keep my cottage very warm and cosy and we'll have a cup of tea and a chat.'

Caroline stood up. 'Thank you, I'll remember that. Take you up on it some time, perhaps.'

'You'll be most welcome.'

When Grandmama answered her door bell that afternoon, she hoped it might be Caroline but she found Peter standing there. The reproachful look in his eyes shamed her. Why did the man always expect the best and look so sad when he didn't find it? They were all of them only human.

'What a lovely surprise, Rector, do come in.'

She offered him the best and biggest chair and sat herself down on the sofa. Peter sat with his forearms resting on his knees and his hands locked together.

'Mrs Charter-Plackett. I've come to say how sorry I am that you told everyone about Dicky and Bel. The last time you started up a piece of gossip it was totally unfounded and would have been very damaging not to say heartbreaking to Caroline if she had heard it. This time what you said is true, but you didn't know for certain it was the truth when you said it, and how I wish you hadn't.' He looked so sadly at her that her heart began to thump. 'I really do wish you hadn't. What do you have to say to me about it?'

This was it. This was when he was going to bring the best out in her when she didn't want him to. She'd only spoken the truth. But, as he said, maybe it would have been best left unsaid. 'Well, I . . . I'm sorry to have disappointed you. I didn't think.'

'Exactly. You see there isn't a Scout troop in the whole of Great Britain with a more dedicated leader than Dicky. He's excellent with the boys, quite excellent. We have boys attending from all three of the villages and way beyond and they are very lucky to have him. And so too is the church lucky to have him. He started the troop from scratch and has built it up in no time at all and he has the most tremendous influence on those boys, a wonderful influence for good. You only have to look at Rhett Wright to see how much good he can do. If you'd known the old Rhett you wouldn't believe the change in him and it's in part due to Dicky and his hard work. I will not, will not ask him to resign.'

'I see.'

'Do you though?'

Grandmama picked an invisible thread from her skirt to give herself a moment to think. 'You mean he stays for the greater good?'

'That's right.'

'But he's living in sin.'

Peter studied what she said. 'Indeed, yes I suppose he is. But what difference does that make to his work?'

'None. I suppose.'

'Obviously it would be better if he wasn't living with Bel and why they don't marry I don't know . . .'

'It's the deceit of it, wearing a ring when they aren't.'

'But it is *their* business not yours nor mine. So am I any nearer to persuading you to withdraw your signature? You see Mrs Charter-Plackett, you have such an influence in this village.' Grandmama smiled somewhat smugly. 'Oh they wouldn't admit it for the world, they wouldn't want you to get above yourself you see, but you have. It's partly through Jimbo, he's so well liked for he's such a generous kind-hearted man, and partly through yourself. Your style . . . and bearing and of course your intelligence. You're no fool. You could be such an influence for *good* you see if you let yourself.'

By the time Peter had finished this speech Grandmama was glowing with pleasure. The dear man. He'd got right to the heart of the matter. Right to the nub. 'I withdraw my signature. They'll all be disappointed but there you are. Common sense and the greater good has prevailed.'

'I can't thank you enough. That's wonderful, I knew you were too liberal-minded not to see my point of view. Now, can you do one more thing for me?'

'Whatever you ask.'

'Persuade the others to withdraw their signatures too?'

Alarmed, Grandmama said, 'Oh, I don't know about that. They were very adamant.'

'Could you invite them round for a strategy meeting? I'm sure it wouldn't be beyond your powers of persuasion to encourage them to agree with your point of view.'

'I could try. Yes, I could try. I'll do that. It'll be a hard nut to crack, but yes I will. I'll tell them they've got to for the boys' sakes. Don't you worry, Peter, you'll be able to tear up that letter by the end of the week. Leave it to me.'

'Thank you.'

'I'm sorry for Georgie though, you know, she is very distressed. She's so sickened by Bryn, and Dicky's brought such happiness and excitement to her life. It's all gone wrong between her and Bryn you see, and I can't think of anything more terrible than being in a marriage which has gone rotten to the core. I don't believe in divorce, you know for better or worse and all that, but I do feel very sorry for Georgie. A bad marriage must be hell. I beg your pardon, Rector, but it must be.'

Peter shook his head. 'I don't believe in divorce either, but I do begin to think that there must be times . . .'

'I can't believe the good Lord wants his children to be unhappy and if they've given it their best shot . . . Well. I've told her to grab happiness when she has the chance.' She stood up. 'Don't let me keep you, a young man like you doesn't want to listen to an old lady's ramblings. Off you go. I promise to do as you wish.'

Peter looked down at her with such a loving smile on his face and said, 'No, as *you* wish, surely?'

There was nothing else she could say but, 'Yes, that's right, as I wish.'

16

The week's respite which Peter had got the four of them to agree to, wasn't working as far as Bryn was concerned. He hadn't had an inkling that Georgie was unhappy, not an inkling and out of the blue he had been presented with Dicky in courting mood and Georgie enjoying his attentions; to say he was stunned was an understatement.

He'd a sneaking feeling that maybe somewhere along the line he'd let her down but it was all too late to retrieve himself. She was sleeping in the other bedroom and providing his meals and working in the bar but there was no rapport between them. Barely even politeness, certainly not any conversation. Takings had slumped dramatically since Saturday, once the initial excitement was over, nobody wanted to drink in a pub where the landlord appeared to be capable of murder. Which he had been that day. Bryn could have thrown Dicky over, gone down carried him back up and thrown him over again for the sheer satisfaction of it. He'd been mad. Completely mad. He didn't know how much longer he could continue like this. What was the point of being tied to someone who wished they were with someone else and a thousand miles away from you?

He'd come to recognise his mistake in not nurturing his marriage, thereby causing it quietly, unobtrusively, to die. It was a long time since he'd given Georgie any real thought. Oh, he'd paid for her clothes, admired her hair, enjoyed her bubbly personality, appreciated her hard work and her willingness but not thought about love. That was it. Love. Somehow he'd left that out of the equation and here he was with a wife being courted by an upstart of a dandy of a man, who'd captured her heart.

Perhaps if they moved away like he'd suggested. Bought another pub, or even heavens above, got that job running a bar on a cruise liner that he'd seen advertised in the trade paper last week. It was a cruise line which worked on the basis of cheap and cheerful and pack 'em in, but it would be a start. That might excite her. Not only might, it would. He seized on the idea like a drowning man a life raft. Yes, that just might . . . Bryn heard her coming down the stairs. He didn't greet her because he didn't know what to say any more. When he heard the thud of something heavy being put down on the stone floor of the passage he turned to see.

Georgie was dressed for going out. Beside her was a large suitcase.

'It's no good, is it? I'm . . .'

'You're not leaving? What about the bar?'

Georgie's face crumpled. ' "What about the bar," he says. That just about sums it up. You'll jolly well have to find someone else won't you? There's always Alan and that girl from Penny Fawcett who keeps pestering for a job. Alan will do more hours, he needs the money.'

'That's not fair, we're in this together you know, we both took it on, you're abandoning me.'

'That's true we did take it on together, but it's your name over the door and I'm afraid you'll have to get on with it.' She pulled on her gloves and bent to pick up the case. 'I'm abandoning you only after you've abandoned me.'

'Don't, please, don't go Georgie. Nothing's changed I still feel . . .'

'You're scoring well today Bryn. That's the second bull's eye in less than five minutes. "Nothing's changed", how right you are.'

'I don't know what you're talking about, it's all riddles to me.'

'Exactly. You're so turned in on yourself you can't see beyond the end of your nose. I shall be at Mrs Charter-Plackett's for the time being if you need me, not that there's anything to say between us.'

'Mrs Charter-Plackett's? Not Dicky's?'

'No, not Dicky's. There's enough gossip without me doing that, and there is Bel to consider. I'm having a respite, to sort myself out.'

'But Mrs Charter-Plackett! That old bat. Why her?'

'She's a kindred spirit.'

'What's that mean?'

'Somehow she understands what it means to be miserable, when you're married.'

'Is that how you think of it? Miserable?'

Georgie looked sadly up at him. 'I'm afraid I do and for some time now. I'll be off then.'

Bryn watched her go. Habit made him offer to carry her case for her, but she shook her head and left by the back door. He stared at the door after she'd closed it. The sound of it shutting struck him right to the heart. That was it then. Marriage, Georgie, the pub. Ashes. All ashes. He might as well not have lived the last twenty-two years. It had all been for nothing. There was a banging at the back door. Three bangs. That was the brewery delivery. He picked up his keys and went to open up the cellar.

Georgie might have escaped, but he still had ordinary everyday life to face. Still had to keep going with the nitty-gritty of a daily grind he was beginning to loathe. Bryn felt weighed down with cares. He looked down at his feet surprised to find there was no ball and chain fastened to them. How could there not be when it was so difficult to walk?

'This bedroom's lovely, Mrs Charter-Plackett. Lovely! So warm and . . . well lovely!'

'I'm glad you like it. These turquoise shades give such warmth to a room don't they? Elegant but welcoming I always think. There's plenty of space in the wardrobe, look.' She opened the mahogany doors and displayed the empty coathangers. 'Fill it up, there's plenty of drawer space too, if you need it. Settle yourself in and I'll make a coffee shortly and we'll sit by the fire and talk.'

Georgie thanked her. 'It's most kind. I shan't stay long. Just till I get my head sorted.'

'Of course, I'm giving you a breathing space. I think it would be nice if you called me Katherine. It seems silly in this day and age to be calling me Mrs Charter-Plackett when we're living in the same house. Come down when you're ready.'

They sat by the log fire, a speciality of Grandmama's. She had trained Greenwood Stubbs, the estate gardener, to keep her well supplied. Mr Fitch had said he didn't mind and she paid him for them so it was all fair and square.

Georgie found the fire comforting. Like the two of them had said before, you can dream dreams in front of a fire. What were her dreams?

'So what are your dreams?' Georgie jumped at the question, surely she wasn't a mind reader? It took her a moment to find an answer.

'In the best of all possible worlds what I'd really truly like is to be in a nice house with Dicky, each with our own careers and coming home in the evenings to spend time together and . . .'

'That sounds very ordinary. Very unadventurous.'

'What would you have us do?'

'I had thought of a new life together in Australia or New Zealand or Canada or somewhere. The colonies, of course, not the USA, far too brash for permanent living.'

Georgie laughed. 'Me? In Australia?'

'Why not. You and Dicky would make a wonderful pair for managing a bar. You with your knowledge, Dicky with his jokes and his outgoing personality. Excellent!'

'I've had enough of the licensed trade to last me a lifetime. Thank you very much.'

'Ah! but is it the combination of Bryn and the licensed trade you hate, or is it just the licensed trade. You've got to distinguish between the two.'

'Ah! Right.' She gazed into the fire and said 'I hadn't thought someone like you would be so understanding. You don't appear to be an under-standing person at all.'

Grandmama shuffled a little uncomfortably in her chair. 'Well, I do have my good moments. I've made a few mistakes since I came here, but I am trying hard. For instance tonight I've got a meeting of the people who put their signatures to that letter I wrote about Dicky.'

Georgie stared at her. 'You wrote that letter then?'

'I'm afraid so. The Rector made me see the error of my ways and I'm having a try at changing their minds. So I'm afraid tonight you'll have to stay in the bedroom or go out. It wouldn't do for you to be seen to be here.'

'Thank goodness for that! You will do your best? Dicky wouldn't be Dicky without his Scouts. They are his life's work. Whatever I do I mustn't part him from that.'

'No, indeed, I think you're right. Perhaps Australia wouldn't be such a good idea. How's Bryn?'

'Shattered.'

'I see.'

'Do you know what his first words were when he realised I was leaving?' Grandmama shook her head. 'He said "What about the bar." If ever I needed confirmation that was it. "What about the bar." I couldn't believe it.'

'Oh dear! What about Bel?'

'Dear Bel. She's been so nice about it all. So understanding. She's the one I feel guilty about, more than Bryn. Bel's not at all upset about Dicky being in love with me, she's very philosophical about it. What will be will be she says. I might go across there tonight and have a talk, though we've promised Peter we wouldn't see each other, so perhaps I'd better not.'

'Don't rush into decisions. You know how impulsive Dicky can be.'

Georgie grinned. 'I certainly do. He's the loveliest man, you know. He sees the world through child's eyes, yet when he's with the boys he kind of grows in stature, literally. One click of his fingers and they're all lined up, no nonsense. There's such *strength* there as well as all the joking and laughter. I do love him. He's such fun. The light of my life you could say.'

'He sounds lovely.'

'Oh, he is!'

'You're very lucky.'

'It doesn't feel like luck at the moment. Bryn's guilty of attempted murder, and Dicky and I drove him to it. It was only the Rector's being so persuasive that prevented Dicky from pressing charges, after all, who could blame him? He'd had a terrible fright, the poor love. Perhaps I'll stay in the bedroom while you have the meeting, maybe I should leave Bel and Dicky to talk things out on their own.'

*

Dicky came in from work desolate. He'd promised Peter a whole week of thinking things over and only two days of it had gone by, and he longed to see Georgie and what was worse he was no nearer a solution.

'Bel! It's me.' He could smell his dinner cooking, pork, he thought and stuffing. The kitchen was its usual haphazard self just like it always was when Bel was cooking. She had the most casual approach to the subject anyone could have, but it always turned out well. She worked on a bit of this and a bit of that basis and wouldn't have been able to find the scales if she looked for them for a week. The kitchen was tiny and it was best to keep out when she was in there. He squeezed himself round the door and got them both a lager from the fridge. 'I won't pour yours just yet.'

'Right. Five minutes.'

'Right.' Dicky seated himself in an easy chair and looked round the room. Bel had made this such a comfortable home. They hadn't the money for all the frills but she'd done a marvellous job with what they'd had available. It had been a bare barren tip when she'd come and somehow out of nothing a home had materialised. Whatever happened, he wasn't abandoning the Scouts, because the Scouts was where he made a real contribution. It was where he counted. It was where no-good loser Dicky Tutt could stand tall. He couldn't count the boys he'd helped over the years, this was the second troop he'd started and it was the best.

His job? Well, he did it, he did it to the best of his ability but it was a useless, waste-of-time, cog-in-a-machine, kind of job. No future, no way. But the Scouts, he gave them and they gave him such energy, that was when he came alive. Now he'd got the band going! He had a vision of them entering competitions, not just entering but winning. He raised a clenched fist and punched the air.

Bel came in and saw him. 'Daydreaming again?'

Dicky grinned. 'I suppose so. You know me, Bel! Always moving on to the next thing, I can't stand still.'

'You're right there, you can't.' Bel put the hot plates down on the table. 'Get stuck in.'

'Can't resist. It looks wonderful, Bel, I don't know how you do it.'

'Hard graft?'

'Yes, of course. You do work hard. I've always admired you for that.' Dicky put his knife and fork back down again. 'It's no good, I've no appetite. Whatever am I going to do?'

'You're going to eat your dinner and get washed and changed and go to Scouts. It's Scout night and that's what you're doing.'

'OK! OK! Why are you always so practical? Can't we just talk for once?'

'When I've eaten my dinner, we'll talk for half an hour and then you've got to go.'

She silently carried on eating her dinner without so much as even a glance in his direction. She ate her tinned fruit and ice-cream, finished her lager and sat back. 'First and foremost I want you to be happy . . .'

Dicky shook his head. 'There's you to consider, can't leave you out of it.'

'If you being happy makes me happy then we're all right, aren't we? You won't be happy without those boys. They're your life's work, not some piddling office job in a factory, though you can't manage without the money it's still not what you really want to do. So you've got to stick at that and you've got to stick at Scouts. Question is do you want Georgie so much that you're willing to give it all up?'

'I want the lot. You, Georgie, the job and the Scouts. Greedy aren't I?'

'No, you're a man, it's to be expected.'

'Bel!'

'With my two jobs I could just about manage, so don't worry about me. You do your own thing.'

'But where would you live?'

'Haven't worked that out yet. But what about Georgie? How could she live here, with Bryn just down the road. It wouldn't be easy.'

Dicky finished his drink, put down the glass and heaved a great sigh. He got up, went round the table and put his arm round Bel. 'Where would I be without you?'

Bel pushed him off. 'Don't go all sentimental it doesn't suit you, Dicky. You've fallen in love with a married woman and she can't live here and you can't leave easily because we've a mortgage as long as your arm for this place, and I don't want to lose you, and you don't want to lose me and altogether you've made a damned mess of things, and all you're doing is wanting me to solve it for you. Well, I can't. Frankly I wish at the bottom of me that we'd told the truth about not being husband and wife when we first came here. Don't you?'

'With hindsight, yes I do. But we both felt so vulnerable it seemed the safest thing to say nothing at all at the time.'

'They'd have got used to us, we know that now but we didn't then.'

'That's right. Not at the time. So we've made the mess and I don't know how to get us out of it.'

'Neither do I!' She burst into tears, jumped up and struggled up the spiral staircase to the bedroom, leaving Dicky bewildered. He couldn't remember the last time he'd seen Bel cry. She must hurt very badly indeed. All this trying to be reasonable. It was her kind heart that was making her try to see it from his point of view. She didn't want to stand in his way because she loved him so much. But she didn't want it to happen; didn't want to lose him.

So much for a week to think things over. He was getting nowhere. Every word Bel had said was true. While he cleared the dishes into the kitchen he thought about it. The easiest thing to do would be to give up Georgie, the pain this idea caused made him almost double up with anguish. He couldn't! He couldn't! Not Georgie! Not to see her again. Ever again. No, that wasn't the way. He checked the time on the kitchen clock, the duck was almost at seven o'clock. When it reached half past it would be in the pond. He'd bought that ridiculous clock for Bel years ago and she'd never been parted from it. His mouth trembled. Dear Bel! Dear Bel! How he loved her, how he relied on her. And here she was giving up everything so he could be happy. He didn't deserve her.

Dicky went upstairs to get washed and changed. As he got to the top his spirits began to lift. In his mind he started running over all the things he had planned for tonight for the boys. When he got back he'd ring Georgie, just to say good night. Saying good night wouldn't be breaking his promise, would it? Peter had said don't see each other, well, he wouldn't be, would he? A whole week without being with her, his spirits dipped again. Nothing would be solved and he'd go circling round, pulled this way and that for the rest of his life. One thing he did know he'd regret it for ever if he didn't get Georgie. Those two days they'd spent away together had been the happiest he could remember in all his life. Being with her had added such zip and excitement; every step they took, every stair they climbed, every view they admired had that extra zest.

He examined his face in the bathroom mirror. Somehow it didn't seem the kind of face that should be able to be in love, or indeed still less inspire it in anyone else. As he shaved he remembered her fingers trailing through his hair, her lips kissing his, her hands caressing his body. The ~~eastasy his memories brought him caused him to double.~~ He'd done it before with others, but never with such joy, such abandonment and such honest *truth*. Love! You thought about it, imagined it, had even convinced yourself in the past that you were in love, but when you were, really truly in love, then there was no mistaking it. Briefly he wished it would be Georgie in there in the bedroom when he went to get his uniform out of the wardrobe. Then the sense of disloyalty to Bel this brought about made him feel guilty.

When he got in the bedroom, Bel had gone. He listened and could hear her running the kitchen taps. Dear Bel. How could he manage without her?

That afternoon Peter had called to see Muriel and Ralph about a reading they were doing for him in church the following Sunday.

'Do come in, Peter. Tea?'

'No thanks, I've drunk enough tea today to float a battleship. Everywhere I go they all seem to think I'm in need of restoration, but I think it's much more likely they're after an eye witness report of Saturday's events!'

Ralph chuckled. 'Well, you must confess you were the hero of the hour. It was absolutely shocking and the ripples haven't stopped yet, have they?'

Muriel joined them just as Ralph finished speaking. 'It's about the reading is it, Peter?'

'That's right.'

Ralph said, 'Dicky and Bel not being married was a complete surprise to you too, was it?'

'Oh yes, it was.'

'Muriel and I were asked to sign the petition, they thought it would carry more weight, but we declined.'

'I'm glad.'

'Though they do have a point.'

Muriel said, 'I don't think it matters, we can't afford to lose him.'

Ralph, surprised by her emphatic support of Dicky, said, 'I thought you agreed with me?'

Muriel looked embarrassed. 'Well, I kind of do, but he does love her very much.'

'Does he?'

Muriel fidgeted with her beads, crossed her knees, looked anywhere but at either of them and then said, 'He told me.'

Ralph astonished at her duplicity said, 'You spoke to him after I'd said you should keep right out of it? When?'

'A while ago.'

'I see.'

'It's very hard, Ralph, when you love like he does and after all he's not entirely wrong in doing so is he, him not being married?'

'No, I suppose not, but when you talked to him you didn't know that did you?' She didn't answer him. 'Did you?'

Muriel looked to Peter for support. 'I . . . I . . . perhaps I should have said.'

Peter asked her what it was she should have said.

'That I guessed they weren't married. Dicky told me in a kind of a roundabout way, when I spoke to him. Perhaps I should have told you.'

Ralph was appalled. 'So you've known for weeks and never said a word.'

She'd been looking at the floor during her revelation, but now Muriel brought her eyes up to look straight at Ralph. 'Yes. I have.'

'But, Muriel, what about his loyalty to Bel? He can't just throw that away without a backward glance, now can he?'

Muriel shook her head.

Peter said, 'Everyone's making a lot too much fuss about all this. It would have been better if it hadn't come out, no one would have been any the wiser and the village would have carried on without a thought of asking Dicky to resign. As it is, Mrs Charter-Plackett spilled the beans, and it's all too late. Don't worry, Muriel, at least you have the virtue of having kept it to yourself. Now about the Bible reading.' He got the paper out of his briefcase and pressed on with his explanation of how he wanted things done on Sunday.

After he left, Muriel said, 'I need to finish the ironing,' and stood up to leave.

'Muriel!'

'Yes!'

'My dear, I'm not angry, just surprised. I thought we had no secrets.'

'We haven't, not really. But you'd said we should keep out of it and the chance came up and I feel for people who are in love. Before I met you again, I would have been shocked, truly shocked at all this, but I can understand now, and it is hard when you love and you mayn't and you want to and you can't help it and you can't keep quiet about it and you want all the world to know when you know it shouldn't.' Her voice trailed off rather lamely and she finished by saying, 'If you know what I mean.'

'I do know what you mean, and I love your dear kind heart and I'm proud you see the world in such a kindly manner, and I can understand how you understand how Dicky feels. I'm honoured that having met me and loved me, you understand the passions involved. You're a very understanding loving person and I love you all the more for it. Dear me, that's almost as confused as what you have just said but we both know what each other means don't we?'

'Oh yes! I thought you would have been annoyed if I'd told you I'd spoken to him so I . . .'

Ralph stood up and put his arms round Muriel. 'No more! have done! Muriel we both know we love people to be in love like we are, and have the happiness we share.'

'The trouble is I don't know how the four of them can possibly solve it. Something or someone will have to be sacrificed.'

'Only they can solve it my dear, we're lucky. Not everyone finds the path to love as easily as we did.'

'Oh yes, Ralph! What a good day it was when you came back and found me.'

He kissed her and then said, 'We came very close to drifting apart, my dear, remember, you refused me first of all.'

'Don't remind me.' Muriel sighed. 'I must have been mad. That's what I mean, about knowing about love, I didn't then, but now I do. I do sincerely hope that they find a solution to all this, though what it will be I can't really think. It alters your vision of things doesn't it? Love?'

17

Grandmama had rung all the people who'd signed her petition and finally convinced them that they needed to attend a meeting at her cottage to discuss strategy, that very night. They'd never actually assembled all together before, because when she'd sought support for her petition she'd simply called at their houses and they'd willingly signed as a result of her persuasive tongue. Now she had to get them to make a volte-face.

She was surprised to find Sheila Bissett one of the first on her doorstep.

'Come in, Sheila, do. So lovely of you to make the effort and struggle round. How many weeks now before the plaster's off?'

'Two weeks, with any luck. Shall I be glad! Just to be able to take a bath will be a luxury.'

Mentally Grandmama wrinkled her nose at the prospect of Sheila not taking a bath.

'What is it you want us for? I thought we'd done our bit?'

'I'll tell you when they've all arrived. Now, where is it best to put you?'

'I'll sit here with this little footstool for my leg. Can you take my crutches?'

'Of course. Sit down. I'll make coffee in a moment, when the others come.'

'Georgie's not here then?'

'Georgie? Why should she be?'

'I saw her in your garden. I spend a lot of time looking out of the window you see. Nothing much else I can do at the moment.'

Grandmama swallowed hard. 'Well, yes, she is, just for a little while. She needed somewhere to hide.'

'And she *chose* to hide here with *you*?'

Overtones of their previous battle could be heard in Sheila's voice but Grandmama was saved from answering because the doorbell rang and Thelma and Valda were in the sitting-room almost before Grandmama had invited them in.

As they seated themselves, Vince Jones arrived and Venetia and so the little cottage sitting-room was filled to bursting point.

Grandmama rapped with the poker on the brass fender. 'Excuse me. Thank you! I think we'll discuss the business of the meeting first and then I'll serve coffee.'

The ensuing conversation took all of Grandmama's diplomatic skills, and then some to resolve anything at all. Her complete change of heart took them all totally by surprise. She finally had to talk to them about their Christian duty, a course of action which made her uneasy, because she wasn't sure it was or maybe it was, after all Peter wanted her to do it and he couldn't be more Christian if he tried.

At last she'd persuaded Vince Jones and the Senior sisters, leaving Sheila Bissett who was being awkward on purpose and Venetia Mayer who saw it as her mission in life to protect the young since she'd become assistant youth club leader and attended every morning service without fail after her fright over the witchcraft incident.

Venetia fluffed her thick jet black hair, crossed and re-crossed her slender legs much to Vince Jones' delight and uttered the one question she, Grandmama, couldn't answer. 'But Mrs Charter-Plackett, it is only days since you gave us a very convincing argument for signing the petition, who or what has changed your mind? I haven't changed mine, so why have you? You haven't yet *really* told me why I should.'

'Charity. Christian charity. Plain, simple back-to-basics, Christian charity. We're changing our minds for the greater good. Yes, definitely the greater good. Dicky is the best scout leader any troup could hope to have. There can't be a troup in the whole county with so many boys and such a long waiting list. You try getting a boy in at the moment. The question is if he goes can we find someone to replace him? Any volunteers?' She looked round them, challenging them to offer their services.

Sheila wouldn't surrender. 'Well, I disagree. What is the good of having a Scout leader who doesn't conduct himself as he should. Things are so lax nowadays, standards should be upheld and I'd be amazed if the Rector wants to keep him anyway. I'm sure he must have fallen on our letter with a sigh of relief.'

Too quickly Grandmama said, 'He didn't.'

Quick as a flash Sheila saw the situation. 'Oh I see, it's the Rector who's behind all this, isn't it? He's made you see the error of your ways, hasn't he?'

'I did agree with his point of view.'

Sheila sighed. 'I know just what you mean. I swear he could make me say black was white if he'd a mind.' Not to be too easily persuaded however she said, 'I wish you'd been more honest from the beginning of this meeting, wish you'd admitted it was him behind your change of heart.'

Grandmama's lips pressed into a straight line, what an aggravating woman this Sheila really was, seeing everything so clearly just at the wrong moment. 'Right. Well, it's all out in the open then. Seeing as the Rector wants us to withdraw the letter then we must. We've no alternative.'

Sheila, musing on the times when Peter had persuaded her to do things she'd never intended, decided to give in because she knew faced with Peter himself she'd have given in immediately. 'Very well then. So be it. But you must understand it's only because the Rector wants it that I'm giving in, not because of you. I withdraw my signature as from now.' Mischievously aware she was scoring a point off Grandmama, Sheila said, 'Those in agreement with me raise a hand.'

She looked round the group and they signified their capitulation so the meeting was taken clean out of Grandmama's hands.

Well satisfied, Sheila cried. 'Carried! Now for the coffee. Sorry I can't help. My leg, you know.'

So the following morning Grandmama called at the rectory to tell Peter he could tear up the letter. Caroline answered the door. 'Do come in Mrs Charter-Plackett, how nice to see you. Is it Peter you're wanting? He's not in I'm afraid.'

'Well, yes, but I'm sure you could pass the message on for me.'

Caroline smiled, 'Well, I'll try!'

'Tell the Rector that I've managed to get every one of the signatories to withdraw and he can tear up the letter. It took some doing let me tell you, but we made it in the end.'

'Come in and sit down, I'm feeling quite lonely, Sylvia's gone home to supervise the washing-machine repair man, Peter's out, the children are at school and well, I'd enjoy having someone to talk to.'

Grandmama accepted. Caroline took her into the sitting-room and invited Grandmama to sit on the sofa while she took one of the chairs.

'It was Sheila Bissett, we don't see eye to eye after what happened you see, you know about the Harvest meeting. The others were easy to persuade, except for Venetia she proved more difficult. She's changed hasn't she, such a lot.'

'Yes, she has. Peter will be glad. He's so concerned about the four of them.'

'Aren't we all. Georgie . . .'

'Someone said she was staying with you.'

'She is. I feel so sorry for her trapped in a bad marriage. I know we make these promises for better or for worse and you mean them at the time but heavens above there is a limit to suffering. You're looking a little better than you have.'

'Mostly, yes, thank you, this blessed chemotherapy is crippling me though I'm afraid. Absolutely knocking me for six. I'm having some really dreadful times, so bad I sometimes really wonder if it's worth it. Far worse than the operation. You know about it then?'

'Yes, I had breast cancer some years ago, I was terrified. It leaves you with a dreadful frightened feeling right inside, doesn't it? As if nothing can be permanent any more and you think it could all so easily slip away. But stick it out, in the end it will all be to the good.' Grandmama noticed that Caroline was looking puzzled. She leaned over and patted her knee. 'I know people think of me as an old trout but I have got my understanding side too you know. Cancer can't be shrugged off like appendicitis or something, it stays hanging around in your mind making you anxious and cautious about everything you do, even when they've given you the all clear. The thing is to get on with life, put it behind you and be positive, it's the only way.'

'I've to go back in December, and hopefully then they'll give me something positive to be going on with. Fingers crossed . . .'

'If I'm any judge you're getting a healthier glow about you, I think you're going to be OK.'

'Thank you. It's been a terrible shock for us. So, how is Georgie?'

'Middling. She can't bear to be idle with having been so busy all these years, in fact one night she nearly went to give Bryn a hand she was so restless, feels guilty you see.'

'Naturally, it's been her life for so long. Are they any nearer a solution?'

Grandmama shook her head. 'No. Give him his due, Dicky has kept away. I wouldn't have him in the house in any case, that wouldn't be keeping his word, would it? I'm in enough trouble from Jimbo over having Georgie staying. But someone had to give her refuge and it couldn't have been you could it?'

' 'Fraid not. That would definitely have been taking sides.'

Grandmama got up to go. 'I won't tire you. You need your rest and you won't get any when those two little ones get home.'

'You're right about that. But I love them dearly.'

'Of course. They're absolutely delightful. You're very lucky.'

Caroline looked very directly into Grandmama's eyes. 'Yes, we are.'

It was Grandmama who lowered her eyes the first. Did Caroline know about the rumour she'd spread? She hoped not. 'Bye-bye, then my dear, take care. I'll see myself out, don't get up. Don't forget to give Peter the message will you?'

She shut the rectory door behind her and went to the Store to collect her fresh rolls for the freezer. The bakery had usually delivered by this time and if the van hadn't come she'd sit in the Store on the customer's chair and talk to Harriet or Jimbo till it came.

'Not here yet, Mother. I've rung, they say it's a new man who doesn't know the area so he's on his way but they don't know when he'll arrive.

Last heard of the other side of the bypass delivering to the petrol station there, so he shouldn't be too long.'

'I'll sit here and have a coffee if I may. Oh, there you are Bel. Now how are things with you?'

Bel put down the gadget she used for pricing stock and smiled cautiously. 'Fine thanks. Just fine.'

'I'm sorry about all this business.'

'So am I.'

'Yes, of course. And Dicky?'

'Stiff upper lip, you know.'

'Of course.'

'And Georgie, how's she?'

Grandmama, feeling discomfited by Bel's directness, said, 'Like you said, stiff upper lip.'

'I'll get on then.'

'Yes, of course.' Jimbo had forgotten the sugar and Grandmama got up to get it for herself as Jimbo had disappeared into the back. Sometimes it was useful to sit in the Store watching the customers and keeping an eye on Linda and the other staff. You learned a lot from keeping quiet and just watching and listening.

Through the window she saw the delivery van pull up. The driver leapt out, opened up the van doors at the rear and lifted out a large bright green baker's tray. A customer opened the door for him and he came in looking very apologetic.

'Bel! The bakery man's here!' Grandmama called out. Bel came from where she'd been pricing tins of soup as she filled the shelves and cleared a place for the baker's man to put the tray down.

'Sorry I'm late, better late than never though, I'll get quicker once I know the route . . .' His voice trailed away and he stared at Bel in amazement. 'Why! It's Bel Tutt isn't it? I'd know you anywhere. Well, would you believe it! Well, I never. I didn't know you'd moved here. What a lovely surprise.'

Bel looked stunned. She put down the order book and blushed bright red. She dabbed her top lip with her handkerchief and said, 'Why, it's you, Trevor. Long time no see. How are you?'

'Very well indeed, now I've got this job. Been out of work nearly six months, glad to have anything that's going. And how's that brother of yours, tricky Dicky? Eh? My we used to have some fun with Dicky in the Prince Albert, I'll tell them all I've seen you. Bye, Bel, see yer tomorrow. Bit earlier I hope. I'll get better at it. We'll have a chat when I'm not in such a rush.'

Bel watched him leave then her eyes were drawn to Grandmama's who'd rapidly risen to her feet. 'When he said "that brother of yours, tricky Dicky" you didn't correct him.'

Jimbo dashed in from the back. 'Oh great! The bread's come. And not before time. I'll put it out for you, Bel.' Jimbo busied himself emptying the tray blissfully unaware of the tension under his very nose.

'Well. I'm waiting.'

Jimbo misinterpreted what she meant. 'Well, come on then, Mother dear, help yourself. Here's a couple of bags.'

His mother ignored him. 'Well?'

Bel's face had gone from bright red to deathly white. She dabbed her top lip again and babbled an answer Grandmama couldn't hear.

'Speak up! Jimbo, are you listening then I can't be accused of rumour-mongering again.'

Bel looked at Jimbo. 'I can't explain here, not in the Store.'

Jimbo looked up from the baker's tray and asked, 'Explain what?'

'I'm still waiting for your explanation. Why are you masquerading as Dicky's wife when that man claims you are Dicky's sister?'

Bel burst out in desperate tones, 'It's none of your business. None of your business. It's private.'

'No, it's not, not any more. He's just shouted it out all over the whole shop. My son has a right to know.'

'Now look here, Mother . . .'

'No, I won't look here. There's something going on here we should all know about. I want the truth.'

'Well, you're not going to get it, you interfering old busybody. You've caused more harm in this village in the time you've been here than all the rest of us put together.' Bel fled into the back and returned in a moment with her coat and keys. 'School. Sorry.'

As the door slammed shut Grandmama said, 'I told you there was something very funny going on when the sewing-machine man was so odd when I mentioned her name. I knew it. I should have persisted then, but you warned me off.' She paced rapidly about the Store. 'So I was right.'

'Mother, for heaven's sake, you're at it again. How many more times. The man's mistaken.'

'She didn't deny it did she? Oh no! Put my rolls on one side. I'll be back shortly.'

She stepped smartly from the Store and headed for the rectory. As she turned into Church Lane she glanced to check the road for traffic and caught sight of Glebe Cottages, and the thought hit her like a sledgehammer. Oh God! Surely not! It couldn't be true! That confirmed what she suspected. Of course! Those cottages only had one bedroom. That could definitely only mean one thing! Dicky and Bel must be lovers . . . they couldn't be . . . could they? But that was . . . yes, that was . . . incest . . . they were committing incest! Well, there was one thing for certain then, that letter was not getting torn up, for she meant every word of it now and she'd make the others change their minds again if it killed her. Someone had to preserve the reputation of this village and keep it a good place to live. If the mantle had fallen on her then so be it.

Peter's car was outside so the moment could not be more opportune. Breathlessly, she hammered on the rectory door.

Sylvia answered the door. 'Good day to you, Mrs Charter-Plackett.'

Instead of answering in her normal well enunciated manner, Grandmama stuttered and stammered. 'The Rrrector, he's in, is he in, in is he?'

'He is, but he's having an early lunch. Can it wait?'

'Wwwait. No, it can't. Tttell him, tell I'm here. Ts'urgent.'

'Step in, then. Wait there.' Sylvia went into the kitchen where Caroline and Peter were eating lunch. Peter looked up. 'Rector, it's Mrs Charter-Plac—'

'It's me, Rector.' Grandmama stood in the doorway. Peter got up from his chair.

'It must be urgent for you to . . .'

'It is. Your study if you please.'

'Won't you join us for coffee? Get another cup, Sylvia, would you, please?'

Grandmama waved her hand impatiently. 'No, there's no time for that. Have you torn up that letter I sent?'

'The petition?'

Grandmama nodded.

'No, not yet.'

'Good, well don't. Things are far worse than we thought.'

Peter raised his eyebrows. 'Are they indeed!'

'Oh yes. I have just found out that Dicky and Bel are brother and sister and Glebe Cottages have only one bedroom. It doesn't take much intelligence to see which way the cookie crumbles. That's the answer to the wedding ring. A complete cover-up. I knew there was something fishy. I knew it.' She slapped her closed fist into the palm of the other hand and looked triumphantly at the three of them.

All of them registered first shock, then disbelief and then downright scorn. Peter was the first to find his voice. 'Come into the study will you?' He led the way and left Sylvia and Caroline staring at each other.

Sylvia gave a croaky little laugh and muttered, 'I don't believe this, she's finally gone balmy.'

'Balmy? She needs certifying. What a perfectly dreadful thing to say about anybody. How can it be true?'

'It can't.'

'Of course, it can't. Not Dicky and Bel. That's ridiculous. Quite disgusting in fact. I just hope Peter is giving her what for. Jimbo and Harriet will be distraught. She can be so perceptive and considerate and then there's this other side to her . . . She defies belief. What I can never quite comprehend is the way she always appears at the right place at the right time and picks up on all the gossip before anyone else does.' Sylvia flashed her a questioning look, afraid there might be more to what she said than first appeared, but Caroline continued by saying, 'I'll clear up. Might as well keep myself occupied while I wait to hear the full story.'

'Certainly not. You go and rest. You had a dreadful day yesterday with that chemo business so you deserve a rest.'

'Sylvia! You're spoiling me.'

'I'm not. Off you go.'

'Very well. But I won't lie down, I'll sit and watch TV.'

'OK. But feet up. That blessed woman. Where does she get her mad ideas from?'

After a quarter of an hour watching TV Caroline heard Peter opening the front door. Though he was trying to keep his voice low it was impossible for her not to overhear him say, 'Not a word until I have verified it one way or the other. Remember! Not even to Georgie. *No one at all.*'

She heard Grandmama answer in subdued tones. 'Very well.'

'Promise?'

'Promise.'

'Good afternoon, then. I'll be in touch.'

Caroline heard him shut the front door, and turned expecting him to come into the sitting-room but he didn't. Then she heard him shut the study door. In that case then it was serious. When he shut the study door like that, no one not even she unless the house was on fire, dared to interrupt. Then there must be grounds for what Grandmama had said. Heaven help Peter if it was true. Heaven help the village, too, if it was true.

'More custard, darling? There's still plenty left. I'm sure you're not eating enough, I want to see you putting on more weight.'

'No, thanks. You know full well I've gained half a stone since my op. If I keep on like this I shall be as big as Bel Tutt.'

Peter didn't take her up on that which she'd rather hoped he would. He hadn't said a word about Grandmama since the door had slammed on her. Caroline was bursting to know, and he normally told her everything but there were times when he shut up like a clam and she knew not to trespass. After all it was the same for her with her patients. Confidentiality and all that. She sighed.

'You're overtired, I can tell.'

'Peter! Stop mollycoddling me! I know whether or not I'm tired. And I'm not. I'm quite simply impatient to know what went on this afternoon.'

'I can't . . .'

'I know you can't, but I'm still bursting to know.'

'I am aware we promised ourselves an evening in on our own but I'm afraid I've got Dicky coming round tonight, it's rather important. We said eight o'clock.'

Caroline glanced at her wristwatch. 'He'll be here in five minutes, then.'

'Heavens I didn't realise how the time had flown. Can you manage the dishes?'

'Of course. Will you want tea or anything?'

'I think the parish whisky might be more appropriate.'

'OK. I'll be in the sitting-room if you . . . There's the door.'

'Help! Is there ever a right way to broach this kind of subject?'

'I have no doubt the Lord will provide the answer.'

When he and Dicky were settled in the study Peter said, 'I've asked you to come to see me tonight because of what happened this morning. I expect Bel has told you that the new bakery man is someone you knew before you moved here? And no doubt you know what he said, which unfortunately was heard all over the Store.'

Dicky didn't answer.

'Come, Dicky, I'm trying hard not to get impatient. I struggled last weekend with your close encounter with death, now it's allegations of a very serious nature and I need answers if I am to be expected to back you up.'

Still Dicky didn't answer.

'Please.'

'It's a long story.'

'Then shall we begin?'

Dicky rested his elbow on the arm of his chair and without looking at Peter began to speak, his voice was far from being the jolly laughing one everyone knew. It was quiet and distant and very thoughtful, and his words were chosen with such care. Peter braced himself for what might be going to be revealed.

'That chap, Trevor, is quite right. Bel is my sister. I make no bones about that. She's older than me by eleven months, so we've grown up together just like twins. She doesn't remember a time when I wasn't there. We don't remember our parents at all, because apparently so we've been told, when Bel was just two and I was just one year old someone, perhaps our mother, left us in our twin pushchair outside a doctor's surgery and walked away. We've seen neither hide nor hair of her since. Why she left us there I'll never know. Desperation I suppose, well at least Bel and me hope it was desperation and not . . . not because she didn't love us. They named Bel and me after the two doctors on duty that morning, and we got the name Tutt because the surgery was in a suburb called Tutt End. So it began, in a home first and then foster parents. All our lives we've looked after each other. There isn't a bond quite like that of children who've never known their parents. You stick like glue. You're all each other's got you see. You're mother, father, sister, brother, aunt, uncle, grandparent. There isn't anyone else to stand up for you.'

Dicky locked the fingers of both hands together very tightly and looked up at Peter. 'See what I mean? Like that. So close. They talked about separating us at one time, Bel for adoption and me to another foster home, but we ran away and spent two miserable nights hiding in a shed till they found us. Bel screamed and cried so much and did such dreadfully bad things that they decided she wasn't suitable for adoption so we went together to another foster home. It's hell, without roots. Not knowing who or what you are. Like living on shifting sands. When you're young you study the faces of the people in the street just in case you catch a glimpse of someone who looks like you and they might be the mother or the father you've been waiting for all through the years. Daft isn't it? We don't do that any more of course. Then when we were sixteen I got the job at the factory where I work now and Bel went into service, but didn't sleep in and we had a little tiny two-roomed flat and it was home. In capital letters it was home. The first real home we'd ever had. We could call it ours and we could lock the door and we were untouchable. We ruled our own lives, we ate what we wanted, we went out when we wanted and we were accountable to no one.'

'Whisky, Dicky?'

'Don't touch the hard stuff, Rector, thank you.'

'Right. Carry on, I'm listening.'

'About three years ago, Bel met this chap. To me it seemed like a gigantic earthquake, my whole world felt as though it was falling apart. There'd been just the two of us, still in the same flat, all those years, and here was an intruder disturbing our very foundations. For Bel's sake, for I could see she was smitten by him, I had to keep quiet, because I thought maybe my prejudice was rooted in the fact that I didn't want to lose my Bel. And it well could have been, for I loved her and she was my anchor in the storms of life like in the hymn. I always will love her, it's not difficult to love Bel.'

He looked up at Peter unable to continue, then he cleared his throat and carried on speaking. 'She's a gem. She knows me back to front and inside out. Every move. I've no secrets from Bel. Anyway he said he had a flat for them and he would persist that they should marry. Bel asked what I thought and well, what could I say? I couldn't stand in the way of her happiness, just like she won't stand in the way of mine now. Selfish love isn't real true love is it?'

Peter shook his head. 'No, it isn't.'

'So they had a wedding. It was a poor do, he said he'd no family and we certainly hadn't so it was just friends and a do at the Prince Albert after. I don't think they'd been married three months when I started getting suspicious things weren't right. They lived in their own flat, and I was definitely feeling the pinch trying to pay the rent for our home all by myself, so Bel used to ask me over quite often for a meal to help me out. Did my washing and that. Called one night unexpected, I was feeling lonely, fancy me Dicky Tutt feeling lonely! Ridiculous isn't it? Even before I knocked on the door I could hear the shouting. They didn't hear my knock so I walked straight in and he was thumping her, like nobody's business. She was thin then, like me and she wasn't half taking a battering. He was a big chap and there wasn't anything I could do to stop him. So a neighbour called the police and he was arrested.'

Dicky's hands were twisting together round and round, this way and that. He swallowed hard two or three times. 'Sorry, I can't forget how she looked when we got her to hospital. I kept saying "why didn't you tell me, why ever not?" '

'Long and the short of it was she came home to our flat, changed her name to Tutt again and that was that. Then she started putting on weight, couldn't stop eating you see, comfort or something I expect. I hadn't the heart to say anything. He started calling again and pestering her, wanting her back, apologising for this and that you know, usual rubbish. He wouldn't lift a finger to her ever again and all that nonsense. She thought perhaps she should go back, I said no she shouldn't, a leopard doesn't change its spots and I think it was the first time in our lives that we'd disagreed. It broke our hearts when we realised what had happened to us. We both hung on to each other crying our eyes out. We decided there and then we wouldn't allow anyone else to come between us, it wasn't worth it. Upshot of it was I persuaded her to go for a divorce and we decided to move. Buy a home of our own. Something of *ours*. We saw the advert for Muriel's, you know Lady Templeton's house being up for sale and by adjusting this and that and bargaining the price down a bit we realised that between us we could just about manage to buy it. Couldn't afford anything bigger you see, and it was isolated and we'd feel secure. We loved the village as soon as we saw it. We're mortgaged up to our eyebrows, believe me, it's been a struggle. Anyway the lady Bel was housekeeper to was taken very ill and Bel couldn't leave her. So I came here and she stayed at the lady's house till she died. We'd had no promises made at all but we both rather hoped that the lady would leave Bel something in her will, but, as I've no doubt you know blood is thicker than water when it comes to wills, and all she got was the lady's gold watch and bracelet, so that was that.'

Peter nodded his head. 'I know, it happens so often, the ones who do all the work get nothing and those who've swanned in once or twice a year get the lot.'

'Exactly. You know Bel, she worked all hours those last months, kindness itself she was, but there we are. So Bel came here. This is the difficult bit now. You know how small the house is, Rector. But it's ours or it will be when the mortgage is paid off, our very own home, every stick and stone, we're impregnable. So now we come to this question of people thinking we share a bedroom. As God is my witness and I don't say that lightly, as you well know, Bel and me we do not share a *bed* like everyone thinks. We share the wardrobe simply because there's nowhere else to hang clothes, but at night I sleep on the sofabed downstairs and Bel has the bedroom.'

Peter thanked him for being so frank.

Dicky took a deep breath. 'We don't and I repeat that, don't . . . that is . . . we're not . . . like man and wife. We observe all the niceties. We share the wardrobe like I've said, so I do go in Bel's bedroom to get my clothes but I don't sleep in there. However, mud sticks, so if you want me to resign from anything at all I will, but I won't have Bel's life ruined over this. I simply will not. I'll sell up and go elsewhere rather than that.'

'I see.'

'That bloody Trevor, I could murder him. Turning up like that, just when we thought we were safe and secure like. It's not fair, it just isn't fair.'

'But letting everyone think you were married.'

'What else could we do? But we never told lies, we simply let everyone assume we were married. We never lied. Just never mentioned it. They'd have hounded us out in two ticks if we'd let on. We both talked about it the other night and we agreed we should have been more honest and open about it all, but we weren't because we were scared of what they would all think. It's our dishonesty that's brought all this about. Now there's Georgie. My darlin' Georgie. And here's Bel being so kind and thoughtful and considerate. I don't deserve her. I don't.'

Peter saw the distress in his eyes. Dicky drew out his handkerchief and blew his nose.

'There's nothing more to tell. Except I love Bel and don't want her hurt and I love Georgie and want her for a wife if it doesn't hurt Bel too much, which it will, but she won't let on. I love this place, know that? Not been here long but I love it, for all its tittle-tattle and feuding I love it, 'cos it's part of old England you see and I can respond to that. But' – Dicky sighed and shook his head – 'I'd better put the house on the market and say goodbye to dreams and happiness and my Scouts, and absolutely damn all that I love.'

Peter shook his head. 'I don't want that. No, that's no solution.'

'There isn't another one. We'll have to uproot and start all over again.' Dicky took out his handkerchief and blew his nose again.

In a voice more upbeat than he felt, Peter said, 'One person I do feel sorry for is Bryn. In a way none of this has been brought about by him, but he's suffering too.'

Dicky looked up at him. 'I know I have to confess I've been feeling bad all the time about Bryn, really bad. All he's guilty of is neglecting Georgie, and there's plenty of husbands guilty of that. At first getting him riled made me laugh, but after a while I began to feel ashamed but by then I loved Georgie too much to give her up. If he'd listen to me I'd apologise to him, but there's small chance of that. He can't stand the sight of me.'

'There must be a solution somewhere to all this. Don't do anything for the moment. Nothing at all. But now the cat is out of the bag so to speak, and everyone knows, we are going to have to do *something* but I don't know what. Thank you for being so frank. The village will react quite violently to this situation and quite understandably, after all to those who don't know the facts, it appears to be incest you're guilty of, and neither they nor I could condone that. But it isn't, and somehow we've to demonstrate that everything is above board. I don't want to be guilty of ruining yours and Bel's lives. Are you absolutely certain in view of your close relationship with Bel that you've got room in your life for Georgie?'

Dicky studied this question for a long while, so long in fact Peter thought he wasn't going to get an answer, and then Dicky said, 'I'm sure there is. All round, in the long term, it would be better for Bel and for me. Perhaps then we could each get on with our own lives instead of being so . . .' He gestured helplessly with his hand and could find no words to describe the closeness of his and Bel's relationship.

Peter nodded. 'Well, then, Dicky, go home and give Bel some support. After all she has everyone to face, you can escape to the office, she can't.'

'And the Scouts? Shall I cry off tomorrow night? The others can cope for one night I'm sure.'

'Cry off. Keep a low profile. That's the best.'

Dicky stood up. 'I've taken up enough of your time, Rector, I'll be off. Thanks for listening and being so understanding.' A vestige of the Dicky Peter knew crept into his face, and Dicky smiled. 'If much more happens I shan't be able to leave the house. I've been banned from the pub, I'm never climbing a church tower ever again, I can't go to Scouts, there's not much left is there?'

'Not at the moment, but we'll sort something out. You'll see. There's always the Jug and Bottle in Penny Fawcett!'

Dicky grinned. 'Of course. There is.' Then his face became stark and full of pain again and he said, 'I've no solution, I hope you have.'

'I'll have a good try. Good night Dicky.'

'Good night, Peter, and thanks.'

'Come any time, you and Bel, the door's always open to you.'

Dicky, standing out in the road with the outside light shining directly on his face, looked up at Peter and said, 'God bless the day you came here, I don't think my story would have been so understandingly received by anyone else. You're one in a million. Good night, and thank you, from the bottom of my heart.'

Peter nodded his thanks and then shut the door. He found Caroline watching TV. She switched it off with the remote control as soon as he entered the room. Peter didn't speak or even glance at her, he flung himself down in a chair and rubbed his forehead with his hand, as though it would help to clear his head.

She stood up and said, 'Tea?'

Without looking at her he said, 'I have faced a lot of very difficult problems in my life as a priest but I think this one is above and beyond anything I've tackled to date.'

'Tea it is, then.'

18

The next morning, it being Friday, the children from the school were scheduled for morning prayers in the church. Normally, by the time they'd done the register and got everyone assembled for the walk across to the church all the mothers had dispersed, but this Friday morning there was a large group still talking by the gate.

Kate Pascoe, heading the crocodile of children, called out, 'Excuse me ladies, could we squeeze by?' The mothers pushed their prams out of the way and made room for them all to pass through the gate.

One of the mothers asked quietly as Kate passed her, 'Could I have a word at lunchtime?'

Kate nodded. 'One o'clock in my room?'

'Thanks.'

Kate knew exactly what the appointment was for and she didn't know what to do. After morning prayers were over, she asked Hetty Hardaker and Margaret Booth to take the children back and she wouldn't be a moment, just needed a word with Peter.

'My advice is to say that you have absolutely no reason for asking Bel to leave. Which I take it you haven't?'

Kate shook her head. 'None at all, she does the job equally as well as Pat did, if not better, I can find no possible reason for sacking her. She's done nothing wrong at all, she's patient with the children, she keeps everything spotless, she's pleasant with the staff. She couldn't be bettered.'

'I thought not. Tell them you won't, and that she's coming to the school until you are told differently. Be quiet, but firm and don't let them sidetrack you into it being a question of her morals. As far as I am concerned she and Dicky are doing nothing wrong at all, I have that knowledge directly from Dicky and I believe him.'

'Thank you for that assurance.'

'I can't give details, obviously it's entirely confidential, but I can assure you it's all right.'

'Thanks. Lovely service. Much appreciated. Bye!'

With half an eye on the clock so she wouldn't be late for the conference with the mothers' representative, Kate went into the Store at lunchtime to buy a frozen vegetable lasagne. She needed something quick for her evening meal because she was off into Culworth after school and hadn't time for cooking for herself.

'Hello, Jimbo! How's things?'

'None too sprightly.' He looked down in the mouth and at odds with himself.

'I think you have the same problem as I have?'

Jimbo asked if Bel was her problem.

'Yes. I think my mothers are up in arms. I refuse to be intimidated by them, though. Peter's given me his assurance that everything is OK about Bel and Dicky. They're a scandal-mongering lot, my mothers, when it comes down to it. Anything for a bit of excitement.'

'I have every sympathy for Bel, but I will not allow my business to suffer. Village Stores are difficult enough to make viable at the best of times, so my business acumen may have to take precedence over my sympathy for her.'

'What are you going to do then?'

'We've agreed she's shelf-filling in the evenings when we're shut, not mornings. Even so I can't give her the hours she normally does without customer contact of some sort, so she'll have to be on the till if I get desperate.'

Kate paid for her lasagne and went back to school, the light of battle in her eyes.

Peter endeavoured to keep the light of battle from his eyes when Grandmama appeared at his request in his study. He'd been ready to call upon her in her cottage but thought that he would take the initiative by summoning her to see him. Might just blunt her sharp edges if she wasn't on her own home territory he'd said to Caroline.

'I agree. The difficulty about this situation is that she's so *right* on the surface. One can't condone incest at all, it is just so downright immoral, to say nothing of unlawful. But it isn't incest, but it looks like it.'

Peter groaned. 'You obviously haven't come up with one of your admirable commonsense solutions. I feel a large dose of it would be very useful.'

'I'm afraid not. Sorry. You'll have to play it by ear.'

Grandmama sat rigidly upright in the easy chair. Peter sat sideways at his desk, facing her. Whatever age she was she kept herself remarkably smart and youthful looking. She had such a strong life force he was in danger of being overcome by it. However, he wasn't going to be intimidated by this almighty formidable lady, and he was determined to keep the upper hand.

'Mrs Charter-Plackett, thank you for finding the time to come to see me. I promised I would get back to you and here I am doing that very thing.'

She nodded. 'Not at all, Peter, I just want the whole matter cleared up. This village won't tolerate the situation for much longer. They all know, not through me but because people were in the Store when that bakery man made his revelation. They all think it's disgusting, absolutely disgusting and they want them out. Scouts, the school, they're both being tainted by it.'

Peter leant back in his chair. 'How about coffee?'

'That would be welcome. Thank you.'

They chatted about the weather, about the plans for Christmas about everything but the matter in hand. Sylvia brought the coffee in and Peter couldn't help but notice that Grandmama's cup was slapped down a little too sharply for his liking. He caught her eye as she gave him his and she couldn't miss the reproof in his face. Sylvia tossed her head and marched out. When Peter tasted his coffee he found it was only instant and not percolated. A sure sign that Sylvia disapproved.

He let Grandmama have a few lifesaving sips of her coffee and then he began. 'I have a story to tell.' By the time he had finished telling her the reasons for the situation Bel and Dicky found themselves in, Grandmama was on the verge of tears. She fumbled in her bag for a handkerchief and surreptitiously dabbed her eyes.

'So you see, Mrs Charter-Plackett, I have Dicky's absolute affirmation that there is nothing untoward at all; he has given me his word and I believe him completely. However, the world at large doesn't know that and neither does anyone else except Caroline and you and me. I have shared this information with you because you are involved and I know, yes I know that, having given you my confidence you will not betray it.' Peter paused, took a final drink of his coffee, put down his cup and looked Grandmama straight in the eye. They looked at each other for a moment and then Peter broke the silence by saying the very last thing he'd ever intended to say. 'What I want is for you to help me to arrive at a solution.'

'Me?'

'Yes, you. There's the situation between Georgie and Bryn and Dicky to solve which is bound up with the situation between Dicky and Bel. Now, do you have any ideas?'

'Well, no I don't. Not at the moment. But I shall give it my earnest consideration.'

'I admit, I'm completely at a loss.'

'So am I.'

'Has Georgie enlightened you at all about what she wants?'

'Not at all. She doesn't know herself.'

Peter allowed a silence to develop. Grandmama checked her cup and found to her disappointment she'd drunk it all. She looked at Peter and said, 'We can't do anything till they all declare what they want to do. Does

Georgie want to go back to Bryn? Does Bryn want her back? Does Dicky want to marry Georgie? Does Georgie want to marry Dicky? If they marry then what does Bel want to do? It sounds like something from a musical comedy.'

'It's far from being that.'

'Exactly. When you know the story you can't help feeling sorry for Dicky and Bel. It must be quite dreadful to grow up knowing your mother, whoever she was and for whatever reason, abandoned you. No wonder they've clung together all these years. The poor things. We all need someone don't we? You can't believe a mother could be so cruel, can you?'

'You can't. Look, I won't take up any more of your time. Think about it and if you come up with any ideas, let me know, but directly, not through a third party.'

'Of course. Absolute secrecy.'

'Meanwhile I'll be thinking too.' Peter stood up and smiled down at Grandmama.

Her heart flipped. If she could solve this for him she would. Given time there was no problem unsolvable. 'Of course. It's partly my fault all this trouble, I'm sorry I've been so . . .'

Peter smiled at her again. 'To err is human.'

Thankfully Grandmama smiled and said, 'Between the two of us we should be able to sort it out, after all we're not fools are we, either of us?'

'Certainly not.' He showed her out and then went to find Caroline. She was pottering in the garden.

'Caroline, you won't dig or anything will you?'

'Of course not, don't worry.' She turned to look at him. 'Do you think I should move those peonies to this side? I think they'd look more effective here, don't you?'

Peter put an arm around her waist and pulled her close. 'Happy?'

She turned towards him and put her arms round his neck. 'I am, couldn't be happier.' Caroline kissed him. 'I love you.'

'I love you. You're always happy in your garden. How about taking a garden design course, carve out a whole new career for yourself? You're very good at it.'

'If I were I wouldn't be asking you about the peonies.'

'Follow your instincts. Move them. I'll dig them out for you.'

'Peter! Sometimes you are absolutely transparent!'

'I don't know what you mean.'

'You do. You're worried I'll have a go myself, so you get in quickly with an offer to do it for me. Well, I shan't. I know what I'm permitted to do.'

'I should trust you more, shouldn't I?'

'Yes, you should. Well? How did you get on with her?'

'I've taken the most awful gamble.'

Caroline listened to what he had to say and replied, 'Rather you than me.'

'Do you think I've got it wrong? You said play it by ear.'

'It will either come off quite splendidly or the situation will be ten times worse. A gamble as you say.'

'I rather hoped you'd agree with me. She's the sort of person who could solve it, you know. Grandmama's no fool as she so rightly said.'

'They might manage to solve it all by themselves if left alone.'

'They're all too deeply involved to see the wood for the trees.'

'I just hope you're backing the right horse. Despite your support, the village may still not approve. There's one thing though, they'll all have plenty to talk about. It'll keep everyone going for weeks and weeks!'

Over the weekend the bar at the Royal Oak hummed discreetly with the gossip about the four of them. In particular the discovery that Dicky and Bel were brother and sister. Discreetly because of Bryn. They didn't want to hurt his feelings, but on the other hand the gossip was far too good to miss. What couldn't be reconciled was the fact that Dicky and Bel had deceived them for so long. Why had no one twigged what was going on? What seemed even more incredible was that the Rector appeared to be condoning it. They couldn't understand that, him being so particular about things, and him having the church's attitude to take into account.

Vera had dragged Don in for a drink seeing as Jimmy was always busy driving his taxi on Saturday nights and Pat hardly ever came in since she'd married Barry. So, not wishing to spend the evening alone, Vera had persuaded Don to accompany her. 'We won't stay long, it's just to find out what's happening, that's all. You can get back to your telly as soon as.'

To her delight Willie and Sylvia were there and they'd secured her favourite table.

'Willie! Sylvia! Don's just getting the drinks.'

'How's things, Vera?' Willie asked her.

'Fine, just fine. In fact brilliant. My wages have gone up again. Thank Gawd.'

'Why's that?'

'Can't get people to work the hours. I should worry. What with Don's money, our Rhett's and mine, everything in the Wright household is great.' Vera nodded her head in the direction of Bryn. 'He's still working then?'

'There's him and Alan and wait till you see the new help.'

'New help? Who's that then?'

'Wait and see.' Willie, out of the side of his mouth, muttered, 'Here she comes.'

Vera was totally unprepared for the vision which appeared through the door marked *Private*. The woman was as tall as Bryn, with a mass of unnaturally red hair, curling and swirling around her head and well down her back. You couldn't call her fat but she was voluptuous. More than enough of her top half was exposed, the part that wasn't, was encased in a sparkling, glittering top which, cropped at her waistline, exposed a tanned midriff each time she stretched for anything the slightest bit out of reach. They'd seen short skirts on some of the teenage girls in the village, but the skirt this apparition was wearing came only just short of covering her knickers.

Vera was scandalised. 'Never in all my born days have I seen anything as disgusting as that. Georgie would never have set her on. Not in a million years. Where the Dickens is she from?'

'Penny Fawcett.'

'Penny Fawcett? That dead alive hole. Giddy godfathers. I bet she sets tongues wagging.'

Sylvia giggled. 'More than tongues believe me! She's one of old Bertie Bradshaw's daughters.'

'No! Not the one the Rector caught . . .' Vera lowered her voice and whispered the rest of the story to Sylvia, finishing with 'Was it Kenny or Terry, I can't remember.'

'The very one.'

'It's disgusting. She'll be putting Don off his orange juice.' Vera moved along the settle to make room for him. 'Don't you make any of your awkward remarks tonight, Don Wright, the last one caused enough trouble. I don't want *you* being thrown from the top of the church tower, well, not before I've checked your insurance anyhow! Thanks. Cheers.' Vera raised her glass to her mouth and drank thirstily.

'Me? As if I would!'

Vera, still appalled by the sight of the new barmaid, said, 'She'll be Elektra.'

'Right name for her too.' Don made one of his rare excursions into the world of laughter which made the others look at him in surprise.

Sylvia thought it was a ridiculous name. She asked Vera what the others were called. 'Can't remember 'em all, the youngest one's called Mercedes I do know that. Reckon their mother must have had a brainstorm each time they popped out. She died years ago before they all grew up. Mind you, with five girls like Elektra there's no wonder she died young, it was the surest way to escape the lot of 'em!'

Willie, still ogling Elektra, declared she was much older than she looked. 'See her neck, yer can't disguise that, nor her 'ands. I bet she's fifty if she's a day. Pity Jimmy's not here, do 'im good to have an eyeful of her.'

Vera tut-tutted. 'Well, I'm disgusted with Bryn. Georgie always kept the place with such style, never a word out of place, everything classy like.'

With a deadpan face Don muttered, 'She'll be in his bed before long.' He waited until Bryn was looking in his direction and he called out, 'Not taken long for yer to find someone to keep the bed warm, Bryn, in a manner of speaking like.'

Elektra answered him because Bryn, caught unawares, couldn't think of an answer. 'Jealous are yer? Expect that dried up old prune sat next to yer is your wife. Bet you've forgotten what it's like.'

Don, the wind completely taken out of his sails by this bold retort, didn't know where to look.

Vera went a kind of purply red, struggled out from the settle and confronted Elektra. Being small Vera's eyes were on a level with Elektra's cleavage which made it difficult to speak with authority.

'You're a tart. That's what you are, a tart. Don't you dare speak to my husband like that. Decent people don't want the likes of you in here, with yer cheeky remarks and yer black lace knickers.'

'You old cow. Bet your knickers aren't black lace, they'll be pink inter-lock with them long legs with elastic. Sexy I must say. No wonder that husband of yours is jealous.' She pulled at the cropped sparkling top and exposed even more of her assets.

Vera, unable to come up with a smart response to this further evidence of Elektra's unsuitability to be barmaid in the Royal Oak, picked up her glass of lager which was still half full and emptied what was left down Elektra's chest, banged the empty glass down on the nearest table and said, 'Don, we're going 'ome.' As they crossed the bar towards the door Vera said, 'Now look what you've made me do with your uncalled-for remarks.' They left in a kind of triumphant flurry.

Elektra was yowling, plucking at her top as the lager trickled down her cleavage, down her midriff and then her imitation leather skirt and thence to the floor. Bryn came from behind the bar armed with a tea towel and began dabbing at Elektra's front.

Uproar ensued. The customers were cheering him on with enthusiasm, making bold hints about their relationship and inferring what a lucky man he was, and did he need a hand?

At that moment Peter walked in. Bryn unaware what had caused the ribaldry to trail off into silence continued mopping Elektra.

'You'll have to go in the back and get changed. You're absolutely wet through. Alan! Get a cloth and a bucket and . . .' Bryn saw Peter and stopped in mid-sentence. Immediately he knew that he looked all kinds of a fool. It would contribute nothing to his case as far as Peter was concerned. But did he care? No, he didn't. Hail-fellow-well-met was the best attitude to adopt. 'Good evening, Rector! What can I get for you?'

'I'll have a mineral water thank you, Bryn. Busy tonight.'

'That's right. Just had a bit of a fracas with two of the customers. All part of life's rich pattern. Eh?'

'Indeed. I've just popped in to see about arrangements for a meeting. I didn't know how you were fixed for help in the bar but I see you've got someone. Eighty pence, that right?'

'That's right, Rector.'

'Sunday evening after service I thought, in the rectory. It's fine with the others. Is it all right with you?'

'I'll get Elektra to change shifts, her and Alan should be able to manage.'

'Good.' Peter stood at the bar, one foot on the brass rail and looked at the crowd. He acknowledged Willie and Sylvia and a few more from church, and drank his mineral water. There was a lot of furtive giggling amongst the customers and an occasional burst of laughter.

Elektra returned. Sylvia gasped. Nudging Willie she whispered 'I'm certain that's one of Georgie's tops. I remember her wearing it. It's not on is it?'

'It's not blinking decent, it isn't. You wouldn't think Georgie was living only yards away, you'd think she was dead. I'm amazed at Bryn. He's lost his marbles, that's what.' Willie went to the bar to buy another drink. 'Good evening, Rector. I'm afraid things aren't what they were in these parts.'

Peter smiled wryly and said, 'I agree.'

Two of the customers called good night and went, and those left behind settled down to a quiet evening. There was a game of dominoes in progress at the table by the fire, someone got up and shouted to Bryn should they put another log on, and he agreed, not caring much either way as he was chatting to Elektra. Two chaps from Culworth decided to have a game of darts and Elektra exchanged some coarse chit-chat with them. Bryn glanced at the clock. An hour to closing. And then . . . He admired Elektra's rampant red hair and thought about burying his hands in it, grasping great handfuls of it, twining it round his fingers, luxuriating in the thickness of it and . . . would she let him though? As she'd said her father had turned her out and she'd nowhere to go, he'd delightedly agreed to her having Alan's old room. Everything somehow had fallen neatly into place. As he contemplated with relish the possibility of some extra-mural activity once the bar was closed, he heard the outside door open. He looked up to see who'd come in.

It was Georgie carrying her case. She'd come back.

Bryn went hot right from his bow tie down to his brown suede shoes. His head swirled till he felt so dizzy he had to clutch hold of the bar to steady himself. Through the mists which, to his surprise, had filled the bar he saw the look of fury on Georgie's face when she spotted Elektra.

He watched her eyes taking in the whole of the saloon, Peter at the bar, the flames hungrily crackling away at the new log, the plastic flowers Elektra had put on the counter, which now appeared to him to be in the worst possible taste, and finally her eyes reached him. If it was possible he went even hotter. Her look floored him. He felt compelled to turn his eyes away, he couldn't meet hers, those lovely blue eyes which had so captivated him all those years ago; it was the horrendous sadness he saw in them he couldn't face. Georgie didn't speak. Not even to Peter. She walked across, went behind the bar and through the door marked *Private*.

Had she come back for good then?

Sylvia asked Willie this very question and he couldn't answer it, neither could anyone else. In fact the question never did get answered for it was 'Time, ladies and gentlemen, please' before they knew where they were. So they all went home, Peter included, none the wiser.

19

Grandmama was taking her turn organising the after morning service coffee in the church hall. With the service commencing at ten o'clock she was already there by quarter past nine putting out the cups. Willie had switched on the heating and the water heater so there was nothing much else to do but put out the cups, get the big coffee jugs out, spoon some sugar into bowls, put the pretty tablecloths on which Muriel had made when the hall had been renovated, get the spoons out of the locked cupboard, where was the key? Drat it, Mrs Jones had that. Where was she?

She heard the outside door shut and Mrs Jones calling out, 'Anyone here?'

'Good morning!'

'Oh! Good morning Mrs Charter-Plackett, I thought I was the first. You've done everything. You must have been early.'

'I was. I had a bad night so I decided to get up early and make the best of the day.'

'Not sleeping well then? I have some blinking good herbal stuff I use when I'm having one of my sessions when I can't sleep. Yer sleep but yer don't feel drugged when yer wake up. I've got a new bottle in my bag, 'ere you 'ave it.' She searched about in her cavernous bag and produced a bottle of tablets still in the herbalist's bag. 'Take it, go on, buy me a new bottle next time you're in Culworth. I've still got some left in my old bottle.'

'Oh, well thank you. I could give them a try, couldn't I? I don't usually have any problem, just an off night now and again. Have you the key for the cupboard, I need the spoons.'

'Coming to something when yer have to lock up church cupboards. Things aren't what they were, are they?'

Grandmama gave her a quizzical look but as Mrs Jones didn't respond in any way she thanked her for the spoons and went round putting one in each saucer.

Mrs Jones, between counting the spoonsful of coffee needed for each jug said 'You won't have seen the new barmaid?'

'No.'

'Our Kenny was in there Friday, he says she's a tart and he should know.'

'Is she?'

'Oh yes. Between you and me she's been around rather longer than she'd like us to know. Dresses fifteen when she's nearer fifty. But as Kenny says she has a heart of gold, so we all know what that means.' Slyly she brought the conversation round to Georgie. 'Must be awful for Georgie having that tart in her lovely pub. How's she keeping? Don't see much of her nowadays. Has she said anything about going back to him? Or is she staying with you a bit longer?'

Sorely tempted to relate the conversation she'd had with Georgie which had gone on far into the previous night Grandmama remembered Peter's admonition and said briefly, 'I'm only giving her a refuge till she sorts out what she wants to do, she doesn't confide in me.'

Oh no, thought Mrs Jones, I should cocoa. 'Well, it must be very difficult for 'em, them being business partners, not like if they were managers and the brewery owned it. Different when it's a free house. More complicated money-wise isn't it?'

'There that's that. I'll be off to church. See you afterwards. I don't expect there'll be many there today. We shouldn't be too busy.'

But she was wrong. The church was filled, not so many as for a special service but there were plenty there, and they all poured into the hall afterwards too. Grandmama and Mrs Jones were kept very busy, so busy they hadn't time for gossip, but judging by the loud hum of conversation and the hoots of laughter everyone else had plenty of time for it.

After the first surge of activity Grandmama took a moment to look around. Her eyes lighted on Peter first, because he was a head taller than most of the others. He was talking to Georgie. Poor Georgie. She'd made that brave decision to go back to Bryn and make a real effort to improve their lives together and what had she found? That disgusting woman serving in *her* bar, wearing one of *her* favourite tops, and Bryn looking like the cat who'd been at the cream. What had made matters worse was her realising, once she'd gone upstairs, that Elektra was living there, something she would never have allowed. Alan, yes, but then they'd known him since he'd first started work with them at eighteen, and been pleased to offer him a home, but Elektra . . . She was a different kettle of fish altogether.

Grandmama had been secretly appalled by Georgie's reaction. It seemed to her that Georgie had still had a lot of feeling left for Bryn, but that it had been destroyed in an instant by what she'd found. Apparently they'd had a frightful row, with Georgie telling Bryn exactly what she thought of him, something she'd never done before. Bryn had grown defiant, and told her what else could she expect when she'd left him to cope by himself, and if she didn't like the new barmaid she knew what she could do.

'Which is?'

'Just leave and let me get on with it my way.'

'We'll have no business left, our punters won't like' – she'd given Elektra a scathing glance – 'someone like her, we've a better class of pub. She's more the Jug and Bottle type.'

Elektra had taken umbrage at that remark. 'The Jug and Bottle! I wouldn't work there.'

'No? Perhaps you're right, they wouldn't want you, you're not even good enough for *them*, and that's saying something.'

Bryn had protested. 'Now come on, Georgie, there's no call to be downright nasty.'

'Isn't there? Don't forget, Bryn, I'm a partner in this business and I shall want my profit share. If she stays there'll be no profit to have. People like Sir Ralph and Jimbo and the Duchess and the Rector won't patronise us with her in here. She'll attract all the wrong kind of people.'

Elektra tossed her hair back and hands on hips retorted, 'Stuck-up lot they are, anyway, with their mineral waters and their gins and tonics.' She mimicked someone sipping delicately from their glass and laughed. 'There's plenty that will come 'cos I'm here. Give me men like Kenny Jones and their Terry, they know how to spend money . . .'

Georgie had looked Elektra up and down and said, 'You should know . . .'

'Well, really, you horrible old . . .'

'Old? Me, old? Try looking at your birth certificate some time.' So Georgie had then turned on her heel after firing that shot, picked up her case and left. She'd heard Bryn calling 'Georgie! Georgie!' but she'd ignored him.

So now poor Georgie was in even more turmoil than before.

Peter was talking and Georgie was listening and nodding her head. Grandmama noticed that Mrs Jones had drawn close ostensibly collecting used cups, but Grandmama could recognise her subterfuge. The choirboys came for their orange squash and her attention was taken making sure they didn't take all the biscuits. St Thomas à Becket choirboys were renowned for their ability to clear the plates of biscuits if you took your eyes off them even for a moment.

By the time she looked up again Dicky had joined Peter and Georgie and Mrs Jones was coming back without a single cup on her tray, and her lips tightly nipped together.

'Didn't hear a thing. They both stopped talking when I got near enough to hear.'

Grandmama saw it was her place to be shocked. 'You don't mean you were trying to eavesdrop?'

Mrs Jones grinned. 'Oh no, of course not! You know there's more than one had a word with the Rector about this business with Bel and Dicky. They've not taken kindly to knowing they share a bedroom. It's all very well the Rector saying he has Dicky's assurance there's nothing going on, but I ask yer? Stands to reason. He's a man isn't he, and a randy one at that by all accounts, so it must come over him sometimes, like it does with 'em all. Yer know.' She nudged Grandmama and gave her a wink.

Grandmama blanched. She wasn't accustomed to gossip at this level. She protested but Mrs Jones carried on. 'Who're they kidding? Not me for one. Much as I like Bel, it's not right. Just think of it. It's disgusting! Mr Charter-Plackett'll 'ave no compunction about sacking Bel. He's a lovely chap but when it comes to business . . . But there, you don't need me to tell you that. If he finds himself with a boycott it'll be curtains for Bel quick sharp. And the mothers at the school have asked if Bel can be sacked and that Kate won't do it. Says she's no cause for sacking her and she won't, not so long as she does a good job. They had a deputation or whatever they call it one lunchtime, but they met their match with Miss Kate Pascoe. Oh, I didn't see you waiting, Dr Harris. Sorry. Coffee?'

Caroline nodded her head. 'Yes, please.'

'Milk?'

'Yes, please. Good morning, Mrs Charter-Plackett.'

'Good morning, Caroline, my dear. Beautiful morning.'

'It certainly is. I don't know why, but when the two of you make the coffee it always tastes much better than everyone else's. Do you have some secret recipe or something?'

Grandmama and Mrs Jones preened themselves.

'TLC, that's our secret ingredient, isn't it Mrs Jones?'

Rather nonplussed, Mrs Jones agreed.

Caroline looked around the hall. 'I see! Oh, there he is. I've a message for Peter. See you.'

The two of them watched Caroline squeezing her way through the throng to Peter. She stood quietly beside him waiting to deliver her message.

Georgie was speaking. 'Well, Rector, there's no two ways about it, I'm not going back. Ever. I wouldn't go back even if he crawled from there to here on his hands and knees begging me every inch of the way.'

'Tonight at the meeting . . .'

'I shan't be there.'

'Georgie!'

'I'm sorry, but I shan't. As far as I am concerned there's nothing to discuss. I'm seeing my solicitor in the morning and I'm going for a divorce and making certain of where we stand with the pub, money-wise. That's that.'

Peter in the face of her resistance could only say, 'Well, if you're determined on that then there's no more to say. I may as well cancel the meeting. So this means you and Dicky . . .' He looked at the two of them in turn.

Dicky took the initiative. 'We haven't discussed what we want to do. Not yet. Georgie only made her mind up last night, so we haven't had time to talk. And there's Bel.'

Peter nodded his sympathy. 'Of course, there's Bel. I'm encountering a lot of opposition on that score, I'm afraid.'

Dicky sighed. 'I know. It'll all come out in the wash.' He saw Caroline standing patiently waiting. 'Good morning, Dr Harris. You're looking well. Better than you did.'

'Indeed I am, thank you. Much better. If you've finished I've a message for you, darling.'

'OK. Yes. I'll tell Bryn the meeting's off. Right?' He turned away and bent his head to hear what Caroline had to say.

Georgie turned to Dicky and said, 'We need to talk.'

'We'll have our dinner with Bel like she's planned and then we'll go out somewhere, just you and me. I'm sorry it's come to this.'

'I'm not.'

'Well, I am. But on the other hand it means we've got the go ahead.'

Georgie squeezed his arm. 'Oh yes it does, and what's more, no regrets now, none whatsoever.'

When they'd finished their Sunday dinner, Bel and Georgie went into the kitchen to clear up. There was scarcely enough room for the two of them but it brought about a kind of intimacy which they hadn't experienced before.

Bel said 'I want to thank you for coming to dinner today. Dicky needed a boost. I don't expect he's told you but you ought to know, we've had some very nasty letters.'

'You never have. Oh Bel!'

'Just pushed through the door, not signed or anything. Dicky's been very upset. There were two more this morning.'

'I'm so sorry. They can be very vindictive. Right from us first coming here we realised that. Very, very nasty if something doesn't suit. All this medieval village bit, you know. But poison pen letters! That's dreadful. Have you told the Rector?'

'Dicky won't. Says the shame would kill him, Dicky I mean, if the Rector was to read 'em. But it's so awful. We've done nothing and I want you to know this Georgie, we've done *nothing wrong*. Truly we haven't, nothing at all.'

'I know that Bel, I know. You're not those kind of people. Dicky told me at the very beginning when we first got attracted to one another that you were his sister, so I've always known you see, but never let on to a living soul. I couldn't love Dicky like I do if what they're saying was true. He wouldn't be like he is, would he now? What's more, neither of you would be so kind and lovely. You don't need to convince me. But I do think the Rector ought to know about the letters, after all those who wrote them are his parishioners.'

'Well, Dicky doesn't want him to know, so that's that. Don't tell anyone will you?'

Georgie reached up and kissed Bel's cheek. 'Of course not, I think too much about you to say anything if that's what you both want. You can rely on me.'

Bel handed Georgie a clean tea towel and said, 'Thanks. We'll say no more. They'll stop eventually I expect. I'm glad about you and Dicky. Very glad. He needs someone like you. A sister's not the same at all.'

'That's very generous of you, Bel. I've been worried about that. Truly worried. I didn't want to come between you.'

'It's time he branched out. I love him dearly, always will, but he needs to move on. I wouldn't say to him but it's true. Between you and me, he clings to me you see, it's not good for him.'

'But what will you do? Where will you live. Here?'

'Let's wait and see. Leave the pans, I'll do those. You take him out and . . .'

'Look Bel, I shan't want him all to myself. We're not kids. There'll still be room for you.'

Bel gazed out of the window. 'We'll see how things work out. Let's not make promises we shan't be able to keep.'

Georgie reached up and placed another kiss on Bel's cheek. 'If it's any comfort I do love him, he's just wonderful, such fun and so thoughtful. He's kind of just right for me, he makes me so happy and I hope I make him happy too. Thanks for being so generous.'

Bel laughed. 'Generous! I shall be glad to see the back of him! You can have him lock stock and barrel! I mean it!'

When they were ready to leave Bel stood at the door to wave them off. She watched them walk down the front path with an indulgent smile on her face, but her lovely green eyes began to fill with tears. They were so absorbed in each other they didn't turn back to wave goodbye, so they didn't see her weeping and she was glad.

That night there was no moon, so without street lighting because everyone had vigorously opposed its installation ten years ago, the village was in almost total darkness. There was a light on in Linda and Alan's bedroom because Lewis was teething and unable to sleep, and there was a light above the Store where Jimbo was still working. He had spent hours sorting and planning his Christmas displays, carrying boxes of attractive packing materials and fancy cardboard boxes down into the mail-order office ready for Mrs Jones to pack the Christmas hampers, getting out the Christmas decorations from last year, planning his windows which at Christmas were his pride and joy, and generally sorting his life out for the ensuing festive rush. He rubbed his eyes and forehead and went to stand at the window looking out over the Green. Besides the Store and the mail order doing so well, he had more catering business this Christmas than ever before. If things went on as they were he'd soon be a wealthy man. So wealthy in fact he'd be able to leave much of it to his staff and elect to be in a supervisory capacity instead of at the sharp end. But when he thought about it that idea didn't appeal. Working in the Store and meeting with these good people was the best tonic he could have. He thrived on it. So did Harriet and so did the children. Such genuine whole hearted folk they were. Half past midnight. He'd better leave.

Jimbo turned off the lights, locked the stockroom door and went downstairs. He let himself out and having reassured himself that everything was secure he stood for a moment in the shadow of the doorway looking at the village. Jimbo knew he was privileged to live here. Fancy if he lived in a high-rise block somewhere. Jimbo shuddered. It didn't bear thinking about. Walking home he passed the Bissetts' house, poor Sheila, he couldn't quite forgive his mother for leaving her helpless in the church hall, he passed the Senior sisters' house, the poor old things, and then his mother-in-law's old house. The chap who'd bought it seemed nice enough. As he was about to put his key in the lock of his own home he thought he heard a noise.

Jimbo stood quite still and listened. There it was again, it seemed to be coming from the direction of Church Lane. Looking across the Green he saw a small group of shadowy figures moving stealthily along towards the church. Jimbo lost sight of them so he walked as softly as he could onto the Green so he could follow their progress. But the royal oak despite its lack of leaves blocked his view. As he walked further onto the Green he heard the smashing of glass. At first he thought they must be attacking the church but as he ran and the church and Glebe Cottages came into view he saw they were attacking Dicky and Bel's windows. Without a thought for his own safety he ran into Church Lane shouting 'Hey! Hey, there! Stop it. Do you hear! Stop it!'

The noise made by the breaking glass masked his voice. He ran down Church Lane shouting, 'Stop it! Stop it!' Lights began coming on in bedrooms, windows were opened, shouts were heard. The four men were wearing balaclava type head gear which made it impossible to recognise any of them. Jimbo knew they must be able to hear his voice but they continued throwing missiles at the windows, by now Jimbo had drawn level with the churchyard wall where it ran down the side of the cottage garden, as he stepped onto the front lawn two of the men darted down the side of the cottage and Jimbo could hear glass breaking at the back. His mobile phone. Damn it! He'd left it in the Store.

The other two men were spraying paint on the brickwork at the front. Jimbo rushed at them but the taller of the two pushed him away. 'Buzz off, Jimbo! Before you get hurt!'

Then they too darted down the side of the house and Jimbo could just see them vault the churchyard wall and disappear. He followed them to the wall in time to see the other two leap it further down and speed away across the churchyard, skimming the gravestones and disappearing helter-skelter round the back of the church hall. There was no way he could catch them, fit as he was, so he went back to the cottage and called up to the broken upstairs window, 'Dicky! Bel! It's Jimbo. Are you all right?'

After a moment Dicky's head appeared. 'We're OK. Have they gone?'

'Yes, there was no way I could catch them. Come on down and we'll see what we can do.' Jimbo went round to the front door, stepping carefully because of the broken glass littering the path and the front lawn.

Dicky unlocked the door, though it seemed a pointless exercise: only jagged pieces of glass were left at the edges of the door frame.

'Careful where you step, Dicky. Where's Bel? What a shock. I just wish I could have caught them. Are you sure you're OK?'

Peter came up the path, his cloak over his pyjamas, and trainers on his feet. 'My God! What on earth is happening? Did you see who it was?'

' 'Fraid not. They were wearing masks over their faces, there were four of them, I know that.'

Bel came to the door, a vast red dressing-gown over her nightclothes, her happy face creased with fear, and white as a sheet. 'Oh dear. What are we going to *do*? I was so scared.'

Dicky put his arm round her. 'Don't you worry, love, we're not going to let a pack of hooligans frighten us away. They've done their worst, but the insurance will take care of it.'

A crowd of villagers had gathered, some carrying torches and most of them appalled at what had happened.

'Who do you reckon it was, Rector?'

'What a wicked thing to do.'

'They need horsewhipping.'

As well as the sympathetic cries Peter distinctly heard someone saying none too quietly 'Serves 'em right. The mucky pair.' And another one muttering 'Just deserts, that's what, we don't want 'em 'ere.'

Peter stood facing the cottage to estimate the damage. 'At this time of night there's no way we can set about making the house safe.'

Jimbo agreed. 'Look, how about it, Dicky, if I lend you my mobile phone and you stay in the house, and someone could offer Bel a bed for the rest of the night? You can't leave the house unprotected but at least if you have my phone you can ring me or Peter for help. No good ringing the police, they'll take ages to get here from Culworth. Bel, what do you think?'

'I don't like leaving Dicky, but I'm too frightened to stay.'

'Serves yer right, yer should be frightened.'

Peter fixed the speaker with a stern look, and they shamefacedly turned their gaze away from him. 'Very good idea. Look Bel, Caroline always keeps clean sheets on our spare bed, you can stay there for the night. What do you say, Dicky, to doing as Jimbo suggests?'

'Can't do any other. I'll get the glaziers to come first thing. What a damned mess. Who on earth could it have been?'

Jimbo, startled into recollecting what had happened when he'd first arrived on the scene, said, 'They were locals. That's right, they were locals.'

Dicky looked up at him. 'How did you know, if their faces were covered up?'

'They called me Jimbo. That's right they told me to go before I got hurt, and said "Buzz off, Jimbo." So they knew me. I'll ring their necks if ever I find out who it was.'

Peter, vastly disappointed that it was local men, looked sadly at the faces of the villagers gathered in the garden. 'We may as well all go home, there's nothing we can do except keep our eyes and ears open in the next few days and tell Dicky if we suspect we know who's done this dreadful thing. And remember if the press come asking questions we none of us know *why* or *who*. We don't want them getting on to it. This is where we all remember "silence is golden". Please don't let me . . . nor Dicky and Bel down, will you? Mum's the word. Good night everyone and thank you for your concern. God bless you all.'

Most of the villagers said 'Good night, Rector', even those who'd been less than kind in their remarks. A few went to comfort Bel and offered to come round to help clear up in the morning. 'Least we can do. Dreadful, really dreadful.'

Jimbo went back to the Store for his mobile phone and Peter went with Bel to the rectory.

Caroline came down the stairs when she heard the door open.

'Darling?' Then she saw Bel. 'Why Bel? Whatever's happened?'

Peter explained and Caroline, full of understanding, put her arms around Bel and hugged her. 'How perfectly dreadful. We'll make a cup of tea and you can take it to bed, the sheets are on.'

Bel protested but Caroline hushed her with a finger to her lips. 'No trouble at all, that's what we're here for.'

'I shall have to be up early because of the school.'

'Don't fret on that score, we're always up early because of the children, and Peter saying prayers. That's no problem. You do your best to sleep, it won't be easy I know. Just remember those dreadful people are to be pitied. Let's be thankful Jimbo was working late, and caught them at it. It could all have been a lot worse.'

When they got to bed Peter said, 'I don't want to call the police.'

'You don't?'

'No. I hope Dicky doesn't either.'

'Why not?'

'If the police know then the press will get to know and then it will all come out. Can't you just see the headlines? Turnham Malpas will turn overnight into a den of iniquity.'

'Of course, because of Dicky and Bel you mean. The one bedroom.'

'Exactly. All he's worked for will be gone overnight.'

'Well, we've had good reason to be thankful for them keeping quiet before, let's hope they can do it again. Good thing we've lost our own police station, the Sergeant would have been here in a flash.'

Peter nodded. 'I was sorry we lost him, but tonight I'm quite glad. He'd have been honour bound to report it. Good night, darling.'

'Good night. There's someone crying. It doesn't sound like the children, it must be Bel. I'll go see.'

20

The following morning Jimbo was feeling considerably below par. He ploughed on day after day carrying the burden of the business and most often he loved it, but today, somehow, a week away with Harriet, on their own, sounded like paradise. Last night had been the final straw. The papers were late, he'd had a load of vegetables to throw out because they hadn't kept over the weekend, the baker's van hadn't arrived, his accounts were getting behind hand, and to top it all he'd had a letter from a company in Culworth complaining about the food he'd provided for their company promotion meeting, when he knew all the time it was because they hadn't really been able to afford such a big splash. It wasn't the food at all. The fact that the promotion hadn't been well attended wasn't his fault, he'd only done the food and done it superbly well.

To add to his troubles it looked as though Linda would be late again. Jimbo decided that if she was that would be that. He could put up with so much, but she really was getting to be a trial. From experience he knew babies could be difficult, but he rather felt that Linda made more fuss than poor subdued little Lewis truly warranted.

He looked at his watch at ten minutes past nine and she still hadn't arrived. Running between till and post office counter he wished Harriet hadn't decided to do the farm run straight from taking Fran to playgroup. They were always busy first thing with the mothers when they'd left their children at school. He needed her right here this very minute.

The doorbell jingled and in rushed a breathless Linda. She called across, 'Sorry Mr Charter-P. Isn't it dreadful about Dicky and Bel? We hardly got any sleep and just to put the lid on it the girl who looks after Lewis on Mondays hasn't turned up, so Alan's having to look after him, and I'm all behind.'

'In that case then go back home and catch up.'

Linda stopped in her tracks. 'What do you mean?'

'Watch my lips, I shall say this only once! If you've a lot to do, go home and do it and don't bother coming back. It's obvious that you've no time for work. So you can be free of it, free to devote your time to Lewis and Alan. I've got a note of how many times you've been late, and how many times you've taken more than an hour for lunch and then left early into the bargain and I'm sorry I can no longer employ you. It's happening far too often and I'm not willing to put up with it. I'm running a business here not a charity. I shall send the money due to you as soon as I get a chance to calculate what I owe. Sorry, Linda, but that's that.'

Jimbo carried on taking the money at the till ignoring Linda's horrified expression. When she finally found her voice she said 'Oh! What a joke, for one awful moment I thought you meant it. Now, Lady Templeton, what can I get for you?'

As Muriel opened her mouth to ask for ten first-class stamps and could Linda send this letter recorded delivery, Jimbo said, 'Stop! I meant it! Don't bother to undo your coat, just leave.' He stabbed a forefinger in the direction of the door. 'That's the way out.'

'Well. After all these years. I don't believe it. You can't sack someone who's worked for you for years. You can't do it. It's not allowed.'

'I have done it, and damn the consequences I say. That's ten pounds and ninety-five pence, please. Thank you. Five pence change. Good morning and thank you for shopping with us.' Jimbo looked at Linda with a surprised expression on his face. 'You're still here, Linda. I've shown you where the door is.'

Linda burst into tears and headed for the door, just as she was about to reach out to grasp the handle Alan burst in.

'Oh, Alan! How did you know?' She flung herself into his arms but he pushed her off.

'The keys. Where are the keys? I can't get in the pub. It's all locked up! I've hammered on the door, back and front, and there's no reply. I can't understand it, it's never happened before! I think Bryn must have been taken ill. Where've you put the spare keys? Eh?'

Because he was ignoring her predicament Linda cried louder still. She burbled out between her sobs, 'In your sock drawer, right underneath.' As he was turning to leave and go home to procure the keys a thought struck her, and gazing frantically about she screamed, 'Where's the baby?'

'The baby? The baby? Oh my God, I've left him outside the pub by the bins.' The two of them raced out leaving the door wide open.

Muriel, who hated confrontation and was standing by the post office section in a state of shock, began to tremble, it was all too much. In a faint voice she said, 'I'll help myself to a coffee if I may, Jimbo.'

'Of course, you do that.'

Muriel stepped round to the shelf where the coffee machine stood, but it was empty. 'Oh dear.'

At that moment Mrs Jones strode in. 'What's the matter with Linda and

Alan? I've just seen them streaking across the Green as if the devil himself was after them.'

Jimbo sighed. 'It's a long story. I'll tell you later. Be on the till five minutes while I do the post office will you?'

'Well, all right but if I make a mistake . . .'

'I'll accept full responsibility.'

'OK, but on your own head be it.'

Jimbo strode across. 'Now Muriel . . . You didn't get your coffee.'

'No, there isn't any.'

Jimbo took off his boater and smoothed his bald head. 'I wonder if I could put back the clock and start Monday all over again? Perhaps it wouldn't be any better if I did. Shall I . . . ?' He nodded his head in the direction of the coffee percolator.

Muriel shook her head. 'Not for me, you've enough to do. Shall I come back later for my stamps?'

'I'll do it now. Who'd be an employer? I ask you? Now, let's see.'

They found the baby safe and sound though somewhat surprised, and Alan took a tearful Linda back home grateful in some ways that she'd been sacked, then he wasn't saddled with the baby to look after when he obviously had a crisis on his hands. Socks flew in all directions as he searched for the keys, grabbing them he rushed back to the pub. Opening the main door he strode into the bar and listened to the silence. It was profound. Either Bryn was laid dead somewhere or he wasn't here at all.

He searched the bar, the public lavatories, the dining-room and the kitchens, the storerooms at the back, and then climbed the stairs. Knowing that Elektra had been making a bid for the lonely Bryn he was cautious which bedroom doors he opened. The door to his old room was ajar. He peeped round the door and saw the bed hadn't been slept in. Or if it had she'd made the bed first thing. Drawing a blank he went to the main bedroom. That door was shut, so taking hold of the knob firmly he gently turned it and opened it just enough to put his head round. The bed had been slept in. Both sides. He tried the third bedroom which had always been more of a boxroom than anything, that too was empty. It occurred to him to look out onto the car park. He went to the window and realised Bryn's Triumph sports car had gone.

There was no one in the lounge nor the kitchen. Obviously Bryn had packed up and left. Alan panicked. He couldn't run it on his own. He'd have to get Georgie. Would she come back though? She'd have to.

When he got to Grandmama's the two of them were just finishing a leisurely breakfast, in a lovely marigold yellow cosy country kitchen Linda would have died for. Grandmama was wearing a splendid housecoat and

Georgie was in trousers and that purpley sweater Linda liked, with the pearl decoration on the front.

Georgie stood up in alarm when she saw Alan. 'What's the matter?'

'Bryn's gone.'

'Gone? Gone where?'

'Don't know. But he's not there.'

'He isn't?'

'No. Not in the pub.'

'He's slept in.'

Alan shook his head. 'No, he hasn't. I've had to get my spare keys to get in. I've been to have a look.'

'Been to look in the bedrooms you mean?' Georgie's heart began to thud.

Alan nodded. 'That's right. Elektra's not there either.'

'She's not?'

'No.'

Grandmama took a hand. 'Best get over there. Have a good search yourself.'

Alan protested. 'I've looked, I know that place like the back of my hand, I lived there. He isn't there, I tell you.'

Georgie's mind was whirling with questions. 'His car?'

'Gone.'

Georgie abruptly sat down again, dropping onto the chair with a thud. Inspired, she asked, 'His clothes. Has he taken his clothes?'

'I don't know, I didn't look in the wardrobes.'

'No, of course not. It's not like Bryn just to disappear. He'll have gone into Culworth for something urgent. Or, I know, the cash and carry, we've run out of something. Yes, that'll be it.'

Grandmama and Alan exchanged sceptical looks.

Georgie sprang to life. 'He'll be back soon. But I'd better come over. He hasn't left a note?'

Alan shook his head. 'It looks like more than just going shopping to me.'

'In that case then we'll have to get ready to open up. Has the chef arrived yet?'

'No, but it's still early for him.'

'Damn it, and I was going to the bank this morning and the solicitors, well that'll have to wait. Blast him. Blast him. And her. I'll get my coat.'

Georgie turned up her nose when she saw the state of the kitchen. Whatever Elektra was good at, it wasn't housekeeping. The sink and draining board were cluttered with dirty dishes, the waste bin was overflowing, and she noted lipstick smothered cigarette ends in a saucer on the kitchen table. Bryn was accustomed to a scrupulously clean kitchen, it surprised her what men were prepared to put up with. In exchange for what?

She saw the bedroom and realised.

Stiffening her resolve Georgie marched downstairs. 'Alan! Now look here, there's no way we can manage without some help. If we've to cover for Bryn then we need someone to clean, temporary, as of today to fill the gap. You'll have to work extra hours which I know you'll quite like. We'll manage till we find out what's going on.'

'Don't you worry we'll cope, remember that time Bryn went into hospital for his hernia, we managed then didn't we?'

'You're quite right we did. Who is there in the village could clean? Today, right now?'

'Linda could. Jimbo sacked her from the post office this morning. She could, temporary, we'll need the money. She'd have to bring the baby though, today.'

'Well, she can for now. Give her a ring. Pay's good tell her, she'll get a bonus for coming in promptly. Right, let's get cracking.'

That night the bar was crowded. The news had flashed round Turnham Malpas and the surrounding farms and villages in no time at all. All the regulars and plenty of customers who only came occasionally had found reason to be in there. Alan and Georgie were, to use an expression of Bryn's "pulled out of the place". Dicky, now that Bryn was no longer around, had called in for a drink but seeing how busy the two of them were he'd volunteered out of sympathy for their predicament and out of love for Georgie to be potman for the night.

'Eh! Dicky, you're back then, now the coast's clear?'

'So how's love's young dream tonight then?'

'We shall miss Elektra, and not half!'

'Don't suppose you wear black lace knickers?'

Dicky took it all in good part, and began to enjoy himself. He liked people and that was something he knew you had to do if you were in the licensed trade. He started telling a few jokes if a particular table was receptive, and before he knew where he was he had an audience and there was nothing Dicky liked better than an audience and he played it to the hilt.

There was a round of applause after his impromptu performance and Alan and Georgie winked at each other with approval.

'See, Alan, I knew I was right. Bryn didn't know everything.'

'Well, I agreed with you at the time. He's a bit of all right is Dicky. Everybody likes him, you see.'

A germ of an idea formed in Georgie's head, but she'd have to think hard first before she put it into words. Business decisions had to be well thought out before you took action. But it might just be the answer to a lot of problems.

Surprisingly it was Grandmama who came up with the complete solution.

She called on the Thursday of the week Bryn had disappeared on the Monday, when she knew they would be quiet.

'Georgie! Georgie!' After a moment a tired-looking Georgie appeared. 'Now my dear, get us both a drink and come and sit down before you fall down. I've had an idea.'

Grandmama placed herself in the comfortable wing-chair by the fireplace. It was the middle of the afternoon and the lunchtime crowd had gone but the evening crowd had not yet arrived.

'Whisky?'

'Not at this time of day and in any case I need a clear head. I'll have a lemonade, thank you, my dear.'

Georgie plumped herself down. She was exhausted.

'My dear, you look worn out.'

'I am. Bryn did all the books and the bulk of the ordering. I never realised just how much time it took. And there's the dining-room to keep an eye on, they're short-handed in there, I've found that one of the part-timers has been taking food home so she's had to go. I feel sorry for her, but it's no good, once one does it the rest will follow.'

'I agree. Now, have you heard from Bryn?'

'No. Not a word.'

'And when you went to the bank and the solicitor's? You'll pardon me asking but I have a rescue plan and I need to know where you stand.'

'He's taken almost all the money from our private joint account. I intended getting there first and taking half which I consider is my rightful share, but being faced with the crisis on Monday, of course, I didn't get there did I? So he's hopped it with almost all of it and I'm seething about it.'

'The devil he has! You'll have to get your share back. Quite definitely yes, you will. And the business account?'

'That's safe he hasn't touched that, but then we only leave enough in there for trading, paying invoices and wages and such. Bryn always takes out whatever can be spared every month and puts it in our own account.'

Grandmama sipped her lemonade, put down the glass and cleared her throat. 'I have a plan. Do you have a plan?'

'Haven't had much time to think but I've a germ of an idea which hasn't formed yet really.'

'Well, listen to my idea first and see if it matches yours. Until you find Bryn, financially you can't do a thing. Can't sell up, can't sell his half of the business, can't get a divorce yet, that's if you want one.'

'I want one right enough. It's insulting, downright insulting and humiliating that he's gone off with that *bitch*.' Georgie's face twisted into a grimace and her eyes glittered with tears. 'I wanted out but this . . . If she walked in now I'd murder her, believe me. It'll be her idea to take all the money, Bryn's got a bit more honour than that. But what's he doing letting her dictate to him like that?'

'Besotted?'

'I expect so. I should have thrown her out when I came back last Saturday . . . Anyway it's all too late now. You've a plan?'

'Yes. It solves all sorts of things. I understand you've been having some great times in here with Dicky helping out?' Georgie nodded. 'He's made for this kind of place you know. He could belong here.'

Georgie smiled. 'He could, you're right.'

'So, you've told me he doesn't like his job where he is, but he does do accounts, now, with a bit of tuition from my Jimbo I'm sure he could take over the accounts and ordering and things and still have enough energy left over for helping in the bar every day too, just like Bryn does, well, did. So he could give up his job, and you could employ him.'

She saw interest sparking in Georgie's eyes and pressed on with her proposal. 'Now, it wouldn't be a good idea for him to live here, there's been enough tittle-tattle, and you don't want any more of that, but that's no problem with him living just up the road. But I don't think it's right that you should live here all on your own, in a public house. Not right at all. Not safe, so how about if Bel comes to live here with you. That then would solve the problem of everyone thinking Bel and Dicky are up to no good.' Grandmama blushed with guilt as she said this and hoped Georgie hadn't noticed. 'The whole village would then forget all about the scandalous situation which they believe exists at the moment in Glebe Cottages.'

'I do believe you might be on to something here.'

'Oh I am! I know I am. Believe me! Now should there come a time when Bryn is wanting out and wants to sell his half of this,' she waved a regal hand around her head, 'Dicky could buy him out and the two of you could marry when you've got your divorce. There!' She sat back and waited for Georgie's reaction.

'Well, it all sounds excellent, wonderful in fact, but you've forgotten one thing, even if Dicky sold his house he has such a big mortgage he wouldn't have enough money left over to buy the half share and the bank certainly wouldn't lend him it because without the house he wouldn't have any collateral. So that's a bit impossible. I couldn't lend him it either because Bryn's got what's ours.'

Grandmama shook her head. 'No, it's not impossible. I've no doubt at all that with you and Dicky here keeping up your kind of high standards the Royal Oak would go from strength to strength. It would become an excellent investment for anyone. So why not me? I have capital which I would be willing to lend him as and when the time arrives.'

'No, Katherine, I can't let you do that!'

'You can't stop me. It will be all legal and properly drawn up, believe me

Jimbo has got his business brain from me not his father, I'd have it all absolutely legal and I *want* to do it. If Bryn should come back full of remorse this way nothing would be changed, Dicky and Bel would still have their house, and you could make your decisions from then on. Only Dicky would have taken a risk with giving up his job.'

'I can't believe this. I can't. That would be wonderful! The whole plan makes everything so right.'

'Exactly!'

'But what about Bel? What would she do?'

'Oh, she'd carry on with her life as it is now. No one could object to that, could they? It would leave Dicky and her whiter than white wouldn't it, her living here and doing what she usually does. She could still help Dicky with the mortgage couldn't she?'

'Oh yes. But what if Bryn comes back? He might.'

'We can't do anything legal till he makes contact anyway, so financially everything would be status quo. He can't object to Bel living here and he can't object to you employing someone besides Alan to give you a hand. The hours are crippling, you need both Dicky and Alan and a barmaid part-time too.'

Georgie stood up. 'All I can say is a big thank you. I've been puzzling my brain about the whole problem but I'm so busy I can't give it my full attention and here you are, you've come up with it all neat and tidy.' She bent forward and kissed Grandmama soundly. 'There! What more can I say, but a big thank you. I'll talk to Dicky and Bel tonight.'

'Talk to them together, Bel mustn't think we've all been plotting and planning her life behind her back.'

'Of course. Got to go, lots to do.'

'And I must be off too. We'll keep in touch.' Grandmama kissed Georgie and as she was leaving she turned back to say rather sadly, 'It'll be lonely in my cottage without you, you know, quite lonely. Bye-bye, my dear.'

Walking up Stocks Row to her cottage she saw Peter pulling up outside the rectory. She called to him the moment he got out of his car. 'Rector! Have you a moment?'

Peter nodded. 'Good afternoon, Mrs Charter-Plackett. Lovely day!'

'Can I have a word?'

'Of course, come in!'

'No, I won't do that, thank you. There's a programme I like to watch at five o'clock. You remember you asked me to solve the problem of Dicky and Bel and Georgie?'

'I did indeed.'

'Well I have, that's if they all agree.' She outlined her plan and was gratified to see the delight on Peter's face. 'I'm not telling anyone except Jimbo about the financial side of it, that's private, I'm telling you because I know I can rely on you to keep a confidence. What do you think then?'

'Brilliant. If they all agree it solves everything at one fell swoop and I know Dicky would be good for the business and he'd still be able to carry on with the Scouts. Wonderful! Thank you so much.'

'All we have to hope is that Bryn turns up some time soon.'

'Georgie hasn't heard then?'

Grandmama shook her head. 'No, not a word. Still it's early days, he might tire of Elektra quite quickly, or more likely she might tire of him! I'm glad you're pleased. Must go. See you soon, Peter!'

With his forearms resting on the roof of the car he watched her stride off to her cottage. She really was an outrageous mixture of a person. Domineering, belligerent, determined, bullying, wilful, imperious, kind, understanding, sympathetic, genteel, intelligent, the list was endless. But the debt he owed her if it all worked out! He rather hoped she wouldn't call it in one day.

21

'So you see, Jimbo, they've agreed to my plan. Now you won't mind tutoring Dicky will you?' Jimbo opened his mouth to protest but his mother continued to speak. 'Dicky only has a month's notice to give and they say they'll have him back any time if it doesn't work out, but it will, I know it will. Now about the money . . .'

'What money?'

'My money.'

'Your money?'

'You are in danger of repeating yourself, the money I'm lending Dicky when Bryn decides he wants to sell his half.'

Jimbo went into shock. 'You haven't promised them *money*?'

Grandmama sensed opposition. 'It is *mine*.'

'I know, but you can't just go throwing it about.'

'I'm not throwing it about. Not at all. It's going to be a proper business arrangement. I'm not some foolish doddery old lady, I do know what I'm doing.'

'Do you though? It seems to me you've had a rush of blood to the head, or the heart, I don't know which. One doesn't invest one's capital on a whim. Think of the risk!'

'You're a fine one to talk about risks. What about the risk you took with this place? Couldn't be called a blue chip investment could it when you bought it? A disgusting one-room shop with no stock to speak of, two dilapidated cottages, and tantamount to nil turnover. You wouldn't listen to me though would you? At least the Royal Oak is an established business with prospects, and that's what I'm investing in.'

'I invested in myself and Harriet and knew I was right. You're investing in Dicky, in truth. You'll have no shares in the business.'

Grandmama paused while she considered this fact. 'Yes, I see what you mean. I need to think about that. That won't do, will it?'

'Well, not for me it wouldn't. That is too risky by far.'

'But I want to help. After the other night Dicky and Bel need all the help they can get. They deserve it. I never heard a thing. I'd taken some dratted herbal sleeping concoction Mrs Jones gave me and I went out like a light. I wish I had, I'd have shown them what for. I don't suppose they've found out who it was?' Jimbo shook his head. 'Pity. I'm so sorry for Georgie too, there's nothing worse than a dead marriage. And I should know.'

Jimbo, who while she'd been speaking had been scribbling on a piece of paper hazarding a shrewd guess at the sums involved, looked up surprised. 'What do you mean? "You should know"?'

'That's what I had. Four years of comparative happiness and then phut! it all went up in flames.' She watched the screen-saver on Jimbo's computer while he absorbed what she'd said.

Eventually he asked quietly, 'What do you mean?'

'I never told you before, the habit of shielding you from it is deeply ingrained, but I expect you're old enough now to understand. It was because of your father that you went away to school so early, it broke my heart but it seemed better than you knowing.'

'What exactly did he do?'

Looking him fearlessly in the eye for a moment before making up her mind Grandmama said decisively, 'He had a mistress and they had three boys and he juggled himself between us. When you were home from school he spent his time with us, and then when you went back he went back to her. Had some mad idea I think, that if he kept faith with you and you never knew, it absolved him from guilt. Made everything all right he imagined, with never a thought as to how I might feel about it. I could have killed him many a time, believe me. The lying, cheating toad.'

Jimbo was appalled. Appalled that all the years of his life he'd never been aware of the misery at the heart of her. 'Mother! I'm so sorry, so very sorry. I had no idea. I just find it so hard to believe.'

'You'd better believe it! It's true! Now you're making me feel I shouldn't have told you. Maybe you're not old enough yet.'

'Mother! Not old enough? For heaven's sake. He was away working a lot, I knew that, but I didn't realise the real truth, not once. Not even when I was at Cambridge. I must have been incredibly blind, and he, and you, incredibly careful.'

'Good, I'm glad. I stuck with him you see, old-fashioned principles and all that.'

'Well, I admire you for that. I really truly do. But three half-brothers! It takes some assimilating. So that's why I'm an only one?'

Grandmama nodded. 'It is. I pretended it was because I didn't like childbirth, which truth to tell what woman does, but I would have liked more children. I couldn't take the risk in case he left me for good, you see. What was more, I didn't fancy him when he'd been with someone else.

However, the son I've got more than makes up for not having more.' She smiled at him.

Jimbo got up from his chair and planted a kiss on his mother's cheek. 'Why have you never told me this before?'

'Pride, I'm afraid. Too proud that's me.'

'I see, I can understand that. I'm so sorry about him. So very sorry. So when he died what happened then, you've never seemed short of money?'

'She got some money and the house she lived in, but the bulk of his money and our house were mine. He did at least have the good manners to reward my tolerance of all those years, and was old-fashioned enough to acknowledge I was his legal wife. I'll give him that. Also I expect he was thinking about his son and heir.' Jimbo grimaced at that. 'A few flirtations with the stock market have increased it way beyond my wildest dreams . . . and his!'

'Where are they now? The other woman and the children? Well, they're not children now, of course.'

'I haven't any idea and I care still less. Somewhere you have three half-brothers all around your age, let's hope they never turn up by chance. I wouldn't know what the odds are on that, but I don't care.'

Jimbo went to stand at the window. There was no view, and the window was barred which limited his vision, but he wasn't looking out at anything, he was absorbed in his thoughts. 'He was always good fun my father. That's one of the things I remember best from childhood.' He turned away from the window to look at his mother. 'It must have coloured your outlook, all this going on.'

'It felt like a smack in the face with a giant, stinkingly dead cod every time he came home: smiling and laughing with his presents and his kisses. He must have felt something for me though, after all, he came home to me to die. The worst of it was I cried when he died. I wept. Grieved. I looked, and was, the genuine distraught widow at his funeral.' Jimbo nodded sadly in agreement. 'But he'd made me tough over the years and I soon got over it. I'd learned not to cry for long.'

They were both silent for a while and then Jimbo said, 'About Dicky, of course I'll teach him. It's all quite simple. And if the need to lend the money does arise then I'll help out with advice about that, too. Like you said, all legal and above board. You can't afford not to be.'

'Oh, I shall be. Now come and give your mother a kiss and I'll be off. You must get on. I see Linda's back.'

'She is indeed and not without a climb-down on my part, believe me. I have to confess I was extremely rude to her, but she caught me on a bad day. I grovelled, positively grovelled, to entice her back. However, the rustle of money finally won the day, well, my charm too, I suppose. God, did I apologise! But, we quite simply could not manage without her. She may be a poor time-keeper but she knows post office procedures through and through and she's never a penny wrong. She's got a different child-minder and she's promised to improve her time-keeping so we'll wait and see. Let's hope she learned a valuable lesson, I know I have. Harriet can't do it, she needs to be with the children.'

Grandmama stood up and collected her handbag and gloves from Jimbo's desk. 'What a lucky man you are. She's a perfectly splendid mother and a wonderful wife to you and I hope you know that and demonstrate it, daily.'

'Oh I do.'

'Good. I don't say much, Jimbo, but I am proud of you. So proud. No one but you could have made such a success of this business. Right, that's enough of sentimentality for one day. I'll be off.'

Jimbo kissed her on both cheeks and opened the door for her to leave. As she passed him she patted his cheek and said, 'At your age you won't let it affect you will you? He was just that kind of a man and in some ways you've inherited his love of the human race, except *he* didn't know when to call a halt.'

Harriet, who'd been in the kitchens supervising the staff preparing for a dinner that night, went in search of Jimbo and found him standing in his office looking lost.

'Jimbo? What's the matter? Are you all right?'

He didn't answer her immediately.

'Well?'

'Close the door, Harriet.' He paced back and forth for a moment and then looked at her. 'Do you know, I've just found out the most amazing news. Incredible really. I've got three half-brothers I never knew I had.'

Harriet was flabbergasted. 'What on earth are you talking about? Have you been at the whisky?'

'No, it's Mother, she's . . . well . . . she's . . .'

There was a split second of silence and then Harriet, eyes wide with shock, shouted '*Your mother? My God!*'

'Honestly Harriet! Of course not. For heaven's sake. No, it's she who's just *told* me. It was my father, he was playing away nearly all the time they were married, and I never knew. What am I, forty-seven, forty-eight? And she's only just felt able to let on.'

'For one dreadful minute I thought . . . that would have been a laugh. Oh dear! Sorry, darling, it must hurt. I must be serious. Tell me then, if you will, or want to or can.'

So he did and Harriet was horrified. 'No wonder she's like she is. How could she have put up with that all those years? Thirty years? Right? Now at least we know the reason why she's so tough and uncompromising. Well, from now on I shall try very hard to be more understanding, she doesn't deserve to have had a husband like that.'

'No one does.' Jimbo opened wide his arms and Harriet went to him and put her arms around his neck and Jimbo hugged her tightly. 'Not even Mother!' They laughed. 'Must press on. We'll talk about it again tonight, right. The children musn't know, for her sake, and also for mine. OK? By the way, she says you're a wonderful wife to me.'

'Does she indeed? Well, well, well. It's certainly been a morning for revelations! I shall definitely have to be more understanding then.'

'We both shall. Kiss?'

22

'Peter? Oh there you are. I'll be off then. My appointment's at eleven so I've no time to spare.' Caroline pulled on her gloves and smiled at him.

He got up from his desk and looking gravely down at her, he smoothed her cheek gently with the back of his hand. 'I'm coming.' He raised his hand to silence her as soon as he saw protest coming into her face. 'I won't brook any argument. I am coming. I will not have you face this alone. That is what being married is all about. Support. Just need to wash my hands, the print's come off all over my fingers. Won't be a minute.'

'I'm better facing things on my own.'

'This time I'm not listening. I've put an end to that, like I said.'

While he washed his hands and got his cloak Caroline stood looking out of his study window at the village. It was a bitterly cold day, with a cruel breeze blowing. She could just see Grandmama battling her way along, with her fur hat on and boots, and a huge scarf around her shoulders on top of her fur coat. Grandmama was blessed annoying with her interfering ways, but at least she'd solved the problem of Dicky and Bel. The Royal Oak was going from strength to strength with Georgie at the helm and Dicky enlivening everyone. Bel living there seemed to be working out too. She recollected hearing Bel crying in their spare bedroom the night their house had been attacked, and going to sit on the end of her bed and talking to her for what seemed hours. Poor Bel! Such a quandary for her. A variation on the eternal triangle in a way. The three of them just needed Bryn to make contact and then perhaps they could finally sort things out.

Caroline heard Peter coming racing down the stairs. 'I'm ready. Come on. We'll go in my car. Sylvia's cleaning upstairs, I've told her we're both going.'

'I expect she's pleased.'

Peter looked at her as he fastened the clasp on his cloak. 'Is she?'

'She will be. Don't pretend you don't know what I mean. It's a conspiracy between the two of you.'

Peter had the grace to look embarrassed. 'Well, yes, you're right. She does approve of me putting my foot down.'

'We'll go in the Volvo shall we? Mine's too small for comfort for you.'

'That's what I thought. In any case you haven't got the all-clear for driving yet. Right.'

Just as they were taking the sharp left turn at the signpost for Culworth Caroline put her hand on Peter's thigh and said quietly, 'Thank you for coming with me. I appreciate it. Suddenly I've gone dreadfully afraid.'

'That's understandable, but whatever the outcome, whatever the specialist says, you've always got me. I'm right up there with you, I just hope it helps.'

'It does, more than you know. I can't bear being told there's only a small chance that I shall see the children growing up. I do want to be able to live long enough to see how they turn out.' The hand resting on his thigh clenched and thumped him lightly. 'There's still so much left to do, and I want to see you when you're sixty, and seventy and eighty. What a lovely dignified old gentleman you will be.'

'That was one of the questions I tested myself with when I first met you. I realised you were the first woman I had ever known whom I wanted to know in old age.' He paused for a moment and followed on with 'And we shall, grow old together.' Taking a hand off the steering wheel he took hold of hers and squeezed it tightly. 'That's a promise.'

'I wish I had your confidence. All mine has ebbed away this morning. Every last drop has gone.'

They were silent for the next few miles and then Peter said. 'Faith that's what you have to have, faith that you'll get the all-clear and having got the all-clear, you and I will go away on our own for a few days.'

'How on earth could we manage that?'

Peter braked at the lights. Looking straight ahead he said, 'I've organised it.'

'How?'

'I've arranged for your mother and father to come down. Your mother can't wait to have the twins to herself.'

'Peter! She's never said a word! I should have been consulted. I knew nothing about it. You never asked me.'

'I know I didn't. It's a decision I made for your sake, and for mine. We both need to recuperate. It's been a long haul these last three months.'

'You can't possibly go away at this time of year so close to Christmas. What about all the work there is to do with the Midnight Service, and the old people's Christmas Lunch and the Scouts' Christmas Party and Christmas morning and things and there's . . .'

'Yes?'

'You've so much to do.'

'I haven't, it's all done. Anne Parkin has got all the typing done, the order of service, the special carols, everything, I've checked it all and it's ready for printing out, Sheila Bissett has organised all the decorations, with I might add Grandmama's invaluable assistance, although I understand from Gilbert that Sheila's file is firmly in her hands and Grandmama is not allowed even a peep . . .'

Caroline laughed. 'Really?'

'Yes, there's a kind of armed truce, how long it will last I don't know. Gilbert has arranged the choir anthems with my enthusiastic approval, Mrs Peel and I have had a long consultation about the organ music, Willie has got his lists ready and all I have to do is go away and enjoy myself.'

'How on earth have you managed to do all that so early?'

'Determination, my darling. Determination that you and I were having a week in Crete together, all on our own, re-establishing ourselves.'

'Crete? How wonderful! I've always wanted to go there.'

'I though it might be fairly warm still and not too far away. We shall be able to leave all our cares behind us and just wander about, just the two of us. Together. On our own.'

With an amused grin on her face Caroline replied, 'If I didn't know you better I'd think you were talking in terms of a second honeymoon.'

'I am. I can't wait. It's been so long. I'll park in my place and then we'll walk through.'

He stood up when he saw her come back into the corridor. Her eyes searched for him amongst the waiting patients and having found him they looked at one another long and hard. He'd spent the hour and a half she'd been away praying like he'd never prayed before. The confidence she'd lost he had also lost, but he had feared to admit to her he was as much at sea as she. He daren't smile before she did, in case the news was grim. Then as she walked towards him he realised her eyes were shining with joy, and relief ran through every vein in his body and filled him with profound rejoicing.

Caroline came close to him and looking up she said, 'I can't quite believe it but . . . it does appear things are looking quite good.' Her face shone with love. 'You were right to be confident after all. I'm so grateful to be . . .' The rest of what she had to say was smothered by Peter's cloak as he hugged her tight.

'Thank God. Thank God. Let's leave this place. Quick. I've had enough to last a lifetime.' He grasped her hand and hastened her out. As they crossed the car park he released his hold on her hand and with clenched fists raised above his head punched the air shouting, 'Hallelujah!'

'Peter, don't, everyone will hear you.'

'And why not? What news! What a relief.'

'Another check-up in three months and then six months after that. I'm just so grateful. It really was touch and go.'

'More than you realise.'

'Of course I realised, I am a doctor after all. I knew more than most.'

'But they never told you that your heart stopped did they?'

'Did it?'

'Yes, about an hour after you came out of theatre.'

'Oh God, I didn't know. Oh heavens. I'd no idea. My legs have gone all weak.'

He opened the car door. 'Here let me help you in. You frightened the life out of me.'

'You were there?'

'I was. Mind your coat. That's it.'

'I had no idea. No wonder they were so very particular about me. I thought it was because I was a medic, you know, one of their own as you might say. Peter, we need that holiday don't we? Is it booked?'

'I've an option on it, which I shall confirm this very day. So it's bells on Sunday and we leave Tuesday.'

After lunch Peter called in at the Store to cancel his papers whilst he was away.

Jimbo wrote it down in his order book and as he snapped the book shut he said, 'Seems to me things have taken a turn for the better if you're going away.'

'They have. They're very pleased at the hospital, the operation appears to have been a success and she doesn't have to go again for three months. In consequence of which we're taking a holiday. Her parents are coming down to stay with the children while we go, but they don't take a morning paper.'

'I'm delighted, absolutely delighted. Harriet will be beside herself, she's been so worried.'

'So have we. I shan't want to go through all that again. Never again.'

'I should say not. Big day on Sunday. I'm feeling very nervous, this bell-ringing lark has really got to me. We've a rehearsal tonight and tomorrow night and then the real thing Sunday. We intend making enough noise to wake the dead.'

'You've no idea how I'm longing to hear the bells. This business of having recordings and pretending it's real, well . . .'

'Exactly. We've got quite a team together you know. There's ten of us fighting for a chance to ring.'

'Brilliant. Wonderful. That's excellent news.'

'Don't suppose, Peter, you've had any news about who attacked Dicky and Bel's have you?'

'None at all. Except, between you and I, I bumped into Mrs Jones . . . is she here?' – Jimbo shook his head – 'into Mrs Jones and I gave her a long look when I asked her if she'd heard any rumours about who'd done it and she avoided my eye. She was obviously very uncomfortable and dashed away as soon as she could. What do you think?'

'She's been very cagey with me about it too. Could be Kenny and Terry know something, they're those kind of people. But if we get the police involved then the press will get to know and then the balloon will go up, oh yes. Excuse me. Bel, the bakery van's here. See to it will you. One day he'll arrive on time.'

Bel called across as she went to open the door, 'They're a man short; he's having to do two rounds.'

'That's not our fault.'

Peter took his leave. 'I must be away. Lots to do before Sunday. I'll give Caroline your good wishes.'

'Thanks.' Jimbo touched his boater and then turned his attention to the delivery man. 'Now, Trevor, this won't do. It's three times this week alone that you've not got here till the afternoon. Most of my bread trade is in the mornings you know. It's too late now and I hate selling yesterday's bread. If it's late again, I shall refuse to accept the order.'

'Sorry, Mr Charter-P. We've a new roundsman starting tomorrow, so everything will be back to normal. I don't like delivering late any more than you. I'll be here in good time tomorrow. Ta-ta for now.' Jimbo caught him winking at Bel. So . . . that was the way the wind was blowing.

'He's left the delivery note in the tray, Bel, I'll check it off for you.' Jimbo picked up the note and unfolded it. '*Dear Bel,*' it read. He quickly refolded it. 'Here, this is yours I think. Nice chap, you could do worse!'

He laughed and Bel blushed bright red as she recognised the writing. 'He's an old friend. That's all. A friend of Dicky's. There's nothing going on.'

'Come on, Bel, why not? You've as much right to a life as anyone else. Go for it, I say.'

'It's only about him coming to hear the Scout band on Sunday. Dicky's organised a performance after the service.'

'I know. Our boys have been practising for years, well not years, but certainly weeks. I swear I could play the trumpet myself I've listened to the tunes so many times. It's going to be great, what with the bells and the band. What a day.'

Though Turnham Malpas got is fair share of rain it was almost accepted as a matter of course that if they had anything special happening the weather would be fine. This Sunday was no exception. A fact which people in Penny Fawcett and Little Derehams accepted with bad grace. The element of rivalry between the three villages had been rumbling on for generations and good weather on a special day always brought out the animosity all over again. As bedroom curtains in the two villages were drawn back that morning and they all saw the clear cloudless skies and the pale winter sun, they said, 'Might have known. It's a lovely day, not a drop of rain in sight. How do they do it?'

Turnham Malpas smug in its own self-righteousness put on its Sunday best and went to the ten o'clock service, but this time for the first time for more years than they could remember the bells rang out across the fields beckoning them to church. Pure and sweet and triumphant.

Perhaps it was the novelty of the bells, or their gratitude for Caroline's good news, or a simple need to praise their Maker, but whatever had motivated them they stretched Willie's extra seating to the maximum. Just as he was beginning to think the last ones had found seats the Nightingales arrived, all seven of them. He remembered the old bench which usually stood in the churchyard, wiped the bird dirt off it with an old cloth from the boiler house storeroom, and he and Ralph carried it in and placed it right at the back near the font. Even so two of the children had to sit on the step below the font. The bells rang their final peal, and the ringers wiped their sweating faces and smiled their satisfaction at each other, and Peter and the choir entered and the service began. Peter stood on the altar steps to announce the first hymn. Behind him beside the altar was a beautiful display of flowers arranged by Sheila Bissett, and the old church silver was on display too, gleaming and twinkling in the light from the candle in the wonderful silver candlestick.

In pride of place at the front in the rectory pew alongside Caroline sat Mr Fitch. The role of benefactor sat well on his shoulders, and he couldn't resist a gracious smile in Ralph and Muriel's direction when Peter spoke of his generosity in paying for the restoration of the bells.

Peter also thanked everyone who had contributed to the Scout Band Fund. 'We are all so proud. Scout bands are quite rare nowadays, and we are very privileged to have one of our own. I understand that in the future they are planning to compete in brass band competitions. We wish them all success. Dicky?'

Dicky's face lit up with pride. He stood up and went to the altar steps to speak. 'Unaccustomed as I am to public speaking . . .' – he was interrupted here with a huge laugh – 'I should just like to say how very, very grateful all the Scouts are for the generosity of the people of Turnham Malpas, and Little Derehams and Penny Fawcett and lots of other people in the surrounding area. Without their money and without their gifts of instruments they no longer had a need for, this band would never have got off the ground. In particular a big thank you to Sir Ralph for buying us such an absolutely spanking big drum, the Royal Marines would be proud to own it. If I was a bit taller I'd have a go myself!'

There came another burst of kindly laughter.

'After the service the band will be giving a short concert, very short actually because we're still beginners, to which you are all invited. We were going to perform in the churchyard but there's so many of you here that we've moved the venue to the Green. There are lots of people I should thank, too numerous to mention, but I wish specially to thank Gilbert Johns, for all his wonderful help. Thank you, one and all.'

The congregation gathered in the road by the gate to the church hall and the band stood in formation on the Green facing them. Gilbert climbed onto an old upturned wooden crate from the Royal Oak, and with his baton raised he gathered the boys' eyes and brought them in on a clashing of cymbals and a roll on the drum. Sheila Bissett who happened to be standing beside Grandmama felt very emotional. Dear Gilbert, he was such a lovely son-in-law and here he was conducting for all the world as if he was in the Albert Hall. He'd make a lovely father in the summer when the baby came and she'd be a grandmother and wouldn't it be fun. She felt Grandmama give her a nudge. 'Isn't this wonderful? They're really quite good considering.'

Thinking there was about to be a slur cast on Gilbert's name Sheila asked sharply, 'Considering what?'

'How new to it they all are. Your Gilbert's done wonders.'

Sheila preened herself, and smiled fondly at Gilbert's energetic back. 'He has hasn't he?'

'But the bells, that'll have to stop.'

'The bells?'

'Yes, I know you'll support me, I'm going to object.'

'What is there to object about?'

'The noise. We don't need bells to remind us what time it is, we have all got clocks.'

'Shhhh! I'm listening.' Sheila thought well here's one who won't be objecting. She wouldn't allow herself to be persuaded, not by the Duchess, never again. Sheila took considerable pleasure in saying, 'Don't count on me for support, I love 'em.'

Grandmama was disappointed. When the concert concluded she joined in the applause and general admiration of the boys and as the crowd dispersed to their Sunday dinners or a pint in the Royal Oak she caught up with Dicky. 'Splendid, quite splendid. We're lucky to have you Dicky. Everything working out all right now you're full-time?'

'Wonderful, quite wonderful, we're so happy, Georgie and I.'

'Heard from Bryn yet?'

''Fraid not. Got to go, see to the boys yer know. Thanks for everything.'

'My pleasure.' She spotted Jimbo and Harriet talking to Peter.

As she drew close she could hear Peter saying, 'Who would have thought five years ago that we would have such a wonderful service as we've had this morning. The bells rehung, the church filled with young people, the band! Wonderful. I'm so thrilled. Everyone's made such an effort.'

Jimbo clapped him on the back. 'Not far to go to see why. It's you, you know. All of it's happening because of you.'

'It's the village itself that's doing it in truth.'

Grandmama interrupted. 'No, no, no, we owe it all to you, Peter. All to you. We're putty in your hands, one look from those eyes of yours and our souls are laid bare and we do exactly what you want of us.' She tapped his arm and looking up into his face she said, '*But* I'm calling in a favour.'

Peter's heart sank. He'd known from the first there'd be a day of reckoning for her sorting out Dicky and Georgie and Bel. 'Yes?'

'The bells. They're far too noisy and I expect you intend them ringing for the eight o'clock service too after today, well, I'm sorry, but it won't do. They'll have to be muffled or something or the peal shortened. They're enough to wake the dead.'

Peter was appalled. 'But . . .'

Jimbo, remembering all his hours of practice, was outraged. He grasped her arm and said through clenched teeth, 'Lunch, Mother? Now!'

'Let go my arm, dear.' She pushed at him to make him release her, but he wouldn't. 'Jimbo!'

Jimbo still gripping her arm said, 'Sorry about this, Peter, just ignore her. Come along, Mother. Lunch, right now. *Please.*'

Grandmama, furious at Jimbo's manhandling of her, tried again to thrust off his hand. Reluctantly he let go.

Peter feeling genuinely upset said quietly in his saddest voice, 'Mrs Charter-Plackett, I've longed for those bells to ring, and to have found someone willing to provide the money for their restoration, seemed heaven-sent, and I want them to ring for many many years to come. They proclaim the message of the church in a supremely special way. I wouldn't be surprised if they can hear them as far away as the bypass. There can't be anyone alive who fails to be touched in one way or another by the sound of church bells.' He smiled down at her. 'So you do see the wider implications of our bells don't you? They're for the world to hear, not just for us, are they not?'

Jimbo, his lips pressed together, his face white with temper, waited for her reply. He swore if she still objected after Peter's impassioned plea, he would personally throttle her out here on the Green in front of everyone, because despite her revelations to him, he really couldn't take any more of her aggravating ways.

Harriet, trying hard to be kinder like she'd promised she would, laid her hand on Jimbo's arm to comfort him and waited in hope.

Grandmama looked up at the splendid young man that was Peter: six feet five, with his halo of red-blond hair, and his all-seeing bright blue eyes, and that special charisma that was his and his alone, and decided she wouldn't, indeed couldn't, call in her favour. Couldn't disappoint him.

She smiled at him and said, 'My dear Peter.' She swallowed hard. 'My dear Peter, put like that how could I object to such a wonderful witness. You're quite right, the whole world needs reminding of what you stand for.' She patted his arm and turned to Jimbo saying with an imperious note in her voice, 'Lunch, I think you said, well come along then, the children will be home before us. Don't dilly-dally.'